Folktales of Newfoundland

Publications of the American Folklore Society
New Series
Patrick B. Mullen, Series Editor

WORLD FOLKTALE LIBRARY—VOL. 3

Garland Reference Library of the Humanities—VOL. 1856

THE WORLD FOLKTALE LIBRARY presents the oral art of the greatest and most representative storytellers from diverse folk traditions. Each volume, assembled by a leading expert in the field, features authentically collected and painstakingly transcribed texts designed to capture the personal styles of the oral artists. Introductory materials offer historical background on the folk community, describe the contexts for taletelling, and provide biographical information on the storytellers. Each book is annotated with comparative notes that help place the tales in relation to international oral traditions. The series is designed both to meet the highest scholarly standards and to reach all readers who take delight in the limitlessly rich art of oral storytelling.

General editor
Carl Lindahl, University of Houston

Volume 1. *Cajun and Creole Folktales: The French Oral Tradition of South Louisiana.* Collected, transcribed, translated, annotated, and introduced by Barry Jean Ancelet.

Volume 2. *Hungarian Folktales: The Art of Zsuzsanna Palkó.* Collected, transcribed, annotated, and introduced by Linda Dégh. Translated by Vera Kalm.

Volume 3. *Folktales of Newfoundland: The Resilience of the Oral Tradition.* Collected, annotated, and introduced by Herbert Halpert and J.D.A. Widdowson, with the assistance of Martin J. Lovelace and Eileen Collins. Music transcription by Julia C. Bishop.

Volume 4. *A Turkish Folktale: The Art of Behçet Mahir.* Annotated and introduced by Warren S. Walker. Collected by Ahmet E. Uysal. Translated by Necibe Ertaş.

Folktales of Newfoundland

The Resilience of the Oral Tradition

Herbert Halpert and J.D.A. Widdowson

Volume I

With the Assistance of
Martin J. Lovelace and Eileen Collins

Music Transcription and Commentary by
Julia C. Bishop

Garland Publishing, Inc.
New York and London 1996

Library of Congress Cataloging-in-Publication Data

Halpert, Herbert.
    Folktales of Newfoundland : the resilience of the oral tradition / Herbert Halpert and
J.D.A. Widdowson ; with the assistance of Martin J. Lovelace and Eileen Collins ; music
transcription and commentary by Julia C. Bishop.
        p. cm. — (World folktale library)
    Includes bibliographical references and index.
    ISBN 0–8153–1736–0 (alk. paper)
    1. Tales—Newfoundland. I. Widdowson, J.D.A. (John David Allison) II. Lovelace,
Martin J. III. Title. IV. Series: World folktale library (New York, N.Y.)
    GR113.5.N54H35 1996   96-3648
    398.2'09718—dc20

Western Brook, Gros Morne National Park

Photo: Sharon Buehler

Hauling wood in Bonne Bay

Photo: Sharon Buehler

TABLE OF CONTENTS

ACKNOWLEDGEMENTS

A work which has been so long in the making inevitably incurs considerable debts of gratitude. The fieldwork on which this collection is based began in the mid-1960s. From the outset the project was supported by a series of grants from the Canada Council. When transcription and preliminary editing began in 1976, the Council again provided financial assistance over a two-year period. We gratefully acknowledge this initial support, without which the project would not have got off the ground.

From 1979 onwards the work has received generous and continuing financial support from the Memorial University of Newfoundland. Here we wish to record our thanks to several members of the University's senior administration, who collectively and individually encouraged and underwrote the costs of the enterprise. Specifically we thank the late M. O. Morgan; and Leslie Harris, Iain Bruce, Michael Staveley, and Terrence Murphy.

The late E. R. Seary had the vision and foresight to develop a program in Newfoundland language and folklore at Memorial University in the 1960s, and we are grateful to him for his guidance and support. Our thanks are also due to the successive heads of the University's Department of Folklore for their co-operation over many years: Neil Rosenberg, the late Kenneth Goldstein, the late David Buchan, Gerald Thomas, and Paul Smith. Michael Staveley, Terrence Murphy, and Paul Smith also gave us their unstinting support during the prolonged negotiations which in due course led to the publication of these volumes.

Our colleagues and students in various departments of the University have given valuable assistance and advice on a wide variety of topics. In particular we wish to thank Raoul Andersen, Geraldine Barter, Anita Best, Iain Bruce, Sharon Buehler, George Casey, Robert Hollett, William Kirwin, Martin Lovelace, Thomas Nemec, Patrick O'Flaherty, Peter Narváez, Harold Paddock, Neil Rosenberg, Shannon Ryan, Lawrence Small, Gerald Thomas, and Wilfred Wareham. We are grateful to Sharon Buehler and Jane Hutchings, and to the storytellers and their families, for providing original photographs. We thank our colleague Philip Hiscock, Archivist of the University's Folklore and Language Archive, for his invariably courteous and professional help with the location, copying, and transcription of archive material, and for his efficient handling of the photographs. We also thank Gordon Handcock for his expert advice and practical assistance in the production of the map.

We owe a special debt of gratitude to our friend and mentor, the late George Story. He was closely involved with every aspect of the interrelated research and publication program in Newfoundland language and folklore from its inception. He was always on hand to advise, encourage, warn, support, and cheer us along the way.

Over the years, the secretarial staff in the Department of Folklore have given us considerable help. In particular we should like to thank Winifred Martin, Cynthia Turpin, and Sharon Cochrane. Our thanks are also due to Magda Moyes and Heather Williamson, who typed successive stages of the earlier versions of the manuscript. The preparation of the final copy has been in the very capable hands of our Publications Assistant, Eileen Collins. She has cheerfully and expertly transformed an unwieldy and complicated manuscript first into typescript and then into final form for publication. Quite apart from the unbelievable speed and accuracy of her work, her dedication and commitment have been an inspiration to us both. We are also grateful to Judith McCulloh for editorial advice and assistance.

We have benefited immensely from the enthusiasm and commitment of Carl Lindahl, the series editor of the Garland World Folktale Library. His invariably cheerful and conscientious advice and support in preparing the work for publication have been truly inspirational. We are equally indebted to Gary Kuris, Vice-President of Garland Publishing, for his unswerving faith in the project.

All the musical transcriptions and notes have been contributed by Julia Bishop. We greatly appreciate the care and attention to detail which she has brought to this exacting task. Margaret Griffel and Stuart Frankel were most helpful in the typesetting of the music transcriptions. In addition to giving us valuable assistance on a variety of other practical matters throughout the preparation of the manuscript, Martin Lovelace has singlehandedly compiled the listings of motifs for each narrative. His mastery of this complex and arduous procedure is amply demonstrated here, and we are most grateful for his conscientiousness, good humor, and enthusiasm.

We are indebted to many scholars from outside the province, who have assisted with various aspects of annotation and bibliographical reference. These include Roger Abrahams, Bo Almqvist, the late Alan Bruford, the late Helen Creighton, Melvin Firestone, the late Kenneth Goldstein, Robin Gwyndaf, the late Wayland Hand, Hamish Henderson, the late Bengt Holbek, Reimund Kvideland, the late Luc Lacourcière, Margaret Low, Donald Archie MacDonald, Seamus Ó Catháin, Ríonach Uí Ógáin. Lillian Krelove and the late Alfreda Bilner kindly located and supplied a number of important books on narrative previously unavailable to us.

Our fieldwork was greatly facilitated by the contacts suggested by many of our students. Several friends and colleagues took the trouble to accompany and introduce us to most of the storytellers in this collection. We especially thank Fred Earle, Jane Hutchings, Roland Hutchings, Walter Lyver, Thomas Nemec, Ronald Noseworthy, Harold Paddock, Pierce Power, Zachariah Sachrey, and Harold Squire.

We are grateful to our colleagues and students at Memorial University who gave us their permission to include in this publication a number of texts and tape recordings which they themselves had collected. Melvin Firestone generously made available to us tape recordings and transcripts of four stories, told in a unique style by Az McLean of Payne's Cove. George Casey kindly supplied two extensive tape-recorded texts from Ambrose Reardon of Croque, along with transcriptions and admirable contextual information. Other texts, whether in manuscript or tape-recorded form, were contributed to the Folklore and Language Archive by: Geraldine Barter, Corman Brown, Sharon Carter, Eric Colbourne, Jesse Fudge, Kenneth Goldstein, Vivian Greening, Helen Halpert, Nicholas Halpert, Claude Hamlyn, Leslie Harris, Harold Healey, Helen Hoskins, Doris Janes, Zita Johnson, Oliver Langdon, Carol McGrath, Ronald Noseworthy, Andrew O'Brien, Harold Paddock, Christina Pynn, Hugh Rowlings, Mercedes Ryan, Zachariah Sacrey, Thelma Sansome, Doris Saunders, Catherine Sheehan, Loretta Sjoen, Harold Stroud, Karl Sullivan, Gerald Thomas, Gladys Thomas, Boyd Trask, Baxter Wareham, Catherine Whelan, Iris Whelan, Madonna Wilkinson, and Melvin Yetman.

To the families, friends, and neighbors of those we interviewed we extend our heartfelt thanks for their warm welcome, their hospitality, and their patience. We are also indebted to many of them for providing us with details of their family history.

Our greatest debt of gratitude is to the storytellers themselves. They welcomed us into their homes, and were happy to share with us their wealth of Newfoundland traditional narrative, only a small proportion of which is included in this collection. On behalf, not only of ourselves but also of all those who may read and enjoy these tales, we especially thank those whose stories are presented here: Becky Bennett, Clarence Bennett, Everett Bennett, Freeman Bennett, John Edward Bennett, Peter Benoit, Elizabeth Brewer, William Chapman, Harold Chaulk, Dick Dalton, Leo Donahue, Richard Furlong, Nathan Goodyear, Heber Greening, Ralph Hewitt, William Hewitt, Jack Hibbs, Blanche Hutchings, Charles Hutchings, Daniel Hutchings, Henry Hutchings, Martha Hutchings, Ellen Johnson, Heber Keeping, Mike Kent, Frank Knox, William Langdon, Lester Lockyer, Fred March, John Martin, Dan McCarthy, Az McLean, Gus Molloy, Mike Molloy, Stan Molloy, Ron Murray, John

Myrick, Allan Oake, Wilson Osbourne, Thomas Pardy, David Payne, William Pittman, Alfred Pollard, David Power, Walter Power, Patrick Quann, Ambrose Reardon, Arthur Rich, John Roberts, Garfield Rogers, Alma Sansome, Rita Sheehan, Stephen Snook, Carol Solberg, Norman Stone, Harold Stroud, Jerome Sullivan, Mose Troke, Thomas Walters, John Whelan, Raymond White, Frank Woods, and Albert Yetman. We respectfully dedicate this collection to them and to their families.

To anyone whom we have inadvertently omitted from these acknowledgements we offer our apologies. Any other errors or omissions are entirely our responsibility and we would appreciate having them called to our attention.

ABBREVIATIONS

a.	adjective
adv.	adverb
det.	determiner
f.	female
Int.	interviewer
m.	male
n.	noun, note
OE	Old English
pl.	plural
ppl.a.	participial adjective
pron.	pronoun
rep.	repeated
rpt.	reprint(ed)
sb.	substantive
trans.	translated, translation, translator
v.	verb

SERIES EDITOR'S PREFACE

Even by the most superficial measure, *Folktales of Newfoundland* represents the work of a lifetime: a sum of sixty years of scholarship, thirty years each from two remarkable folklorists. Sixty years would be too brief for most scholars to complete a project of this magnitude, but the careers of Herbert Halpert and J. D. A. Widdowson illustrate an attraction for—and remarkable success with—impossible tasks (motif H1010).

Each man's contribution to this collection is merely part of a multivalent and multidisciplinary career. Each man in the course of pursuing rigorous personal goals as a researcher and author has also demonstrated his conviction that well-grounded folklore research is a group enterprise demanding carefully coordinated teamwork: each has created a folklore program from scratch and converted it into an internationally recognized research center.

Folktales of Newfoundland could only have been created by such a team: two men with impeccable personal research standards, deep mutual respect for each other's skills, and a shared sense that all the skills at their disposal would often be inadequate to address the enormous challenge they had chosen for themselves: recovering and characterizing the extant märchen tradition of English-speaking Newfoundlanders.

For more than half a century Herbert Halpert has been a commanding presence in North American folklore scholarship. Born in New York City in 1911, a folklorist by inclination since childhood, and a published folklorist since 1936, Halpert had by 1979 produced a scholarly vita of 173 items (Rosenberg 1980). Prominent in the list of his publications is folksong, a field which he has mastered very nearly to the extent that he has mastered folk narrative. Indeed, many of the folktales in this collection were recorded during evening entertainments in which folksongs dominated.

Halpert's vita barely alludes to two of his most substantial contributions. First, the enormous extent and great quality of his fieldwork are nearly unequaled: only such legendary collectors as Alan Lomax and Kenneth Goldstein have traveled as many miles, visited as many folk performers, spent as many years in the field, and shown as much sensitivity to the contexts of collection as Halpert has. Second, Herbert Halpert founded the folklore program at Memorial University of Newfoundland, which now ranks as one of the leading folklore centers in the world. The folklore program grew largely from his inspiration: its archive—among the richest in the English-speaking world—is built from his collections as well as those of his colleagues and the many students he has trained.

As Herbert Halpert was arriving in Newfoundland from the United States, J. D. A. Widdowson, an Oxford graduate specializing in English language and literature, was arriving from England to assume the position of Lecturer in English at Memorial University. Some thirty years later, Widdowson would be known as the author or editor of some ninety publications in the fields of folklore and linguistics, including such monumental team projects as the *Linguistic Atlas of England* (1978) and the *Dictionary of Newfoundland English* (1982; 2nd ed. 1990). In subsequent years Widdowson would serve as founder and editor of the British folklore journal *Lore and Language*, as president of the English Folklore Society, and as Co-Director of the Institute for Folklore Studies in Britain and Canada.

Like Halpert's, Widdowson's most enduring achievements include the foundation of an entire center for folklore studies. In 1964, Widdowson became the Director of the Survey of Language and Folklore, headquartered at the University of Sheffield; within a few years, this would be designated the Centre for English Cultural Tradition and Language, then and now England's only major university-based folklore program.

Shortly after Halpert and Widdowson met, they embarked upon the thirty-year collaboration which created this collection. The introduction to this volume conveys something of the difficulties they faced in visiting the rugged environments of the storytellers as well as the intensive fieldwork methods necessary to bring these remarkable tales to a wider audience.

Folktales of Newfoundland is notable not only for the number and quality of its narratives, but also for the format in which they are presented. As explained in the introduction, Widdowson developed for this collection a special transcription system designed to convey to the reader the accents and rhythms of each performance. The transcriptions strive for a previously unobtainable balance of accessibility and linguistic accuracy. Close attention to the tellers' language is a major facet of this book; the introduction contains a close consideration of Newfoundland English, and the endnote to each tale features an analysis of the narrator's language. This extraordinary examination of the linguistic features of oral art sets this book in a unique position among English-language folktale collections: only the studies of such Native American narrative scholars as Dell Hymes treat the speech of oral artists with equal care.

A final point of major importance is the masterful scholarly treatment of each tale. Following each transcription is an analysis of its performance style and context as well as a comparative note discussing the text's relations to related tales from worldwide tradition. Each note concludes with a thorough and geographically organized bibliography of related tales from around the world and an exhaustive index of the tale types and motifs represented in the tale.

For more than fifty years Halpert has been writing comparative notes for English-language folktale collections, and he is generally acknowledged as the world's foremost expert in this art. No previous collection can equal the exhaustiveness or usefulness of this one as a resource for the comparative study of folk narrative in English.

Halpert and Widdowson began this project, respectively, as teacher and student, as narrative scholar and dialectologist, as folklore bibliographer and phonologist. In thirty years of collaboration, their roles have overlapped to the point that they have become virtually indistinguishable. Folk narrative scholarship has a history of extraordinary partnerships. From the times of Grimm and Grimm and Asbjornson and Moe, to those of Bolte and Polívka, many of the most monumental and enduring narrative collections, catalogues, and comparative studies have been duets. This landmark work—collection, catalogue, and comparative study all at once—will take its place beside the other great team-works just listed.

Gerald Thomas has called *Folktales of Newfoundland* "the most important folktale collection since the Grimms'." Having had the honor of examining this remarkable collection, I can only agree.[1]

Carl Lindahl
General Editor
World Folktale Library

[1] I thank the University of Houston for awarding me a Limited Grant in Aid to support work on this series, and Katherine Oldmixon for her expert editorial help.

Professors Halpert and Widdowson have acknowledged the many people who helped them assemble their text, but I feel a special need to acknowledge those who have helped Garland publish it: Paul Smith, Head, Folklore Department, Memorial University of Newfoundland, for his patience, perseverance, and continued faith in this project and his willingness to spend the time and resources necessary to complete it; Eileen Collins for her skill, extraordinary endurance, and superhuman good humor in assembling the entire manuscript; Shalom Staub and Patrick B. Mullen of Publications of the American Folklore Society for expediting the preparation of camera-ready copy; Patrick B. Mullen, Pack Carnes, Carole Carpenter, the late Kenneth Goldstein, and Gerald Thomas for their sensitive evaluations and strong support of this work.

Work Cited

Rosenberg, Neil V. 1980. "The Works of Herbert Halpert: A Classified Bibliography." In *Folklore Studies in Honour of Herbert Halpert*. Ed. Kenneth S. Goldstein and Neil V. Rosenberg. St. John's: Memorial University of Newfoundland Folklore and Language Publication Series, Bibliography and Special Series, No. 7, pp. 15-30.

INTRODUCTION

This collection of Newfoundland folk narratives grew out of extensive fieldwork in folk culture in the province, beginning in 1962. In that year a major program of folklore teaching and research, one of several in a number of disciplines designed to investigate aspects of Newfoundland culture, was inaugurated in the Department of English Language and Literature at Memorial University. Led by E. R. Seary, this program pioneered research into the province's regional speech and onomastics, and from this there developed an increasing awareness of the wealth of local traditions, which, except for folksong, had received comparatively little attention. It was therefore a logical step to initiate a folklore program, and, with the appointment of Herbert Halpert in 1962, the first stages of assembling material for a folklore archive began.

Halpert's intention was to collect as broad a spectrum of traditional material as possible. Recognizing that the limited number of trained fieldworkers could not hope to undertake a comprehensive survey of all the traditions, he developed a program of student fieldwork such as had already been undertaken under his direction at several universities in the United States. This was based on the premise that, with proper guidance, students steeped in their own tradition can not only report the insider's view of their culture but can also become aware of the scope and value of their heritage and the importance of studying it. The development of the Memorial University of Newfoundland Folklore and Language Archive (MUNFLA) provided a localized data base to complement the theoretical and methodological aspects of the academic course work. In addition to the collecting by students in folklore courses, several hundred other students in the Department of English were encouraged to take home a series of extensive exploratory questionnaires on specific aspects of folklore and language. They used these to glean information from family, neighbors, and friends in a wide selection of communities throughout the province. The surprising richness of the responses made available a wider cross-section of major and minor genres of Newfoundland folklore than would have been collected by any other means in so short a time.

Today MUNFLA has become one of the major folklore archives in North America and contains extensive material on film, videotape, and audiotape, along with manuscript collectanea and questionnaire responses. Its scope is broad, and it includes, for example, a considerable amount of data on individual life histories, family, local and oral history, and popular culture.[1] The depth and significance of the tape-recorded documentation in MUNFLA of Newfoundland speech in full context have already been demonstrated in the *Dictionary of Newfoundland English,*[2] which draws extensively on the tape and manuscript resources of the archive.

While these new initiatives were developing, field trips were undertaken to various parts of the province by trained fieldworkers to explore the range of available traditional materials. Though intended as merely exploratory, these early forays that we ourselves made, whether jointly or individually, yielded a substantial amount of data, most of it tape-recorded in the field, which considerably augmented that being collected by other means. This field data, supplemented by other material deposited in MUNFLA, became the basis for the present study. Collecting has of course continued on a more extensive scale since the completion of our own fieldwork. MUNFLA now has a wealth of new material, including some Märchen, collected more recently not only on audiotape but also on videotape.[3] For practical reasons, however, we decided to limit the main focus of this study to narratives collected between 1964 and 1979, concentrating on the longer, internationally known stories but including a number of shorter tales, again mostly international, to illustrate one aspect of the range and variety of the storytelling tradition in Newfoundland.

Our first field trips were to localities where student reports suggested that fuller information on specific folklore genres might be forthcoming. We interviewed and tape-recorded many people on a broad range of topics, paying particular attention to mummering and its associated folk drama, to aspects of folk belief, and in due course to the rather less immediately accessible traditional narratives and songs. Since these trips were intended as pilot surveys of unknown territory, we tried to collect material on other topics, our inquiries being based in part on responses to the early questionnaires. We were also especially interested in recording local dialects and other traditional linguistic forms and inquired systematically, for example, about linguistic variation, weather sayings (dites), and aspects of traditional verbal social control.

It soon became clear, even at this early stage, that there was a remarkable depth and breadth of oral tradition in the province. We therefore decided to collect the full range of what people wanted to talk about, and our conversations usually focused on the community, past and present. We were consciously collecting linguistic data as well as folklore and oral history, since we were aware that outport life in Newfoundland was changing radically and there was an urgent need to monitor these changes while those who had experienced the older ways of life were still able to talk about them.

All tape-recorded speech is of course useful to the linguist. This is especially so in areas such as Newfoundland where the complex patterns of dialectal usage offer unique opportunities for investigation. The collecting of linguistic data inevitably led to the recording of information on many aspects of folklife and material culture, such as details of local fishing technology and other occupational lore. The fullest possible biographical information was also recorded, including details of age, sex, religion, occupation, and family origins.

Once the range of the available material became clearer, we planned our field trips more systematically and extended them farther afield to many small and often isolated communities. We were fortunate to visit these outports while the older traditions were still being actively practiced. As visiting strangers, we first had to overcome our hosts' attempts to treat us as guests by showing us into the sitting room rather than inviting us to join in the informal, friendly atmosphere of the kitchen. However, once it was realized that we were genuinely interested in the local life-styles and traditions, we were welcomed into the kitchen, which was, and in many places still is, the center of social interaction within the home.

As visitors were comparatively rare, people were usually pleased to see us, and once they had satisfied themselves about us and about the purpose of our visit, they were more than generous in their hospitality and their willingness to share their traditions with us. Only rarely did our request to use a tape recorder meet with resistance. People were eager to help us record the spoken word in this authentic form. Most of them readily understood, particularly after they heard their own accounts replayed, how useful the tape recorder is in preserving what they had to say.

In retrospect, this somewhat haphazard method of collecting took the fieldworkers to many of the less accessible areas of the province but neglected some of the communities near at hand that could probably have yielded equally important materials, as later student contributions to the archive indicate. As it happens, however, this was perhaps the last opportunity to visit many of the outlying communities before they were drastically changed by the advent of electrical power and improved communications, or in many cases before they themselves were uprooted by the government's Resettlement program.

HISTORICAL BACKGROUND

Newfoundland, the oldest overseas English colony, uniquely preserves many aspects of older traditions from England, Ireland, Scotland, and France that have remained relatively unchanged in coastal enclaves, although modified by their new environment. The early English settlers came predominantly from the West Country, first as migratory fishermen and eventually as settlers, mainly along the east coast of the province. Later they were joined by immigrants from Southern Ireland. There was a tendency for English Protestants and Irish Catholics to maintain separate identities during the early period of settlement, and this often resulted in the development of distinctively English or Irish enclaves.[4] In some localities, however, the two groups lived side by side, though often in separate areas of the same settlement. Occasionally a small early community of English settlers was overwhelmed by Irish immigrants, while in others the reverse was true. What usually happened was that the minority group was assimilated into the dominant one, affecting such aspects of culture as religion and speech. In the eighteenth century French fishing stations were to be found in numerous locations around the island. Today, however, settlements extensively or predominantly French are virtually confined to the Port-au-Port Peninsula on the west coast, while Scots Gaelic-speaking settlements extend from the southeast of that peninsula down through the Codroy Valley, one of the richest farming areas in the province. The indigenous native peoples, the Inuit or coastal Eskimo and the Montagnais and Naskapi Indians of Labrador, and the Micmac Indians, concentrated in such enclaves as those in the Baie d'Espoir region of the south coast of the island, continue to maintain a degree of distinctive cultural identity despite the superimposition of immigrant European cultures, which became predominant in the course of time.

All the immigrant communities had to be self-sufficient. They therefore supplemented their fishing with hunting, growing crops, keeping animals, and exploiting the resources of the forests for housebuilding, boatbuilding, and domestic fuel, and later on a more commercial scale for exporting timber and timber products. Some of these activities, especially working in the lumberwoods and those tasks that kept groups of men together in relative isolation for periods of time, gave opportunities for maintaining storytelling and singing traditions in addition to such customs as asking riddles, dancing, and other traditional activities commonly practiced in the home. The maintenance of these home-based traditions has been reported from other somewhat isolated groups of English origin in North America, such as those in the southern Appalachians and the Ozarks.

The patterns of settlement in Newfoundland, scattered all around the coastal perimeter, have been conducive to the preservation of older life-styles and until recently have presented something of a barrier to change. At the time when the bulk of the fieldwork for this book was undertaken, many communities could still be reached only by sea and often preserved some distinctive elements of language and tradition that reflected earlier settlement patterns. Local people were often aware of differences in speech between themselves and their neighbors in settlements only a few miles away. Most of our fieldwork was carried out when roads were only just being built to many parts of the island. These improved communications were part of the process of rapid change that followed Confederation in 1949 and that was accelerated by the advent of electrical power and the far-reaching effects of the Resettlement program.

Though Newfoundland settlement goes back to the seventeenth and eighteenth centuries, there has been a constant influx of new immigrants, frequently from those parts of the British Isles and Ireland from which the original settlers came. So we find, for example, a large number of folksongs from the nineteenth century but somewhat fewer of the older songs. Nevertheless, certainly at least until the early 1950s, much of outport Newfoundland retained speech patterns, customs, beliefs, legends, and material culture processes that were basically those of Britain and Ireland around 1880. This situation was radically altered by the influence of the American bases in World War II. Other major changes took place after the war. These included greatly increased educational opportunities, the complex political and social results of Confederation, much greater accessibility by rail, road, and air, and the impact of new technology on outport life. The advent of electrical power, radio, television, and the telephone helped to break up many of the close-knit social and family structures. Until that time, the older traditions had flourished and had been preserved longer than in most if not all of the other English-speaking areas of the world. This is not to say that these older elements of the culture were preserved merely as relics, since Newfoundlanders have proved themselves to be creative in their adaptability to changing situations. This has meant, among other things, that the traditions brought by the original settlers have been modified over the years to reflect the Newfoundland environment and have developed a unique set of characteristics.

Nevertheless, Newfoundland has preserved many aspects of English and Irish folk tradition, some of which are apparently no longer active in the countries of their origin and are now also under the threat of extinction in the province. Working from the premise that traditions virtually unknown in England might still survive in active form in Newfoundland, we set out to discover if this was in fact the case. Could it be that the longer folktale, which nineteenth-century scholars claimed could no longer be found in England, might perhaps still exist in the isolated coastal communities of Newfoundland and still be observed and studied in its social context? The material presented in this book goes some way toward answering these questions.

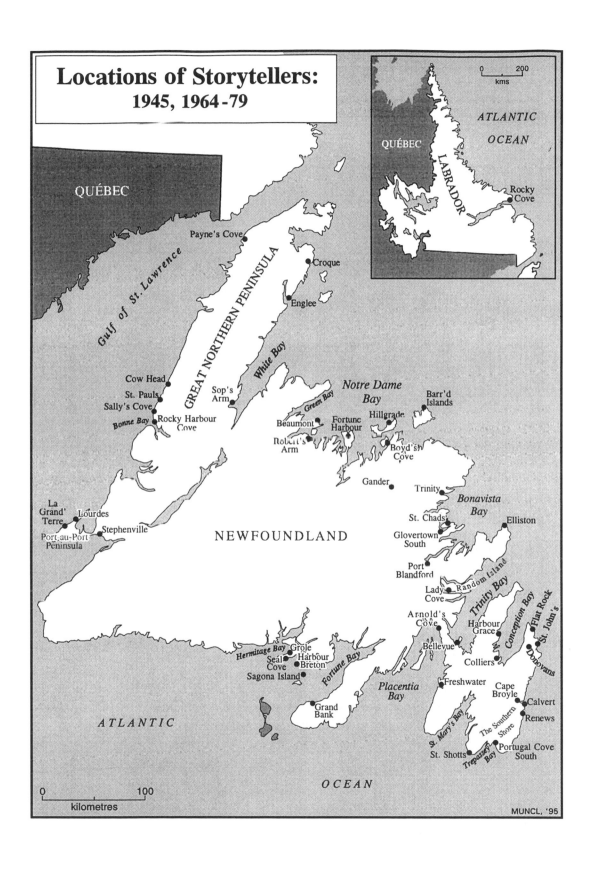

Locations of Storytellers: 1945, 1964-79

QUÉBEC

ATLANTIC OCEAN

QUÉBEC

LABRADOR

Rocky Cove

0   200
kms

Payne's Cove

Croque

Englee

Gulf of St. Lawrence

GREAT NORTHERN PENINSULA

White Bay

Notre Dame Bay

Barr'd Islands

Cow Head

St. Pauls

Sally's Cove

Bonne Bay Rocky Harbour Cove

Sop's Arm

Green Bay

Beaumont

Robert's Arm

Fortune Harbour

Hillgrade

Boyd's Cove

Gander

Trinity

Bonavista Bay

St. Chads

Elliston

La Grand' Terre

Lourdes

Stephenville

Port-au-Port Peninsula

NEWFOUNDLAND

Glovertown South

Port Blandford

Random Island

Lady Cove

Trinity Bay

Arnold's Cove

Harbour Grace

Conception Bay

Flat Rock

St. John's

Bellevue

Colliers

Donovans

Hermitage Bay Grole

Seal Cove Harbour Breton

Sagona Island

Fortune Bay

Freshwater

Cape Broyle

Calvert

Renews

ATLANTIC

Grand Bank

Placentia Bay

St. Mary's Bay

The Southern Shore

St. Shotts

Trepassey Bay

Portugal Cove South

OCEAN

0   100
kilometres

MUNCL, '95

Our fieldwork revealed a number of Märchen, although the total repertory is apparently limited. Our failure to find more such stories might be explained by the somewhat random and unrepresentative coverage of the widely scattered communities throughout the island, our investigations being hampered at that time by difficulties of travel, the absence of other trained fieldworkers, and the limitations of time. Our visits to many outports were brief and exploratory and must inevitably have overlooked potential storytellers. More recent fieldwork in other communities has revealed a few additional storytellers. However, although our coverage is in no way exhaustive, it amply demonstrates that the Märchen tradition was to be found in many parts of Newfoundland. This is also true of the French-speaking tradition, as recently published collections show.[5] On the other hand, of the many hundreds of students who have contributed material to MUNFLA from all parts of the province over the past twenty-five years, only a handful have collected any of the longer tales. Those we collected were concentrated in three main areas: the Great Northern Peninsula, the Notre Dame Bay/Green Bay region, and the south coast from Trepassey Bay to Ramea. There are therefore many gaps in the regional representation, but colleagues and students have helped to fill out the picture with their own collecting.

Although our fieldwork has taken us to most parts of the island, we have found that the longer tales apparently survive only in a few widely scattered communities. Of these, only in one, St. Pauls, on the Great Northern Peninsula, did we find a family tradition of telling such stories. Elsewhere the individual storytellers we found seem not to have passed on their skills and knowledge to a younger generation. It is clear, however, that until recently this tradition was much more vigorous, though now it is practiced mainly by the older generation. This contrasts with the French-speaking tradition on the Port-au-Port Peninsula on the west coast, where the telling of Märchen, though not as active in public performance as in years gone by, still flourishes within families, where the younger generation still listen with pleasure to the tales and in some instances continue the tradition by telling them themselves.[6]

The themes and motifs of most tales in this collection are international. Certain aspects of their setting and flavor, however, are distinctive to the Atlantic provinces in general and to Newfoundland in particular. Although a number of the stories are from the Irish tradition, the majority appear to be from England. What is more, comparatively few have been reported at any time from England itself and even fewer from English-speaking North America. The stories demonstrate that the vitality and breadth of an earlier English tradition have been maintained in this region of the New World.

The claim by folklorists at the turn of the century that the English tradition had practically no Märchen[7] was disproved by the publication in 1966 of Baughman's extensive type and motif index.[8] In the 1960s and 1970s a few compilations of tales recently collected in England were published,[9] and there were new revelations about the unexpectedly large number of chapbooks and broadsheets known to have been printed. This implies a consistently higher level of literacy in England than had been assumed hitherto. In the same way, a new generation of collectors, of different training and social background from their predecessors, have found that the folksong tradition in England is still alive despite the claim that it was dying out in the early years of this century.[10] They have also proved that quite apart from songs, the folktale tradition is still within living memory and that legends and other narratives with Märchen motifs are recoverable today.

Cecil Sharp and Maud Karpeles discovered a more vigorous tradition of older English ballads and songs in the isolated Southern Appalachians during World War I than they had found in England.[11] Since that time American collectors have found that the English folk narrative tradition had been maintained not only in the Appalachians but also in the Ozarks, the eastern United States, parts of eastern Canada, and sporadically elsewhere in both countries. The isolation of communities in all these regions, however, had certainly broken down by the end of World War II. Returning to the Appalachians in 1951, Maud Karpeles was dismayed by the many changes that had taken place since her earlier visit.[12] Very few of the older songs were still to be found in the localities where the tradition had once been particularly vigorous. New roads and schools and the advent of the phonograph and the radio, among many other developments, had contributed to the modification and decay of the older tradition.

In most parts of Newfoundland, however, roads came much later, along with education and the other social consequences of Confederation. Therefore it was still possible, even as late as the 1960s and early 1970s, when most of the tales in this collection were obtained, to find storytellers and singers who were only just beginning to lament that there were none of the traditional adult audience to listen to them. Money and work became more available, and these factors, among others, hastened the breakdown of the old patterns. When fieldwork was being carried out in the province in the 1960s, for example, many outport homes were still self-sufficient in garden vegetables and animal products.

Because of Newfoundland's isolation, Cecil Sharp suspected that it too might have retained the older English folksong tradition.[13] It was not till the early 1930s that his associate, Maud Karpeles, had the chance to come to Newfoundland to test this theory. By chance, her visit coincided with that of Greenleaf and Mansfield.[14] All three indeed discovered an active and vigorous folksinging tradition in the province, as is amply demonstrated in their published collections.

Similarly, Halpert, who had already collected extensively in several parts of the United States, suspected that there might also be in Newfoundland a folk narrative tradition that could include English Märchen and thus augment the limited collections published in England and North America since the mid-nineteenth century. During several brief visits to the United States air bases in Stephenville and Gander in 1945 he found that it was possible to collect a variety of tales from Newfoundlanders working there. Because of this he felt sure that, in addition to folksongs, there could well be an active folktale tradition in the province, including the longer Märchen, as indeed proved to be the case.

When we began our fieldwork, we were already aware that surprisingly little of the rich traditional heritage of Newfoundland had been studied in depth apart from the custom of mummering at Christmas.[15] Of the several major published collections of Newfoundland folksongs,[16] only two, those of Greenleaf and Mansfield and of Leach, discuss the role of the songs in the life of the people. Although several other collections of Newfoundland songs have appeared,[17] no one has attempted to collect, analyze, and present the longer folk narratives from the English-speaking tradition in the province, many of which are internationally known. The telling of such stories was formerly common in many parts of the island, though probably less widespread as a form of entertainment than the singing of songs. By the time we collected these tales, however, they seemed to be part of a declining tradition, despite some more recent evidence that this decline may not be complete. A few of the storytellers whose tales are presented here are still alive, and others have since been discovered.[18] Some younger Newfoundlanders, having heard these stories from their elders, are now beginning to tell them again.

The bulk of the narratives in this collection are transcribed from tape recordings made in the field. Our primary aim has been to preserve the actual speech of the storytellers along with many features of their oral styles. The presentation of this recorded material therefore differs in many respects from the usual literary treatment of folktales, which are often either completely rewritten or at least edited to satisfy certain preconceived literary standards. Folklorists often pay lip-service to the ideal of the faithful recording of their informants' speech. In practice, however, this frequently results in the reinterpretation of the teller's actual words to fit the editor's and reader's preconceptions of how a story should be presented in writing. In attempting to overcome this problem we decided to see how far it is possible to set down in written form not only the exact words of speakers but also some idea of the structure of the narrative as indicated by pauses, emphases, and other linguistic and rhetorical features.[19] It soon became clear, however, that this form of presentation has its own shortcomings, not the least of which are the difficulties such detailed transcriptions pose for the reader who expects the normal conventions of the printed word.

Quite apart from the immediacy of the spoken texts, the collection itself reveals the remarkable variety of the older Newfoundland narrative tradition, though not all regions of the province are represented. Nevertheless this comparatively small number of tales demonstrates that, as in other aspects of folk tradition, these narratives are part of the international stock of tales and have not only persisted here but have also been adapted by the tellers to the Newfoundland cultural environment. In their stories and songs Newfoundlanders prove themselves to be part of a highly oral culture, rich in inventive language, colorful names, vivid proverbial sayings, ingenious riddles, and other forms of verbal art. For theirs is a verbal art—a dramatic art—and for that reason hard to capture on paper. The same, of course, is true of such minor literary forms as the riddle, which also loses much when removed from its social context. The telling of riddles, like singing and storytelling, is a performance art with a style of its own.

As noted above, in contrast with the folktales, folksongs have been extensively collected in Newfoundland and published together with their tunes. In addition to the substantial collections by Greenleaf and Mansfield there are those by Karpeles and Peacock and also by Leach for Labrador. The apparent ease with which many Newfoundlanders compose local songs to express their feelings on a variety of topics is remarkable. These songs include many about wrecks and other disasters and also satirical songs about merchants and other local individuals or about some humorous occurrence. Because of their specific local references, however, many such songs are difficult for the outsider to understand and appreciate. This problem does not arise in the case of folktales. Although the stories in these volumes reflect many aspects of Newfoundland culture, they are more accessible than some of the local songs and more universal in their appeal.

To most people unfamiliar with performances in a predominantly oral culture the term *folktale* calls up memories of the multi-colored fairy books of Andrew Lang or the polished accents of a professional telling stories to a captive audience of children. However, in many cultures, including Newfoundland, the folktale has been and often still is primarily an adult pursuit, children being present only on sufferance. It is the adults who are the critical responsive audience that the storyteller addresses.

The wonder tales or Märchen that adults have listened to and admired all over the Indo-European world were most unfortunately called *Die Kinder- und Hausmärchen,* the children's and household tales, by the Brothers Grimm,[20] no doubt because even in early nineteenth-century Germany the longer tales had already begun to lose their high place as adult entertainment. In Hungary, Russia, Ireland, and Gaelic-speaking Scotland in the last century this was not so—nor was it so in much of Newfoundland as recently as between the two world wars. There are still many Newfoundlanders who remember hearing the long tales told at night in a logging camp, in the forecastle of a schooner, or by the kitchen stove on winter nights before an attentive group of friends and neighbors. As already mentioned, a few of these tellers of long tales can still be found among the French, the Irish, and even the English settlers of the province. We stress the last because for a long time folklorists assumed that England had somehow missed having its share of these international Märchen known all over Europe and eastward.

To be frank, however, searching for and finding Märchen in the province nowadays is subject to the law of diminishing returns. Today very few Newfoundlanders have to face the long winter nights in houses lit only by kerosene lamps and with a total absence of competing entertainment that once made listening to long ballads and stories such a welcome way of passing the time. Nevertheless, quite apart from their interest in present-day traditions, folklorists continue to search for these older forms in order to secure a fuller record of the past. Occasionally they make some surprising discoveries. For instance, in our fieldwork we came across versions of a story that, no doubt in some printed form, was known to Shakespeare. Scholars agree that the main plot of *The Merchant of Venice* was based on an Italian story, either in the original or in a lost English intermediary. In the original published version[21] the hero must pass a test by which he gains the lady's hand and fortune. In *The Merchant of Venice* the test is a choice of three caskets, gold, silver, and lead. This test, however, is not the one found in Shakespeare's presumed source. There the test is more startling. The suitor is given a chance to sleep with the lady, a test that a series of suitors have failed. As with previous suitors, this pleasant prospect for the intending lover is twice frustrated by his being given a drugged glass of wine before going to bed. He falls into a heavy sleep and on awakening is told he has lost not only the lady but also his ship and cargo. On the third occasion, thanks to the advice of a serving maid, he only pretends to drink the sleeping potion and to fall asleep, then successfully passes the bed test—to the lady's great satisfaction.

As Spencer has pointed out, such a test "is obviously unsuitable for dramatic presentation and strains credulity."[22] He suggests that Shakespeare therefore substituted the casket test. So far as we know, the original test has not been reported from oral tradition except in one published collection from Chile.[23] The Chilean version is apparently an oral retelling of the original Italian story from Ser Giovanni's *Il Pecorone.* Nevertheless, between 1964 and 1971 no fewer than eight examples of this episode (see Nos. 36-43) were collected as part of a completely different tale from five storytellers on the Great Northern Peninsula of Newfoundland. The survival of the episode in this comparatively isolated part of the English-speaking world obviously leads to speculation about its origins and transmission. It seems unlikely that someone who had read a translation of *Il Pecorone* would then tell the story in Newfoundland. Nor, in view of its indelicacy, would a story including such an episode have been readily told to British folklorists in the nineteenth century. It is more probable that tales incorporating this episode may have been in oral circulation in many cultures, including the British Isles, and the accident of its transmission to this part of the New World provides us with a unique clue to its wider provenance and distribution in former times. For this reason alone the recensions presented as Nos. 37-43 ("Hard Head," etc.) are among the more interesting narratives in this collection, quite apart from the opportunities they offer for studying variation in form and style among the narrators, two of whom were recorded telling the story on more than one occasion.

Two other AT types presented here also have Shakespearean parallels. One of them, No. 54 ("The Faithful Wife"), has not been reported from folk tradition in the British Isles or Ireland. It has an essential element of the plot of *All's Well That Ends Well,* namely the fact that a woman has a child by her husband without his knowledge. A second folktale parallel to a Shakespearean plot is found in Nos. 45-48 ("Jack and the Slave Islands"). The basic element of the plot of *Cymbeline,* i.e., AT882, "The Wager on the Wife's Chastity," is also central to the plot of these Newfoundland recensions. This folktale form, however, though reported from Scotland and Ireland, has been found only in Gypsy tradition in England.[24]

The fact that Shakespeare and many other writers have drawn on the folk narrative tradition has led to an interest in the relationships between folklore and literature. Historically, folk narratives and ballads were primarily studied by scholars who accepted the canons of literary taste. Even though many of the great nineteenth-century collectors of folktales in Germany, Scandinavia, and elsewhere maintained that they were interested in the language of the common people and were presenting faithful versions of the stories they had collected from them, we now know that their claims were unjustified. These scholars usually rewrote the tales to fit their own Romantic concepts. If some of the stories were fragmentary or incomplete, as is inevitable in field collections, they conflated different versions to create an apparently complete story in keeping with their views of what stories should be like. The result was a stylized literary production that has been accepted in the western world as the authentic tradition and now forms the corpus of tales constantly reprinted and made available to a popular audience, especially children, with whom they are primarily identified.

Ironically, even those later folktale scholars who used the historic-geographic and other "scientific" methods to study the distribution of tales consciously or unconsciously preferred the more neatly rounded, literary versions. At that time and even today many folktale scholars in Europe view the tales from the literary angle rather than examining them as oral performance in a traditional context. It is certainly easier to find identifiable types and motifs in "good" literary versions than in the less polished oral performances.

Whereas folktales were originally transmitted orally and were intended for an adult audience, in western urban society today they are mainly known through printed collections intended for children.[25] These stories follow the normal conventions of print and therefore create the impression that each has a single established form. This is a far cry from the Newfoundland oral tradition where until recently, as we have stressed, stories were performed by adults largely for an adult audience. Nor are they an isolated genre. They are intermixed with numerous other traditional forms such as songs, rhymes, and riddles in the normal course of social interaction.[26] Conversely, beliefs, songs, rhymes, riddles, and proverbs that occur independently in other contexts are often incorporated into stories. They form part of a complex of floating elements which recur in various traditional genres and are familiar both to the storytellers and to their audiences.

STORYTELLING IN NEWFOUNDLAND

Although we have stressed the isolation of many Newfoundland communities, this does not mean they lacked influence from outside. Certainly the singing tradition, although it retained many of the older songs, was also permeated by the printed tradition from the Canadian mainland and beyond, for example, through such newspapers and journals as the *Family Herald*,[27] which found their way into many outport homes. Furthermore, when people went to the "Boston States" or to New York they often brought back broadsides and copies of popular song collections.[28]

Even more important is the wealth of locally composed songs. As noted earlier, there are many songs about shipwrecks and other disasters as well as some of a humorous nature. Although most of these local songs maintain an existence in the oral tradition, accessible to the collector only through fieldwork, some of them have appeared in newspapers, broadsides, and songsters. The composing of such songs is not limited to the outports. St. John's, the capital city of the province, had its own lively broadside and songster tradition.

There is no equivalent printed tradition for the stories told in Newfoundland. Even so, the storytellers, like the singers, are remarkably creative. This creativity is seen in the many variant recensions of folktales such as those presented in this collection, in which the narrators combine and recombine episodes and motifs in many different ways in several performances of the same story while retaining the basic plot. It is also to be found not only in the dramatic performance of vivid personal experience narratives but in the wit, satire, and social comment of humorous tales, anecdotes, and jokes.

The most popular venues for the performance of songs were primarily in the home and also at local "concerts" and other entertainments. Performances at the more public of these occasions included not only songs but also plays, recitations, and stories. Many of these were locally composed, but many were drawn either from the older traditional repertory or had been learned more recently, sometimes from printed sources. Newfoundland has retained many older aspects of tradition alongside more recent importations. What is more, Newfoundlanders are highly skilled in the imitation and adaptation of both old and new forms so that they have a more specific or localized significance for their audiences.

Throughout the island the twelve days of Christmas, the major festive season, provide one of the best opportunities for bringing together these traditions. This is the time when many outport families and neighbors visit each others' houses. These may simply be social visits, but sometimes the visitors are disguised as mummers or "janneys." On these occasions, after the game of guessing identities is over, hosts and visitors may dance and exchange stories and songs. These house-visits and the "concerts" and "times" that also took place mainly at Christmas have received little attention until recently. Their importance should not be underestimated.[29]

It was in fact our attempt to collect mummers' plays that provided the initial motivation for the field trips during which most of the tales in this collection were recorded. Our first joint field trip in June 1964 took us to the communities of Eastport, Salvage, Happy Adventure, and St. Chads in Bonavista Bay on the east coast. Among the older men we recorded at St. Chads was Uncle Mose Troke, aged eighty-five, who not only remembered much of a mummers' play he had heard in neighboring Salvage many years before but also talked about his seventy years as a fisherman, about weather lights, luck, the Christmas hobby horse, and other topics. When one of us inquired about stories, he told a brief tale about Pat and Mike. When asked about longer tales, he at first apparently could not remember any, though he told us about a man he had known at Salvage who "could begin in the morning and tell you stories all day." Suddenly he said, "There was a king one time _ I'll tell you this one now," and immediately launched into a version of what we later realized was the Endless Tale known as "The King Loses Patience" (No. 140), which he told with great animation and enjoyment. Immediately after this he told a fine version of one of the great international Wonder Tales, "The Princess on the Glass Mountain" (No. F4). Again the story was told with obvious delight, which was an exciting experience for both collectors, since it proved to us for the first time that, like the mummers' play, the longer folktales were still known in Newfoundland. The excitement of this discovery was later tempered by the realization that our tape recorder, the first all-battery-operated model used in fieldwork locally, had developed a fault and recorded only the first section of the tale. More unfortunate still, when Mr. Troke was visited again some years later, he no longer remembered the stories. Such are the pleasures and perils of fieldwork!

Encouraged by these discoveries, we decided to search more systematically for other examples of these two genres, the mummers' play and the longer folktale. In the summer of 1965 one of the editors therefore traveled to the Burin Peninsula and the south coast and again collected a wide variety of material including several Märchen among many other kinds of narrative. In the following year we heard a report about the performance of "plays" at Christmas time on the west coast of the Great Northern Peninsula. Thinking this might be some form of mummers' play, we planned a brief exploratory trip to the area. Our local contact, Jane Hutchings, the district nurse who lived in Cow Head, introduced us to many people in that community and then took us to St. Pauls to meet members of the Bennett family. We knew that the Bennetts had been recorded some years previously by Kenneth Peacock of the National Museum of Canada and that they had a notable singing tradition. However, we had no idea of what other traditional materials might still be in their active repertory apart from the so-called Christmas plays. As it happened, these were not mummers' plays but a variety of dramatic games. These included performances of various ballads such as "When Jones's Ale Was New" and a cante fable, "Little Dicky Melburn," which was dramatized in the fashion of the Elizabethan jigs as discussed by Baskervill.[30]

After we had recorded these, we asked about songs and stories. In our very first conversations with Everett Bennett and his son Clarence we were given the outline of a long story about Jack, the first time we had heard the name mentioned in all our fieldwork up to that time. The tale obviously had Märchen characteristics. At intervals during the next two weeks we revisited the Bennetts several times. It soon became clear that this family was as remarkable for its storytelling as for its singing. We recorded some two dozen stories, including ten long Märchen, from four members of the family and also a variety of narratives from people in neighboring communities. The tape recordings from this and our other field trips were deposited in MUNFLA, which already contained a substantial amount of other data.

The folktales in this collection are drawn from MUNFLA, primarily from tapes recorded in the field by the editors between 1964 and 1972, supplemented by tape recordings and manuscripts submitted to the archive up to 1979 by colleagues in the Department of Folklore and the Institute of Social and Economic Research and also by several folklore students. We have included two of the tales collected by Halpert in 1945 that were the initial stimulus for his interest in Newfoundland folklore in general and in the province's narrative tradition in particular. These add a historical dimension to the collection.

In the first stage of the research we decided to bring together all the versions of the longer fictional folk narratives then available in the archive. The very existence of a hitherto undiscovered corpus of longer English folktales in oral tradition at this late date is itself significant. The stories are of sufficient importance both to an understanding of Newfoundland culture and to the history of folklore studies to warrant detailed transcription, annotation, and discussion. Virtually all those we interviewed told us numerous legends, anecdotes, jests, and personal experience narratives. These and the thousands of such texts deposited in the archive, however, would clearly require large-scale and lengthy investigations. For practical reasons alone a study of the legends and other kinds of stories must therefore be postponed.

We recorded most of the stories on tape, some in several versions by different tellers. We also revisited a few of the tellers on a number of occasions over several years and recorded some of the tales again. This offered an unusual opportunity to present not only the variation in stories and storytelling among tellers from different parts of the province but also to illustrate the variation in the retelling of specific tales by the same tellers over a time span of several years. What is presented here is therefore a departure from most previous published collections of tales from the English-speaking tradition.[31] It concentrates attention on tape recording as a technique for the collection of folk narrative and the recording of variations in form, style, and language on specific occasions as they actually occur in the living context of storytelling.

It is unlikely that such tales as these could now be recorded in Newfoundland in many of the original contexts that the storytellers describe. In the old days, for example, tales were told in the lumber camp at night, on fishing trips and sealing voyages, at wakes, and on other occasions when entertainment was necessary to pass the time. The most obvious venue nowadays, which was of course equally popular in the past, is the family kitchen. Our storytellers are either speaking to an audience of family and neighbors in addition to the collector or the collector is the sole audience in what is at least an induced natural context. The storytellers we recorded were glad to have an interested listener. Given good rapport with the teller, the collector becomes accepted as one of the audience. Even the tape recorder did not unduly disturb the storytelling situation once such relations were established.

Of the 150 recensions and 15 fragments presented here, 102 were tape recorded and 7 taken down in manuscript form during our own fieldwork. The remaining 56 were collected by colleagues and students, 35 on tape and 21 in manuscript. The tales and fragments were collected from a total of 65 individuals in 40 communities in Newfoundland and Labrador.

The majority of the texts (137 out of a total of 165), including almost all the longer narratives, were therefore transcribed from field tapes. The 150 full recensions represent 81 AT types, whether singly or in combination, a further 2 types being identifiable among the fragments. Most of the recensions are classifiable according to the AT type index[32] and are presented in the numerical order of that index. Of the 18 recensions not listed in the AT index, 14 are classifiable by reference to Ó Súilleabháin and Christiansen, *The Types of the Irish Folktale*,[33] and to Hoffmann, *Analytical Survey of Anglo-American Traditional Erotica*,[34] the remaining 5 being unclassified. The fragments are mostly either parts of longer tales or sketches or outlines of them.

Almost a third of the full narratives belong to the class of Wonder Tales, AT300-AT699. The remainder comprise examples of most other categories in the AT index, with the exception of Religious Tales. We have tried to include as many as possible of the international tales recognized by the index, ranging from Animal Tales to Formula Tales. Toward the end of the collection we have grouped a few examples of tales recognized by other indexes and 2 recensions of a Märchen that seems not to have been listed in any index of English-language tales published to date. This final group of stories is presented in the following sequence: first, 2 recensions of Irish Type 2412 and 1 of Irish Type 2412B, which follow on directly from the AT numbers of the preceding tales and which have all the characteristics of legends; second, 3 versions of the tale of Black George, Nos. 144-146, a legend with folktale characteristics, collected only from one family; third, 2 brief single-episode tales, Nos. 147 and 148, which, though not fully fledged types in the AT type index, can be classified by motifs; fourth, 2 versions of the Märchen "Little Jack," Nos. 149 and 150, which lacks an AT type number. It should be emphasized that these 165 recensions represent only a small fraction of the narrative tradition in the province recorded since the 1960s. However, whereas virtually all those interviewed knew legends, anecdotes, jokes, and personal experience narratives, very few of them remembered the longer international folktales.

Most of the stories in this collection flourished some two generations ago, after the turn of the century. The narrators we recorded usually learned them from the older generation, notably uncles, grandfathers, and others in those age groups. At that time the Newfoundland tradition was still comparatively isolated and enclavic. Although the outports themselves were largely self-contained, the men's seasonal occupations often took them away from the community. Many fishermen, for example, took part in the Labrador fishery and went on sealing trips "to the ice." In both cases they met men from other communities. The same was true of those who worked in the lumber camps, the mines, and other occupations. Some went even further afield, like Captain Albert Heber Keeping of Grand Bank (see Nos. 2, 30, 88, 89), who was one of many sailors who went "foreign." Like others, he had skippered sailing ships carrying fish to Europe on numerous occasions and could talk freely about the Mediterranean countries he had visited. Whenever men worked together in occupations such as these, there were many opportunities for making their own entertainment. A man who knew a long story that would pass the time was a welcome addition to any group. The majority of the storytellers we recorded, however, first became interested in the tales and in learning them when they were young and at home.

Most of those we recorded had retired from active work. The very fact that we were interested in them and what they knew about the old days gave them a rare opportunity to tell some of the things they knew. When the contributors themselves were young, older people had been admired for their storytelling abilities. However, the younger generation nowadays has become disaffected from the old ways and is seeking new experiences. Consequently the older storytelling and singing skills are less eagerly sought by the young, and the status formerly enjoyed by the older tellers and singers has declined. We experienced this change at first hand when we were interviewing Everett Bennett and his son Clarence at St. Pauls. As the two men talked, the room gradually filled with children and teenagers, who sat quietly in the background. When one of us remarked that it was encouraging to see the youngsters taking an interest in the storytelling, Clarence laughed and said that far from coming in to hear the stories, the youngsters had in fact simply come to see us, the visiting strangers! This quickly disabused us of any romantic notions we might have had about the status of the storyteller. Even so, some of the younger generation are interested in these and other aspects of the oral tradition, and on occasion we found that a younger member of a storyteller's family consciously adopted the role of narrator. What is more, the skillful singer or storyteller of whatever age group is still accorded due respect in the community.

As already noted, the bulk of the tales in this collection were recorded in three main areas: the Great Northern Peninsula; Notre Dame Bay/Green Bay; and the south coast. Our intention was to explore the potential for further research in areas most distant from the capital, with the expectation that localities nearer St. John's would be easily accessible for later investigation. At that time communications by road were very difficult and travel was often limited to the coastal boats or local vessels. This imposed limitations on the fieldwork, as did also initially the lack of adequate portable recording equipment, personnel, and funds. A few of the storytellers were already known to us by reputation or otherwise before we went on particular field trips. One or two had been suggested to us as possible narrators by students. Most were interviewed only once, but the Bennett family of St. Pauls were revisited several times over a period of some ten years. One storyteller at Grand Bank was visited twice. Another, who lived at Beaumont, was re-interviewed by a folklore student when convalescing in hospital at Springdale nine years after the original recordings were made.

The tellers were usually interviewed in their own homes, often with other members of the family, neighbors, or friends present. Occasionally a teller was interviewed alone with only the fieldworker as audience. Almost all the narrators were men. Only six women were represented, three of them contributing cante-fable material. This confirms our fieldwork experience that women in Newfoundland are recognized more as singers than as storytellers, and that the cante fable is, as it were, a compromise between the two genres—a common ground of performance shared by men and women. Many of the stories were recorded from families where we also collected songs from women as well as men. Nevertheless, it may be that some women continue to tell the longer folktales in communities from which we did not collect them.

The storytellers we ourselves recorded in the field were in the age range forty to ninety, most being over sixty, but some of the shorter tales contributed to this collection by students were from a much younger age group, including a few in their twenties. The majority of the tellers are typical of the everyday working occupations of Newfoundlanders. Those who had retired when we recorded them had mostly spent their lives in the seasonal tasks of fishing and woods work. One teller who had been a blacksmith and two others who had been captains of ocean-going vessels were regarded as having a superior status in their home communities. Although we interviewed people of other classes and occupations, including merchants, clergymen, teachers, nurses, and lighthouse keepers, for example, none of them told us any of the longer folktales. Again it may be that those in such occupations also know such stories, but our evidence suggests that the tradition is at its strongest among ordinary working families where a whole complex of older household traditions is also maintained.

Most of those interviewed were of English or Irish descent and retained many features of their parent languages in their speech. A notable exception was the Bennett family, whose ancestors were French (some branches of the family maintaining the older surname Benoit) but whose speech is now predominantly West Country English in its distinctive features, which they share with those of the Great Northern Peninsula communities in which they live.

Most of the narrators we recorded had a reputation as storytellers in their communities, sometimes restricted to their families, friends, and neighbors. Almost all of them had repertories that included legends, riddles, personal experience narratives, songs, and information on local history and the ways of life in their community. Interestingly enough, though the Märchen are full of supernatural, magical motifs, few of our storytellers talked openly or frequently to us about other aspects of the supernatural. It seems likely that the Märchen and other longer tales were recognized as appropriate for public performance, while other aspects of the supernatural were more a matter of private or personal belief and would require a deeper level of rapport with the collectors than was usually possible on our brief exploratory field trips.

When the interviews took place, there were on average two or three people present in addition to ourselves, usually members of the family already in the house, and/or visiting friends and neighbors. Most interviewing contexts were therefore of a fairly close and intimate nature. They were invariably informal, though the narrator was always in control. On some occasions, however, the interviews provided an opportunity not only for a larger audience of family, friends, and neighbors to listen to the storyteller but also for these visitors to come and see what was going on—to satisfy their curiosity by seeing the "strangers" (ourselves), witnessing the recording, seeing the tape recorder (itself then very much a rarity), and occasionally listening to the playback of part of an interview, which was more often requested by the audience than by the teller. On a few occasions this more extended audience numbered at least a dozen. In general, all audiences were relatively passive participants in the interviewing context, listening quietly and attentively to the stories and responding with nods, smiles, laughter, and occasional interjected remarks. Only very rarely were members of the audience persuaded to tell stories or sing songs themselves, often at the instigation of the storyteller. However, on a few occasions, when several narrators and singers got together at one venue, they took turns performing, each following the other with no prearranged pattern or sense of competition. These larger gatherings were prompted by individual informants suggesting that both they and the collectors should visit other acknowledged narrators and singers. In this way the collectors became part of the traditional house-visiting customs of the community and provided a welcome and convenient excuse for such visits, which were obviously enjoyed by the families and their friends. These situational contexts were therefore controlled by the narrators and their families, who called for certain songs and stories that they knew the new hosts could perform. They even asked the hosts' permission for the collectors to use the tape recorder and ensured that there were breaks in the sequence of performance so that tapes could be changed when necessary. On these occasions we ourselves as collectors were relegated to a much more passive role, for the most part simply being allowed to eavesdrop on a typical social gathering that was largely unconstrained by either us or our machine. This relieved us completely of the need to engage in the usual preliminaries to an interview or of establishing a simulated natural context, since we were vouched for by those who took us along to the new venue.

The typical composition of the audience was predominantly male, ranging in age from young children to people in their fifties—that is, generations usually considerably younger than the storytellers. In general, the women of the house, after staying long enough to greet and offer hospitality to us and other visitors, usually withdrew and busied themselves with their everyday household chores and left the men to their storytelling, reappearing only to bring tea or other refreshments. Sometimes small children were present. If they became noisy enough to disrupt the interview, their parents or an older relative would quiet them, often by taking them on their knee. If the noisy behavior persisted, the children would be told to leave the room. On one occasion one of the fieldworkers was directly used as a threatening figure by a member of the household to help ensure the obedience of very young children. Teenagers, on the other hand, listened attentively like the adults.

There was, of course, inevitably some artificiality about the contexts of recording in that the fieldworkers were strangers, usually visiting only briefly either on a single occasion or on widely separated occasions, along with their recording equipment. It must also be borne in mind that many of the older-established contexts for telling the longer tales such as the Märchen had virtually disappeared by the time the fieldworkers visited these communities. There was no longer the need for the storyteller to play an important part in filling up long periods of enforced leisure, especially on dark winter evenings or when work finished for the day, whether at the fishing, in the lumber camps, or in other occupations. Also at that time most homes in many communities lacked electricity. Although portable radios were relatively common, television was confined to a few urban centers. Nonetheless, because the collectors asked questions on a wide variety of folklore topics during their visits, the interest they showed helped to stimulate individual memories to recall many forms of tradition that had been slowly disappearing. Among these, the older longer tales, including the Märchen, eventually came to the surface. After all, the Märchen is a rather specialized genre, told by comparatively few people. Even Freeman Bennett, whose repertory was the most extensive we recorded, had forgotten many of the longer tales because of lack of opportunity to tell them: "Oh, I used to know a lot of stories one time...wonderful lot of stories, but...I forgets a lot of 'em now 'cause...I don't TELL stories not very often now. And...no one is not interested into 'em an' I don't tell stories very often."[35]

It has apparently always been the case that the home was the most usual venue for much of the storytelling, as several narrators made clear: "tell them in the houses, oh yes. ...Any time o' the year at all you get in th' house for a little party or anything...well they'd...start tellin' those stories, see. ...perhaps somebody else might tell a SHORT story but...there was me father an'...me uncle, well now...they knowed a lot of stories, see. ...They [i.e., other people] 'd come to get 'em to tell those stories, see."[36]

Further evidence that the enjoyment of hearing such stories had not died out completely came from Allan Oake of Beaumont: "Well there's an odd one now sometimes, a feller'll come in and the first thing he'll say, 'Tell me a story.' Now there's a scattered [i.e., occasional] feller comes in now wants me to tell un a story right away you know. Well there's a lot of young fellers, oh my son, nearly all the young fellers around here they'd be interested in even now hear...hear me tell a story."[37]

Even so, the telling of such tales is no longer a normal part of house-visiting customs and family entertainment in Newfoundland. For many of the narrators the collectors were the interested audience that they had once known but that had gradually slipped away. The interest the fieldworkers showed in the tellers and their tales helped overcome any minor problems of rapport. As far as we can judge, the only difference between the storytelling context of our recordings and that which might often have obtained when a larger audience was present in former years is that some of the narrators felt it necessary to explain certain of the technical terms and details in the stories. This apart, we felt that the tellers retold the tales in much the same way as they had done in the past and with equal enjoyment. Their welcoming hospitality and willingness to talk meant that even on such short visits rapport was easily established and maintained. The storytellers appreciated the fact that the collectors were so interested in them and in what they knew about the old days.

The rapid cultural changes following Confederation reduced the need, the opportunities, and even the venues for storytelling sessions. However, once the collectors asked for such tales, narrators whose once extensive repertories had been inactive for many years became encouraged to try to "get the stories together," as they put it. This process of recall sometimes took days rather than hours, though some tellers first sketched the story out and then suddenly remembered and told it in full. Others told the tales hesitantly, piecing them together, and were able to improve them in later retellings. In so doing, their enthusiasm for the story and renewed confidence in their ability to tell it brought back the old fire and vividness into the narration.

The interviews were usually held in the kitchen or "house-place," though sometimes they took place in the main sitting room or parlor—mainly to escape the noise and activity of the kitchen. Extraneous noise was a constant problem during fieldwork, whether from the normal household activities, such as cooking and washing, or from the stove or furnace, children, animals, visitors, and all the everyday domestic happenings. On one occasion a narrator felt most at ease sitting in a rocking chair in his garden shed, and this was where he was recorded. On another occasion, we were asked by eighty-nine year old John Roberts to take him by car to a neighboring community, and we were able to record two long stories from him in the car en route.

It is difficult to generalize about the storytelling events as a whole, because each is unique and each differs in a variety of ways—location, storyteller, interviewer, audience, situation, occasion, time of day, and so on. However, to give the reader some insight into the events as we actually witnessed them during fieldwork, it may be useful at this point to outline a specific example that captures something of the flavor of such an occasion. We emphasize that while other tales in the collection may share some of the contextual features described here, this is merely a sample of the many different storytelling events in which we participated as audience members. The relevant contextual information for each storytelling session will be found in the notes to the tales themselves.

The particular example we have chosen is the occasion when we first met Freeman Bennett on our initial field trip to St. Pauls on the west coast of the Great Northern Peninsula in the late summer of 1966. As with all our early trips, this is an exploratory foray, and we are interested in collecting information on the full range of traditional material. We learn something of Freeman Bennett's reputation as a storyteller from his younger brother Everett, whom we had first interviewed a few days previously. On the afternoon of August 31 we return to St. Pauls from a brief trip further north along the coast and again call in to see Everett and his son Clarence. They sing songs and tell stories and riddles for two or three hours, after which Clarence takes us over to introduce us to his uncle Freeman, aged seventy, and his aunt Rebecca (Becky), aged fifty-eight. Clarence explains what we are interested in and smooths the way for our arranging a visit later that day. When we return at about 7:45 P.M., after supper, Freeman and Becky welcome us and immediately make us feel at home. Freeman sits down in his accustomed chair in a corner of the living room, with Becky at his side. We sit near him, one of us immediately alongside his chair and the other a little to one side to minimize any potential distraction caused by the tape recorder, which is conveniently placed on a small table between us. As often happens on these preliminary visits, we have little opportunity to observe more than the essential details of the venue. The living room, some twelve or fourteen feet square, is comfortably furnished, and there is plenty of seating space for the many people, young and old, who call in to see Freeman and Becky. Such "open-house" arrangements are common in Newfoundland, with relatives, neighbors, and their children habitually calling on each other to chat, exchange the news, and, as happens on this occasion, become part of the active or passive audience for any traditional performance that might take place. The visitors simply walk into the house as if it is their own, with the minimum of ceremony and without knocking at the door. During our visit, which lasts for more than five hours, we form part of a constantly changing audience. When we arrive, a young man who we understand is a relative is already sitting in the room, and he stays for much of the session. A number of children come into the house from time to time, including the grandson of Freeman and Becky. On one occasion a crowd of young boys arrive but are not allowed to stay for long. Later in the evening a second, somewhat older, local man calls in and stays until we finally take our leave in the early hours of the following morning.

After very few preliminaries, during which we mention their local reputation as singers, Halpert asks Becky how and when she heard the songs she knows. We discover that she learned her first song at the age of eight. Our usual practice, which we follow on this occasion, is for one of us to ask questions and the other to become part of the attentive audience and to do the actual recording. We find that this "double act" works very well in practice. A lively conversation soon develops with husband and wife about their singing, their ancestry, and the strength of the singing tradition, which they quickly trace back to their grandparents' generation, Freeman mentioning Becky's grandmother as "the best singer o' the whole lot." The conversation then turns to the question of what makes a good traditional singer, and both agree that a clear voice, especially in articulating the words, is a first essential. Whether songs are old or made up on the spur of the moment, Becky feels that "a true song is the best," a song such as "Flora" (Peacock, 2, pp. 445-46), in which you "can see the life of a person."

Halpert then asks about comical songs, and Becky, who is about to go out to a local garden party, suggests to Freeman that they sing "Whisky in the Jar" before she leaves. This they do, their highly individual voices not so much blending as accompanying each other in a strongly contrasting way—Becky with her powerful, strident voice, at the top of the register, reminiscent of the southern gospel singing tradition in the United States, and Freeman with his distinctive harsher, throaty vocal quality, very much at the lower end of the register. As they sing, Becky takes her lead from her husband, sitting at his side, turning toward him with affection and encouragement. She breaks the ice of this first interview by singing with him, first supportively, then with the full-throated power for which she is locally renowned. When the song ends, Freeman recites a long rhymed toast and Becky reminds him of a second one, which he also recites. At this point several young children come in, and Becky goes with them into the adjoining kitchen, their voices being heard in the background for several minutes before they go outdoors again and Becky returns. Freeman then asks if we have heard the story of "Peter and Minnie," adding that it is a real old story, but "'tis only a joke, 'tis not true, you know." He immediately launches into the narrative (No. 4 in this collection), and we hear for the first time the vivid and racy style of his storytelling, the animated dialogue with its constantly changing tonality and color compelling the rapt attention of the listeners. A small, quiet, unassuming man, he is suddenly transformed as he takes on the persona of each character in the tale, distinguishing one from the other by subtle changes of pace and vocal tone, notably in the extraordinarily lively and fast-moving dialogue. We immediately become aware, too, of his ability to dramatize incidents through facial expression, gesture, and bodily movements. Though remaining seated, he acts the part of Jack creeping up to spy on the giants, he shows us how Jack points his gun, and with facial expressions and head movements, at once graphic and amusing, he allows us to visualize each of the giants in their quarreling. All this animation complements and extends the dramatic impact that the remarkably skillful use of dialogue has on his audience. Freeman uses little direct eye-to-eye contact, relying instead on the sheer virtuosity of his dialogue and dramatization of events. We also become aware of the humor that is an essential feature of his storytelling style. His infectious, engaging laughter invites us to smile at the incongruity of Jack's firing his little gun at the giants. When the old woman tries to prevent Jack from telling his story in the hotel, we are treated to an amusing vignette by means of the excited, fast-spoken dialogue, which instantly brings this minor character to life. Freeman's obvious pleasure in telling the story is again seen in his laughter, which immediately follows the end formula and once more invites the audience's amused response.

Becky, who slips quietly back into the room to listen to the story, now recites the opening two lines of a song, by way of rehearsal, recalling that she used to sing it to her son when he was a child. Freeman encourages her to sing it, and this she does, commenting afterward on it with affectionate memories of how her son loved to hear it. She encourages her husband to sing two other songs, but he says one is too hard and the other too long, adding that he would rather sing us a short song. Becky expresses her disappointment at this, but it soon becomes clear that she knows his repertory of songs, and she perseveres in encouraging and helping him to remember and sing them by reminding him of titles and first lines and by singing snatches of tunes to prompt his response. His deafness tends to inhibit conversation. At this point the session is temporarily interrupted by the arrival of a crowd of youngsters—"about twenty-five half-growed boys," as Becky puts it—whom she eventually asks to leave so as not to disrupt the proceedings.

Halpert then asks about "The Tarry Sailor." Becky reminds Freeman how it goes by singing the first few lines at a fast pace, whereupon he recalls and sings it with gusto and tells us from whom he learned it. Remembering our recording of Freeman's brother and nephew telling riddles earlier in the day, we ask him if he knows any. He immediately tells "In come two legs," and then he and Becky in turn tell a neck riddle.

After a break while the tape is changed, Halpert asks about the title of "Peter and Minnie," and this leads on to a second tale, "Jack and the Giant" (No. 114). The same animated style is immediately in evidence again, a memorable instance of acting out the incidents. To demonstrate how Jack stuffs the pig's bladder inside the front of his clothes, Freeman first mimes this process with his hands and then raises them to throat level, fingers curled, as if grasping the pipe into which Jack pours the soup. A rare moment of audible audience response is heard when the young man visiting the house, who otherwise remains silent throughout the session, interjects an appreciative "Hm!" in an undertone when the king tells Jack that if he brings him the strongest giant in the world Jack can have his daughter.

The story takes some twelve minutes to tell. In the meantime, perhaps prompted by the riddles told earlier, Becky is trying to remember what she knows of "The Golden Fiddle." She asks Freeman if he knows it, then prompts him by singing a lively first verse of the song, tapping out the rapid beat with her foot. Freeman quickly responds with a neat definition of the cante fable: "...that's a...kind of a story an' a...song all together." Becky claims she has never heard the whole piece and suggests it is "a smutty one." Freeman disagrees, saying, "'tis not blackguard [i.e., vulgar], nothing like that, no," and then tells the story in full (No. 49), laughing as he does so, hugely enjoying its humor.

From this point onward the session becomes more and more relaxed. Freeman tells us how stories come to mind, though they are often less easy to recall when he is asked to tell a specific one. He is concerned that he might have to pause during the recording of a story if he cannot remember all of it, but we reassure him that this presents no problems and that the recorder will pick up the story whenever he resumes it. Becky now sings a snatch of the song "The Devil that Came to Me Door." After a brief pause Freeman remembers its title and sings the song, first making sure that we are ready to record it—aware of the machine but in no way inhibited by it. When the song is over, Becky tells us that there are better singers locally than herself and Freeman and says her sister is a better singer than she is. Freeman emphatically disagrees. He praises his wife's singing, especially the fact that she has a higher voice than her sister. Becky prompts him to sing another song, then says, "These little songs are some nice though, aren't they?" Confirming her role in helping Freeman to maintain his repertory, she adds that she cannot always remember songs but she can "name 'em out for th' ol' man." Freeman suggests that she sing the next song she recalls, while he sits back and has a smoke. We always have cigarettes with us, and the men we interview are usually very pleased to be offered some. At this point we also realize that Freeman has already been talking and singing for a long time on this warm summer evening, so we open one of the bottles of beer we have brought, and he sips from the bottle, as Newfoundlanders habitually do, while Becky sings a slow, measured, and moving version of "Young Reilly."

The arrival of their young grandson prompts Freeman to tell the story "Abraham, What Hast Thou Got in Thy Bosom?" (No. 128), which includes a "little feller" like the grandson. He follows this with a second humorous anecdote in which a young boy is also the protagonist. Becky and Freeman then sing several more songs, helping each other to remember them. Becky mentions how she and Freeman's brother Everett recently "picked up" [i.e., pieced together] a song, which indicates a similar mutual maintenance and reinforcement of the singing tradition among other members of the family. In spite of her earlier intentions to attend the garden party, it is only at this quite late stage in the session that Becky leaves, having participated fully and helpfully for much of the evening.

Our appetites whetted by the tales we have already heard Freeman tell, we ask if he knows any more about Jack. He says no, but he knows one about Black George. This interesting and more realistic story (No. 144), some seventeen minutes in duration, nevertheless has many characteristics of the folktale, with its stock opening and closing formulas and rhetorical repetitions. By this time darkness is falling. Freeman maintains his graphic style of narration, for instance using the edge of his hand to simulate Black George's splitting the end of the pole on which a message is to be passed to the girl captured by the Indians. He demonstrates how the note is inserted into the split end of the pole and snakes his hand and arm slowly across the table in front of him, oblivious of the tape recorder, to show how Black George silently pushes the pole toward the girl. He chuckles at the mention of the young furrier, incidentally called Jack, "having a time with" the girl before her capture, and he "breaks frame" to say it is only natural that Jack wants to see his girl friend, laughingly telling the audience, "Course, you would too, and so would me!"

Now that he has got fully into his stride and feels relaxed and confident enough to tell us some of the longer tales, Freeman talks away tirelessly, occasionally sipping from his bottle of beer. By now it is difficult to see well enough to change tapes on the recorder, as has to be done halfway through "Black George." Even the longer time needed to change tapes causes no problem to Freeman, who simply resumes the story. The semi-darkness seems to bind teller and audience closer together, the ears and eyes of the listeners concentrating on the voice and actions of the narrator in the gathering dusk.

The conversation again turns to songs. Freeman confirms that his repertory is extensive but adds that he now finds it more difficult to remember songs and stories on the spur of the moment. He tries to recall a story about "Hard Head" but instead tells "The Basketmaker" (No. 53), no doubt reminded of it by the similarity of its opening episodes to those of "Hard Head," which also begins with the marriage of two people when they were children. Just before he begins the story, he notices that one of us seems to be trying to avoid a cloud of tobacco smoke, and he waves his hand to clear the air. The narration itself is again full of graphic detail, a memorable instance being the incident when the girl's hat blows off and Jack is set adrift in the boat. With the sheer power of words, complemented by gesture and facial expression, Freeman makes us visualize the fast-moving scene.

When the tale is over, Freeman gives us an insight into his narrative technique by commenting that stories and songs are similar in that "every word'll tell ya the next word, see." This gives us the opportunity to question him more closely about how he learned his stories. He tells us that in his younger days he only had to hear a tale once and he could tell it himself immediately afterward. He learned some of his stories from an older man from the neighboring community of Sally's Cove, Jack Roberts, whom he knows we have already interviewed (see Nos. 36, 45, and 62), and asks if he told us the story of "Little Jack." When we say he did not, Freeman is more than happy to tell it himself (No. 149). It proves to be a delightful tale, which he begins by pointing to the young boy who is listening to indicate Little Jack's size and age in the story. The dialogue between Jack and the king's daughter about the pretty fish he catches is particularly engaging, its contrasting vocal tones effectively characterizing each of them in a gently humorous way that immediately arouses the listeners' sympathetic response. This is another lengthy story, more than twenty minutes in duration.

After a brief humorous excursion into "The Three Questions" (No. 57), which he thoroughly enjoys telling, he is at last prepared to tackle two more of the longest stories of the session, "The Green Man of Eggum" (No. 8) and "Hard Head" (No. 37), each of which extends to just under twenty minutes. In the first of these, despite the fading light that prevents us from taking any more notes on the event, we are still able to see that when Jack is called upon to recognize his future bride by the identity test of recognizing her crooked finger, Freeman stretches out his hand in front of him, his extended little finger pointing downward to demonstrate what the girl is doing.

At this late hour a second visitor comes into the room and Freeman asks him to tell a story. When the invitation is not taken up, Freeman says, "You can tell some kind of a joke, can't you?" but gets no response. Even so, the visitor contributes significantly at a later stage by reminding Freeman of names and other details that he cannot immediately call to mind. Halpert now asks about other Jack tales, all of which Freeman has known but cannot remember in sufficient detail to tell. However, he then tells us the story "Hard Head," learned from his uncle who passed on to him the house in which we are now sitting. As with the other long stories, a particular instance of dramatization stands out: when Jack is given sleepy drops to drink, Freeman falls suddenly back in the chair, head back, mouth open, arms hanging loosely at his sides, imitating Jack snoring!

By this stage we are getting increasingly concerned about the lateness of the hour and the possibility of outstaying our welcome. Freeman, however, is still warming up! Nor do we wish to disrupt the intimate atmosphere of which we are now so much a part. We go on to ask him about mummering—a central focus of our inquiries around the province. He gives us information on the dress and behavior of the janneys, as the mummers are called in the locality, and then shows us in vivid detail exactly how a hobby horse, a favorite mummering device, is made. It is here that we see his remarkable skills of demonstration fully displayed. Using only a piece of kindling from the woodbox near the stove, he shows us exactly how to construct the horse. At this point we again recognize how crucial these same skills are to his abilities as a storyteller. In the absence of film or video camera we are reduced to commenting aloud on his demonstration in an effort to make it intelligible on the audiotape.

Our questions then range widely over other customs and aspects of folk belief—witchcraft, ghostlore, the fairy world, supernatural lights, fortune telling, and the like, as well as the social control of children. In general, Freeman expresses scepticism about such beliefs and the stories attached to them. When pressed to comment on a story of a man who was said to be able to move his spirit from place to place, he simply replies, "I don't know. I...don't hardly listen [to] stuff like that." On the other hand, he then gives us a detailed account of a notorious local murder of two furriers. Although it is now well past midnight, he sings part of a song about Robert Kidd, at which point Becky returns and they resume singing songs and snatches of songs, tell us about traditional explanations of natural phenomena, and recite feature-naming rhymes and the tongue twister "Two ducks and a fat hen." Prompted by the visitor, they round off the session with some of the "plays" or singing games that had originally attracted us to that part of the island in our search for variant forms of traditional drama. Our tape recordings end with a spirited rendering of "When Jones's Ale Was New."

With a journey before us later that same morning, we take our leave at 1:20 A.M., feeling somewhat exhausted, and certainly more exhausted than Freeman and Becky! It is quite some time before we realize what a remarkable session this has been. Apart from the songs, riddles, and the wealth of other information that he and his wife have regaled us with over some five hours, during most of which we were tape recording, Freeman has told us no fewer than ten of the stories presented in this collection, only three of which are short, the remainder ranging from twelve to twenty minutes each. Having previously encountered only one or two such stories or fragments here and there in our fieldwork, we at last have conclusive evidence of the former strength of the storytelling tradition in Newfoundland.

While many aspects of this particular session are unique and it should not be regarded as typical, numerous facets of it are echoed in our fieldwork experience elsewhere in the province, as will be seen by comparing the contextual notes to these and other tales in these volumes. Even so, this remarkable occasion seems redolent of storytelling and singing sessions as they once were in the then isolated outports of Newfoundland, when Freeman and his brother Everett first learned these tales from their father and uncle, lying in front of the wood stove in the evenings of their boyhood. As night fell in the quiet room, we caught a glimpse of that former time and for a moment we became part of it.

During fieldwork we learned of other venues for storytelling outside of the house in former days. These included the bunkhouse in the lumber camp, on board ship (whether fishing, sealing, or trading vessel), during roadmaking, and in woods camps during hunting trips and other activities. Many of the narrators had learned some of their stories in such locations in their younger days. We also had the impression that the essentially informal nature and also the very length of many of these stories made them less suitable for telling at more formal social gatherings such as weddings, wakes, concerts, or "times" in the local halls and similar venues, although such occasions might lend themselves to the telling of legends and shorter tales, jokes, and recitations, along with the singing of songs. For instance, one of the narrators from St. Shotts mentioned an old man who told stories at a wake in Ferryland on the Southern Shore:

> There was a wake there an' he went in, ol' Bill Molloy. He didn't know anyone at the wake. But when he was in there awhile there was one o' the women said, "You looks like an old man now'd be able to tell a story for the night, pass away the night." That was about twelve o'clock. An' he was tellin' stories from that till daylight. They never heard the like of 'em—ghost stories. He frightened some of 'em! [*laughs*] Old Irish stories. When he was leavin' in the morning they asked him when would he come again. He said, "The next wake!"[38]

Apart from the common denominators of age and maleness the narrators displayed no remarkable similarity in personality. Some were more outgoing and demonstrative than others, but many of those whose everyday personality was rather quiet became dramatically involved in the stories they told, using animated language, gestures, mimicry, and a wide range of other rhetorical devices. These skills of self-expression were unsuspected when we observed their undemonstrative everyday behavior. Most knew only one or two of the longer folktales, while a few knew about half a dozen, and one as many as fourteen, not to mention several shorter tale types. Of the 137 tape-recorded stories in this collection, 68 (50 percent) were of less than five minutes in duration and 91 (66 percent) were told in under ten minutes. Twenty-five tales (18 percent) extended beyond fifteen minutes, of which 8 (6 percent) took more than twenty minutes to tell, 5 (4 percent) took over twenty-five minutes, and only 2 (1 percent) continued for slightly more than thirty minutes. The longest tale recorded lasted for thirty-two minutes, fifteen seconds,[39] while the shortest, a fragment, took a mere seventeen seconds. This appears to contrast sharply with repeated claims both from the tellers themselves and from many other people interviewed that in the older traditional contexts, such as the lumber camps, stories used to take up to three or four hours:

> When they'd tell these stories they all get around as a group, you know, if they be sittin' down perhaps on a seat here, an' well all the rest'd gather around, whatever was there, get as handy as they get to hear what...the story was all about... Oh he was a long story. ...Well...three or four hours you know... He'd be...sat down tellin' a...story all night see... Well 'bout from round about eight o'clock up till about eleven o'clock you turn in, round there, you know, twelve o'clock like that, well now whenever a long story be on well...I mean to say...'d amuse 'em, they'd...stay up, you know, for to listen to this... ...there wasn't much goin' on then in the woods, see.[40]

> At night time when we all get back to camp. Big goin'-on then—songs—some singin' songs an' next feller then he'd tell a riddle, probably next feller tell a story... Oh you'd be longin' for the nights to come to get to camp then because there'd be songs an' jokes an' stories an'...all kind o' pastime then till around ten o'clock'd be bunker down time; well, turn in then—lights 'd go off an' that be all for the night...we'd have from suppertime till around ten o'clock, and Saturday nights well probably might be twelve or one.[41]

It was claimed that stories would take a day or more to tell. Everett Bennett vividly recalled John Roberts' prowess in this respect:

> He started tellin' us one Sunday after dinner, an' he told till supper time. An' he come out after supper, and he start tellin' of un again, an' he never finished un. His son was into one o' th' other camps, an' he took sick. They come for un, an' he had to go and...in where his son was. An' the next Sunday he finished that story. An' time he had un told, I knowed un all. But you know I never told that after I learned it see, an' I forgot it. Oh, took him a full day...it'd take him a full day to tell un, an' I knowed un all, every bit of un. I told un once or twice afterwards an' I give un right up; I didn't bother.[42]

Some tales were so long that they would continue on successive nights with much the same audience. This was true of Freeman Bennett from St. Pauls, for example:

> he was pretty good, you know. He told an awful lot o' stories an' sing songs, one time, in the nighttime. Well he might tell ya a story perhaps every night. ...his story wouldn't...continue on one night but...it be on couple o'nights, ya know, 'fore he...finish the story.[43]

> I've heard un tell stories around eight hours, for sure, eight hours long, tellin', taked eight hours to tell it. That was on a Bowaters camp up in...Pynns Brook. Oh it was around twenty-eight years ago. He was cuttin' wood. In the night, after we'd get our supper, he'd get out; he'd tell an hour, hour an' a half or a couple o' hours like that, of a night. Then he continue from there...till he finish the story. ...everybody'd crowd around an' listen to the story...in the bunkhouse...round from seven until eight thirty. Nine o'clock we'd turn in. Same story for a week 'fore he finish it. ...story after story; it wouldn't come hard on un even. ...some o' them were short, some of 'em were real long, take [an] hour, couple o' hours too, some of 'em. Well some long ones well he wouldn't finish 'em in a night; he'd go on...night after night, you know, an' continue. But mostly you could get un to tell a short story, you know, like a hour, like that, you know, for to [*laughs*] get the kick out of![44]

Although we recorded no fewer than twenty-six narratives from Freeman Bennett, only two extended just beyond twenty minutes, most of the others being between twelve and twenty minutes in duration. Even allowing for some degree of exaggeration in remembering the conviviality of bygone days, it is difficult to account for the considerable discrepancy between the reported length of stories in the older tradition and those we recorded.[45] While the different storytelling contexts might prompt narrators to be less expansive when telling the stories to comparative strangers in a fieldwork situation, the inescapable conclusion is that the tradition has changed radically with respect to the duration of the tales, no doubt partly in response to the sharp decline in their primary function, that of an entertaining pastime that helped to while away the empty hours of leisure or enforced inactivity.

Whenever possible, the collectors tried to discover the source of the stories they recorded. In many cases a teller remembered no specific source but would say that he heard it from the older generation when he was young, whether in the family or his own community, when visiting other communities, or while at work on board ship, in roadmaking, and especially in the woods camps. Just as often, however, the narrators could trace a given tale to a particular individual, usually named, or at least to a very specific location. What we found especially interesting was that some storytellers could also be quite specific about how they actually learned a certain story. These accounts provide valuable insights into the whole process of learning and transmission. On the Great Northern Peninsula we had the unique experience of recording tales told by the two Bennett brothers, when in their sixties, and later by John Roberts, when in his nineties, who they claimed was their source for those stories. In turn the son and nephew of these two brothers had an extensive repertory of tales, many also learned from John himself as well as from Everett and Freeman. Although we have not attempted it in detail here, close comparison of these versions of the same tale told by narrators of three different generations offers a rare opportunity to explore the complex patterns of transmission and variation.

When asked about the sources of his extensive repertory, Freeman Bennett told us:

Oh when I...first learned stories like this I was...a boy about...eight or nine year old. I...first heard 'em from me uncle...Charles Bennett. ...I heard un tell un at home... 'cause I used to live with he when I was home, see. ... They [i.e., Freeman's parents] couldn't get me to go home, see, 'cause I used to stay down there with he now...nighttime. Nighttime...he'd lie down by the stove, an' I'd lie down 'longside of un, an' he started tellin' me stories, see, start in tellin' me stories. Oh he knowed a wonderful lot of stories. Yes, I learned a lot of 'em from un.[46]

In addition to learning tales from his uncle and from John Roberts, Freeman also learned them from his father, Cornelius Bennett, and from John Roberts' brother Eli, both of whom, like Charles Benoit, had been dead for many years before we arrived to record their successors. Although Freeman's brother Everett had access to the same sources, he stressed that he also picked up many of his tales in the lumber camps. It was interesting to discover that Everett's son Clarence, like his uncle Freeman, learned his stories, songs, and riddles in the house when he was young. He even followed the pattern Freeman described of lying down on the floor alongside an older relative, in this case his father, whose repertory he learned in its entirety:

I knew *all* his stories. Well the first story I learned...was from my uncle. He's dead now for years. That's Charl, Charlie Benoit. Oh...he'd be dead now probably what, twenty-five, thirty years, I guess. That's oh when we were only youngsters. We wasn't allowed be out around, runnin' around the roads later in the night an' all this. An' home, my father in there he'd lay down in the next room an' we laid 'longside of him, he'd sing songs, song after song. An' this is how I come to get songs, an' stories. I was more interested in songs than I was in stories till after I learned quite a few songs. An' then we got at the stories. So I learned...three nice long stories. But I forgets 'em in parts, an' that'll make no sense.

...well in fact that's where I learned all my riddles from—th' ol' man [i.e., his father] ya know, my uncle livin' here, an' uncle Charlie Benoit... But ol' man knowed a awful lot of riddles one time, but I...probably don't know any hardly now.[47]

In fact both Clarence and his father remembered many more riddles than they had expected when we recorded them in a riddling session together.

Many of those we interviewed gave us other fascinating insights into the way they learned stories. Typical of the accounts of how quickly the narrators picked up a story from hearing it told only once or twice is this from Everett Bennett:

At that time I only want to hear a story once. ...Just once. Over twenty year ago you could sit there and tell me a story at twelve o'clock today, and the night twelve o'clock I'd know it. Any length—if it took [a] spell from six in the day to twelve at night I'd know the works [i.e., all] of it, word for word. As soon as you had that story told, I wouldn't know none of it, but the next time he'd come in me mind during the day I could tell you the same story you told me. When he come in my mind I'd think the story over, and I could sit down and tell you the same story you told me. That's the kind of memory I had one time, but I haven't got the memory now.[48]

Even allowing for some degree of exaggeration, this ability to learn a story from a single hearing was a common claim.

Everett Bennett also discussed the difference between hearing songs and stories, always maintaining that songs are more difficult to pick up:

> Took me a little longer to learn songs. ...When Freeman an' me was two boys, home, poor mother'd be always singin' songs, course poor father too. An' he'd...he [Freeman] was learning a song, well I wouldn't learn one Freeman was learnin'. No I wouldn't...I didn't want to learn he at all; I had to learn one of me own. I'd have one learned and he'd have one.[49]

> Now I wasn't so quick on a song. I had...wanted to hear a song couple o' times before I could know un, see. Take me a long time to learn 'em now though.[50]

The suggestion here that songs are more difficult to learn is also of crucial relevance to the differences between the actual performance of songs and stories. As one narrator from the Anglo-Irish tradition at St. Shotts put it: "With songs it's different. ...But when ya...when you're singing a song, if you miss you *can't* make up something [to] fill in. You either have to...leave [it] out and forget about it [or] pick up the next verse. But with a story it's different. You're tellin' something an' if you miss a part of it, if you're quick enough to, put in something yourself."[51]

Such comments corroborate our recognition during fieldwork of the extraordinary flexibility in the narrative texts that allows the storytellers to exercise their ingenuity and creativity in different ways at each performance.[52] Such flexibility is much more possible in a story than in a song, since the narrator retells the basic structure of a tale, though not necessarily including all the same motifs or presenting the episodes in the same order, each telling being unique[53] and the variants differing in detail if not in more substantial ways. As Allan Oake puts it: "You never hears two stories alike. Never hears one feller tell...one story the same. Always a little different."[54] Those narrators such as the Bennetts from whom we recorded more than one telling of the same story obviously felt free to vary motifs and episodes and to omit, combine, and recombine them at will, as the variant recensions themselves demonstrate. Since the individual styles of storytellers and the contexts of performance also vary, it follows that each interpretation reflects this. For example, a teller may expand or contract the narrative according to a variety of constraints such as audience response, problems of recall, tiredness, and numerous other factors.

Individual styles of storytelling range from the measured, leisurely pace of such narrators as Ron Murray and Allan Oake through the animated delivery and colorful dialogue of the Bennetts to the extraordinarily breathless pace of Az McLean. All of the latter's four stories in this collection are a tour de force of rapid speech, and all of them incidentally are of a remarkably even length, their average duration being seven minutes, thirty-two seconds, with the longest (eight minutes, four seconds) taking only one minute, twenty-two seconds more to tell than the shortest. This contrasts markedly with the much wider variation in the duration of tales by other narrators and with the deliberately unhurried delivery of such tellers as Ron Murray, who utilizes frequent and lengthy pauses. The timing of the duration of oral narratives thus reveals important differences between individual storytelling styles, quite apart from what it can tell us, for example, about the average timespan of various narrative genres performed in different situational contexts.

While we have stressed the continuity of the oral tradition in the transmission of folk narratives in Newfoundland, it seems likely that a few of the tales in this collection were learned from printed sources. For example, comments by the narrators in Nos. 65, F5, and F10 clearly indicate a printed source, and the very close textual parallels between Nos. 141 and 142, "Mr. O'Brien from the County of Cork," together with the formulaic delivery of each version, suggest that the tale's origins may well lie in the relatively fixed form of a recitation. On the other hand, of course, formulaic delivery is part of the oral narrator's stock-in-trade. Many of the tales begin with a traditional opening formula, some of the simple "Once upon a time" variety and others more elaborate, such as those of Albert Heber Keeping of Grand Bank: "Once upon a time an' a very good time it was, not in your time, 'deed in my time _ in olden times. When quart bottles hold half a gallon an' house paper[ed] with pancakes, an' pigs run about, forks stuck in their ass _ see who wanted to buy pork." The same is true of end formulas, which range from Allan Oake's down-to-earth variants of "For I had a cup o' tea an' left for home" to the more complex rapid-fire runs such as those with which Az McLean ends his stories. Formulaic elements in the body of a tale may take the form of a rhyme, as in Nos. 65 and 66, "The Fox Riddle," for example, or may simply consist of segments or phrases, often repeated, that are uttered with a markedly strong rhythm. Such formulaic elements have parallels with the verse/song elements of the cante fable. They break up the text and give variety on one hand, and they allow the audience to recognize and respond to certain core sections of the story on the other. In this respect they resemble the refrains of ballads, especially when they include repetition. They are focal points with which the audience can identify and which the narrator may well use as markers on the cognitive map necessary for remembering and telling the tale. Like the "runs" characteristic of Irish tales, their formulaic nature, which at times leads to their being intoned almost ritually by the teller, may be one way of continuing to remember the tale. Just as the repetition of actions, quests, and other elements is governed by Olrik's "Law of Three," the formulaic passages provide both teller and audience with set pieces that mark stages in the development of the plot and are part of the underlying structure of the tale.

The various tape-recorded recensions in this collection are of three main kinds. First, there are retellings of the same story by the same tellers at intervals over an extended period of time. Second, there is the telling of the same story by various members of a family and/or the person from whom it was originally learned. Third, there are narratives that have the same or a similar plot structure and/or constituent episodes told by two or more unrelated storytellers from different communities, often from widely dispersed regions of the province. The variants of each tale under a given AT type number are presented here in order of fullness, the most extensive and elaborate recensions appearing first, followed by shorter, less fully rounded texts, minor fragments being relegated to a separate section toward the end of the collection. This allows the reader to compare the variants, utilizing the more detailed notes that accompany the first recension of each tale type. Quite apart from the fragments, we have also retained a few unfinished recensions of longer tales, not only for the purposes of comparison but also to provide further evidence of the problems of collecting full texts in the field and of the difficulties that narrators themselves have from time to time in the storytelling situation. The twenty-one manuscript texts include written versions of several AT types also recorded on tape, either by the same teller or by someone else. They therefore provide additional comparative data.

Many of the narratives, especially those of the longer Märchen type in which Jack is the protagonist, are frequently characterized by certain underlying patterns of structure and plot that by their very repetition establish in the mind of both listener and reader a certain predictability about the course of a given story. With only the most superficial analysis, for example, one becomes aware of certain recurrent basic patterns:

(beginning formula) + unpromising hero (+ meeting future bride) (+ encounter with adversary) (+ assistance (human or supernatural)) + task/quest accomplished (+ recapitulation) + dénouement/resolution (+ end formula)

It should be pointed out that this is a generalized schema and that the sequence of episodes is not fixed. While the beginning formula, when used, is obviously in initial position and the recapitulation and dénouement/resolution perforce immediately precede any end formula, the sequence of other constituent episodes is variable. Furthermore, those elements in parentheses are optional, whereas the remainder, in whatever sequence, are typical of many of the tales and might be regarded as core episodes, if not essential ones. Thus these episodes will be found in a majority of the longer stories about Jack. In some of the tales, however, and especially in the shorter ones, one or other of the core elements may be absent. For example, Nos. 99-103 lack the task/quest and its accomplishment, since in these tales Jack himself is the trickster who gulls others into behaving foolishly.

Those stories that include a lengthy recapitulation preceding or as part of the dénouement make it easier for listeners to learn the narrative themselves. Since the recapitulation briefly and effectively retells what has already been narrated, it helps to fix the tale in the listener's mind because the main events of the plot are repeated. In No. 13, for example, the recapitulation actually begins with the traditional opening formula "Well once upon a time." However, the recapitulation sometimes causes problems for the narrator, not least because it involves a series of shifts from direct to indirect speech. This in turn demands a complex shift of pronouns and tenses that some tellers have difficulty in handling. At times, too, especially if interrupted, the narrators forget whether they are telling the main body of the story or its recapitulation, a confusion all too apparent, for instance, in No. 5, one of three versions of "Peter and Minnie" recorded from Freeman Bennett.

The quest/test element frequently involves a journey or a voyage and provides a point of stability in the narrative that lends itself to the generation of a variety of journeys, voyages, and difficult or impossible tasks. Structurally it is a pivotal point in the narrative where the teller may exercise ingenuity in developing the plot in a number of different ways. It therefore provides a focus for studying variation between recensions and may well offer clues about the development of new oicotypes. It also offers opportunities for the heroes to demonstrate their skills and capabilities, and since the action in each narrative centers on them, they are the prime focus of the audience's attention. Their character and activities are essentially the vehicle through which the worldview implicit in the tales is communicated. Since the audience for the most part identifies with their character, or is at least in sympathy with it, these deeper levels of meaning in the tales are readily apprehended and absorbed by the listeners, whether consciously or unconsciously.

The characterization of Jack emphasizes certain typical traits. He is the archetypal hero of no fewer than 63 of the 150 full recensions, including a high proportion of the longer narratives of Märchen type. The heroes of many of the other stories share the essential features of his character and often differ from him only in name. He is normally presented as fairly good-natured, although offhand, truculent, and cheeky. When being maligned or treated badly he behaves quietly, resignedly, almost stoically, and appears to accept whatever misfortune comes his way. Once he is able to outwit his tormentors or those who mistreat him, however, his nature changes completely. He often becomes aggressive, decisive, and ruthless, meting out punishment and death with apparent unconcern as he seeks revenge, and especially when those who have wronged him are people with power and/or authority and who exploit that power and authority for their own ends. He thus becomes a kind of "people's champion," fearless and invulnerable, crusading against oppression. The audience may recognize in him a vicarious means of venting their own frustrations at what they perceive as social injustice. From a Marxist standpoint such tales could be viewed as a device for maintaining the status quo of social stratification within culture by offering people a safety valve through which their aggression can be expressed.

Occasionally Jack's behavior is quite unnecessarily cruel, even in pursuit of revenge, as for example in No. 96, "Jack and the Goose." If this is out of character, it may simply be a survival of the unnatural cruelty common in other international folktales that has simply become attached to him. On the other hand it could be seen as revealing the darker side of human nature—Jack representing "the common man"—unpromising, ordinary, quiet, unperturbable unless provoked—and even then slow to anger, outwardly calm, but inwardly resourceful, optimistic, having native cunning, instinctive commonsense, a sense of duty, and so on. However, he is also mischievous, capable of trickery, physically and mentally agile and dexterous, witty and alert, and capable of ruthlessness, cruelty, and disregard for others, especially when seeking revenge and redress. Above all, though, he is perceived as an achiever, as someone who always wins through against the odds—essentially the embodiment of the principle of optimism in our constant struggle for survival and progress. As Freeman Bennett puts it: "There was a feller, course his name was Jack, all their names was Jack those fellers in the stories 'cause they (were)...they was all smart men they'd always come out on top."[55] The only tale in this collection in which Jack behaves like an outright scoundrel for no apparent reason is No. 111, "Jack Lives without Eating." However, it may be that this is only part of a longer narrative in which the old man who starves to death may have done some injustice to Jack. He is certainly a very similar character to the old men and farmers who mistreat Jack in other tales, such as No. 96, "Jack and the Goose."

When Jack offers to undertake the tasks in which his two brothers have failed, he is often mocked for even suggesting that he wants to make the attempt, as, for example, in several versions of "Hard Head" (Nos. 37-41) when he asks to see the daughter's sum. This mocking attitude, which is part of the stereotyping of Jack as the unpromising hero, dramatizes the situation and hints to the audience that the form and outcome of Jack's quest are likely to be different from those undertaken unsuccessfully by others who attempted the quest before him in the tale. It also arouses the sympathy of the audience toward him as someone who is unjustly disregarded and denied due opportunities to prove himself. At the same time it raises the listener's hopes and expectations not only of his eventual success but also of the unforeseen and unexpected way he is likely to achieve it.

Although Jack, or a male protagonist of similar character, is the hero of most narratives in this collection, females play important roles in several of the tales. The most prominent of these is the fully fledged personality of Peg(g) Bearskin, the heroine of those stories that have her name in the title, Nos. 17 and 18. It is interesting to note that these two recensions were both told by a female narrator. On the other hand, a woman plays the dominant role, for example, in Nos. 45-48, "Jack and the Slave Islands," and in No. 54, "The Faithful Wife," and is seen to have considerable power and authority in Nos. 29-33, notably toward the end of the story. Perhaps even more important is the powerful role of women as advisers and enablers who direct and/or assist the heroes in overcoming the obstacles in their path. This is seen to good effect, for instance, in Nos. 7-13, 35, and 36-43, particularly in those episodes where Jack is at first totally defeated by the impossible tasks imposed upon him. At such times the female helper, usually the daughter of Jack's adversary, not only brings her ingenuity and magical powers to bear in directing or advising the hero but also rekindles his volition and willingness to tackle the task again. She is thus the prime mover in maintaining that persistence and tenacity that we admire in the hero and that enable him ultimately to succeed against the odds. In many tales this female helper is also the hero's future bride but is by no means perceived as a merely passive partner. While the fact that most of the storytellers represented here are male may account for the overall predominance of a male protagonist, the role of women in these stories, not only in their own right but also as crucial to the hero's success, must not be underestimated.

The characterization of the heroes and their interaction with both helpers and adversaries is heavily dependent on the high proportion of lively and informative dialogue that also adds color and animation to the tales. It is largely through the dialogue that the audience gets to know about the protagonists. Its immediacy and dramatic quality allow the listeners to become as it were eyewitnesses to the events as they happen. Its appeal is instant and direct since it incorporates all the vernacular conventions such as greetings, leavetakings, and countless other idioms of the local speech with which the audience is familiar and with which it identifies. It is often through dialogue and brief comments spoken to the audience aside from the narrative that the storyteller conveys much of the humor inherent in the tales. The mixing of direct and indirect speech, typical of many of the narrative styles illustrated in this collection, also has the effect of bridging from past to present time, especially in recapitulation. This again makes the events appear more immediate and gives the impression that what took place earlier in the story is in fact happening at the present moment. Indeed, the way in which time is handled by the narrators would repay further investigation. For example, they rarely employ specific time references such as *soon, directly,* or *presently.* They prefer much less precise local usage such as *by an' by,* or mark the end of a given episode with *very good, anyway, alright,* etc. The passage of time is signaled by references to having breakfast or supper, going to bed, etc., the next morning often marking a new stage in the development of the plot. Major forward movements in time, however, are often more specific, being prefaced by such phrases as *after...nine months, 'bout a...twelvemonth afterwards, in a hundred and one year.*

Iterative constructions are frequently employed to convey a sense of time passing or of distance traveled: *she cooked away and cooked away; an' he rode all day. Rode all day; walked away again; she walked an' walked, walked on again an' walked on.*[56] The passage of time is also of course implicit in a sequence of events, such as when three brothers in turn undertake a journey or quest, implying that time elapses, even though the timespans are usually vague and indeterminate. This also applies to such stories as No. 82, "The Heelstick," and to those about Black George (Nos. 144-46, F14, F15), which are given a more realistic setting. These particular narratives, while exhibiting some of the characteristics and motifs of folktales, are in many ways more characteristic of legends. This is especially true of the stories about Black George, which are obviously legends and of literary origin. However, they are told by the Bennett family along with Märchen and other long tales, and despite their greater realism and credibility they have much in common in theme with the more fantastic stories and even include the exotic and unlikely reference to a camel rather than a buffalo in one version. Although the tellers regard them as "true stories," they incorporate many of the structural features identified in the longer tales of Märchen type elsewhere in this collection. It is important to add that in Newfoundland many of the latter are told with a degree of verisimilitude more typical of the novella or the legend, in that they are deliberately set more in the real world than might be expected of international Märchen and include correspondingly fewer elements in which magic or "wonder" plays a significant part.[57] The shift from the wonderful to the realistic is emphasized by the localizing of many episodes, elements, and details, including of course the use of familiar vernacular words and idioms. However, the storytellers rarely deviate significantly from their normal speech style during performance. They make little or no attempt, for example, to mimic the voice quality of a woman when speaking the dialogue of a female character in a story.[58] Instead they content themselves with varying the speed, pitch, stress, and pause structure of the narration, for the most part within the limitations of everyday speech.[59]

The linguistic cues that signal the passage of time and the forward movement of the narrative appear to be similar in both the English- and Irish-based narrative traditions in Newfoundland. However, the Irish tradition may have penetrated more deeply into Newfoundland storytelling than may at first appear from the comparatively few Irish tales in this collection. Note, for example, that Nos. 8, 9, and 10, "The Green Man of Eggum," AT313, and Nos. 62, 63, and 64, "Jim Slowan" and "The Black Chief of Slowan," strongly suggest an Irish origin, both on linguistic grounds in their titles and through their analogues. This penetration of the Irish material into English enclaves is found, for instance, on the Great Northern Peninsula, where the historical Irish influence on the east coast of the peninsula could have been transferred to the west coast relatively easily. Evidence for this might be found, for example, in the recensions of the Irish by-form of AT611, Nos. 36-43, which were collected from communities on both coasts of this fairly narrow peninsula—and from no fewer than five different storytellers: Ambrose Reardon on the east, John Roberts, Freeman and Everett Bennett, and Az McLean on the west. It is interesting to note the use by the predominantly English narrators on the west coast of the peninsula of certain superficial Irish linguistic forms such as *begar/begobs, don't be talkin'*, etc. Furthermore, like many other narrators from predominantly West Country English-speaking communities in the province, these storytellers also knew a number of tales about the Irish comic characters Pat and Mike. It therefore appears that the West Country English and the Anglo-Irish storytelling traditions in Newfoundland have much in common, even down to the lexical level. It is mainly at the phonological level that the two traditions differ, and most of this distinction is lost in any nonphonetic transcription.

TRANSCRIPTION

In contemporary folk narrative collection and publication in the English-speaking world there exists a marked disjuncture between theory and practice in the presentation of the printed texts.[60] On the one hand there are the ideals of modern theory; on the other hand standard practice largely ignores the ideals in actual publication. Modern theory holds that the narrative should be secured in full context; the tape recorder is essential; there is no one definitive text or performance; a published text must be an exact record of the performance. On the first two points, most folklorists nowadays translate the theory into practice quite effectively. On the third point, that there is no one text or performance that represents the tale fully, the publishing practice is mixed. It is on the fourth point, that a text should be an exact record of a performance, that most collections fail. The majority of published folktales have been edited considerably, and their editors do not state clearly just how they have changed the material. Often they have edited it according to literary conventions. The very punctuation of the tale demonstrates that it is no longer truly oral.

In the past, the editors of folktales have felt it necessary or desirable to polish the texts, to a greater or lesser degree, in order to enhance their "readability" and in deference to accepted literary conventions. In recent years, however, many of the characteristics of oral style, such as repetitions, hesitations, and misencodings, have become increasingly recognized as typical of normal speech and therefore as having a role to play in narration and in the interaction between teller and audience. Despite claims to the contrary, no one has hitherto presented verbatim transcriptions of English-language folktales in such a way as will allow the detailed study and analysis of these characteristics of spoken style.[61] Indeed, for better or worse, these features have been normalized or ruthlessly excised, even by those who claim minimal editorial interference in their texts.

Although many folk narrative scholars today stress that one must use the tape recorder to record the folktale as a living entity, in practice the transcription of the tales they have recorded provides ample evidence that they have not escaped the trammels of the literary tradition. Their transcripts are often in neat, well-punctuated, literary form, with nicely turned sentences, even-lengthed paragraphs, and also a tendency to normalize and/or stereotype features of pronunciation and lexis. They may retain a few elements for "local color," though these are in many cases obviously too consistent to be truly representative of the enormous capacity for individual variation exhibited even by a single teller, let alone a group of tellers of different age and sex from widely dispersed communities.

The texts presented here are not literary reworkings but are transcribed verbatim from oral tradition.[62] As such, they include all the normal characteristics of spoken usage, such as false starts, re-encodings, unstable "sentence" structure, various pause and intonation patterns signaled in different and more complex ways than can be achieved by the standard rules of punctuation in written narrative. It is impossible to convey every nuance of the variety and complexity of such spoken usage in print, but we attempt to give as much of the authenticity and flavor of the speech here as is feasible in the circumstances. The linguistic notes provide the reader with more detailed information about both the speech and the transcription. As already noted, the tape recordings are deposited in MUNFLA, and may in due course be made available for scholarly reference.

To the reader, many of these tales will seem incomplete. They often omit details and stages of the plot in a way that would normally be unacceptable in print. Their written expression is sometimes ambiguous and lacks conventional grammatical and syntactical consistency. However, despite the absence of "correct" formal structure particularly evident in any precise transcript, it is important to note that during the performance the audience has no difficulty in following the story line, as is obvious from their response. In the storytelling situation itself none of these apparent shortcomings acts as a barrier to the understanding and enjoyment of the tales. Of course, the interaction between narrator and audience includes many reciprocal features of intonation, gesture, facial expression, and the like, which can only be hinted at even in a detailed transcript. These would require skillful recording on film or videotape—and even more skillful and complex transcription and analysis if one were to attempt a full contextual description in print. As we have participated as listeners in most of the recording situations, we attempt wherever possible to convey to the reader a sense of the physical, social, and linguistic context of the storytelling event within the limitations of the tape-recorded medium. Some account of the physical and social context is also presented briefly in the notes. Where relevant, something of the conversation preceding and following a tale is given to indicate the setting and the tone.

What we are attempting to do here is essentially to extend to English-language texts some of the conventions of verbatim transcription, analysis, and commentary employed so successfully by the translators and editors of tales collected from the oral tradition of many native peoples.[63] In those cultures, as until recently in Newfoundland, the telling of such stories is primarily an adult pursuit—part of a rich oral vernacular tradition that has a rhetoric and vigor of its own, untrammeled by the often stultified conventions of literary form and style. While recognizing that it is impossible to transfer more than a fraction of this multi-faceted oral performance to the unidimensional medium of print, our principal aim in this collection is to explore some of the possibilities of such transference. Not even film can capture the pure essence and the magic of the storytelling event as experienced by the participants, but we believe it is possible, even through the imperfect medium of print, to present a much fuller and more accurate record of the event than has been attempted hitherto for folktales in the English-speaking tradition. This at least provides a starting point for more objective and rigorous analysis in the future, which will in due course no doubt reveal much about the form, structure, and conventions of oral narrative style and provide a key to its universal appeal.

Those stories in this collection that are transcribed from tape reproduce as closely as possible the full text of each oral narrative as recorded in the field, apart from certain concessions inevitable in transferring the spoken word to the printed page. The transcriptions attempt to put in writing the actual sounds and some intonational and contextual features of what is essentially a dramatic oral performance, in much the same way as an ethnomusicologist transcribes a folksong. This facilitates a more detailed and authentic representation not only of the storytellers' speech but also of many aspects of oral narrative style. The transcriptions employ a system of conventions that permits the original speech to be transferred verbatim to the printed page but that is not so complex as to hamper accessibility. By means of this system it is possible not only to provide an accurate rendering of the language itself, including many features of pronunciation, vocabulary, grammar, and syntax, but also to convey some idea of the narrative structure, as indicated by pauses, emphases, and other linguistic and rhetorical means.

This fuller account of the oral and linguistic features of the storytelling event is presented within a framework of contextual features—some deduced from the evidence on tape and some drawn from fieldwork notes and shared experiences of the recording situation. In addition we have been able in some instances to obtain further interpretative and contextual information from other fieldworkers in those cases where we ourselves did not record the tapes.

One immediate effect of this more detailed system of transcription is that it reveals numerous linguistic forms that invite further attention. Since the oral medium of transmission depends primarily on language, we have included an extensive linguistic commentary to complement the notes on the context and international parallels of the tales. This again is something of a departure from previous studies and draws attention not only to the central importance of language in storytelling but also to those forms that characterize the unique amalgam of Newfoundland speech. As lexical items from these tales were excerpted for the *Dictionary of Newfoundland English,* the linguistic notes in the present volumes complement and extend the record of local usage available in that work. At the same time they demonstrate how the creativity and versatility of Newfoundland storytellers have adapted these older international tales to the local culture, environment, and idiom.

Since these are primarily oral texts, recorded during performance in a semi-moribund tradition, it follows that while some of them read quite well and are reasonably fluent, others are disjointed and/or hesitant, as tellers strive to recall them, often after not having told them for many years. We must therefore re-emphasize that we are not presenting polished and edited texts here, but rather the most accurate representation possible of a declining tradition. This in itself presents problems enough, but it is also necessary to confront the added difficulties of transcribing from tape—a process by no means as easy or straightforward as some scholars might suggest. On the positive side, however, the Newfoundland tellers are so skilled that they are able to hold the attention of their audience even if they make mistakes or omit or vary the sequence of episodes. They concentrate their efforts on holding the audience's attention, come what may, and seem less concerned than scholars might think about telling a story consistently, fully, or accurately to conform with some preconceived "ideal" or "complete" version. They themselves are usually aware that they have made a mistake or omission and occasionally even apologize for so doing. However, the audience is equally responsive whether or not such errors or omissions occur. The listeners do not usually question the minutiæ of motivation or plot but are well content simply to listen to the performance. Minor hiatuses cause little difficulty to the audience, whose attention is maintained by the overall flow of the narrative. Any brief, temporary difficulties are soon forgotten. Even the coughs, hesitations, and other hindrances to reading the transcriptions are often significant in that they involuntarily delay the progress of the spoken narrative and are sometimes used deliberately by the teller as a means of creating suspense, humor, and expectation.[64] Someone reading the story for its own sake should note these features in passing, since they are part of the performance and its context but extraneous to the narrative. Like the original audience, the reader will soon become accustomed to relegating them to an inconsequential position when following the story line itself. In view of this, perhaps folklorists are wrong to insist on the production of a fully rounded and totally fluent text, since what is being told is on each occasion a unique recension influenced by audience, physical context, mood, and many other factors, some of which are evident from our transcriptions and notes, but which are conspicuously absent from most folktale collections from the English-speaking world, though available in some of those from exotic cultures where the interpretation of linguistic and contextual features is, for whatever reason, felt to be more necessary.

The notes on transcription following the tales discuss the kinds of problems faced by all transcribers of archival material, especially that which is recorded in fieldwork conditions that are far from ideal. Transcription is therefore analogous to the deciphering of ancient documents from which the most complete and definitive text possible is reconstructed, with the process of reconstruction discussed so that further interpretation, analysis, and refinement may be possible at a later stage. The notes on transcription also allow us to comment on the tellers' individual use of language, the idiosyncrasies of their delivery and style, and the most likely interpretation of cruces in the narration that are inevitable when the transcriber is listening only to a tape recording rather than participating fully in the actual storytelling context, where there would be no difficulty in following the gist of the narrative without any need to take account of the minutiæ of enunciation and the interpretation of sounds, words, grammar, and syntax essential to the transcription process.

No matter how narrow and careful the transcription, the transcriber is often forced to make decisions in minor matters such as whether a word lacks a given sound or syllable or whether it includes an additional sound or syllable, because by the very nature of tape-recorded data it is not possible by normal auditory means to be 100 percent accurate in representing speech. We aim here to be as accurate as possible within these limits, allowing ourselves repetition of a taped excerpt until a decision can be made about its form, but not having recourse to other mechanical means of analysis such as loops, sound-stretchers, and segmentators.

Although the tape recording of folktale texts gives us actual speech in partial context, indicating by changes of intonation some of the dramatic features of the storytelling situation, the tape recorder proves to be a mixed blessing. One of the greatest present-day illusions in fieldwork is that the tape recorder effectively secures the exact words of a speaker, which can then be easily transcribed and presented in written form. Our transcriptions reveal a plethora of misencodings and indistinguishable speech from storytellers whose narratives are not only dramatic and entertaining but also quite understandable to the audience in context. When the voice drops to make some ironical or other "aside," the listeners get the point, but the tape recorder may give only a muffled reproduction of vowels and consonants, whose meaning can often only be guessed at. The problem is compounded by the fact that the speakers are using their local dialect. Older speakers may not enunciate words clearly or may turn aside to address another member of the audience (and so lose clarity in the recording) or otherwise, as they put it, "swallow their words."

The very length of these narratives causes troughs of poorly expressed stretches of speech as the tellers try to remember details, adapt to their audience, or simply become tired. Our experience in transcribing such performances suggests, as noted earlier, that the elegantly phrased stories presented by some scholars as exact transcriptions have been edited, consciously or unconsciously, into a more intelligible and literary form, whether this is done in the understandable attempt to make the story clear to a reading audience, or whether the editors feel confident that they know what the speaker intended to say but in fact did not. Such an approach produces not a literal translation of the actual tape recording but a version that has passed through several stages of "improvement."

It may well be true, of course, that tellers whose stories appear in other collections were more "in practice" than many of those we have recorded in Newfoundland and that their tales may have been told more fluently and with fewer misencodings, omissions, and inconsistencies than are found in our material. If this is the case, it may be that comparatively little editing was necessary and the tales could be printed more or less as they were. However, if they were taken down from dictation, the editor would of course edit and normalize them to some extent when writing them down in the first place.

Our approach represents a compromise between the supposed "ideal" situation in which storytelling events are filmed and recorded in an "objective" and comprehensive fashion and the situation formerly common in the publication of folktales in which the editors cleaned up versions of narratives taken down from dictation (itself very artificial) or reconstructed versions from plot outlines noted down during a performance. In fact the "ideal" or optimal recording situation is impossible to achieve, and even reasonable approximations to it would be virtually impossible to reduce easily to accessible printed form. Tape recorders, for all their virtues, must be recognized as no more than a unidimensional means of recording speech, the context being merely hinted at and guessed only by rare inferences. Furthermore, while film or video recordings might compensate to some extent for the lack of visual and contextual features, they still need interpretation by transcribers skilled in phonetics, lipreading, paralinguistics, kinesics, and proxemics and in providing a full choreography of the storytelling event. In such an "ideal" situation the attitudes and responses of every listener would also require investigation and analysis, along with the teller's own taxonomy and perceptions of the tale and the storytelling context. Even if such information was forthcoming, it would be difficult, if not impossible, to analyze the material objectively, including, as it might, the reflections of numerous local, social, and individual patterns of behavior, both overt and covert, within the reference group.

In transcribing the Newfoundland audiotapes, it proved impossible to do more than hint at the many nuances of vocal expressiveness used by tellers, especially in the dialogue. For example, the hero Jack's blatant, cocksure manner when he denies facts that the audience already knows and that his opponent also has correctly guessed, is clearly indicated during performance by subtle changes in the voice quality, speed of delivery, pitch levels, stresses, and other linguistic and stylistic devices. These can be apprehended only by the ear (and incidentally the ear of someone familiar with the dialect) and cannot be represented in a written recension. The transcriptions presented here are analogous to a musical score, the flesh being put on the bones only in an actual performance, where the interaction between teller and audience essential for this verbal art form generates the combination of factors that give it its unique flavor and power.

Most who have used a tape recorder to collect narratives employ it as a convenient secretarial adjunct to the editing process. They allow it to function primarily like a shorthand notebook in providing the basic text for editing, in a similar way to its use by some music transcribers, who tend to normalize the recorded tunes and to create a basic form that approximates or reflects their idea of "what the singer is trying to sing." These transcribers minimize and often totally ignore any detailed ornamentation of a tune, which tends to vary not only from verse to verse but also from one line to another. Thus they obscure or destroy the individuality and creativity of the actual performance. In other words, like so many transcribers of folk narrative, they have simplified and regularized the heterogeneous and complex nature of the original, providing what is essentially an "emic" rather than an "etic" transcription. This is unquestionably much more accessible to a general readership but lacks the essential features of the dynamic context of performance.

We recognize that such an edited text is easier to read. But if folklorists insist that one should take down the text exactly and indicate features of performance and context as fully as possible, one must attempt to transcribe texts as they were actually spoken, in the same way that the ethnomusicologist may seek to represent exactly what notes the singer sang as distinct from an idealized or standardized form. In short, in our texts we strive for the maximum verisimilitude within certain obvious limits. For example, it is impossible to indicate with any precision the actual sounds a speaker utters merely by using normal orthography. However, since comparatively few people read phonetics, it is necessary to make this compromise, among others, simply to make the texts as accessible as possible. Our augmented orthographical transcription demands few of the considerable skills required in reading more complex transcripts such as those that include phonetics and/or a more elaborate display of linguistic, paralinguistic, and contextual features.

Similar problems obviously also occur in the representation of typical features of a given regional dialect. In Newfoundland speech, for instance, as in many dialects of English, the initial aspirate, /h/, is frequently dropped, and words beginning with a vowel, especially under strong sentence stress, may have an initial aspirate added. For reading purposes, however, it proves impracticable to omit all the initial aspirates dropped by a given speaker, especially as these omissions may be inconsistent. To transcribe such omissions in normal orthography makes for a great deal of confusion and potential ambiguity, not least in words that in consequence fall together in pronunciation and become homophones. To take another example, in words ending in -ing, to indicate the substitution of final /n/ for -ng, /ŋ/ by adding an apostrophe would be to pepper the text with an unacceptable number of punctuation marks.

Despite these and other necessary compromises in our editing procedure, we have constantly borne in mind our intention to present a text as close to the original speech as is both possible and practicable, always erring on the side of accurate representation rather than on the kind of editing which, in both obvious and more subtle ways, changes the original text radically in its insistence on presenting a text more acceptable from the literary viewpoint.

We have retained the original lexis, grammar, and syntax because these are essential to the dialect, particularly since they also reflect the regional character of the tales. As we have pointed out, we have endeavored to represent the actual flow of the speech, especially the pauses that are so important in the interaction between speaker and audience. The differences between the styles of two narrators are readily apparent by observing the flow of speech and the patterns of pauses used by each.

Orthographical transcription is inevitably impressionistic and involves constant exercise of judgment, which is bound to be arbitrary in many cases. Phonetic transcription also involves similar empirical decisions and impressionistic interpretations, especially in the running text and more particularly in rapid (allegro) speech.[65] A truly comprehensive transcription of the actual speech would include detailed symbolization of such intonation features as pitch, stress, juncture, and terminals. Again, this proves impracticable in presenting a text to a general academic readership. However, we have indicated in boldface type those words and phrases particularly emphasized by the speaker, confining this to those instances when the teller's voice gives particular prominence to a word or phrase within the intonation pattern of an utterance. When a tale is being performed, the listener is constantly aware of these subtle features of oral style that signal important emphases and contrasts in the narrative and give valuable clues about the progress of the plot, the teller's attitude toward the characters and events and interpretation of the material, which in turn condition or at least influence the reactions and attitudes of the audience. The reader, on the other hand, lacks the benefit of most of these cues. Other important means of signaling emphasis to an audience—including, for example, sudden changes in pitch and voice quality and a shift into rapid speech in those stretches of dialogue that demand particular animation—cannot be represented in normal orthography, except by verbal comment and in incidental fashion, in texts of this kind. We have kept such indications to a minimum, using them only occasionally to point out especially striking features of the narrator's style.

Since the language of folktales is essentially simple and the lexical range is limited, the tellers are proportionally restricted in the means at their disposal to provide emphases and contrasts and otherwise exploit the rhetorical devices in their repertory. Instead they must rely for much of their impact on subtle variations of intonation, pause, rhythm, and tone of voice. Such features are therefore of crucial importance in the interaction between teller and audience. To some extent they are predictable because of the basic simplicity of the narrative structure, with its usually straightforward syntax, simple vocabulary, and transparent form. Its very simplicity and directness make for a certain consistency and predictability. There is no hidden, covert, or obfuscating use of language. Its stereotyping gives both hearer and reader useful clues about the ways in which it is to be told, read, heard, and interpreted. The only problems in interpreting the language arise from dialectal usage or from misencodings and similar inaccuracies of narration and articulation. What looks fussy or difficult in setting these down on the printed page causes much less difficulty in the actual context of oral narration because these intonational and paralinguistic features help to convey the *intended* meaning irrespective of dialectal forms, false starts, misencodings, and the like.

Technically, it would be feasible to present a translation of the text with some of these linguistic, rhetorical, and contextual features mapped or otherwise symbolized. However, while the result might be useful for analysis, it would be as difficult to read as specialized musical notation. One cannot sing a song even from the most complex transcription exactly as it was sung by the traditional performer. Similarly, one could not fully replicate the original performances of the stories presented in these volumes, even if the transcriptions were more detailed and elaborate. The texts merely reproduce orthographically the full sequence of sounds spoken at a given storytelling event, together with a basic interpretative apparatus. In attempting this degree of verisimilitude and commenting on the event itself, it is inevitable that the texts are of a different order from even the simplest of "normal" writing and are not referable to the rules of written usage.

Transcription is such a difficult and uncertain art that each transcriber inevitably produces a different text insofar as minor details and interpretations are concerned. One particular difficulty arises from the fact that the transcribers naturally want to make sense out of obscure or unclear speech and in so doing run the risk of creating even more problems. Indeed they may revise their transcriptions after a further hearing under different conditions and hear or not hear things they thought they had heard during the original process of transcribing. In the texts presented here, however, there is some measure of consistency. Virtually all the original orthographical transcriptions were made by professional typists, all of whom were Newfoundlanders familiar with local usage. Helpful though these transcriptions were, however, they were not intended to offer more than a reasonable approximation of the exact words used. It was therefore necessary to return to first principles in preparing detailed transcriptions of the texts. The original transcripts were submitted to many hours of scrutiny by one of the editors while he listened to all the tapes. Then difficult points of transcription were repeatedly listened to and scrutinized by both editors before the final editing, during which the transcripts were rechecked and on occasion the tapes listened to yet again, to resolve specific transcriptional and/or textual problems. Even so, we are aware that the transcribing process is one of continual emendation and refinement that is rarely, if ever, final or fully satisfactory. The transcriptions presented here might well benefit from further polishing and elucidation.

We began transcribing with only an outline system of typographical conventions.[66] These were modified and developed as time went on, in light of the variations and problems encountered in the texts themselves. To a considerable extent they were therefore generated from within the structure of the tales as perceived during the transcription process. In this process of trial and error, we bore in mind the difficulties a reader might have in following a text that by its very nature is unlike conventional literary prose. In summary, we aim to present full and accurate renderings of tape-recorded narratives, using a specialized format, normal orthography, a somewhat modified punctuation system, and certain other typographical conventions. At the same time we are concerned to make the texts as accessible as possible and have therefore kept the editorial apparatus to a minimum so that the stories may be read without undue interruption. In opting for as little editorial intervention as is consonant with our aims we have nevertheless found it necessary on occasion to explain unfamiliar words, to resolve ambiguities, and to supply words and phrases essential for understanding the story. Such interventions have been restricted to those felt to be essential, and each is clearly identified by appropriate typographical symbols. We have consciously minimized editorial interpolations and have consigned the bulk of the commentary to the accompanying notes. Recognizing the impossibility of presenting every facet of the variety and complexity of spoken usage in print, we attempt merely to convey the flavor of the speech, allowing the linguistic notes to provide a more detailed reference source for exploring the nuances of the vernacular language.

In many of the transcripts short segments of conversation before and after a given tale provide important information about the narrative and are essential to the storytelling context. The brief editorial comments, glosses, elucidations, indications of the speaker's vocal quality, tone, gestures, and the immediate physical context pertaining directly to the narrator, along with other minor interpolations incorporated into the text, are enclosed in brackets. Brackets are also used to identify the speech of the interviewer and other speakers present. Additionally, they are used to mark asides spoken by the narrator to the audience by way of explication. New paragraphs are initiated for significant forward movement of the narrative and also for the successive utterances of each character in the dialogue. Comments on the contextual background and other brief general elucidations are transferred to marginal notes (within slant lines), as are misencoded words (glossed within slant lines in the text) and more than three repetitions of a given word (often due to hesitation on the part of the speaker). Material transferred to marginal notes is signaled by appropriate symbols in the text. The apostrophe is used in the standard way to indicate the possessive case or to mark the omission of sounds, except in such contractions as *ant* or *aint* and in the realization of final /n/ as /ŋ/ in words ending in *-ing,* which is so frequent that we felt the apostrophe to be redundant.

In attempting to indicate something of the form and structure of the narrative, as reflected in the pauses, rhythms, and flow of the speaker's utterance, which has its own pace, cadences, focal points, contrastive features, rhetoric, local color, and "punctuation," we have adapted some of the standard conventions of punctuation and added a few other symbols and devices:

† Denotes a title supplied by the editors.

[ ] Brackets have four functions:
    (a) enclosing brief editorial interventions;
    (b) denoting reconstructions of muffled or semi-inaudible forms, the reconstructions being preceded by a question mark if tentative;
    (c) identifying speech by the interviewer or others present;
    (d) marking the narrator's asides to the audience.

( ) Parentheses denote tentative transcriptions of unclear speech, conjectural transcriptions being preceded by a question mark.

/ / Slant lines mark the substitution of corrected forms for misencodings, conjectural substitutions being preceded by a question mark; orthographical representations of misencoded forms are transferred within slant lines to the margin. Slant lines also enclose broad phonetic transcriptions in the linguistic notes.

.   The period usually denotes a pause following a falling intonation at the end of an utterance or following a distinctive rising tone requesting agreement. Occasionally the period is used, like the comma, to signify a sense break before the transition to a new idea, but only if a brief pause is detectable (otherwise a comma is used). The use of the period is often justified by an intonational shift following a minimal pause. When the speech flows on without a pause, the period is not used.

,   The comma is used to separate segments of speech for syntactical clarity and to resolve possible ambiguity where phrases are run together in speech without a pause and the sense of the utterance may be unclear when transferred to print; it does not indicate a pause. Its positioning is often suggested by a shift of vocal tone demarcating a pivotal change from "end of thought" to "transition to new idea."

_   A single underlining symbol, preceded and followed by a space, denotes a brief pause, often for breath.

...   Three ellipsis points represent a brief pause preceding correction or re-encoding of a false start, usually involving hesitation. They are also used in conjunction with an asterisk to indicate more than three repetitions of a form, the total number of repetitions being noted in the margin. Such repetitions again usually involve hesitation.

....   Four ellipsis points indicate when a speaker is interrupted and is unable to complete an utterance.

--   The double hyphen signals a longer pause, usually for dramatic effect, aimed at involving the audience more closely in the action, often at a suspenseful point when the narrative takes a significant step forward.

***   Three asterisks denote that the preceding or following segment of the utterance was not recorded.

*   One asterisk refers to marginal notes concerning an item in a given line of text.

+   A plus sign refers to marginal notes concerning a second item in a given line of text.

BOLDFACE   Denotes strong emphasis.

It should be emphasized that we attempt to transcribe and set down in printed form all the sounds we can actually hear, and only these sounds. In the storytelling situation itself, the speaker may say, for example, "He was able man," and, whereas the listener may well supply the indefinite article before *able,* the transcript simply records what was said and no more than that. Our main concession to helping the reader to understand some of the more difficult sections of the oral text has been to use parentheses to elucidate the probable sound(s) actually spoken and brackets to bridge minor linguistic gaps in the narrative or to resolve possible ambiguities.

Similarly, when the speaker omits a grammatical marker, such as [d] in *they('d) walk,* the listener normally expects to hear a requisite set of grammatical forms, for maximum communicability, and therefore mentally supplies the missing elements. It requires very careful listening on the part of the transcriber to ascertain whether the grammatical markers are actually spoken or not. The situation is complicated by the fact that a speaker may say neither *they walk* nor *they'd walk* for *they would walk,* for instance, but an intermediate form where some kind of closure or other phonetic element is articulated, giving the impression of, say, a [d]-marker, but not actually articulating one in a form transcribable by articulatory means. The impression that such a sound has been articulated may also be given by a pause feature or the lengthening of the final sound of the preceding word. This shadowy area of transcription involves crucial decisions about *actual* versus *impressionistic* transcribing. Compromises are inevitable, but here we have erred on the side of articulatory evidence and tried to avoid supplying intuitive or impressionistic emendations or reconstructions of putative speech forms. We have not attempted to show the elongation of words or syllables that has diverse functions in spoken usage, including emphasis and expressing surprise.[67]

While it is impossible to give an accurate representation of speech sounds without phonetic transcription, we have retained certain typical features of Newfoundland usage and pronunciation wherever these occur on the tapes. These include informal syncopated forms such as *'tis(n't), 'twas(n't), aint, we'll, wouldn't,* etc.; aphesis, e.g., *'wards* (towards), *'fore* (before), *'nother* (another), *'tween* (between) etc.; the realization of /ŋ/ as /n/ in final position in words ending in -*ing;* the omission of final -*d* in *and* and *old,* final -*th* in *with,* final -*f* in *of;* the elision of the vowel in *the* before a following vowel, e.g., *th' other;* and the use of the close front vowel in *me, meself* (my, myself) in unstressed position. It should be noted, however, that these forms have not been normalized throughout the transcription. Variant forms, such as those that retain final /ŋ/, /d/, etc., are transcribed in full to indicate that typical features are not constant but may differ in certain linguistic contexts and also from speaker to speaker. Similarly, such variant pronunciations as in *fellow, fella, feller* are differentiated in the text.

It is only comparatively rarely, however, that such phonological features can be translated easily and consistently into print. We have not extended these special modes of spelling to other dialectal pronunciations that, though characteristic of much Newfoundland speech, are less consistent in their operation. A case in point is the typical absence of the initial aspirate, /h/, referred to above and also its prefixing to words beginning with a vowel, often under strong sentence stress. Again, the final /r/ sound that normally follows and colors many vowels in the primarily rhotic (i.e., maintaining historically earlier -*r* finally in syllables) dialectal speech of Newfoundlanders is not always present and so is difficult to represent consistently in print. As with the aspirate, this would cause confusion and ambiguity in the text and problems of interpretation for the reader. Similar problems occur with the sporadic appearance of intrusive consonants and offglides such as the final [t] in *clifft* (cliff). Another kind of difficulty becomes apparent when one attempts to indicate pronunciation in any detail in normal orthography, namely the danger of creating confusion by even the simplest of spelling changes. A good example is found in our early efforts to indicate the characteristic pronunciation of *by* as *be* in unstressed positions. While such a minor change presents few problems in conveying the pronunciation of unstressed *my* as *me,* the potential for confusing the prepositional form *be* (by) with the verb that has the same spelling forced us to abandon the attempt. Nevertheless, such spelling changes as we have been able to make contribute to an overall impression of the dialectal speech. In addition, many dialect words and phrases, with interpretative glosses, are included in the texts, their pronunciation being indicated in orthographical form. Readers who wish to learn more about the pronunciation of words and phrases will find numerous phonetic transcriptions in the linguistic notes. For greater accessibility, these transcriptions, which use the alphabet of the International Phonetic Association,[68] are "broad" rather than "narrow." Similar transcriptions of many Newfoundland words and expressions whose pronunciation is unusual may also be found in the *Dictionary of Newfoundland English.*

In order to illustrate possible modes of transcription we present below three contrasting versions of tale No. 140, "The King Loses Patience" (AT2301A). The first is edited in a conventional way but with minimal alteration of the original. The second exemplifies our own transcriptional practice in this collection. The third combines our system of representing the original with an interlineated phonetic transcription.

140. The King Loses Patience[†]
Conventionally edited version

There was a king one time who had a daughter, and whoever could tell him a story without an end was to marry his daughter and have half of the kingdom. And whoever tried but could not tell him such a story would have their heads cut off.

There were several fellows who tried it; they thought they would go and get the king's daughter. And one fellow said he would try it, so he started out and he told his story.

And he said, "There was a certain rich man who had a lot of corn growing, and he built a big barn to put this in. And the locusts came and began carrying away the corn."

And the old king told him that was enough now about the locusts and that he should tell him something else.

Now the locusts only carry away one grain of corn at a time, you see, and when the old fellow wanted to get clear of the locusts to get the rest of the story, the man who was telling it says, "Hold on, sir. I am not finished yet. They have only got just a little bit carried out of one corner of the barn, and when the locusts get all the corn carried away out of the barn that will be the end of the story."

And the old king got tired of listening to the story.

"Ah!" he said. "That will do. That is enough about the locusts. Take my daughter and go away with her."

140. The King Loses Patience[†]
Verbatim edited version

A king one time _ I'll tell you [th]is one now. Er...a king one time _ he got a...a daughter. An'...whoever _ 'd tell un a story without a end _ was to marry his daughter _ an' have a half o' the kingdom. An' whoever couldn't tell un _ they had...they had their head cut off. Ah there was several fellers tried it _ thought they'd go an' get the king's daughter.

An' one feller _ said HE'D try it. /So/ _ he started out _ an' he made his story. An' _ he said there was a...a certain man _ rich man _ he had a lot o' grain growin _ corn _ growin. An' he built a big barn (to) put this in. An'...the locusts come _ an' begun carryin away (o') the corn. An' _ th' ol' king asked un, told un that was enough now about the locusts _ tell un something else. Now the...the...uh...the locusts only carry away one grain o' corn at a time _ ya see? An' when...the ol' feller wanted to...gets clear o' the locusts now (to) get the rest o' the story, "Hold on sir _ " he says "I'm not finished yet. They've only got.../just/ a...little bit carried out o' the one corner (o') the barn. An' when the...the locustes gets all the corn _ called out...carried away out o' the barn _ that'll be the end o' the story." -- An' th' ol' man got tired listenin to her [i.e., *the story*] "Ah!" he said "That'll do _ that's enough about the locusts, take me daughter an' go on with her." [*laughs*]

/fo/

/bit....bis/

140. The King Loses Patience[†]
Interlineated verbatim and phonetically transcribed version[69]

A king one time _ I'll tell you [th]is one now. Er...a king one time

²ə kıŋ wʌn taim⁴↗²ail tɛl jə ıs   wʌn næu³↗² əɪ ə kıŋ wʌn taim³↗

_ he got a...a daughter. An'...whoever _ 'd tell un a story without a end

²ii gʌt əʔə 'dɒ·ʈəɪ↘²ɐn ou'ıvəɪ²⁺ əd tɛl n̩ ə 'stoən wi'ðæut ə hɛən²⁺

_ was to marry his daughter _ an' have a half o' the kingdom. An' whoever

² wɐz 'mɑri iz 'dɒ·ʈəɪ³↗ æn æv ə ræʃ ə ðə ³kıŋdəm¹↘²æn ɷ'ıvəɪ

couldn't tell un _ they had...they had their head cut off. Ah there was

³kɷdn̩ tɛl n̩³↗²ðɛi æd ðɛi æd ðəɪ ³i̥d kɷ̈ʈ ɒ·f¹↘² ɑ ðə wəz

several fellers tried it ‿ thought they'd go an' get the king's daughter.

'sɪvrəl 'fɛlɑɹz treid it? tɒ·t? ðëid gou ən get? d̬ə kɪŋz 'dʊ·t̬əɹ³↗

An' one feller ‿ said HE'D try it. /So/ ‿ he started out ‿ an' he made   /fo/

²an wɒn 'fɛlɑɹ²→²sɛd ɪ·d trɑi ɪt?¹↘²fo·ɯ²→² ɪɪ 'stæɹt̬əd æ̈ɑt?²→²ŋ hɪ· meid

his story. An' ‿ he said there was a…a certain man ‿ rich man ‿ he had

izs 'stθɔɔən³↗²an ²→²ɪɪ sɛd ðɔ̈ə wəz ə? ʔə 'sə·ɹt?ŋ mæ°n³→³ntʃ mæ°n²→²ɪ̈· æd

a lot o' grain growin ‿ corn ‿ growin. An' he built a big barn (to) put this

ə lɒt̬ ə grein 'groɯən¹↘²kɒ·ɹn²→²groɯən¹↘²ən ɪ bɪld ə bɪg bɑ·ɹn pʌt? ðɔis

in. An'…the locusts come ‿ an' begun carryin' away (o') the corn. An' ‿

i·ɪɪ¹↘ʔɛɪɪ·³→²də 'loɯkʌs kʌm² ²ən bɪ'gʌn 'kɒɹən ə'wei °dɔ̈° kɒɹn³↗²æn?²→

th' ol' king asked un, told un that was enough now about the locusts

²ð° oɯl kɪŋ æ·st? ŋ toɯld ŋ̩ næt? wəz i'nʌf naɯ ə'buɑt? də 'lo·kʌs·⁴↗

‿ tell un something else. Now the…the…uh…the locusts only carry away

²tɛl ŋ̩ 'sʌmθɪŋ ëls¹↘² naɯ ðə? ðə? ə? ðɔ̈ə 'lo·kʌs 'ounli 'kɛɹ ə'wɛɪ

one grain o' corn at a time ‿ ya see? An' when…the ol' feller

wʌn græn ə kɒɹn ət̬ ə ³tɒim¹↘²ju sɪɪ³↗²æn wën·? ʔoul 'fɛlɑɹ

wanted to…gets clear o' the locusts now (to) get the rest o' the story, "Hold

'wɒnəd t̬ə?²→²gets klɪɑɹ ə ðɔ̈ə 'loɯkʌs næu dget? d° rɛst ə ðə 'stoəɹt²→²oɯld on sir _ " he says "I'm not finished yet. They've only got.../just/ a...little bit   /bit...bis/

³ɒ·n sɑɹ ι s̞ĕz ʁim nɒt? 'finiʃ j̞ĕt¹\²ðɛiv 'ounι gŏt? bι? bιs ə? 'tl̞ιt̞l bιt

carried out o' the one corner (o') the barn. An' when the...the locustes

'kɒrid əu̞t ə d̂ðə wɒn 'kaɔɹnəɹ d̂ðə baɔɹn¹\²æn wĕ·n də? kjə? də 'loukŏstəs

gets all the corn _ called out...carried away out o' the barn _ that'll be

gets ɒ·əl ðə kaɔɹn²⁻²kɒ·ld ³æ̈u? 'kæ̈rid ə'wɛi æu̞t ə d̂ðə ba·ən²⁻²ð̞æt̞l bii

the end o' the story." -- An' th' ol' man got tired listenin to her [i.e., *the*

ð̞ι ɛnd ə d̂ð̞ə 'stoən¹\ æn d̂ðoul mæn gɒt? 'taiəɹd 'lιsnin tʊ ɔɹ²⁻

story] "Ah!" he said "That'll do _ that's enough about the locusts, take me

²ɑː ι s̞ĕd ³d̂ðætl dʉu¹\²ðæts ι'nʌf ə'bʁu? də 'loukŏs tɛik? mι

daughter and go on with her." [*laughs*]

'dɒ·təɹ ən gou ɒ·n wið əɹ¹\

It is readily apparent from a comparison of these three texts that the more detailed the transcript the more misencodings, repetitions, and hesitations are represented. While these may be a hindrance to readers who may respond by identifying what they see as deficiencies in the storytelling style, such responses seriously misjudge the very nature of the oral tradition. In the actual storytelling context, as we have said, the misencodings are scarcely noticed by the audience, the repetitions often serve as punctuating devices, and the hesitations have the advantage not only of giving the tellers time to collect their thoughts but also of allowing the audience to anticipate the clarification that follows. What is more, it will be noticed from the transcripts of many of the tales that, as with any other speaker, the interviewers' speech is equally hesitant and fragmented, with similar misencodings, false starts, and the like.

Reading the hesitations and misencodings inevitable in oral storytelling, transcribed here more fully than in most published collections, tends to mislead because these surface manifestations may obscure the deep structure of the tale. Such superficial details may at first obtrude too much on the reader's attention, and therefore detract from the importance of the storyteller's personality and individuality as they operate in the context of telling. They also tend to draw attention away from those fundamental dramatic features of the teller's style, which, like the content, are paramount. The audience present at a storytelling event has the incomparable advantage of being able to follow and respond to all or most of the largely untranscribable linguistic and paralinguistic features that are an essential part of the interaction between teller and audience and for which there is no substitute, especially in print. In reading verbatim transcriptions of speech we must therefore adopt a completely different approach, one that not only puts aside much of our habitual response to printed texts and especially to works of literature, but that also accepts the transliteration of the oral tradition and its context as valid and important in its own right. The Newfoundland storytellers themselves emphasize that it is the manner of telling, or as they put it, "the way he's told," that makes a story successful, in the same way as the singers we interviewed emphasized the importance of both the clarity of words and the ornamentation of the tune in a song's performance.

LANGUAGE

At this point it may be helpful to present an overview of some of the typical features of the storytellers' language. The following discussion takes up some general points and then considers the speech of the narrators at each of the accustomed levels of linguistic analysis: phonology, lexis, grammar, and syntax. This is perhaps the first attempt to provide a summary of the range of such features to be found in Newfoundland speech, based on a specific and substantial corpus of narrative material drawn from many different parts of the province. The summary gathers together some of the essential information presented in the linguistic notes to individual tales throughout the collection. The notes themselves are structured consecutively in the same way as the summary below, so that in a given section of the notes the reader may identify the features outlined in this summary and see how they are illustrated in a particular tale. The reader is therefore advised to consult the notes for exemplifications of the points mentioned here and for more detailed comments on the language, at each level, from phonology to syntax.

As noted earlier, the language of the tales is essentially simple and straightforward. This is particularly true of the vocabulary and much of the sentence construction. It has been necessary to provide glosses for remarkably few words and phrases. Most of these are dialectal and/or archaic. For the outsider first listening to a Newfoundland storyteller, however, there are many difficulties in interpreting the speech, mainly due to unfamiliar phonological and grammatical features of local dialect. The speed of delivery of the more animated of the narrators raises problems of interpretation, not least in the blurring of word boundaries and the fragmentation of syntax inevitable in allegro speech. Since our transcriptions closely reflect the inconsistencies of actual spoken utterance, they not only reveal to the reader something of the mechanics of speech production but also provide a substantial body of data for the linguist to study in greater depth. Even so, the reader may have difficulty in interpreting unfamiliar words such as *quintal* ['kænt] (a measure of fish, usually 112 lbs.), the spelling of which offers no immediate clue to pronunciation.

The monosyllabic nature of much of the narrative is striking, the proportion of monosyllables on occasion being as high as twenty words in an utterance of twenty-two or twenty-three words. As a corollary to this, many of the longer words such as *abed, adown, afore, bestraddled, bluejackets, bosom, consent(ed), damsel, forsaken, guineas, merchandise, pacified, passion* (fury), *perished* (died), *recommend, satisfied* (agreeable), *twelvemonth, yonder* and such monosyllables as *ails, aught, breeze* (strong wind, gale), *eyed* (observed, looked at), *poll* (head), *scoff* (mock), *slay, steed, strand* (shore, country, etc.), *sway* (control) are more typical of formal and/or archaic literary usage. They are part of an often somewhat self-consciously used word stock also found, for example, in folksong and traditional drama.

Allied with the straightforwardness of the vocabulary is a marked restraint in the use of risqué or vulgar expressions. Expletives and exclamations, for instance, are usually kept strictly within the limits of decorum. With very few exceptions, euphemism is employed, often coupled with innuendo and humor, to maintain propriety, especially with reference to sexual matters, e.g., *to have a time with, lay around with.* Some of these euphemisms, e.g., *to get aboard,* are drawn from a wide range of nautical expressions characteristic not only of these tales but of Newfoundland speech in general. This is very natural in such a maritime environment, but it is particularly interesting to note that many of these words and expressions have been transferred from a nautical to a general usage in the province. Examples in the stories include *all hands* (everyone), *crew* (crowd, company), *grog* (drink of rum/spirits), *grub* (food), *hatch* (trapdoor), *rig* (clothes, dress), *ship* (hire, employ, etc.), *sing out* (shout), *skipper* (respectful term of address to older man), *stow away* (hide), *turn in* (go to bed). Many more of these expressions and their vernacular counterparts are of course used with their normal reference in the numerous accounts of voyages and other seafaring activities in the tales.

Although some evidence exists for the identification of certain localized dialectal variations in Newfoundland and Labrador, it is at present inconclusive. However, in the anglophone population we can identify two distinct major types of speakers, according to whether their speech predominantly reflects its origins either in West Country England or in southern Ireland. For the purposes of commentary and notes in these volumes we refer to these two types as *West Country English* and *Anglo-Irish* respectively. It must be emphasized that these are very general labels, as will be clear from the transcripts themselves. While each of these types is in many cases still concentrated in certain communities, most settlements on the Southern Shore, for example, being predominantly Anglo-Irish, the speech of individuals frequently manifests a mixture of forms. Some Anglo-Irish speakers may use certain features more typical of West Country English and vice versa. As might be expected, the mingling of the two traditions is rather more common in the relatively few urban centers, though even here the two speech types tend to remain distinct in all but a few features. Typical examples of the infiltration of one dialect type by the other in these narratives include the occasional appearance of West Country English *un* (he, it) in the predominantly Anglo-Irish speech of some narrators and of *begar/begobs, don't be talkin, his/my ownself* in that of predominantly West Country English speakers. Such transference, however, is very limited and superficial, and in some cases it may be that a form thought to be characteristic of one dialect type also has a history in the other. This appears to be true, for instance, of the utterance-final tag *sure,* which is typical of Irish speech but also a feature of West Country English. A few unusual lexical items also betray their origins in either England or Ireland. It is therefore difficult to generalize about the narrators' speech, not least because it is also of course subject to variation from one individual to another, especially in pronunciation. However, it is true to say that although Newfoundland speech may not differ completely from that of the other Atlantic provinces of Canada, it manifests numerous distinctive characteristics at all levels—phonological, lexical, grammatical, and syntactical. The linguistic heritage of the province, drawn principally from English and Irish sources, and augmented by the Scottish, French, Inuit, Micmac, Naskapi, and Montagnais cultures, is a unique amalgam that scholars have only recently begun to explore. The following discussion will concentrate on those aspects of language in Newfoundland that differ from the more standard forms of English currently in use.

Attention has already been drawn above to the importance of intonation in storytelling, much of the impact of a tale depending on subtle variations in vocal tone. Nowhere is this more evident than in the frequent passages of direct speech punctuated by the ubiquitous *he/she said.* The frequency of the latter often causes ambiguity in that the referent or antecedent is not always clear, especially when the teller uses *he* with a female referent, or vice versa, and when *he* or *she* is substituted for *they.* The confusion of *he* and *she* is often precipitated by two principal factors: first, the teller's anticipation of a change of speaker in the dialogue from male to female or female to male; and second, the intrusion of a male character into the narrative at a point when a female is speaking, or vice versa. The situation is further complicated by the fact that *he* and *she* may also refer to an inanimate item and that *un* may apply to male, female, and inanimate referents. As is the case with most regional dialects, the reader will therefore find that the pronominal system is more complex than that of Standard English and is accompanied by a greater variety of verb forms and their nonstandard inflections.

Another aspect of intonation worthy of note is the syllable stress in certain disyllabic and polysyllabic words that differs from standard British or Canadian usage. Examples include: [ˌkænənˈbɑ·əl] cannonball, [ɡɒdˈsɛnd] godsend, [ɡɒlənˈtiːnd] gullentined (guillotined), [ˈoʊtɛl] hotel, [ˈɪnsein] insane, [ɪntəˈrɛstɪd] interested, [ˈpɔ·ɪtɪɡi·] Portuguese, [ˈkwiːbek] Quebec, [sɛpəˈreit(id)] separate(d), and also in the phrasal compound [ˈɪnsaid klouz] inside clothes, underwear. Of these, *interested* and *separate(d)* suggest Anglo-Irish influence, the malapropistic *gullentined* maintains the French stress on the final syllable, and the stress in *godsend* is almost equally strong on each syllable, the second perhaps being marginally more prominent.

Phonology

In the absence of a comprehensive phonological description of Newfoundland speech it is useful to draw attention here to some of the more prominent features commonly found in these narratives, and in particular those that differ from Standard (British) English and/or general (world) English. They include the following:

Aphesis

The loss of the initial syllable of words is a recurrent feature in both the West Country

English and the Anglo-Irish dialects of Newfoundland. Examples include *'board* (aboard), *'bout* (about), *'canter* (decanter), *'cause* (because), *'cordin'* (according), *'cquainted* (acquainted), *'cross* (across), *'deed* (indeed), *'fore* (before), *'gain(st)* (again[st]), *'gar* (begar, begorrah), *'gree(d)* (agree[d]), *'greement* (agreement), *'lectric* (electric), *'long* (along), *'longed* (belonged), *'longside* (alongside), *'lowed* (allowed, supposed), *'magine* (imagine), *'nitials* (initials), *'nother* (another), *'pose* (suppose), *'self* (herself), *'sleep* (asleep), *'spects* (expects), *'stead* (instead), *'stificate* (certificate), *'tween* (between), *'ward* (toward), *'way* (away), *'while* (awhile). It is interesting that a majority of these forms begin with *a-* in Standard English, while others, e.g., *before, between,* formerly had alternative first-syllable forms with *a-* that are now archaic. To the above list one might add the following phrases which are not strictly aphetic but manifest the loss of an initial unstressed vowel: *'tis(n't)* (it is[n't]), *'twas(n't)* (it was[n't]), *'twill* (it will), *'twont* (it won't), *'twudden* ['twɒdn̩], ['twɔdn̩] (it wasn't), *'twould(n't)* ['twɔdn̩] (it wouldn't). The initial consonant is also lost in *'ee* (thee, ye) in the speech of the West Country English narrators in this collection.

Consonants

Initial: *h*-deletion is extremely common in word-initial position, though inconsistently from speaker to speaker. The aspirate is also added initially in words beginning with a vowel, usually for emphasis, e.g., ['hɔunlɪ·] only, ['hɔːɹlɪ] early, [ho·ɔɹ] oar. The addition of *h-* is also inconsistent and far less common than its deletion. As noted earlier, for practical reasons it has not been possible to indicate these features in the transcriptions, but attention is drawn to intrusive initial /h/ in several of the linguistic notes.

Fricative consonants in initial position are sporadically voiced by a few of the West Country English narrators, this feature being almost entirely absent in the Anglo-Irish speech. Examples are [vɒ·l] fall, ['vaɔɹmɔɹ] farmer, [vel], [vɛl] fell, ['vɛlɔɹ] fellow, [vaind] find, ['vɪŋɔɹ] finger, ['vaiɔɹ] fire, [vɔːɹst] first, [vɒt] foot, [vaɒnd], [vaɒn] found, [vɒl] full, ['və·ɹðɔɹ] further, [zeim] same, [zɒːd] sawed, saw, [zez] says, [ziː] see, [zɔɹ] sir, [zoɒ] so, ['dretʔn̩d] threatened, [dræʃ] threshold. This characteristic feature of West Country English is in rapid decline in Newfoundland and in these stories is largely confined to four speakers: William B. Hewitt of Barr'd Islands, Allan Oake of Beaumont, John Roberts of Sally's Cove, and Mose Troke of St. Chads.

Initial /ð/, voiced *th-*, is realized as /d/ in such words as *that, the, them, there, this, these, they, those,* in both speech types. /θ/, voiceless *th-*, is realized as /t/ in *thick, thief, thievin', think, thought, thousands,* etc., apparently borrowed from Anglo-Irish into the West Country English speech variety. Initial /kw/ appears in [kwɒil] coil, and the initial onglide /j/ is found in [jə·ɹ] hear, ear, and ['jʌðɔɹ] other.

Medial: Medial /t/ is normally voiced by the West Country English narrators, but much less so in the Anglo-Irish type of speech, where it often has a breathy quality. The medial consonant is lost in *e'r, ar* (a, a single, any), *ne'r, nar* (no(ne), not a, not one), *whe'r* (whether). /d/ is lost in ['ʃaulɔɹ] shoulder. /n/ is realized as /l/ in *chimley,* /ð/ as /d/ in *father, mother,* /ð/ as /t/ in ['bæ·tɪŋ] bathing, /ð/ as /v/ in *sive* (scythe), /v/ as /f/ in *shuffed* (shoved), *wifes* (wives), /z/ as /ð/ in *scithers,* scissors. Occasionally /z/ is realized as /d/ in *('t)wudden* ([it] wasn't), ['idn̩] isn't. Medial intrusive /h/ is heard in a few isolated instances: [dis'hoɒnd] disowned, [wɪd'hæɒt] without, where it appears in syllable initial position under strong stress.

Glottalization and/or gemination sometimes occur medially in *twothree*. Intrusive /t/ is found before /f/ in *infants*. /s/ follows /r/ in *cerstificate* and is retained as the first sound in the aphetic form *'stificate*. /h/ follows /r/ in *overhalls,* perhaps through folk etymology—**overhauls*—but see comments on medial intrusive /h/ above.[70] The onglide /j/ precedes the final vowel in *livyer(s)* (inhabitant(s)), *mowyers* (mowers). Metathesis of /k/ occurs in *aks,* ask, and of /r/ in the distinctively West Country English *gert* (great) and *perty* (pretty). Syncopation is found in [bɒim'bɒi], [bʌm'bɒi], [bɪm'bɒi] by and by, ['skænləs] scandalous, [spouz] suppose, and many other words and phrases in allegro speech. Before nouns beginning with a vowel the preferred form of the indefinite article among the West Country English type storytellers is *a* where standard English would have *an*. Examples include *a aunt, a awful, a axe, a egg, a eye, a hour* (no initial aspirate), *a office, a old*. However, the form of the determiner with /n/ does occur, e.g., in [ən oɒl] a hole, initial /h/ being deleted in the noun.

Final: Newfoundland speech is predominantly rhotic, and the /ɹ/ continuant occurring finally in syllables strongly colors the preceding vowel. In the tape-recorded narratives, however, there is little evidence for the survival of the retroflex continuant -*r,* /ɽ/, with its characteristic pharyngovelar quality in word-final position that is typical of much West Country speech in England. On the other hand, narrators of the Anglo-Irish type retain the distinctive breathy quality of word-final or penultimate retroflex continuant -*r,* /ɽ/, for example in such words as *her, sir, stirred, sure*.

In the speech of West Country English type, frictionless continuant /ɹ/ also occurs finally in ['fɛlɒɹ], ['vɛlɒɹ] fellow, alternating with ['fɛloɒ], ['fɛlə], and in ['pɪləɹ] pillow, ['wɪndəɹ] window, while in some pronunciations of *tomorrow* the final syllable is assimilated: [də mæɒɹ]. Unlike British English, there is no assimilation in the first syllable of *forecastle* ['fɔɹkasl].

Final /ŋ/ is normally realized as /n/ in present participles and other words ending in -*ing*. However, /ŋ/ is found in *evening* and sporadically in other -*ing* words. The normal pronunciation of this final syllable varies from [ɪn] through [in] to [ən] and [n̩], the latter two forms evidently contributing to the widespread assimilation of the syllable with a preceding /n/, as in [bə'gɪn] begin(ning), [dæəɹn] darn(ing), [mæəɹn] morn(ing). A similar kind of assimilation occurs in some -*ed* words where the vowel is lost and the final /d/ is virtually articulated synchronically with the preceding glottalized voiceless dental, notably before a following vowel, as in [beɪt͡ʔd] beated, [kʌt͡ʔd] cutted, [iːt͡ʔd] eated, [fɪt͡ʔd] fitted, [lɒɪt͡ʔd] lighted, [skwəːɹt͡ʔd] squirted. Along with such truncated forms as the verb *empt* (empty), this provides fascinating evidence for studying the historical phonology of such past tense markers.

In final position, voiceless -*th,* /θ/, is often realized as /t/ or /t͡ʔ/, the latter being heard especially before a following dental. In an isolated example from Allan Oake, final /θ/ becomes /f/ in ['blæk͡ʔsmɪf] blacksmith. The penultimate labiodental fricative in plural reflexives is frequently voiceless, as in *ourselfs, theirselfs,* and the same is true of *lifes*. Note also *diamont* (diamond), [rɒɒst] roused, and [ʃʌft] shoved. Final /d/ is commonly lost in *and, child, crippled, find, found, old, told,* final -*th* in *with,* final /v/ in *give, of,* and final /t/ in *tuft* constant unless a subsequent metronome marking suggests otherwise. It should be borne in mind that such changes in tempo appear sudden because of the way in which they have been notated, but they are in reality gradual and usually imperceptible.

Finally, the bars have been numbered consecutively throughout each performance, except where the same stanza is repeated, for ease of reference in the short commentaries that follow each transcription. These latter focus on the individual performances, noting the presence of variation of any kind and describing unusual, interesting, or typical features of the music and the way it is sung. Wherever possible an attempt has been made to suggest reasons for the phenomena observed. While these must remain largely conjectural in the absence of corroborating evidence from singers themselves, we hope that they will at least stimulate further debate on the music of folksong and its interpretation. Only in this way will it be possible to venture beyond the technical description of folk music and tackle the deeper question of its meaning.

We have used the following symbols in the musical transcriptions:

↑   up to a quarter tone higher than written

↓   up to a quarter tone lower than written

∪   slightly shorter than written

∩   slightly longer than written

✓   breath

/   glissando

x   spoken

x^1 note that expresses a rhythmic element but is not actualized in sound due to the shortness of the vowel or voiced consonant

♪ ♫   grace notes

>   accent

accel.   gradually quickening in pace

[ ]   editorial insertion where a note is inaudible due to background noise or where part of the song is missing from the recording

Types and Motifs

Type and motif summaries for the narratives are based on the standard works: *The Types of the Folktale,* the *Motif-Index of Folk-Literature,*[74] Baughman's *Type and Motif-Index.*

words as [fəɹ] for, [jə] ya, you, [jəs], [jəz] yous. The vowel of the definite article is usually elided before a following vowel: *th' attic, th' axe, th' end, th' evening, th' island, th' office, th' old, th' only, th' other(s), th' owner, th' under,* including those words in which initial *h-* is absent in pronunciation: *th' hammer, th' harbour, th' heart, th' hole, th' horse, th' house.* In all these pronunciations the initial consonant(s) [ð], [d͡ð], [d] of the determiner effectively become the initial consonant(s) of a single unit of speech. Alternatively, if elision does not take place, the transition from *the* to the initial vowel of the following word is effected by brief glottal closure. There are occasional instances of the reduction of *the* to /t/, e.g., *t' other*. A similar elision is also found in the preposition *to: t' heaven.* Numerous other examples of individual pronunciations will be found in the linguistic notes. As one might expect, the versions of tales presented here from manuscript sources convey comparatively few dialectal features, especially as regards phonology. Much of the vernacular pronunciation and lexis has been filtered out by the collectors in response to the conventions of written usage, and the attempts by student collectors to represent dialectal forms are sometimes idiosyncratic and/or questionable.

Lexis

The simplicity of the lexicon in these tales has already been remarked upon. This straightforwardness is of course characteristic of folk narratives in many languages. Technical and complex words are singularly absent, and this in itself makes such stories maximally accessible. Those lexical items in the transcripts that are unusual or may cause difficulty in reading and/or interpretation are glossed in the text. Virtually all these items are dialectal, and since the speech of the majority of the storytellers is of the West Country English type, most of the unfamiliar words are characteristic of dialects in the southwest of England. Typical examples are *abroad* (in pieces), *arg* (argue), *crunnick* (weather-beaten tree), *drivin' works* (causing a commotion), *duckish* (dusk), *either* (any), *empt* ([v] empty), *flux* (snatch), *handy* (near), *handier* (nearer), *livyer* (settler, inhabitant), *lodge* (put, place), *neither* (none), *planchin'* (floorboards), *skirred* (flew rapidly), *spell* (pause for rest), *the once* (directly, right away), *turn* (load), *twitin'* ['twɒit͡ʔn̩] (teasing).

Anglo-Irish examples include: *begar* [bɪˈgaəɹ], [bɪˈgɑəɹ], [bɪˈgɒəɹ] (begorrah), *begobs* (by god), *boniffs* (piglets), *gutter* (mud), *rightified* (corrected, put right), and perhaps also *boy* [bɒɪ] as an informal term of address for males, and *scords* (gashes). Rather more problematical are a number of dialectal items that could be of either English or Irish origin. As with the phonology, in establishing the provenance of individual items it is often difficult to distinguish between the two principal sources, West Country English and Southern Irish, because of the longstanding historical links between the two, both in their places of origin and also in Newfoundland. The problem is compounded by the fact that a number of these words are also well attested in other regional dialects of English. Among these items are *(al)lowed* (supposed, reckoned), *dodge* (move slowly, saunter), *flat* (level piece of ground), *forelaid* (lay in wait for, got there ahead of), *frounge* (?complain), *gawks* (fools [friendly term of address]), *gugglin* (gurgling), *hypocrite* (cripple), *intermined* (determined), *learn* (teach), *oreweed* (seaweed), *persuadance* (persuasion), *rattle* (rustle), *rampsin'* (tumbling, romping with), *scrunchins* (fried cubes of pork fat), *siss* (hiss), *twothree* (two or three), *trickled* (raised [to facilitate movement]), *uncle* (respectful term of address to older man), *unstrip* (undress), *without* (unless), *wonderful* (great, tremendous).

The long history of settlement in Newfoundland has given rise to numerous terms that are particularly associated with the province, many of them having a specifically local reference and/or a somewhat different meaning in their adopted environment. Among these are *blackguard* (vulgar, risqué), *buddy* ([pron.] this man/fellow), *chinched* [tʃɪnʃt] (full, tightly packed), *country* (inland area, interior), *cracky* (small mongrel dog), *dagger* (whetstone), *fitout* (outfit, equipment), *flake* (raised wooden platform for drying fish), *heelstick* (wooden last for mending shoes), *lunch* (snack eaten between meals), *marshberries* (small cranberries), *mug up* (cup/mug of tea), *scattered* (occasional), *scribbler* (exercise book), *smart* (in good health), *smopped* (drew [at a pipe]), *stage* (covered wooden platform for processing fish), *tilt* (temporary shelter, hut), *time* (party, celebration).

To the reader unfamiliar with the dialect, the vocabulary of course contributes to the somewhat archaic flavor of the narratives and helps to distance them from the real world. The reader's impression that the tales are set in another time and another place is strengthened by the frequent use of archaic and/or specialized words and phrases. Some of these have also been retained in other regional dialects of English, while others were once part of the standard language but have become obsolescent or fallen into disuse. They include *bide* (stay, remain), *clergy* (clergyman), *daybed* (couch), *dout* (put out [candle, etc.]), *fresh* (not salty [of food]), *heighth* (height), *little small* (small), *make away with* (kill, remove), *mind* (remember), *minded* (inclined, disposed), *put up* (put away), *pitch(ed)* (land[ed], alight[ed]), *puncheon* (large wooden cask), *quintal* (a measure of fish), *right* (very), *sack* (hit, beat), *shift* (change [clothes]), *slack o' the poll* (nape of the neck), *start naked* (naked), *take (re)marks* (observe, take notice), *tant* (tall), *turned (the door)* (closed). A few alterations of a malapropistic nature also occur, e.g., *grand aviser* (?grand vizier), *gullentined* (guillotined), *manogany* (mahogany).

The pronominal system in Newfoundland retains many archaic and dialectal features, notably in the West Country English speech type. In these narratives, for instance, we find *her, 'ee, us, ye, yous,* and *'em* in subject position: *where her was, have 'ee got ar 'nother son, how's us goina get, how long are ye here, yous 'll be killed, how is 'em goin' to find out, what would 'em do, where's 'em to. I, 'ee, he, she, un, we, ye, yous, they* may occur in nonsubject position: *only got I, no more of I, get aboard 'ee, give 'ee three chances, got he shaved, that wasn't he, the devil can have he, you'll always mind he, he'll kill he, didn't know she, dig she up, try to get she out, soon bring she to life, give she a lot, pilot un in, nobody couldn't save un, never see un no more, lost a needle into un, keep ye awoke, there's no men like yous, two o' we, stay with we, had they goin', 'tis not they, one/some/three o' they.* A rare example of *you* as a vocative in sentence-final position occurs in *sure take all night sure [to] cut it off, you.* Most of these nonsubject forms occur under strong, secondary, or tertiary stress. It must be emphasized that the examples here, as elsewhere in this section, are selected for their deviation from the standard. Many of them are found comparatively rarely, as alternates for their more standard equivalents.

As mentioned briefly above, the third person singular pronouns *he* and *she* may have both animate and inanimate referents. Typical of the latter are the use of *he* with reference to *barn, basket, chain, chest, kettle, newspaper, ring, story (I learned he),* and of *she* with reference to *chest* and of course attributively with *boat, ship,* etc. This extends to the object forms *him* with such referents as *egg,* and *her* with such referents as *devil, gun.* The pronoun *un* may be substituted for all three nonsubject case forms of the third person singular pronouns *him, her, it,* though substitution of *un* for *her* is less common. Occasionally, *it* has a plural referent, e.g., *clothes.* The forms *ar, e'r, either, arn, ne'r, neither (one)* function as positive and negative indefinite pronoun substitutes, meaning *a, any, not a, no(ne)*—a semantic grouping that is further complicated by double or multiple negation. The reflexives *meself, hisself, ourselfs, theirselfs/theirselves* are augmented by *me own self, his own self,* especially in emphatic utterance. These last are evidently Anglo-Irish but are also found in the speech of the West Country English narrators.

The demonstrative *those* is sometimes replaced by *them* or *they: them fellers, them two, they cakes/candles/three.* The function of *this* is shifted from adjectival to pronominal or adverbial in *we leaved this,* i.e., this place, here. The plural forms *these* and *those* may have a different time reference from that of their use in the standard language, *those days/times* referring to the present and *these days/times* (or *them days/times*) referring to the past. Note also the preposition *into* (in), the prepositional phrase *off o',* the preposition and adverb *'gain* (against), and the intensifiers *awful, right, terrible, wonderful.* Further information on many of these words and about Newfoundland lexis in general will be found in the *Dictionary of Newfoundland English.*

Grammar

As in any regional dialect of English, the speech of Newfoundlanders preserves numerous grammatical features that have been lost or become obsolescent in the standard language. In the following summary account attention is drawn to some of the more outstanding of these features in the narrators' speech.

Nouns: A few nouns whose singular form ends in -*st* retain -*e*-, pronounced /ə/, in the plural inflection, e.g., *beastes, locustes, toastes.* A double plural common in many other regional dialects is found in *belluses* (bellows). Isolated examples of a similar phenomenon occur in marking the possessive singular: *Jackses, motherses, worldes.* On the other hand the possessive marker is absent in *Paradise', Pierce',* and in one instance of *horse'* (horse's). A parallel example is the lack of plural marker in *corpse* (corpses), *mile, story, year,* and in single instances, e.g., *cow, question.*

Verbs: Many archaic and dialectal verb forms are found in the speech of the storytellers and reflect the extent and variety of such features in Newfoundland usage as a whole. In the simple present tense the -*s* inflection is predominant throughout the paradigm in all three persons, singular and plural, in both of the speech types identified above: *I comes, you carries, we wants, they pitches.* The verb *have* may also add -*s* in the present tense. Occasionally, the -*es* form is retained, e.g., *you askes,* (he) *knockses, you wantes.* The various forms of the verb *be* also warrant attention, e.g., the Anglo-Irish *don't be talkin', I don't be tellin',* and the West Country English variants, *I is, I's, I aint* [ent͡ʔ], [ɛnt͡ʔ], [eint͡ʔ] (I am not), *so be I, aint I* [en ɑi], *aint 'ee* [en ɩ·], [ën ɩ·] (aren't you), *you'm, you is, is you/ya, he be, we'm, we 's, is we, they bes* [bɪz], *they is.* Note also such present tense forms as *he do, How much do the moon weigh?, she/it don't, you does* (pronounced [dʌz] and sometimes [duːz]), *I ant* [ænt͡ʔ], (I haven't), *up go the pigeon.* The absence of final /ŋ/ in the present participle *being* leads to difficulty in distinguishing it from the past participle *been*. Occasional instances of the *a-* form of the present participle are found, e.g., *agoin', asingin'*. Note also the pronunciation of ['lɒsən] losing.

A major characteristic feature of Newfoundland dialect and especially of the West Country English speech type is the high proportion of nonstandard forms in the past tense and past participle of verbs. This feature is well illustrated in the texts presented in this collection. Several categories of nonstandard past tense forms may be distinguished:

1. Forms that lack a final marker of tense, such as *ask, bake, become, begin, blind, bring, build, catch, climb, come, drift, eat, fit, get, give, happen, hide, hold, invite, keep, leave, light, live, load, meet, persuade, point, pound, post, ride, send, slip, spit, start, stoop, twist, visit, want.*

Of these, some two-thirds end in a dental or alveolar consonant, notably /t/ and /d/. As noted above in the comments on pronunciation, final *-ed* following these consonants is very susceptible to assimilation. It should also be borne in mind that many of these unmarked past tense forms alternate with marked forms in the speech of the narrators. Furthermore, the frequent switching of tenses, especially from past to present in dialogue, encourages the blurring of inflectional distinctions between the two. In a number of cases, therefore, verb forms embedded in a predominantly past-tense context of utterance may be construed as "vivid present" in function if not in form.

2. Forms with nonstandard additional past tense marker, often alternating with another variant: *beated, bursted, drowneded, owneded.*

3. Forms in which the historically "strong" or "mixed" classes of verbs have followed the "weak" pattern with dental suffix: *blowed, buyed, catched, choosed, comed, creeped, drawed, drinked, eated, falled* (fell), *flied* (flew), *gid* (gived, gave), *growed, hided, knowed, leaved, meaned, rised, runned, seed* (saw), *shined, sleeped, swimmed, throwed, winned.*

4. One or two verbs that in contrast with the standard language indicate tense by vowel change, in much the same way as "strong" verbs: *bid* (stayed, waited), *hod* (hid), *hove* (heaved), *ris, rose* (raised), *sot* (sat), *sove* (saved), *sprod* (spread), *squez* (squeezed), *upsot* (upset).

5. Occasional instances of past tense forms with the prefix *a-: abroke, afalled* (fell).

Other nonstandard past tense forms include: *(I) been, begun, builded, confound* (confined), *done, fled* (flew); *(he) have been, heared, laid* (lay), *losed, maked, rung, seen(ed), sond* (sent), *sung; he/she were; you/we/they was.* Note also such past continuous forms as *was stood.*

Nonstandard past participles appear to be rather more limited in number in these narratives but have a great deal of affinity with the past tense verb forms outlined above. Examples include *beat, borned, broke, cutted, drowneded, eat, frit* (frightened), *gi(ve), growed, leaved, lied* (lay), *lineded, look, paste, runned, sot* (sat), *saven, sove* (saved), *stole, took, tore, wore*. More significant, however, is the comparatively large number of past participles prefixed by *a-*, such as *abarred, abeen, ablowed, abought, aburned, acome, acured, adone, adrinked, afeared, afind, afired, afound, agive, agot, aheard, ahung* (hanged), *akilled, aknowed, aleaved, alost, aput, arobbed, aruined, ascared, aseen, aserved, aslep', asold, astalled, astart(ed), astole, astruck, atold, atook, atried, awent, aworked*. The frequency of such forms raises tantalizing questions about adverbs in such phrases as *apast me labour, to make asure,* and *keep ye awoke;* the second of these perhaps allows such alternative transcriptions as *to make sure* and *to make her sure*.[71]

Adjectives and adverbs: The archaic weak inflection *-en* survives in *glassen*. Nonstandard adjectival forms are found in the double comparatives *more contenteder, more handier, more hungrier* and the superlatives *beautifullest, firstest*. Uninflected adjectival forms occur in adverbial position, e.g., *he spoke cross, he gets un done good*. The genitive *-s* inflection persists in certain adverbs and adverbial phrases: *anyhows, anywheres, a long ways, somewheres*.

Syntax

Much of the syntax in these Newfoundland narratives, as we have seen, is characterized by short, simple sentences. This is especially evident in the compression and economy typical of many of the storytelling styles, as the following examples demonstrate: *Soon have enough; Got the ring; Mixed up a big cake; Still couldn't learn; Lost everything; Off jacket; Sat down; Wasn't enough see; Go across ocean; Just got in port; Went over; She found out; So they left; Come to my turn; Got up; Bed empty, nobody in; No breakfast; Frightened her; Went on up; Next man came; Looked everywhere; Went home; Come ashore; Sot up*. The numerous sentences and clauses of this type are often used as a rhetorical shorthand by the narrators to sketch in some of the pivotal points in the forward movement of the plot. Their elliptical form is reminiscent of various types of block language such as that used in telegrams, in which not only function words are frequently omitted but also adverbs and especially the pronominal subject of the utterance.

Ellipsis is also of course inevitable in allegro speech, in which determiners, prepositions, connectives, relatives, auxiliaries, and pronouns are sacrificed without detriment to overall communication. Typical examples of each are: *in boat, in cabin, knock me in head, in ship, what is into orange, practisin' with gun, get little mare; course* (of course), *what's goina happen us, had plenty money, dout they ten...candles the one shot; one thing another; the man [who/that] done it, the feller [who] was with me; I [was] tryin' to catch her, he wouldn't [have] done it, what [did] Pa(ppy) say, She mixed [it/un] up, brought [it/un] down, she put [them/they] on the step*. With reference to these latter three examples, the omission of the object pronoun after *brought* and *put* is common and, as with *mixed*, may be due in part to the assimilation of *it* with the final /t/ of the verb. The subject pronouns *he* and *she* are often lost before *said* in the structural framework of direct speech, while the definite article is sometimes omitted before the modifier or head of a noun phrase, e.g., *other fellow*.

The syntax of the verb phrase invites further investigation. It must suffice here simply to draw attention to a few of the more interesting features. Those storytellers whose speech is of the Anglo-Irish type continue to employ the construction auxiliary + *after* + present participle to indicate a completed action in the past tense. This is a translation from Irish and is a hallmark of the English spoken in Ireland.[72] Examples include *they were after bein' out in the barn; we were after droppin' our beans; the poor old horse is after eatin' oats; I been after fallin'; he was after gettin' a berth; I was after gettin' jammed in; they're after growin' that tall; we're after killin' our brother; he's after makin' a bad job of it; the boy was after overhearin'; he was after sellin' hisself; you're after sleepin' longer than you thought; I'm after spendin' a very weary night here.* Occasionally, as mentioned earlier, narrators of the West Country English speech type also use this construction. Other verb phrases that seem to be exclusively used by the Anglo-Irish storytellers are seen in the elliptical *without be cuttin'* (without being cut), and *I suppose be a Welsh* (I suppose would be a Welsh).

Among our West Country English-speaking storytellers there is some ambiguity in the pronunciation of *used to* and *was to*, which often fall together and are indistinguishable, especially in the speech of Allan Oake. Certain verb phrases have the form auxiliary + participle + *of*, especially in the stories of Everett and Freeman Bennett: *they was eatin' of it, beans is hurtin' o' me, I'm not stealin' of it, she was takin' of it all down.* This construction can lead to some unusually complex syntax: *if you're tellin' of me a lie; I was tellin' of ya about today.* By contrast, *of* is lacking in *she took un hold, he got the door hold,* and *goin' to catch me hold,* but with similar effects on the syntax as in the examples immediately above. Also of note are the frequent use of the archaic purposive *for to* before infinitives, and such constructions as *I'd like for, he had like to kill 'em,* and *I don't think* (I don't think so). At times the syntax can be simultaneously complex and cryptic, contrasting sharply with the normally straightforward structure of clauses and sentences. Typical examples are *more I don't* (nor do I), *more can't you* (any more than you can), *they missed un gone* (they noticed he was missing). Once in a while the normal rules of syntax are strained, no doubt partly as a result of the teller's striving to remember, articulate, and concatenate a complex string of forms under the stress of the performance and its context. Even here, however, the audience has no difficulty in unraveling the syntax or apprehending the meaning and may even respond to the rhetorical effect of the suspension of sense by means of which the resolution of the utterance is postponed until the final word as in *there was goin' to be three o' the prettiest fish was in the sea caught.*

Mention must be made of the remarkably large number of double negatives in these texts, in both the West Country English and the Anglo-Irish speech types. Indeed, one becomes so used to them in hearing the tales or reading the texts that it is easy to forget that such negative constructions have long ceased to be used in the standard language. Examples are so plentiful that it must suffice merely to offer a sampling of them here to illustrate their range and variety: *don't know no stories, don't eat/do it/fire/tell no more, don't want no dinner, didn't make no matter, couldn't get no further, can't eat/don't know nothing, couldn't learn un nothing, don't know/won't take/won't tie up none, don't miss ne'r step, couldn't get nar drink, couldn't see no one, don't/wouldn't let nobody, aint been nowhere, nobody is not goin' to, nobody couldn't save un, nobody don't recognize him, nobody never done it, nobody never came/could catch, never let nobody know, never done/fired/got/had/stole/thought nothing, ain't got/didn't know/haven't done/won't know nothing, never made no noise, never thought no more, never had nar punt, no other man'll never live here.* Multiple negatives are rare, but such forms as *no, never seen nobody* occur occasionally, as does the archaic *or no* (or not): *whe'r 'tis he/you or no.*

Note also, among many other phrases typical of local usage: *(a)way to go* (off we go, let's go), *last goin' off, on the last of it, in (the) latter end* (finally), *pod auger days* (bygone times), *they'd take week on week* (they'd take turns on alternate weeks), *where's he to?* (where has he gone [to]?, where is he?), *knocks to the door* (knocks at the door), *(ac)cordin' as, so big as, so well as, 'stead on* (instead of), *light in/make in a fire.* Dates normally have *and* between the century and the year: *eighteen and ninety-six.*

METHOD OF PRESENTATION

The 150 recensions presented here are numbered serially and follow the order of the AT index, from AT130 to AT2301A, the final 10 versions not being listed in that index. These are followed by 15 fragments (Appendix A), numbered F1-F15, again presented in the order of the AT types. The recensions of a given tale type are therefore grouped together, the first version in each group being the fullest and/or the most complete. Each numbered recension bears a title, either learned from the narrator, or, if the narrator offered no title, assigned by the editors. Those titles editorially assigned are distinguished by the symbol [†]. Immediately below the title the reader will find the name of the storyteller, the place and date of recording or collection, together with the AT type number(s), the MUNFLA reference number, and the name of the fieldworker(s) or collector(s).[73] In those instances where we ourselves are the collectors, our initials are used for identification.

The text of the story then follows, sometimes preceded by a brief preamble, usually of conversation relevant to the tale and/or its context. A similar transcription of the conversation immediately following the tale is also often included, not least for its contextual importance. After each transcript a series of notes provides further information, commentary, and references, presented in the following sequence:

1. Duration
2. Source
3. Location
4. Audience
5. Context, style, and language
6. Music
7. Types and motifs
8. International parallels

Of these notes the sixth set is of course included only when the narrative incorporates a song or perhaps just a few words that are sung. Where these songs or song fragments occur, a transcription of the music is provided, together with commentary and notes. Where the same basic tune recurs in a group of two or more variants, the transcription appears in the notes to the first of these. The eighth set of notes, those on the international parallels, is normally found under the first recension of a given AT type. The notes on language in set No.

5 include an account of the principal characteristics of each storyteller's speech. These accounts appear in the notes following the first recension told by that individual in the numbered sequence of texts. Thus, for example, the major discussion of Freeman Bennett's linguistic usage is found in the notes for tale No. 4. In the linguistic notes to subsequent stories by the same teller, additional comments are made about the language, but the reader is referred back to the earlier general account for the essential basic characteristics of that teller's speech. In those cases, therefore, the notes on language are cumulative, and taken as a whole, they provide a detailed commentary on a storyteller's usage. Individual linguistic items are noted only on the first occasion they appear in the sequence of stories told by a given narrator.

To assist the reader in using the notes and their accompanying apparatus each of the eight sets listed is discussed briefly below.

Duration

These short factual notes provide information on the precise length of time, measured in minutes and seconds, that a tape-recorded story takes to tell on a given occasion, excluding any preamble or conversation after the narrative ends. No information of this kind, of course, is available for those recensions drawn from MUNFLA that were collected in manuscript form.

Source

These notes give whatever information is available concerning the source from which the storyteller originally learned the tale. This may include the name of an individual, the place where the tale was first heard, and often an approximate date for that first hearing.

Location

Brief details are given here of the specific place in which the story was recorded—usually a particular room of a house—together with the time of day when the interview took place.

Audience

Whenever possible, we include here a list of all those present at the storytelling session. This is of course relevant to the complex interaction between teller and audience and also provides clues about the role of the fieldworker(s) as participant observer(s) in a "natural" or "induced natural" context.

Context, Style, and Language

This set of notes is much more extensive than the first four. Where the evidence is available, we first expand on the brief description of the physical and social context given in notes 3 and 4 above and then move on to discuss both general and specific aspects of the storytelling style. This leads into the linguistic notes proper, which begin with general comments and then successively consider phonology, lexis, grammar, and syntax. At each of these levels of analysis, the examples used in this commentary are presented in the order in which they appear in the text of the story itself. To make the linguistic notes as accessible as possible, we have avoided detailed phonetic transcription. However, general guidance on pronunciation will be found in the discussion and in certain spellings that closely reflect the vernacular speech. More specific information on the pronunciation of individual words is provided by means of broad phonetic (strictly phonemic) transcriptions set between slashes. The symbols used in the linguistic notes and also elsewhere in this introduction are again those of the International Phonetic Association alphabet, items in narrow transcription being enclosed in brackets. Many characteristic linguistic features of the tales are also identified and discussed in the section on language in this Introduction.

Where we present more than one version of a story by the same teller, the fullest linguistic notes appear following the first recension. The linguistic notes on the later recension(s) are supplementary. In the cross-references the number of the first recension is in boldface to remind the reader to consult the notes to that version for a fuller discussion of the language.

Cross-references to the language of previous tales by a given teller in this collection appear at the end of each set of linguistic notes. However, it should be emphasized that these notes are by no means exhaustive. Although they take up many of the significant features in a given tale, they make no claims to be comprehensive and the reader may wish to pursue interesting points of detail further by close reference to the text.

Music

The twelve music transcriptions included in this collection were made by ear from sound recordings played back repeatedly at both full speed and half-speed. Pitch was gauged by means of a tuning fork and an electric piano, while tempo was measured against a metronome. The resulting transcriptions were then checked for accuracy in every respect. As is usual in the transcription of Anglo-American folksong, they are written in conventional musical notation, despite its shortcomings for "descriptive music-writing," for ease of comparison and more immediate accessibility. The notation is supplemented by diacritical marks that are introduced to suggest, albeit impressionistically, subtleties of intonation and singing style. Nevertheless, the standard qualification regarding the partial and approximate nature of musical transcriptions in relation to what is sung must be reiterated here, and the limitations of the system of musical notation and the human ear acknowledged. Ideally, these transcriptions should be used in conjunction with, and not as a substitute for, the sound recordings themselves.

In contrast with most publications containing folksongs, it has been feasible to transcribe the music of these songs in full and in as much detail as possible due to their comparative brevity. The original pitch of each performance has also been preserved to the nearest semitone in transcription as potentially significant, and any shifts in pitch level are noted in the accompanying commentary. There has similarly been no attempt to standardize the length of individual bars, which are sometimes subject to extension or abbreviation in response to such variables as text, breathing, singing style, and the circumstances of the performance. Thus, the time signature at the beginning of each song acts as a general but not inflexible guide to the overall meter. Care has been taken to notate the exact placing and duration of the rests, as these may also furnish important clues to the performer's notion of phrasing and singing style. All breaths are likewise marked where audible. Metronome markings at the beginning of each stanza indicate its approximate tempo, which may be taken to be fairly and such past tense/participle forms as *aslep'* (slept). As in several regional dialects of England, *trough* is pronounced [troɷ]. The Survey of English Dialects identified only this form of the word in Somerset, Wiltshire, and Dorset. It was also predominant in Devon and Hampshire, though recorded from only one locality in Cornwall. Clear [l] in final position, e.g. ['mɪkl̩] Mickel, Michael, and the strong aspiration of final plosives are characteristic of the speech of the Anglo-Irish storytellers.

Among the West Country English narrators, glottalization of /t/ occurs frequently in syllable final and word final position: [bæɷt͡ʔ] 'bout, [iːt͡ʔ] eat, ['iːt͡ʔn̩] eating, [miːt͡ʔ] meet, ['skwɒt͡ʔn̩] squatting, ['træɷt͡ʔn̩] trouting.

Offglides /t/ and /d/ are fairly common in final position, e.g., *acrosst* (across), *clifft* (cliff), ['kʌzənd] cousin, [gaɷnd] gown, [rə'vɒlvəɹd] revolver, *sermont* (sermon), [taɷnd] town, *underneatht* (underneath), *unknownst* (unknown—cf. *unbeknownst*), *whole(d)* (whole). Note also *heighth* (height).

Vowels and diphthongs

The variety and complexity of the vowel sounds in this collection are such that few valid conclusions can be drawn concerning dialect boundaries. While it is clear, for example, that the Anglo-Irish narrators commonly use a centralized form of the half-open back rounded vowel, e.g., in [hɔ̈ɹ] her, [sɔ̈ɹ] sir, in contrast with the West Country English [(h)əɹ], [səɹ], [zəɹ], the pronunciations of the diphthong in such forms as [bɛɪt] beat, [klɛind] cleaned, [grɛɪs] grease, and [spɛɪk] speak are more problematical since their origins may well lie in both English and Irish dialects. Among the vowels and diphthongs of stressed syllables that have clear parallels in the dialects of West Country English one might note the following: [iː] in [(h)iːz] his, [iːn] in, [ʃiːn] shin, ['spiːʃəl] special; [ɪ] in [bɪn] been, [kɪtʃ] catch, [klɪm] climb, ['knɪtʃiz] crutches, [kɪp] keep, [mɪts] meets, [sɪtʃ] such, ['wɪzl̩] weasel; [i] in ['flɪniʃəz] flinches, ['ridl̩ɪ] riddly (the territory of /i/ ranges from the half-close to the half-open central position); [ɛ] in [kɛtʃ] catch; [ʌ] in [hʌv] hove, [sʌns] since, [ʃʌk] shook, [tʌpt] tipped, [tʌk] took; [ɷ] in [bɷt(s)] boot(s), [tʃɷkt] chucked, [fɷd] food, ['fɷlɪʃ(nəs)] foolish(ness), [rɷf] roof, [rɷm(z)] room(s), [spɷnz] spoons; [ɛɪ] in [kɛɪ] quay; [æə] in [æəɹ] any, [(ə)'kæəɹdn̩] (ac)cording, [æəɹg] argue, [bæəɹn] born, ['kæəɹnəɹd] cornered, [kæəɹps] corpse(s), ['mæəɹn(ən)] morn(ing), [næəɹ] no(ne), not one, [stæəɹm] storm, [də mæəɹ] the morrow, tomorrow; [aɷ] in ['ʃaɷlɔɹ] shoulder; [ɒɪ] in [nɒɪt] night. It must be emphasized that these pronunciations are by no means consistent among the West Country English storytellers.

Other nonstandard pronunciations of vowels in stressed syllables that are characteristic of their speech include [beig] bag, [dɒɷt͡(ʔ)] dout, [eiv] heave, [lænʃ(t)] launch(ed), [leːvd], [leɪvd], [lɛɪvd] leaved, [noɷn] none, ['oɷvn̩] oven, [stɛɪd], [stɛd] steed, ['rækin] wreck. Also of note are ['buːtlɔɹ] butler (cf. French *bouteillier*), ['kænəvəs] canvas, ['hɛɪgoɷ] eagle (the final diphthong developing from the typical West Country English dark [ɫ]), ['hɛləm] elm, from individual speakers of the West Country English type, and ['kʌvətjuəs] covetous, [aɷld] old, [plɛiz] please, from those of the Anglo-Irish type.

In unstressed syllables /ou/ is realized as /ɪ/ in ['barɪd] borrowed, ['fɒlɪ(d)] follow(ed), ['hɒlɪ(z)] hollo(s), shout(s), ['hɒlɪən] holloing, shouting. /ɪ/ is found in the final syllable of ['bɷlɪk] bullock, ['stʌmɪk] stomach, and /ə/ occurs under weakest sentence stress in such

Hoffmann's *Survey* was used for a few stories, and three tale types were identified by reference to *The Types of the Irish Folktale*. Where appropriate, the dominant tale type designation is supplemented by one or more additional types. Usually these are either fully or substantially represented in the story. Occasionally, both in the main type heading and the supplementary ones, additional designations, preceded by *Cf.*, are given, in order to draw the reader's attention to cognate types. In a few instances revised motifs personally communicated to Halpert by Baughman have been employed; these are preceded by an asterisk. The list of motifs accompanying each tale is intended to be as complete as possible in order to facilitate comparison between versions of the tales by different tellers, and of varying recensions by an individual. Even so, the nature of motif analysis is such that there will inevitably be a number of omissions. Lacunæ will also occur, of course, when the various indexes used do not list a relevant motif, or offer an appropriate motif which is either directly or indirectly germane to an episode or element in a given narrative. In certain cases, for example in such commonplace events as the baking of buns, bread, or cakes for the hero as provisions on his quest, there appears to be no appropriate motif, and we have resisted the temptation to create new ones. However, in order to make clear the precise relevance of certain motifs to a given element in the tale we have occasionally added a specifying word or phrase, enclosed in brackets, to Thompson's original. A particular motif may differ slightly in these specified variants from one story to another. The reader should note that individual motifs are not repeated within the motif list for a particular recension, even though the teller may have repeated them in his narration of it. A full listing of all the motifs will be found in the Index of Motifs.

International Parallels

The information on the international parallels to each tale type in this collection forms the bulk of the remaining notes. These notes will usually be found under the first recension of a specific tale type, though occasionally some shorter commentaries occur under a later recension in a given group. We assume that the reader will first consult the relevant information on the tale type(s) in the AT index. This information is normally not repeated in the references presented here.

The notes, which are essentially comparative in nature, begin with an introductory discussion and commentary and proceed, where relevant, to a brief listing of studies and notes, usually supplementing those in the AT index. These are presented in chronological order. These listings are not comprehensive, but are works we have found useful. Fuller studies for many of the types will be found in the *Enzyklopädie des Märchens*. The remainder of the notes comprise an extensive listing of the international parallels to the tale, sometimes interspersed with further discussion of specific by-forms. These comparative references are presented systematically by geographical distribution.

The primary aim of these notes is to set the Newfoundland tales in their wider historical and cultural context. Only in this way is it possible to demonstrate the importance of this hitherto undiscovered storytelling tradition to the international stock of narratives. As the Newfoundland tradition is mainly derived from Great Britain and Ireland, we have concentrated on parallels from those countries and from North America. For several important tales in this collection we fortunately also have English translations or substantial

English abstracts of tales originally told in Scottish Gaelic or Irish. At the same time, the notes add a further dimension to our discussion of how Newfoundland storytellers utilize the full resources of their unique expressive culture to give these tales a distinctive local flavor and significance.

The discussion, commentary, and references strongly emphasize the English-language tradition, wherever found, supplemented by information about the tale type from other languages and cultures, whenever this has been available to us either in translation or in reasonably complete English abstracts. Although our references are quite full for North America, Great Britain and Ireland, those for mainland Europe and the other continents, while fairly extensive, are certainly not exhaustive. There are many translations on our lists to which we have not had access. We have stressed English-language materials and translations primarily for the general English-language reader and for both undergraduate and graduate folk-narrative students in English-speaking countries. Those interested in wider-ranging international parallels in other languages will be able to follow up some of the references in more detail in those languages with which they are familiar.

In addition to the AT index and the Baughman index, we have utilized extensively the Coffin *Index* for the *Journal of American Folklore*,[75] Parsons' extensive annotations in her published collection of black folklore from the Antilles;[76] and where available the indexes to other American folklore journals; the Robe index for Mexico, Central America, and the Hispanic United States;[77] Hansen, *Types*,[78] for the Caribbean and South America; *Irish Types*[79] for Ireland; Hodne, *Types*,[80] for Norway; the Rausmaa catalogue[81] for Finland; Thompson and Roberts, *Types*,[82] for the Indian subcontinent; and Klipple's unpublished doctoral dissertation for Africa.[83] We have also consulted where pertinent the Boggs index for Spain,[84] the Hoffmann survey for erotic tales, and the Rotunda motif index for Italy.[85] For details of these short-title references see the Bibliography.

For references to Franco-American tales from North America we are greatly indebted to the late Professor Luc Lacourcière and his associate, Dr. Margaret Low, for making available to us detailed information on parallels to the Newfoundland stories from their unpublished catalogue, as well as on those in the Lacourcière index. The latter, a set of file cards, includes references to the recordings and manuscript collections of Les Archives de Folklore at Université Laval, Québec, and other archives, as well as to printed sources. These are the only full archival references in our notes besides those from the Newfoundland archive, MUNFLA.

The discussion and commentary preceding the lists of references take up a variety of topics. These may include problems of classification; variations in theme, theme content, structure, and patterning; the international and regional distribution of the tale type, its episodes, incidents, and elements, with particular reference to North America, the British Isles, and Ireland; the historical development of folktales and their relationship with mythology, literature, and the printed tradition; the interrelation between folktale, legend, and folk belief; aspects of the function of traditional narratives, including their relevance to social class, gender, race, religion, ethics, and worldview, and their utilization of mockery, humor, and other devices as a mechanism for entertainment and/or social control; the localization of certain story patterns and elements to particular regions; the contrast between the archetypal Märchen hero and the male protagonist in other tales who is primarily a trickster figure; and the drawing of attention to various other aspects of international folktales that so far as we know have received little attention elsewhere.

The lists of comparative references are arranged geographically by continent and region. Their order of presentation may be summarized as follows:

A. North America
   1. Canada: east to west
   2. United States: New England; Middle Atlantic; Midwest; Western Great Lakes; South; Southern Mountains; Southwest; North Dakota, South Dakota, Nebraska, Kansas; Colorado, Wyoming, Montana, Idaho, Utah, Nevada; West Coast, California to Alaska.
   3. Mexico: east to west on a north-south axis
   4. Caribbean Islands

B. Central and South America

C. Europe and Asia
   1. British Isles and Ireland
      England: West Country; Southeastern counties, including London; South Central counties (Oxfordshire, Bedfordshire, and Cambridgeshire); East Anglia; East Midlands, West Midlands; North Midlands; Lincolnshire; Yorkshire; the Borders; Lake District; Lancashire and Cheshire; the Marches
      Wales: South, West, Mid-, North
      Scotland: Southern Uplands; Lowlands; Northeast Coast; Highlands; Inner Islands; Outer Isles; Orkneys and Shetlands
      Isle of Man
      Ireland, North and South: Ulster, Leinster, Munster, Connacht
      Channel Islands

      [The few references to the English-language folktale tradition in Australia are inserted at this point.]

   2. [The tale numbers of J. and W. Grimm, *Kinder- und Hausmärchen,* together with translated titles and annotations from the Hunt edition, where relevant, are inserted at this point to facilitate comparative reference to European and Asiatic tales.]
   3. Iceland, Norway, Denmark, Faeroe Islands, Sweden
   4. France, Basque, Catalan, Spain, Portugal, Mallorca
   5. Italy, Corsica, Sardinia
   6. The Netherlands, Belgium, Luxemburg, Germany [Pomerania], Austria, Switzerland
   7. Finland, Estonia, Latvia, Lithuania
   8. Poland, Czechoslovakia [Bohemia, Moravia, Slovakia], Hungary, Rumania [Bukovina], Yugoslavia [Slovenia, Croatia, Slavonia, Bosnia, Serbia, Montenegro], Bulgaria, Albania

9. Macedonia, Greece, Turkey
10. [Lappland], Russia, U.S.S.R. (general), White Russia, Ukraine, Bessarabia, Moldavia, Caucasus, Dagestan, Georgia, Armenia, Komi A.S.S.R., Bashkir A.S.S.R., Votyak A.S.S.R., Tatar A.S.S.R.
11. Siberia, Mongolia, Manchuria
12. Arabia (general), Syria, Lebanon, Israel, Jordan, Iraq [Mesopotamia], Saudi Arabia, Iran [Persia], Afghanistan
13. Tibet, Pakistan, India (following the regional order in *Types of the Indic Oral Tales*), Ceylon
14. Burma, Thailand, Indo-China [Vietnam, Laos, Cambodia]
15. China, Korea, Japan [including the Ainu]
16. Indonesia (general), Malaya, Sumatra, Java, Borneo, Sarawak, Philippines, Celebes

D. Africa

For further information on the individual storytellers and their social background the reader is referred to Appendix B, Biographical Profiles. The indexes of titles, tale types, motifs, and narrators following the Bibliography will help identify specific information on these aspects throughout the collection.

Finally, it has become clear to us during our work on this collection that as information on tales and the number of available texts increases, the need for a systematic index of cross-references within the AT index becomes more and more important. Certain tale elements and motifs migrate much more freely than others from one type to another. Such elements are less tied to a given type and are often more generalized than others in theme. They can therefore fit easily into slots in the element structure of a number of different types. It follows that a number of types are particularly receptive to the incorporation of such "free-floating" motifs, elements, and episodes, just as beginning and end formulas can be attached to or detached from stories at will. As some of the stories in this collection demonstrate, certain types lend themselves more readily to combination with others. All these types are therefore especially susceptible to change, variation, lengthening, or truncation.

If one concentrates too much on the validity or discreteness of a type and its number, the AT index is too constricting. It tends to limit scholars in their interpretation and classification of tales because, being an index, it is necessarily static. It appears to be final, enshrined, infallible, and scholars tend to base many of their judgments too exclusively upon it.

To make the AT index work more functionally, it is useful to take account of the ways in which the types interact—which of them are similar to or different from others and in which specific ways. This should be done over the full range of types within the AT index rather than merely within a given type and its immediate variants.

What is needed at this point in the development of folk narrative scholarship is a move away from such static models of reference and annotation as the AT index, and similar numerically based lists, toward a more dynamic interpretation of the folktale text. In so doing the indexes can be utilized in a new and more functional way, by linking them to a fuller discussion of performance, context, style, and language. This is a move away from content analysis as such—an approach already regarded as passé by many scholars—toward the study of narrative as a complex social and psychological phenomenon. Such an approach would also reflect the underlying traditional taxonomy of narratives: what the storytellers are actually doing, their perception(s) of what a story should be. This aspect of the traditional aesthetic may not be a conscious process on the part of the narrator, but such a process is clearly at work in each and every performance.

Folktale scholars and annotators should base their texts and analyses increasingly on the tellers and their performance, rather than solely on indexes to whose fixed numbered categories narrators and narratives are somehow expected to conform. Fieldworkers all too easily seek a specific AT type when they should be recording the fullest possible range of tales. Only when this has been done is it relevant to ask whether such narratives have a place in an index or whether they require some alternative treatment and classification.

This leads us ultimately to question the validity and function of such indexes. While we acknowledge their usefulness in categorizing specific international types and in demonstrating the comparability of these types across cultures and their distribution within a given culture, it is clear that they have their limitations. Our own analysis of this collection of Newfoundland tales relies heavily on such indexes and on the AT index in particular. Nevertheless, like many others in recent years, we have become increasingly dissatisfied with the restricting and inflexible nature of such an approach, as indicated in our discussions of several of the types represented here.

Following in the footsteps of most other presenters and commentators on folktale texts, we naturally felt it would be both logical and helpful to present these tales in the numerical order of the AT index and to base our comparative notes on the index and other established works of that kind. While this obviously has many advantages, especially when discussing international parallels, it proved inadequate in other respects. We soon discovered, for example, that though such an approach is useful in annotating fully rounded and "edited" texts, it is less appropriate for analyzing structure, variation, and linguistic features in narratives transcribed verbatim from tape in a declining tradition. This realization led us to augment the index-based comparative analysis with commentaries on context, style, and language that provide a fuller insight into the storytelling event. Together with our attempts to set down the actual words of the storytellers, these tentative and exploratory efforts to move beyond the constricting influence of the indexes offer considerable scope for further development.

Drawing on a revised, expanded, fully cross-referenced, and computerized AT index, augmented by all other extant indexes in a single comprehensive data base, scholars of the future may also wish to explore traditional narratives as a living art. Such an approach, combining updated international classification systems with analyses of actual performance, would break down the artificial barriers that separate the two approaches and enable scholars to study the full range of traditional narrative more effectively. In optimistic anticipation of such developments we offer in the texts and notes in this collection a few hints and suggestions on possible ways forward. A more holistic and interdisciplinary approach to the study of narrative would in itself effect a rapprochement between folklorists, historians, literary scholars, linguists, other social scientists, and all those who share an interest in this perennially fascinating subject.

NOTES

1. See H. Halpert and N. V. Rosenberg, "Folklore Work at Memorial University," *Canadian Forum* 53, no. 638 (March 1974), 31-32, and "MUNFLA: The Development of a Folklore and Language Archive at Memorial University," *Laurentian University Review* 8, no. 2 (February 1976), 107-14, rpt. together as *Folklore Studies at Memorial University: Two Reports* (St. John's: Department of Folklore, Memorial University of Newfoundland, 1978).

2. G. M. Story, W. J. Kirwin, and J. D. A. Widdowson, eds., *Dictionary of Newfoundland English* (Toronto: University of Toronto Press, 1982; 2d ed., with Supplement, 1990). Cited as Story, Kirwin and Widdowson, *Dictionary.*

3. Among these are several tape-recorded folktales in the Goldstein-Wareham Collection, MUNFLA (1980-), and fifteen tales (twelve Märchen and three novelle) collected from Pius Power of South East Bight, Placentia Bay, by Anita Best between 1977 and 1987. Gerald Thomas has collected numerous folktales on tape, in both French and English, from the French-speaking tradition on the Port au Port Peninsula. These latter tapes are deposited in both MUNFLA and the archives of the Centre D'Études Franco-Terreneuviennes (CEFT) at Memorial University. Many of these narratives were collected from Emile Benoit of L'Anse-à-Canards, including a full-length videotape in English of a version of AT313 recorded in 1985.

4. For a discussion of settlement patterns see K. Matthews, *Lectures on the History of Newfoundland, 1500-1830* (St. John's: Maritime History Group, Memorial University of Newfoundland, 1973); J. J. Mannion, ed., *The Peopling of Newfoundland: Essays in Historical Geography* (St. John's: Institute of Social and Economic Research, Memorial University of Newfoundland, 1977).

5. G. Thomas, *Les Deux Traditions: Le conte populaire chez les Franco-Terreneuviens* (Montréal: Les Éditions Bellarmin, 1983); M-A. Desplanques, coll. and ed., *Folktales from Western Newfoundland,* told by Angela Kerfont (Rouen: Université de Rouen, 1985).

6. See G. Barter, "The Folktale and Children in the Tradition of French Newfoundlanders," *Canadian Folklore Canadien,* 1, nos. 1-2 (1979) 5-11.

7. See, e.g., E. S. Hartland, comp. and ed., *English Fairy and Other Folk Tales* (London: Walter Scott, [1890?]), Introduction. For a brief discussion and commentary on the absence of field collections of folktales in England, see H. Halpert, Appendix, in R. Chase, coll. and ed., *The Jack Tales* (Cambridge, Mass.: Houghton Mifflin, 1943), pp. 183-88. Cited as Chase, *Jack.*

8. E. W. Baughman, *Type and Motif-Index of the Folktales of England and North America* (The Hague: Mouton, 1966).

9. See, e.g., W. H. Barrett, *Tales from the Fens,* ed. E. Porter (London: Routledge and Kegan Paul, 1963); W. H. Barrett, *More Tales from the Fens,* ed. E. Porter (London: Routledge and Kegan Paul, 1964); K. M. Briggs and R. L. Tongue, *Folktales of England* (London: Routledge and Kegan Paul, 1965); K. Palmer, *Oral Folk-Tales of Wessex* (Newton Abbot: David and Charles, 1973).

10. See C. J. Sharp, *English Folk-Song: Some Conclusions* (London: Simpkin, 1907), pp. 119ff.

11. See O. D. Campbell and C. J. Sharp, *English Folk Songs from the Southern Appalachians* (New York: Putnam's, 1917), Introduction; C. J. Sharp, *English Folk Songs from the Southern Appalachians,* ed. M. Karpeles (London: Oxford University Press, 1932), Preface. Cited as Sharp-Karpeles.

12. Sharp-Karpeles, 2d imp., 1952, Note to Preface.

13. M. Karpeles, coll. and ed., *Folk Songs from Newfoundland* (London: Oxford University Press, 1934), Introduction. Cited as Karpeles, *Folk Songs* (1934).

14. See E. B. Greenleaf, coll. and ed., and G. Y. Mansfield, *Ballads and Sea Songs of Newfoundland* (Cambridge, Mass.: Harvard University Press, 1933). Cited as Greenleaf and Mansfield, *Ballads.*

15. H. Halpert and G. M. Story, eds., *Christmas Mumming in Newfoundland: Essays in Anthropology, Folklore, and History* (Toronto: University of Toronto Press for Memorial University of Newfoundland, 1969). Cited as Halpert and Story, *Christmas Mumming.*

16. Greenleaf and Mansfield, *Ballads*; Karpeles, *Folk Songs* (1934); K. Peacock, coll. and ed., *Songs of the Newfoundland Outports* (Ottawa: National Museum of Canada, 1965); MacE. Leach, *Folk Ballads and Songs of the Lower Labrador Coast* (Ottawa: National Museum of Canada, 1965); M. Karpeles, coll. and ed., *Folk Songs from Newfoundland* (London: Faber, 1971).

17. See, e.g., Gerald S. Doyle, ed., *Old-Time Songs and Poetry of Newfoundland* (St. John's: Gerald S. Doyle, 1927), and subsequent revised editions with varying titles; J. White, comp., *Burke's Ballads* [St. John's: John White, 1960?]; O. Blondahl, comp., *Newfoundlanders, Sing! A Collection of Favourite Newfoundland Folk Songs* (St. John's: E. J. Bonnell, 1964); S. Ryan and L. G. Small, *Haulin' Rope and Gaff: Songs and Poetry in the History of the Newfoundland Seal Fishery* (St. John's: Breakwater Books, 1978); W. J. Kirwin, ed., *John White's Collection of the Songs of Johnny Burke* (St. John's: Harry Cuff, 1982). For other bibliographical references, see P. Mercer, comp., *Newfoundland Songs and Ballads in Print, 1842-1974: A Title and First-Line Index* (St. John's: Memorial University of Newfoundland, 1979).

18. See n. 3 above.

19. For important and cogent discussions of these and other aspects of style, see J. Ball, "Style in the Folktale," *Folk-Lore* 65 (1954), 170-72. See also W. H. Jansen, "A Folktale—On Paper?," *Mid-South Folklore* 3, no. 3 (Winter 1975), 83-87; D. R. Preston, "'Ritin' Fowklower Daun 'Rong: Folklorists' Failures in Phonology," *Journal of American Folklore* 95 (1982), 304-26; E. Fine, "In Defence of Literary Dialect: A Response to Dennis R. Preston," *Journal of American Folklore* 96 (1983), 323-30; D. R. Preston, "Mowr Bayud Spellin': A Reply to Fine," *Journal of American Folklore* 96 (1983), 330-39; E. A. Fine, *The Folklore Text: From Performance to Print* (Bloomington: Indiana University Press, 1984). These are cited as Ball, "Style"; Jansen, "Folktale"; Preston, "'Ritin'"; Fine, "Defence"; Preston, "Mowr"; Fine, *Text.*

20. J. Grimm and W. Grimm, *Die Kinder- und Hausmärchen* (Berlin: Realschulbuchhandlung, 2 vols., 1812 and 1815).

21. I.e., "The Story of Giannetto of Venice and the Lady of Belmont," in the late fourteenth-century Italian collection *Il Pecorone,* attributed to Ser Giovanni, published in 1558; for a commentary and translation, see T. J. B. Spencer, *Elizabethan Love Stories* (Harmondsworth: Penguin, 1968), pp. 28-29, 177-96.

22. Ibid., p. 28.

23. Y. Pino-Saavedra, ed., *Folktales of Chile* (Chicago: University of Chicago Press, 1967), pp. 189-94.

24. See K. M. Briggs, *A Dictionary of British Folk-Tales in the English Language, Incorporating the F. J. Norton Collection,* Pt. A, 2, pp. 451-52.

25. See E. S. Hartland, *The Science of Fairy Tales* (London: Walter Scott, 1891), Chap. 1, "The Art of Story-Telling." This chapter includes some remarkably perspicacious and farsighted comments on both the telling and the collecting of stories.

26. See notes to No. 67.

27. The *Family Herald and Weekly Star,* a weekly newspaper published in Montreal, included a feature entitled "Old Favourites" from 1895 to 1968. See E. Fowke, "'Old Favourites': A Selective Index," *Canadian Folk Music Journal,* 7 (1979), 29-56. Everett Bennett of St. Pauls told Halpert in an interview: "An' lots of times there would be songs come in the newspaper, you know, 'Family

Herald'—we [were] takin' the 'Family Herald' at that time. A lot o' songs in the 'Family Herald' then. Well we'd learn 'em that way, see. ...we'd most always put tunes to 'em ourself, ya know. Get a...tune'd suit the song good, well put that tune to it." MUNFLA tape, TC971, 71-50, edited transcript.

28. Among these were the publications of the Wehman Brothers of New York. We can verify that at least one of their song compilations, *Six Hundred and Seventeen Irish Songs and Ballads* (n.d.), found its way to one of the outports near St. John's.

29. Halpert and Story, *Christmas Mumming*.

30. C. R. Baskervill, *The Elizabethan Jig* (Chicago: University of Chicago Press, 1929), pp. 310-11.

31. For examples and analysis of the retelling of stories over a period of time, see P. B. Mullen, *I Heard the Old Fishermen Say* (Austin and London: University of Texas Press, 1978), pp. 130-48; P. B. Mullen, "A Traditional Storyteller in Changing Contexts," in R. Bauman and R. D. Abrahams, eds., *"And Other Neighborly Names": Social Process and Cultural Image in Texas Folklore* (Austin: University of Texas Press, 1981), pp. 266-79; R. Bauman, *Story, Performance, and Event* (Cambridge: Cambridge University Press, 1986), pp. 78-111; R. Bauman, "Ed Bell, Texas Storyteller: The Framing and Reframing of Life Experience," *Journal of Folklore Research* 24 (1987), 197-221.

32. A. Aarne and S. Thompson, *The Types of the Folktale: A Classification and Bibliography,* 2d rev. ed. (Helsinki: Academia Scientiarum Fennica, 1961).

33. S. Ó Súilleabháin and R. Th. Christiansen, *The Types of the Irish Folktale* (Helsinki: Academia Scientiarum Fennica, 1963). Cited as *Irish Types*.

34. F. Hoffmann, *Analytical Survey of Anglo-American Traditional Erotica* (Bowling Green, Ohio: Bowling Green University Popular Press, 1973).

35. Freeman Bennett, St. Pauls, MUNFLA tape, TC1063 72-4, edited transcript. This and other excerpts from transcripts quoted in the Introduction have been edited in a more conventional way than the transcriptions of the tales themselves. For greater accessibility these quotations omit hesitations, repetitions, interjections by the interviewer, and other less pertinent material. The original and the edited transcripts are on file in MUNFLA.

36. Ibid.

37. Allan Oake, Beaumont, MUNFLA tape, TC309 66-25, edited transcript; see comments following No. 26.

38. John Myrick, St. Shotts, MUNFLA tape, TC528 68-43, edited transcript.

39. More recent fieldwork confirms that some of the narratives collected from other tellers were very much longer in terms of performance duration. The version of AT313 told by Emile Benoit of L'Anse-à-Canards and recorded on videotape by Gerald Thomas extends to approximately one hour, twenty-seven minutes, and the longest tale recorded on audiotape by Anita Best from Pius Power of South East Bight took one hour, fifty-five minutes to tell.

40. George Payne, Cow Head, MUNFLA tape, TC1062 72-4, edited transcript.

41. Clarence Bennett, St. Pauls, MUNFLA tape, TC1050 72-4, edited transcript.

42. Everett Bennett, St. Pauls, MUNFLA tape, TC970 71-50; see comments following No. 48.

43. David Payne, Cow Head, MUNFLA tape, TC1062 72-4, edited transcript.

44. Frank Bennett, St. Pauls, MUNFLA tape, TC1065 72-4, edited transcript.

45. See, however, n. 38 above.

46. Freeman Bennett, St. Pauls, MUNFLA tape, TC1063 72-4, edited transcript.

47. Clarence Bennett, St. Pauls, MUNFLA tape, TC1050 72-4, edited transcript.

48. Everett Bennett, St. Pauls, Halpert field notes, 11 September 1971.

49. Everett Bennett, St. Pauls, MUNFLA tape, TC971 71-50, edited transcript.

50. Everett Bennett, St. Pauls, MUNFLA tape, TC245 66-24, edited transcript.

51. Frank Knox, St. Shotts, MUNFLA tape, TC527 68-43, edited transcript.

52. See, e.g., notes to Nos. 96, 97, 102, 103, 149.

53. The same is true of oral epic. Lord notes that "every performance is a separate song; for every performance is unique, and every performance bears the signature of its poet singer." A. B. Lord, *The Singer of Tales* (Cambridge, Mass.: Harvard University Press, 1960), p. 4.

54. Allan Oake, Beaumont, MUNFLA tape, TC309 66-25, edited transcript.

55. See the opening lines of No. 97. For a corroboration of this view of Jack as lucky and successful from another North American tradition see the comment by Sam Harmon of Tennessee quoted in Chase, *Jack* (1943), Halpert appendix, p. 187.

56. For a discussion of parallelism and repetition in performance, see R. Bauman, *Verbal Art as Performance* (Prospect Heights, Ill.: Waveland Press, 1984), pp. 18-19.

57. This is also true of some stories in other North American English language collections. See, e.g., Chase, *Jack*; R. Chase, *Grandfather Tales: American-English Folk Tales* (Boston: Houghton Mifflin, 1948); R. Chase, *Jack and the Three Sillies* (Boston: Houghton Mifflin, 1950); V. Randolph, coll., *Who Blowed Up the Church House? and Other Ozark Folk Tales* (New York: Columbia University Press, 1952); V. Randolph, coll., *The Devil's Pretty Daughter and Other Ozark Folk Tales* (New York: Columbia University Press, 1955); L. W. Roberts, *South from Hell-fer-Sartin: Kentucky Mountain Folk Tales* (Lexington: University of Kentucky Press, 1955); R. Chase, comp. and ed., *American Folk Tales and Songs, and Other Examples of English-American Tradition as Preserved in the Appalachian Mountains and Elsewhere in the United States* (New York: New American Library, 1956); V. Randolph, coll., *The Talking Turtle and Other Ozark Folk Tales* (New York: Columbia University Press, 1958); V. Randolph, *Hot Springs and Hell and Other Folk Jests and Anecdotes from the Ozarks* (Hatboro, Pa.: Folklore Associates, 1965); L. Roberts, coll. and ed., *Old Greasybeard: Tales from the Cumberland Gap* (Detroit: Folklore Associates, 1969); L. Roberts, *Sang Branch Settlers: Folksongs and Tales of a Kentucky Mountain Family* (Austin: University of Texas Press, 1974); V. Randolph, *Pissing in the Snow and Other Ozark Folktales* (Urbana: University of Illinois Press, 1976).

58. An exception to this is Emile Benoit, a storyteller from the French-speaking tradition of the Port-au-Port Peninsula, on the west coast of the Province, whose narratives have been extensively recorded and discussed by Gerald Thomas. See G. Thomas, *Les Deux Traditions* (Montréal: Les Éditions Bellarmin, 1983), pp. 178-79. Emile Benoit adopts various female speaking roles in his videotaped version of AT313, through both mimicry and the use of disguise.

59. For a discussion of these and other paralinguistic features, see Bauman, *Verbal,* pp. 19-20.

60. For a discussion of this problem, see Ball, "Style"; Jansen, "Folktale"; Preston, "'Ritin'"; Fine, "Defence"; Fine, *Text*; H. Halpert and J. D. A. Widdowson, "Folk-Narrative Performance and Tape Transcription: Theory versus Practice," in R. Kvideland and T. Selberg, eds., *The 8th Congress for the International Society for Folk Narrative Research,* Papers, 1 (1984), pp. 225-32, and rev. and rpt., *Lore and Language* 5, no. 1 (1986), 39-50. Cited as Halpert and Widdowson, "Folk Narrative."

61. The increasing recognition of the need for verbatim transcription of English language texts may be seen, e.g., by a detailed examination of the texts presented in H. Creighton and E. D. Ives, colls., "Eight Folktales from Miramichi as Told by Wilmot MacDonald," *Northeast Folklore* 4 (1962); P. Greenhill, *Lots of Stories: Maritime Narratives from the Creighton Collection* (Ottawa: National Museum of Canada, 1985) (cited as Greenhill-Creighton, *Narratives)*; Fine, *Text*.

62. For comments on and/or discussion of verbatim transcription of English-language narratives see, e.g., Chase, *Jack,* Halpert appendix, pp. 187-88; H. Halpert, "American Regional Folklore," *Journal of American Folklore* 60 (1947), 360-61; H. Halpert, "Problems and Projects in the American-English Folktale," *Journal of American Folklore,* 70 (1957), 60-62; Halpert and Widdowson, "Folk-Narrative" (1984/1986); Greenhill-Creighton, *Narratives*; Fine, *Text*; B. Ellis, "Why Are Verbatim Transcripts of Legends Necessary?," in G. Bennett, P. Smith, and J. D. A. Widdowson, eds.,

Perspectives on Contemporary Legend, 2 (Sheffield: Sheffield Academic Press for the Centre for English Cultural Tradition and Language, 1987), pp. 31-60.

63. See, e.g., D. Tedlock, "On the Translation of Style in Oral Narrative," in A. Paredes and R. Bauman, eds., *Towards New Perspectives in Folklore* (Austin: University of Texas Press, 1971), pp. 114-33; D. Tedlock, *Finding the Center: Narrative Poetry of the Zuni Indians* (New York: Dial Press, 1972); B. Toelken, "The Pretty Languages of Yellowman: Genre, Mode and Texture in Navaho Coyote Narrative," in D. Ben-Amos, ed., *Folklore Genres* (Austin: University of Texas Press, 1976), pp. 145-70; D. Hymes, *"In vain I tried to tell you!" Essays in Native American Ethnopoetics* (Philadelphia: University of Pennsylvania Press, 1981); B. Toelken and T. Scott, "Poetic Retranslation and the 'Pretty Languages' of Yellowman," in K. Kroeber, ed., *Traditional Literatures of the American Indian: Texts and Interpretations* (Lincoln: University of Nebraska Press, 1981), pp. 65-116; W. Bright, "A Karok Myth in 'Measured Verse': The Translation of a Performance," *Journal of California and Great Basin Anthropology* 1 (1979), 117-23; B. Swann, ed., *Smoothing the Ground: Essays on Native American Oral Literature* (Berkeley: University of California Press, 1983); for ethnopoetic transcriptions of English language materials, see J. Titon, transcriber, "Son House: Two Narratives," *Alcheringa: Ethnopoetics* 2, no. 1 (1976), 2-9; J. Titon and K. George, transcribers, "Dressed in the Armor of God," *Alcheringa: Ethnopoetics* 3, no. 2 (1977), 10-31; J. Titon and K. George, "Testimonies," *Alcheringa: Ethnopoetics* 4, no. 1 (1978), 69-83; Greenhill-Creighton, *Narratives.*

64. For comments on the significance of hesitation, pause, misencoding, and other features of individual storytelling style see B. Almqvist, "The Narrative Performance of an Irish Storyteller," paper presented at the Centenary Conference of the Folklore Society, Egham, Surrey, 1978. See also Ball, "Style," and Preston, "Mowr."

65. R. Hollett, "Allegro Speech of a Newfoundlander," in H. J. Paddock, ed., *Languages in Newfoundland and Labrador,* 2d version (St. John's: Department of Linguistics, Memorial University, 1982), pp. 124-70.

66. These conventions were first suggested to Halpert by Dr. George Herzog for the transcription of cante-fable recordings made on phonograph disks; see H. Halpert, "The Cante Fable in New Jersey," *Journal of American Folklore* 55 (1942), 133-43. Coincidentally, Newfoundland versions of three of the cante fables collected in New Jersey also appear in this collection.

67. See Fine, *Text,* esp. pp. 166-203.

68. See *The Principles of the International Phonetic Association* (1949, rpt. 1982), obtainable from the Association at University College, London. This alphabet is also used in Story, Kirwin, and Widdowson, *Dictionary,* to indicate a number of Newfoundland pronunciations that differ significantly from those recorded in the principal English and North American dictionaries.

69. This fairly narrow phonetic transcription incorporates aspects of intonation: four levels of stress (´ primary, ˆ secondary, ` tertiary, and ˘ minimal), and four levels of pitch (ranging from ^{1} low, to ^{4} high, accompanied by arrows denoting lower, higher or level direction of pitch), adapted from W. N. Francis, *The Structure of American English* (New York, Ronald Press, 1958), pp. 152-55.

70. The asterisk here indicates a putative form.

71. See the entry for *a-^{1}* (reduced form) in C. T. Onions, ed., *The Oxford Dictionary of English Etymology* (Oxford: Clarendon Press, 1966).

72. See the entry for *after* in Story, Kirwin, and Widdowson, *Dictionary.*

73. In a few cases where material might be thought risqué or otherwise sensitive, or at the request of the contributor, the name of the storyteller and/or collector is omitted or a pseudonym is used. Brief biographical information about these individuals, if known, is nevertheless made available in Appendix B. The spelling of place-names follows that of the *Gazetteer of Canada: Newfoundland and Labrador* (Ottawa: Canadian Permanent Committee on Geographical Names, 1968). The geographical

distribution of place-names is based on the system in Halpert and Story, *Christmas Mumming*, pp. 224-29.

74. S. Thompson, *Motif-Index of Folk-Literature: A Classification of Narrative Elements in Folktales, Ballads, Myths, Fables, Mediaeval Romances, Exempla, Fabliaux, Jest-Books and Local Legends*, rev. and enl. ed. (Bloomington: Indiana University Press, 1955-58).

75. T. P. Coffin, *An Analytical Index to the Journal of American Folklore* (Philadelphia: American Folklore Society, 1958).

76. E. C. Parsons, *Folk-Lore of the Antilles, French and English*, Pt. 3, ed. G. A. Reichard (New York: American Folk-Lore Society, 1943).

77. S. L. Robe, *Index of Mexican Folktales, Including Narrative Texts from Mexico, Central America, and the Hispanic United States* (Berkeley: University of California Press, 1973).

78. T. L. Hansen, *The Types of the Folktale in Cuba, Puerto Rico, the Dominican Republic and Spanish South America* (Berkeley: University of California Press, 1957).

79. *Irish Types*.

80. Ø. Hodne, *The Types of the Norwegian Folktale* (Oslo: Universitetsforlaget, 1984).

81. P-L. Rausmaa, ed., "A Catalogue of Anecdotes: Addenda to the Aarne-Thompson Catalogue of Anecdotes in the Folklore Archives of the Finnish Literature Society," in *Catalogues of Finnish Anecdotes and Historical, Local and Religious Legends* (Turku: Nordic Institute of Folklore, 1973, pp. 3-).

82. S. Thompson and W. F. Roberts, *Types of Indic Oral Tales: India, Pakistan, and Ceylon* (Helsinki: Academia Scientiarum Fennica, 1960).

83. M. A. Klipple, "African Folk Tales with Foreign Analogues," Ph.D. diss., Indiana University, 1938.

84. R. S. Boggs, *Index of Spanish Folktales* (Helsinki: Academia Scientiarum Fennica, 1930).

85. D. P. Rotunda, *Motif-Index of the Italian Novella in Prose* (Bloomington: Indiana University, 1942).

The Tales

TEXTS AND NOTES

1. THE ANIMALS FRIGHTEN THE ROBBERS[†]

Allan Oake   AT130
Beaumont, Green Bay, Notre Dame Bay   TC309 66-25
10 September 1966   Collectors: JW and Harold Paddock

Well that was uh...first startin o' that one was a donkey I believe. You know they was goin to...goin to be...your donkey we'll say he...got lazy now then uh...he was no good, they was goina make away with un, well he started off _ you [know] on his own. An' once he come across a...a dog the same way, an old dog you know was uh...past labour _ was...goin to be made away wi'. Well ('twas) dodge on wi' the...wi' the donkey.

Well (the) once it came to...(like) a cat _ you know in the same way that they was probably goin to...make away with her well she...got out an'...and folly these. An' then we'll say it come to the...rooster. He was goin to have his head chopped off _ probably for dinner next day. Well 'twas skin out too _ an' join the crowd.

Well they dodged on, when they come to this robbers' house you know. Well they...'twas...'twas reach up you know, the dog got up on the...[*coughs*] on the donkey's back an' the...cat got up on the don...on the dog's head an'...an' the dog got an' the...dicky bird...the...the rooster we'll say got up on the cat's head. Well they could look in the winder [i.e., *window*] now an' they [*the robbers*] was just havin a s...they...they were just havin their...their meal.

Well of course now they...they all began in their own language you know, the donkey, the dog an' the...cat an' the...an' the rooster. Well as soon as they [*the robbers*] heard that they all went through the door frightened to death. Well now then we'll say they...when they was all gone they went in and eat what they wanted.

Well now then 'twas lie down in the best place you know that they...they wanted to lie down. Well the rooster got up on the shelf down the corner _ the cat we'll say laid down there in the front of the stove _ (there) under the stove _ an' the dog back in the corner, well uh...the donkey out in the YARD laid down.

By an' by uh after everything got quiet an' everything...they [*the robbers*] come back, one feller come back. An' he went in th' house you know. [*coughs*] And uh...well first thing he seen you know was thi[s]...those...those sparklin eyes there under the stove. An' he...went to put down his hand see an' the cat made a big siss an' a...claw at un. An' uh...he jumped up you know an'...he jump...slewed around to get out through the door an' the dog jumped up behind we'll say and bit his leg _ an'...and with a bark. An' then he runned out in the yard you know an' the...donkey jumped up an' kicked un. An' here the rooster in...he started to crow in there on the shelf.

1

An' he went back an' told th' other fellers there was a…there was a man under the stove _ that uh…clawed un he said an' there was another feller back there made a chop at un with a leg…with a…wi' stick. An' he said there was a feller out in the out in the yard gid un a kick. An' he said there was something in there on shelf sayin "Who done that? Who done that?" [*laughter*]

That's uh…that's all I got o' that _ you know.

Duration: 2 min., 59 sec.
Location: Store in garden of teller's house, afternoon.
Audience: Interviewers.

Context, Style, and Language: Relaxed, informal, almost intimate situation, the teller preferring to tell his stories there, rather than in the house. The little wooden store is a favorite retreat where youngsters and others seek him out for conversation and occasional storytelling. The interviewers, one of whom is well known to the teller, are able to slip easily and naturally into the normal context of his narration.

Of all the storytellers represented in this collection Allan Oake had the fullest repertoire of Märchen. Sixteen different tales were recorded altogether, fourteen of these in 1966 and a further two in 1975. The student collector sent to record Mr. Oake in 1975 found him convalescing in Springdale hospital and was able to collect five of the original stories for the second time. These retellings, separated from the earlier versions by nine years, offer interesting opportunities for comparison. In the 1966 interview Allan Oake mentioned that he rarely told stories except when "a scattered [i.e., occasional] young feller" asked him. He therefore had to make considerable efforts to recall them and inevitably had some difficulty over the order of events in the plots and other details. On the second occasion he was interviewed, although not at his best physically—his speech tending to be slurred or mumbled at times—he was relaxed and otherwise articulate and enjoyed the chance to retell the stories to while away the time. In 1966 he was recorded in a small shed at the bottom of his garden, where he sat in a rocking chair and obviously felt at ease in that environment; the comforting sound of the chair rocking to and fro is clearly heard on the tapes. He was very unwilling to tell the stories in the house and clearly preferred the privacy of the shed, where he could act as he pleased.

Most of the stories on that occasion were recorded by one of the editors and a colleague who acted as the local contact. Once the introductory recording session was over, the editor continued the interview alone and was often the only listener present. The recordings in 1975, however, took place in very different conditions. Apart from the fieldworker, a number of people were in the hospital room during much of the storytelling session, some of them asking questions and otherwise contributing to the interaction. There is a considerable amount of talking and background noise that sometimes causes problems for the transcriber. However, some of the tales were recorded in quieter moments by the teller himself, after receiving instructions from the fieldworker on how to operate the controls on the machine. There is no noticeable difference in the storytelling style, whether or not an audience is present. This corroborates Allan Oake's comments to one of the editors in 1966 that he often used to run through the stories in his mind to keep his repertoire active in spite of the lack of opportunities to tell them to an adult audience. Indeed, he "got together" more tales and fragments of tales from his memory and told them on the second day of the field trip, after being asked if he knew certain stories he had not told on the previous day. It may well be that the 1966 field trip contributed to the reactivation of his repertoire, and this possibility is strengthened by the collection of two tales in the 1975 interview that he did not tell in 1966.

Allan Oake's storytelling style is characterized by a rather slow, measured delivery, with few contrasts of pitch or intonation and none of the breathless excitement and verbal pyrotechnics of such narrators as John Roberts. An occasional strongly stressed word or phrase is the main contrastive feature of the style, its rarity being more than enough to make such words or phrases stand out markedly from the otherwise somewhat unanimated narration. The consequent evenness of the style, however, has its merits. The absence of highlights and obtrusive rhetorical effects demands the listener's close attention to the details of the undemonstrative, quietly spoken narrative, with its underlying humor and matter-of-fact tone. These characteristics are mirrored by the simplicity of the syntactical construction of the tales, sentences tending to be short, with clear pauses at frequent intervals, again contrasting sharply with the longer run-on sentences typical of the stories of the Bennett family and others. This episodic style may be partly due to the effort to recall stories from an inactive repertoire after a long period of time. Further evidence of this may be found in the very frequent use of *we'll say* as a punctuating phrase, not simply to mark a stage in the narrative but also as a kind of insurance against the audience's recognition of errors in the storytelling. The phrase suggests that the teller is not absolutely certain of this or that detail in the story and his frequent use of it glosses over such inaccuracies by implying that the precise details are unimportant. As noted elsewhere, the phrase, which is a hallmark of Allan Oake's style, also serves as a constant reminder to the audience that the events and situations in these folktales are not "true." Such a device is at the opposite extreme from those employed in narrating a legend, where they are explicitly intended to create a sense of reality or plausibility. In a similar way, Allan Oake often pays scant attention to exact pronunciation, tending to mispronounce words or sections of words with an apparent disregard for their importance. This puts a further strain on the relationship between teller and audience. Not only must the audience listen intently to the quiet, undemonstrative delivery, with its frequent pauses, hesitations, corrections, and repetitions, but must also interpret the misencodings in order to follow the narrative. In these respects Allan Oake's style is the least distinctive of the tellers represented in this collection. He seems detached from the tale rather than involved in it. He uses little dialogue or embellishment and scarcely any rhetorical devices. Even his descriptions are sparse and laconic. Yet with the minimum of distinctive rhetorical features he succeeds in interesting his audience and holding their attention.

Allan Oake's speech leans towards the West Country English variety, as seen here and in all his other tales in the frequent use of *un* (it, him) and in such forms as *dodged on* (sauntered, strolled). Also of note are the absence of final *-th* in *wi'*, the final /i/ in *folly*, the loss of initial vowel in *'twas*, the final *-er* in *winder* (window), the archaic *make/made away* *with/wi'* (kill[ed]), and *mind* (remember), dialectal *skin out* (escape), and *siss* (hiss), along with the past tense forms *they was, laid* (lay), *seen, runned*, and *gid* (gived:gave).

Type and Motifs:

AT130. *The Animals in Night Quarters.*
B296. *Animals go a-journeying.*
K335.1.4. *Animals climb on one another's backs and cry out, frighten robbers.*
Cf. K1161. *Animals hidden in various parts of a house attack owner with their characteristic powers and kill him when he enters.*

International Parallels: As the notes in the AT type index indicate, the tale of the mistreated animals who leave their homes and travel together is widely known in Europe and also, though less commonly, across Asia. Several domestic animals who have grown old go on a journey together to escape death. They come to a house and frighten away the robbers in it. They lie down in various parts of the house and yard, and when one of the robbers returns, they attack him and frighten him off. He reports his experience to his comrades, and as a result the animals are left in peace. In some versions the domestic animals frighten away wild animals and take possession of the lair, and then in a similar way scare off one of the inhabitants who ventures to return. As Thompson (*Folktale,* p. 223) points out, "It is the animal versions that have usually been carried to America."

In certain versions of the story a young man, often called Jack or Little John, is the leader of the group of animals. These versions occur in the English-language tradition in the United States, in the Franco-American tradition, and also in Ireland. In all of these the animals invariably frighten away robbers. Wild animals are presumed to be those frightened away unless the notes below specify otherwise. Where robbers are frightened away, this is specified. In those tales in which Jack is the leader of the traveling band of domestic animals he is named in the notes; in these instances it is robbers who are frightened away.

The gist of the story—that aged animals flee to escape death, form a co-operative group, aggressively fight off robbers, and take over their home—has a continuing social relevance. There is an implicit notion in the tale that the animals, like people, should not be written off after a lifetime of faithful service. Their very domestication has fostered a spirit of co-operation on which they can draw to better their circumstances. The animals discover that they can act collectively, not only to stay alive but to secure a new home in which they can live together. Unlike many aged farm laborers in the past, and indeed other groups today, they are able to choose a place to live together on their own terms despite the fact that all their years of service have been disregarded. This solution to their problems, however, can hardly be regarded as revolutionary in the true sense, as portrayed, for example, in George Orwell's novel *Animal Farm.* Although the animals act lawlessly, it is not against their former masters but against another lawless group.

Studies and Notes

Gerber, *Animal,* pp. 74-75, no. 34; Bolte and Polívka 1, pp. 237-59, no. 27; Aarne, *Die Tiere auf der Wanderschaft, FFC* no. 11; Chase, *Jack,* p. 191, no. 4, notes; Thompson, *The Folktale,* p. 223; Espinosa, *CPE,* 3, pp. 386-97; Roberts, *South,* pp. 209-10, no. 1, notes; Delarue, *Borzoi Book,* pp.

4

391-92, no. 1, notes; Dorson, *Folktales,* pp. 230-31, note 152; Baughman, *Index,* Type 130, p. 4; Ranke, *Folktales,* pp. 197-99, nos. 3-4, notes; Robe, *Index,* Type 130, p. 28; Delarue and Tenèze, *Catalogue,* 3, pp. 396-98, 404-6.

Canada

Lacourcière-Low, "Catalogue," cites 24 Francophone versions of AT130 from Canada: 3 (New Brunswick), 19 (Quebec), 2 (Ontario).

United States

Newell, *JAF* 1 (1888), 228-30, 2d version [with Jack], heard in Ohio (Massachusetts).

Newell, *JAF* 1 (1888), 230-34, 3d version, with notes (Massachusetts).

Parsons, *Islands,* 1, pp. 187-88, no. 61 [robbers], English trans. of Portuguese text, Cape Verde Islands, black (Massachusetts).

Newell, *JAF* 1 (1888), 227-28, 1st version [with Jack], heard in Massachusetts (Connecticut), and rpt. with changes in Jacobs, *English,* pp. 20-27, no. 5, and rpt. in summary from Jacobs in Briggs, *Dictionary,* A1, p. 313.

Reaver, *SFQ* 12 (1948), 262-64, no. 3 [robbers], Lithuanian, in English trans. (Illinois).

Dorson, *Folktales,* p. 189 [animals frighten man], black (Michigan), and rpt. in Dorson, *American,* pp. 350-51, no. 215.

Chase, *Jack,* pp. 40-46, no. 4 [with Jack], and notes, p. 191 (Virginia).

Perdue, *Devil,* pp. 57-59, no. 11 [with Jack] (Virginia).

Boggs, *JAF* 47 (1934), 294, no. 7 [with boy], incomplete (North Carolina).

Rodenbough, *NCF* 19 (1971), 181-83 [robbers] (North Carolina).

Fauset, *JAF* 40 (1927), 258, no. 12 [animals frighten man], black (Louisiana).

Roberts, *South,* pp. 14-15, no. 1 [robbers] (Kentucky).

Roberts, *Greasybeard,* pp. 28-31, no. 2 [robbers] (Kentucky).

Roberts, *Settlers,* pp. 236-37, no. 112 [robbers] (Kentucky).

M. Campbell, *Tales,* pp. 226-28, no. 7 [robbers] (Kentucky).

Carrière, *Tales,* pp. 19-21, no. 1 [with little John], French text with English summary (Missouri).

Thomas, *Good,* pp. 3-7, no. 1 [with little John], French text and English trans. (Missouri).

Dobie, *PTFS* 6 (1927), 33-37 [with Jack], has notes (Texas).

Robe-Jameson, *Folktales,* pp. 47-48, no. 14 [robbers], pp. 46-47, no. 13 [animals frighten other animals], 2 versions, Spanish tradition, in English (New Mexico).

Robe, *Index,* Type 130, cites 6 Spanish-American texts from New Mexico (Espinosa, *Folk-Tales,* nos. 102-4; Rael, *Cuentos,* nos. 361-62, 365-66), 2 from Colorado (Rael, *Cuentos,* nos. 363-64), and 6 from Mexicans and Mexican Indians. In all of these the protagonists are animals.

Lacourcière-Low, "Catalogue," cites 2 Francophone versions of AT130 from the United States: 1 (Louisiana), 1 (Missouri).

The Caribbean

Parsons, *Andros,* p. 135, no. 83 [robbers], black (Bahamas).

Hansen, *Types,* Type 130, cites 5 Hispanic-American versions from Puerto Rico; thieves figure in all of them.

England

Gomme, *FL* 20 (1909), 75-76, no. 1 [animals frighten prospective robbers] (Co. Durham), and rpt. in Briggs, *Dictionary,* A1, p. 174.

Scotland

Williamson, *Tales,* pp. 73-80 [robbers], Scottish traveller (Argyllshire).

Campbell, *Popular Tales,* 1, pp. 194-201, no. 11 [thieves], Gaelic text and English trans. (Islay).

Ireland

MacManus, *Heroes,* pp. 1-14 [with Jack] (Co. Donegal).

Kennedy, *Fictions,* pp. 4-11 [with Jack] (Co. Wexford), and rpt. in Jacobs, *Celtic,* pp. 112-20, no. 14, and again in O'Faolain, *Children,* pp. 332-39.

Ó Duilearga, *Béal.* 1 (1927), 94 [robbers], English summary of Irish text (Co. Kerry).

Ó Danachair, *Béal.* 17 (1947), 204-6, no. 3 [with Jack] (Co. Limerick).

Danaher, *Folktales,* pp. 123-27, no. 38 [with Jack] (Co. Limerick).

Irish Types, Type 130, 83 versions.

Continental Europe and Asia

Grimm no. 27, "The Bremen Town Musicians" in Grimm-Hunt 1, pp. 114-17, no. 27, composite text (Germany), 1, pp. 375-76, no. 27, notes, and for other trans. see Grimm-Magoun, pp. 105-8, no. 27, and Grimm-Zipes, pp. 105-7, no. 27.

Hodne, *Types,* AT130, 22 versions (Norway).

Delarue, *Borzoi Book,* pp. 285-87, pt. 2, no. 1 (France), and pp. 391-93, notes.

Cf. Massignon, *Folktales,* pp. 179-81, no. 52 (France), and p. 279, no. 52, notes.

Cf. Caballero, *Bird,* pp. 204-8 (Spain).

Cf. Crane, *Popular Tales,* pp. 272-74, no. 88 (cf. 210, with cf. 130) (Italy), and p. 377, n. 22, references.

Cf. Ranke, *Folktales,* pp. 6-8, no. 3 (with 15, 210), pp. 8-17, no. 4 (with 41, 104), 2 versions (Germany), and pp. 197-99, nos. 3 and 4, notes.

Cf. Gerber, *Animal,* p. 29, no. 34 (Russia), and pp. 74-75, no. 34, notes.

Cf. Afanas'ev, *Fairy Tales,* pp. 188-91, pp. 455-56, 2 versions (Russia).

Davidson and Phelps, *JAF* 50 (1937), 37-39, no. 14 [thieves], English trans. from Portuguese (New Goa, Bombay, India).

Cf. Zŏng, *Folk Tales,* pp. 160-62, no. 70 (cf. 130, with cf. 210) (Korea).

Cf. Eberhard, *Folktales,* pp. 143-46, no. 63 (cf. 130, with cf. 210) and p. 233, no. 63, notes (China).

Cf. Mitford, *Tales,* 1, pp. 264-66 (Japan).

Cf. Seki, *Folktales,* pp. 16-20, no. 6 (cf. 130, with cf. 210) (Japan).

Cf. Miyake, *Folktales,* pp. 30-35, no. 6 [animals and objects punish animal] (Okayama, Japan).

Cf. Mayer, *Guide,* pp. 302-5, nos. 325-27 [animals and objects punish animal] (Japan).

Africa

Cf. El-Shamy, *Folktales,* pp. 203-4, no. 52, last part of story [woman and animals punish thief] (Egypt).

Honeÿ, *Folk-Tales,* pp. 28-32 [robbers], Bushman people (South Africa).

2. THE OLD WOMAN AND HER THREE SONS

David Power
Harbour Breton, Fortune Bay
31 August 1967

AT300
TC444 65-21
Collector: HH

[recorder off]*** she had three sons.
[Int: So…what…was this? Yeah.]
Three sons.
[Int: An old woman?]

She had three sons _ Jack, Bill an' Tom. So _ Tom said "Bake me a cake mother, [*laughing tone*] roast me [a] (hen) till I goes off [to] seek me fortune."

So she baked a cake an' he went off _ travelled away an' sailed away, he come to a brook. Sat down to get a…drink. A little bird come down…uh get a mug-up [i.e., *snack*], a little bird come down an' pitched [i.e., *landed*] on a…tree while he was eatin

He said _ "Give us a /crumb/ uh…that fall from the mouth Tom"   /crump/
"No" Tom said "not a damn bit."

So he went off. He stooped down to get a drink it turned all into blood. Couldn't get (nar drink).

Tom travelled, travelled, bimeby [i.e., *by an' by*] he _ come [to] the king's palace, he looked up.

An' he said "What can you do?" Told un. "Come in."

Went in, give him his supper. Went to bed, next morning /called/   /carl/
uh…called un up, they give un _ twenty-five cows [to] carry off you know for to feed see. Anyhow _ Tom carried 'em off an' twelve o'clock Tom got up the tree an' went to sleep. 'Long comes th' ol' giant an' grabbed up five of his cow an' carried away.

Oh Tom woke up when th' evening come. Cows is gone. Comes down an' th' ol' giant…drove his cows down, /the king/ asked where the cows   /th' ol' giant/
was to.

Didn't know.

"Well" he said _ carry un out on the hea[d]…on the…choppin block, cut off his head an' put (it) up on a spear.

So _ Bill says "Bake me [a] cake mother, roast me [a] (hen) till I goes off to see where Tom is."

"Ah ya young fool" she said "you know that Tom is gone."

"Devil might care!" he said "I'm goin."

So he went off. He's travelled away till he come to this brook. He see there was somebody there so he…sat down to get a mug-up, along come the bird _ pitched. "Give us the /crumbs/ that fall from the mouth Bill."   /cums/

7

"Not a damn (sight)" he won't give.

So he stooped down to get a drink an' he turned it all i...into blood, the same thing.

Tom travelled away uh...Bill travelled away till he come to this...king's palace. Called un in ‿ what he could do. Anyhow ‿ got up the next morning, get...cows an' went off, same thing happened. Come home with six or seven of his cows gone. So he brought un out on the block an' cut off his head an' aput up on a spear. (Yes).

Jack said ‿ "Mother bake me a cake an' roast me a (hen) till I goes off to see where Bill an' Tom are to."

"Ah" she said "you're the only boy we got left I can't let ya go."

"(Well) devil might care mother, I'm goin."

So anyhow she baked un cakes an' he went off. Come to the brook. Huh! [*laughs*] Start havin a mug-up an' the little bird come down an' fled down.

/me/   "Give me the crumbs that fall from /the/ mouth"

"Yes" Jack said "you can have half what I got here."

Anyhow ‿ he ‿ eat away ‿ stooped down to get a drink it turned all into wine.

An' Jack travelled away an' bimeby it got dark on Jack. Looked up see the light an' went in. Ol' woman there.

And uh...an' she said "You have to hide away see 'cause I got a giant comin with seven heads" ‿ no three heads.

Anyhow ‿ he hided away till the giant got...bimeby the giant had his supper an' got out the chair ya know an' ‿ fell off to sleep. Th' ol' woman called un up. She give him a red ball.

"Now" she said "Jack. Wherever you goes or wants to go you chuck that red ball an' wherever he goes you folly un."

/la/   Jack done it. Went down. Bimeby he folly the ball. By...bimeby he come across this king's palace. Went in. The king said.../looked/...he looked up goin along an' he seen (un). He see Jack's head an' Tom's head uh...Bill's head ‿ they're Tom an' Bill's head[s]. So that...went in.

King said "What can you do?"

"Well" he said "I come to look for a job." He give him his supper an' he went to bed.

Called un up the next morning to give un the cows. He went off. An' they ‿ come up but there's a great big...farmstead, they couldn't get in, 'twas all ‿ build you see ‿ with concrete right around, all the hay was up everywhere ‿ (for it to have) Jack hove this little ball, **DOWN** comes the concrete hill (behind). In walks Jack's cows into the middle.

Jack got up in the tree 'bout twelve o'clock an' ‿ havin a nap (an') he see th' ol' giant comin with the...with his hands an' he took up three o' Jack's cows (ya know he...) Jack jump...jumped down out o' the...out o'one...he says "Fair play mister" he said "fair play, you're not goin to get my cows for nothing."

"Oh" he said "you DAMN rascal" he said "I scoff (at you)."

But Jack took his little ball an' _ down comes th' ol' giant. [bangs with hand to indicate fall] Jack runned up an' cut out his three tongue[s] an' put [them] in his pocket. Went up an' got his cows [Female listener: Mm.] that...brought 'em home. An' they milked everywhere, they couldn't put the milk away what they ha[d]...what come out the cows.

Anyhow his daughter was goin to be married. An' there was a...man goin be married, an' there was fiery serpent was comin in*...was goin (to)...kill her if...if he...if uh...ya know if he did (?that later) but uh...the butler he was goina...he was goin to save (her).

*rep. 4

So anyhow _ Jack (met her by) _ an' off she goes then (boy) _ right down on the beach an' sat down. Ol' butler went...about FIVE MILE from where she was to _ on a big hill. Sat down /front/ o' this _ crunnick [i.e., *stunted tree*].

/fraid/

Anyhow twelve o'clock _ Jack...Jack went down. He laid his head in her lap.

"Oh" she said [*urgent tones*] "you'll have to get out of it" said "'cause the fiery serpent's comin."

Jack said "Ah! Don't care about the fiery serpent." He laid down an' whilst he was laid down an' she...he cut a lock...she cut a lock o' hair out _ of his (head). Bimeby she's holly out to him the fiery serpent was comin. An' he come, (well then come fire) but Jack run down with his little ball. Hove _ hit th' ol' fiery serpent, killed un. Went down, cut out his tongue put [it] in his pocket an' went on.

Bimeby he come to th' ol' se...ol' uh...butler acome down off o' the hill "Aha!" he said "I saved ya!" An' she'd never said nothing but she went home an' _ next morning they got up to be married.

Well she said _ "I'm not...I'm not marrying nobody only so...(who)... whoever I marries" said "this lock o' hair 'll fit their head _ whoever it is."

Butler come in an' put down his head, ah nothin (doin). All the people was around you know like they had uh...servants.

An' uh...th' ol' woman said "I wonder 'twould be our Jack?"

Th' ol' man [said] "Our JACK! [*scornful tones*] You knows 'tis not our Jack."

She said "Devil might care!" she says. "Bring in...bring un in."

He went in an' laid down on (her)...on her lap an' _ took out the lock of hair, fit...goes to Jack's head.

"Ah" she said "that's the man I'm goina marry."

An' they got married, they had children in /baskets/ (?that sheltered five apiece) till I come away. [*laughter*]

/baskins/

9

[Int: What do you call that...story Uncle Dave?]

Eh?

[Int: What...does that story have a name? Do you have...]

Yes "Th' Ol' Woman an' her Three Sons" is...well that's uh...that's uh...they went off to seek their fortune then.

[Int: Ah ha. Where did you hear that story?]

God know where I did hear un, when I was down round home, when I was a...small kid down round home.

[Int: And that was back in...you...]

Back in...in...seventy years ago.

[Int: Mm hm. Uh on Burin?]

Eh?

[Int: Was it...where was it...where was your home an'...]

Down St. Bernard's.

[Int: St. Bernard's.]

Yes. At THAT time it 'll call Cross Cove [?] see wasn't it?

[Female listener: Yeah] They'd have...you...rename it _ St. Bernard's. (Well) that was about seventy, seventy odd year ago.

Duration: 6 min., 15 sec.

Source: Cross Cove (St. Bernard's), Fortune Bay, "seventy years ago."

Location: Living room of teller's house, evening.

Audience: A shifting group of up to eight people, including the teller's daughters, visiting adults and several children, interviewer.

Context, Style, and Language: House party, at which the interviewer sits in the living room with the teller. Various people, especially children, come in from the party in the kitchen to listen to the stories and songs. During the recording there is considerable background noise from the party. One of the teller's daughters twice responds in agreement by way of encouragement during the narration.

David Power's speech is of the West Country English type in pronunciation, although the long high back vowel in *butler,* pronounced as in *boot,* suggests comparison with the French *bouteillier* from which the English word derives. His lively storytelling style is evident in his gestures and the frequent changes in tone of voice which add vividness to the narrative. Several words and phrases are given strong emphasis which provides further vocal contrast and the dialogue is particularly racy and effective, even when the colloquial and the formal are in juxtaposition as in "Oh" he said "you DAMN rascal" he said "I scoff (at you)." It is unfortunate that because of his age some of Mr. Power's speech is difficult to transcribe, especially as the speed of delivery tends to blur the boundaries between words. This causes particular problems in the transcription of repeated formulas and phrases and especially the rapidly spoken end formula. In these the gist is obvious, but the exact sounds and words are at times impossible to transcribe with any real precision. The tentative transcriptions in

10

parentheses are therefore in this case more guesswork than a representation of the sounds actually spoken. This tale as a whole is a good example of the difficulties encountered in setting down on paper speech that is more readily understandable in the actual storytelling context. Breath groups tend to be of short duration, perhaps again due to the teller's age, and function words and other phrases are frequently omitted—e.g., "Looked up see the light an' went on. Ol' woman there." This gives a cryptic and economical flavor to the narrative style.

A similar economy of expression is seen in such aphetic forms as *'long* (along), *'cause* (because), *'bout* (about), in the loss of initial vowel in *'twas* (it was), *'twould* (it would), *'tis* (it is); and in the syncopation of *by and by* to *bimeby*. In the formulaic sentence "Give us a /crumb/ uh...that fall from the mouth Tom" and its two variants, the pronunciation of unstressed *the* before *mouth* strongly suggests it would originally be realized as *thy*. Also of note are the pronunciation of *follow* and *hollo* as *folly* and *holly*, the dialect words *pitched* (landed), *mug-up* (snack), and *crunnick* (weatherbeaten tree), the past tense forms *fled* (flew), *hided* (hid), *hove* (heaved), the omission of the plural inflection in *cow* in *grabbed up five of his cow* (para. 8), the archaic past tense forms *aput* and *acome*, and the purposive *for to feed*.

Type and Motifs:

AT300. *The Dragon-Slayer.*
P251.6.1. *Three brothers.*
B211.3. *Speaking bird.*
D478.4. *Transformation: water becomes bloody.*
H1199.17. *Task: guarding.*
F531.6.7.2.1. *Giant steals from man (fish, sheep, sword) [cattle].*
H901.1. *Heads placed on stakes for failure in performance of task.*
Q2. *Kind and unkind.*
D477.1. *Transformation: water becomes wine.*
G530.5. *Help from old woman in ogre's house.*
F531.1.2.2.2. *Three-headed giant.*
D821. *Magic object received from old woman.*
D1313.1. *Magic ball indicates road.*
Cf. D2093. *Walls overthrown by magic (Jericho).*
Cf. G152. *Giant herdsman.*
G512.8. *Ogre killed by striking [with magic ball].*
Cf. D1652.3.1. *Cow with inexhaustible milk.*
B11.12.3. *Fiery dragon.*
B11.11. *Fight with dragon.*
R111.1.3. *Rescue of princess (maiden) from dragon.*
Cf. H105.1. *Dragon-tongue proof.*
Cf. K1932. *Impostors claim reward (prize) earned by hero.*
Cf. H75.6. *Recognition by missing hair.*
L161. *Lowly hero marries princess.*
Z10.2. *End formula.*

International Parallels: The story of the hero who rescues a princess by killing a dragon and then gets her in marriage is well known in European literature from the classical legend of Perseus and Andromeda and the Christian legend of St. George and the Dragon. The archetypal form of the folktale includes a lady about to be killed/eaten/taken by a dragon; the hero comes to her aid when others desert her; he falls asleep in her lap, and only she can awaken him from his magical sleep; she obtains some identification from him while he is asleep; after she awakens him, he kills the dragon, cuts out its tongues, and then disappears; an impostor finds the dragon slain and the slayer gone, so claims credit and the princess in reward, using the cut-off heads as proof; the hero appears in disguise before the wedding and proves he killed the dragon by producing its tongues; the princess identifies him by a lock of hair, ring, missing fingertip, etc. In the Newfoundland version presented here, although the hero cuts out the tongues of the giant and the fiery serpent, they are not used as proofs against the impostor's claim.

The many legends on this theme often lack certain elements found in the folktale. For example, they rarely include the hero's magic sleep and awakening or the exposing of the impostor by the exhibiting of the dragon's tongues that the hero has cut out and preserved. No doubt because of its title, AT300 is used in many collections as a catchall for various local dragon legends. Consequently, references in many indexes and lists are not completely accurate. For this reason many of the references below are marked *cf.* to indicate that they diverge from the archetypal form. Although we are aware that there are many more analogues that might be classified under Cf. AT300, we present only a sampling here to indicate something of the range.

In our version of the story the hero does not have the assistance of helpful dogs, as found in many analogues of AT300, but obtains a magical ball. For discussions of those analogues in which dogs help the hero, see the extensive studies by Ranke and Espinosa below.

Supplementary comment is called for in connection with one feature of the version of Cf. AT300 found in No. 23: the employment of an animal that can store and eject a vast amount of water to assist the hero in his fight against a fire-spouting dragon. On rechecking the North American, British, and Irish analogues to AT300, we found only three versions that had this feature. In all three of these, as in No. 23, the hero acquires three differently colored sets either of armor or of rich clothing and differently colored horses. In all three versions, and also in No. 23, the heroine is to be taken or killed by a dragon or giant, and on each of three successive days the hero comes to her defense wearing a differently colored suit of armor or clothing and riding a different horse. The number of giants defeated by the hero to obtain these sets of armor or clothing and the horses varies in the three versions we are examining. It is three in the Aberdeenshire version as in the Newfoundland text, two in the County Donegal tale, but only one in the Welsh Gypsy tale.

In the Aberdeenshire story in Buchan, *Tales,* pp. 55-58, the hero fights the dragon on the first two days but cannot defeat it because of the fire it emits. On the third day the hero takes with him a camel, first having it swallow a great quantity of water. When the dragon appears, it again spouts fire at the hero. The camel in return spouts water to quench the fire, and this enables the hero to kill the dragon and cut off its head.

In the County Donegal tale in MacManus, *Heroes,* pp. 55-70, the hero conquers only two giants and in consequence acquires only two mares. The hero asks each of them what her capabilities are. The first claims that she is remarkably swift, while the other tells him that she can drink a lake of water and with it drown fires of any size. In this tale the hero fights a giant, rather than a dragon, on three successive days. In the second day's fight, the giant begins to belch fire at the hero, whereupon his mare runs to a nearby lough, drinks it dry, then rides against the giant. As fast as he belches fire, she casts water at it and drowns the fire. Curiously, on the third day the giant does not belch fire, and the battle ends with the defeated giant running away through the ocean.

In a Welsh Gypsy story in Sampson and Yates, *Folk Tales,* pp. 1-8, there is only one giant. He dies in a most unheroic fashion when he swallows the pins a helpful dwarf gives to the hero to put in the giant's drink. Here once again we have three sets of clothing and three horses, so that the hero has a change of both clothing and horses for each of the three days on which he fights the fiery dragon. The dwarf has a leading role in the tale. Each day he gives the hero a key to the giant's castle, instructing him to dress in the clothing and take the sword he finds there. Then he is to mount the waiting steed and take it to the river to let it drink before he goes forth to protect the lady and vanquish the fiery dragon. In each day's battle, when the dragon vomits fire at the lady, the horse vomits the water it has drunk and puts out the fire. Then, while the hero strikes the dragon with his sword, the horse pounds it with his hoofs.

On the first day the hero wears black clothing and rides a black horse; on the second day, the clothing and the horse are white. On the third day the complete sequence is repeated, with the hero wearing red and riding a red horse. This time, however, when the third horse stops at the river, he drinks it completely dry. In the battle the horse protects the lady by vomiting all the water over the dragon's fire and then with his hoofs fells the dragon to the ground, enabling the hero to kill the dragon by cutting off its head.

Although the water regurgitation scenes add a touch of humor to all three versions, the storytellers do not dwell on these scenes. In the first analogue the camel has been given its store of water before the battle; in the second the horse runs to the lough during the battle and promptly drinks it dry before returning to the fight. The third tale is unlike the others in that there is a strong element of humor in having a dwarf stage-manage the hero's actions, including the unheroic disposal of the giant. But even though the horses regularly drown the fiery dragon's flames and the third horse even drinks the river dry, these actions are combined with the very active part the hoofs of the horses play in the defeat and eventual killing of the dragon. In short, the Welsh Gypsy tale mixes humor with the serious Märchen action, but the humor does not predominate as it does in the treatment of the battles in the Newfoundland recension, No. 23.

Studies and Notes
Cox, *Cinderella,* pp. 521-22, n. 72; MacCulloch, *Childhood,* pp. 381-490; Campbell and Henderson, *Dragon,* pp. xi-li; F. Boas, "Notes on Mexican Folk-Lore," *JAF* 25 (1912), 258 and n. 4; Bolte and Polívka, 1, pp. 534 (Incident C), 547-51; Thompson, *European,* pp. 323-34, no. 1; Rose, *Handbook,* p. 273; Ranke, *Die Zwei Brüder, FFC* no. 114; Gardner, *Schoharie,* pp. 106-9, no. 2, notes; Parsons, *Antilles,* 3, p. 236, no. 245, headnote; Thompson, *The Folktale,*

pp. 24-33; Espinosa, *CPE,* 3, pp. 9-26; Graves, *Myths,* 1, p. 240; Delarue, *Catalogue,* 1, pp. 102-3, p. 108, and pp. 149-50, 162-63; Christiansen, *Studies,* pp. 33-80, 240, 242; Baughman, *Index,* Type 300, p. 6; Robe, *Index,* Types 300, 300*C, 300*D, pp. 42-44; El Shamy, *Folktales,* pp. 279-81, no. 34, notes.

Canada

Fauset, *Folklore,* pp. 13-14, no. 7, black, pp. 41-43, no. 18, Variant (with 563), 2 versions (Nova Scotia).

MacNeil, *Sgeul,* pp. 342-57, no. 52, Gaelic text and English trans. (Nova Scotia), English trans. only, in MacNeil, *Tales,* pp. 174-81, no. 52.

Cf. Mechling, *JAF* 26 (1913), 234-47, no. 4 (cf. 300, with 650A, 1640, 1000, 301B), Maliseet Indian (New Brunswick).

Cf. Creighton and Ives, *Folktales,* pp. 13-20, no. 1 (511A, with cf. 300) (New Brunswick); for another transcription of pp. 14-18, see Greenhill-Creighton, *Narratives,* pp. 15-27.

Speck and Beck, *JAF* 63 (1950), 286-94 (with 302), and useful discussion, Mohawk Indian (Quebec).

Radin and Reagan, *JAF* 41 (1928), 119-20, no. 24, Ojibwa Indian (Ontario).

Skinner, *JAF* 29 (1916), 330-34, no. 1 (with 303), Plains Ojibwa Indian (Manitoba), and rpt. in Thompson, *Tales,* pp. 201-5, no. 78, see also pp. 358-59, n. 289.

Skinner, *JAF* 29 (1916), 364-67, no. 9 (with 303), Plains Cree Indian (Saskatchewan).

Teit, *JAF* 29 (1916), 307, no. 2 (with 301A), summary, Upper Thompson River Indian (British Columbia).

Teit, *JAF* 50 (1937), 185-89, no. 6, Thompson Indian (British Columbia).

Thomas, *Types,* cites 4 versions of AT300 from Newfoundland French tradition.

Lacourcière-Low, "Catalogue," cites 128 Francophone versions of AT300 from Canada: 35 (Acadia), 75 (Quebec), 18 (Ontario).

United States

Parsons, *Islands,* 1, pp. 261-63, no. 87, pp. 263-68, no. 88 (with 303, 567), pp. 268-72, no. 88a (with 303), 3 versions, English trans. of Portuguese texts, Cape Verde Islands, black (Massachusetts).

Gardner, *Schoharie,* pp. 103-6, no. 2, and pp. 106-9, notes (New York).

Hoogasian-Villa, *Tales,* pp. 202-10, no. 22 (with 314, 502), pp. 266-73, no. 34 (with 550, 301A), 2 versions, Armenian tradition, in English trans. (Michigan).

Mathias and Raspa, *Folktales,* pp. 179-92, no. 12 (with cf. 592), Italian tradition, in English trans. (Michigan).

Glassie, *TFSB* 30 (1964), 97-102 (511A, with 300) (North Carolina).

Parsons, *Sea Islands,* pp. 83-88, no. 74 (with 315, 327), black (South Carolina).

Saucier, *Folk Tales,* pp. 29-31, no. 4 (with 326), French tradition, in English (Louisiana).

Musick, *Hills,* pp. 107-12, no. 24, Polish tradition, in English trans., pp. 113-18, no. 25 (with 303), Hungarian tradition, in English trans., 2 versions (West Virginia).

M. Campbell, *Tales,* pp. 132-39, no. 1 (with 313C), pp. 216-20, no. 2 (with 316), 2 versions (Kentucky).

Carrière, *Tales,* pp. 37-43, no. 9, French text with English summary (Missouri).

Thomas, *Good,* pp. 8-20, no. 2, French text and English trans. (Missouri).

Campa, *WF* 6 (1947), 323-26 (with 910B, cf. 559), Spanish tradition, in English, with notes (Texas or New Mexico).

Parsons and Boas, *JAF* 33 (1920), 50-55, no. 5, Laguna Indian (New Mexico).

Espinosa, *Folk-Tales,* p. 197, no. 22 (with cf. 301A), p. 197, no. 23 (with 303), 2 versions, English summaries of Spanish texts (New Mexico).

Lea, *Literary,* pp. 197-99 (with 910B, cf. 559), Spanish tradition, in English (New Mexico).

Rael, *Cuentos,* pp. 726-27, no. 246, English summary of Spanish text (New Mexico), and English resumé in Espinosa, *Folklore,* pp. 181-82.

Weigle, *Two Guadalupes,* pp. 53-60, Spanish tradition, in English (New Mexico).

Cf. Weigle, *Two Guadalupes,* pp. 66-68 (303, with cf. 300), Spanish tradition, in English (New Mexico).

Dorsey, *JAF* 5 (1892), 297-98, Ponca Indian (Nebraska).

Rael, *Cuentos,* pp. 727-28, no. 247 (with 315), pp. 765-66, no. 338 (with 1640), 2 versions, English summaries of Spanish texts (Colorado).

For further North American Indian references see Thompson, *European,* pp. 323-34, no. 1; Thompson, *Tales,* pp. 358-59, n. 289.

See Robe, *Index,* Type 300, for additional references to Hispanic American versions.

Lacourcière-Low, "Catalogue," cites 5 Francophone versions of AT300 from the United States: 3 (Louisiana), 2 (Missouri).

Mexico

Dobie, *PTFS* 12 (1935), 194-200 (with 650A), Spanish tradition, in English, Yaqui Indian (Mexico).

Foster, *Folklore and Beliefs,* pp. 226-28, no. 37 (with 327A, cf. 315), Spanish tradition, in English, Sierra Popoluca Indian (Veracruz).

Wheeler, *Tales,* pp. 126-32, no. 57 (with cf. 510B; girl kills monster), pp. 235-39, no. 92 (with 650A, 1551*A), pp. 286-89, no. 103 (with cf. 570), cf. pp. 293-95, no. 106 (with 1551*A), pp. 332-36, no. 114 (with cf. 506), pp. 355-58, no. 121 (with cf. 303), 6 versions, Spanish texts with English abstracts (Jalisco).

Paredes, *Folktales,* pp. 134-41, no. 43 (with 910B, 1551*A) (Jalisco).

See Robe, *Index,* Type 300, for further Mexican references.

The Caribbean, Central and South America

Crowley, *Talk,* pp. 114-16, Tale 139, pp. 113-14, discussion, black (Bahamas).

Cf. Crowley, *Talk,* pp. 93-94, Tale 152, cf. pp. 117-18, Tale 189 (with cf. 301), 2 versions, black (Bahamas).

Milne-Home, *Stories,* pp. 67-69, black (Jamaica?).

Jekyll, *Song,* pp. 54-57, no. 17, black (Jamaica).

Beckwith, *Stories,* pp. 113-15, no. 89, black (Jamaica).

Tanna, *Folk Tales,* pp. 113-15 (with 1535, V), black (Jamaica).

Dance, *Folklore,* pp. 30-31, no. 21, black (Jamaica).

Johnson, *JAF* 34 (1921), 77-80, no. 35 (with 303), black (Antigua, British West Indies).

Parsons, *Antilles,* 2, p. 409, no. 13 (with 303), black (St. Martin, Lesser Antilles).

See Parsons, *Antilles,* 3, pp. 236-44, no. 245, A-R, for English summaries of 18 French texts (often with 303) from many island locations, black (Lesser Antilles); headnote to no. 245 has additional references to texts from Europe, Asia, Africa, and Brazil.

Gossen, *SFQ* 28 (1964), 237-50, with a comparative survey (Costa Rica).

See Hansen, *Types,* Type 300, for references to the Dominican Republic, Puerto Rico, Colombia, and Chile.

England

Groome, *Folk-Tales,* pp. 205-8, no. 53 (with 511A), recorded by John Sampson, Gypsy (North Country), and rpt. in Yates, *Book,* pp. 155-58, no. 37, and rpt. from Yates in Briggs, *Dictionary,* A1, pp. 380-82, also cf. Jacobs, *More English,* pp. 172-76, no. 79, from John Sampson's collection in *Gypsy-Lore Journal,* but adapted, rewritten, and euphemized.

Cf. Henderson, *Notes,* 1866, pp. 247-52 [The Lambton Worm] (Co. Durham), and rpt. in Henderson, *Notes,* 1879, pp. 287-89, and rpt. from 1879 ed. in Hartland, *Folk Tales,* pp. 78-82, and also rpt. but rewritten in Jacobs, *More English,* pp. 198-203, no. 85, and rpt. from Jacobs in Briggs, *Dictionary,* A1, pp. 373-76.

Cf. Briggs, *Dictionary,* A1, pp. 382-83 (with 511A), summary from *Thompson Notebooks,* Gypsy (Lancashire).

Cf. Leather, *Folk-Lore,* pp. 174-76 (cf. 300, with 1640, II, 1115, 1088, Jack the Giant-Killer), learned from an old chapbook when a small boy (Herefordshire), and rpt. in Briggs, *Dictionary,* A1, pp. 331-33.

Cf. Jacobs, *English,* pp. 99-112, no. 19 (cf. 300, with 1640, III, II, 1115, 1080, cf. 507A, Jack the Giant-Killer), compiled and adapted from 3 sources, including 2 chapbooks (England).

Cf. Hartland, *Folk Tales,* pp. 3-17 (cf. 300, with 1640, III, II, 1115, 1088, cf. 507A, Jack the Giant-Killer), collated from sundry chapbooks (England), and rpt. in summary in Briggs, *Dictionary,* A1, pp. 329-31.

Cf. Briggs, *Dictionary,* A1, pp. 474-76 [St. George], summary from chapbook, *The Seven Champions of Christendom* (England).

Cf. Johnson, *7 Champions,* pp. 1-23, 58-138, Pt. 1, chapters 1-3, 10-19, differs from preceding chapbook in that George does not retire to Coventry (England).

About a dozen British dragon legends, many of which are stories about dragon killings (cf. 300), are reprinted in full or in summary from a variety of sources in Briggs, *Dictionary,* B1, pp. 159-72. A few of them are also reprinted in Briggs, *Sampler,* pp. 141-49.

Wales

Sampson and Yates, *Folk Tales,* pp. 1-8, English trans. from Romani, Gypsy (Wales), and cf. Groome, *Folk-Tales,* pp. 252-53, no. 61, for a rephrased version.

Briggs, *Dictionary,* A1, p. 333, from *Thompson Notebooks,* incomplete summary, Gypsy (Wales).

Scotland

Briggs, *Dictionary,* A1, pp. 144-47, rpt. from Douglas, *Scottish Fairy and Folk-Tales,* p. 58ff. (Scotland).

Cf. Chambers, *Rhymes,* pp. 89-94 (cf. 300, with cf. 303), from the original Peter Buchan MS. with verse repetitions condensed (Aberdeenshire), and rpt. in Briggs, *Dictionary,* A1, pp. 463-70, with Chambers' condensations extended in full, also rpt. with many changes in Jacobs, *English,* pp. 131-37, no. 23; cf. Buchan, *Tales,* pp. 13-17 (cf. 300, with cf. 303), an anglicized and rewritten version of the presumed original given in Chambers (Aberdeenshire).

Buchan, *Tales,* pp. 55-58 (Aberdeenshire), and rpt. in Briggs, *Dictionary,* A1, pp. 569-72.

Cf. Buchan, *Tales,* pp. 61-64 (cf. 300, with 400) (Aberdeenshire), and rpt. in Briggs, *Dictionary,* A1, pp. 448-51.

Cf. Briggs, *Dictionary,* A1, pp. 507-9 (cf. 300, with cf. 577), from School of Scottish Studies recording with dialect modified, Scottish traveller (Aberdeenshire).

MacDonald and Bruford, *Tales,* pp. 54-59, no. 18 (300, with 303) (Ross-shire).

Bede, *Wife,* pp. 19-27 (300, with cf. 327E) (Argyllshire).

Cf. Campbell, *Records,* p. 220 (Argyllshire).

MacInnes, *Tales,* pp. 278-305, no. 8, Gaelic text and English trans. (Argyllshire).

Campbell, *Popular Tales,* 1, pp. 71-93, no. 4 (with 302, 303), Gaelic text and English trans. (Argyllshire), 1, pp. 93-96, no. 4, 2d version (with 302) (South Uist), 1, pp. 97-98, no. 4, 3d version, summary in English (Argyllshire), 1, pp. 98-100, 4th version (with 302), summary in English (Berneray).

J. F. Campbell constructed a composite Celtic dragon myth in English trans. using elements from many of the stories he had secured from the Hebrides. The basic form is AT303, with the separate adventures of each of the brothers given. For AT300 see Campbell and Henderson, *Dragon,* pp. 44-47, sections 32-175, with notes, pp. 129-48, and Gaelic texts, pp. 149-72.

Ireland

The county is not specified for:

Curtin, *Myths,* pp. 157-74 (Ireland).

Cf. Curtin, *Myths,* pp. 114-28 (Ireland).

For Ulster see:

MacManus, *Heroes,* pp. 55-70 (300, with cf. 1063, cf. 1640, III) (Co. Donegal).

MacManus, *Corners,* pp. 1-19 (300, with 511A), pp. 37-53 (300, with cf. 551), 2 versions (Co. Donegal).

Kerr and McQuillan, *Béal.* 19 (1949), 185-87 (300, with 511A) (Co. Antrim).

For Leinster see:

MacGréine, *Béal.* 2 (1929-30), 268-72 (300, with 511A) (Co. Longford).

Cf. Gmelch and Kroup, *Road,* pp. 131-36 (1640, I, with 650A, cf. 300), Irish traveller (Co. Longford).

Cf. Ó Tuathail, *Béal.* 7 (1937), 46-47 (cf. 511A, with cf. 300) (Co. Carlow).

For Munster see:

Cf. Lover and O'Donoghue, *Legends,* 2, pp. 134-50 (cf. 300, with 1640) (Munster), and rpt. in Graves, *Fairy Book,* pp. 128-41.

Britten, *FLJ* 1 (1883), 54-55, no. 3 (Co. Tipperary).

Murphy, *Tales,* pp. 11-21 (Co. Cork).

Ó Cróinín, *Béal.* 35-36 (1967-68), 350, no. 1 (300, with 700), English summary of Irish text (Co. Cork).

Cf. Curtin, *Hero-Tales,* pp. 373-406 (cf. 300, with 302) (Co. Kerry), and rpt. in O'Faolain, *Children,* pp. 91-115.

Cf. Curtin, *Hero-Tales,* pp. 242-61 (300, with cf. 551) (Co. Kerry).

An Seabhac, *Béal.* 4 (1933-34), 45, English summary of Irish text (Co. Kerry).

Cf. Jackson, *Béal.* 4 (1933-34), 310-11, no. 1 (300, with 511A), English summary of Irish text (Co. Kerry).

Ó Duilearga, *Béal.* 5 (1935), 209-10 (300, with 301A), English summary of Irish text (Co. Kerry).

O'Sullivan, *Folklore,* pp. 35-43, no. 4 (300, in Finn mac Cool tale) (Co. Kerry).

Cf. Curtin, *Hero-Tales,* pp. 335-55 (Co. Limerick).

Ó Duilearga, *Béal.* 4 (1933-34), 226-27 (300, with 302) (Co. Clare).

Ó Duilearga, *Béal.* 30 (1962), 2-10, no. 1 (Co. Clare).

Ó Duilearga, *Béal.* 32 (1964), 50-59 (300, with 511A) (Co. Clare).

For Connacht see:
Cf. Larminie, *Folk-Tales,* pp. 130-38 (Co. Galway).
Cf. Gregory, *Poets,* pp. 138-42 (with 511A) (Co. Galway).
Gregory, *Wonder Book,* pp. 166-73 (with 303) (Co. Galway).
Synge, *Aran Islands,* pp. 78-84 (300, with 1640, I) (Co. Galway).
Ó Gríobhtha, *Béal.* 1 (1927-28), 297, English summary of Irish text (Co. Galway).
Nic Dhonnchadh, *Béal.* 1 (1927-28), 393-94, English summary of Irish text (Co. Galway).
O'Faolain, *Children,* pp. 135-46, trans. from Irish (Co. Galway).
Cf. O'Faolain, *Children,* pp. 287-98 (cf. 300, with 303), trans. from Irish (Co. Galway).
Dillon, *King,* pp. 53-76 (Co. Galway).
Gmelch and Kroup, *Road,* pp. 88-95, Irish traveller (Co. Roscommon).
Cf. Larminie, *Folk-Tales,* pp. 139-54, 196-210, 2 versions (Co. Mayo).
Ó Moghráin, *Béal.* 8 (1938), 224, brief English summary of Irish text (Co. Mayo).
Irish Types, Type 300, 652 versions.

Continental Europe and Asia
See Grimm no. 60, "The Two Brothers" in Grimm-Hunt 1, pp. 244-64, no. 60 (with 567, 303) (Germany), for other trans. see Grimm-Magoun, pp. 226-43, no. 60, and Grimm-Zipes, pp. 230-47, no. 60, and see also Grimm-Hunt 1, 418-22, no. 60, for other references.
Thorpe, *Yule-Tide,* pp. 300-312 (with cf. 303, 513B) (Norway).
Dasent, *Popular Tales,* pp. 180-94, no. 20 (with 303, cf. 513B) (Norway).
Cf. Dasent, *Fjeld,* pp. 261-73 (Norway).
Hodne, *Types,* AT300, 55 versions (Norway).
Thorpe, *Yule-Tide,* pp. 189-91, no. 2 (300), cf. pp. 175-88 (cf. 300, with 301A), 2 versions, and 2 abbreviated versions, cf. pp. 188-89, no. 1 (cf. 300, with 301A), cf. pp. 191-92, no. 4 (cf. 300, with 301A) (Sweden).
Delarue, *Borzoi Book,* pp. 147-56, no. 17 (with 315) (France).
Massignon, *Folktales,* pp. 34-39, no. 8 (France).
Webster, *Legends,* pp. 22-32 (with 502), pp. 33-38, pp. 87-94 (with 303), 3 versions (Basque).
Bødker, *European,* pp. 174-75 (Spain).
Cf. Cameron, *FL* 21 (1910), 349-50 (Italy).
Calvino, *Folktales,* pp. 147-52, no. 48 (with 315), composite text (Italy).
Calvino, *Folktales,* pp. 189-96, no. 58 (with 303), composite text (Italy).
Basile, *Pentamerone,* 1, pp. 64-77 (Day I, 7th Diversion) (with 303), with notes, literary (Italy).
Straparola, *Nights,* 2, pp. 182-90 (Night X, Fable 3) (with 315), literary (Italy).
Ranke, *Folktales,* pp. 53-59, no. 29 (with 303, 304) (Germany).
Coxwell, *Folk-Tales,* pp. 944-45, no. 3 (Lithuania).
Jones and Kropf, *Folk-Tales,* pp. 110-17, no. 20 (with 303), pp. 196-206, no. 38 (with 302), cf. pp. 39-46, no. 9 (304, with cf. 300), 3 versions (Hungary).
Nicoloff, *Folktales,* pp. 19-22, no. 13, pp. 22-26, no. 14 (with 301A), 2 versions (Bulgaria).
Wheeler, *Wonder Tales,* pp. 247-80 (Albania).
Dawkins, *More,* pp. 123-28, no. 21, tale combined with ballad of "St. George and the Dragon" (Greece).
Cf. Rose, *Handbook,* p. 273 (cf. 300) [Perseus and Andromeda], literary (Greece).
Cf. Graves, *Myths,* 1, p. 240 (cf. 300) [Perseus and Andromeda], literary (Greece).
Bain, *Fairy Tales,* pp. 126-40 (with 303) (Russia).

Afanas'ev, *Fairy Tales,* pp. 314-20 (with 551, 301A) (Russia).

Druts and Gessler, *Tales,* pp. 7-17 (with 314), Gypsy (Russia).

Cortes, *Folk Tales,* pp. 31-35, pp. 96-99, 2 versions (White Russia).

Cf. Bilenko, *Folk Tales,* pp. 88-93 (Ukraine).

Cf. Rédei, *Texts,* pp. 136-37, no. 37, Zyrian dialect text and English trans. (Komi, A.S.S.R.).

Bogoras, *Tales,* pp. 12-14, no. 3, Yukaghir tribe (Siberia).

Indian Subcontinent

Dracott, *Village,* pp. 61-67 (300, with 567) (Simla).

Cf. Steel, *Tales,* pp. 129-43 (cf. 300, with 567), pp. 245-50 (cf. 300), pp. 289-96 (cf. 300, with 425D Ind.), 3 versions (Punjab).

Cf. Swynnerton, *Tales and Entertainment,* pp. 471-82, no. 96 (cf. 300, with 938B, 381A Ind.) (Punjab).

Cf. Day, *Folk-Tales,* pp. 64-92, no. 4 (cf. 300, with 302) (Bengal).

McCulloch, *Household,* pp. 255-82, no. 26 (300, with 566) (Bengal).

Elwin, *Folk-Tales,* pp. 178-83, no. 7, pp. 430-31, no. 5, pp. 452-55, no. 6 (300, with 910, 182), 3 versions (Mahakoshal, Central India).

Cf. Bodding, *Folk Tales,* 2, pp. 284-87, no. 62 (cf. 300), pp. 288-315, no. 63 (300, with cf. 182), 2 versions, Santal texts and English trans. (Santal Parganas, Central India).

Bompas, *Folklore,* pp. 274-76, no. 91 (300, with cf. 182) (Santal Parganas, Central India).

Cf. Emeneau, *Texts,* 3, pp. 96-131, no. 24 [boy kills tiger and python], Kota text and English trans. (Nilgiri).

Thundy, *Folktales,* pp. 77-79, no. 45, Kadar tribe (Kerala, South India).

Parker, *Village,* 1, pp. 137-45, no. 15 (300, with 502, 531), 2, pp. 162-71, no. 111 (300, with cf. 301B, 516B, 302B Ind.), and notes, 3, pp. 373-79, no. 260 (300, with 302B Ind.), 3 versions (Ceylon).

For other analyzed Indian versions see Thompson and Roberts, *Types,* Type 300.

Eastern Asia

Cf. Zŏng, *Folk Tales,* pp. 166-69, no. 72 (cf. 301A, with cf. 300) (Korea).

Cf. Eberhard, *Folktales,* pp. 161-73, no. 67 (cf. 300, with cf. 301A, 554) (China).

Cf. Seki, *Folktales,* pp. 33-36, no. 15 (300, II, cf. IV) (Japan).

Cf. Seki, *Folktales,* pp. 43-47, no. 18 (650A, with 513A, cf. 300) (Japan).

Cf. Mayer, *Guide,* p. 5, no. 2 (650A, with cf. 300) (Japan).

Africa

Cf. El-Shamy, *Folktales,* pp. 3-14, no. 1 (303A, with 518, cf. 304, cf. 300, 302) (Egypt).

Cf. El-Shamy, *Folktales,* pp. 14-24, no. 2 (cf. 300, with 875D, 590), cf. pp. 159-60, no. 34, 2 versions, and pp. 279-81, no. 34, notes (Egypt).

Fuja, *Cowries,* pp. 50-67 (300, with 303), Yoruba tribe (Nigeria).

Cf. Weeks, *Cannibals,* pp. 200-204, no. 1, Bolokoi tribe (Congo).

Cf. Baskerville, *King,* pp. 1-4 (Uganda).

Cf. Mbiti, *Stories,* pp. 118-20, no. 40, Akamba tribe (Kenya).

Cf. Kirk, *FL* 15 (1904), 319, no. 2, Ishak tribe (Somali Republic).

Cf. Chatelain, *Folk-Tales,* pp. 84-97, no. 5 (cf. 300, with 650A, 301B, 303), Ki-mbundu text and English trans., Mbamba tribe (Angola).

See Klipple, *Folk Tales,* pp. 254-68, for English summaries of additional African versions of AT300.

3. DADDY REDCAP

Dan McCarthy   AT301A
Bellevue, Trinity Bay   TC1175 72-51
25 November 1971   Collector: Helen Hoskins

[*aside to listener*: well (Donna) my story is called "Daddy Redcap."]
[*laughter*]
Once upon a time _ [a family] had three brothers _ Jack _ Mike _ an' Bill. The three of 'em happen to be sailing on the one ship. An' they got shipwrecked. They drove ashore on a lonely island. That's all was sove out o' ship, the three brothers. So finally _ they made camp. They had lots of provisions _ lots of everything. They got the sails an' ropes and everything off o' the ol' wreck. They made a...camp. And _ settled theirselves away for awhile. They didn't know how long they were goin to be there. They had luh...guns an' ammunition. So _ they said they'd kill [game as] a part of their livin. There's some birds around.

So -- the first day _ when they were ready, had their camp...had a home we'll call it built _ they said they'd leave the two o' the brothers home to cook. [Male listener: (One)] One o' the...yes _ one o' the brothers home to cook. An' the other two 'd go huntin.

So -- they leaved _ Mikes _ home to cook. An' Jack an'...Bill went off _ huntin. So uh...he said "I wonder what am I goin to get for the boys' dinner. Well" he says "I'll put...I think I'll put on a pot o' pea soup."

*male listener
speaking in
background

[*laughter*] Well very good he put on his pea soup an' he had it*...he got it about cooked there was a knock come to the door. Opened the door. An' this was a little ol' man _ very small man _ with a red cap on. So he called un Daddy Redcap.

Uh...so very good he said "What are you cookin?"

He said "I'm cookin soup."

"Is there any chance of a bowl?"

"Yes" he said. "You can have a bowl o' soup." Passed over. So he drank the bowl o' soup. An' he ask for another.

He said "Yes. I'll give you another bowl." So he drank that one an' ask for another.

"Well" Mike said..."I got two brothers" _ he said "out huntin" an' he said "I can't give you all me soup. If I do" he said "they'll have none for their

/I go/

dinners when /they come/ home." [*laughing tone*]

Uh...he said "Alright. [If] you don't give it to me" he said "I'll TAKE it." [*laughter*] So finally _ he give Jack an' awf...Mike an awful trimmin. An'

/they/

/he/ drink what soup was there _ an' went off, left uh...poor Mike in under the table half killed. [*laughter*]

(So) finally Jack an'…Bill come. Poor Mike in under the table ‿ fire out ‿ no dinner. [*laughs*] So ‿ he said "What happened ‿ Mike?"

"Ah" he said "there was a /man/ come here" he said "with a…red cap on, little feller" he said "and uh…he said "he wa[nted]…I give un three bowls of soup ‿ [*laughing tone*] an' he wasn't satisfied. (Anyway)" he said "what should he do only give me a hugging, (thee) sees now" he said "what happened."

/lan/

An' they said "You're an awful man to leave home for cookin." [*laughs*] "Little ol' man like that" he said "give you a trimmin" he said "big man like you!" An' said "Alright."

"Alright" Bill said "I'll stay home tomorrow, he won't get MY soup!" [*laughs*] Very good.

Bill stayed home the next day. So ‿ when they had the soup just about cooked Daddy Redcap come again.

"Now ‿ what ya cookin Bill?"

"Soup! Want a bowl?"

"Yes. /I/ wants a bowl o' soup." [*laughs*]

/You/

"Alright" he said "you (can) have bowl o' soup." (An') ‿ so ‿ he drank the bowl o' soup. He drank TWO. "(Look)" /Bill/ said "you're not gettin no more." Says uh…[*laughing tone*] "I'm not goin to give you all me soup. The two brothers is comin an' I'll have none"

/Bip/

"Well" he said "I'll serve you now" he said "like I served Mike." [*laughs and coughs*] Uh…very good. That's what happened. An' he served Bill now the same as he served Mike.

So ‿ so when ‿ Mike an'…uh…Mike an' Jack come home ‿ poor ol' Bill [*laughing tone*] /in/ under the table half killed! [*laughs*] Fire out ‿ no soup ‿ no nothing.

/im/

An' ‿ "A nice fellow 'tis no mistake" Jack said "ye too! [*laughs*] Anyway ya can't trust ya to stop home an' cook a drop o' soup for me. [*laughs*] An' a little ol' man" he said "with a red cap on come in an' [*laughs*] (take it all away)." Very good.

"Alright" said Jack said "then…then I'll stay home tomorrow, he won't get my soup." [*laughs*]

(Bill)…Bill…Mike an' Bill said "That's what you thinks. I never got such a trim[min in] me life ‿ (?not like that see)" [*laughs*].

Well anyway ‿ next morning they got up an' two of 'em went off, they leave Jack home. Got on his soup. Put on a good big boiler o' hot (water), boiler, boiled that. (Hell) ‿ by an' by he come.

"(What) ya cookin Jack?"

"Soup. (Like) a bowl?"

"Yes. Want a bowl o' soup" ‿ he said.

"Alright" so he give un a bowl o' soup ‿ an' he give un TWO. Will he give un three?

"Now" he said "that's all you're gettin. An' now don't think you're goin to serve me like you served the...like...[*laughing tone*] Bill" he said "because you're not."

Uh...uh...th' old man said "That's what you thinks." Huh! [*laughs*] An' he jumped up. An' when he did Jack jumped up too an' he picked up the hot wa[ter]...the boil water, he dumped un down over his head an' away she goes. [*laughs*] Cap _ hair _ the whole lot down on the floor. [*laughs*] An' th' ol' man took off _ an' Jack after un. Very good.

He went off. An' Jack chased un. An' begar he went out through a great big hole [in] the ground, down he goes _ down into the hole. An' Jack thought he was [?there] (a little [?while] look). Huh! Go(t)..."Well" he said "where the hell did he go?" [*laughs*] Alright.

Uh...the two brothers come home an' _ they had the _ feed cooked for 'em.

"Did ol' man...bu...ol' Daddy Redcap come today?"

/they/   "Yes" he said "he come" he said "/there's/ his cap there, his hair there." [*laughs*] Yes. [*laughs*] Yes.

"Know you didn't scald the head off un."

"No. I sure didn't." [*laughs*] "He won't be back here no more." [Male listener: Yeah.] "An'" he said "that's not the best of it." He said "He went down there, went out in a hole" he said "now we('ve) got to _ [*laughs*] now" he said "we got to find out what's down there." [*laughter*] Yeah.

Anyway they's uh...had lots o' rope. Now they had lots o' rope that they sove out o' _ wreck you know. [Female listener: Mm.] So he said _ "We'll go out an' get a quoil now _ sixty fathom." An' he said "That'd go to a bottom anyway!" [*laughs*] Now uh...so they went out an' they got a quoil o' rope. Got in _ an' they lowered...lowered down _ with a rock on un now, lower down to see how far 'twas see. Lower down quoil. No bottom. Get another sixty fathom. [*laughter*] Lower down. Begar they got bottom _ now.

Oh anyway "Now" they say "who's goin down? [*laughing tone*] Who's goin down (an') find out what's down (there)?" [*laughs*] Well Jack said "'Tis no good to send ye now, one o' ye." He said "Because _ ye were afraid o' Daddy Redcap" an' he said "you don't know what you're goina meet down there!" [*laughter*] Yeah. "So I think I better go meself." Uh...alright. Alright. He tied the rope on Jack. Now he was supposed to give a signal (ya) see. He was supposed to give a signal _ for anything he WANTED when he get down you know an' _ if he want to get up there was a certain signal he give 'em now to hoist un up.

So they lowered un down. Got down an' when he got down he got into a big _ fine...(it was)...cattle _ the lord know what was down there _ now. Uh...travelled away an' he come into a house an' knocked to the door. Woman come out. Well he thought she was the best lookin woman ever he seen in his life. Well she was SOME BEAUTY _ now. When Jack said "Alright." (He) went in. So _ he asked her what was…huh…where they were to an' all this

"Now" she said "there's only three…brothers here" _ said "an' they are three giants" _ she said "an'" she said "they're goin to kill YOU _ [Male listener: Yes] (well) soon as ever he comes now my husband will kill ya" _ /she/ said. /She/ said "He can't bear the blood of an Englishman anyway." [laughter]   /he/ /He/

Oh…so _ she said "Alright" said "get something to eat now." An' they got something to eat an' _ Jack was in love with her now. Oh she was a beauty _ alright. [laughter] "Uh…now" she said "John" _ she said "I'm goina give ya something to drink now make you THREE times as strong as my husband." /She/ said "So you needn't be afraid of un _ when he come[s] (in)."   /He/

So by an' by he come. Come in. An' he comes to sniff round an' _ he said "I smells the blood of an Englishman" [laughter] he said. /She/ had Jack stowed away now. Now by an' by begar he…he decide just as well to come out. He had…uh…come out. Well he was goin to have un right off o' the bat then an' she said "No, no. We'll uh…(let)'s give un his supper now _ have a bit of fun with un" they said out in the yard you know, before he'd _ make away with un. Alright.   /He/

So anyway after they got their supper he said "Jack we'll go out in the field now" _ (he) said. He said an' uh,..he said "I'm a strong man" he said "how strong [are] you?"

"I'm not very strong" he says [laughing] "I'm not." Said "Only s…weak man" said "[that's] all." "Got a big rock over in the field" he said, went over. Great big rock. Picked un up th' ol' giant did an' he FIRED un at Jack you know. [laughter] So Jack jumped away clear of un. Huh.

Uh…he said "Pick un up now" _ he said "an' heave un at ME!"

"Oh" Jack said "/I'm not/ able to lift that rock" he said "a big rock like that _ lift un uh…"(Now) Jack waited till he got his chance when the ol'…giant come over handy to un he picked up the rock an' let fly and killed un. [laughter] That's very good.   /I don't/

Go back now…[laughs] (now) the wife. [laughs] Alright. Get back.

Well the next mornin _ he said he'd take a walk around now _ have a look. Begar he went over _ to this yuther [i.e., other] house. Went in there. But if the first woman was beautiful, THIS wud [i.e., was] one be beautiful now. See this look, oh she was LOVELY this one. [laughs]

Well he said "If I get 'nother one [laughs] _ (now) I'd had one for Bi[ll]…one for Ned an'…one for…Mike an' one for Bill, if we ge[t]…if we get 'em up out of it." [laughter] So _ very good.

Now this man had two heads on un now. The other fellow only had one. Very good.

"Now" she said "John _ my husband is awful strong. Awful strong man, now" she said "I'm goin to give you something (to) make ya three times as strong now as he is." Now she had (?trip) like [*laughs*] _ he was six times so strong now as that old un. [*laughs*] Uh...very good. He come. An' we'll make the story now so short as we can anyway, the same thing happened, he was goin to make away with un right off o' the bat and she said "No. Get un out in the field now an' _ have a bit of fun with un, play with un" ball or something another you know. (Yeah). Anyway they went out...playin around, by an' by there was a great big bull there, the old giant picked up the bull, he let fly at Jack _ the bull! [*laughter*] Uh...Jack got clear. That was all of it.

/I/ So /he/ said "Jack heave un at me!" Yes [*laughs*] _ (?at the giant). Big horns on un _ you know (so)...so _ Jack said he wasn't able to lift a bull! What [did] he think he was to lift a bull! An'...uh...anyway he waited till he gotten a chance an' he got the bull head-on to un you know. He said "If I..."when he got...pretty handy to it he give the bull a shove. [*laughs*] An' of course he made away with the giant. (Now). He had TWO now. So _ very good.

So the next day _ he said "I had to go to look for the other fellow _ now." Huh. So _ very good, they went out. Begar _ went over to the house. Knocked to the door. Woman come out. Well you talk about beautiful, oh my! She was a good lookin one! [*laughs*] Uh...this one. Uh...she was the beauty _ altogether.

An' Jack said "Now if I ever get aboard 'ee [I] tell ya!" [*laughs*] He said "This is the one I'm goin to have for meSELF." [*laughs*] Huh! Very good. An' then _ told un.

She said "Now my husband got three heads" she said. An' she said _ "I'm goin to give you stuff now to make yous three times so strong as HE is. But" she said _ "now when he comes he's goin to ask ya is ya any good to fight? You tell him yes _ you'll fight. An' he's goin to give you a choice _ of a sword or fist _ e'r one of it. You can take your choice. Now" she said "he got TWO swords _ a rusty one an' a bright one _ new one. But" she said "you take the rusty one. Fight wi' sword now" she said "an' you take the rusty one."

So when he come he...oh he was goin to have un right off o' the bat for his supper. [*laughs*] Goin to have Jack right off o' the bat _ no foolin

"Oh no" she said "oh no, no _ no...l[ike]...like _ kill un like that" _ said (then).

So anyway they got their suppers an' _ he said "Jack any good to fight?"
"Yes (a real) devil to fight." [*laughter*] (Oh yeah).
"Ever fight with fists?"
"Yes I can fight with fist."
"Ya fight with sword?"

"I can fight" he said "not much good though" _ he said "with the sword."
Never seen one (in) his life! [*laughs*] (Yeah.) Yeah.

"Alright then" he said. (They'll) fight. Fight now with the sword. An'
they brought out the two swords _ rusty one an'...the bright one an' Jack
looked at 'em, viewed 'em over an' (over).

"Ah" he said "I'm goina die anyway an' 'tis just as well to take the rusty
one" _ he said.

"Damn your leader!" he said. He knowed now the wife 's after tellin un
_ [Male listener: (Right).]

Anyway they got out...they got at it. An' after a spell he got one head off
of un. [*laughter*] Yeah. Now they were a good while at it but he got the
second one.

An' Jack said "(I got) one to go!" [*laughs*] Anyway _ we'll make the story
short. He got the other one off of un. Now very good. THREE women now
_ all [to] hisself, what in the devil (was) he goin to do? How...how are they
goin to get UP _ out o' this.

So anyway _ he went back _ he told 'em an' he had thousands o'
money...saven. (The) three ol' giants they had lots o' money. Well they said
uh...the only way they knowed if /they/ could get back, get up you know   /we/
where Jack belonged, where he come from, [Male listener: Right.] said
they'd...come up. "(So I'll)" said Jack "we'll try it anyhow."

Now they got the gold _ an' agot the three women, (we) got 'em out to
the hole. They made the signal. An' have uh.../?send/ down the rope. So --   /(blend)/
he tied on one o' the women _ first, send 'em up. An' she got up _ the other
men start fightin over her! Huh. [*laughs*] They got up onto the...out o' that.
(Now) you could hear now what was goin on (you know). So one was goin
to have her an' the other was goin to have her. Now she'd...(quieten) 'em
she told 'em that there was three of 'em. [Male listener: Mm.] Now that's
it, there [was] three of 'em up. So anyway _ (he throwed) up another one.
An' they start fightin over her now, she was better lookin than the other one.
[*laughs*] So very good. They hauled up the other one. Well NOW the row
started! See they got HER up. Very good.

Now Jack was a...sen[d]...he send up word to 'em he said "(They're out)
there now an' they're foolin at all" he send down the rope an' haul up the
money now _ you see. Well alright. (Haul up) the money. An' very good,
they haul up the money. Now to go down after Jack _ now _ send rope down
after Jack. Mm. They got down.

Uh...Jack says "So sure as the devil they're goina make away with me
now, that's what they're goina do with me!" he said. (Yeah.) "They got the
women, they got the money. They('ll) make away with me, I'm goin (to) try
'em now _ what they do." So he tied on a big rock _ onto the rope. An'
they'd roused [i.e., *hoisted*] away.

/lope/   Now then when they got up, pull uh…the /rope/ along Jack heard un comin _ now _ (down) SOUSE! The big rock down _ the hole. Huh _ thought they had Jack killed now.

"Huh! I knowed darn well what they were goina do alright." (Yes). [*laughs*] (Said) "You can't trust your brother." [*laughs*] Very good.

"Now" he said "how in the hell am I goin to get up out of it? How?" So _ one of th' ol' giants had a big eagle. Uh…he had un tamed _ able to talk. Now _ so come across the eagle. An' uh…an' he said _ "I'LL bring you up." He said "I think I'm able to carry ya. You're not a very big man" _ said "but you got to carry grub" he said "to feed me, 'tis a long ways up there" _ he said.

Now Jack said that was easy got _ grub, because (there) was lots o' cattle there. So anyway he killed a bull. An' he cut off a quarter _ o' the bull. An' got on th' eagle's back an' his quarter o' beef.

Now th' eagle said "Every time I bawls you got to give me a piece o' beef." [*laughs*]

So _ now Jack said "Alright." So _ he thought he had lots but he didn't spare it now _ see. Every time the eagle 'd bawled he give un a bit _ see (in its beak) It went all up. By an' by begar he got up far (enough) to see the

/weef/   light. Jack's /beef/ get pretty short now! [*laughs*] An' anyway he got up _
/vull/   pretty up handy to /?find/ all beef gone. So th' eagle commenced to bawl.
/they/   So /he/ said "What in the devil am I goin to do _ at all." An' he've atake knife, cut piece off backside. [*laughs*] Take a…took piece off backside. Give it to th' eagle. Up he gets. Got up. Got up. Got up _ to (anyway) [*laughs*]

Tom an' Bill…Tom uh…uh…Mike an'…an' Bill was enjoyin theirself to the full now, they got up _ frightened 'em to death when he come up. (Didn't know) where in the name o' god HOW he got up. And he never told 'em. So they were livin very happy when I leaved.

Duration: 18 min., 38 sec.
Location: Kitchen of teller's house, evening.
Audience: Fieldworker and several friends or relatives of both sexes.

Context, Style, and Language: Skipper Dan McCarthy, who is married to the fieldworker's grandmother, is sitting on the couch, smoking his pipe. Intermittent microphone noise suggests that the interviewer is unable to maintain a specific position during the recording. Although made informally in the teller's home, the tape recording reveals a certain degree of nervous tension, strongly indicated by the frequent laughter of both narrator and audience. Nevertheless, the teller succeeds in involving the audience in the story, especially in its humorous aspects, and there is constant interaction not only through laughter but also by no fewer than five monosyllabic verifying responses by a male listener. The teller often adds short words such as *yeah* in an undertone between sentences. Because of the nature of the recording it is difficult if not impossible to transcribe these with any real accuracy. These quiet words are nevertheless a means of punctuating the narrative, emphasizing certain points, and providing brief pauses during which the audience has an opportunity to react to the preceding words and to keep up with the events of the plot as they unfold piece by piece.

The rather slow delivery of this tale suggests that the teller is probably calling it to mind after a considerable lapse of time. The opening aside to a member of the audience implies that the title has just been recalled following earlier unrecorded discussion of the tale. After the conventional opening formula the names of the three brothers are spoken hesitantly, with quite lengthy pauses between them, again strongly hinting at a degree of uncertainty regarding the precise details of the story. There is considerable vocal interaction between narrator and audience, the story being addressed primarily to one of the female listeners identified by name in the opening aside. A male listener quietly corrects the teller by interjecting the word *One* in the second paragraph—a correction immediately accepted by the teller and incorporated into the tale. The same man also frequently interjects words of agreement in an undertone as the story proceeds. These are rare examples in this collection of the audience's direct influence on the narrator. There is also a great deal of laughter from both teller and audience, especially the former, which is an important part of the interaction, not least because the teller's laughter encourages the listeners not to take the story too seriously and thus strongly influences their response. Perhaps the laughter is due in part to the nervousness of the teller. This is the first tale recorded on this tape, and the audience is a little uncertain how to respond at this early point in the interview. The laughter causes difficulties in the transcription as is seen in the material in parentheses in the text, where we have attempted to decipher the words obscured by laughter or unclear speech. Dialogue is used rather sparingly and is less vivid and dramatic in quality than that in many other tales in this collection.

Dan McCarthy's accent is predominantly of the Anglo-Irish type, as seen for instance in the construction *after tellin,* but like many other similar speakers he uses such West Country English features as *un* (him). He employs the punctuating form *alright* to mark stages in the narrative, and also the phrase *very good,* which is frequently used with the same function by such West Country English type speakers as the Bennetts. Of particular interest are the pronunciation of *none* (rhyming with *own*), *quoil* (coil), *yuther* (other), *wasn't* (pronounced *wodden*), the devoicing of the final consonant in *roused,* and the typically English West Country voicing of the voiceless initial consonant in *so* at the beginning of the final sentence. At the lexical level we find *trimmin* (hiding, thrashing), *make away with* (kill), *fired at* (threw at), *handy* (near), *'ee* (thee), the intensive *awful* (very), *e'r one* (either), and the vivid exclamation *souse* (crash). The asseveration *begar* is used frequently, and nautical terms are also in evidence, e.g., *stowed away* (hidden), the euphemistic *get aboard 'ee,* and *grub* (food). Also of note are the dialectal *off of* and the pronominal forms *theirselves/selfs, yous,* and *hisself.*

The quality of the recording is poor and the teller's voice consequently muffled, adding to the problems of transcription already noted above.

0825847

Redcap is defined in the *OED* as "the name of a sprite or goblin" and appears to have had a long history in both legends and proverbs. Various goblins of that name are described in Henderson, *Notes on the Folklore of the Northern Counties,* 1879, pp. 253-55. The first of these (p. 253) has several characteristics in common with the Daddy Redcap in Dan McCarthy's tale: "Redcap . . . is cruel and malignant of mood . . . . He is depicted as a short thickset old man, with long prominent teeth, skinny fingers armed with talons like eagles, large eyes of a fiery-red colour, grisly hair streaming down his shoulders, iron boots, a pikestaff in his left hand, and a red cap on his head."

Type and Motifs:

AT301A. *Quest for a Vanished Princess.*

Z10.1. *Beginning formula.*

P251.6.1. *Three brothers.*

Cf. F451.2.7.1. *Dwarfs with red heads and red caps.*

Cf. F451.5.2. *Malevolent dwarf.*

Cf. G475.1. *Ogre attacks intruders in house in woods.*

Cf. H1471. *Watch for devastating monster. Youngest alone successful.*

Cf. F102.1. *Hero shoots monster (or animal) and follows it into lower world.*

F92. *Pit entrance to lower world.*

F96. *Rope to lower world.*

G530.1. *Help from ogre's wife (mistress).*

D1335.2. *Magic strength-giving drink.*

G84. *Fee-fi-fo-fum.*

H1562.2. *Test of strength: lifting stone (fireplace, etc.).*

F628.2.3. *Strong man kills giant.*

F531.1.2.2.1. *Two-headed giant.*

F624.1. *Strong man lifts horse (ox, ass).*

F531.1.2.2.2. *Three-headed giant.*

L210. *Modest choice best.*

G512.1. *Ogre killed with sword.*

N538.2. *Treasure from defeated giant.*

R111.2.1. *Princess(es) rescued from lower world.*

K2211. *Treacherous brother.*

K677. *Hero tests the rope on which he is to be pulled to upper world.*

K1931.2. *Impostors abandon hero in lower world.*

K1935. *Impostors steal rescued princesses.*

B211.3. *Speaking bird.*

F101.3. *Return from lower world on eagle.*

B322.1. *Hero feeds own flesh to helpful animal.*

Z10.2. *End formula.*

International Parallels: This is our only full-length version of a tale that is popular with storytellers in many parts of the world. The notion of an underground country reached by descending on a rope through a hole, as coalminers go down into the mine in a cage, has obviously intrigued people in many cultures. Sometimes, however, the otherworld country is on a plateau up a high mountain and therefore equally inaccessible.

The diminutive man, or occasionally woman, who in most versions appears on successive evenings asking for food, attacks and defeats the much larger elder brothers but on the third night is defeated by the youngest. The diminutive being, Redcap in our version, then disappears down a hole in the earth. In turn each of the two elder brothers is lowered part way down the hole but in fright asks to be hauled back up again. Only the youngest brother has the courage to complete the descent. One suspects that the humiliation latent in the defeat of the older and presumably stronger men by this diminutive being is felt to be humorous. Similarly, the bravery of the youngest brother in descending to the underground country is frequently contrasted with the cowardice of his two elders.

After the youngest brother has overcome giants or other monsters in the underground country, he obtains great riches and beautiful women, and he has the brothers haul these to the surface. The brothers then decide to take all the credit, along with the riches and the women. They leave Jack to his fate, often by cutting the rope, which is his only apparent means of escape. Nevertheless he does escape by another route, frequently on an eagle's back. In most versions he then regains his possessions and is acknowledged as a hero. In the Newfoundland version, however, he merely startles his brothers by his unexpected reappearance.

In the notes below we have also referred to versions of AT301B. These differ from AT301A primarily in that the hero's companions, who are not related to him, possess unusual strength, but the hero's supernatural strength easily surpasses theirs.

Studies and Notes

MacCulloch, *Childhood,* pp. 270-71, 350-52; Boas, "Notes on Mexican Folk-Lore," *JAF* 25 (1912), 254-58; Bolte and Polívka, 2, pp. 300-318; Thompson, *European,* pp. 334-44, no. 2; Chase, *Jack,* p. 194, no. 12, notes; Thompson, *The Folktale,* pp. 53, 85, 147; Espinosa, *CPE,* 2, 498-504; Espinosa, "Western Hemisphere Versions of Aarne-Thompson 301," *JAF* 65 (1952), 187; Randolph, *Church House,* pp. 219-20, notes; Roberts, *South,* pp. 210-12, no. 2, notes; Szövérffy, "From Beowulf to the Arabian Nights (Preliminary Notes on Aarne-Thompson 301)," *MF* 6 (1956), 89-124; Delarue, *Catalogue,* 1, pp. 112-14, pp. 132-33; Barakat, "The Bear's Son Tale in Northern Mexico," *JAF* 78 (1965), 330-36; Baughman, *Index,* Type 301A, p. 6; Robe, *Index,* Types 301, 301A, 301B, pp. 44-47.

Canada

Cf. Leland, *Legends,* pp. 311-19 (301B, with 650A), Micmac Indian (Nova Scotia).

Samson, Joseph D. "Joseph D. Samson Tells an Old Tale," *Cape Breton's Magazine,* no. 39 [1985], 55-61, versions in Acadian French and in English told by the same storyteller. [Editor notes: "The English should not be considered a direct translation."] (Nova Scotia).

Cf. Mechling, *JAF* 26 (1913), 234-47, no. 4 (301B, with 650A, 1640, 1000, cf. 300), Maliseet Indian (New Brunswick).

Radin and Reagan, *JAF* 41 (1928), 113-16, no. 21 (301A), Ojibwa Indian (Ontario).

Hallowell, *JAF* 52 (1939), 170-73, no. 3, Berens River Saulteaux Indian (Ontario).

Thompson, *Tales,* pp. 205-7, no. 79, rpt. from Lowie, *The Assiniboine,* 1909, pp. 147-49, no. 6a, Assiniboine Indian (Alberta).

Cf. Teit, *JAF* 29 (1916), 307, no. 2 (301A, with 300), summary, 308-12, no. 4 (301B, with 650A), 2 versions, Upper Thompson Indian (British Columbia).

Cf. Teit, *JAF* 39 (1926), 450-59 (301B, with 650A), Thompson Indian (British Columbia).

Teit, *JAF* 50 (1937), 189-90 (301A), Thompson Indian (British Columbia).

Cf. Russell, *JAF* 13 (1900), 11-13, no. 1 (301B, with 302), Loucheaux Indian (Northwest Territory).

For further North American Indian references see Thompson, *European,* pp. 334-44, no. 2; see also Thompson, *Tales,* p. 359, note 290.

Thomas, *Types,* cites 2 versions of AT301A from Newfoundland French tradition.

Lacourcière-Low, "Catalogue," cites AT301A among 105 Francophone versions of AT301, AT301A, and AT301B from Canada, provinces not specified.

United States

Parsons, *Islands,* 1, pp. 30-39, no. 12, pp. 39-42, no. 13, 2 versions, English trans. of Portuguese texts, Cape Verde Islands, black (Massachusetts).

Goldstein and Ben-Amos, *Tales,* pp. 45-51 (with cf. 327E, 2250), from Irish family tradition (New York), see pp. 156-57, notes.

Cf. Goldstein and Ben-Amos, *Tales,* pp. 53-57 (301B), from Irish family tradition (New York).

Cf. Goodwyn, *JAF* 66 (1953), 143-54 (301B, with 650A, 860), English trans. of Spanish text, learned in Mexico (Illinois).

Hoogasian-Villa, *Tales,* pp. 266-73, no. 34 (with 550, 300), cf. pp. 273-90, no. 35 (301B, with 302), 2 versions, Armenian tradition, in English trans. (Michigan).

Cf. Perdue, *Devil,* p. 67, no. 15B (cf. 301A) (Virginia).

Cf. Chase, *American,* pp. 71-73, composite text, truncated version (Virginia and Kentucky).

Carter, *JAF* 38 (1925), 341-43, no. 1 (North Carolina).

Chase, *Jack,* pp. 106-13, no. 12, and p. 194, notes (North Carolina).

Cf. Claudel, *JAF* 58 (1945), 210-12, no. 2 (301B, with 313, III), Spanish tradition, in English (Louisiana).

Roberts, *South,* pp. 17-19, no. 2 (Kentucky).

Roberts, *Greasybeard,* pp. 53-58, no. 11 (Kentucky).

Roberts, *Settlers,* pp. 212-16, no. 104 (with 1358C) (Kentucky).

M. Campbell, *Tales,* pp. 78-82, no. 2 (with 550), pp. 89-92, no. 6, 2 versions (Kentucky).

Cf. Carrière, *Tales,* pp. 44-50, no. 10 (301B, with 650A), cf. pp. 50-64, no. 11 (301B, with 650A), 2 versions, French texts with English summaries (Missouri).

Cf. Thomas, *Good,* pp. 21-33, no. 3 (301B, with 650A), French text and English trans. (Missouri).

Randolph, *Church House,* pp. 148-50, and pp. 219-20, notes (Arkansas).

Cf. Skinner, *JAF* 38 (1925), 480-81, no. 20 (301B, with 650A), Iowa Indian (Oklahoma).

Cf. Barakat, *JAF* 78 (1965), 331-32 (650A, with 301B), English trans. of Spanish text, learned in Chihuahua, Mexico (Texas).

Cf. Paredes, *Folktales,* pp. 63-78, no. 29 (301B, with 650A, 302), Spanish tradition, in English trans. (Texas).

Campa, *WF* 6 (1947), 329-32 (301A, with 314, VI), Spanish tradition, in English trans. (Texas or New Mexico).

Espinosa, *JAF* 24 (1911), 403-8, no. 3 (301A, with 314), cf. 437-44, no. 12 (301B), 2 versions, Spanish texts with English summaries (New Mexico).

Cf. Boas, *JAF* 35 (1922), 92-95, no. 6 (301B, with 650A), Zuñi Indian (New Mexico).

Parsons, *Tales,* pp. 151-58, no. 81 (301A, with 302), Taos Indian (New Mexico).

Espinosa, *Folk-Tales,* p. 196, no. 20 (301A), pp. 196-97, no. 21 (301A) [woman, not man, is hero], 2 versions, English summaries of Spanish texts (New Mexico).

Cf. Espinosa, *Folk-Tales,* p. 195, no. 17 (650A, with 301B, cf. 300, 314), English summary of Spanish text (New Mexico), English resumé in Espinosa, *Folklore,* p. 181.

Cf. Espinosa, *Folk-Tales,* pp. 195-96, no. 18 (650A, with 301B, 570), cf. p. 196, no. 19 (650A, with 301B, 302), 2 versions, English summaries of Spanish texts (New Mexico).

Cf. Rael, *Cuentos,* pp. 682-83, no. 171 (301B, with 314) English abstract of Spanish text (New Mexico).

Cf. Barakat, *JAF* 78 (1965), 334 (cf. 301A), English trans. of Spanish text, learned in Chihuahua, Mexico (New Mexico).

Robe-Jameson, *Folktales,* pp. 59-62, no. 27, pp. 62-65, no. 28, 2 abbreviated texts, Spanish tradition, in English (New Mexico).

Weigle, *Two Guadalupes,* pp. 60-66, Spanish tradition, in English (New Mexico).

Rael, *Cuentos,* pp. 684-85, no. 173 (with 314), p. 715, no. 228 (with cf. 300, 314) [on plateau, not underground], p. 721, no. 236 (with 314, 570), 3 versions, English summaries of Spanish texts (Colorado).

Cf. Rael, *Cuentos,* p. 681, no. 170 (650A, with 301B), cf. pp. 683-84, no. 172 (650A, with 301B, 314), cf. pp. 685-86, no. 174 (650A, with 301B), cf. pp. 686-87, no. 175 (650A, with 301B), 4 versions, English summaries of Spanish texts (Colorado).

For references to some additional North American Indian versions see Hallowell, *JAF* 65 (1952), 418.

See Robe, *Index,* Types 301, 301A, 301B, for other Hispanic American references.

Lacourcière-Low, "Catalogue," cites 2 Francophone versions of AT301, AT301A, AT301B from the United States: 2 (Missouri).

Mexico

Cf. Dobie, *Tongues,* pp. 211-27 (301B) (Mexico), and summarized in Hudson, *SFQ* 15 (1951), 152-54.

Cf. Barakat, *JAF* 78 (1965), 333-34 (650A, with 301B) [no rescue of princess], English trans. of Spanish text (Chihuahua).

Foster, *Folklore and Beliefs,* pp. 229-30, no. 38 (301A), Sierra Popoluca Indian (Veracruz).

Cf. Mason and Espinosa, *JAF* 27 (1914), 208, no. 14 (301B), English summary of Spanish text, Tepecano Indian (Jalisco).

Wheeler, *Tales,* pp. 239-40, no. 93 (cf. 301A), pp. 280-82, no. 101 (cf. 301A, cf. 300) 2 versions, Spanish texts with English abstracts (Jalisco).

Cf. Wheeler, *Tales,* pp. 240-46, no. 94 (301B, with 560), cf. pp. 247-59, no. 95 (650A, with 301B), cf. pp. 259-71, no. 96 (650A, with 301B, 314), 3 versions, Spanish texts with English abstracts (Jalisco).

Cf. Boas, *JAF* 25 (1912), 241-45, no. 1 (301B, with 650A, 326), Tehuano Indian (Oaxaca).

See Robe, *Index,* Types 301, 301A, 301B, for other Mexican references.

The Caribbean and South America

Cf. Parsons, *Andros,* pp. 142-43, no. 93 (2 condensed variants of first part of 301A with animal characters), black (Bahamas).

Cf. Parsons, *Andros,* p. 144, no. 94, animal characters, black (Bahamas).

Parsons, *Antilles,* 2, p. 396, no. 4 (301A, interrupted cooking scene only), black (St. Bartholomew, Leeward Islands).

Cf. Parsons, *Antilles,* 3, pp. 292-95, no. 294 (301B), English summaries of 3 French texts, A, C, D, black (Martinique/Guadeloupe, Lesser Antilles), see pp. 292-93, headnote no. 294, for international references, including some African ones.

See Hansen, *Types,* Types 301A, 301B, for references to versions from Puerto Rico and Chile.

Pino-Saavedra, *Folktales,* pp. 9-19, no. 3 (301A, with 408), and see pp. 250-51, no. 3, notes (Chile).

England

Although two English versions of AT301A have appeared in print, neither has all of the elements of the Type. In both, the passage to the underworld has become rationalized as a well.

Cf. Sternberg, *Dialect,* pp. 196-97 (has interrupted cooking scene only) (Northamptonshire), and rpt. in Briggs, *Dictionary,* A1, p. 393.

Cf. Addy, *Household,* pp. 50-53, no. 50 (Derby), and rpt. in Briggs, *Dictionary,* A1, pp. 391-93.

Wales

Groome, *Folk-Tales,* pp. 243-47, no. 58 (with cf. 300) [brothers are not treacherous], Gypsy (Wales).

Sampson and Yates, *Folk Tales,* pp. 37-40, English trans. from Romani, Gypsy (Wales).

Scotland

McKay-Campbell, *Tales,* 2, pp. 190-214, no. 62 (with 329), collected from man from Skye, Gaelic text and English trans. (Glasgow).

Douglas, *King,* pp. 93-97 (with 2250) [all 3 brothers go underground; no treachery], Scottish traveller (Dunbartonshire).

Cf. Campbell, *Popular Tales,* 1, pp. 236-50, no. 16 (301B, with cf. 513B), Gaelic text and English trans. (Argyllshire).

Campbell, *Popular Tales,* 3, pp. 1-35, no. 58 [basket up crag, not underground], Gaelic text and English trans. (Islay).

Ireland

Curtin, *Folk-Tales,* pp. 14-24 (with 550, 329) (Ireland), and rpt. in O'Faolain, *Sagas,* pp. 219-31.

MacManus, *Book,* pp. 207-30 (Co. Donegal).

Kennedy, *Fictions,* pp. 39-48 (with cf. 313) (Co. Wexford), and rpt. in Graves, *Fairy Book,* pp. 1-14.

Gmelch and Kroup, *Road,* pp. 168-75, Irish traveller (Co. Westmeath).

Ó Duilearga, *Book,* pp. 6-23, no. 11, and pp. 23-45, no. 12 (with 300), 2 versions (Co. Kerry).

Gregory, *Poets,* pp. 172-79 (Co. Galway).

Curtin, *Hero-Tales,* pp. 262-82 (with 550) (Co. Galway), and rpt. in Graves, *Fairy Book,* pp. 143-60.

Mac Giollarnáth, *Béal.* 4 (1933-34), 423-24, English summary of Irish text (Co. Galway).

Cf. Gmelch and Kroup, *Road,* pp. 79-81 (cf. 301A, with 551) (Co. Roscommon).

Irish Types, Type 301A, 193 versions.

Continental Europe and Asia

Grimm no. 91, "The Elves," Grimm-Hunt, 2, pp. 24-28, no. 91 (with cf. 300) (Germany). For other trans. see Grimm-Magoun, pp. 333-36, no. 91, and Grimm-Zipes, pp. 334-37, no. 91, and see also Grimm-Hunt, 2, pp. 387-90, no. 91, for variants.

Cf. Dasent, *Popular Tales,* pp. 360-69, no. 55 (cf. 301A, with cf. 300) [not underground] (Norway).

Hodne, *Types,* AT301, 52 versions (Norway).

Thorpe, *Yule-Tide,* pp. 175-88 (with 300) [princesses are in mountain caves, not underground] (Sweden). See also pp. 188-89, no. 1, and pp. 191-92, no. 4, for 2 abbreviated versions.

West, *Folk-Tales,* pp. 124-26 (Faeroe Islands).

Cf. Delarue, *Borzoi Book,* pp. 45-64, no. 6 (301B, with 650A) (France).

Webster, *Legends,* pp. 77-87 (301A, with 302, 327B, 328) (Basque).

Cf. Cabellero, *Bird,* pp. 88-98 (301B) [helpers not treacherous] (Spain).

Cf. Do Douro, *FLR* 4 (1881), 142-51 (301B, with 650A, 513A) (Portugal).

Crane, *Popular Tales,* pp. 36-40, and p. 336, n. 13 (Italy).

Calvino, *Folktales,* pp. 284-88, no. 78, composite text (Italy).

Bódker, *European,* pp. 90-91 (Germany).

Cf. Zobarskas, *Folk Tales,* pp. 79-88 (301B) (Lithuania).

Schwartz, *Violin,* pp. 215-21, Jewish tradition (Eastern Europe).

Cf. Schwartz, *Violin,* pp. 169-75 (813, with cf. 301A, cf. 400), Jewish tradition (Eastern Europe).

Cf. Schwartz, *Violin,* pp. 202-8 (cf. 301A, with cf. 400, cf. 300), Jewish tradition (Eastern Europe).

Baudiš, *Folk Tales,* pp. 129-41 (Czech).

Groome, *Folk-Tales,* pp. 151-54, no. 44 (with 300), Gypsy (Moravia).

Cf. Jones and Kropf, *Folk-Tales,* pp. 244-49, no. 46 (301B, with 650A, 513A, cf. 300) (Hungary).

Ortutay, *Folk Tales,* pp. 180-92, no. 6 (with cf. 300) (Hungary).

Dégh, *Society,* pp. 288-89, no. 1 (with 552A), notes (Hungary).

Cf. Dégh, *Folktales,* pp. 3-15, no. 1 (cf. 511A, with 650A, cf. 301B) (Hungary).

Cf. Creangă, *Folk Tales,* pp. 67-81 (301B, with 650A), literary (Romania).

Cf. Sturdza, *Fairy Tales,* pp. 113-25 (301B) (Romania).

Cf. Sturdza, *Fairy Tales,* pp. 301-13, literary (Romania).

Cf. Groome, *Folk-Tales,* pp. 74-80, no. 20 (301B, with 650A, 513A) [lacks rescue of princess], pp. 85-90, no. 23 (301A, with cf. 566), 2 versions, Gypsy (Bukovina).

Cf. Mijatovies, *Folk-Lore,* pp. 123-45 (301B, with 650A) (Serbia).

Nicoloff, *Folktales,* pp. 22-26, no. 14 (with 300), cf. pp. 78-83, no. 25 (301B), 2 versions (Bulgaria).

Wheeler, *Wonder Tales,* pp. 19-42 (Albania).

Cf. Abbott, *Folklore,* pp. 351-57, Greek text, and pp. 268-78, English trans. (cf. 301A, with cf. 300) (Macedonia).

Dawkins, *Modern,* pp. 140-44, no. 26 (Greece).

Paton, *FL* 10 (1899), 495-98, no. 1 (with 300) (Greece).

Cf. Dawkins, *MGAM,* pp. 370-75, no. 9 [lacks rescue of princess and treacherous brothers], pp. 448-53, no. 4 (with 300) [lacks treacherous brothers], 2 versions, Greek dialect texts and English trans., see pp. 274-76 for notes (Turkey).

Bain, *Folk Tales,* pp. 84-96 (with cf. 300) (Turkey).

Kúnos, *44,* pp. 77-86 (Turkey).

Cf. Walker and Uysal, *Tales,* pp. 10-24, no. 1 (cf. 301A, with cf. 551, cf. 300) (Turkey).

Ralston, *Folk-Tales,* pp. 86-92, no. 15 (with cf. 300), pp. 92-96, discussion, pp. 153-55 (with cf. 300), 2 versions (Russia).

Curtin, *Myths and Folk-Tales,* pp. 1-19 (with cf. 300) [kingdoms are on mountain, not underground] (Russia).

Strickland, *Stories,* pp. 61-66 (with 554, 302) [kingdom is above mountain] (Russia).

Curtin, *Fairy Tales,* pp. 15-23 (with cf. 300) [brothers not treacherous] (Russia).

Magnus, *Folk-Tales,* pp. 225-29 (cf. 301A) (Russia).

Afanas'ev, *Fairy Tales,* pp. 49-53 (301A), pp. 314-20 (with 300, 301A, 551), 2 versions (Russia).

Cf. Afanas'ev, *Fairy Tales,* pp. 375-87 [the three kingdoms are above a mountain, not underground], pp. 457-62 (301A) [companions are not treacherous], 2 versions (Russia).

Cf. Afanas'ev, *Fairy Tales,* pp. 262-68 (301B, in part) (Russia).

Cf. Cortes, *Folk Tales,* pp. 36-43 (with cf. 300) [prince rescues his sisters; castles are not underground] (White Russia).

Strickland, *Stories,* pp. 22-26 (with cf. 300) (Ukraine).

Cf. Zheleznova, *Mountain,* pp. 48-64 (301B) (Ukraine).

Cf. Bilenko, *Folk Tales,* pp. 20-31 (301B, with 650A) (Ukraine).

Cf. Wardrop, *Folk Tales,* pp. 68-83, no. 12 (301B, with 650A, cf. 300) (Georgian S.S.R.).

Dirr, *Folk-Tales,* pp. 36-44, no. 8 (with cf. 300, 302) (Georgian S.S.R.).

Cf. Papashvily, *Yes,* pp. 81-103, no. 9 (303, I, with 313, II, 301B, 516) (Georgian S.S.R.).

Seklemian, *JAF* 6 (1893), 150-52 (Armenia).

Wingate, *FL* 22 (1911), 351-61, no. 6 (301A, with 300, 314) (Armenia).

Surmelian, *Apples,* pp. 41-52, no. 1 (with cf. 300) (Armenia).

Rédei, *Texts,* pp. 424-31, no. 188, Zyrian dialect text and English trans. (Komi, A.S.S.R.).

Cf. Busk, *Sagas,* pp. 36-53, Tale 3 (301B, with 650A, cf. 300) [no rescue of princess], Kalmuck people, literary (Kalmuck A.S.S.R.), also trans. in Coxwell, *Folk-Tales,* pp. 188-92, no. 5.

Cf. Coxwell, *Folk-Tales,* pp. 363-67, no. 7 (cf. 301A, with hero tale) [no rescued princesses], Kirghiz tribe (Kirghiz S.S.R.).

Bushnaq, *Folktales,* pp. 104-6 (with cf. 300), Arab tradition (Syria).

Lorimer, *Tales,* pp. 251-55, no. 38 (Persia).

Indian Subcontinent

Not all of the Indian versions of this tale that we have examined have the underground country entered through a hole in the ground; we have indicated those that have it.

Cf. Steel, *Tales,* pp. 42-60 (301B, with 302, 516B, 302B) (Punjab).

King, *FL* 37 (1926), 81-84, no. 13 (301A, with 302, 567) (Punjab).

Cf. Devi, *Pearls,* pp. 151-57 (301B, with 650A, 302B) (Bengal).

Shakespear, *Clans,* pp. 178-82 (301A, with 313, III) [underground] (Assam Hills).

Elwin, *Folk-Tales,* pp. 3-13, no. 1 (301A, with 551, 1061) [underground], pp. 24-28, no. 5 (301A, with cf. 408, 302) [underground], 2 versions (Mahakoshal, Central India).

Emeneau, *Texts,* 2, pp. 334-75, no. 21 (301A) [underground], Kota text and English trans. (Nilgiri).

Parker, *Village,* 1, pp. 160-66, no. 20 (301A, with 300, 302B), cf. 2, pp. 162-71, no. 111 (cf. 301B, with 300, 516B, 302B) with notes, 2 versions, Singhalese texts and English trans. (Ceylon).

For additional analyzed references see Thompson and Roberts, *Types,* Type 301A and 301B.

Eastern Asia

Cf. Zŏng, *Folk Tales,* pp. 166-69, no. 72 (cf. 301A, with cf. 300) (Korea).

Cf. Eberhard, *Folktales,* pp. 161-73, no. 67 (cf. 301A, with cf. 300, cf. 313, II, 554), (China).

The Philippines

Cf. Fansler, *Tales,* pp. 17-23, no. 3 (301B, with 650A, 513A) [lacks underground episode and rescue of princess], pp. 23-29, notes; pp. 29-31, no. 4a (301A) [interrupted cooking episode only], 2 versions; pp. 155-65, no. 17 (301A, with 313C), notes, pp. 165-67, include a prose summary of a printed Tagalog verse romance, 3 versions.

Africa

We have indicated which versions have the underground country.

Cf. Herskovits, *JAF* 50 (1937), 95-97, no. 24 (301A, I, II), Pidgin English text, Ashanti tribe (Gold Coast).

Cf. Barker and Sinclair, *Folk Tales,* pp. 147-53, no. 29 (301A, I, II) (Gold Coast).

Cf. Nassau, *Animals,* pp. 159-63, no. 20 (301A, II only), Benga tribe (West Africa).

Cf. Nassau, *JAF* 28 (1915), 38-41, no. 14 (cf. 301A), Batanga tribe (Gabon), and rpt. in Goldstein and Ben-Amos, *Tales,* pp. 135-45 and p. 157, notes.

Cf. Tremearne, *Superstitions,* pp. 354-57, no. 71 (301A, I, II), cf. pp. 414-17, no. 88 (301B, I, II), 2 versions, Hausa people (Nigeria).

Nassau, *JAF* 28 (1915), 38-41, no. 14 (301A) [underground], Batanga tribe (Congo).

Cf. Chatelain, *Folk-Tales,* pp. 84-97, no. 5 (301B, with 303), Ki-mbundu text and English trans., Mbamba tribe (Angola).

Tracey, *Lion,* pp. 15-21, no. 4 (301A, with cf. 315A) [underground], Shona people (Rhodesia).

Klipple, *Folk Tales,* pp. 272-74 (301A), English summary of tale from Renel, *Contes de Madagascar,* Tanala tribe (Madagascar).

Cf. Stayt, *Bavenda,* pp. 358-59, no. 23 (cf. 301, II), BaVenda tribe (Northern Transvaal).

Thomas, *Stories,* pp. 71-75, no. 29 (301A) [underground], Bushman people (South Africa).

4. PETER AND MINNIE[†]
(Jack and the Three Giants[†])

Freeman Bennett   AT304
St. Pauls, Great Northern Peninsula   TC269 66-24
31 August 1966   Collectors: HH and JW

Well once upon a time in olden times you know ‿ there was a...well there...perhaps there'd [be] a family livin here an' perhaps in another...thirty mile there'd be another family see? Well now 'twould be a long ways 'fore they'd get to the...to the settlement. Well anyhow there was a family we'll say he was lɪ[vɪn]...they was livin HERE. An' uh...only just uh...their uh...only just the three of 'em, they had one son. Now their son's name was Jack.

It got poor times, well they never had very much an'...an' uh...he said to his father well he said uh..."We got to shift out o' this place" he said "we can't stay here" he said "we'll have to go out" he said "to the...to the city" he said "that we can...so we can earn a livin" he said "we got nothing to eat." He said "An' we can't stay here."

Ol' man said "Yes" he said "we'll have to go. Well" he said "we'll pack up tomorrow morning" he said "an' we'll go."

So by god ‿ next morning ‿ they packed up. Now all they had when they left home ‿ they had three little buns ‿ to take with 'em. Now they had uh...over a day...uh...they had a day's walk. Well very good, now the...Jack ‿ he had uh...one o' those little uh...twenty-twos we calls it now. A little gun about that long [*indicates length*].

So they started. An' they travelled till ‿ 'bout twelve o'clock. An' they got hungry. Well they decided they'd set down 'longside this little brook an' they'd eat one o' their buns. Well that's what they done. They sat down an' eat one o' their buns. An' they got up an' they travelled again.

Well now it's comin on 'wards dark and ‿ "Now" Jack said ‿ he said "yous can go on" he said "this way" he said "yous is on the road" he said "to the settlement." He said "An' I'm goin to leave yous."

35

Oh all they...his mother said "You can't do that. You can't do that 'cause you'll be lost, we'll never see you no more."

"Oh yes." He said "I'll get on alright" he said

"An' ya..." she said "an' you got no grub"

"Oh well" he said "I got me little gun" he said "I'll kill something for my lunch."

So anyhows he leaved. An' they leaved _ an' he went on. An' he travelled an' about dark _ he looked down in a little valley an' he seen a light. Said to hisself "There's somebody down there." An' uh...said to hisself "I'll go down."

An' he went down an' he got down _ in the valley, well he...he lost the light he couldn't find un. Tuh...he decided he have to come back on the little hill again an' uh...see could he see un. He come back again an' he seen the light AGAIN. He started again, he got down in the valley an' he STILL couldn't find the light. Well he said he'd go back on the hill THIS time, he'd find un THIS time. So he went back on the hill again. An' ne[xt]...he started. An' he went down by god _ come across the light an' he seen the light. Now he didn't know who 'twas. At THEM times there used to be what they used to call giants around see? He didn't know what uh...'twas, anyhow _ he creeped up to the door _ an' there was a little hole in the door. An' when he did there was uh...three o' the big giants _ one on each end o' the table an' the other one to the side. Now they had a big leg o'...o' meat up on the table an' they was eatin of it.

He thought to hisself he'd take his little gun an' he...he'd have a shot at th' ol' feller. Huh! [*laughs*] So he took his little gun an' he fired at un an' he struck un here on the arm.

An' he said to the other feller he said "What you uh...uh...fire that at me for?" [*angry tone*]

He said "I never fired nothing at ya."

He said "Yes you did" he said "an' don't fire no more" he said "lest I chop your head off " he said "wi' this big knife." [Jack] said to hisself that /to/ was alright. Shoved this little gun in /through/ again an' he fired at un again. He [*the giant*] made no more ado, he grabbed up the big knife an' he chopped his head off. [Jack] said to hisself that was alright there was one of 'em gone anyhow. An'...has he...he...said to hisself he'd have ANOTHER shot. He fired at un again.

"Now" he said "I chopped off that yuther [i.e., *other*] feller's head, now" he said "YOU'RE startin at it."

He said "I never fired nothing"

He said "Yes you did fire it." Said "I knows you fired it." So -- he eat away an' uh...Jack shoved his little gun in through an' he fired at un again. He [m]ade no more ado but he grabbed up the big knife an' he chopped HIS head off. Now he had two of 'em gone, there's only his own self now.

An' uh...Jack thought to hisself he'd have **ANOTHER** shot at un. An' he fired at un again. Yeah, looked all around, he thought to his...said to hisself well he'd akilled the two of 'em, 'twasn't they **NOW**.

He jumped up an' he went out through the door an'...Jack whipped behind the door. He looked all around an' he couldn't see no one an' _ by an' by he hauled the door open "Hah me son" he said "I got ya!" He said "I got ya! Come out" he said "I'll kill you!"

"Hold on a bit now" Jack said "hold on a bit now" he said uh..."I got me little gun here" he said uh..."I can do a lot wi' this little gun."

"Now" he said "Jack come in." He said "Come in." He said "I'm goina put up ten candles now" he said "right along a string." He said "An' if you can knock down they ten candles" he said "the one shot _ dout they ten...ten candles the one shot" he said "I won't kill ya." /He/ said "I'll save your life." /I/

"Well" Jack said "I can do **THAT**!" An' sure enough he light the ten candles all along wi' a string _ all in breast o' one another an' Jack got...that's on the other side of his house with his little gun an' he fired at 'em an' he dout all the candles.

"Alright" he said "Jack" he said "you're just the man" he said "I wants." He said "I...I been tryin to get the king's daughter" he said "this long spell" he said "an' I...uh...I can't get her." He said "They got a cat there" he said "an' every time I goes to th' house" he said "the cat wakes 'em. An'..."he said "you're the man" he said "I wants. Now" he said "you can kill that cat."

"Yes" [*laughing tone*] Jack said "it's no trouble for me to kill **THAT** cat."

"Alright" he said "Jack" he said "now by twelve o'clock" he said "you an' me 'll go."

So twelve o'clock that night _ away they goes. Went up to the house an' got out in the city an' got up to the king's palace an' _ there was a hole in the door see? Looked in through the door an' the cat was lied (down) on the table see?

"Now" he said "Jack" he said "there's the cat" he said "on the table, now" he said "if you can kill the cat _ " he said "we'll go in" he said "an' get the king's daughter."

"Huh! By god" Jack said "I can soon kill **SHE**!" So Jack shoved this little gun in through the door an' he fired at the cat an' he killed her.

"Alright" he said "Jack." "Now" Jack sai[d]..."now" he said "Jack _ " he said "you go in th' house" he said "an' look around" he said "see the room she's in." He said "An' I'll get up to the window" he said "an' you'll pass her out to me."

"Alright" Jack said.

Well Jack went in th' house an'...he went in twothree rooms you know an' he looked all around an' by an' by he opened a room door an' he went in an' when he went in _ the king an' his wife was in the bed _ **SOUND** asleep. He looked up over the bed an' there was a sword hung up over the bed. Took the sword down. An' he went out. An' he went up...stairs in the top storey. An' the first room he went into _ here was the king's daughter lied down on the bed **SOUND** asleep. Huh! [*laughs*] Jack looked out, lowered down the window, looked out through the window, Jack said "Here she is here!"

"Alright" he said "Jack" he said "I'll get the ladder now" he said "an' I'll get up to the window." He said "An' you pass her out to me."

Got the ladder an' he got up to the window an' Jack said "Now" he said _ "you shove your head" he said "right in through the window" he said "'cause she's too heavy" he said "I can't lift her."

An' _ "Alright" he said an' your...giant shoved his head in through the window like that an' when he shoved his head in through the winder Jack took his sword an' he chopped his head off. His head falls down in the room an' his body falled down outside.

Anyhow Jack went on. Jack went on an' he went back to the other giant's house an' he...he took all the money he had. Uh...he had the three of 'em killed. An' he stayed there all night.

An' the next morning _ the king woke. "Oh my!" he said "The giant" he said "got our daughter this morning" he said uh..."the cat...somebody have a...he've akilled the cat" he said "an' uh...he got her." Jumped out o' bed an' away he goes up _ in her room an' when he went up in her room the first thing he seen was the giant's head down there. An' looked out through the window an' his body was outside.

"Oh" he said "somebody been here tonight" he said "our daughter 's alright, somebody been here tonight" he said "an' killed the giant. Now" he said "how is we goin to find out" he said "the man done it?" He said "If I can find out the man done it" he said "they got to marry my daughter." Well now _ they didn't know how to find out, now Jack /be out/...out with his mother an' father now.

/bou/

So they stayed out in the city for uh...'bout ten year. An' uh...well they have money enough now they was goin back home again, now Jack had a nice bit o' money too an'...they was goin back home again.

Now they...the...king was sizin up how he was goina find out _ the man that killed the...the giant. An' his daughter said to un "Well" she said "now" she said "father, the only way" she said "we can find out that _ " she said "you build" she said "a big hotel _ " she said "an' put out over the door _ " she said "'Meals All Hours Free.'" She said "An' every man comes in" she said "I'll get 'em to tell a story."

She..."Yes" he said "I guess" he said "we'll find out like that."

So that's what he done. He build this big hotel an' uh...this is what he post up over the door: "Meals All Hours Free." An' _ he had un there for a...oh he had un there for about...ten year. An'...people comin an'...tell a story, well he...not...still it never got the man.

So very good uh...Jack an' his mother an' father they leaved now, they was goin back home. An' _ when they got out in the city they...was gettin hungry an' they...passin along by this...place. Jack looked up over the door an'..."Meals All Hours Free."

Jack said "Let's go in (here)" he said "an' get a lunch."

Th' ol' man said "I suppose" he said "we'll have [to] pay five or six dollars for a lunch here."

"No!" he said uh..."Free meals in here look" he said "up over the door."

An'...the ol' man said "We'll go in." So they went in.

Went to lunch, sot down to the table, well uh...king's daughter come out an' uh...girl 's...gettin a lunch on the table, she said "Now" she said uh..."before yous haves a lunch _ " she said "yous got to tell a story."

"Hah!" [*laughing tone*] th' ol' man said, he didn't (have) no story to tell.

"Well" she said "you got to tell SOMETHING!"

So anyhow, well he said uh..."Sooner [than] I'll do without a lunch" he said "I'll tell SOMETHING." Well he...told his story, I don't know what his story was now.

Now come to the ol' woman SHE had to tell one. So SHE told one.

Then come to Jack. An' Jack said "I don't know no STORIES to tell" he said "that's something I never learned in me life" he said "a story" he said "I don't know no stories [to] tell" he said "only something" he said "I done me OWN self."

"Well" she said "that's [the] kind of a story" she said "[we] wants to hear."

"Well (see)" Jack said "I can tell ya THAT."

"Well" he said uh..."about ten year ago" _ he said uh..."we lived" he said "about thirty miles" he said "from this." He said "An' we got down an' out" he said "we never got nothing...had nothing...had to eat" he said "an' we had to come out" he said "to the city" _ he said "for to GET something to eat. An'" he said "we (do)...was travellin all day" he said "all we had" he said "when we left home" he said "was a bun apiece. An'" he said "dark" he said "I leaved 'em." He said "An' I went off /by/ meself. Well now" he said "I...I was searchin around" he said "an' I come across" he said _ "three giants. An'"

/for/

"Go ahead" she said "Jack, tell away" she said "that's (the) story I wants to hear."

An' ol' woman said [*fast excited tone*] "Now" she said "Jack" she said "don't tell no more. Don't tell no more" she said "I knowed" she said "you was goin to get we in trouble."

An'..."No" she [*the king's daughter*] said "go ahead" she said "you got to tell un."

An' uh...Jack said _ "I creeped up to the door" he said "an' I uh...had twothree shots at 'em." Well he said he KILLED two of 'em.

"Go ahead" she said "Jack" she said "that's [the] story" she said "I wants to hear."

Now ol' woman said "Jack" [she] said "let's go on" she said "don't tell no more" she said "'cause" _ /she/ said "I knowed you was goin to get we in trouble today."

/he/

"Oh no" she [*the king's daughter*] said "ya can't go" [she] said "till we hear...till I hears that story."

An' Jack said uh..."Well uh..." Jack said "I had another shot at un uh...after he...after they killed 'em, well" he said "he come out, well" he said _ "he was big enough" he said "to EAT me. 'Cause" he said "I didn't look very big 'longside of un. Well he was goin to kill ME!" Jack said "An'...*he told me to come in" he said "an'...he stuck up ten candles" Jack said. "An' uh...if I could dout the ten candles _ the one shot _ he wouldn't kill me. An'" _ Jack said "well" he said "I can do that. An'" _ Jack said "I fired at the ten candles" he said "an' I...dout them all. 'Now' he said 'Jack' he said 'I'm after the king's daughter.'"

*listener coughs

"Come on" she said "Jack, that's [the] story [we] wants to hear."

Th' ol' woman said "Now" she said "Jack" she said "come on" she said "'cause" she said "you're goin to get we in trouble today" she said "an'...an' let's go on" she said "(?don't stop)!"

She says "Oh no" she said "he can't go" (she) said "till he tells that story."

An' Jack said "We started" he said "twelve o'clock" he said "for the king's palace." He said "An' when we went there" he said "the cat was lied down on the table." He said "An'...course" he said "I fire at the cat" he said "an' I killed her. An'" he said "I went in th' house" he said "an' I searched around" _ he said "I searched around" he said "an' the...the last room I went into in the under storey" he said uh..."the king an' his wife was there" Jack said "an' uh...I looked around" he said "an' there was [a] sword hung up over the bed."

Said "Jack" she said "that's just the story" she said "I been after."

"Now" th' ol' woman said "Jack" she said "come on, don't...don't tell no more" she said "don't tell no more 'cause" she said _ "you're goin to get us in trouble."

Uh..."Oh yes" she said "Jack" she said "finish your story."

An' uh...[*coughs*] Jack said "I took down the sword" he said "an' I...come out o' that room" he said "an' I went upstairs" he said "an' when I went upstairs" he said "the king's daughter" he said "was lied down on the bed" he said "sound asleep, well" he said "I /?loved/ to had time with her. An'" he said uh..."I looked out through the window" he said "an' I told un." He said "An' he got up to the window" _ he said "an' I told un" he said "to shove his head in through" he said uh..."an' help me get her out." He said "An' when he shoved his head in through" he said "I chopped his head off."

/left/

Said "That's the story" she said "I wants to hear"

She jumped up an' she went out an' she locked the door. 'Way she goes after the king.

"Oh" she said, "father" she said "I got the man!"

He said "Have ya?"

"Yes." Said "I got un."

Over the king comes. "Well now" _ the king said _ "I been after that man" he said "this ten year." He said "An' I got un" he said "this morning. Now" he said _ "Jack" /he/ said "you got to marry my daughter" _ he said "an' I'm goin to give yous this hotel" he said "an' yous can live in un" an' when I leaved they had two children. That ends the story. [*laughs*]

/she/

[*recorder off*] I heard that uh...I learned that story from a ol' man up to Sally's Cove. Ol' Eli Roberts we calls un, he's dead now. He would be...he'd been ninety odd year ol' if he was livin.
[Int: Is he any relation to Uncle Jack Roberts?]
Yes. Uncle Jack Roberts's brother. Uncle Jack Roberts's brother.

Duration: 13 min., 38 sec.
Source: Eli Roberts (John Roberts' brother), Sally's Cove, Great Northern Peninsula.
Location: The darkening sitting room of the teller's house, in the late evening.
Audience: Mrs. Rebecca Bennett (teller's wife), male visitor, several children, interviewers.

Context, Style, and Language: This lengthy recording session begins around 7:45 P.M. after the evening meal. In the early stages Freeman and his wife Rebecca take turns to sing songs and when Rebecca leaves to go to a garden party Freeman continues to tell stories for several hours, the interview ending at 1:20 A.M. the next morning, by which time Rebecca has returned and recited many of the adult singing games which were referred to locally as Christmas plays. As darkness falls, Freeman tells story after story without intermission, occasionally sipping from a bottle of beer, his lively narration characterized by frequent gestures and bodily movements, now acting the part of Jack creeping up to spy on the giants, then taking the part of the whole group of them quarreling, his face constantly animated and his hands frequently gesticulating. Such a setting as night falls in the otherwise quiet room must have been typical of many such storytelling sessions from the time that Freeman and his brother Everett first learned these tales from their father and uncle, lying in front of the wood stove in the evenings of their boyhood. The authentic nature of the storytelling context nevertheless poses problems for the interviewers, not least in the changing of tapes on the recorder in virtual darkness, and the fact that it was impossible to take adequate notes.

The repertory of Freeman Bennett is the most extensive in this collection. In a series of interviews over a period of some five years we recorded a total of nineteen different story types in twenty-six recensions, most of them told only once, but a few repeated twice or three times which allows us to gain some impression of the consistency of his style and technique.

His repertory is comparable with that of his younger brother, Everett, who told a total of seventeen story types, also in twenty-six recensions, over a similar time period. As the two brothers had learned most of their stories from the same sources it is inevitable that identical titles and similar versions appear in the repertory of each. However, Freeman's stories are in general much longer, fuller, and more elaborate than those of Everett, and he tells twelve tales which were not told by the younger brother. His style is rather less demonstrative and flamboyant and he seems a little less concerned to involve his audience directly in the events of the story through dramatic interplay, eye-to-eye contact, rhetorical questions, gestures, and other proxemic features, although all these features are found in his stories. His physical presence is less charismatic and he shows a greater degree of detachment than Everett, relying on the sheer pace and technique of his narrative to capture and hold the audience's attention. Like that of his brother, his delivery is very animated, with frequent changes in pace and skillful contrasting of pitch, stress, and other tonal features. Unfortunately, the subtle nuances of these techniques are virtually impossible to transfer to print without resorting to a full phonetic transcription accompanied by some formal means of representing the intonation. Even if such a transcription were possible—and no satisfactory notation system for intonation has yet been devised—it would exclude most readers from access to the tale. The transcriptions presented here can therefore only hint at the rich and subtle variety of vocal tone.

Freeman Bennett's storytelling skills are seen to greatest effect in his fast-moving dialogue, which is remarkably energetic and realistic, the variation of color and tone not only contributing immeasurably to characterization but also demanding and sustaining the attention of the listeners. The dialogue is punctuated very frequently by *he/she said* which serves as a conventional marker for segments of direct speech. It is often immediately followed by a hesitation form before the quoted words, and this feature is so frequent that it may well be regarded as a mannerism he has developed to allow himself time to devise and control dialogue to the best advantage. A similar device is seen in the frequent use of *And,* often followed by a pause and/or hesitation form, at the beginning of sentences. This not only gives the teller an opportunity to construct the sentence which follows but also provides a constant means of creating a certain degree of suspense and anticipation in the audience who have to wait for a few seconds before hearing the next segment of the narrative. These devices are also used by Freeman's brother, Everett, though to a lesser extent, and may have been picked up from those members of their family and neighbors from whom they first learned the stories.

The speed of delivery, especially in the dialogue, sometimes results in the confusion of pronouns in *he/she/they said* and their referents, and this also shows itself in similar ambiguities in the narrative sections of the tales. Freeman's enunciation, however, is usually very clear and distinct, aided by the crisp and incisive quality of his voice. It is rare for him to mispronounce or slur a word and in this he presents a notable contrast to many other tellers in this collection whose voice qualities and/or narrative styles are less distinctive. Like his brother Everett, Freeman makes use of the mingling of direct and indirect speech, with its associated shifts of tense and pronouns—a most effective stylistic device which brings added vividness and immediacy to reported speech by investing it with the intonation patterns and other characteristics of spoken usage. Another feature of style which the brothers share is the punctuating of the narrative with such set phrases as *(well) very good, (so) anyhow, alright,* marking the end of a segment, and *by an' by* which marks the passage of time—usually of an indefinite period of time so typical of folktales. By contrast, he and all the other tellers in this collection very rarely use expressions such as *soon, directly, presently,* which have more specific reference to time in the real world. The use of *we'll say* gives him license for vagueness of reference in the glossing over of imprecise details, a feature found much more frequently in the tales of Allan Oake.

Freeman Bennett's speech is of the West Country English type as is evident at all levels of linguistic analysis. At the phonological level the vowel system has numerous West Country English features such as /ar/ in *born, morning,* etc., aphesis is common, and schwa is often elided in *the* before a following vowel. Many lexical items reflect the same origin, especially the frequent use of the object pronoun *un* (him/it). Determiners, pronouns, prepositions, and auxiliary verbs are often omitted. The grammar is characterized by typical survivals and developments in Newfoundland of West Country English forms, especially in the tense structure and negation of verbs. Although the syntax is usually straightforward, it is occasionally reminiscent of various regional dialects of English, including the West Country, and the punctuation of dialogue with *he/she said* sometimes results in aberrant syntactical forms when these markers disrupt the normal flow of spoken usage.

Many of the features of style and language are exemplified in this the first of Freeman Bennett's stories in this collection. The tale was recorded on three occasions over a five year period and the versions are substantially similar. However, the third (No. 6) recorded in 1971, is the fullest, and the second (No. 5) ends unsatisfactorily when the teller has difficulty resuming the narrative after a tape is changed on the machine. Certain minor variations in expression make each telling unique (e.g., the family go for a *lunch* (snack) in versions one and three, but *dinner* in version two, and they have it in a *hotel* in versions one and two, but in a *restaurant* in version three), and the giant calls Jack *me son* (typical of Newfoundland speech) in version one, *me lad* (colloquial British usage which sounds rather out of place in the local context) in version two, but simply says *'Tis you* in version three. Some significant differences occur in the content and chronology of which the principal ones may be summarized in the following table:

Version one (No. 4)	Version two (No. 5)	Version three (No. 6)
1.	preamble mentions "pod auger days" and local place-names	preamble begins with biographical data and joking claims that the teller was a boy some five or six hundred years ago
2.		family has breakfast

3. family takes three buns	family takes two buns	family takes two buns, and more details are given about them
4. Jack has gun to kill something for lunch	Jack has gun	(gun mentioned briefly later)
5. Jack invited in by giant after saying he can do a lot with his gun	Jack invited in by giant—no reason	Jack is hungry and is invited in by giant to have something to eat
6. (mentioned later in recapitulation)		Jack's size compared to that of giant
7.		quest for king's daughter mentioned before Jack shoots at the candles
8.	Jack has supper before leaving with giant for the palace	
9.	king's daughter described as a "wonderful smart lookin girl"	king's daughter described as a "handsome girl"
10. (mentioned later in recapitulation)	Jack would "like to have a time" with king's daughter	
11.	Jack returns sword to king's and queen's room	Jack returns sword to king's and queen's room
12. (Jack reunited with parents later)	Jack gets up next morning to go to look for parents	
13. hotel open for ten years, but hero not found	hotel open for four or five years	restaurant open for "a twelvemonth"
14. Jack offers to tell a story about his "OWN self"		Jack offers to tell a story about his "OWN self"

15. king's daughter responds immediately to Jack's offer to tell a story		king's daughter responds immediately to Jack's offer to tell a story
16. (recapitulation) details of Jack finding light at place where giants are, after three attempts		(recapitulation) full details of Jack finding light of place where giants are, after three attempts
17. less detailed recap of episode with three giants	fuller recap of episode with three giants	full, detailed recap of episode with three giants
18. remaining recap less detailed than original	remaining recap confused and curtailed by change of tape	remaining recap full and detailed
19.	daughter goes to tell king she has found Jack	daughter goes to tell king she has found Jack
20. king gives Jack hotel	king builds house/castle for Jack	king builds house for Jack's mother and father, and asks Jack to live with him
21. couple have two children		Jack is seventy or eighty years old and has lots of money

This comparison reveals the omission of several elements in the earliest version, the curtailment of an otherwise promising narrative in the second, and the fullness of the third version with its detailed recapitulation. All three versions repeat certain focal sections of the narrative in very similar words, e.g., the description of the king and queen lying in bed, the setting up of the hotel/restaurant, and the dialogue of the king's daughter and Jack's mother in the recapitulation.

Although all three tellings begin "Once upon a time. . . ," the third dates the events as "five or six hundred year ago" and the teller puts himself humorously into the tale as remembering it, and adding that he was then not very old. The second telling makes a proverbial reference to the date: "away back in pod auger days," and seems to locate the story locally: "a...family living well...we'll say up to...Sally's Cove, that's about ten mile from this. Oh further than that, so far as to this to Bonne Bay." This is probably an expression of the distances involved in concrete terms, rather than a claim that the events took place locally. The 1966 and 1972 tellings both use the phrase "a family living here," though again, it is

45

likely that the teller is only trying to exemplify the distance between Jack's home and the city. Nevertheless, St. Pauls is a long way from the city and the teller's use of local analogies suggests he may have the local terrain in mind as a background for Jack's journey. These variations in the opening formulas are matched by a similar variability in the endings of each version, indicating that the teller does not regard a particular set of formulas as sacrosanct.

In Nos. 4 and 6 it is Jack who has the idea that they should leave home and find work in the city; in No. 5 it is his father, seconded by the mother. As noted above, there is some variation as to the number of buns they have for provisions; in No. 4 they have three, one of which they share (at noon, sitting by a brook—a realistic touch), but in the other tellings there are only two buns for the journey. The important point for the story, however, is to arrive at a situation where there are only two buns between three, thus precipitating Jack's generous giving up of his share to his parents and sending them towards the "settlement" (Nos. 4 and 5) or the city (No. 6).

When Jack sees a light in a valley and tries to walk toward it, he twice loses it and has to go back to the hill to get his bearings again. This heightens the listener's anticipation as to what he will meet, and gives a supernatural cast to the situation (a Newfoundland audience might have Jack o' Lanterns in mind). In Nos. 5 and 6 we have a representation of the woodsman's method of direction-finding: "he sized it up an' he took good notice. . . ." (No. 5); "he took good marks" (No. 6). It is notable that in No. 6, when telling his story to the princess, Jack says he "took out a paper...an' maked out kind of a map of it. . . ," almost as if Jack was embellishing his rustic skills with a veneer of literacy when in her presence.

Nos. 4 and 6 use almost identical phrases to introduce the giants: "At THEM times there used to be what they used to call giants around see?" (No. 4); "there used to be giants around them times see _ they used to call 'em" (No. 6). In No. 5 the teller says "there was _ three giants," and then confirms with his audience, "You've heard tell o' the giants." The stability of the phrase in Nos. 4 and 6 implies that this is a key structural element in his memory and delivery of the tale. No. 5 specifies that the giants are father and sons; this may be implicit in the other tellings where it is "the old feller" that Jack shoots at. In each telling the giants have meat on the table but the most graphic version is in No. 4 where it is "a big leg o'...o' meat" they are eating. The first is the only telling which specifies that Jack's "little gun" (all tellings) is a .22. With his first shot he hits the old giant on the arm (No. 4), on the head (No. 5), and on the ear (No. 6). Otherwise the sequence of shots, dialogue, and beheadings is fairly consistent.

Nos. 5 and 6 emphasize the contrast in size between Jack and the giant when they confront each other: "Jack got behind the door. Now he was...only small, the giant was a great big man who weighed about _ four hundred pound see." In all three the giant, though threatening, asks Jack in; in Nos. 4 and 5 the test of his shooting skill follows at once; in No. 6 Jack has his supper first.

There is variation in the number of candles and their manner of placement for the shooting test. In No. 4 ten candles are mounted on a string; in No. 5 three candles are set up on the table; in No. 6 six candles are set on the table, and the teller reduces this number to four in the next paragraph. The number of candles is obviously inconsequential.

The detail of the cat on the table, seen through a hole in the door, is consistent in all tellings. In Nos. 4 and 6 the narrator seems eager for the audience to picture the scene: "...there was a hole in the door see? Looked in through the door an' the cat was lied (down) on the table see?" (No. 4). In No. 6 the giant asks Jack if he can see the cat:

> ..."look in through that hole" he said "see can ya see the cat." Jack looked in through the hole an' the cat was lied down on the table see. An' he said "You see her?"
> Jack said "Yes" he said "I sees her."
> "Now" he said _ "see can you kill her."

The word *see* occurs five times here and, while this is due to its ubiquitous usefulness as an interrogative or connective tag in Newfoundland speech, it also has the effect of forcing us to imagine the scene, as we participate with Jack.

When Jack goes into the castle there is a fusion of Newfoundland ordinariness and Märchen detail; he opens a "room door" and takes down a sword from the wall, and in No. 6 he tidily replaces it after using it to cut off the giant's head. It should be noted too, that the king, queen, and princess are in a normal sound sleep, not a "magic" one, so motifs F771.4.4. and N711.2. should not be taken as implying magical influence. Other details also suggest a large house of an outport merchant rather than a medieval castle: the giant needs a ladder to get up to the top storey, and in No. 5 the giant tells Jack to "rise the window," which suggests a wooden-framed window as in the clapboarded houses typical of Newfoundland.

The first telling modestly makes no comment on the sleeping princess's beauty except in Jack's telling of the story, where he says (somewhat flirtatiously in the context) "I /?loved/ to had time with her." This is like the comment in No. 5 where the narrator says "she was a wonderful smart lookin girl" and Jack thinks "I'd like to have a time with ya." No. 6 mentions "she was a handsome girl too."

There is a concern to account for where characters stay the night, which may have to do with these being essentially stories of journeys. Vivian Labrie's essay on "The Itinerary as a Possible Memorized Form of the Folktale," is relevant here, especially the informant's remark, p. 101, that, "When somebody tells you a tale, you keep your attention until the hero sets out for another place and then, you notice again where he stops if you want to be able to tell it back."

There is some difference in the depiction of Jack's father: in No. 4 he is much more the 'bayman' in the big city, dubious about going in to eat: "I suppose" he said "we'll have [to] pay five or six dollars for a lunch here." In Nos. 5 and 6 he has become a connoisseur: "Yes" he said "it's a very good place."

The device of storytelling within the tale allows Freeman Bennett some sardonic remarks about storytelling, especially in No. 6 where the old man declares he "wasn't interested in stories," and in No. 4 where Jack says "that's something I never learned in me life" he said "a story." The princess's enthusiasm for the tale may also be seen as a reflection of a real audience's encouragement of real storytellers. Jack's querulous old mother, afraid his story will get them into trouble, is played to the hilt in all three tellings.

In No. 5 the teller is confused by the interruption when the tape is changed. When he resumes he finds himself narrating the start of his story, not Jack's retelling of the events. This is a significant illustration of how relatively "fixed" sections of the tale are in his memory and performance. A small detail, possibly related to the question of how fixed the words are, is that in No. 5 the king says "You sove my daughter," but in No. 6 it is Jack who reveals this information, using almost the same words: "He said 'Sove your daughter.'"

These three tales include some interesting patterns of light and darkness, and specifically of lighted interiors seen from the darkness outside, and of penetration into those warm, comfortable surroundings. These patterns begin with Jack on the hill looking down into the dark valley at the light from the giants' house, which proves so elusive. When he creeps up close he looks in through a hole in the door or window, through which he then intrudes his gun. The shooting test also involves points of light—candle flames—in darkness. Then the theme of looking in through a hole is repeated at the king's castle (the cat on the table implying peace and comfort). After the shot through the hole Jack penetrates an interior once more, going into bedrooms, desiring the princess. When the giant attempts to imitate Jack's intrusion, however, poking his head through the window to receive the princess, his head is cut off. Finally, Jack enters the hotel or restaurant confidently, and this results in his entry to the king's family and to the princess as her husband. All this, of course, is in keeping with the theme of a family seeking to escape its poverty in a bleak, outlying country by moving to the bright, wealthy city.

Analysis of this kind may no doubt be applied as much to the Märchen as genre as to this tale in particular; Lüthi comments on the fondness of tales for enclosed spaces ("Aspects of the Märchen and the Legend," 166). However, if one of the qualities of a storyteller is to make his or her audience picture the scene, then Freeman Bennett is very successful here, and these aspects of his style contribute to that success.

The dialogue is handled in masterly fashion, especially in the highly complex use of speech within speech in the recapitulations. It is very animated and true to life, notably in the episode with the three giants where one accuses the other who in turn protests his innocence, and in the querulous and agitated tones used to characterize Jack's mother when she tries to prevent him from telling the story in the hotel. Equal skill is seen in the portrayal of Jack as bold and cocksure when talking to the giant. There is particularly effective use of strong stress to highlight individual words, and the punctuating expressions discussed above mark stages in the development of the plot—sometimes incorporated into the speech of a character and thereby disguising that function, rather than calling attention to them at the beginning of sentences. The occasional ambiguity of pronominal reference causes no difficulty for the listeners, not least because the pace of the narration is so fast that there is no time to pause for such quibbles and attention is quickly refocused on the next segment of narrative.

Despite the conventional opening formula *Once upon a time* the preamble affects an air of plausibility in its account of families living in scattered locations *in olden times,* and this is even more obvious in No. 5 which mentions local place-names as examples of such locations. A similar pretense of historicity is found in the explanation that giants used to be around in those days. On the other hand, expressions such as *in olden times, made no more ado,* have a more formal, literary ring. Notice also the rhetorical device of repeating brief segments of the narrative, using identical or very similar words, partly for emphasis and partly to allow the narrator a brief space of time to gather his thoughts before moving on. This is both effective and necessary in the complicated detail and chronology of the recapitulation, e.g., "'I searched around' _ he said 'I searched around' he said", and also the slightly more progressive "'an' I went upstairs' he said 'an' when I went upstairs' he said." Further, the repetition of *he/she said* is at times so obtrusive as to suggest it is not simply a means of punctuation which breaks up the quoted speech into short segments, but an almost obsessive mannerism which, together with the pauses which often accompany it, may also be used partly to gain time for the mental processes of planning and articulating the complex and fast-moving dialogue. Two examples will suffice to indicate this and to draw the reader's attention to it elsewhere in this teller's repertory:

"Now" he said "Jack" he said "there's the cat" he said "on the table, now" he said "if you can kill the cat _ " he said "we'll go in" he said "an' get the king's daughter." [6 *he said* forms, delimiting 7 segments].

"Alright" he said "Jack." "Now" Jack sai[d]..."now" he said "Jack _ " he said "you go in th' house" he said "an' look around" he said "see the room she's in." He said "An' I'll get up to the window" he said "an' you'll pass her out to me." [8 *he/Jack said* forms, delimiting 9 segments].

The enigma of the story's title unfortunately remains unresolved, perhaps because Freeman Bennett is evidently unsure about the precise circumstances in which he first heard the tale told by Eli Roberts. In the tape-recorded discussion which follows No. 6 he seems to suggest that Peter and Minnie were the names of someone's mother and father, although whose is unclear. In an earlier interview following the version which is presented here as No. 4, he offers a somewhat different explanation:

An' I said uh..."Eli" (I) said "tell us the story." An' he said "Yes" now uh...uh...'twas Peter an' Minnie's house we was to see, his wife's name was Minnie an' his name was Peter. An' he said "I'll tell ya a story _ about Peter an' Minnie." An' so he up an' told a story about Peter an' Minnie _ which I learned. [*laughs*]

Here the implication is that the story is named after the people in whose house Freeman first heard it told by Eli. Neither explanation is satisfactory, but it appears that the story is named after a married couple who presumably lived in the vicinity. Local records suggest a possible origin in the names of Peter Payne (born 1860, died 1936) and his second wife Amelia Elizabeth ("Minnie") Decker (born 1876, died 1959) who lived in the neighboring community of Green Point. It may be that the story became identified with their names if their house was a venue for its telling, as Freeman Bennett implies.

Turning now specifically to linguistic matters, at the phonological level we find the diphthong /ei/ in *leaved,* the long close front vowel in /kriːpt/ *creeped,* intrusive onglide /j/ in *yuther,* the realization of /z/ as /d/ in *'twasn't,* and of the second syllable of *window* as *-er* in one instance; the loss of final /t/ in *'twasn't, hotel* lacks the initial aspirate and there is strong stress on the first syllable, while *twothree* has geminated medial /t/; aphesis is common, e.g., *'fore, 'bout, 'longside, 'wards, 'cause, 'Way;* the initial consonant is lacking in *'twould, 'twasn't;* the final consonant is lost in *wi'* (with), and schwa is elided in *th' house* (initial aspirate omitted) and *th' ol'*. In morphology we have the plural inflection in *yous,* the possessive first element in *hisself,* the addition of final *-s* in *a long ways, anyhows,* and the lack of plural marker in *mile, year.* Apart from the frequency of West Country English *un,* dialectal vocabulary includes *set* (sit), the nautical *grub* (food), the demonstratives *them/they* (those), the familiar term of affectionate address *me son,* the pronouns *she* and *we* in the object position, archaic *dout* (put out), the compound *twothree,* the use of *this* in the sense of "this place, here" in *thirty miles...from this,* and the purposive *for to,* along with the asseverative *by god,* and *in breast of* (abreast), while a hint of Anglo-Irish appears in *his/my own self.* Nonstandard verb forms include the present tense *I knows/wants/goes/hears, yous is, you haves, is we,* the past tense *done, leaved, seen, come, creeped, eat, light, I been, falled* (fell), *build, knowed,* the past participles *akilled, lied,* and the past continuous *they was eatin of it.* There are many double negatives: *never see you no more, don't fire no more, never fired nothing, couldn't see no one, didn't (have) no story, don't know no stories, never got nothing, don't tell no more,* confirming the strength of this feature in current Newfoundland usage. Apart from the frequent omission of determiners, we also find that pronouns, prepositions, auxiliaries, and other words are dropped, no doubt partly as a result of the pace of the narration and the tendency towards abbreviation, e.g., *[with] the one shot, the man [who has/that] done it.* Foregrounding of a rhetorical or poetical nature is found in the syntax of *Over the king comes.* In all three tellings the king wakes and exclaims "Oh my!"—a typical expression of surprise in Newfoundland speech.

In conclusion one might note Freeman Bennett's use of gesture to indicate to the audience the length of Jack's gun, and also the obvious pleasure he finds both in the telling of the tale and in the tale itself, as shown in his laughter which indicates the incongruity of Jack's shooting his little gun at the giants, the laughing tones which convey Jack's cocksure attitude when he boasts he can kill the cat, the suggestive laughter which follows Jack's discovery of the king's daughter lying asleep (compensating here for the lack of overt expression of Jack's wish to *have a time* with her which is mentioned only in the recapitulation), and the exclamatory refusal of Jack's father to tell a story, the tone of which suggests he is simply dismissing the very idea as laughable, since he knows no stories.

Type and Motifs:

AT304. *The Hunter.*

Z10.1. *Beginning formula.*

Cf. N772. *Parting at crossroads to go on adventures.*

Cf. F771.4.1. *Castle inhabited by ogres.*

F661. *Skillful marksman.*

K1082. *Ogres (large animals, sharp-elbowed women) duped into fighting each other.*

N2.2. *Lives wagered.*

B576.1. *Animal as guard of person or house.*

Cf. F771.4.4. *Castle in which everyone is asleep.*

N711.2. *Hero finds maiden in (magic) castle.*
Cf. K912. *Robbers' (giants') heads cut off one by one as they enter house.*
R111.1.4. *Rescue of princess (maiden) from giant (ogre).*
N538.2. *Treasure from defeated giant.*
T68.1. *Princess offered as prize to rescuer.*
Cf. Q481. *Princess (queen) compelled to keep an inn.*
Cf. H152.1.1. *Woman entertains every traveller in the hope of finding her husband.*
M231. *Free keep in inn exchanged for good story.*
Cf. H11.1.1. *Recognition at inn (hospital, etc.) where all must tell their life histories.*
L161. *Lowly hero marries princess.*
Q53. *Reward for rescue.*

International Parallels: In North America this tale is apparently better known in the Franco-American tradition; the only published English-language version known to us is from Kentucky. We have found no reports of the story from the British Isles, although the recently published Scottish-Gaelic text from Nova Scotia is evidence that it must have been known in Scotland. In Ireland only eleven versions have been reported, in sharp contrast with the more than 600 versions found for better-known tales such as AT300, "The Dragon-Slayer," and AT313, "The Girl as Helper in the Hero's Flight."

The marksman's shooting at the giants while they are eating is a theme found in other versions of the tale, but only in the Newfoundland texts by Freeman Bennett and the one published by Desplanques does it lead to the killing of two of the giants by the third—a motif more familiar as Incident III of AT1640, "The Brave Tailor."

Unique to the Newfoundland versions is the giant's test of Jack's marksmanship. In our first recension the giant challenges him to shoot out the flames of a row of ten lighted candles hung from a string. This reminds us of the test of Penelope's suitors in *The Odyssey* of Homer, who were supposed to string the mighty bow of Odysseus and then shoot an arrow through the handle ring holes of twelve axes set in a row, a feat that only Odysseus himself accomplished. The resemblance between the two feats is even closer in the Desplanques text in which the boy uses a bow and arrow, not a rifle, to shoot out the flames of a row of twelve lighted candles.

Near the end of the tale when in payment for his free meal Jack tells of his personal experiences, recapitulating the main events of the story, his mother excitedly interrupts repeatedly to deny that he is telling the truth because she fears his telling will lead to serious consequences. This amusing scene is also stressed in the Desplanques version. It is not, however, unique to Newfoundland. We also find it, though less prominently, in Delarue's text from France, and again, with great emphasis, in Groome's Gypsy version from Moravia. In each of these the mother clearly demonstrates the fear that peasants and gypsies have for the power that the upper classes may exert to punish unsanctioned behavior by legal means.

Worth commenting on is Jack's remark about the beauty of the sleeping princess that he would have "loved to had time with her." According to the Type description of the tale, in other versions the hero does not limit himself to wishing but lies with the princess and makes her pregnant. This is exactly what takes place in a different story in our collection, No. 29.

What is more to the point is that it also occurs in the Desplanques version of AT304 collected from a Newfoundland west coast storyteller in the French tradition, and it is the stock pattern in the majority of the small group of European versions of this tale available to us in English translation. While the hero does not sleep with the princess in the composite version of the tale found in the Grimm collection, the Grimms' notes to their Tale no. 111 indicate that it does occur in several of the German versions they summarize.

It should be added that except for the Desplanques version the hero does not sleep with the princess in any of the other published North American versions of the tale, those from Nova Scotia, Kentucky, and Missouri. This is not from the laudable self-restraint Jack displays in Freeman Bennett's versions, but because the other storytellers present their tales in such a way that the temptation does not arise.

Although Delarue lists eleven versions from France and Ranke reports thirty-one German versions, we are not certain that all of the recensions listed in the AT index from across Europe and through the Balkans into Turkey belong to the exact Type description. Both Bolte and Polívka and W. R. Halliday before them called attention to a different version of the story, one which, rather surprisingly, was not included in the AT index. In our own notes this secondary version, which we have identified by the label *cf. 304,* is found in Hungary, Romania, Yugoslavia, Serbia, Bulgaria, Greece, Turkey, Georgia, Armenia (in recensions from Michigan), the Bashkir A.S.S.R., and Persia, plus two reports from Africa.

This related tale version lacks the magic gun or magic bow and arrows and the display of marksmanship listed in Incidents I and II of AT304. Here is an outline of the plot. Three princes, who are brothers, are on a trip, usually in search of wives. Each in turn stands guard at night while the others sleep. While on guard duty each kills a dragon or other monster but says nothing about it to the other brothers. When the third brother in his turn kills the largest dragon, its blood puts out their camp fire, and he goes in search of fire to start it again. As in our Newfoundland tale, he sees a light in the distance and finds a band of giants or robbers sitting around the fire. He joins them boldly, often exhibiting his great strength, and agrees to help them steal a princess from the king's castle. Through trickery he kills each of them in succession by cutting off their heads. This is AT956, "Robbers' Heads Cut off One by One as they Enter House," and is a standard element in AT304.

In the castle he finds three beautiful princesses asleep and exchanges the rings they wear for his brothers' and his own—a form of marriage engagement. In the castle he also sees and kills a huge snake which is about to attack the sleeping king, pins it to the wall with his sword, and then leaves. An interesting theme found in many versions is that while on the search for fire, he meets and ties up the personage(s) whose task is to wind up the dark and unwind the dawn. He does this in order that daylight should be delayed until he secures fresh fire. (AT723*, "Hero Binds Midnight, Dawn and Midday.") On his return from his adventure he releases this personage and gets back to start the fire before his brothers awake. Like them, he says nothing about his night's adventures.

When the king awakes, he finds the snake pinned to the wall, his guards report finding the headless giants, and his daughters report that their rings have been taken and replaced by men's rings. To find the unknown hero who did all this, we have the conventional offer of free meals given to all comers in return for which people must tell their life histories, or the free bath-house where there is the same requirement. This is a version of AT425D, "Vanished Husband Learned of by Keeping Inn (Bath-House)," another stock incident in AT304. The hero of the adventures is usually discovered when he tells his story, or when it is seen that there is no sword in his scabbard. The story concludes with the three princes marrying the king's three daughters.

Studies and Notes

MacCulloch, *Childhood,* pp. 367-70; Dawkins, *MGAM,* pp. 272-73, notes by W. R. Halliday; Bolte and Polívka, 2, pp. 503-6, no. 111; Thompson, *The Folktale,* p. 34; Espinosa, *CPE,* 3, pp. 108-10; Dawkins, *Modern,* pp. 121-23, no. 23, headnote; Roberts, *South,* p. 213, no. 4, notes; Delarue, *Catalogue,* 1, pp. 163-64, 166-67; Ranke, *Folktales,* pp. 208-9, no. 29, notes.

Canada

Desplanques, *Folktales,* pp. 19-21 (with cf. 1640, III, 2250) [bow and arrows], French tradition, told in English (Newfoundland).

MacNeil, *Sgeul,* pp. 258-69, no. 38 [bow and arrows], Gaelic text and English trans. (Nova Scotia), English trans. only, in MacNeil, *Tales,* pp. 132-37, no. 38;

Hallowell, *JAF* 52 (1939), 161-67, no. 1b (304, I, II, with 313A) [bow and arrows], Berens River Saulteaux Indian (Ontario).

Lacourcière-Low, "Catalogue," cites 21 Francophone versions of AT304 from Canada: 5 (Acadia), 14 (Quebec), 2 (Ontario).

United States

Cf. Hoogasian-Villa, *Tales,* pp. 77-84, no. 1 (cf. 304, with cf. 552A, 723*, 956, 302), cf. pp. 96-102, no. 4 (cf. 304, with 315, 956), cf. pp. 102-9, no. 5 (cf. 304, with 956, cf. 306), 3 versions, Armenian tradition, in English trans. (Michigan).

Roberts, *South,* pp. 23-25, no. 4 [rifle] (Kentucky).

Carrière, *Tales,* pp. 69-72, no. 13 [bow and arrows], pp. 72-80, no. 14 [bow and arrows], 2 versions, French texts with English summaries (Missouri).

Lacourcière-Low, "Catalogue," cites 3 Francophone versions of AT304 from the United States: 1 (Louisiana), 2 (Missouri).

Ireland

Irish Types, Type 304, 11 versions.

Continental Europe and Asia

Grimm no. 111, "The Skilful Huntsman," in Grimm-Hunt, 2, pp. 102-8, no. 111, composite text (304, with 300, cf. 900) [air-gun], and see 2, pp. 412-13, for the Grimms' notes on the tale and some variants [bow and arrows in fourth version]; for other trans. see Grimm-Magoun, pp. 404-9, no. 111, and Grimm-Zipes, pp. 402-6, no. 111.

Hodne, *Types,* AT304, 4 versions (Norway).

Delarue, *Borzoi Book,* pp. 233-36, no. 30 [gun; mother protests when son tells of his adventures], and p. 384, no. 30, notes (France).

Cf. Boggs, *Index,* Type 302*A, pp. 42-43 (cf. 304, with cf. 518, 302), English summary of Spanish text (Spain).

Ranke, *Folktales,* pp. 53-59, no. 29 (304, with 303, 300) [bow and arrows], and pp. 208-9, no. 29, notes (Germany).

Groome, *Folk-Tales,* pp. 144-51, no. 43 [gun which makes no sound; mother protests when son tells of his adventures], Gypsy (Moravia).

Cf. Busk, *Legends,* pp. 167-69 (cf. 304, with cf. 300, 723*, cf. 956, 425D, cf. 554, 302) (Hungary).

Jones and Kropf, *Folk-Tales,* pp. 39-46, no. 9 (304, with cf. 304, 300, 723*, 956) [bow and arrows] (Hungary).

Dégh, *Society,* p. 290, no. 2 (with 723*, 401A, 402), notes only, no text (Hungary).

Cf. Sturdza, *Fairy Tales,* pp. 51-63 (cf. 304, with cf. 301A, 300, 723*, 956, cf. 519, IV) [bow and arrows] (Romania).

Cf. Ćurčija-Prodanović, *Folk-Tales,* pp. 184-210, no. 26 (cf. 304, with 552A, cf. 300, 956, 425D, 302) (Yugoslavia).

Cf. Mijatovies, *Folk-Lore,* pp. 146-72 (cf. 304, with 552A, cf. 300, 956, 425D, 302) (Serbia), and rpt. in Petrovitch, *Hero Tales,* pp. 247-67, no. 8.

Cf. Yates, *Book,* pp. 78-85, no. 16 (cf. 304, with 552A, cf. 300, 723*, 956), Gypsy (Bulgaria).

Cf. Garnett, *Folk Poesy,* 2, pp. 171-76 (cf. 304, II, with cf. 554, 956, cf. 302) (Greece).

Cf. Dawkins, *Modern,* pp. 121-31, no. 23 (cf. 304, with 552A, cf. 300, 723*, 956, 425D, 302) (Greece).

Cf. Dawkins, *MGAM,* pp. 354-57, no. 3 (cf. 552A, with cf. 304, cf. 300, cf. 723*) [lacks the killing of robbers and snake], cf. pp. 378-83, no. 11 (cf. 304, with cf. 552A, 956, 302), pp. 272-73, notes, 2 versions, Greek dialect texts with English trans. (Turkey).

Cf. Bain, *Folk Tales,* pp. 112-33 (cf. 304, with 300, 723*, 956, 425D, 552A, 302) (Turkey).

Cf. Kúnos, *44,* pp. 102-16 (cf. 304, with 300, 723*, 956, 425D, 552A, 302) (Turkey).

Cf. Wardrop, *Folk Tales,* pp. 112-18, no. 2 (cf. 304, with 552A, cf. 300, cf. 723*, 956), Mingrelian tradition (Georgian S.S.R.).

Cf. Coxwell, *Folk-Tales,* pp. 457-60, no. 8 (cf. 304, with 300, 957, cf. 425D), Bashkir tribe (Bashkir A.S.S.R.).

Cf. Lorimer, *Tales,* pp. 169-75, no. 27 (cf. 304, with 956, cf. 507C) (Persia).

Africa

Cf. El-Shamy, *Folktales,* pp. 3-14, no. 1 (cf. 304, with 303A, 518, 956, 302, cf. 300, cf. 301A) (Egypt).

Cf. Klipple, *Folk Tales,* pp. 288-90 (cf. 304, with 300), English summary of Tiling, "Jabarti-Texte" (Somali Republic).

Addendum

One element in AT304 that is also found in combination with a variety of other stories is AT425D, "Vanished Husband Learned of by Keeping Inn (Bath-house)." For some examples see:

Webster, *Legends,* pp. 120-30 (Basque).

Wolf, *Fairy Tales,* pp. 129-45 (Germany).

Nicoloff, *Folktales,* pp. 57-66, no. 21 (Bulgaria).

Dawkins, *Modern,* pp. 56-60, no. 12, pp. 85-88, no. 16, 2 versions (Greece).

Megas, *Folktales,* pp. 65-70, no. 28 (Greece).

Bain, *Folk Tales,* pp. 166-75 (Turkey).

Kúnos, *44,* pp. 243-49 (Turkey).

Walker and Uysal, *Tales,* pp. 104-11, no. 11 (Turkey).

Campbell, *Told,* pp. 105-8, Arab tradition (Palestine).

Bushnaq, *Folktales,* pp. 188-93, Arab tradition (Palestine).

Stevens, *Folk-Tales,* pp. 45-57, no. 11 (Iraq).

Bushnaq, *Folktales,* pp. 94-104, Arab tradition (Iraq).

Freeman Bennett

5. PETER AND MINNIE[†]
(Jack and the Three Giants[†])

Freeman Bennett
St. Pauls, Great Northern Peninsula
18 July 1970

AT304
TC965, 966 71-50
Collectors: HH and Helen Halpert

[Int: What...what's the name of the story?]
"Peter an' Minnie."
[Int: "Peter and Minnie?"]
"Peter and Minnie" yes.

Well once upon a time ˗ in uh...i...in olden times ya know, that's away back in pod auger days that is ˗ there was a...well there...there was a...family living well...we'll say up to...Sally's Cove, that's about ten mile from this. Oh further than that, so far as to this to Bonne Bay. Well they...they lived there for...oh good many years an' they uh...got on alright. An' last goin' off [i.e., *finally*] uh...the times got so bad ˗ they got down an' out an' uh...nothing to eat see? Well uh...th' ol' man said, he said "Well" he said uh..."we'll have to leave" ˗ he said "an' go out" he said uh...* "go out" he said "to the (city)." [*aside to child*: Shu[t]...shut up Kevin] "Go out" he said "to the city." An' well ˗ th' ol' woman said "Yes" she said "we'll have to do something ˗ 'cause" she said "we got nothing to eat." Well uh...Jack ˗ they had a little feller there, his name was Jack, they only had one...one...boy ˗ one child. "Well" he said "alright" he said "tomorrow morning" he said "we'll go."

*teller's wife and others talking in background

Well ˗ in the morning they got up an' they packed up. Well now (then) all they had to take with 'em ˗ was two...two little buns. That's all they had to take. Well now they had a long ways to go.

Well they started. An' they walked ˗ uh...well ('twas) around... twelve o'clock. An' they begin to get hungry. An' ˗ they walked on. An' begin to get...duckish ˗ gettin on awards dark. And ˗ well they were...they were starvin. They never had nothing to eat.

An' ˗ Jack said "Well now" he said ˗ "we got two buns." He said "Yous take the two buns" ˗ he said "an' go on" he said uh..."an' I'll go my way." Oh well they couldn't do that, they couldn't go away an' leave un.

"Oh yes" he said "you take the two buns" he said "yous take two buns" he said "an' go on" he said "yous are not (far)...far" he said "from the...from the settlement." He said "An' I'll go my way." Well very good, they took the two buns an' away they goes.

Now Jack ˗ he had a little gun see? Jack did. Well he ˗ turned off an' he went down ˗ towards the forest. An' he walked down a piece ˗ an' he seen a little light.

An' he thought to hisself "Well there's something down there. I'll go down." An' _ he went down _ an' when he got down _ off o' the hill _ he lost the light an' he couldn't find it.

"Well" he said "have to go back on the hill again." He went **BACK** on the hill again an' when he went back on the hill again he could see the light again. "Well now" he said to hisself "I'll try it again." An' _ he tried it again. An' he still couldn't find the light. Well he...he went back to the hill again. An' he said "I'll find un this time." He went back to the hill again an' he sized it up an' he took good notice and _ he started. Away he goes. By god _ he come to the light. An' he looked in through the keyhole o' the door -- he never made no noise. He looked in through the keyhole o' the door an' uh...there was _ three giants. You've heard tell o' the giants. They was sot to the table an' they was...they was eatin. Now there was...there was a...ol' feller there an' his uh...his two sons. They was eatin an' uh...they had a...they had uh...some fresh meat on the table. Now he thought to hisself _ his little gun, there was a hole in the door, his little gun'd go in through the hole. An' _ he'd fire at th' ol' feller. An' _ 'twouldn't kill un. An' _ anyhow he shoved this little gun in through the hole _ an' he fired at un.

He [*the old feller*] put his hand up to his head like that [*gestures*] an' he rubbed his head an' he said _ "What did you strike me for?" he said (to)...feller was sot 'longside of him, one of his sons.

He said "I never struck ya."

He said "Yes you did. Struck me."

And _ he [*Jack*] said to hisself "That's good enough." An' _ they...eated away and _ he shoved this little gun in again an' he fired at un again, he struck un in the head again.

He said "Yes you did" he said "struck me" he said. "That's twice" he said "you've astruck me" he had a big knife on the table an' took the big knife _ he chopped his head off.

"Good enough" he said "there's..." to hisself "there's one gone." An' _ he shoved his little gun in through again. An' he fired at un again.

Put his hand up to his head like that [*gestures*] an' he rubbed his head. He said "Now" he said _ "I just killed that feller" he said "an' you've astarted at it!"

He said "I never touched ya"

He said "Yes you did touch me."

He said "No I didn't."

"Now" he said "don't do it no more" he said "or else I'll serve you the same as I served the other feller."

Jack thought to hisself "That's alright. He uh...he'll kill he directly." (Well) shoved this little gun in through again _ an' he fired at un again. He made no more ado but he grabbed the knife an' he...he chopped his head off. An' the two of 'em fall down.

57

Well now _ he was sot down to the table eatin an' Jack shoved this little gun in through the door there _ an' he fired at un again. He put his hand up to his head an' he rubbed his head an' he looked all around an' he thought...he said to hisself "Well _ 'tis not they at all. I got to go outdoors." Now _ Jack was only a little feller, now he was a...a great big man he was, the giant was.

[Int: How big were the giants?]

[*Teller misunderstands question*] Yes. An' uh...he looked all around everywhere, now Jack...Jack was behind the door. He looked all around everywhere an' by an' by he uh...he looked behind the door an' he seen (un).

"Ah" he said "me lad" he said "I got ya now!" He said "I'll soon fix you!"

"Hold on now" he said "a bit" he said "don't uh...(no)...don't...don't be too quick."

He said "Come in." He said "Come in." An' he went in an' he had this little gun. He said uh..."Now" he said "I'm goina stick up three candles" he said "on that table." He said "Now if you can...knock them...dout they three candles" he said "with the...the first shot" _ he said "I won't hurt ya."

"Alright" Jack said. So he stuck up the three candles on the table an' Jack got back wi' this little gun an' he fired at the three candles _ an' he dout the three of 'em the one time.

"Now" he said "you're just the man" he said "I wants." He said "I been after" he said "the king's daughter" he said "this long spell." He said "An' I can't get her." He said "They got a cat in the house." He said "They got a cat in the house" he said "an' soon as I goes to the door" he said "that cat is on the table." He said "And soon as I makes a noise" _ he said "that cat" he said "'ll go in an'...an' call 'em." He said "An' if...we can get down" he said "an' uh...you can kill the cat" _ he said "we'll get the king's daughter."

"Oh well" _ Jack said "I can...I can kill the cat."

Well alright. Got Jack some supper an' he had his supper. "Now" he said "we'll go." He said "They're turned in now" he said "we'll go." 'Way they goes. Went down to the...king's house. An' looked in through the...keyhole [o'] the door, the hole in the door an' sure enough the cat was lied down on the table.

"Now" he said "Jack" he said _ "you try, see what you can do." An' Jack shoved this little gun in through the table...in through the hole. An' he fired at the cat _ an' he killed the cat.

"Good enough" he said. "We'll go in now." They went in. An' Jack search...Jack went in an' he searched all around an' uh...went in all the rooms an' by an' by _ the...second room he went into _ the king an' the queen was in there _ lied down sound asleep. An' he looked all around, looked all around, by an' by he looked over...up over the...king's bed. An' there was a sword there. An' he took the sword down - an' he went out.

"Now" he said uh...ol' giant said to un, he said "we'll go" he said uh..."the king's daughter" he said "is up...in the top storey." He said "You go up" he said "an'...an' rise the window." He said "An' uh...an' pass her down to me."

"Alright" Jack said. So - up Jack stair...goes upstairs an' sure enough when he went in the room she was lied down on the bed, well she was a wonderful smart lookin girl.

Jack thought to hisself - "Well I'd like to have a time with ya." An' - he got her...he rose up the window - an' th' ol' giant he got a ladder an' he put up.

"Oh" he said "you'll have to get up" he said "further than that" he said "you'll have to get up" he said "an' put your head in through the window" he said "'cause - I can't handle her" said "she's too...she's too heavy for me to handle." An' ol' giant - got up an' he shoved his head in through the window - an' when he did - Jack took the sword - an' he chopped his head off. An' his body falled down an' his head falled uh...down in the room.

Well Jack - goes along an' he...he went out an' he...he went in the king's room an' he hung the sword up over the bed again an' away he goes. Now he went to the ol' giant's house. Well now he had a lot o' money there. An' - he took all the money he had there an' he stayed there that night. An' the next morning he got up, started - to go to look for his mother an' father.

Well now daylight -- the king an' the queen they woke.

"Oh my!" he said, the king said uh..."Somebody been...they been here tonight" he said "an' killed the cat" he said "an' they're gone away" he said "with our daughter. Giant is gone with our daughter." An' he jumped out o' bed an' upstairs. An' when he went upstairs what should be down in the...in the room - but th' ol' giant's head. An' he looked out through the window an' his body was down...by the window.

He said "Somebody been here tonight" he said. "An' killed the giant." He said "Killed the giant" he said "an' our daughter 's" he said "she...she's still in the bed" he said "to sleep." He said "Now" he said "how 's we goina find that out" he said "who done it?" Well she got up. "Well" he said "we got to find out" - he said "who killed him."

Well now - "Well" she said "father" she said "the only...way" she said "we can find it out" she said - "is you be...build a big hotel." She said "An' put up over the door - 'Meals All Hours Free.'" She said "Well" she said "everybody comes in" she said "I'll be there." She said "An' everybody comes in" she said - "to get something to eat" she said "I'll make 'em tell a story."

"Yes" he said. He guessed they find out like that.

Well very good, he started in, he got a crowd o' men an' they build a...a big hotel an' uh...she went in, got...three or four girls in there [to] cook and _ she went in. She used to be there every day. Well _ pretty well every day there'd be some uh...three an' four come in. And _ well they had (to) tell a story 'fore they'd get anything to eat. Well they'd tell the story, well _ no good.

Well now _ after _ four or five year _ th' ol' man an' th' ol' woman an' uh...Jack his son _ well they got money enough sove up _ that they was goin back again to their own home. Well they started. An' _ when they was goin an' walkin along on the street _ Jack looked up _ an' he said uh..."Meals all hours in there look" he said "free. You get a meal in there" he said "for nothing." He said "Let's go in" he said "an' get our dinner."

An' ol' man said "Yes" he said "it's a very good place." He said "Yes" he said "let's go in an' get our dinner." They went in an' uh...want some dinner.

"Yes. Oh yes. Get some dinner. But uh...'fore you gets your dinner _ yous got to tell a story."

Well -- old man said he didn't know much about tellin stories. But uh...he'd tell something. Well anyhow _ ol' man told a little story. An' _ now th' ol' woman she had to tell one. Well she told a little story. Well now come to Jack.

"Well" Jack said "I'm not...very much posted up" he said "in tellin' stories but" he said uh..."'fore I'll do without me dinner" he said "I'll tell a story. Well" he said uh..."in five or six year ago" _ he said "we lived" he said "in a little place" he said "by ourselfs." He said "Well" he said uh..."we got down an' out" he said "nothing to eat." He said "An' we had to leave."

An' ol' woman said "Now" she said "Jack" she said "don't tell no more."

"Yes" she [*the king's daughter*] said "go ahead." She said uh..."Tha[t] uh...ahead" she said "I wants to hear that story."

An' _ ol' woman said "You're goin to get us in trouble" she said "today Jack."

"No" she said. "Go ahead" she said uh..."I got to hear that story."

An' _ "Well" Jack said "w[ell] all we had when we leaved in the morning" he said "was two little buns." He said "Well" he said "we travelled till almost dark." He said "An' I give...th' ol' woman an' ol' man the two buns." He said "An' I leaved 'em." He said "An' I went down through the forest." He said "An' I seen this little light." He said "An' I went to go to the little uh...to the light" he said "an' I couldn't find un." He said "An' I tried it three times." He said "Well" he said "the third time" _ he said "I found the light." He said "Well" he said "when I found the light" he said "I looked in through the hole in the door." He said "An' there was three giants" he said "sittin to the table."

And _ "Go ahead" she said "Jack" she said "that's the story" she said "I wants."

"(Now)" ol' woman said "now" she said "Jack" she said "don't tell no more." She said "'Cause you're goin to get us in trouble" she said "I knowed you was goin to get us in trouble" she said "when you uh…when you started at it."

"No" she [*the king's daughter*] said. "You got to tell that story" she said "'fore you leaves."

"Well" Jack said _ "I shoved…I had a little gun" he said "an' I shoved her in through the hole in the door." He said "An' I fired at th' ol' feller." He said "An' he start to rub his head." He said "An'…an' into a row" he said "with the other fellers." He said…"An' I…had another shot at un. Well" he said "he had a big knife there" he said "an' he took the knife" he said "an' he chopped his head off."

"Go ahead" she said "Jack" she said "that's the story" she said "I wants."

Now th' ol' woman said "You're goin to get us in trouble Jack. You're goin to get us in trouble" she said "an' the best thing we can do" she said "is go on."

"No" she said. "You can't go" she said "'fore I hears that story."

An'   "Well" Jack said _ "I shoved me little gun in through again." He said "An' I had a shot at un again. Well" he said "he made no more to do" he said "he b…but he grabbed the knife" he said "he chopped the other feller's head off. Well" he said "the two of 'em was gone. (An') now" he said _ "I was goin to have the…the…another shot at un. Well" he said "I had another shot at un, well" he said _ "when…when I had the other shot at un, well" he said "he found out" he said…. [*recorder off; tape changed*]

[*aside:* go ahead…go back…go where…where I start from.]
[Teller's wife: No.]
[Int: No. Where the…'bout the giants, shooting at the giants.]
[Young boy listener: 'Bout the giant. You were shootin at the giant.]
[*aside:* Eh…uh…uh…(where)…what…at the first of un.]
[Teller's wife: No. No.]
[Young boy listener: Where (he's) shootin at the giants, where he tells the story about shootin the (other) giant.]
[Teller's wife: The last time.]
[*aside:* Oh yes. Yes. Yes. Yes.]
Well uh…after he uh…after he had the two of 'em killed _ he thought to hisself well he'd have another shot at un. An' _ he fired at un again. He rubbed his head like that an' he found…he said…to hisself "Well 'tis not them fellers at all, there's somebody out there
[Teller's wife: Oh now you…you're goin back too far.]
(Eh?)
[Int: No it's alright.]

[Teller's wife: (It's alright.)]
There's somebody out there." An' he...out he goes. An' when he went out [*aside:* no I'm wrong.]
[Int: Alright.]
[*recorder off*]*** (went out) _ Jack was behind the door [*aside:* yes I...I...I'm...I'm wrong. I'm wrong. I never...I'm not back to where I leaved off to. I'm not back to where I leaved off to.] [*recorder off*]*** (there's)
[Int: Yeah.]

*teller's wife speaks in background

An' uh...he come in. Got un in. Now he was goin to stick up three candles on the table.* Well now he had to dout...dout they three candles the one time. [*aside:* yes I've atold that once see.] [Int: Mm-hm.] [*aside:* an' all bothered up now.]
[Teller's wife: You got to tell where...they was talkin to the princess.] [Int: He...he...] [*aside:* Yes. Yes. Yes. Now I knows.]

An' he said...he said uh..."I uh..." he said "I been after the king's daughter" _ he said _ "this three or four year" he said "an' I can't get her." He said "There's a... [*aside:* no. He (didn't)...I'm wrong, still wrong.] [Teller's wife: (Now be) he's goina have her all fooled up.] [*aside:* I got un mixed up. I...yes I got un all fooled up now. I got un all fooled up now. [*recorder off*] This is...this is where I knocked off to.]

The...th' ol' king got up _ an'...went up in the room _ an' th' ol' giant's head was down in the room. An' his body was outside. An' uh..."Someone ha' been here tonight _ an' killed the giant" and _ [*aside:* no. I'm still wrong.] [*recorder off*]
[Int: They...they come back.]
[*aside:* Yes. That's right. Yes. Yes. That's right.]

An' uh...she said uh...the...his daughter said uh...foun[d]...king's daughter said, she said "Go ahead" she said "that's the story" says "I wants to hear."

"Well" he said uh..."I...I got upstairs" he said "to take her down. Well" he said uh..."when I did" _ he said "he shoved his head in through the window" he said "an' I chopped his head off." He said "An' his head falled down" he said "an' his body falled outside."

She said "That's just the story" she said "I wants to hear" she said "that's the man" she said "I been after" she said. "That's the man we been after" she said "this two year." Now she...she jumped up an' she locked the door.

An' uh...th' ol' woman said "Now" she said "Jack" she said "you got us in trouble. You got us in trouble" she said uh..."we're...there's no one knows what's goin to happen to us today"

An' down comes th' ol' king. Down comes th' ol' king. "Now" he said "Jack." He said "You killed the giant." He said "You sove my daughter." He

said "Now" he said "I'm goin to build a...I'm goin to build a house for yous"
he said "a castle." He said "You can take your mother and father _ 'long with
ya." He said "An' you can have me daughter." (See) an' that end the story.

But uh...he...he...he's all mixed up see.
[Int: Did he marry...so he married the daughter?]
Yes. Married his daughter.
[Int: Ah-huh. Well then he could...then he had a good time with her after
all.]
Eh? Oh yeah. Well they...they...they lived...they lived there then an'...
[Teller's wife: Yeah. (Had) the good time after all!] [*laughter*]

Duration: 18 min., 5 sec.
Source: Eli Roberts (John Roberts' brother), Sally's Cove, Great Northern Peninsula.
Location: Sitting room of teller's house, afternoon.
Audience: Mrs. Rebecca Bennett (teller's wife), young boy (Kevin), interviewers.

Context, Style, and Language: The story is told in a natural context in which the
interviewers are merely part of the audience, and the teller "breaks frame" on one occasion
to tell the young boy to be quiet, although quite a lot of talking continues in the background.
The narrator either does not hear or does not understand the interviewer's question
about the size of the giants, and simply continues with the story. As in most of his tales, he
uses gesture to bring events to life, as for example in the vigorous rubbing of his head to
simulate the response of the giants to Jack's shooting at them.

This second version of three recorded from Freeman Bennett begins promisingly
and develops well, with considerably more detail and elaboration than the first (No. 4).
Unfortunately, however, it is necessary to change the tape on the recorder shortly after
the teller has begun the recapitulation. He has great difficulty in picking up the threads
when he tries to resume the narration, and in spite of reassurance from the interviewers
and several further breaks in the recording during which they, the teller's wife, and a
young boy in the audience try to help him to find the appropriate restarting point, he
still makes several more attempts before finally struggling through a much shortened
version of the recapitulation. These difficulties provide an object lesson in the skills
needed for successful storytelling, and especially for such complex narrative as that in a full
recapitulation like this in which the teller has to tell a story within a story, maintaining
the chronology and detail of the original, but putting all the information into the mouth
of one of the characters, which necessitates a completely new level of expression, particularly
in the dialogue, and calls for resourcefulness and alertness in manipulating the convoluted
interactions of plot, style, and language. The problems posed by an unexpected hiatus of this
kind not only demonstrate the need to avoid such interruptions but also reveal that the
storyteller must maintain the thread and flow of the tale if he is to complete it satisfactorily.
He does in fact restart at the appropriate place in the narrative, as one of the interviewers

tries to point out, but apparently is unsure whether this is the first part of the story or the recapitulation. The fact that he suffers from partial deafness also makes it more difficult for him to pick up the cues offered by the listeners.

Aside from these problems, however, this is an otherwise quite full and interesting version which displays all the principal features of the narrator's style and language. The dialogue is very lively, as is seen, for example, in the angry and argumentative exchange between the giants, and the excited and reproachful tone of Jack's mother's interruptions of his story. The storyteller shifts easily from direct to indirect speech, e.g., the king's response to the idea of building the hotel: "'Yes' he said. He guessed they find out like that." The narrative is punctuated by the typical expressions *(well) very good, (well) anyhow, good enough, alright, by an' by,* and the dialogue frequently segmented with many more occurrences of *he/she said* than are strictly necessary to identify the speakers. There are a number of very short utterances, e.g., *I'll go down, Away he goes, Well she got up, Oh yes. Get some dinner,* the latter also exemplifying the ellipsis common elsewhere in the tale. Function words are frequently omitted, especially the definite article before the head of a noun phrase. The repetition of brief segments of the narrative for rhetorical effect and consolidation of the plot is found for instance in the following: "He said 'They got a cat in the house.' He said 'They got a cat in the house' he said"; "'Oh' he said 'you'll have to get up' he said 'further than that' he said 'you'll have to get up' he said"; "He said 'Somebody been here tonight' he said. 'An' killed the giant.' He said 'Killed the giant' he said." These examples also demonstrate the extraordinarily frequent interjection of the marker *he said,* which breaks up the narrative into short segments and helps to give the impression of almost breathless pace in much of the dialogue.

Jack is portrayed as nonchalant and self-assured even when confronted by the giant. The contrast in their size is suggested by the loud menacing tones of the giant's speech, while Jack's response is calm and unperturbed. The tone of voice used by the storyteller invariably characterizes Jack as someone whose speech and temperament are so matter-of-fact that he simply shrugs off the giant's threats and all other obstacles to his progress in an offhand way which emphasizes his cheeky self-confidence. Although the audience gathers that the giants are huge and menacing, their size remains vague and Freeman Bennett misunderstands the interviewer's question about them, no doubt partly due to his deafness. However, it is clear from No. 6 that a giant was "a great big man who weighed about _ four hundred pound," rather than a being of truly enormous proportions.

Points of linguistic interest include the loss of final consonant in *child,* aphesis in *'tis, 'long,* and the retention of voiceless /f/ in *ourselfs;* the West Country English *duckish* (dusk; see *DNE duckish* n.), *awards* (towards), the intensive *wonderful,* the phrases *pod auger days* (bygone days; see *DNE pod auger* n.), *last goin off* (finally; see *DNE last* n.), the nautical *turned in* (went to bed), the asseveration *Oh my!,* and *posted up* (famous, well-known; cf. *OED Posted* ppl. a.[3] 2. Pasted or fixed up in a prominent place as a public notice). The subject pronoun *they* occurs in complement position in *'tis not they* and as a demonstrative in object position in *dout they three candles,* while *them* appears as a demonstrative in *'tis not them fellers, her* is used with the neuter referent *gun,* and the object pronoun is omitted in *he got a ladder an' he put up.* Among dialectal verb forms we find the present tense *they goes, rise* (raise), *you gets,* the past tense *rose* (raised), *give, sove,* the past participles *sot, eated, astruck, astarted, sove, atold,* and the past *ha' been* which because of the elliptical sentence structure might also be interpreted as *abeen* in *Someone ha' been here tonight.* Additional double negatives are *never had nothing* and *never made no noise.*

See also the notes to No. **4.**

Type and Motifs:

AT304. *The Hunter.*

Z10.1. *Beginning formula.*

Cf. N772. *Parting at crossroads to go on adventures.*

Cf. F771.4.1. *Castle inhabited by ogres.*

F661. *Skillful marksman.*

K1082. *Ogres (large animals, sharp-elbowed women) duped into fighting each other.*

N2.2. *Lives wagered.*

B576.1. *Animal as guard of person or house.*

Cf. F771.4.4. *Castle in which everyone is asleep.*

N711.2. *Hero finds maiden in (magic) castle.*

Cf. K912. *Robbers' (giants') heads cut off one by one as they enter house.*

R111.1.4. *Rescue of princess (maiden) from giant (ogre).*

N538.2. *Treasure from defeated giant.*

Cf. Q481. *Princess (queen) compelled to keep an inn.*

Cf. H152.1.1. *Woman entertains every traveller in the hope of finding her husband.*

M231. *Free keep in inn exchanged for good story.*

Cf. H11.1.1. *Recognition at inn (hospital, etc.) where all must tell their life histories.*

Q53. *Reward for rescue.*

L161. *Lowly hero marries princess.*

International Parallels: See No. 4.

6. PETER AND MINNIE[†]
(Jack and the Three Giants[†])

Freeman Bennett   AT304
St. Pauls, Great Northern Peninsula   TC1064 72-4
14 September 1971   Collector: HH

My...my name is _ Isaac Freeman Bennett. An' I was borned _ in eighteen
an' ninety-six.
[Int: What's the name o' this story you're goina tell?]

Um?

[Int: What's the name of the story? What do you call this story?]

What's he say?

[Teller's wife: What do you call the story?]

Uh...uh...the..."Peter an' Minnie."

[Int: Who did you learn it from?]

I learned he from uh...Eli Roberts. That's us...ol' Jack Roberts's uh...brother.

[Int: How long ago?]

Oh that's about uh...oh I guess that's about forty year ago.

[Int: Was Eli older than Jack?]

[Teller's wife: Yeah.]

Yes Eli was older than Jack. Yes.

[Int: Uh-huh. Was he also a good storyteller?]

Yes. Yes he was a good hand for tellin stories yes. Good hand for tellin stories.

Well once upon a time _ in olden times ya know well might be uh...perhaps five or six hundred year ago _ well uh...I can...I can only just mind that anyhow! I wasn't very ol'. [*Teller's wife chuckles*] Not...not five or six hundred year ago! But anyhow I...I...I can mind a little bit about it. There was a...one time see ther...there used to be a...a family livin here, well now they'd be a long ways see from the...from the city, they might be _ two days' walk. Well now this family was livin here he had one son. An' his name was Jack. An' there was only the three of 'em, well _ they lived there for uh...twenty-five or thirty year. Well the times got so bad _ [Male listener: (Yes)] they uh...never got much to eat. He said to his uh*...father an' mother, he said "I think" he said "we'll _ go out to the city" he said "an' see" he said "can we get a job out there" he said "an' a place to stay" he said "'cause we can't live here" he said "no longer." He said uh..."We can't live here."

"Well" she said "alright" she said "we'll go."

Well now _ they got up in the morning to have their breakfast _ an' when they got up they only had _ a couple o' little buns for their breakfast see. Well now they...they eat uh...one apiece _ an' they had two to take with 'em. Well now they had...they had uh...over a day's walk see. Well anyhow _ they locked up their house an' they leaved. An' _ they was walkin till about twelve o'clock. An' about twelve o'clock _ they got hungry.

"Well now" he said _ "yous can eat the two buns." He said "If yous go your way" _ he said "an' I'll go mine."*

Oh no they couldn't do that. They couldn't leave un.

*teller's wife speaks in background

*talking in background

66

"Oh yes. Oh yes* I'm goin by meself" he said. "Yous go on uh...this way" he said "yous 'll come out in the city. Well now" he said uh..."I'm goin this way."

*noise in back-ground

(Well) anyhow they leaved an' Jack _ he went this way. An' he travelled till [it] begin to get dark. And _ he never had nothing to eat, he was gettin hungry now. An' _ he got...he was up on a little hill an' he looked down in a valley _ an' he seen a little light. An' he thought to hisself "Well there's somebody livin down there." An' _ he start to go down _ to it _ to the light. An' when he got down in the valley 'twas dark. He couldn't fi[nd]...couldn't see the light an' he couldn't find un.

"Well" he said "I got to go back" he said "to the hill again." An' he went back to the hill again an' he _ looked down an' he...he...he could still see the light. He said to hisself "Well I'm goin to try it again." An' _ he started again. An' when he got down in the valley again _ he couldn't find the light again. An' he had to come back to the hill again. An' he come back to the hill again an' he.../he/ took good marks an' he said to hisself "Well now I'll find un this time." Well he _ started in an' he went down. An' by god _ when he got down in the valley he seen the light. An' _ he walked up an' he creeped up to the door. An' he looked in through, there was a hole in the door an' he looked in. Now they used to...there...there used to be giants around them times see _ they used to call 'em.* An' there was three _ sittin down to the table. An' they had a...a...quarter o'...o' meat on the table _ cooked an' they was eatin of it. An' yeah now Jack had a little gun see _ a small gun. An' _ he said to hisself he'd have a shot at one an' he shoved (it) in through the hole _ an' he fired _ an' he struck one feller...he struck the ol' man there on the ear.

/the/

*noise in background

An' he said "What do you fire at me?"

He said "I never fired nothing at ya."

"Yes" he said [rapid angry tones] "you did." He said "You fired something" he said "an' you struck me there." He said "But don't do it no more 'cause" he said "if you does it any more" he said "I'll kill ya."

He [Jack] thought to hisself that was very good. Well he shoved this little gun in through again an' he fired an' he struck th' ol' man in the same place again. An' ol' man jumped up, he had a big knife an' he jumped up an' he _ chopped his head off _ and hove un [to] one side. Jack thought to hisself that was very good, there was ONE gone.

Well now he...shoved this little gun in through the window again an' he...he fired to the old man again, he...he he took un down. He said "Now" he said "I've akilled one feller _ one of un" _ he said "an' you've astart just the same thing"

He said "I never touch ya."

He said "Yes you did." He uh...said "[If] you does it any more now" he said "I...I'll...I'll chop your head off."

So _ Jack thought to hisself "That's very good, he'll kill that one directly." An' _ shoved his little gun into again an' he fired _ an' took th' ol' man there again. He jumped up an' he took the knife an' he chopped IIIS head off _ hove un to one side. Uh...very good, he had the two of 'em killed.

Now he sot down to the table an' he start eatin an' Jack shoved this little gun in through again an' he struck un down.

[S]aid to hisself "No there's somebody around here. There's somebody here tonight _ and I got to find 'em."

Jack got behind the door. Now he was...he was only small, the giant was a great big man who weighed about _ four hundred pound see. An' uh...he got behind the door. An' he [*the giant*] got out lookin around. By an' by _ * shoved the door open an' uh...Jack was stood up be...Jack was stood up before the door see.* Jack was stood up before the door.

An' uh..."Hello" he said. "'Tis you" he said "been doin all this uh...this uh...firin tonight. Now" he said _ "I'm goina kill you."

"Hold on a bit now" Jack said. "Hold on a bit now" Jack said uh..."take your time" he said uh..."the...uh...let me...let me come in" he said "I'm hungry."

"Alright" he said "come in" he said "an' _ have something to eat."

An' he...Jack went in an' he had uh...sot down and _ he had his supper.

"Now" he said "Jack" _ he said "I goin to tell ya" _ he said "I'm tryin to get" he said "the king's daughter." He said "Now" he said uh..."I'm goina stick up six candles" he said "on the table" _ he said "an' light 'em." He said "An' if you can dout all they candles the one time" _ he said "I won't kill ya."

"Well" Jack said "I can do that."

An' (said) light the four candles (see) an' lined 'em all up on the table an' _ Jack got with his little gun an' he _ point at the candle an' he fired at 'em, he douted all the candles the one time.

"Just the man" he said "Jack" he said "I wants. Now" he said "we got to go tonight" he said "an' get the king's daughter."

"Alright" Jack said.

"Now" he said "the king" he said "got a cat" _ he said "on the table." He said "Now" he said "when anybody goes to the door" _ he said "this...this cat" he said _ "goes in an' wakes him. An' now" he said "there's a hole in the door" he said "if you can fire" he said "an' kill the cat" _ he said "we'll get the king's daughter."

Well Jack said "I can do that."

Very good, about twelve o'clock _ they started. They went out...in the town to the king's...palace _ an' uh..."Now" he said "Jack" _ he said "let's get up to the door" he said "they're all abed." He said "Now" he said uh..."look in through that hole" he said "see can ya see the cat." Jack looked in through

*microphone noise

*microphone noise

the hole an' the cat was lied down on the table see. An' he said "You see her?"

Jack said "Yes" he said "I sees her."

"Now" he said _ "see can you kill her." Jack shoved his little gun in through the...the hole in the winder [i.e., *window*] an' he fired at the cat an' he killed her.* Said "You kill her?"

Jack said "Yes" he said "I got her killed"

"Alright" he said. "We're goin to get the king's daughter now."

And _ went in the house an'...Jack went in then an' looked in...three or four...twothree rooms an' _ round one place [or] another, by an' by _ he opened a room door _ an' when he opened the room door the king _ an' his wife was lied down in the bed see. An' he looked all around like that an' uh...there was a sword hung up over his head. An' he took down the sword _ an' he come out.

"Now" he said uh..."Jack" he said "you go upstairs" _ he said "the king's daughter" he says "is up there" he said "lied down in the bed." He said "You go upstairs" /he/ said "an' I'll get the ladder" _ he said "an' get up to the window" _ he said "an' you take her out" he said "an' pass her down to me."

"Alright" Jack said.

(Well) Jack went upstairs _ an' uh...opened the room door, sure enough the king's daughter was in lied down on the bed sleepin away, well she was a handsome girl too. An' uh...Jack said uh...he was up in the ladder, Jack said "Now" he said _ "you'll have to come in" he said "an' help me" he said "'cause _ she's too heavy for me" he said "I can't...I can't start her" he said "you get up" _ he said "an'...an' put your head in through the window" he said "an' help me get her out."

An' uh...he said "Yes." (So) he got up _ an' he shoved his head in through the window an' whe[n]...soon as he shoved his head in through the window Jack took the sword an' he chopped his head off. An' his head falled down in the room an' he...his body falled out. An' course _ Jack went out _ Jack went downstairs an' he went in the king's room an' he hung up the sword again. An' he went down to the ol' giant's...uh...place, well he...oh he...he had lots o' money down there _ an' _ he sleeped all night.

An' _ the king woke up in the morning. "Oh my!" he said "The ol' giant been here" he said "an' got our daughter" he said "tonight." He said "Somebody uh...somebody have awent in" he said "what's wrong with the cat?" He went out an' when he went out the cat was dead on table, he said "Somebody been here an' killed the cat" he said "an' they got our daughter."

Runned upstairs an' when he went upstairs _ th' ol' giant's head was down on the floor an' his body was down...there an' his...his daughter was lied down in the bed sound asleep. "Well" he said "somebody been here tonight" he said "an' killed the giant" _ he said "an' killed the giant" he said

*crockery rattling in background

/she/

69

"an' our daughter" he said "is up there to sleep" he said _ "now" he said "how is we goin to find out" he said "who 'tis?"

An' she got up _ an' SHE didn't know nothing about it. "Well" he said "we got to find out" he said "who done it." He said "Whoever done this" _ he said uh..."they're goina...they're...they're...goin to marry my daughter."

Well now _ she said "Father" she said "the only way" she said "we can find out" she said uh..."who done it" _ she said "is uh...build a big restaurant" she said _ "an' _ we'll put so many chuh...so /many/ girls into it" she said "an' I'll go in there." She said "An' put it up over the door _ 'Meals All Hours Free.'" She said "Well now" she said "everybody comes in there" she said "I'll get 'em /to/ tell a story."

"Yes" he said "we can find out like that alright."

A[n'] that's what he done, he build this big restaurant and _ he put a couple o' girls in there, well now the king's daughter she used to spend her time in there see. And uh...everyone 'd come in _ well they'd ge[t]...she 'd uh...get 'em tell a story. Well uh...everyone 'd tell a story, well _ not the right man, well they had it there for _ a twelvemonth.

By an' by Jack _ an' th' ol' woman an' his father they uh...got money enough they was goin back home. An' _ anyhow they leaved _ next morning to go back home _ an' uh...when they was walkin along on the street they was begin to get hungry, Jack look up over the door _ an' he said "Look" he said "we can get uh...our meals in here free." He said "Let's go in" he said "an' have a lunch."

He said "Yes." Th' ol' man said "Yes" he said "very good place."

So they went in _ an' uh...king's daughter was in there an' she said uh..."Yous wants a lunch I suppose."

An' uh...Jack said "Yes" he said "that's what we come in for" he said "we...looked up over the door" he said "an' uh...'meals all hours free'"

She said "Oh yes" she said "free meals" she said "here."

"Well" he said uh..."we'll have a lunch"

Well the...girls got their lunch on the table an' they sat down to the table "Now" she said _ "'fore yous uh...eats" _ she said "yous got to tell a story."

Well the ol' man said he didn't know uh...no stories to tell, he said he wasn't interested in stories

"Well" she said "you got to tell something."

Well now he started in, he told a story, a little story to 'em, I don't know the story he told. When he had his story told now _ th' ol' woman SHE had to tell one.* Well she started in an' she told 'em a little...little story. But I don't know what one 'twas, so it come to JACK'S turn.

/mony/

/an'/

*crockery rattling in background

70

Well Jack said _ "I'm not...very much post up" he said "in tellin stories" he said "I...I don't know much about stories" he said uh..."I don't know no stories" he said "only about me OWN self" he said "what I done meself."

"Well" she said "that's the story" she said "we wants to hear _ (sir), what you've adone yourself."

"Oh well" he said "I can tell ya a story like that."

"Well" she said that's [the] story she wants to hear.

An' _ "Well" Jack said _ "that's me mother an' father there" Jack said "an' we...now" he said "we're goin back home" he said "we lived in a...a place" he said uh..."about uh...twenty mile from this" he said "by our own selfs" he said "an' uh...we never had much to eat" he said "we got short...the times got so bad" he said "we got short o' grub." He said "An' we leaved." He said "We leaved" he said "an' come out in the city." He said "Now" he said "we been out here" he said "for...for three year. Well" he said uh..."we got money enough" he said "that we're goin back home again."

He said "When we left in the morning" he said "we had _ two buns" he said "that's all we had" he said "for a day's walk. Well" he said "twelve o'clock come" _ he said "an' I give the...me mother an' father" he said "the two buns" he said "an' they went their way" he said "an' I went mine. Well" he said "I walked" he said "till _ almost dark." He said "An' I was up on a little hill" he said "an' I looked down" _ he said "an' I seen a little light."

She said "That's the story we wants."

"Now" she said "Jack" she said "don't tell no more" th' ol' woman said "don't tell no more" she said "you're goin to get us in trouble today."

"No" she said..."let un go on" she said "an' tell the story."

An' uh...she said "I knowed" she said "you was goin to get us in trouble."

"No" she said. "/He/ got to tell the story."   /She/

"Well" he said "I...I uh...started to go down to the light." He said "An' I got down the valley" she said...he said uh..."an' I never seen the light." He said "I couldn't find un. An'" he said _ "I had to go back on the hill again." He said "I had to go back on the hill again" he said "an' when I got uh...back on the hill" _ he said "I looked at the light" _ he said "an' I...started again" he said "an' when I got down in the valley" he said _ "I couldn't...uh...I still couldn't find the light. Well" he said "I had to go back to the hill again." He said "THIS time" he said "when I went back" he said "I _ took good notice" he said "an' I took out a paper" he said "an' I...took out a...kind...an' maked out kind of a map of it" he said uh..."an' I started again." He said "The...an' I found the light that time." He said "An' when I got down to the light" _ he said "I...I looked in through the door" he said "there was a little hole in the door" he said "an' there was three giants" he said "sot down (to) the table."

71

"Now" she said "Jack" she said "don't tell no more." She said "Don't tell no more" she said "'cau[se]…'cause you're goin to get us in trouble."

An' "No" she said. "You got to tell on" she said "that's the story" she said "we wants."

"Well" Jack said ‿ "I had a little gun with me" he said. "An' I shoved me little gun in through the hole in the door" ‿ he said "an' I fired at th' ol' feller" he said "an' I struck un there. [*indicates his ear by hand movement*] An'" he…said "he looked at the other feller an' they…he said 'What did you fire that at me for?' He said 'I never fired nothing at ya.' He said 'Oh yes you did.' He said 'An' don't do it no more' he said 'or else I…I'll kill you.' And" ‿ Jack said "they sot down an' they…'s eatin away" he said "an' I shoved me little gun in through again" ‿ he said "an' I fired again." An' he said "He jumped up" he said "an' he took this big knife he had an' he chopped his head off " he said "an' he hove un to one side. An'" he said "he sot down eatin away an' uh…" Jack said "I thought to meself that's was…that's very good. He got one killed." He said "I shoved my little gun in through again" ‿ he said "an' I fired again." He said "I /struck/ th' ol' man in the same place again. An' now he said 'I've akilled the…that feller' he said 'an' **YOU'VE** astarted on it.' He said 'I never fired nothing.' He said 'Yes you did.' He said 'Don't do it no more' he said 'else I'll chop your head off.'" Jack said "Very good" he said "he'll kill he directly." An' ‿ Jack said "He sot down" he said "an' I shoved me little gun in through" he said "an' I fired again" he said "an' struck the ol' man" he said "in the same place again." Said "He jumped up" he said "with the knife" he said "an' he chopped his head off" ‿ he said "an' shoved un to one side." Said "He shoved un to one side an' ‿ he sot down" he said "an' he started eatin away an'" he said ‿ "I fired again" ‿ he said "an' struck un in the same place. An' he said 'No' he said 'there's somebody here.' He said 'I got to go out' he said 'an' afind un.'" An' Jack said "I got behind the door. Now" he said "I wasn't very big" he said uh…the…uh…"'gainst the giant. Well" he said "he looked all around" he said "he couldn't see nobody" he said "an' he…he shoved the door open" he said "an' I was stood up behind the door. 'Ah' he said 'I got ya now' he said. 'I got ya now' he said 'I goin to kill you' he said 'tonight.' Hold on a bit now" Jack said "take your time" he said uh…"I'm hungry." He said "I'd like to have a lunch. 'Well' he said 'come in' he said 'an' have a lunch.'" He went in an' he…he had a lunch, Jack sat down an' he had a lunch.

"Now" he said "Jack" ‿ he said "I got…I'm goin to sti…uh…stick up six candles" he said "I'm tryin to get uh…" he said "the king's daughter. An'" he said "I goin to stick up six candles" he said "in a line on the table" ‿ he said "an' if you can dout they candles ‿ the one time" ‿ he said "I'll save your life."

"Well" Jack said "I can do that."

/shook/

72

"Well" he said "he stuck up the…the candles" he said "on the table" he said "he…lined them up." He said "I took me little gun" he said "I fired at 'em" he said "I dout(ed) all the candles. He said 'You're just the man I wants. Now' he said 'tonight _ about twelve o'clock' he said 'we'll go. Well' he said 'twelve o'clock in the night _ now' he said _ 'the king' he said 'got a cat' he said 'on the table.' He said 'An' when anybody goes to the door an' makes a noise _ the cat goes in an' wakes him.' He said 'Now' he said 'if you can kill that cat' _ he said 'we can get the king's daughter.' Well" Jack said "I can do that.

An' [coughs] uh…anyhow" Jack said "we started. An' we got to the king's house" he said "an' I looked in through the hole in the door" he said "an' the cat was lied down on the table." He said "An' I shoved me little gun in through." He said "An' I fired at the cat" he said "an' I killed her. An' _ 'Now' he said _ 'we'll get the king's daughter' he said 'we'll go in.' We went in" Jack said "I went in" he said "an' I…went in…couple o' rooms" he said "an' by an' by" he said "I went in a room" he said "and uh…the king an' his wi[fe]…wife was in there" he said _ "in the bed" he said "to sleep." He said "An' I looked all around" he said "an' uh…I seen a sword" he said "hung up over their heads" he said "an' I took the sword down" he said "an' I come out." Said 'Now' he said _ 'the king's daughter' he said 'is upstairs.' He said 'You go up' _ he said 'if the…an' I'll get a ladder' he said 'an' get up to the window an' rise the window' _ he said 'an' you pass her out to me' he said 'an' I'll take her.'"

"Alright" Jack said.

An' Jack said "I went in" _ he said "well" he said "the king's daughter was lied down in the bed" he said "an' _ she was a handsome girl. An' uh…" Jack said uh…"I said to un 'Well now _ you'll have to get up _ in the ladder an' shove your head in through to help me get her out' he said ''cause _ she's too heavy for me to handle.'"

An' _ Jack said "He got up" he said "an' he shoved his head in through the window an' when he shoved his head in through the window" he said "I took me sword" he said "an' I chopped his head off" _ he said "an' his head fall down in the room" _ he said "an' _ his body falled down _ outside."

"JUST the story" [Teller's wife claps to indicate the king's daughter's delight] she said "Jack I wants to hear."

The ol' woman said "Yes" she said "Jack" she said "you got us in trouble now" she said "I knowed you was goin to get us in trouble." [Teller's wife claps in background]

An' she [the king's daughter] got up an' she locked the door. Over she goes over to the king. An' she said "Father" she said "I got the man" she said "that uh…killed the giant."

She said "You…" he said "you have?"

"Yes" she sai[d]…she said "I got un."

An' the king come over. [She] said "Here he is here!"

An' she say...he said "You're the man" he said "that killed the giant."

He said "Yes" he said "I'm the man" he said "that killed the giant." He said "Sove your daughter."

/She/   "Well now" he said "Jack _ you got to marry her." /He/ said "Now I'm goin to build a house" he said "for your...mother an' father" _ he said "an' you got to marry my daughter" he said "an' live with me."

An' when I left they had three children an' ol'...an' ol' man, well they was gettin ol' then, they was 'bout seventy or eighty year ol' then. [B]ut Jack had...lots o' money then, he was alright, well _ that end the story. [*laughs*]

[Int: It's a wonderful story. It's [*untrans.*]...]

Yes that's one I learnt from Eli Roberts.

[Int: What do you say the name is?]

Eh?

[Int: Do you remember what the name of that story is?]

Uh..."Peter and Minnie."

[Int: Why is it called "Peter and Minnie"? Who...?]

Why uh...well that's...that's...that was their...uh...their father an' mother's name see. That was his father an' mother's name, Peter an' Minnie see.

[Int: I see. Mm-hm. And Eli told this story? El[i]...Eli was an older man than Jack Roberts?]

Oh yes he was older than Jack. Yes.

[Int: Were you down at Sally's Cove when you heard that?]

Yes. He lived at Sally's Cove yes. Yes.

[Int: Ah-ha. Were you...is that where you heard the story?]

Yes that's where I heard the story.

[Int: How did you happen...?]

No. No I heard the story...he used to be uh...them times see we used to uh...be workin on the road. We had our own Government, Responsible Government see. An' they used to send us so much money every year to work on the road, well now _ he was on the road board see. We was up here to the Western Brook, you remember about that bridge you crossed up there. We was buildin a bridge there. Well now every time we'd go to our dinner _ he'd tell us a story see. Well now this is...the...this is the one he told us see.

[Int: How old a man was he about when you heard that story?]

How old was I?

[Int: How old were YOU and how old was HE? How old were the (two)?]

Well I should say he was a man uh...I should say he was a man about uh...about forty year old _ then. 'Cause I was only about uh...I wasn't no more than uh...no more than twenty-five year ol' then.

[Int: So that would be about fifty years ago?]

That'd be about fifty years ago yes.

[Int: An' how many times did you hear him tell that?]

I only heard him once.

[Int: An' you...an' you've been telling it since?]

Yes. I've been tellin that one ever since.

[Int: Wish I had your memory.]

Yes. Yes I got a good memory. Yes.

[Int: Did you ever hear him tell any other stories _ Eli?]

No that's the only one ever I heard he tell. That's the only one ever I heard un tell.

[Int: H[ow]...how many stories did you hear Jack Roberts _ tell?]

Well now I heard Jack tell another one about uh...'bout uh...'bout Little Jack.

[Int: Little Jack?]

Yes Little Jack.

[Int: Is that one that you still remember?]

Yes. Yes.

[Int: It...it's another...it's another long story though isn't it?]

Yeah, well the...he's a longish story yes.

[Int: Yeah.]

He's longish story but I...I don't believe he's so long as that one just [the] same.

[Int: Well _ what was the most...most times that people...what time of the year would people tell st...tell stories mostly?]

Any time at all.

[Int: Really?]

Any time at all uh like...like they come in your house an' uh...tell those stories or when you was out anywhere huntin perhaps _ huntin an' sit down an' have a lunch, well they start in tell story to ya see.

[Int: An'...an' this was always the grown men, not the children, who were listening?]

Oh no. No.

[Int: Uh-huh. Mm-hm. How about in the lum[ber]...did...you worked in the lumber camps didn't you?]

Oh yes I worked in lumber camps yes.

[Int: Were there any storytelling there?]

Yes. Well now the...this is what I heard Jack Roberts tell uh...tell this story about Little Jack, in a lumber camp.

Duration: 20 min., 32 sec.
Source: Eli Roberts (John Roberts' brother), Sally's Cove, Great Northern Peninsula.
Location: Sitting room of teller's house, afternoon.
Audience: Mrs. Rebecca Bennett (teller's wife), Frank Bennett (teller's nephew), interviewer.

Context, Style, and Language: Frank Bennett has joined his aunt and uncle for the midday meal and stays to listen to the stories. He sits on a sofa on the opposite side of the room to where his uncle and the interviewer are sitting, and responds verbally to this story, as well as later contributing very useful information about his uncle's storytelling in the lumber camps. From time to time he and his aunt exchange a few quiet words in the background as the story proceeds, crockery is heard rattling, there is the sound of wood crackling in the stove, of the poker being used every so often to keep the fire blazing, and of more wood being put into the stove. All this activity is immaterial to the narrator, who brings the story to life by his animated delivery and gestures, even getting to his feet to demonstrate how Jack looks for the king's daughter, and leaning his head back to indicate her sleeping posture as he sits in his chair. This dramatic style is echoed in the dénouement when his wife claps her hands not only to indicate the king's daughter's delight but also her own obvious enjoyment of the story. On this occasion, as also in the recording of No. 38, the interviewer takes the opportunity to note down some of the more significant proxemic and gestural features of the storytelling context. For example, Freeman Bennett stands up to show Jack on the hill trying to see the light in the valley; he rubs his head behind his ear vigorously with his hand in humorous imitation of the giant's response to Jack's shooting at him; he gets to his feet and looks around while telling about the giant searching for Jack and mimes the setting up of the candles in line; finally he uses his hands, one behind the other, index fingers outstretched, to simulate Jack's little gun as he prepares to fire at the candles. These more detailed observations provide a rare insight into the dramatic nature of the performance context, much of which is inevitably absent from a tape recording.

This is the fullest of the three versions told by Freeman Bennett and the recapitulation is especially detailed. The same stylistic and linguistic features noted in Nos. 4 and 5 are again evident here, especially the lively dialogue in the recapitulation when the king's daughter is encouraging Jack to tell his story but his mother is discouraging him. The insistence on punctuating dialogue so frequently with *he/she said* results in some awkwardness in the syntax, e.g., "'I'm tryin to get' he said 'the king's daughter,'" where the interpolated phrase causes an unnatural hiatus. The dialogue again shows Jack to be bold and cheeky when he dissuades the giant from killing him. The giant's response is to offer Jack a surprising degree of hospitality. This foolhardy generosity is unexplained but the inference is that the giant admires Jack's audacity.

As with most other narratives recorded on this field trip in 1971, Freeman Bennett begins this version with a full statement of his name and age. Having been asked to do so by the fieldworker on one occasion he then adopted it as a means of identification at the beginning of other stories through which he expresses a certain personal pride as his own name is implicitly linked with the telling of each story whose title he also announces. His increasing deafness is compensated for by his wife's helpful relaying of the interviewer's questions and by her encouraging responses to the narration.

On the linguistic side we find a single instance of the voicing of initial /s/ in *same* and room(s) pronounced /rum(z)/ as in West Country English; the second syllable of *window* is pronounced *-er* on one occasion (lowered close front vowel in first syllable), the final consonant of *douted* is syncopated in one occurrence, and partially so in another, to produce a form between *douted* and *dout*—a further example of how such reduction probably takes place in the past tense of verbs whose name-forms end in /t/; the long close front vowel appears in *sleeped* /sliːpt/, the third syllable of *interested* bears the strong stress, and aphesis occurs in *'gainst.* At the lexical level we have the nautical *hand* (man/person), *mind* (remember), *marks* (notice), *directly* (immediately; see *DNE directly*, av.), and the archaic *abed;* note also the archaic *to sleep* (asleep), the typical local way of expressing the date in *eighteen and ninety-six,* and the use of the masculine pronoun *he* with the neuter referent *story,* and also in the object position in *I learned he.* Present tense forms include *you does, I sees, yous wants/eats, we wants,* past tense forms are *begin, hove, point, sleeped, runned, post up* (known/famous), *maked,* while *look* might be construed as present or past. Past participles are: *borned, astart, awent, afind,* while *begin* in *they was begin* appears to be a syncopation or assimilation of *beginnin.* Additional double negatives are *can't live here. . .no longer, don't do it no more,* and *didn't know no stories.*

See also the notes to Nos. **4** and **5.**

Type and Motifs:

AT304. *The Hunter.*
Z10.1. *Beginning formula.*
Cf. N772. *Parting at crossroads to go on adventures.*
Cf. F771.4.1. *Castle inhabited by ogres.*
F661. *Skillful marksman.*
K1082. *Ogres (large animals, sharp-elbowed women) duped into fighting each other.*
N2.2. *Lives wagered.*
B576.1. *Animal as guard of person or house.*
Cf. F771.4.4. *Castle in which everyone is asleep.*
N711.2. *Hero finds maiden in (magic) castle.*
Cf. K912. *Robbers' (giants') heads cut off one by one as they enter house.*
R111.1.4. *Rescue of princess (maiden) from giant (ogre).*
N538.2. *Treasure from defeated giant.*
T68.1. *Princess offered as prize to rescuer.*
Cf. Q481. *Princess (queen) compelled to keep an inn.*
Cf. H152.1.1. *Woman entertains every traveller in the hope of finding her husband.*
M231. *Free keep in inn exchanged for good story.*
Cf. H11.1.1. *Recognition at inn (hospital, etc.) where all must tell their life histories.*
Q53. *Reward for rescue.*
L161. *Lowly hero marries princess.*
Z10.2. *End formula.*

International Parallels: See No. 4.

7. GREENSLEEVES

Stephen P. Snook
Sagona Island, Fortune Bay
30 August 1967

AT313A + AT329
TC438 65-21
Collector: HH

Now you wants the story.
[Int: Right]
What's that "Greensleeves" is it?
[Int: Um-hum.]
That's another bit of sweat [i.e., *fog*] goin away again. I couldn't see in Harbour Breton other night. I suppose I must start un eh? You listen to un eh? (Till I's tryin to mind un at...in the...)

*i.e., people
talking loud-
ly in kitchen
*i.e., kitchen
door
†i.e., stove

[Int: I'll listen] listen to that. Do that* hurt out...interfere out there (or not)?
[Int: It won't help.]
Shove that* to. That's† awful warm aint it? Well I find it warm (in here). It will after a bit. Stories goes 'once upon a time' what?
[Int: If that's the way it begins.]

Mm. Well once upon a time...[*aside to Int:* anyone gets something good (to say)] a very good time it was not in yours not in mine there was a' ol' man he had one son named Jack. Well -- that was very well. They...he sleep...he kept...at (or) goin with the ol' woman so last goin off they (carried un on) an' they got this little...boy. An' while it was in the cot an' he'd be playin with the blankets now an' again an' haulin off one thing an' th' other _ the ol' woman said "Now" she said to her ol' man she said "I'm wonderin now" she said "what can we get for the...for the boy to play with."

"Oh" he said "I can get something" he said. Oh he went off, (only) took a hundred dollars with him, went off down...down town. He pick up a few little articles. No nothin he didn't...didn't trouble with 'em. So he said "I think I'll get un a pack o' cards. See if he'll learn how to play cards." So anyhow when he comes back he brought back two or three articles he wouldn't look at it. The very minute they put the cards in he was pickin on 'em right straight.

"Well now" he said "that's just what he DO want." Only a YOUNGSTER now.

"Well" she said "my son" she said…"if you give un the cards" she said to th' ol' man she said "you knows cards" she said "is wonderful…is a wonderful game…uh…chum." She said "He agot be come to some bad end" she said "if you use un to play cards."

"Ah the devil may care" he said "I'm goina give 'em to un." So he give 'em to un. He played with the cards an' played with 'em till he got up (to) four five years old an' he was still playin the cards an' he could beat anything (that) come along.

"An' now" she said uh…to th' ol' grand /vizier/ "now" /she/ said "you'll haves…you'll have to sent un out" /she/ said "an' to try (to) do some work." /She/ said "We got…a lot o' hay to mow too" she said. "Well" she said "I suppose the boy can mow?"   /avise/   /he/   /he/   /He/

"No I don't know _ whe'r [i.e., *whether*] he can whe'r he can't. He never…seed a scythe."

So anyhow so he went on out an'…looked at where he was goin to. Little boy toddled on then, I can see un now. I was there same time see? Mm. [i.e., *yes—confirming his presence there*] Went down and he sot down on the grass an' he (played with un). When he went an' sot down, hauled out his pack o' cards. Had a little tablecloth about that long I suppose. Cleared away by hisself.

"Well" she said "no" she said "old man" she said uh…"we'll have to try to break he o' that."

"No" he said "an' that we can't break un o' that. That's something he's got into now" /he/ said "an' no clear. So let un bide." So she's let un bid he said an' he was there _ playin away, he bide there to…back for dinner an' supper out in the field playin away.   /she/

An' one day she said _ 'bout twelve o'clock _ there was a little ol' man come down 'longside of un. "Oh" /he/ said "John my son" /he/ said "what are ya doin?"   /she/   /she/

"Havin [a] game o' cards" he said "but" he said "I get (no)…I can't get nobody to play with" he said "seem(s) awful lonesome by meself."

"Oh" he said "what about a game" he said "John?"

"Go away" [*dismissive tone*] Jack said. "You goin be beat."

"Well" he said "I don't know, I never was beat yet."

"Well" he said "you'll be beat today."

So anyhow (so) he went 'long up an' told his…mother then that uh…there was a man down there, he never seen come an' never seen go. An' he said "He wants a game o' card[s]."

"Well" she said "that's Greensleeves. He comes here once every twelvemonth an' he takes a man" she says "an' carried away, we never years [i.e., *hears*] tell of (him) after(ward)." An' "Now" she said "what did I tell you Pa?" She said "That John was goina ma[k]e away with use them cards."

"(May) the devil may care" Jack said "I'm goin to try un. If he comes tomorrow" he said "I'LL have a game with un." So he went on again the same thing. Next mornin he got up an' went on down, he wasn't down five minutes now 'fore he...playin away wi' the cards. Up he jump 'longside him, he said "Where you come from?"

"Well" he says "I uh...I can turn meself into a bird" he said "an' fly in the air an' I can turn meself into a fish an' swim in the sea" he said "where you won't see me come an' won't see me go."

"Well" Jack said "me poor old mother says" Jack said "I be come some bad end playin cards."

"Oh no" he said "you won't." He said "What about a game" he said "John?"

Jack..."Sure" Jack said "you goina be beat. I told you yesterday you'd be beat."

Alright. Off jacket an' sat down 'longside. "Why" he said "goina have a fight?"

"No" he said "no John. No my son" he said "no I just have a game o' cards." Alright. Sat down. An' he dealt up his cards an' he...he'd [*demonstrating by gesture*] lick 'em with his tongue.

"Oh" he said "what ya...what ya makin cards dirty for?"

"Oh" he said "not makin cards dirty" he said "I'm just havin good luck."

"Well" he said "you can have all the luck you want but you're goina be beat."

So anyhow they hove out an' they had a first thirty.

"Now" Jack said "what did I tell 'ee _ was goin to be done with (un)?"

"Now" he said "I see" he said "you got the first game."

"Yes" he said "an' I'll have the next one too uh...(if) you isn't smart." So anyhow he got up by god an' the next time he hove out he...got twenty five.

"Now" he said "'tis comin back."

"Yes" Jack said "but this game is not ended" he said "ol' man."

"Oh" he said "the first two out o' three" he said "John."

"Yes" Jack said "I know that." So anyhow he hove out again. Now he said "I'LL lick the pack this time, try it. See what luck is in that."

"Now" he said "it'll be no good to you." Anyhow go for (to) deal up. And he had a full house _ again.

"NOW" he said, Jack said "you're licked. What I tell 'ee?"

"Well now" he said "John" he said "my son there's...there's three things now" he said. "You got to go off now" he said "an' uh...on go off now" he said "an' find uh...the oldest man is in the...in the country."

Jack said "Find th' oldest man in the country! [*coughs*] Well" Jack said "certainly...(that's something [to] be done)."

"Oh" he said "you...you can...no trouble to find un" he said "I show 'ee the road to go. But" he said "I'll be on your right hand side anyhow" he said "[if] you gets in any trouble."

An' Jack said "(It) be alright" Jack said "'cause you can...turn yourself into a bird an' fly in the air an' turn yourself [into] a fish swim in sea" Jack said "you can do anything."

Well anyhow he goes off. An' he went up an' he got...th' ol' woman bake up some grub for un, go off for his journey. An' th' ol' man give him a pair o' nine mile boots too _ with that _ (so) he can walk nine mile every stride, by Jesus, agoin too now! [*sneezes and coughs*] He said "You got a long walk." Anyhow he walk away. He said "You got to walk twelve month an' a day now _ 'fore you come to the first man."

Jack said "For...twelve mile...an' twe[lve]...a hundred...a hundred...a hundred mile!"

"No" he said "you got a...twelvemonth an' a **DAY**" I say "you got to go." [*sneezes and coughs*] Very well. He give him the boots _ nine mile boots an' away he go. [*has a drink*] Walked on an' he walked on till he...come to a big hill.

"Now" Jack says "it's gettin dark" Jack (said) "an' I'm gettin sleepy." So anyhow Jack laid down for to have a little nap -- an' when he laid down he seen a little blue light. [*coughs*] [*aside to Int:* I got a cough that bad so I can't talk.] [*coughs*]

Jack said "Where there's light there's hopes. Anyhow" Jack said "I must go down." Went down an' uh...knocked to the door, th' ol' fella come out.

"Oh" he said "good night" he said "Jack" _ an'...Jack said

He said "You aint got nothing" he said "give us no haircut nor shave" he said "an' I'm awful hairy _ an' dirty."

Jack said "Yes" Jack said "I'm twelve...I was...agoin a twelve...twelve month an' a day" he said "an'...I brought everything I had." Very well.

He come out, he opened the door, he said "Come in John" he said "my son." An' he had whiskers long enough (to) lodge down here on his belt. First old feller.

"Well" Jack said "well /who am I/ to say you isn't hairy?"   /I'm/

"Yes" he said "old man _ me son I'm kind o'...kind o' dirty." So he got in an' he...sot un up in the chair. He took an old draw _ knife they had there, years ago they used to have draw _ knife(s) _ an' chopped off so much [wi'] that an' he chopped off so much with the scithers [i.e., *scissors*]. An' then he got the clippers an' he clipped it off un. An' then he got the razor an' he give him a shave.

"Now" he said to hisself "now then he looks young." He was 'bout seventy odd years ol'. He looked about twenty _ when he had the shave.

81

"Well" he said "Jack my son" he said "you're lookin for Greensleeves aint 'ee?"

"Yes" Jack said "I AM lookin for un. An' that I'll never find."

"Well" he said "I don't know." He said uh…"I got three brothers" he said. "An' the oldest one got more enchantment than the works [i.e., *all of them*]." He said "Now me other brothers – the next to…meself " he said "lives 'bout thirty mile from this." An' he said "You'll find he alright."

Jack said "[How] in the name o' god [am] I goina find (he)!"

"Oh you'll find (un)." He said "Come on" he said "an' have your…have your supper now an' go to bed" he said "an' get up morrow morn early" he said "an' we'll…I send 'ee off." An' he said uh…"Jack" he said "can 'ee smoke the pipe?"

Now Jack said "I never light one in me life – but I suppose I smoke un."

They got up the next morning, give him some grub "Now" he said "you get on that road look. An' I'll fill this pipe full o' baccy – an' light un. An' you go. An' accordin (as) you draws that smoke an' wherever the smoke goes – you go. (?You don't care a devil) 'bout woods or uh…concrete walls or whatever 'tis but you keep goin wherever the smoke goes."

Jack says "Alright" Jack says "I listen to (thee)."

Oh there was…two or three women milkin cows when he's passin along an' the smoke 'd blow right clean, Jack walks right CLEAN in the wor[ks]…walks straight over the works – never bothered nothin only goin to…[where] the smoke went.

"An' now" he said "John when that smoke stops – you stop. 'Cause" he said "you're handy [i.e., *near*] now."

So anyhow Jack smopped [i.e., *smoked*] an' smopped an' smopped away when it come just 'bout dark an'…couldn't get no smoke. An' Jack said "Ol' man told me" Jack said "whatever I do now an' had (to) go (o)bey orders an' now he…don't go when the smoke stops. That's it – you 's handy." An' Jack said "I don't see nothin." So Jack said he looked down in the valley an' he seen another old green house. "Well" Jack said "begar where there's light there's hope" Jack said "I'm goin down."

Anyhow Jack went down. Knocked to the door he said an' "Good night" he said "John."

"Oh" Jack said "you knows me."

"Yes" he said "I know ('ee)."

"Good night" Jack said "sir. Oh" Jack said "you're kind o' hairy an' dirty."

"Yes" he said, he said "my son" he said "you aint got nothing (to) give us no kind of haircut or shave have 'ee?"

Jack said "Yes sir." Jack said "I'm off for a twelvemonth an' walk" he said. "An' I got all kinds o' that" he said "for cuttin off hair an' one thing an' th' other like that."

"Well" he said "come in my son" he said "an' whatever lies in my power for 'ee I'll do." An' uh...he got in an' he cut it off him with the knife _ an' he hacked it...he done it all. He chopped [it] off wi' the scithers. He cut off fourteen armfuls of hair now _ off his face. Huhuh [*laughs*] [*aside to Int:* this goina be somethin to listen to too!] Fourteen armfuls he carried out 'gain the door an' made away with. And he come in then he give him a shave an' he was 'bout twenty, twenty-five. He was a hundred an' THREE _ that feller!

"Well now" he said "John my son" he said "I got some enchantment an' I guess" he said "you been to me other brother too."

Jack said "(Your) other brother" Jack said "who's he?"

"Oh" he said he named un but uh...he knowed but he...but he wouldn't tell. He said "There must be something wrong" he said. "There's something somewhere. Now" he said "John my son" he said "you want bit of a rest."

Jack said "Yes I'm tired" Jack said "hungry too." So he put just 'bout a quarter o' meat. Jack said "Now don't...just [as] well for you to put ENOUGH on there as put a quarter o' meat up 'cause I can't eat that much anyhow. Oh" Jack said "a SMALL bit now 'll do me tonight."

So anyhow they had their supper an'...he went to bed an' now next mornin "Now" he said "John" he said _ "I got a brother...'nother brother now" he said "me oldest brother lives thirty mile from this. An'" he said "he got more enchantment than I" he said "an' you's lookin for Greensleeve, I knows who you're lookin for."

"Yes" he said "I'm lookin for Greensleeve."

"Well" he said _ he said "any good [to] kick ball?"

"Ball?" Jack said. "Jesus all ever I done" Jack said "to...kick ball!"

"Well" he said "now I'll give you a ball tomorrow morn" he says "an' I'll give un to you an' put you out on the street _ an' you kick un an' wherever that ball goes you goes. An' when he stops on the road _ or wherever 'tis to _ an' you kick an' he don't move, well" he said "you're handy to me other brother. But" he said "now _ Greensleeves -- that's what you're after."

"Yeah." Very well.

So anyhow Jack said he kicked un, Jack wore off...score off wi' th' ol' leather boots onto him. He kicked un like the devil. And he went (a) half mile I suppose.

Jack said "I'll never see un no more." So he walked on an' sure enough he seen un. Give un another rap or two an' he chased un. Now th' ol' man said "Now whenever that ball stops you stop now" he says "'cause it be...you're handy to the...me other brother."

So very well. He stopped an' Jack whacked the boot into un an' he never moved. "Well" Jack said "now that's what th' ol' man said" took an' put un in his pocket. An' looked into the same place again in (a more...) a little he (have) seen a little blue (light).

An' Jack said "By (gar) where there's light there's hope" Jack said "I'm goin down to try he" last one I suppose this (is).

So he went down, knocked to the door "Oh" he said "good night...good night" he said "John. Good night John" he said "my son."

Said "How you come to know Jack?"

"Well" he said "everybody knows Jack sure."

/I/ "Yes" /he/ said "I suppose."

"Well" he said "me other brother sent you here?"

"No" Jack said "I don't know your other brother, don't know (whether) 'ee HAD ar brother or no."

"Well" he said "there must be somebody got...enchantment here" (he) said "[or you] wouldn't got to where I to. Well" he said "John" he said "my son" he said "have 'ee got anything [to] give us any kind o' haircut or shave?" he said "I been hundred year now" he said "wi' this growin."

An' Jack said "Yes I think you have." He was comin an'...um...an' his whisker was draggin out on the floor. Well Jack said "Sure take all night sure [to] cut it off, you. Oh" he said "I got plenty cutters" he said. "All kinds o' cutters." Anyhow Jack got in. Sot up in the chair amongst the hair on all (sides). An' he chopped it off un. An' got in to where he could get at his face. He's...chopped off thirty-seven armfuls off o' that ol' feller _ o' hair now, that's a good...that's a...that's a good bundle too eh? An' he carried out an' heave it over out 'gain the door for un to walk on. An' when he got he shaved up he was a hundred an' thirty-nine _ that feller. An' he looked no more he said than if he were fifty. A real jolly ol' feller.

"Well now" he said "John my son" he said _ "I got the most enchantment. I got two more brothers way back from this."

Jack said "You('ve) two brothers have 'ee? (There're) a lot o' yous in family 'cordin (to) that!" He knew it all (fine but) he wouldn't tell un.

/hent/ He said "I think they must have /sent/ you then."

"No sir" Jack says "I knows nobody" Jack said. "You's th' only one I seen."

"Well" he said "John my son" he said "if we can't get Greensleeves now" he said "(there)...there'd...were nobody in this world get un." He said "Now Greensleeves uh...uh...lives fifty mile from this an' tomorrow" he said "about two o'clock is his day home. He only has **ONE** day home out of twelvemonth, writin. An'" he says "you should see un anyhow. 'Twas but...that's if we can get 'ee across there."

"Now get across this little ocean. Now how's us goina get across there?" An' Jack said "Go across ocean?"

"Yes" he said "you got about fifty mile 'cross that ocean. An' get where Greensleeves is to. Well" he said "John my son" he said "I tell 'ee one thing I got" he said "I got some eagles out there" he said. "I don't know if they could do anything with 'ee."

"Eagles!" Jack said. "Carry men?"

"Oh well" he said "if fatten up they would."

So he give him some money an' he went on down (the) shop an' he brought up six or seven sacks o' meal. An' he went out an' he give it to 'em. An' he /whacked/ it all down into un.   /walked/

"Now" he said "John" he said "get up on un, try un, see what he'll do." By Jeez John got up, put his two arms around his neck an' he give two deep flaps an' he went out around th' house an' he skirred back again, he dropped. Wasn't enough see. Wasn't **STRONG** enough yet.

"Now" he said "John" he said "I guess you'll do it with six more. You go down an' get six more." So he give him the money, he went down got six more meal...bags. And he come up an' they feed away

"Now" he said "tomorrow mornin" he says "seven o'clock I guess" he said "he'll be able to...get 'ee somewhere."

"Oh" Jack said "it be somewhere if I gets halfways 'cross that ocean an' tumbles down! There'll be no more of I!"

"No no" he said "you won't do that. He'll come back before that time." Anyhow he put th' other six bags into un. An' the next morn he got out _ gee whiz he went off over the water an' he come back he didn't know he was on his back.

"Well" Jack said "no I believe" Jack said "there is something to it alright."

"Now" he said "Jack there's something I got to tell 'ee. You got the...I got (to) write out a recipe now for you" he said. "An' he got a daughter, more enchantment than...than Greensleeve got. Daughter Ann she's called. The oldest daughter. An'" he said "if you can only get down tomorrow" he said "by their dinner time now, if we can get you over half early 'cross this coun[try]...'cross this ocean _ that they'll be out swimmin. An'" he said "there's silk, satin uh...a...an'...an'...uh...an' cotton _ the clothes they wear. Now you come to the first lot" he said "an' (if) 'tis cotton _ an' (if) th' other is silk" he said _ "don't touch it. (That's) if you sees the satin _ sit on to it" he said "an' bide there."

"Alright" Jack said "so I will _ if I can live to get there."

An' he says "You wants a bit o' money." He said "You got...want money to see Greensleeves when you do get there. 'Cause" he said "there's so much on every door 'fore you gets to un."

Jack said "I got plenty money."

So very well. Got out next morn, he checked...(watch for) th' ol' eagle -- an' away they go. And /he/ took Jack on his back an' 'way they goes an' Jack...he was flyin right high...in the high...in the air. If she should get tired you know he'd go a long ways 'fore he tumbled. Anyhow Jack was up right clean out of sight. Jack says "By Jesus" Jack says "I feels him goin down." Anyhow he start to drop. You know he couldn't...couldn't bear un see? So he dropped an' dropped an' dropped an' th' ol' eagle /kept/ goin an' /kept/ goin /kept/ goin an' Jack said "Drowneded I got to be for sure." But he didn't. He reached so [close a] distance to the land when Jack struck the bottom he was to this [*gestures to indicate waist height*] in water. "My" Jack said "thank god" Jack said "I'm (to) land." So anyhow Jack found his way ashore an' wrung out his clothes an'...th' old eagle /?detached/ an' away he goes.

So anyhow Jack said he'd walk up an' th' old man told un he had to walk around the pond where they were swimmin to. An' he said _ "You [do] like he tells 'ee" he said "an' boy" he says "you should come out of it alright."

So anyhow Jack after he got his clothes wrung an' got it on Jack went on. Walked on an' Jack said "Now th' ol' man said there was a pond too." Sure enough Jack looked on, there was a pond. Jack said "Well wouldn't I like to have me gun this mornin!" There was three loos [i.e., *loons*] look off in that pond, see 'em divin an' comin up. This was the three girls see.

So anyhow Jack said "Now" Jack said "that wouldn't be his three daughters off swimmin would it?" Jack said. [Unidentified listener: Hm!] "Like th' ol' man told us, my gad" he said "now it could be." So anyhow he walked around the edge o' pond till...an' he's right enough he come to the rag clothes. There's cotton. An' Jack said "By god that's not it." An' then he come to the silk _ clothes _ what they had took off now _ off in the water. "Mm Jeez" Jack said "that's not (they)." So he walked another little distance he said "An' it's fairly /glistenin/. I couldn't hardly look at un, satin. Well now" Jack says "that's what...ol' man is right. I'LL be right. So I'm sittin down on top o' that. An' give...not givin her that 'fore she tells me where (her) father 's to."

So anyhow after they've adone swimmin they come in on side an' they said "Young man get out o' that" /she/ said "you're on my clothes."

"No" Jack said "I'm not gettin out of it."

"Oh" she said "you got to get out."

"Oh not..." (Jack said) "I'm NOT gettin out. (That)'s one thing I'm NOT doin, gettin out of it. Unless you can heave me out of it" Jack said "an' that's something you's not able (to) do."

/she/

/step/

/step/ /step/

/detack/

/glistener/

/he/

86

So anyhow th' others come ashore an' took off their clothes an' Jack was lookin at everything sonny when they (started) to peel off. Jack said to hisself now took a good view at everything. Two of 'em come, put on their clothes an' daughter Ann bid off in (the) water.

"Now" he said, John said "what's **YOUR** name?"

She said "If I tells you **MY** name [an'] Pa gets hold to it" says "I'll be hung."

Well said "The devil may care" Jack says "[if] you don't tell us who it is" Jack said "you'll never get your clothes."

She said "Give me me clothes young man" she said "I'll give 'ee all kind o' money."

Jack said "I don't want no money, I got thousands o' that now." An' Jack said "There's **ONE** thing I do want." An'...let th' other two girls go on, so they went on up an' John could see what they were goin to do.

Jack said "Now I **WANTS** to know where your father is to"

"Well" she said "Pop" she said "'ll be home today" she said "soon be home now" she said "an' that's once out of a twelvemonth. He's writin all day today. An' you'll see un anyhow."

"Well how in the name o' god I goin to see un if I don't know where he's to?"

"Oh" she said "**I'LL** be right to hand now" she said "when you wantes anything (if) you give me /my/ clothes _ call on daughter Ann an' I'll be...uh...the next one to 'ee." Alright. Anyhow she came along an' give Jack a kiss an' Jack kissed she. An' rubbed her a little bit you know he you would when you was co...start courtin, yeah.   /your/

"Well" she said "John my son" she said "you're th' only man ever come this way."

Jack said "Yes I know" an' Jack said "perhaps I'll never turn up no more."

"Oh" she said "you will." So very well.

So he went on in. "Now" she said "my father lives up...three sets o' stairs. An' there's three doors" she says "an' you want ten dollars to every door 'fore you gets in."

Jack says "I don't mind ten dollars."

"When you goes" she says "there's the first door you'll open there 'll be a...footman there" she says "want ten dollars before you gets to the...hand on the knob."

"Alright" Jack said.

"An' the next one is ten dollars. An' the last one" she said "where /father's/ to" she said _ "**IIE** a ten dollar, that's thirty dollar."   /faver's/

"Well" Jack said "I don't care 'bout thirty dollars, I got lots o' that."

"And" she said "if you **DO** get in any mischief" she said _ "call on daughter Ann time enough" she said "an' I'll help you...for sure. Whatever lies in my power for 'ee I'll do." Alright.

So very well. So Jack went an' he...went in to (the) door, a man stood up there.

"Boy" he said "good day" he said "Jack."

Jack said "Good day sir. Greensleeves in?"

"Yes" he said "just come. An' you want to see un?"

"Yes" Jack said "I wants to see un bad."

"Well" he said "John (I want)s ten dollars now."

Jack said "I don't mind ten dollars. Twenty if you want it."

/kept/ "No" he said "ten dollars." An' he said "Go on up, /keep/ goin on the same step." Went on up.

Next feller said "Ten dollars sir please."

"Okay" Jack says.

"Now" he said "keep goin." So he went on up. Sure enough when he got to the last one ten dollars again. Thirty...thirty dollars. Very well.

An' went on up an' knocked the door an' in he goes. "Oh" he said "good mornin" he said "Jack."

"Good mornin" Jack said "sir." Jack said "You wouldn't be the man I had a gam[e]...I had a game o' cards with would 'ee?"

/you/ "Hoo well yes" he said "John me son" he says "/I/ is." An' he said "When we dealed up (?it must)" he said "now" he said "if you didn't

/pry/ /find/ me [in] twelve month an' a day" he said "your head 'd go on a spear an' if you did you'd get clear."

"Well" Jack said "I'm clear now aint I?"

"No" he said "John my son you're not clear yet."

"Not **CLEAR**" Jack said "after goin through what I'd an-went through!"

"Oh no" he said "you're not clear yet. Now" he said "John" he said "my son" he said "you got to go...tomorrow morn" he said "I got to hide away from you. An' if you can find me" he said "you're clear. An' if you can't find me" he said "why your head got to go on a spear."

"Well" Jack said "it's just as well for you to kill me now at first as last. 'Cause" Jack said "you can turn yourself into a bird an' fly in the air an' turn yourself into a fish an' swim the sea, (well) how in the name o' god will I find you?"

"Oh" he said "you **GOT** to find me. That's it."

"Very well." Uh...he said "Alright."

Anyhow Jack goes on down the very first mornin he meet with daughter
/He/ Ann. /She/ said "What Pa say this mornin?"

88

"Well" he said "I...he got to hide away from me now tomorrow mornin" he said. "And" he said "if I can find un I'm clear an' if I can't find un" he said "why" he said..."my head got to go on a spear."

"Ah nonsense" /she/ said.   /he/

An' Jack said "Yes" Jack said "that's a bad...that's a bad game."

"Now" she said "be sure now get up early tomorrow mornin." Alright. He got up for to have breakfast next mornin _ went out /'gain/ the door _ and   /bin/ she was there to meet un right straight. She said she would. Give him a kiss you know like yous, you see, yes.

"Now" she said "John he never come outdoors 's morn. He hided in the yard somewhere."

Jack said "Alright." Anyhow they got breakfast an'...never had no fruit on the table.

"Now" she said "Jack if you gets on the top o' that tree don't forget to take the top one of all right up on the top. Make no difference what apples you knocks down. Get the top one WHATEVER. 'Cause he could be in one [o'] they." [*coughs*] Anyhow they (go) an' get breakfast an' footman...call up footman.

"Now" she said "we want some...fruit for breakfast. Got no apples...oranges."

"Oh" he said "I can't climb un." He said "Perhaps that young man (could)."

"CLIMB!" Jack said "I guess there's no place here" Jack said "(boy) I never go on top of o'...[if] I want to."

"Well me good man" he said "that's just what we want."

An' the...girl went out with a basket an' Jack said "How many ('ee) want?" Oh she wanted a basket full.

"Oh" /he/ said "young man don't knock so many off. You's climbin   /she/ through 'em" he said "way...way to ruin 'em."

"Well" Jack said "devil might care! I'm goin get one on top now 'fore I gives up." So Jack said he mounts right to the top o' the tree. An' the last one on the top that's (the) one he took an' he marked un. Very well. Ate a bit o' rind of un, he knowed...he knowed un anyhow. Everybody come down an' they had their breakfast an'...'twas their style then [to] take a orange an'...cut un in two you know. [*gestures to demonstrate cutting*] Very well they...Jack watched 'em (to) see what they was doin. He was kind o' ignorant you know, only young man just...tryin (un). He've seen they'd agive un a big chop with a knife see an' lay un abroad [*gesture of chopping*] an' (with it) so Jack come to his turn, he done it. Well before they start their breakfast Jack took up his orange like that an' JUST as he were goin to make the chop, (?lay it he...)"Oh" he said "my GOD" he said "John" he said "save my life" he said "you'll have all I'm owner of."

Jack said [*tone of mock surprise*] "Well! Look what is into orange ('s morn)!"

"Well" he said "yes. That's it."

/fyin/   "Phooh ah" Jack said "no (trouble) /tryin/ find you sure!"

"No" he said "'tis no (trouble) to find me now." He said "Daughter Ann must have (a hand in)."

"Daughter Ann" Jack said "what's that (a) cat? A dog or what is it?"

"No" he said "my oldest daughter."

"(Why)" he said "I didn't know you HAD any daughters" Jack [said].

"Well" he said "now then" he said "ol' man" he said _ "I'm clear now sure."

"No" he said "John my son. You's not clear yet."

"Well" Jack says "'tis just as well for you take me now an' put me head on a spear first as last. 'Cause" he said "there's nothing I can do." He said
/Wed/   "/Where/ you can't find me."

"Well" he said "I...you got to hide away from me now tomorrow
/can/   morn" he said "John" he said "my son" he said "an' if I /can't/ find you you
/don't/   be clear _ an' if I /do/ find 'ee" he said "well (that's...luck)."

"Well" Jack said "I take no chances on that" Jack said "'cause if I go to hide away from you (you) knew you got to find me."

"Oh" he said "I (mightn't)."

Very well. Next morn come. And he went down to the door. He said "What Pappy say 's morn (?just)?"

"Well" she said "he come this morn" she said "well I never seed un go this morn" she said "but he went up in stable somewhere." An' she said "Now then" she said "John" she said "we'll go up." So (they) went up. They had (a) little mare up there go nine mile...every stride, little mare.

"An' now" she said "John take...take off your jacket."

"I'll do it" Jack said.

"Oh" she said an' they went up an'...she put her hand up in the mare's mouth an' took out his jaw tooth.

"Now" she...she said "get up. Jack (you)..."

"Oh yes" he'd get up. So she...Jack got up in the hole [o'] the tooth an' they put the tooth back in. Jack fit in there.

An' the ol' man come off seven o'clock, comin home then, come up to look for Jack _ an' make away with un as he thought. Went up an'...looked all round, the froth was comin out of his mouth, no sign, couldn't find nothin. No. Looked everywhere. When it come eight o'clock _ Jack walks out an' walks down. Puts the tooth back in the mare again an' he walks down.

Jack said "I thought last night" Jack said "that you said we had to ship on turns, you had to come an' find me this mornin or I find you."

He said "So I did. Where was you?"

"I was /?nowhere/ at all" Jack said. "I was up there on the…up in the stable" he said "where you told me to go to an' I hung across them cross trees up there _ two legs flickin about" he said "I could s…jumped on you if I'd mind to. I seen you come up" he said "tearin all around an' tearin around this an' tearin that. An' I said you wasn't lookin for me at all. If you did you see me! Well" he said Jack said "there's no odds. Well now" he said "I'm clear." /nurry/

"Well" he said "no. You're not clear yet."

"Not clear YET!" Jack said. "Well" Jack said to…"if you don't clear un now" Jack said "what in the name o' god I goina do then?"

"Well no" he said. I said…I've…he said "We got a stable up there now" he said "forty mile long an' twenty mile wide. An' there were forty head o' cattle in that" he said "this last hundred year. An' you knows what kind of a mess is IN (there)." An' he said "My mother" he said "losed a gold ring in there"…/he/ said "when she was a young girl. An'" he said "you got to find he." /she/

"Hm!" said Jack "What find THAT in THAT! Why I wouldn't walk the length o' that sure in twelvemonth!"

"Well" he said "you got to do it" he said. "Or else your head go on a spear."

"Well" Jack said "take un off now boy an' let's have it done with 'cause I won't do no more."

"No" he said "you go." He said "Daughter Ann must have a hand in this too you know."

"Daughter Ann" [*dismissive tone*] Jack said. "Who the HELL is she, daughter Ann?"

"'s my oldest daughter" he said. "You must 've seen she."

Jack said "I've see no girl _ see no women, see nobody _ clear (o') yous."

So anyhow she come down the next mornin. Sure enough daughter Ann is right to hand.

"Well" she said "Jack what have 'ee got?"

Jack said "I got nothin clear of (a) stick. There's some shovels up there…in…in uh…in the barn."

"Well" she said "you better go on an' try un."

An' Jack said "No" Jack said "I'm damned if I do" Jack said "'cause I knows" Jack said "I'll never find THAT."

"Oh" she says "you might find it." She took a little shovel out of her pocket about that long, a little white hand shovel.

"Now" she (said) "use that."

"THAT!" Jack said "What's good [o'] that to a big shovel up here, you wouldn't miss ten o' they sure."

91

"Oh you try un." Anyhow Jack was (in) only 'bout an hour _ at forty mile long, twenty mile wide an' that's up...up...up...'bout that high (to un) _ [*gestures to indicate height*] 'fore he had it all cleaned out. No sign (o') the ring.

So Jack said "There's one more little knob over there look in that hay now." They walked away an' walked away an' got over an' he hit un with his shovel for [some] (reason), out come the ring. Got the ring. Very well. So Jack said...anyhow Jack slung shovel off [to] one side, Jack said "I knows I'm clear now." So _ very well. So uh...Jack went out an' _ went up to th' ol' man.

"Well" he said "that wasn't uh...the that first shovelful I took up" he said _ "up come the ring."

"No" he said.

"Yes" Jack said "there he is, this is he"

"Yes" he said "right enough. 'Tis he."

"**NOW**" Jack said "I'm clear aint I?"

"No John" said "my son" he said "there's one more thing you got to do _ an' then you'll be clear."

"Well" Jack said "just as well for you put my head on a spear first as last as do this 'cause I'll be wore out sure!"

"Oh no" he said "you got **ONE MORE THING.** [*each word emphasized in measured tones*] I got to hide from you tomorrow mornin again" she said...he said "for the last time." Alright.

(An') Jack come out next morn the very first thing he opened the door an' jumped down on the drash [i.e., *drashol: threshold*] o' the door, daughter Ann was out. She says "What Pa say this mornin?"

"Well" he said "he got to hide away from I again today."

"Well" she said "I tell 'ee what he done this mornin Jack" she said. /he/ "Come out at dawn this mornin he shook hisself" /she/ said "an' turned hisself into a bird an' 'way he goes in th' air (or) somewhere there."

An' Jack said "No..."

"Well" she (said) "the only way you can get he" she said _ "is take the rifle now" she said "an' go, they've got no fresh meat today." An' she said "You go off an' get a turn [i.e., *load*] o' birds _ of any kind, (it) makes no difference what kind of a bird [you] fire at. Are you good to fire?"

"Yes" Jack said "I'm good to fire. I don't miss nothin." Alright.

Anyhow Jack took gun, pockets full o' shells an'...bullets an' 'way she goes. An' he went off an' the little sparrows come out Jack lick it into 'em, kill 'em. Jack just 'bout had a **BAG** full. Everything he fire at he kill. "Anyhow" Jack said "('tis) not he 'cause (I) suppose" Jack said "you'd see un if 'tis in there." So Jack come along by the pond I tell 'ee now an'...they had a (?task)...(well) that's some goin boy this eh? Soon have enough. "Oh" Jack said "by gee look at the loo [i.e., *loon*] look! See the loo off there divin off in the pond." Jack said "If I gets he that WILL be enough." Anyhow Jack worked an'…an' he dived, he walked down an' got down by the pond an' _ got out 'longside of him an' uh…'bout fifty or sixty yards from un that's handy enough. Jack shot the bullet into her. An' JUST as he were goin to draw (the) trigger he hove his hand. [*clapping noise signalling sudden action*]

"For GOD'S sake" he said "Jack" he said "don't…don't…don't shoot me" he said. "You'll have all I own."

"Well" Jack said "well what (trouble to) [i.e., *it's no trouble*] find you!" Jack said "I come off practisin with gun _ an' now" Jack said "an' find you! ANYWHERE at all" Jack said "make no differ(ence) where 's to I can find (you). Well" Jack said "I'm clear now aint I?" He wouldn't say then see 'cause I suppose Jack…thought Jack put a bullet in un.

"Well" he said "come on" he said "John my son" he said "an' we'll go up an we'll see what's goin be done."

"Now" Jack said "I know (that) I'm clear now, there's nothin else can be done."

"Well John" he said "my son sorry to say" he said "but your head got to go on a spear" he said "in two hours from the day."

"What!" Jack said "After doin everything."

"Yes" he said. "We tries 'em out" he said "of all kinds" he said "an' when they does…they sees that you got just so much enchantment as we got ourself we makes away with 'em quick. You see all them heads on the spears what's around here." He said "That's what uh…we been (doin)."

"Alright" Jack said "sir. What time is that?"

"Oh" he said "give him 'bout two hours time."

So anyhow Jack goes down "Yes Jack?" [*lowered anxious tone*] Sit down an' he…an' (said) "We're up again it now" (said). "My head got to go on a spear in two hours" (he says).

"Not at all" [*dismissive tone*] (she said). "Well" she said she went in she got some flour an' she mixed up. Mixed up a big cake. An' put…an' put two songs into un _ into the big cake an' put un in the pan.

"Now" she said "John be(come) [*whispers*] (we're) smart." She took John in, she washed un from top to bottom, th' other end. An' she put un on a sort o'…kind o'…put on a suit of clothes the colour o' the stars _ he fair glisten, an' quiff hat on. "NOW" she said "we'll go an' get little mare _ while he's singin a song."

"Now" she said…"now" he [*the grand vizier*] said to Jack, he said "now when them two songs is fini[shed]…when the first song is finished" said "prepare" he said "'nother half an hour now" he said "your head got to go on a spear when the last one [is sung]." So Jack keeps singin see, he…he THOUGHT 'twas, but 'twas the cake 'twas singin, Jack wasn't singin.

/by/

One of 'em took (the) little mare an' she said uh...and /my/ daughter Ann (an') he goes off.

An' Jack says "By the gee" Jack said "he'll never catch us now." They was gone somewhere 'round fifty or sixty mile now.

/?lie him/

"An' now" she said "John my son" she said "Pa 'll be soon be comin" she said "'cause he got nine mile boots. They'll soon /?arrive/. An'" she said "we goin twelve mile too. Now" she said "you take a lump o' froth now out the ma[re's]...uh...mare's left year _ an' heave [it] over your ri...uh...uh...right shoulder _ an'" she said "there'll be a concrete wall rise up there" she said "what he can't get over _ an' can't walk around. An'"

/hatches/

/he/ /he/

she said uh..."he'll have to go back an' get his steel /hatchets/ _ an' come an' cut his way through" /she/ said "an' by **THAT** time" /she/ said "we goina be a **LONG** ways."

Well anyhow Jack done that see, put his hand in the left year o' the...mare an' he took out a lump o' froth...lump o' wax an' he hove over his left shoulder an' when he looked back they stopped an' looked at it, it was a concrete wall rised up 'twas fifty mile long each way.

"An' now" she says "he goina be a **LONG** time cuttin through that!"

So when he found out he come out for to kill Jack or something _ uh...here was the cake talkin an' Jack gone. An' daughter Ann was gone. And he (?wanted two hours)

She said "Two hours _ now" she said "an' he'll be cut through."

"Cut through!"

"Yes Jack" said "she'll be cut through in two hours' time. And" she said "you keep lookin now an' see if you (can) see a little...black bank risin up

/He/

after ('ee)." /She/ says "If 'tis, he's through that _ after us." So was very well.

So _ she says "Now" he said "'tis...he's pretty well through it now."

She said "You put your hand in the mare's left year now" she said "an' do the same as you done before with a lump o' wax _ an' heave over your left shoulder. And" she said "there'll be a forest o' wood rise up" she said "hundred mile long an' (a) hundred mile square" she said "an' he'll have to go back home again now _ to get his hatch(ets to) cut nine mile 'fore (?he's here) to get through this."

"Hoh well" Jack says "sonny 'll never catch us then." So very well.

She said "He's pretty well through it." So anyhow Jack done that an' it rised up. My son! You could see the big mast sticks growin everywhere.

"Now" she said "we're set fre[e]...we're free. We're goin now." So anyhow Jack...went on _ an' went on an' went on.

"Well" she says "he'll never get us now."

Anyhow Jack went on with...with daughter Ann an' they went to a little place an' uh...an' they had (a) lot...they only had one bed

Well Jack said "That's enough 'cause I only got I an' me wife and uh..."
Jack said "Well now we don't want two beds. We only wants one bed an'
that was it." So anyhow 'twas a hundred dollars a night, that's what he had
to pay. An' Jack said he didn't mind that 'cause he had plenty money an' she
had plenty money. Anyhow they put 'em up for the night. An' when I come
'way they have six children an' they was only a fortnight at it. An' I had a
pie for tellin a lie an' I come all the ways home (an' I'm sober). Good
enough. That's the last of un. Not tell no more.

[Int: Where did you get THAT one Mr. Snook?]
Hey? That's one I got from Uncle John Martin. Fella is dead now.
[Int: Where was he? Here in...]
He belonged Harbour Breton an' I got he up erm...in Connaigre Bay. I only
wants to hear un once an' that settled _ an' I'll get un. Now...song I got to
have un wrote off, I got to look un over he 'bout twenty-five times.
[Int: You mean you heard this only ONE time?]
Only once I got that an' I've atold that I suppose a DOZEN times...perhaps
twenty times at that. An' I don't say there's two words out of it.
[Int: How do...how...?]
Hey?
[Int: How do you...how do you...get it so good?]
I don't know...sir. I learn it just so fast...you sit down an' tell one now I can
go up (?to the Moran's) an' tell un the works. Same way, an' I bet you I
wouldn't miss two words. Now the...the...the...you got your thing* on.   *i.e., tape
What we's talkin now is all true.   recorder
[Int: That's...yes. That's...that's what I wanted to get.]
Yeah.
[Int: Well that's a WONDERFUL story _ there.]
Yes sir I can year [i.e., *hear*] a story now an' I can go out an' sit down
out in house an' tell un o'er. A funny thing boy.
[Int: Hm-mm.]
An' I got memory you know _ my memory's not good. But still it's a long
time ago I learned that thing. An'...'tis a good bit ago. I never told un last
winter at all. Well that ends the story.

Duration: 32 min., 15 sec.
Source: John Martin (Harbour Breton, Fortune Bay), Connaigre Bay, Fortune Bay.
Location: Sitting room of teller's house, afternoon.
Audience: Adult male visitor, young child sitting on teller's knee, interviewer.

Context, Style, and Language: Just before the story begins, Stephen Snook closes the
door leading to the kitchen and reduces the sound of several people talking in there.

Various individuals come in and out of the room, and conversation continues in the adjoining kitchen throughout the narration. On this warm August day, the teller is troubled by a dry throat and cough but overcomes these by drinking occasionally as the tale unfolds over more than half an hour. At the beginning of the narrative, Stephen Snook suggests that anyone who has a good story to tell should begin with "Once upon a time," though this is by no means a universal opening formula in the tales presented here. Even so, early on in the narration he poses as a participant in the events of the plot and his "Mm" acknowledges the nods and silent expressions of acquiescence in this pose on the part of the audience. In most other tales in this collection the claim to be present at the narrated events appears in the closing section of the narrative. He is much more relaxed than in the telling of No. 25, the pace is somewhat slower and the pauses more frequent.

This long and well-constructed story begins rather hesitantly, but the teller soon gets into his stride and the narrative is clearly told and easy to follow. The teller himself is well satisfied with its completeness as is demonstrated in his remarks in the brief discussion at the end of the story. His animated delivery is enlivened by vivid dialogue, and especially in the changing variety of tones of voice, as for example in the dismissive way Jack responds to the little old man's request for a game of cards and to the various tests which Greensleeves sets him, these being some of the many instances in the story where Jack is typically portrayed as being unconcerned for his own safety, cheekily confident of his own abilities, and willing to try anything whether "the devil may care" or not.

Stephen Snook frequently puts strong emphasis on individual words which is a hallmark of his style and which adds effective contrast and variety to the narrative, and he often uses gestures to involve his audience. In addition to several asides and questions designed to involve the audience and encourage their response, the teller indicates his awareness of the tape recorder when he remarks that the story is "goina be somethin to listen to too!" following the amusing account of Jack's shaving so much hair off the second old man. In a similar way, he poses as an eyewitness to the events he is narrating when in the early part of the story he says he can still remember seeing the little boy Jack toddling out to play cards.

As in several of the stories told by Freeman and Everett Bennett, the passage of time is marked by economical references to Jack's having his supper, going to bed, and continuing his adventures next morning. Such parallels are significant in that they suggest common features of narrative style among storytellers from opposite ends of the island, who also tell the same basic story, notwithstanding differences of title and plot, but who have never met or heard each other's tales. Like the Bennetts, Stephen Snook marks stages in the progress of the narrative with such forms as *(So) very well* and *alright,* and often condenses material into the shortest form possible, as for instance in *Off jacket, Sat down, First old feller, Wasn't enough see, Go across ocean, Went on up, Next morn come, Looked everywhere, Got the ring, Soon have enough, Mixed up a big cake.* This cryptic style is paralleled by the omission of function words, pronouns, and auxiliary verbs as in *What Pa(ppy) say, what is into orange, I goina do, practisin with gun, She mixed up* (omission of object pronoun), *get little mare, had plenty money.*

The opening formula is spoken very rapidly, without a break, the word boundaries therefore being blurred, resulting in problems of transcription, though the gist is obvious to the listener. The pronunciation is of the West Country English type, with many conservative features, as for example in *care* (pronounced like *cure*), the short vowels /u/ in *boot(s)* and /i/ in *bid* (bide), *keep* and *climb,* in the initial onglide /j/ in *years* (hears) and *year* (ear), and the voicing of initial consonant in *drash* (threshold). Other noteworthy pronunciation features include the medial consonant in *scithers* (scissors), the half-open back unrounded central vowel in *shook,* /duːz/ (does), and /'wudnt/ (wasn't). The vowel of *the* is elided in *th' ol', th' only, th' other(s),* and *morning* is often realized as *morn.* Aphesis is a common feature, e.g., *'bout, 'longside, 'long, 'fore, 'cause, 'nother, 'cordin', 'cross, 'way,* the initial vowel is lacking in *'tis, 'twas,* the final consonant is lost in *wi'* (with), *whether* loses its medial consonant and becomes *whe'r,* and *today* is realized as *the day.* The pronunciation of "grand vizier" as *grand aviser* suggests a rationalization of the original, perhaps equivalent to "grand adviser."

There is also some confusion between the pronouns *he* and *she* during the conversation between the grand vizier and (presumably) his wife which perhaps suggests uncertainty regarding the precise meaning and specific reference of the term *grand aviser.* The rhetorical device of repeating a verb effectively indicates the passage of time or the intensity of an action, e.g., "Jack smopped an' smopped an' smopped away," "So he dropped an' dropped an' dropped," "So anyhow Jack...went on an' went on an' went on."

At the lexical level Stephen Snook makes use of *'ee* (thee), and of *you* in sentence final position as a vocative form of address, clearly separated from the preceding word by open juncture, in "Sure take all night sure [to] cut if off, you." The West Country English pronoun *un* is especially prominent. He uses many words typical of Newfoundland speech, including the familiar terms of address *my son* and *boy,* along with the intensifier *right, handy* (near), *smopped* (drew [on a pipe]), the asseveration *begar, ar* (any), *this* (this place), *skirred* (flew or glided rapidly [cf. *DNE skirr*]), *abroad* (in pieces), *jaw tooth* (molar [cf. *DNE jaw*]), *ship* (agree to work/act [cf. *DNE ship* v.]), *turn* (load [cf. *DNE turn* n.]), and *mast sticks* (cf. *DNE stick* n. 1). Notice also the facetious use of *draw-knife*—a technical term for the large double-handled knife used in coopering, wheelwrighting, farriery, etc. (cf. *OED Drawing-knife, OED* Supp. II *draw-knife*), *the works* (everything), the nautical *grub* (food), the purposive *for to,* the archaic *make away with* (dispose of, kill), and *quiff hat* (soft felt hat with an indentation in the crown); the reference to this kind of hat, which has long been out of fashion, contrasts bathotically with the suit which glistens and is the color of the stars. An interesting anachronism is the reference to concrete walls, though this is understandable in the Newfoundland context where stone and brick are rarely used as building materials.

At the morphological level we find *hisself, yous,* the singular pronoun *it* used with reference to *clothes* and the masculine *he* with reference to *ring,* and the absence of the plural inflection in *mile.* Pronominal usage is also typical of the West Country English variety of Newfoundland dialect, as for instance in *how's us goina get across, There'll be no more of I, When he got he shaved up, in one o' they,* and *only got I.*

Typical Newfoundland verb forms are also common, as for instance in the present tense *I gets/knows/tumbles/feels/wants/gives, you isn't/knows/gets/knocks,* and the exceptional *you wantes; we tries/wants, they goes*, the present participle *agoin*, the past tense forms *seed, sot, hove, seen, knowed, come, pound, bid, hided, losed, done, rised*, and the past participles *agot, beat, drowneded, agive, wore, adone, atold*, and the aberrant *an-went*. Double negatives abound, as in *can't get nobody, aint got nothing, couldn't get no smoke, don't see nothing, never see un no more, don't want no money, never turn up/not tell no more*.

Finally one might call attention to Jack's saying *"where there's light there's hope(s)"* each time he gets near the house of one of the three old men who help him. It is an ingenious adaptation of the proverb "Where there's life there's hope" which is appropriate to the plot even though the alteration is presumably the result of the confusion of the words *life* and *light* in the process of oral transmission.

Types and Motifs:

AT313A. *The Girl as Helper in the Hero's Flight* + AT329. *Hiding from the Devil.*
Z10.1. *Beginning formula.*
T585. *Precocious infant.*
F660. *Remarkable skill.*
Cf. N221. *Man granted power of winning at cards.*
N4.2. *Playing game of chance (or skill) with uncanny being.*
Cf. S221.2. *Youth sells himself to an ogre in settlement of a gambling debt.*
H942. *Tasks assigned as payment of gambling loss.*
H1319. *Quests for the unique—miscellaneous [oldest man].*
Cf. D1521.1. *Seven-league boots.*
N810.2. *Helper's beard and eyebrows cut.*
N825.2. *Old man helper.*
F571.2. *Sending to the older.*
H1235. *Succession of helpers on quest.*
D822. *Magic object received from old man.*
D1313. *Magic object points out road.*
D1314. *Magic object indicates desired place.*
Cf. D1293.2. *Green as magic color.*
D1313.1. *Magic ball indicates road.*
Cf. G229.7. *Blue lights follow witches.*
F141. *Water barrier to otherworld.*
B455.3. *Helpful eagle.*
B552. *Man carried by bird.*
Cf. D361.1. *Swan Maiden.*
K1335. *Seduction (or wooing) by stealing clothes of bathing girl (swan maiden).*
F156. *Door to otherworld.*
G461. *Youth promised to ogre visits ogre's home.*
K231.2. *Reward for accomplishment of task deceptively withheld.*
G465. *Ogre sets impossible tasks.*
H901.1. *Heads placed on stakes for failure in performance of task.*

K869.2. *Deceptive hide and seek game.*
D638. *Transformation by magician.*
D630. *Transformation and disenchantment at will.*
G530.2. *Help from ogre's daughter.*
Cf. E711.8. *Soul in golden apple.*
Cf. F989.17. *Marvelously swift horse.*
Cf. F535.1.1.10. *Thumbling hides in small place.*
H1102.2. *Task: emptying in one day a barn filled with manure.*
D1205. *Magic shovel.*
D161.3. *Transformation: man to duck [loon].*
K5. *Contest with magician won by deception.*
D1611.8. *Magic cakes answer for fugitive.*
F821.1.5. *Dress of gold, silver, color of sun, moon and stars.*
D672. *Obstacle flight.*
Cf. D2091.16. *Enemy magically enclosed within walls.*
D941.1. *Forest produced by magic.*
T115. *Man marries ogre's daughter.*
Z10.2. *End formula.*

International Parallels: AT313, one of the most widespread of modern folktales, is found nearly all over the world. It is a story steeped in magic; there are persons with magic powers who can transform themselves and others, and who give or produce magic objects. The hero may be courageous and talk with brash assurance, but without the help of others he would be lost. Fortunately for him the daughter of his opponent, a powerful enchantress in her own right, falls in love with him and does not scruple to assist him in every way, much as the enchantress, Medea, compelled by Aphrodite to love Jason, aided Jason in his quest for the Golden Fleece against her own father (Rose, *Handbook,* pp. 202-3).

We have versions of this tale from six Newfoundland storytellers, two recordings from one of them, and will compare and contrast the six texts step by step. No. 13 is a variant of No. 12 and temporarily will be disregarded. Although the stories have a basic similarity, there is considerable variation in the details. In this analysis we have utilized extensively both Christiansen's earlier and later analyses of Scandinavian and Irish versions of the tale and Hamish Henderson's perceptive discussion of a Scots version. For the latter see Henderson, *Scottish Studies* 2 (1958), 47-85, hereafter cited as: Henderson.

To assist us in the comparative analysis of our tales we will utilize, as Henderson did, Christiansen's earlier (*Béal.* 1 [1927-28], 108) division of the structure of AT313 into several parts: A.—Introduction. B.—The Journey, i.e., how the hero reaches the strange castle. C.—The Tasks Set, and how he performs them. D.—The Escape, and E. End: The Forgotten Bride. For our purposes this division is more useful than the list of Incidents in the AT index.

Three of our recensions (Nos. 7, 9, 12) begin with card games. Our hero wins two out of three games in Nos. 9 and 12; in No. 9, the king's son's opponent is The Green

Man of Eggum; in No. 12 he is called "The Head Card Player of the World," but the hero, a young man, is not named. For the lost game our hero is put under the obligation to find where his opponent lives within a stated period of time. No. 7 is more confused: the hero, Jack, wins all three games against Greensleeves: nonetheless he is set three tasks by his opponent. We are only told the first task, which is to find the oldest man in the country, but from the events of the story we learn that Jack is trying to find where Greensleeves lives.

Christiansen observes that the "Playing Episode" is the most common type of introduction in Irish versions of the tale (Christiansen, *Béal.* 1, p. 108). He discusses it in more detail in his later study where he says about fifty percent of the Irish variants open with it, adding that this popular Irish motif "seems to be an Irish characteristic and its occurrence elsewhere, may, with some reason, indicate Irish influence" (Christiansen, *Studies,* pp. 101 and 102). Henderson, whose article was published a year before Christiansen's *Studies,* would probably not agree with the statement about Irish influence. He pointed out that not only is the playing episode found in two lowland Scots versions, but it also occurs in a Scottish Gaelic version from Barra, and in a Romany version collected in central Wales (Henderson, pp. 65-73).

The other Newfoundland recensions, in all of which Jack is the name of the hero, lack the card game. In No. 8, Jack, of his own volition, seeks to find The Green Man of Eggum who is a witch. In No. 10, the Green Man of Eggum visits Jack's family when Jack is only old enough to talk, is interested in the boy, and invites him to pay him a visit when he is old enough. In No. 11 there is no introductory sequence or journey, which are Parts A and B in Christiansen's structure; Jack is already at the king's court and wants to marry the king's daughter.

In the five Newfoundland recensions in which Jack undertakes the journey, he is sent in succession to three persons who help him: three fierce brothers in No. 8; the three giant sons of an old woman in No. 9; three wicked giants in No. 10. In each of these stories he is given cakes or buns as identifying tokens to give to the next person he visits so that these dangerous individuals not only will not harm him but will assist him. In No. 12, he is sent from a 100-year-old man to his 200-year-old brother, then to the one who is 300 years old. In No. 7 he is sent from one old man to his two older brothers, but in this tale he must earn the help of each of the old men by cutting the long hair and whiskers of each and giving them a shave.

In all five versions the last and oldest man tells him how he can get where he wants to go. In all five we also have versions of the swan maiden story. The daughters of the personage he is seeking come, usually in bird form, to bathe (swim) at a certain place. He must hide the clothes of one of them, the youngest one in four versions, the oldest one in No. 7, and not surrender them until the girl promises to help him.

Our hero follows his instructions carefully. In Nos. 8 and 10, the girls come to the pond in the shape of swans, turn into girls, undress, and go swimming, turning back into swans in order to leave. In No. 9 we are not told in what shape they came, but when they leave they fly away. In No. 12 they come in the form of a cloud and presumably leave in the same fashion. In No. 7, when Jack gets to the pond the girls are already swimming in the shape of loons, not swans, a nice Newfoundland localization, and their clothes are on the shore.

In three stories (Nos. 8, 9, and 10) the chief help the chosen girl must give is to carry our hero over an unclimbable "glassen hill" so that he can get to his destination. In Nos. 7 and 12 she must tell him how to find her father. In the former there is an amusing sequence in which he has to pay a doorkeeper at each of three sets of stairs before he is allowed to climb them to reach the hidden Greensleeves. Why there are three charges of ten dollars is never explained.

In No. 12 he has less of a problem. He is told the castle he is seeking is just behind a mountain around which he can walk. In all these five versions the girl warns our hero that he must not mention her help.

At the outset of these comparative notes we said that these stories are steeped in magic. This is particularly true of parts C and D. But it might be worthwhile to point out some of the magical elements found in the earlier sections of the individual versions of the tales. In No. 8, we are told at the outset that the Green Man is a witch, i.e., a magician or enchanter. In his search Jack visits a series of fierce brothers who are mollified in turn by the cakes each brother gives Jack; obviously these cakes are magical. Christiansen (*Studies*, p. 102) suggests: "The cakes and the three giant brothers seem to be an Irish motif. . . ." The swan maidens have the magical power to transform themselves, and the one Jack has selected is also able to carry him over the glassen hill.

In No. 9, the old woman who helps the king's son says she knows ten times more than everything and her giant sons know ten times as much as she does. We may assume that in a story like this knowledge is magical knowledge. She gives the king's son enough identifying magical cakes to give one to each of the giants. We again have the swan maidens, one of whom carries the king's son over the glassen hill.

In No. 10 no mother is mentioned, but we have again a series of giant brothers, each mollified by the magical bun supplied in turn to Jack by each giant he visits, and again the swan maidens, including one who carries Jack over the glassen hill.

In No. 12, our hero is sent in turn from a 100-year-old man to his 200- and 300-year-old brothers. These are more peaceable than the giants and there is no need for cakes or buns. We have the swan maidens again, but Jack only needs information and does not have to be transported.

We have reserved No. 7 to the last because it has a greater number of magical elements. To begin with, Jack's mother knows that Greensleeves is a dangerous character. Greensleeves himself tells Jack that he has the power to turn himself into a bird and fly, and turn into a fish and swim. When Jack starts on his travels he is given a useful pair of nine-mile boots to help him along. All in his series of helpers have magic knowledge and magical equipment.

When he arrives at the first old man's house, the old man knows who he is and calls him by name. He is a man about seventy, but after Jack cuts off his long hair and whiskers and shaves him, he looks about twenty. The old man knows Jack is looking for Greensleeves so he sends him to his older brother. This brother gives him a pipe to smoke and tells him to follow the smoke wherever it leads and he will get there. The second old man also knows him and after Jack cuts off his hair and shaves him, the 103-year-old man looks about twenty-five.

101

This man admits he has some enchantment. He gives Jack supper and a bed for the night. Next day, knowing that Jack is looking for Greensleeves, he sends him to his still older brother who has even more magical power, giving him a ball to kick to guide him there. This third brother also badly needs a haircut and shave, and though he is 139 years old, after Jack has trimmed and shaved him he looks no older than fifty.

The realistic exaggeration of the many armfuls of hair Jack chops and cuts off the elderly brothers and then carries outdoors obviously delights the storyteller. Note, however, that after each of the three brothers is shaved, he looks many years younger. This is not tall-tale humor but a quite different realm, that of magic rejuvenation. (For further notes on this topic, see Addendum 1 below).

The oldest brother admits that he has more magical power than his other two brothers. He knows Jack wants to find Greensleeves, knows where Greensleeves is, and that he will be at home the next day. Jack has to cross fifty miles of ocean. The old man feeds one of his eagles with huge amounts of food and the eagle carries Jack across the ocean and drops him on the other side in waist-high water. Then Jack sees the girls in loon shape swimming and diving in the pond, very much like ordinary loons. Following his instructions, he sits on the clothes of the oldest daughter and from her gets the information he needs.

Greensleeves' greeting in No. 7 is abrupt enough. He tells Jack that if he had not found him his head would have gone on a spear. Similarly in No. 12, the Head Card Player of the World tells our hero that if he had not come, he would have been killed. No such statement is made in No. 9, the only other story in which the hero is obligated to find his card-playing opponent, but the Green Man of Eggum implies that his daughter must have helped him. Of course, the king's son denies this, saying he did not know the Green Man had a daughter.

We should mention here that, in most versions of the story, whenever Jack reports to his opponent that he has completed a task, he is told that someone, usually naming a daughter, must have helped him. Invariably Jack challenges this statement vigorously, frequently denying he has ever met the daughter.

In discussing Irish and Scottish versions of our tale, neither Christiansen nor Henderson comments on an element of the story that occasionally occurs between B.—The Journey and C.—The Tasks Set, and how he performs them—namely the kind of hospitality shown the hero by his opponent. In many of the analogues where hospitality is given it is usually unpleasant: poor and skimpy food, and a very rough bed. Usually in those analogues the daughter, who is already in love with Jack, substitutes a good meal and a good bed, the latter often provided by her magic power. Before her father visits the hero in the morning to set his first task, she makes sure that the hero is back on the rough bed. There are two examples of this rough hospitality in our Newfoundland stories, and each, for different reasons, is worthy of comment.

In No. 9 the hero is made to sleep in a pool of water with only his head out. The girl substitutes a real bed, only putting him back in the pool in the morning. We have found only one other analogue to a similar watery bed: in an Irish version in Curtin, *Myths*, pp. 40-44, the giant puts the king's son to bed in a deep tank of water, expecting him to drown. From this situation the giant's daughter removes him on each of three nights, giving him first a good meal and then a good bed, but returning him to the tank when she hears her father stirring at daybreak.

Even more unusual is the kind of hospitality provided in No. 12, a tale in which the young man gets no help from the Head Card Player's daughter. On the first night he is put to bed with the pigs and gets pig food. On the second night he sleeps with the hens and gets food like theirs. On the third night he is put to bed with a woman; we are not told what food he gets that night. Each morning he is taunted and asked how he liked his bed. The first two times he replies that he found it acceptable. On the third morning, however, he says, "Not very good, sir. I wasn't in bed very long after SHE got there." This unexpected response is meant to startle his host and would probably draw uproarious laughter from the storyteller's audience. We do not recall finding any analogues to this peculiar hospitality sequence.

A major part of our story, following Christiansen's list, is C.—The Tasks and how they are performed. Usually there are three tasks (only two in No. 8), one given each day, and each must be completed on the day it is proposed: the penalty for failure is death. Only one of the tasks is found in all six of the Newfoundland tales, the emptying of a huge barn or stable that has not been cleaned for a long period, sometimes given as a hundred years. In two versions, Nos. 9 and 10, this is the full task; in the others there is the additional requirement that he find a long-lost small object: a ring in Nos. 7 and 12, a needle or a darning needle in Nos. 8 and 11.

In Greek mythology, when Hercules was faced with a similar problem, the cleansing of the Augean stables, he accomplished it by an engineering feat: he turned the course of a river so that it ran through the stables (Rose, *Handbook*, p. 213). Our hero is not given this option: he must do the job with a shovel or a stable fork. In some versions the problem is doubled in that for each forkful he throws out of the stable, another comes in. Usually, after a morning of futile work, our hero gives up; sometimes he most unheroically sits down and weeps. He is unwilling even to eat the meal brought to him by the girl who loves him. She persuades him to eat, and after the meal, in three versions, Nos. 8, 9, and 10, either the barn has already been cleared, or he is then imbued with magic strength and finishes the job. In the other three the girl provides him with a magical tool, described variously as a little white hand shovel, a rusty fork, or a gold shovel, with which the task is completed easily.

One of the other tasks set, to fill a huge bed tick or a feather bed with feathers from birds on the wing, is found only in Nos. 9 and 10. In both, after an unsuccessful morning, he despairs. In No. 9, while he is eating the meal his girl brings him, the bed tick is filled with feathers. In No. 10, after eating he develops the magical speed necessary to complete the task. His task, however, seems somewhat easier than the common Irish version of not only obtaining the feathers from many kinds of flying birds, but also of thatching a stable or other building or building a bridge with them (Christiansen, *Béal.* 1, p. 110; Christiansen, *Studies,* pp. 98, 103). The thatching of a castle with feathers is also found in Buchan's tale from Aberdeenshire (Buchan, *Tales,* pp. 40-47).

Another task, again found in only two recensions, is to catch and tame a wild animal. It is an unbroken wild horse in No. 11, and a wild goat in No. 12. About the latter we should note that in No. 13, another telling of the tale by the same storyteller, he shifted his description in the middle of the story and calls the goat a horse. At any rate, in No. 9 the girl gives him an old bridle and saddle and the horse is then easily caught and becomes tractable. In No. 12 he is given a gold saddle and with it the goat becomes controllable. It is worth observing that here we have different conceptions of how a magic object should look. The storyteller of No. 12, which has the gold saddle, is the one who in the first task had the girl provide a magical gold shovel to clean the stable. The old bridle and saddle in No. 9 are paralleled by the rusty fork used to clean the barn in No. 11.

One set of tasks found only in No. 7 is the magical hiding game in which Greensleeves and Jack hide from each other in turn. Thanks to daughter Ann's help Jack is successful both in hiding from Greensleeves once and in finding Greensleeves twice. This hiding game is a version of AT329, "Hiding from the Devil," and analogues to it are listed below in a separate section. While AT329 is not found too often in combination with AT313, at least a half dozen reports of the combination are listed in *Irish Types* and J. F. Campbell published a version with the two Types that was secured in Argyllshire.

The last task we shall discuss, and the most dramatic, is found in all the Newfoundland recensions of this story except No. 7. Of all the tasks it is probably the one that has the widest distribution, being found nearly everywhere that the tale is told, though of course with a fair amount of variation. The task is for the hero to secure a gold ring from the top of a high glass pole, or alternatively to bring down unbroken the eggs from the nest of a bird that has nested on top of a glass pole. It is a ring in Nos. 8-11, eggs in No. 12. Since the pole is too slippery for Jack to shinny up it, he gives up in despair. The solution, the girl tells him when she appears, is to make a ladder of bones from her body by hitting her on the head with a hammer or an ax. Our hero in horror refuses to do this, but she finally persuades him that it is essential. She warns him, however, that he must step on each rung of the ladder, both when climbing and descending it; otherwise, when she comes to life again she will have injuries. With this help our hero secures the ring from on top of the glass pole in Nos. 8-11, but he fails to step on one rung of the ladder of bones. As a result, when the girl returns to life, the little finger on one of her hands is crooked.

In No. 12 the problem has a different solution. The young man must cut off four fingers from the girl's hand, and these become branches on the glass pole which the man can climb to secure the bird's egg from the nest on top. Then the branches become fingers again and the man sets them back on the hand. Unfortunately he sets the little finger on crooked. Fortunately for the girl and her lover, in none of the stories does her father notice this bodily defect in the girl; otherwise he might have deduced from it how she had helped the hero, and the consequences would have been disastrous for both of them.

The crooked finger serves a useful identifying function in three of our stories, Nos. 8, 10, and 12. Having succeeded in all of the tests, our hero is to select which of the three daughters he wants to marry from the finger and hand each shows through a door. Naturally the crooked finger of his helper is the clue for his choice. In Nos. 9 and 11 the crooked finger is not utilized as a further element in the story.

Despite the fact that our hero has completed successfully all the tasks he was set, and ignoring whether he is the opponent's son-in-law or not, in all of the Newfoundland versions of the story the opponent decides to kill the hero that night, usually after the hero has fallen asleep. The enchantress daughter knows this and she and her lover take flight. A curious preliminary to this part of the story, D.—The Escape, is the tactic she adopts to delay her father's pursuit. In all versions except No. 12, she bakes a magical cake or cakes. Christiansen (*Studies*, p. 104) observes that "To cover their escape Irish stories generally make the Maiden bake three cakes, 'and put speech into them'. . . ." Our Newfoundland recensions show more variety. In No. 7, it is a big cake that sings two songs; in 8, four speaking cakes that respond when Jack is addressed; in 9, three talking cakes, each of which speaks in turn at the end of one, two, and three hours; in 10, a talking cake that replies for three hours; in 11, nine speaking cakes which answer for Jack in turn when he is addressed.

Meanwhile the couple take flight: by land in five versions and by sea in one. They go on horseback in four versions: on the mare that had figured in the hiding sequence in No. 7, on the best horse in Nos. 8, 9, and 10, and on the magically tamed goat in No. 12. Unexpectedly, in No. 11 they do not use the magically tamed horse, but take a vessel. When the father realizes he has been delayed by the speaking/singing cake(s), he pursues: wearing nine-league boots, in No. 7; on horseback, in Nos. 8 and 9; as a cloud, in No. 10; and on a pig, in No. 12. He does not follow them in No. 11, but instead sends a large female dog that is able to tow the vessel they are on back to the place from which it started.

The fugitives on the animal's back delay the pursuit by throwing out small objects which magically become major obstacles. In two stories a twig in No. 9 and a bag of seeds in No. 10 become by sympathetic magic a dense forest, while a bottle of water in both No. 9 and 10 becomes an ocean and also a glassen hill. In No. 8 a bottle of water also becomes a pond, but the second obstacle, an ax, becomes a forest, which is an exact reversal of the normal sympathetic magic seen in the two preceding stories since an ax is a tool used to cut forests. The obstacles in No. 7 are less easy to explain: froth from the horse becomes a concrete wall and wax from the horse's ear becomes a forest. We can only assume that whoever invented this obstacle, which we believe is unique, had observed the working and bubbling when concrete is being mixed and adapted it for the story. On the second obstacle: while wax would impede hearing just as a forest would impede travel, we offer this explanation only as a tentative suggestion. In all of the stories the pursuer must first return home for the tools to cut down the forest or break through the concrete wall. In No. 12, the liquid contents of an egg thrown out of a basket become a pond; the old man has to build a raft to cross it with his pig-steed. A second egg becomes a mountain; by sympathetic magic the roundness of the egg has the shape of a mountain. Here, most amusingly, the pursuer is frustrated because, with its short legs, the pig he is riding cannot run up the mountain to cross it.

Most unexpected of all is the device in No. 11 to forestall the powerful bitch sent after them that can tow the vessel backwards. The couple have taken with them the bitch's nine pups. They throw them out one at a time, and each time the dog carries the pup

105

back to shore for safety. By the time she reaches the vessel after the ninth pup is safe, the couple have landed on the other shore. Christiansen remarks (*Studies,* p. 104): "New, however, is the incident of the savage dogs which are sent in pursuit, which the hero and heroine stop by throwing back their own whelps." While we have not found versions in English which match Christiansen's description, there is a published County Cork version in Britten, *FLJ* 1 (1883), 322, in which the warlock sends an old, big bitch after the fleeing couple. They have taken the bitch's three pups with them, and throw them back one at a time. The bitch takes each pup back for safety and, when she has the third one, she refuses to take up the pursuit again for fear she would lose her pups. This is the closest parallel we have found to the escape in No. 11. We do not recall reading any other analogues in which the couple escape in a vessel.

Part E.—End: The Forgotten Bride, is not relevant to Nos. 7 and 10 because the story ends immediately with the couple getting married. The broken taboo, Jack the hero going home without the girl and, despite her warning against it, being kissed and forgetting her, occurs in the remaining tales. It is a child that kisses him in No. 8, a dog in Nos. 9, 11, and 12. How the girl reawakens his memory is handled in various ways.

In No. 12, like everyone else, she is asked to tell a story at the party which precedes her lover's wedding to another girl. She retells the story of how she had helped him with his tasks but now had been forsaken—and he grabs her. In No. 8, she has two hens and a rooster and is living in a little house. When Jack comes that way, she throws a crumb to the hen and the rooster pecks the hen. She reprimands the rooster, calling it a naughty bird and asking it if it does not remember how she helped with the tasks. Each time she reproaches the rooster it pecks the hen and, after she tells another element of the story, Jack's memory comes back and he kisses her. In No. 11, she takes a golden cock and a golden hen to a big "time" which Jack also attends. As in No. 8, each time she calls the golden cock a naughty bird and asks if it does not remember the individual services she had rendered him. Jack suddenly realizes who she is and says, "You're my wife." In No. 9, after the king's son has forgotten his wife, she becomes a servant in the household. Before the king's son is to be married, she is invited to bring in her golden hen and golden rooster, presumably to entertain the guests. As in Nos. 8 and 11, in the guise of repeated reprimands to the rooster for pecking the hen, she retells each event in which she had helped the king's son. He regains his memory, then addresses the people present saying those were their joint experiences. He will take his old wife and the new one can go back home.

In many of the analogues of this tale (cf. Christiansen, *Studies,* p. 86) it is not the girl but the hen which has the magical power of speech and who reprimands the rooster, repeating each time the succeeding details of the story. This magical element is not found in any of the Newfoundland recensions.

From the earliest years of our transcribing, analyzing, and annotating this group of stories we had been intrigued by the titles "The Green Man of Eggum" and "Greensleeves," each of which is also the name of a protagonist in a version of the story. Was there a relationship between these names and that of "The Green Knight" in the well-known English medieval poem, "Sir Gawain and the Green Knight," or with the many English inns called "The Green Man" and the traditions that lie behind this concept? We were, of course, familiar with Hamish Henderson's 1958 article, "The Green Man of Knowledge," and knew it presented a version of AT313, together with an excellent discussion.

Like everyone else (Henderson, p. 78) we knew that green was a color associated with the fairies. We knew that the word "knowledge" in the title of Henderson's tale can also mean magical power, sorcery, or "enchantment, spell, incantation"; but what, if anything, did *Eggum* mean? We turned for help to the Department of Irish Folklore, University College, Dublin, inquiring if there was any word in Irish that sounded like *Eggum*, which could mean something like magical power.

On 27 November 1979, Ms. Ríonach Uí Ógáin, of the Department of Irish Folklore wrote:

> With reference to your inquiry regarding AT313 *The Green Man of Egham (Hegum)*, there is to my knowledge no word in Irish that sounds like Egham (Hegum) and means magical power or sorcery.

> I have consulted the list of titles for Irish versions of AT313, here in the Department and none of the titles suggest Egham (Hegum). I enclose a list of some of the titles which are found for AT313. Included are titles which contain the word Green/Grey or an indication of the man's origin.

We have rearranged this useful list and omitted the archive manuscript reference numbers. To explain the "grey" in some of the titles it will help if we cite Henderson. He remarks: "In Gaelic, the adjective *glas* can mean either 'green' or 'gray'; this may explain the plethora of 'gray men' in Irish-English versions of 313. . . ." (Henderson, p. 72).

Here is the list:

> The Green Man of Knowledge (Co. Mayo);
> The Green Man of Wisdom's Castle (Co. Kerry);
> The Green Man's House in No Man's Place (Co. Tipperary);
> The Grey Man from the Green Island (Co. Leitrim);
> The King of Grey Norris (Co. Limerick);
> Old Grey Norris and Seán the King's Son (Co. Kerry);
> The Grey Man and the King (Co. Longford);
> The King of the Grey Beard (Co. Waterford);
> An Green Knight (text in Irish) (Co. Kerry);
> Royal John and the Green Yarrow (Co. Roscommon);
> The Green House of Ivy (Co. Kerry);
> The Green Coat of Ivy (Co. Clare);
> The Coat of Green Ivy (text in Irish) (Co. Clare);
> Fair Lady Green Leaf (Co. Westmeath);
> Green Leaf (Co. Monaghan);
> Green Leaf (Co. Clare).

As a convenience for researchers we note here all the other grey/green titles we have given in brackets in the published analogues for England, Wales, Scotland, and Ireland below:

"Daughter Greengown" (Gypsy, Nottinghamshire);
"The Green Man of No Man's Land" (Gypsy, Wales);
"Green Sleeves" (Aberdeenshire);
"The Green Man of Knowledge" (Aberdeenshire);
"Green Man of Speech" (Barra);
"Grey Norris from Warland" (Co. Cork);
"The Queen of the Green Leaf" (Co. Kerry);
"The Plover Green Bawn" (Co. Clare).

However, the enigma of the word *Eggum* remains unsolved and our very tentative etymological suggestions in the linguistic notes to No. 8 can do no more than hint at some possible avenues for further exploration.

Studies and Notes

Lang, "A Far-Travelled Tale," *Custom and Myth,* pp. 87-102; Clouston, *Popular Tales,* 2, pp. 96-98, note, "Sending One to an Older and the Oldest Person"; Newell, "Lady Featherflight: An Inedited Folk-Tale," in: Jacobs and Nutt, *Second Congress,* pp. 40-66, the tale is rpt. with the discussion summarized in Newell, *JAF* 6 (1893), 54-62; Bolte and Polívka, 1, pp. 498-503, 2, pp. 516-27; Thompson, *European,* pp. 366-82; Penzer, *Ocean,* 8, pp. 213-34, Appendix I: "The 'Swan-Maiden' Motif"; Christiansen, "A Gaelic Fairytale in Norway," *Béal.* 1 (1927-28), 107-14; Rose, *Handbook,* pp. 202-3; Aarne, *Die Magische Flucht, FFC* no. 92; Chase, *Jack,* p. 198, no. 15, notes; Parsons, *Antilles,* 3, p. 153, no. 172, headnote; Thompson, *The Folktale,* pp. 88-90, 280; Espinosa, *CPE,* 2, pp. 470-82; von Sydow, *Papers,* pp. 192-93, 210-12; Randolph, *Daughter,* pp. 169-70, notes; Roberts, *South,* pp. 216-17, no. 8, notes; Graves, *Myths,* 2, pp. 236-40, chap. 152; Dorson, *Folktales,* p. 231, note 153; Delarue, *Catalogue,* 1, pp. 203-7, 234-41; H. Henderson, "The Green Man of Knowledge," *Scottish Studies* 2 (1958), 47-85; Christiansen, *Studies,* pp. 81-108, 242-43; Jackson, *Popular Tale,* pp. 9-13, 56-57, 73; Baughman, *Index,* Types 313, 313A, 313C, p. 7; Robe, *Index,* Type 313, pp. 51-55; El-Shamy, *Folktales,* pp. 251-54, no. 8, notes.

Canada

Fauset, *Folklore,* pp. 7-9, no. 4 (313A), p. 9, no. 4, variant (313A, with 327), 2 versions, black (Nova Scotia).

Parsons, *JAF* 38 (1925), 105-8, no. 37 (313A), Micmac Indian (Nova Scotia).

Creighton and Ives, *Folktales,* pp. 21-28, no. 2 (313A) (New Brunswick).

Jones, *JAF* 29 (1916), 386, no. 44 (313A), Ojibwa Indian (Ontario).

Hallowell, *JAF* 52 (1939), 155-61, no. 1a (313C), pp. 161-67, no. 1b (313A, with cf. 304), 2 versions, Berens River Saulteaux Indian (Ontario).

Teit, *JAF* 50 (1937), 177-82, no. 4 (313A, with 563), Thompson Indian (British Columbia).

For other North American Indian references see Thompson, *European,* pp. 366-82, no. 6 (Canada and the United States).

Thomas, *Types,* cites 9 versions of AT313 from Newfoundland French tradition.

Lacourcière-Low, "Catalogue," cites 94 Francophone versions of AT313 from Canada: 28 (Acadia), 58 (Quebec), 8 (Ontario).

United States
   The Baughman *Type Index* gives more than a dozen references for the United States under Types 313, 313A, and 313C, most of which we have not repeated here. To these add:
Parsons, *Islands,* 1, pp. 142-60, nos. 52, 52a, 52b, 3 versions (all 313C), English trans. of Portuguese texts, Cape Verde Islands, black (Massachusetts).
Paredes, *Folktales,* pp. 78-88, no. 30 (313C), Spanish tradition, in English, learned in Guanajuato, Mexico (Indiana).
Cf. Neely and Spargo, pp. 121-23, no. 81 (313, Ib, IId, with cf. 332; no flight), learned from an Irish immigrant (Illinois).
Dorson, *Folktales,* pp. 189-91 (313A), and p. 231, n. 153, black (Michigan), and rpt. in Dorson, *American,* pp. 268-71, no. 142.
Cf. Hoogasian-Villa, *Tales,* pp. 119-24, no. 8 (313A), Armenian tradition, in English trans. (Michigan).
Skinner, *JAF* 26 (1913), 64-72, no. 1 (313, I, II, with cf. 566; no flight), Menominee Indian (Wisconsin).
Chase, *Jack,* pp. 135-50, no. 15 (313C), and p. 198, notes (Virginia).
Perdue, *Devil,* pp. 28-38, no. 6A (313C), pp. 39-44, no. 6B (313A), pp. 45-50, no. 6C (313A), 3 versions (Virginia).
Cf. Parsons, *Sea Islands,* pp. 52-53, no. 37, 2 versions (313, II) [both lack magic flight], black (South Carolina).
Johnson, *Culture,* pp. 150-51, no. 14 (313A), black (South Carolina).
Hurston, *Mules,* pp. 70-77 (313A), black (Florida).
Cf. Fortier, *Folk-Tales,* pp. 68-75, no. 19 (313A), French text with English trans., black (Louisiana).
Saucier, *Folk Tales,* pp. 24-28, no. 3 (313C), pp. 61-65, no. 19 (313C), 2 versions, French tradition, in English trans. (Louisiana).
Roberts, *Greasybeard,* pp. 61-64, no. 13 (313A), pp. 65-68, no. 14 (313C), pp. 68-72, no. 15 (313C), pp. 99-105, no. 23 (313A, with 563, 302), 4 versions (Kentucky).
Carrière, *Tales,* pp. 80-83, no. 15 (313A), French text with English summary (Missouri).
Espinosa, *Folk-Tales,* p. 194, no. 14 (313C), English summary of Spanish text (New Mexico), English resumé in Espinosa, *Folklore,* p. 183.
Rael, *Cuentos,* p. 670, no. 149 (313C), pp. 670-71, no. 150 (313C), pp. 672-73, no. 152 (cf. 554, with 313C), 3 versions, English summaries of Spanish texts (New Mexico).
Weigle, *Two Guadalupes,* pp. 68-71 (313C), Spanish tradition, in English (New Mexico).
Rael, *Cuentos,* pp. 665-66, no. 144 (313C), pp. 666-67, no. 145 (313C), pp. 667-68, no. 147 (313C), pp. 668-69, no. 148 (313C), 4 versions, English summaries of Spanish texts (Colorado), see Robe, *Index,* for other Colorado versions in Rael.
See Robe, *Index,* Type 313, for additional Hispanic American references.
Lacourcière-Low, "Catalogue," cites 9 Francophone versions of AT313 from the United States: 4 (New England), 4 (Louisiana), 1 (Missouri).

Mexico
Aiken, *PTFS* 12 (1935), 61-66 (313C) (Mexico), and rpt. in Aiken, *Folktales,* pp. 66-71.
Mason, *JAF* 25 (1912), 196-98, no. 4 (400, with 313C), Tepecano Indian (Jalisco).
Mason and Espinosa, *JAF* 27 (1914), 207-8, no. 12 (cf. 313C), English summary of Spanish text, Tepecano Indian (Jalisco).

Wheeler, *Tales,* pp. 295-302, no. 107 (cf. 400, with 1551*A, cf. 313C), pp. 302-7, no. 108 (313A), pp. 307-10, no. 109 (313A), pp. 310-14, no. 110 (313C), 4 versions, Spanish texts with English abstracts (Jalisco).

Cf. Parsons, *JAF* 45 (1932), 312-13, no. 18 (313, I, II; no magic flight), Spanish tradition, in English trans. (Oaxaca).

See Robe, *Index,* Type 313, for further Mexican references.

The Caribbean, Central and South America

Edwards, *Stories,* pp. 99-100, no. 38 (313C), black (Bahamas).

Parsons, *Andros,* pp. 54-60, no. 27 (313C), 2 versions, black (Bahamas).

Cf. Parsons, *Andros,* pp. 60-61 (313, II, with 1115; no flight), black (Bahamas).

Parsons, *JAF* 41 (1928), 490-92, no. 6 (313A), pp. 506-7, no. 27 (313A), 2 versions, black (Bahamas).

Lewis, *Journal,* pp. 254-58 (313A), black (Jamaica), and rpt. in Wake, *FLJ* 1 (1883), 284-87, and again rpt. in Abrahams and Szwed, *After Africa,* pp. 115-18.

Beckwith, *Stories,* pp. 135-39, no. 105 (313C), black (Jamaica).

Parsons, *Antilles,* 2, pp. 461-64, no. 4 (313A), black (St. Vincent), 2, pp. 439-41, no. 30 (313C), black (St. Croix), 2, pp. 380-82, no. 5 (313C), black (St. Eustatius), 2, pp. 201-3, no. 109 (313C), black (Guadeloupe), 4 versions.

Cf. Parsons, *Antilles,* 1, pp. 105-8, no. 7 (313, I, II; no flight), black (St. Vincent, Windward Islands).

Parsons, *JAF* 38 (1925), 275 (313A), black (Barbados).

See Parsons, *Antilles,* 3, pp. 153-64, no. 172, for English summaries of 5 English texts (given above) and of 18 French texts from many island locations, black (Lesser Antilles), and see p. 153, headnote to no. 172, for nearly worldwide references.

See Robe, *Index,* Type 313, for references from Panama.

See Hansen, *Types,* Types 313A and 313C, for references to versions from Cuba, the Dominican Republic, Puerto Rico, Argentina, Chile, Venezuela, and Uruguay.

See also Herskovits, *Folk-lore,* pp. 326-31, no. 103 (313A), pp. 332-41, no. 104 (313A), 2 versions, "Taki-taki" texts with English trans., black (Surinam).

England

Briggs, *Dictionary,* A1, pp. 202-3 (313C) [Daughter Greengown], summary from *Thompson Notebooks,* Gypsy (Nottingham), A1, p. 161 (cf. 313, with cf. 315), summary from *Thompson Notebooks,* Gypsy (Lancashire), 2 versions.

Wales

Sampson and Yates, *Folk Tales,* pp. 33-36 (313C), English trans. from Romany, Gypsy (Wales), and rpt. in Yates, *Book,* pp. 11-14, no. 1, and rpt. in summary from Yates in Briggs, *Dictionary,* A1, pp. 376-77.

Cf. Sampson and Yates, *Folk Tales,* pp. 17-23 (313, I, II; no flight) [The Green Man of No Man's Land], English trans. from Romany, Gypsy (Wales), and see Groome, *Folk-Tales,* pp. 254-55, no. 62, for same title and plot, but somewhat different phrasing.

Scotland

Buchan, *Tales,* pp. 40-47 (313C) [Green Sleeves] (Aberdeenshire), and rpt. in summary in Briggs, *Dictionary,* A1, pp. 296-97.

Henderson, *Scottish Studies* 2 (1958), 47-61 (313C) [The Green Man of Knowledge], transcribed from recording, with discussion, Scottish traveller (Aberdeenshire), transcribed text rpt. in MacDonald and Bruford, *Tales,* pp. 18-27, no. 12, and again in Bruford, *Green Man,* pp. 11-27, 104-5, notes, and again rpt. in a long summary in Briggs, *Dictionary,* A1, pp. 290-95.

Cf. Douglas, *King,* pp. 119-21 (313, I, with 817*), Scottish traveller (Aberdeenshire).

Cf. Lang, *FL* 1 (1890), 292-95 (cf. 313C; lacks magic flight) (Morayshire), and adapted with changes in Jacobs, *English,* pp. 33-39, no. 7, and rpt. from Lang in Briggs, *Dictionary,* A1, pp. 424-26.

Cf. Briggs, *Dictionary,* A1, pp. 160-61 (cf. 313, with 1 motif of 1640, III), School of Scottish Studies recording by Hamish Henderson, summary of transcription, Scottish traveller (Perthshire).

Cf. Briggs, *Dictionary,* A1, pp. 565-69, transcription of recording by Hamish Henderson, School of Scottish Studies, dialect modified, Scottish traveller (Perthshire).

Campbell, *Popular Tales,* 1, pp. 25-47, no. 2 (313B and C, with cf. 212, 537), Gaelic text and English trans. (Argyllshire), and see pp. 47-62, for discussion and English summaries of 7 other Gaelic versions from various parts of the Highlands.

MacInnes, *Tales,* pp. 2-31, no. 1 (313C), Gaelic text and English trans. (Argyllshire).

Cf. MacDougall, *Tales,* pp. 145-86, no. 7 (313C, with hero tale), Gaelic text and English trans. (Argyllshire).

Cf. Briggs, *Dictionary,* A1, pp. 483-84 (cf. 313A), School of Scottish Studies recording by Hamish Henderson, summary of transcription, Scottish traveller (Argyllshire).

Henderson, *Scottish Studies* 2 (1958), 71 (313C) [Green Man of Speech], English summary of Scottish Gaelic text (Barra).

Ireland

The tale is well known in Ireland. See:

Curtin, *Myths,* pp. 32-49 (313C) (Ireland).

Curtin, *Folk-Tales,* pp. 25-34, no. 3 (313C) (Ireland).

Kelly, *Custom,* pp. 20-28 (313C) (Ireland).

For Ulster see:

MacManus, *Book,* pp. 251-84 (313A) (Co. Donegal).

Cf. MacManus, *Corners,* pp. 259-81 (313, I) (Co. Donegal).

MacManus, *Heroes,* pp. 15-36 (cf. 313; lacks magic flight), pp. 71-85 (313A), 2 versions (Co. Donegal).

MacAirt, *Béal.* 19 (1949), 53-63, no. 6 (313, I, III, with 314, 329) (Co. Tyrone).

For Leinster see:

Kennedy, *Stories,* pp. 56-63 (313C) (Co. Wexford).

Kavanagh, *Béal.* 2 (1929-30), 19-22, no. 6 (313A) (Co. Kilkenny).

For Munster see:

Britten, *FLJ* 1 (1883), 316-24 (313C) [Grey Norris from Warland] (Co. Cork).

O'Faolain, *Children,* pp. 147-56 (313C), composite text, trans. from Gaelic, but ending from Curtin, *Folk-Tales* (Co. Cork).

Ní Chróinín, *Béal.* 3 (1931-32), 31-35 (313C, with cf. 222) (Co. Cork).

Ó Floinn, *Béal.* 5 (1935), 138, no. 3 (313C), English summary of Irish text (Co. Cork).

Murphy, *Tales,* pp. 48-57 (313C) (Co. Cork).

Ó Cróinín, *Béal.* 35-36 (1967-68), 351-52, no. 3 (313C, with cf. 222), English summary of Irish text (Co. Cork).

Ó Duilearga, *Béal.* 29 (1961), 143, no. 1 (313C) [The Queen of the Green Leaf], English summary of Irish text (Co. Kerry).

Ó Duilearga, *Book,* pp. 50-69, no. 14 (313C) (Co. Kerry).

Ó Duilearga, *Béal.* 32 (1964), 43-49 (313C) [The Plover Green Bawn] (Co. Clare).

For Connacht see:

Gregory, *Poets,* pp. 153-60 (313C), pp. 160-63 (313C), 2 versions (Co. Galway).

Curtin, *Hero-Tales,* pp. 163-81 (313A) (Co. Galway).

Cf. O'Faolain, *Children,* pp. 116-34 (313, I, with cf. 531, 329, 302; no flight), trans. from Gaelic (Co. Galway).

Graves, *Fairy Book,* pp. 182-200 (313A), trans. from Irish by Douglas Hyde (Co. Mayo).

McManus, *FL* 26 (1915), 191-95 (313C, with 302) (Co. Mayo).

Ó Moghráin, *Béal.* 8 (1938), 224-25 (313C, with 302), brief English summary of Irish text (Co. Mayo).

Carleton, *Traits,* 1, pp. 30-66 (313C), literary (Ireland).

Irish Types, Type 313, 644 versions.

Continental Europe and the Near East

Cf. Grimm no. 56, "Sweetheart Roland," Grimm-Hunt, 1, pp. 224-27, no. 56 (cf. 313C, with 327B, cf. 592) (Germany), and for other trans. see Grimm-Magoun, pp. 207-10, no. 56, and Grimm-Zipes, pp. 212-15, no. 56.

Grimm no. 113, "The Two Kings' Children," Grimm-Hunt, 2, pp. 108-16, no. 113 (313C) (Germany), and for other trans. see Grimm-Magoun, pp. 410-17, no. 113, and Grimm-Zipes, pp. 408-14, no. 113.

Dasent, *Popular Tales,* pp. 137-51, no. 11 (313C) (Norway).

Christiansen, *Folktales,* pp. 213-28, no. 78 (313C) (Norway).

Hodne, *Types,* AT313, 62 versions (Norway).

Grundtvig, *Fairy Tales,* pp. 93-100 (313A) (Denmark).

Bødker, *European,* pp. 70-77 (313C) (Denmark).

Thorpe, *Yule-Tide,* pp. 192-204, no. 1 (313C), pp. 205-21, no. 2 (313C), 2 versions, also pp. 221-26, 5 abbreviated versions, plus a 6th in considerable detail (Sweden).

Claudel, *SFQ* 9 (1945), 196-99 (313) (France).

Delarue, *Borzoi Book,* pp. 10-19, no. 2 (313C) (France).

Massignon, *Folktales,* pp. 23-29, no. 6 (313C), pp. 54-60, no. 12 (313C), 2 versions (France).

Webster, *Legends,* pp. 120-30 (313C, with cf. 1730) (Basque).

Consiglieri Pedroso, *Folk-Tales,* pp. 14-20 (313C), cf. pp. 53-59 (313A, with 884A), 2 versions (Portugal).

Dane, *Once,* pp. 105-63 (313C) (Majorca).

Crane, *Popular Tales,* pp. 72-77 (313C), and pp. 343-44, n. 25 (Italy).

Busk, *Legends,* pp. 4-15 (313C, with cf. 310), and notes (Italy).

Calvino, *Folktales,* pp. 65-67, no. 22 (313A) (Italy).

Basile, *Pentamerone,* 1, pp. 179-92 (Day II, Diversion 7) (313C), with notes, and 1, pp. 285-91 (Day III, Diversion 9) (313C), with notes, 2 versions, literary (Italy).

Thorpe, *Yule-Tide,* pp. 441-52 (313C) (Germany).

Wolf, *Fairy Tales,* pp. 234-35 (313C) (Germany).

Bowman and Bianco, *Tales,* pp. 129-40 (313B, with 537) (Finland).

Groome, *Folk-Tales,* pp. 188-97, no. 50 (313A), Gypsy (Poland).

Coxwell, *Folk-Tales,* pp. 953-56, no. 2 (313C) (Poland).

Wratislaw, *60*, pp. 108-21, no. 17 (313C) (Poland), also trans. in Strickland, *Legends*, pp. 95-104.

Baudiš, *Folk Tales*, pp. 103-8 (313A) (Czech).

Fillmore, *Fairy Tales*, pp. 219-39 (313C) (Czechoslovakia).

Jones and Kropf, *Folk-Tales*, pp. 25-35, no. 7 (313A), pp. 188-95, no. 37 (313A), 2 versions (Hungary).

Ortutay, *Folk Tales*, pp. 332-38, no. 16 (313C) (Hungary).

Groome, *Folk-Tales*, pp. 124-28, no. 34 (313C), Gypsy (Bukovina).

Wratislaw, *60*, pp. 278-83, no. 53 (313A, with 329) (Croatia).

Dawkins, *More*, pp. 55-58, no. 9 (313C) (Greece).

Cf. Rose, *Handbook*, pp. 202-3 (cf. 313) [Jason and Medea], literary (Greece).

Cf. Graves, *Myths*, 2, pp. 236-40, chap. 152 (cf. 313) [Jason and Medea], literary (Greece).

Megas, *Folktales*, pp. 42-46, no. 22 (313C, with 310) (Greece).

Kúnos, *44*, pp. 58-63 (313C) (Turkey).

Ralston, *Folk-Tales*, pp. 130-41 (313B and C) (Russia).

Curtin, *Myths and Folk-Tales*, pp. 249-70 (313B, with 222, 537) (Russia).

Hodgetts, *Tales*, pp. 291-308 (313C) (Russia).

Magnus, *Folk-Tales*, pp. 243-55 (313B, with 537) (Russia).

Coxwell, *Folk-Tales*, pp. 687-94, no. 3 (313C, with 537) (Russia).

Afanas'ev, *Fairy Tales*, pp. 427-37 (313C, with 537, 513) (Russia).

Cortes, *Folk Tales*, pp. 44-50 (White Russia).

Bilenko, *Folk Tales*, pp. 44-54 (313B and C, with 222, 537) (Ukraine).

India

Penzer, *Ocean*, 3, pp. 218-35, no. 53 (313A) [has 2 magic flight patterns, the first obstacles, the second transformations], literary (India).

For analyzed references to folktale versions, see Thompson and Roberts, *Types*, Type 313A.

Eastern Asia

Eberhard, *Folktales*, pp. 55-61, no. 27 (313A) (China).

Cf. Seki, *Folktales*, pp. 63-69, no. 23 (313, Ib, IIb,c, with cf. 400) (Japan).

The Philippines

Fansler, *Tales*, pp. 155-65, no. 17 (313C, with cf. 327, 301A), and pp. 165-71, notes.

Africa

Cf. Sibree, *FLJ* 1 (1883), 202-8 (313, I, II; no flight), Malagasy people (Madagascar).

Cf. Brownlee, *Lion*, pp. 121-31 (313, II; no flight), tribe not specified (South Africa).

Cf. Theal, *Folk-Lore*, pp. 78-88 (313) [has 2 magic flights: transformation and obstacle], Kaffir people (Cape Colony).

Addendum 1: Magic rejuvenation by shaving

In No. 7, making the three elderly brothers look many years younger after they are shaved can be classified under motif D1880, "Magic rejuvenation." So far as we are aware, No. 7 is the only English-language version of AT313 that includes this motif.

The closest narrative analogues to such rejuvenation that we have found occur in AT726*, "The Dream Visit." (See the AT index for the full plot summary of this Irish story). Only a few of the 224 versions of the tale listed in *Irish Types* are in English. Some, but not all, of the texts in this group include people's rejuvenation by shaving with a magic razor as a motif in the tale. Here is a summary of this element. An Irishman visiting Scandinavia is given the dangerous task of securing a razor (sometimes other equipment as well) from a fairy fort in Ireland and bringing it back to Scandinavia. He does this. The result of using this magical equipment is reported with some variations in the three County Kerry versions available to us in English.

In Curtin, *Tales,* pp. 102-7, he brings back a basin, towel, and razor, and shaves two old men and a hag. One man turns nineteen, the second eighteen, and the hag becomes a girl of sixteen. In the English translation from Irish in Ó Duilearga, *Book,* pp. 113-14, no. 22, there are an old man, his father, and his grandfather; the latter is being rocked in a cradle. When each of them has shaved himself with the razor the Irishman brought back from Ireland, the eldest appears to be not more than forty. In Murphy, *Tales,* pp. 96-102, an old woman and two old men use the magic comb and magic razor carried from Ireland, and they become twenty-five years old. The appropriate motif for these three versions is D1338, "Magic object rejuvenates." The *Motif-Index* has no reference to a magic razor under this motif. Although there is no suggestion in No. 7 that Jack's razor has magical power, the close resemblance to the similar magic motif in the Irish tale is worthy of comment.

Addendum 2: Other Versions of "The Flight"

International Parallels: Element III, "The Flight," is an important incident in AT313. Its presence is so much to be taken for granted in that tale that we have called attention to its absence from a given recension by the phrase: *lacks magic flight.* But that incident also has had a vigorous independent existence in many parts of the world. It is also widely found in combination with various quite different folk narratives. We thought it would be useful to scholars if we grouped together those versions of AT313, III, "The Flight," which exist outside AT313, "The Girl as Helper in the Hero's Flight."

In all analogues of AT313, III, the persons pursued know their lives are at stake if they are caught by their pursuers. They therefore strive to gain time either by delaying the pursuers or by deceiving them in some way. In most analogues the flight motif takes only one of three forms. In a few tales, however, two of the three forms of flight motif are used.

The first form of flight is realistic: delaying the pursuers by throwing before them some object or objects to distract them. In Greek myth Atlanta delays to pick up the apples of the Hesperides, while Medea delays her father's pursuit by flinging the dismembered body of her brother into the sea. In Norse legend Rolf Kraki strews gold and a precious ring. In American migratory legends a woman fleeing from a panther gains time by throwing off singly each article of her clothing; the panther stops to worry each one. Eventually the naked woman reaches the safety of a pioneer cabin where an armed man often shoots the panther. In both American and European migratory legends a man with a wagonload of meat saves himself from pursuing wolves by throwing out a large piece of meat whenever the wolves are too close; they stop to eat it before renewing the pursuit. Similarly in African tales food or some other item slows down a pursuing cannibal, or pack of dogs, or hyenas.

The second and perhaps most common form is the "magical obstacles" flight. In this, when the pursuers get too close, the individual or one of a fleeing couple (it is frequently either a couple or a group of people) throws out in succession some small objects, each of which magically produces a great obstacle: a twig or piece of wood becomes a vast impenetrable forest, a comb becomes a row of jagged mountains, a drop of water or an egg becomes a wide river or a large sea. Each of these obstacles delays the pursuing ogre or magician, who usually must return home each time to get the proper equipment to break through or overcome the barrier. In most of these stories the third barrier either completely frustrates the pursuer or has given the fleeing couple the time needed to reach safety. Obviously in these stories the principle of sympathetic magic operates, e.g., a drop of water becomes a sea.

A different kind of magic operates in the third form, the "transformation flight." In stories that have this pattern, the pursued individual transforms himself into another person or an object, or if it is a fleeing couple as in versions of AT313, the one with magical power transforms both members of the couple into paired objects that vary considerably but are always clearly related to each other: a lake with a duck swimming on it, a garden with an old man gardening, a church with a chandelier, or a church with a minister, or a bush or tree with one flower on it, and so on. The pursuer, coming up to these transformed beings, is disheartened and returns home, only to be told each time that the transformed beings or objects were the couple being sought.

Thompson has distinguished among the three patterns of flight by establishing three separate motifs in the *Motif-Index:* R231, "Obstacle flight—Atlanta type"; D672, "Obstacle flight"; and D671, "Transformation flight." In the notes below we have inserted in parenthesis: 313, III, followed for two flight patterns with either the designation "obstacle flight" or "transformation flight." For the third pattern, "Obstacle flight—Atlanta type," we thought it advisable to give details in brackets. Where we could easily determine an associated AT Type, we give the AT number in the parentheses preceding 313, III.

Studies and Notes

Ralston, *Folk-Tales,* pp. 151-53; Clouston, *Popular Tales,* 1, pp. 439-43; Cox, *Cinderella,* pp. 497-98, note 33; MacCulloch, *Childhood,* pp. 167-81; Boas, "Mythology and Folk-Tales," *JAF* 27 (1914), 386; Bolte and Polívka, 2, pp. 140-46, no. 79; Thompson, *European,* pp. 347-57, no. 4, pp. 366-82, no. 6; Beckwith, *Stories,* pp. 273-75, no. 86, notes; Pauli and Bolte, 1, pp. 302-3, no. 526, 2, p. 376, no. 526, notes; Penzer, *Ocean,* 3, pp. 236-39, "Note on the 'Magic Obstacles' Motif," also cites other references beyond those listed here; Munch, *Mythology,* p. 219; Rose, *Handbook,* pp. 250, 292; Thompson, *Tales,* pp. 333-34, note 205, "Obstacle flight," p. 334, note 205b, "Transformation flight (transformed fugitives)," p. 342, note 232, "Obstacle flight—Atlanta type"; Aarne, *Die magische Flucht, FFC* no. 92; Krohn, *Übersicht, FFC* no. 96, pp. 62-67; Elwin, *Folk-Tales,* pp. 152-53, Note 1, "The Magic Obstacles Motif"; Thompson, *The Folktale,* pp. 60, 439-40; Thompson, *Motif-Index,* D671, "Transformation flight," D672, "Obstacle flight," R231, "Obstacle flight—Atlanta type"; Graves, *Myths,* 1, p. 266, 2, p. 241; Christiansen, *Studies,* pp. 84-85, 89-90, 92, 97, 99-100, 104-5, 107.

Canada

Parsons, *JAF* 38 (1925), 60-62, no. 3 [woman throws singly two baby diapers and baby's cap into water to delay pursuing witches], Micmac Indian (Nova Scotia).

Fauset, *Folklore,* pp. 23-25, no. 11 (956B, with 313, III, obstacle flight), heard in Gaelic, black (Nova Scotia).

United States

Cf. Parsons, *Islands,* 1, pp. 121-25, no. 43 (cf. 551, with cf. 315A, 313, III, obstacle flight), pp. 125-31, no. 44 (303, with cf. 315A, 780, 313, III, obstacle flight), 2 versions, English trans. of Portuguese texts, Cape Verde Islands, black (Massachusetts).

Dorson, *Bloodstoppers,* pp. 93-95 (313, III, obstacle flight), French Canadian tradition, in English (Michigan).

Dorson, *Bloodstoppers,* pp. 135-37 (313, III, obstacle flight), Finnish tradition, in English (Michigan).

Cf. Fauset, *JAF* 41 (1928), 539-40, no. 20 (513A, with 313, III, obstacle flight), from Virginia, black (Pennsylvania).

Bacon and Parsons, *JAF* 35 (1922), 280-81, no. 36 (313, III, obstacle flight), black (Virginia).

Wright, *JAF* 54 (1941), 197-99 (cf. 315A, with 313, III, obstacle flight), Scotch colony (North Carolina).

Cf. Parsons, *Sea Islands,* pp. 45-49, nos. 32, 33, 34, pp. 51-52, no. 36, no. I, 4 versions (all with 313, III, obstacle flight), black (South Carolina).

Cf. Jones, *Myths,* pp. 82-88, no. 34 (313, III, obstacle flight), black (Georgia).

Claudel, *JAF* 58 (1945), 210-12, no. 2 (cf. 301B, with 313, III, transformation flight), Spanish tradition, in English (Louisiana).

Barbeau, *Narratives,* pp. 32-35, no. 26 (313, III, illusionary obstacle flight), Wyandot Indian (Oklahoma).

Parsons, *Tales,* pp. 64-70, no. 23 (cf. 1653, with 313, III, obstacle flight), pp. 81-83, no. 27 (313, III, obstacle flight), 2 versions, Taos Indian (New Mexico).

Espinosa, *Folk-Tales,* pp. 193-94, no. 13 (432, with 313, III, transformation flight), English summary of Spanish text (New Mexico).

Robe-Jameson, *Folktales,* pp. 65-66, no. 29 (400, with 313, III, obstacle flight), Spanish tradition, in English (New Mexico).

Weigle, *Two Guadalupes,* pp. 71-78 (cf. 465, with 400, 313, III, transformation flight), Spanish tradition, in English (New Mexico).

Spinden, *JAF* 21 (1908), 156-57, no. 17 (313, III, obstacle flight), Nez Percé Indian (Idaho).

For North American Indian references see Thompson, *European,* pp. 347-57, no. 4 (313, III, mostly with 314) (Canada and United States).

See Thompson, *Tales,* pp. 333-34, Note 205, p. 334, Note 205B, p. 342, Note 232. Thompson cites a large number of American Indian references, most of which we have not duplicated in our notes.

Mexico

Opler, *Myths and Legends,* pp. 66-68, no. IV A1 (400, with 313, III, transformation flight), Lipan Apache Indian (Mexico).

Parsons, *JAF* 45 (1932), 312, no. 17 (313, III, obstacle flight), Spanish tradition, in English trans. (Oaxaca).

The Caribbean and South America

Cf. Parsons, *Andros,* pp. 50-51, no. 26, I (313, III, transformation flight), pp. 52-53, no. 26, III (313, III, obstacle flight), pp. 53-54, no. 26, IV (313, III, obstacle flight), 3 versions, black (Bahamas).

Parsons, *JAF* 41 (1928), 504, no. 23 (1115, with 313, III, obstacle flight), black (Bahamas).

Cf. Herskovits, *Folk-Lore,* pp. 340-45, no. 105 (313, III, obstacle flight), "Taki-taki" text with English trans., black (Surinam, South America).

Scotland

Douglas, *King,* pp. 132-37 (554, with 313, III, obstacle flight), Scottish traveller (Dunbartonshire).

Williamson, *Thorn,* pp. 62-71 (cf. 511A, with 313, III, obstacle flight), Scottish traveller (Argyllshire).

Ireland

MacManus, *Stories,* pp. 97-131 (314, with 313, III, obstacle flight) (Co. Donegal).

Kennedy, *Fictions,* pp. 39-48 (301A, with 313, III, obstacle flight) (Co. Wexford).

Continental Europe and Asia

Grimm-Hunt, 1, pp. 200-202, no. 51 (313, III, transformation flight) (Germany). See Grimm-Magoun, pp. 185-87, no. 51, and Grimm-Zipes, pp. 189-92, no. 51, for other trans.

Grimm-Hunt, 1, p. 310, no. 79 (313, III, obstacle flight) (Germany). See Grimm-Magoun, p. 289, no. 79, and Grimm-Zipes, pp. 289-90, for other trans.

Grimm and Hansen, *Tales,* pp. 20-22 (cf. 310, with 313, III, obstacle flight) (Germany).

Cf. Dasent, *Popular Tales,* pp. 290-98, no. 41 (325, with 313, III, obstacle flight) (Norway).

Cf. Grundtvig, *Fairy Tales,* pp. 29-33 (cf. 811C*, with 313, III, obstacle flight) (Denmark).

Cf. Munch, *Mythology,* p. 219 (313, III) [Rolf Kraki strewed gold on ground and then a famous ring to delay pursuing Swedes], literary (Denmark).

Cf. Webster, *Legends,* pp. 111-20 (314, with 551, cf. 313, III, magic horse produces magical obstacles) (Basque).

Basile, *Pentamerone,* 1, pp. 49-55 (Day I, Diversion 5) (621, with 513A, 313, III, obstacle flight), with notes, literary (Italy).

Cf. Bowman and Bianco, *Tales,* pp. 147-60 (cf. 313, with cf. 315, 313, III, obstacle flight) (Finland).

Cf. Mijatovies, *Folk-Lore,* pp. 248-55 (725, with 313, III, obstacle flight) (Serbia), and rpt. in Petrovitch, *Hero Tales,* pp. 322-28, no. 17.

Geldart, *Folk-Lore,* pp. 154-73, no. 26 (725, with 314, 313, III, obstacle flight) (Greece).

Cf. Dawkins, *Modern,* pp. 7-13, no. 2 (450, with 313, III, obstacle flight) (Greece).

Rose, *Handbook,* p. 259 (313, III) [Hippomenes drops or throws singly 3 apples of the Hesperides to delay Atlanta in their race], literary (Greece).

Graves, *Myths,* 1, p. 266 (313, III) [3 golden apples delay Atlanta in race], literary (Greece).

Rose, *Handbook,* p. 292 (313, III) [Medea dismembers body of her brother, Apsyrtos, and flings them piecemeal into the sea to delay her father's pursuit of the Argo], literary (Greece).

Graves, *Myths,* 2, p. 241 (313, III) [dismembered body of Apsyrtus thrown piecemeal into sea to delay pursuit], literary (Greece).

Cf. Dawkins, *More,* pp. 1-4, no. 1 (450, with 313, III, obstacle flight) (Greece).

Kent, *Fairy Tales,* pp. 79-86 (cf. 441, with 425B, 313, III, transformation flight) (Turkey).

Ralston, *Folk-Tales,* pp. 148-52 (313, III, obstacle flight), with discussion (Russia).

Magnus, *Folk-Tales,* pp. 64-69 (313E*, with 313, III, obstacle flight) (Russia).

Dirr, *Folk-Tales,* pp. 29-36, no. 7 (cf. 460A, with 313, III, obstacle flight), Imeretian people (Caucasus).

Seklemian, *JAF* 10 (1897), 135-42 (315, with 313, III, obstacle flight) (Armenia).

Cf. Downing, *Folk-Tales,* pp. 157-67 (433, with 425, 313, III, transformation flight) (Armenia).

Surmelian, *Apples,* pp. 229-50, no. 24 (433, with 425, 313, III, transformation flight) (Armenia).

Coxwell, *Folk-Tales,* pp. 101-3, no. 3 (cf. 315A, with 313, III, obstacle flight), Yukaghir tribe (Northeast Siberia).

Bogoras, *Tales,* pp. 9-10, no. 1 (313, III, both obstacle flight and transformation flight), Yukaghir tribe (Siberia).

Penzer, *Ocean,* 9, pp. 151-52 (315A, with 313, III, obstacle flight), English trans., Pashai tribe (Afghanistan).

Knowles, *Folk-Tales,* pp. 209-10 (313, III) [throws biscuits to delay pursuing dogs] (Kashmir, India).

Elwin, *Folk-Tales,* pp. 147-50, no. 8 (cf. 462, with cf. 707, 302, 313, III, obstacle flight), pp. 197-202, no. 2 (462, with 313, III, obstacle flight), 2 versions (Mahakoshal, Central India).

Frere, *Days,* pp. 38-49, no. 4 (451, with 313, III, obstacle flight) (Mysore, India).

Parker, *Village,* 1, pp. 67-71, no. 5 (328, with 313, III, obstacle flight) (Ceylon).

Htin Aung, *Folk-Tales,* pp. 106-9, no. 12 (313, III, obstacle flight) (Burma).

Zŏng, *Folk Tales,* pp. 171-74, no. 74 (315A, with 313, III, obstacle flight) (Korea).

Seki, *Folktales,* pp. 47-51, no. 19 (313, III, obstacle flight) (Japan).

Mayer, *Guide,* pp. 102-4, no. 100 (313, III, obstacle flight) (Japan).

The Philippines

Fansler, *Tales,* pp. 279-80, no. 36 (cf. 327C, with 313, III, obstacle flight), also see pp. 280-83 (314, with 313, III, obstacle flight), summary of Pampangan metrical romance, literary.

Africa

Cf. Fuja, *Cowries,* pp. 44-49 (313, III) [images of escaping girl placed at intervals to delay pursuing monkeys], Yoruba tribe (Nigeria).

Cf. Nassau, *Animals,* pp. 68-76, no. 15 (313, III) [throwing out peanuts, then gourd seeds, finally gourd of water that turns into a river, delays pursuing leopard], Mpongwe tribe (Gabon).

Cf. Chatelain, *Folk-Tales,* pp. 96-101, no. 6 (313, III) [woman throws in turn a calabash of millet, one of sesamum, and one of Eleusine to delay pursuit of ogre husband], Ki-Mbundu text and English trans., Mbamba tribe (Angola).

Cf. Mbiti, *Stories,* pp. 186-91, no. 61 (313, III, obstacle flight), Akamba tribe (Kenya).

Cf. Sibree, *FLJ* 2 (1884), 161-66 (313, III) [delays pursuing mother by scattering rice, then Indian-corn, finally beans], Malagasy tribe (Madagascar).

Cf. Knappert, *Myths,* pp. 198-203, no. 9 (314, with 313, III, obstacle flight), Swahili people (East Coast of Africa).

Cf. Callaway, *Nursery,* pp. 21-22 (313, III, transformation flight), pp. 144-45 (313, III) [girl repeatedly scatters sesamum seed to delay pursuing cannibals], 2 versions, Zulu text and English trans., Zulu people (South Africa).

Bushnaq, *Folktales,* pp. 158-65 (cf. 400, with 313, III, obstacle flight), Arab tradition (Libya).

Cf. El-Shamy, *Folktales,* pp. 54-63, no. 8 (310, with 313, III, obstacle flight) (Egypt).

Cf. Finnegan, *Stories,* pp. 157-62 (313, III, obstacle flight), Limba tribe (Sierra Leone).

Cf. Barker and Sinclair, *Folk-Tales,* pp. 97-101, no. 18 (313, III) [40 bags of rice scattered on ground keep guardian cock from crowing, large number of cattle bones thrown singly delay pursuing dragon], pp. 123-28, no. 22 (313, III, obstacle flight), 2 versions (Gold Coast).

Cf. Rattray, *Folk-Tales,* pp. 52-55, no. 16 (313, III, obstacle flight), Ashanti text and English trans., Ashanti tribe (Gold Coast).

Cf. Herskovits, *JAF* 50 (1937), 88-91, no. 19 (313, III, obstacle flight), Pidgin English text, Ashanti tribe (Gold Coast).

Cf. Herskovits, *Narrative*, pp. 355-56, no. 92 (313, III, obstacle flight), Dahomey tribe (Dahomey).

Cf. Talbot, *Shadow*, pp. 247-54 (315A, with cf. 1115, 313, III, obstacle flight), Ekoi tribe (Nigeria).

Cf. Theal, *Folk-Lore*, pp. 40-47 (313, III) [boy repeatedly scatters roasted wild roots to delay pursuing cannibal], pp. 78-88 (313, III) [2 flights: first, fat on stones delays pursuing cannibals; second, obstacle flight], pp. 98, 100-101 (313, III, 2 transformation flights), 3 versions, Kaffir people (South Africa).

Cf. Stayt, *Bavenda*, pp. 349-51, no. 15 (313, III) [crushed insect skins delay pursuing hyenas], BaVenda tribe (Northern Transvaal, South Africa).

Cf. Brownlee, *Lion*, pp. 89-91 (313, III, obstacle flight), pp. 146-50 (313, III, obstacle flight), 2 versions (South Africa).

AT329. *Hiding from the Devil* (Tale No. 7).

International Parallels: Although this tale has been reported from Scandinavia and across Europe to Russia then down through Greece to Turkey, it appears to be only moderately popular both on that continent and in the Near East. While there are only single reports from Wales and Scotland, it is reasonably well known in Ireland.

Our Newfoundland text in Tale No. 7 is apparently the first English-language report from the Western Hemisphere. On the other hand, as Massignon points out, while only two versions have been collected in France, it seems better known in Franco-American tradition than in France itself. Similarly, as Pino-Saavedra notes, although the tale has not been reported from Spain, there are two Hispanic American versions from the United States and several more from Brazil, Argentina, and Chile.

Can the explanation for this situation be that the tale was originally more popular in the regions from which the French and Spanish settlers emigrated at the period when they left than it is in the same areas today? We know that the descendants of emigrants have frequently preserved the older folklore repertory their forebears carried with them better than it is retained in the old country.

Most of the analogues we give below fit the AT description of the tale in that only one person has to hide. But in some the game is more elaborate; see the description of Type 329 given in the *Irish Handbook,* p. 561: "A princess or her father sets suitors the task of hiding themselves three times without being discovered (or finding out where the other has hidden three times). . . ." We would qualify this description still further. Sometimes one of them hides three times and then it is the other's turn to do the same. Occasionally, they hide alternately though in the Newfoundland version the father hides twice and Jack only once.

In the analogues to Type 329 the versions in which one protagonist hides three times and then the other takes his turn at hiding are mostly in the Irish tradition, but also in one Scottish Gaelic text.

Studies and Notes

Bolte and Polívka, 3, pp. 365-69; *Irish Handbook,* p. 561, Type 329; Thompson, *The Folktale,* pp. 56-57, 280; Delarue, *Catalogue,* 1, pp. 344-45; Pino-Saavedra, *Folktales,* pp. 254-55, no. 10, notes; Massignon, *Folktales,* p. 285, no. 62, note.

United States

Rael, *Cuentos,* pp. 733-34, no. 261 (with 302), English abstract of Spanish text (New Mexico).

Rael, *Cuentos,* p. 732, no. 258, English abstract of Spanish text (Colorado).

Caribbean

Parsons, *Antilles* 3, pp. 289-90, no. 292B (with 513A), English abstract of French text (Guadeloupe, Leeward Islands).

South America

Pino-Saavedra, *Folktales,* pp. 50-53, no. 10, and pp. 254-55, no. 10, notes (Chile).

Wales

Sampson and Yates, *Folk Tales,* pp. 72-75 (with cf. 1527, cf. 313, III), Gypsy (Wales).

Scotland

McKay-Campbell, *Tales,* 2, pp. 190-214, no. 62 (with 301A), Gaelic text and English trans., collected from a man from the Isle of Skye (Glasgow).

Ireland

MacAirt, *Béal.* 19 (1949), 53-63, no. 6 (with 313, I, III, 314) (Co. Tyrone).

Gmelch and Kroup, *Road,* pp. 138-45 (with 303, 325, IV), Irish traveller (Co. Longford).

Ó Cróinín, *Béal.* 35-36 (1967-68), 353, no. 6 (with 302), English summary of Irish text (Co. Cork).

Curtin, *Folk-Tales,* pp. 14-24, no. 2 (with 550, 301A) (Co. Kerry), and retold in O'Faolain, *Sagas,* pp. 219-31, no. 5.

Ó Duilearga, *Béal.* 30 (1962), 16-21, no. 3 (with cf. 313) (Co. Clare).

Gregory, *Wonder Book,* pp. 153-55 (with cf. 531, I, III) (Co. Galway).

Irish Types, Type 329, 165 versions.

Continental Europe

Grimm no. 191, "The Sea-Hare," Grimm-Hunt 2, pp. 321-24, no. 191, and for other trans. see Grimm-Magoun, pp. 612-14, no. 191, and Grimm-Zipes, pp. 596-99, no. 191.

Cox, *Cinderella,* p. 447, no. 319 (with 511A, 530), English summary of text from Asbjørnsen and Moe (Norway).

Mulley, *FLR* 3 (1880-81), 214-25 (with 550), trans. from Svend Grundtvig collection (Denmark).

Massignon, *Folktales,* pp. 207-9, no. 62, and p. 285, no. 62, notes (France).

Ortutay, *Folktales,* pp. 286-91, no. 12 (Hungary).

Bain, *Folk Tales,* pp. 209-21 (Romania).

Wratislaw, *60,* pp. 278-83, no. 53 (with 313A) (Croatia).

Coxwell, *Folk-Tales,* pp. 705-12, no. 7, in verse (Russia).

Wardrop, *Folk Tales,* pp. 124-29, no. 4, Mingrelian tradition (Georgian S.S.R.).

Dirr, *Folk-Tales,* pp. 1-6, no. 1 (with 554) (Georgian S.S.R.).

8. THE GREEN MAN OF EGGUM

Freeman Bennett   AT313C
St. Pauls, Great Northern Peninsula   TC284 66-24
31 August 1966   Collectors: HH and JW

[*recorder off*]*** you know the...what they used to call "The Green Man of Eggum" one time. [*coughs*]

The Green Man of Eggum well he was a...he was a witch see like...they used to call...at one time they used to have the witches out around. Well now Jack _ he'd heard tell see o' the...the Green Man of Eggum. An' he said _ he was goin to look for un.

An' uh...ol' man said to un "Well" he said "you knows" he said "you'll never find the Green Man of Eggum."

"Well" he said "I don't know." He said "I...I'm goin to try."

So he started. An' he walked ALL day _ an' dark _ he seen a house. An' _ he went up an' he knocked to the door. A ol' feller come out an' he opened the door, oh well he was a...he was a fierce man, he...he looked bad to un. An'...he told un to come in. An' he went in. An' he said uh..."Where ya goin?"

He said "I'm goin" he said "to look" he said "for the Green Man of Eggum."

"Well" he said "you'll never find un. You'll never get there" _ * he said "I don't THINK." He said "But now" he said "I got a brother" he said uh..."lives" he said "he's a day's walk" he said "from me. Well now" he said uh..."HE might be able to tell ya something about un. (But) now" he said _ "he's a fierce man" he said "he is." He said uh..."'Tis hard to say what he'll do" he said "when you...when he sees ya." He said uh..."He might" he said uh..."he might" he said "kill ya. But" he said "I tell ya what I'll do." He said "I'm goin to...give ya a cake." He said "An' when you sees him comin" _ he said "you'll fire the cake at un." He said "An'...when he picks up the cake" he said "he'll know where the cake come from, well" he said "you'll be alright."

*talking in background

So very good. He got up next mornin _ an' he started. He give un the cake an' he started. An' dark _ he seen th' house. An' 'fore he got to the house _ he [*the second brother*] come outdoors an' he seen un comin. Well now he was goin to...he was goin to kill un right away. An' he wait till he got almost to un an' he fired the cake at un.

An' he picked up the cake. "Oh" he said "alright" he said "come on" he said "you was to my brother's" he said "last night."

He said "Yes."

/corn/

*tape speeded
up

Oh very good. Jack thought to hisself, well _ he'd be killed tonight for sure. So he went out. After he got out he start in at /barn/...barn an' 'cordin as he'd heave out one shovelful there'd be another one come in see? An' he *hove out twothree shovelfuls an' uh...as far...'cordin as he hove it out there'd be another one come in, well _ thought to hisself just as well for un to sit an' uh...let un kill un. So he sot***....[*recorder off*]

[*clears throat*] (Well) he _ sot down. He couldn't get out. He thought to hisself just as well for un to sit down an' uh...make up his mind to die.

He sot down an' he was sot down thinkin an' by an' by _ she come down _ with his dinner to un.

"Hello" she said "Jack" said "how ya gettin on?"

"Oh" he said "not very good." He said uh..."I can't get a shovel out" he said "as fast as I shovels out" he said "'twill come in again."

"(Well)" she said "have your dinner."

"No" he said "I don't [want] no dinner" he said uh..."Just as well not for me eat no dinner" he said uh..."I got to die tonight."

"Oh no" she said "eat your dinner" she said "an' after you gets your dinner eat this is..." she said uh..."you'll be alright."

So he eats his dinner _ an' _ she leaved an' when he got his dinner eat he got up an' he start shovellin ('em) uh...oh! 'Twas going out o' the barn just uh...faster an' uh...faster than it come IN there. An'...when he got it...by an' by he had the barn cleaned out an' the first thing he seen down the bottom was the needle. Picked up the needle an' he shoved un in his pocket.

He sot down. Now she said uh...told un not to come back till supper time. Sot down in the barn and _ by an' by ge[tti]n...gettin handy to suppertime _ shoved his hand in his pocket an' away he goes up to th' house. Went in.

"Hey!" he said _ "How ya get on" he said "Jack?"

"Huh!" Jack said "I got on alright" he said uh..."I was only a couple o' HOURS" he said "gettin that out."

He said "Ya get the needle?"

"Yes" Jack said "I got the needle" he said "there he is there."

"Ah!" he said "You got (to) thank me daughter Nan for that."

"The hell with your daughter Nan!" he said "I know nothing about your daughter Nan."

An'..."Well" he said "now Jack" _ he said uh..."tomorrow morning" he said "there's a glassen pole out there." He said "An' there's a ring" he said "right on the top of it." He said "An' if you can get up un" he said "an' get that ring" _ he said uh..."I'll save your life."

Jack thought to hisself well he wouldn't get THAT one for sure. An' _ the next morning he got up an' he had his breakfast an' he went out. An'...he couldn't get up the glassen pole. There's no...no way for a man to

124

get up a glassen pole. He tried to get up an' he get up a little piece an' he slip down and _ he couldn't get up. He keeped at it an' he couldn't get up an' he sot down. Said to hisself well he...he wouldn't get he for sure _ sure he wouldn't get the ring. So he sot down and _ he know...he...no use (to) try no more. "No use (to) try no more 'cause I won't get un."

Sot down an' by an' by dinner time _ out she comes _ with his dinner to un.

"Ah" she said "Jack, how you get on?"

"Ah" Jack said "not very good." He said "I can't get up the pole" he said "I never got" he said "a foot from the ground."

"Ah" said "Jack" she said "have your dinner."

"No" Jack said "I don't want no dinner." Said "I don't want no dinner" he said "I ant goina eat no dinner" he said "'cause _ I got to be killed tonight."

"Oh no" she said "Jack, eat your dinner." Jack _ sat down an' eats his dinner _ an' after he got his dinner eat _ she had a little hammer in her hand.

"Now" she said "Jack." She said "You take that hammer" she said "an' uh...an'...an' hit me in the head."

"Oh" Jack said "I won't do THAT."

"Oh yes" she said "you take th' hammer" she said "an' hit me in th' head."

"No" Jack said "I can't do that" he said "I sooner die meself" he said "than I kill you."

"No" she said "you take that hammer" she said "an' hit me in th' head" she said _ "an' there'll be a ladder" she said "right in the top o' that pole." She said "An' you'll get up" she said "an' get the...the ring off" she said "an' I'll be alright again."

So Jack took th' hammer an' he knocked her down. An' sure enough soon as he got her knocked down there was a ladder right to the top o' the pole an' Jack went up an' he got the ring. An' when he got down _ course _ she was stood up 'longside of un. Very good. Jack had the ring now.

Well now _ the bargain was if Jack could get the ring he was to marry his daughter see? One of his daughters. So -- Jack stayed there till handy round supper time an' he went in.

Said "How you get on Jack?"

"Oh alright" Jack said.

Said "You get the ring?"

"Yes" Jack said "I got un."

Said "Where's he to?"

"Here he is here" Jack said.

"Ah" he said "you got to thank my daughter Nan for that."

"To hell with your daughter Nan" he said "I don't know nothing about your daughter Nan."

"Well now" he said "Jack" -- he said "I promised" he said "you'll marry" he said "one of me daughters. An' _ now" he said "Jack" he said "I'm goina bore three holes" he said "in the door." He said "An' they got to shove out their fingers" he said "an' whatever one...'s finger you catches hold to" he said "that's the one" he said "you got to have."

Now Jack...I'm...kind o' before me story. She told Jack when he'd go up on the ladder _ "Be sure an' not to miss nar rung" see? 'Cause [if] he'd miss a rung _ well one of her fingers 'd be crooked see?

Well now when Jack got down _ he missed th'under rung see? An' when she got up her...her...her finger was crooked see?

"An' now" she said "Jack" _ she said uh..."I'll shove me crooked finger" she said "out through the hole" she said "an' you'll know 'tis me." She said "An' you can catch hold o' my finger."

"Yes." Very good. That's what Jack 'd do.

An'...[clears throat] so very good, he bored th' holes in the door an' Jack got outside _ an' they shoved their fingers out through, now she shoved her crooked finger out through _ an' Jack catched hold to her finger see? Well now he...that's the one Jack had to have.

Well now very good. Jack was goin to marry her, well now that night -- th' ol' feller uh...after he get to bed was goin to kill un see?

"Now" she said "Jack" _ she said "the ol' man" she said "is...is goina kill you tonight." She said "An' I'll tell you what I'll do, I'm goin to bake _ three cakes" she said. "An' I'm goin to put [one] on each /step/ o' the ladder. Four cakes" she said. "An' every one o' they cakes" she said "'ll speak." She said "An' when th' ol' man uh...he uh...by an' by in the night" she said "he'll ask ye" /she/ said "if /you/ 's asleep. Well now" she said uh..."the cake 'll speak.

Now" she said _ "after they goes to bed" she said "I'm goina get the best horse" she said "they got in the barn" _ she said "an' you an' me 'll go."

"Alright" Jack said.

So _ very good. She baked the cakes an' she put [them] on the step o' the ladder _ down on the step o' the ladder an'...they got ready an' _ she got the best horse they had out in the barn an' away they goes.

By an' by the ol' man said "Is ye asleep Jack?"

"No" he said "I'm not to sleep yet."

An' he said "He's not to sleep yet. No."

Ol' man stopped for about another hour _ an' (now) he said "(Is) ya 'sleep Jack?"

"No." Jack said "I'm not to sleep yet."

"Hah! He's not to sleep yet."

Stopped for about another hour, he said _ "Ya asleep Jack?"

"No" Jack said "I'm not to sleep yet."

/struck/ [i.e., ?strike (rung)]

/he/ /she/

126

An' he said "He's not to sleep yet." Said "He's not goin to sleep tonight I don't suppose."

Stopped another hour, he said "'Sleep Jack?"

"No." Jack said "I'm not to sleep yet." Now three hours, they was gettin a long way see with a smart horse. "(Well)" he said "he's not to sleep yet."

Stopped another hour. "Are ya asleep Jack?" No answer. "Yes" said "he's 'sleep." Jumped up to go upstairs _ to kill Jack. Jack was gone. "Oh" he said "Jack is gone! Jack..." get one of his horses. Get one of his horses an' a man an' start after un. Well now they started.

"Now" she said "Jack" she said "th' ol' man" she said "is comin." Said "Th' ol' man is comin." She said "An' uh...now" she said _ "you look" she said "in under the...the...horse's left yur [i.e., *ear*]" she said "an' you'll see a little bottle o' water." She said "An' you heave that bottle o' water" _ she said "an' there'll be a big pond" he said...she said "he'll have to go back" she said "an' get some boots" she said "'fore he can get across that pond." She said "An' that 'll leave us to be a long ways."

(Alright) the...by an' by _ she looked around an' she said "Th' ol' man is comin. Now" she said "Jack, heave the bottle o' water." Uh.../throwed/ the bottle o' water an' when he did there was a big pond see? Couldn't get across, well he come up to this big pond, well he...he had to go back. He had to go back an' he had to get some boots to...get across the pond. Well time he had THAT done, well now they was gettin a long ways. And...anyway he got the boots an' he got across the pond an' he started again. /cowed/

"Now" she said "Jack" she said "'twon't be long" she said "'fore the ol' man'll be comin again." She said "Now" she said _ "the...you look in under the...the...the saddle" she said "o' th' horse" she said "an' you'll find a axe." She said "An' you'll sling that axe" _ she said "an' there'll be a big forest." She said "He'll have to go back an' get men" she said "to...to clear a road" she said "to get through it. Well now" she said "by that time" she said "we'll be clear."

An' _ they went on an' by an' by she looked around she said "Yes" she said "Jack, he's comin." An' _ Jack...got th' axe out an' he slung un an' sure enough there was the biggest kind of a forest, you couldn't get through it at ALL. So he come up to the forest an' he had to go back. Well now _ time he had to go back, well he had to go back, well he said 'twas no good for un to go anyhow.

Well they...they went on then. An' _ well after a spell Jack got to his home, well now on their...on their way she said "Now" she said "Jack" _ she said _ "when you gets home" _ she said "don't..." she said "let none o' your people" she said "kiss ya." She said "'Cause if ya do" she said "they uh...you'll forget all about me." She said "You won't know nothing about me."

"Alright" Jack said, so -- when Jack got home he'd abeen gone so long see, oh well they was so glad to see Jack they was goin over to kiss un and...everything, well Jack wouldn't let none of 'em kiss un, well by an' by...one of his...sisters or brothers runned along an' they kissed un. Well Jack forgot all about her, she...he didn't know nothing about her at all see?

Well now she was there by herself _ a stranger, well now she didn't know WHAT to do see. So anyhow _ she got i[n]...a little...place there and she was livin in. She lived there for a couple or three months. An' she had...two hens. She had uh...two hens an'...an' a rooster see?

An' uh...Jack walked out one day. An' when he walked out _ she was out by the door. An' she hove out a crumb to the hen. An' the rooster runned along an' he picked the hen see?

An' she said "Ah" she said "you naughty bird!" She said "You can't mind the time" she said "I carried you over the glassen hill." An' Jack stopped see? Se...seemed like he could mind something about something.

By an' by she hove out another crumb. An' the rooster went along an' picked the hen again. "Ah" she said "you naughty bird" she said "you can't mind about the time" she said _ "you knocked me down" she said "an' got the ring off o' the glassen pole." God _ Jack stopped. He could mind all about her _ mind all about her. He went over. Went over then, took her hold around the neck an' give her a kiss an' _ when I leaved Jack an' she was livin the best kind an' had three or four children. Huh!
[*recorder off*]*** learned that story from me uncle _ Charl.

Duration: 19 min., 16 sec.
Source: Charles Benoit (uncle), St. Pauls, Great Northern Peninsula.
Location: The darkening sitting room of the teller's house in the late evening.
Audience: Interviewers.

Context, Style, and Language: (For context see notes to No. 4). As this was the first occasion on which we recorded Freeman Bennett we were less aware of his dramatizing of the plot through the use of gestures. However we vividly recall that at the point in the story where the youngest daughter pushes her crooked finger through the hole, Freeman sticks out his hand in front of him, with the extended little finger bent downwards to demonstrate what the girl is doing.

The title of this story poses a problem in that no exact parallels have been found which permit a definitive etymology of the final word. Consistently pronounced /'e:gəm/ by all those narrators whose versions were recorded for this collection, it is represented here in a spelling designed simply to reflect that pronunciation. At an early stage of our investigations it became clear that an etymology based on an actual place-name such as *Egham* could be ruled out, although possible connections with topographical features such as *island* (OE ēg, īeg, iggoð), and especially the dative plural form *egum*, suggested as the origin of the English placename *Eyam*, cannot be dismissed entirely since such parallel figures as the Green Knight in the medieval romance of *Gawain and the Grene Knight* may live in an almost inaccessible fastness (cf. *The Green Man's House in No Man's Place* from Tipperary where the fastness becomes otherworldly). It is also difficult to rule out etymologies from OE *ecg,* bearing in mind the Green Knight's fearsome ax, or even from OE *eggian* (to incite), especially since something of the fierce and threatening nature of such characters persists even in the modern recensions presented here. Perhaps the most plausible derivation, however, is to be sought in parallels from Britain and Ireland, and specifically in the Scottish and Irish versions of the tale in which the Green Man is characterized by certain mental, rather than physical, qualities. It seems likely that designation of this figure as *The Green Man of Knowledge*—a knowledge both natural and supernatural—may provide the most fruitful line of inquiry. An investigation of possible etymological roots for the current pronunciation of the word in Newfoundland led us to consult available dictionaries and glossaries in English, Scots, Irish, Welsh, and Cornish. The only linguistic form which offers a plausible linguistic source is the Irish *eagnaí* (wisdom). This possibility is corroborated by the existence of an Irish version of the tale called *The Green Man of Wisdom's Castle.* Etymologically, the development of *eagnaí* to /ˈeːgɔm/ seems reasonably straightforward: *eagnaí* /ˈeagnə/ > /ˈeagŋ/ > /ˈeːgɔn/ > /ˈeːgɔm/, on the assumption of the application of English sound changes to an exotic word, in which the final syllable of the original is reduced and the final unstressed nasal fronted to a bilabial, the lack of precise referent in the semantics contributing to the vagueness of the current pronunciation in Newfoundland. It is possible, then, that we have here the survival of an Irish word which remains embedded in a translation from the original, perhaps because of uncertainty regarding its precise meaning. It is also not impossible, of course, that a written or printed version may have generated a similar confusion, though the clear line of phonological development makes oral transmission more likely.

There are, of course, other obvious parallels between several of these versions of AT313 and the *Gawain* poem. For example, the hero is reluctant to start his search for the Green Man's house, and does not set off until the very last moment. Gawain similarly remained at court and delayed his journey until the last, and worst, moment, for by then it was winter and he had to endure the frost and cold. Although some scholars see the poem in terms of a fertility cycle, the versions of the story presented here suggest that the *Gawain* poem is written within a far more naturalistic convention. Gawain faced real frost and snow rather than having to climb a glass mountain and had no help from swan maidens. The adultery theme in *Gawain,* with the exchange of winnings, is also to be contrasted with the simple wooing of the ogre's daughter in these tales. In both the poem and the stories the woman is the more active agent in this. Perhaps the *Gawain* poet felt that his sophisticated audience would appreciate courtly amours rather than a simpler peasant wooing.

This is a smoothly told, well motivated, and detailed version of the tale, enlivened by such typical features of this teller's style as the tonal variation, especially heard in the vivid dialogue, the punctuation of the narrative with *(So/Oh) very good, (So) anyhow, by an' by,* and the rhetorical question *(you) see,* and of the dialogue with *he/she said.* This latter feature is again carried to extraordinary lengths, e.g., "'but' he said 'now' he said 'I'll tell ya what...what you'll do.' He said uh...'You'll get there' he said uh...'to this glassen hill' he said 'about uh...' he said 'about two or three hours' he said ''fore dark,'" in which hesitation forms often follow *he said*. This suggests that the reiteration of the phrase is a useful device to aid the teller in recalling and presenting the narrative. Short sentences, frequently elliptical, help to provide contrast with longer utterances and give the impression of crisp, economical, and speedy narration, e.g., *She dressed herself, They went on, He sot down, Went in, No answer. Jack was gone,* and the most effective example at the end of the tale when Jack's memory is restored: *God _ Jack stopped.* Here we also see one of several instances of the rhetorical mingling of direct and indirect speech in which the asseveration might equally well be transcribed as actually spoken by Jack, the storyteller's intonation implying this. The effectiveness of this device is redoubled by the rhetorical repetition of the crucial information in the following sentences which leads immediately to the reuniting of the lovers: "He could mind all about her _ mind all about her. He went over. Went over then. . ." Similar repetition is seen in the second brother's warning that Jack will never get to where the Green Man lives, in his invitation to Jack to come in, in the Green Man's greeting when Jack first knocks at his door, and in the girl's urgent warning that her father is coming after them: "'Now' she said 'Jack' she said 'th' ol' man' she said 'is comin.' Said 'Th' ol' man is comin.'" Individual words of importance to the plot or for stylistic contrast are highlighted by strong stress, their prominence giving cues to the audience to prompt their interpretation and/or response.

The elliptical style causes the loss of numerous function words, especially the definite article, heads of noun phrases, and pronominal subjects. Ambiguity also results from the failure to express or discriminate between the referents for some personal pronouns. There is a problem of transcription caused by the speeding up of the tape due to battery failure during the description of Jack shoveling out the barn. This section of the tale was transcribed by using a slower machine-speed, and apart from some slight overlap when the recording restarts there is no significant interruption of the narrative. The teller gets "before his story" at one point but again this does not materially affect the flow of the plot.

Jack is again characterized as nonchalant and almost offhand in his response to challenge or danger. He is prepared to take on even the most impossible task and the implication here is that one should at least attempt such a test, despite its apparently overwhelming difficulty. This exemplifies the principle of optimism in folk narrative and in other traditional genres, suggesting that if even the unpromising or disadvantaged hero is willing to attempt it, so should the listener, as it may be worthwhile and yield good results after all. In Newfoundland one can observe a similar pattern of behavior in that individuals are more than prepared to tackle difficult tasks, the accomplishment of which is the subject of a natural though understated pride in personal experience narratives and legends concerning such feats. Even a genre as apparently remote from reality as the Märchen may thus have functional relevance to everyday life and behavior.

As a footnote to the teller's skill in signaling the forward movement of the narrative, it is interesting to note that the passage of time is also marked by reference to meals. Jack and other characters are frequently said to eat breakfast, dinner, or a "lunch" in these tales, and this not only implies a time reference but may also be part of the characterization of Jack and his relationship with others, as is the case in this tale when the girl persuades the dejected Jack to eat his dinner. When he agrees to do so, he is immediately able to accomplish his task.

On the language side we find the diphthong /ou/ in *none,* the half-open front vowel in *catched,* the long close front vowel in *keeped,* /kiːpt/, the initial onglide /j/ in *yur* (ear [common in West Country English, see *EDD EAR*]), *set* (sit), *ant* (haven't/aint), aphesis in *'cordin, 'sleep,* loss of initial consonant in *'twill, 'twont,* loss of final consonant in *gi'* (give), elision of schwa in *th' only, th' under, th' axe, th' head, th' hammer* (the latter two also with typical loss of initial aspirate in the noun), and the lack of transitional /n/ in *a ol', a axe.* A specific problem of transcription is illustrated in "'I can do with ye' he said" in which the close front vowel in *ye* probably anticipates the vowel of the following word *he,* especially as the latter lacks the initial aspirate. One would normally expect the unstressed form of the second person pronoun *ya,* in that position. Dialectal vocabulary includes the archaic *glassen, pitches* (land/alight), *handy* (near), *nar* (any), *smart* (vigorous/in good health [see *DNE smart* a]), and *picked* (pecked [see *OED Pick* v.[1] I.1.b. Obsolete—last recorded in 1645]). The preposition is omitted before *dark,* which is used in the adverbial sense to mean "at dark, when it was dark," and before *course* (of course), while the normal Newfoundland use of *to* (at), in *knocked to the door, you was to my brother's,* and *where's he to,* is found, along with *into* (in), e.g., *we lost a needle into un.* The pronoun *it* is used with the plural referent *clothes, he* has the neuter referents *needle* and *ring,* and the third person plural pronoun object is omitted in "She baked the cakes an' she put [them] on the step." Present tense verb forms include *you knows/sees, carries, comes, knocks, they pitches, I/he ant,* and *I don't think* (I don't think so)—a common usage in Newfoundland. Past tense forms are: *start, keeped, sot,* and there is also the past participle *abeen.* Additional double negatives are *don't want no dinner, won't/didn't know nothing.*

See also the notes to Nos. 4, 5, and 6.

Type and Motifs:
    AT313C. *The Girl as Helper in the Hero's Flight.*
G207. *Male witch.*
H1220. *Quests voluntarily undertaken.*
Cf. F150.1. *Way to otherworld hard to find.*
N825.2. *Old man helper.*
F151.0.1. *Hospitable host entertains (guides, advises) adventurer on way to otherworld.*
F571.2. *Sending to the older.*
H1235. *Succession of helpers on quest.*
F751. *Glass mountain.*
D361.1. *Swan Maiden.*
K1335. *Seduction (or wooing) by stealing clothes of bathing girl (swan maiden).*
D531. *Transformation by putting on skin.*
B552. *Man carried by bird.*

G465. *Ogre sets impossible tasks.*

H901. *Tasks imposed on pain of death.*

H1102.2. *Task: emptying in one day a barn filled with manure.*

G530.2. *Help from ogre's daughter.*

D1335.1. *Magic strength-giving food.*

H1114.1. *Task: securing three eggs [gold ring] from top of glass tower.*

Cf. F848.3. *Ladder of bones.*

Cf. E33. *Resuscitation with missing member.*

H331. *Suitor contests: bride offered as prize.*

Cf. H57.0.1. *Recognition of resuscitated person by missing member.*

Cf. T115. *Man marries ogre's daughter.*

D1611.8. *Magic cakes answer for fugitive.*

D672. *Obstacle flight.*

D921.1. *Lake (pond) produced by magic.*

D941.1. *Forest produced by magic.*

C120. *Tabu: kissing.*

D2004.2. *Kiss of forgetfulness.*

D2003. *Forgotten fiancée.*

Cf. D2006.1.3. *Forgotten fiancée reawakens husband's memory by having magic doves [hen and rooster] converse.*

K1911.3. *Reinstatement of true bride.*

Z10.2. *End formula.*

International Parallels: See No. 7.

9. THE GREEN MAN OF EGGUM[†]

Thomas Walters
Rocky Harbour Cove, Bonne Bay, West Coast
1 September 1966

AT313C
TC286, 287 66-24
Collectors: HH and JW

I'll tell ya a story directly.

[Male listener: Tom's goin to tell ya a story.]

[Int: Alright sir.]

[Female listener: Don't ya go tellin that dirty ol' story.]

I'm goina tell you one. 'Tis not [a] dirty story. The...the...th' ol big man that got the king's son.

[Female listener: The what?]

The king's son.

[Female listener: Oh I don't know about that one.]

What one d' ya mean?

[Male listener: Well the...they find...]

What one you mean?

[Female listener: I thought ('twas goin on again)

[*recorder off*]*** yes you better!] [*laughs*]

*[*recorder off*]*** (a man was there) the king's son an' he was a awful gambler _ to play cards. An' uh...an' there was a ol' Green Man of Eggum _ called th' ol' Green Man of Eggum. He was playin. They'd come to meet un an' (they'd) ask him (would he have to) play _ cards. He said "Yes."

*background noise, coughing, etc.

He said "What'll [we] play for?"

"Well" he said "we...we'll play [*untrans.*]" So the king's son beat un. An' he said "What (d'you do)?"

He said "I got a acre o' land out...off by road [*untrans.*] tomorrow morning at sunrise."

He said "Alright." Next morning they got up an' _ directly this /(Eggum)/ (man) was off (to the road) [*untrans.*]

/(Edgar)/

Now the next night they meet again.* An' he said "What'll (we) play for?"

* talking in background

He said "We play for same as (we did) last night. We'll play [*untrans.*]" An' the ol' Green Man there meet un. "Now" he said "what we play for?"

"I'll give ya a t[w]elvemonth an' one day (to) find my house" he said. Alright. An' he was only a young feller, he...(bummed) around he didn't feel good for nothing. An' he said (he'd want) to find th' ol' Green Man o' (Eggum's) house. An' by an' by the last on...last of it (he) thought he'd go [*untrans.*] An' he went to an old woman...to an old woman...lady _ an' he asked her _ an' she said she didn't know (anything at all about un never) heard talk of un.

Well he...uh...(turned round).

"Oh" she said "come back." She uh...[said] "I got three sons" she said "I knows everything an' ten times more then everything" she said. "But I got three sons on _ where I knows one thing they knows TEN times so much [as] I do. (Lord)" she said "my three sons is three giants" she said [*untrans.*] Well he went...[*untrans.*] back an' she _ she baked un three cakes _ carried ['em] out an' give to give the three sons. She come out an' he...when he was goin through the forest he _ oh the...everything was shakin. An' he see this big man comin an' he _ hold his cake out arm's length to un. He's come an' he's looked at un an' he broke un an' _ taste un, smelled un. He said "You come from my mother's house"

He said "Yes."

He said "Alright" he said "come in."

He told un...he asked un about ol' Green Man of (Eggum) "No" he's asaid he's never heard..."Sure I knows everything" he said "an' ten times more then everything _ sir but I...I never heard talk of un." So he went on (upstairs) to have (?lunch).

133

He went on he met by...the other's brother. An' he asked did he know anything about th' ol' Green Man (at Eggum) _ (where he lived to _ which house to.)

Said "Well now" he said "I'd...I've heard something about un" he said "but I know no...nothing about un. But" he said "I knows everything an' ten times more than everything. But I've uh never hear...(don't) know nothing about un. (I have...) yes _ I seem like I've ahear something about this ol'...ol' man...Green Man o' Eggum." But said "I got a...a brother on further _ me oldest brother. He knows everything."

He's travelled on. An' he meet this ol' man _ comin _ and _ hold out (his)...towards this cake, (give) un to un an' _ he seen an' the other fellow was **BAD** _ (was) roarin. An' when he went out...an' he...meet un uh...(?he hold out) cake to un an' he broke un abroad an' he _ looked at un (an') he smelled un an' taste un an' _ he said "You come from my...mother's house."

He said "Yes."

"Well now" he said _ "the Green Man of (Eggum) yes" he said "I knows all about un." He said "But you got uh...you won't ever...you..."

"I got to get there tonight" he said.

Uh..."You'll never get (down) ol' man" he said "tonight." He said "You got to...you got a glassen hill to climb over. An'" he said "on this side the glassen hill there's a pond. An'" he said "th' ol'...the king's st...uh...the Green Man of (Eggum) got three daughters. An' they'll come there to swim. Now" he said "(the one way) to get over uh...you'd l...get in _ an' hide away the youngest girl's clothes. An' don't give 'em her up _ don't give it up to her _ before you...she...she promises you [to] carry you over the glassen hill."

"Well" he said "alright." So when the youngest one _ went swimmin he...hide away her clothes. An' _ the oldest one said vis...she'd go an' fly on 'cause the younger one [was] f...faster than she. An' the second one said _ she'd fly on _ 'cause the...younger one could fly faster then she. So they flied on an' she swimmed round an' she got dressed, she went an' might as well get...go (up)...get her clothes an' by god the clo[thes] was gone. An' she...an' if he...didn't (make show for her). By an' by /he/ showed up.

An' she [said] "You got my clothes."

"No" uh.../he/ said "I haven't."

"Oh yes" she [s]aid "you have."

He said "No I haven't. Well" he said "yes I have got your clothes" he said "an' you don't carry me (out) over that hill you'll never get your clothes." Well she couldn't do that because father 'd kill her _ [if] she go an'...carry him in over the hill. An' he coaxed her an' coaxed her an' (at long la[st]) that she s[aid] "Yes. I'll carry ya over...I'll get ya up an' on

/they/

/she/

134

me wings" she said "an' I'll fly ya over. But don't let nobody know (who) took [ya] over."

So anyway he got down _ he...he got over an' knocked to the door an' went in an'

"Oh wa...well" (the ol' Man of Eggum says) "you're...you're here."

"Yes" he said.

"How d'ya get here? Well" he said "an' thank my daughter for that" he said.

"Daughter" he said "you got daughters?"

"(Yes)" he said "I got three."

"Well" he said uh..."I come in?" So come in an' uh...got something to eat for un. An' (he) thought he'd be in a nice bed that night. An' the ol' woman put un into a...a big pool o' water _ that night an' that's where he sleep to _ with his head...with his head out o' water. An' the girl got up in the night an' took un out an' put un in a nice bed. An' just 'fore daylight _ she got him put un in...in the water again. So the next morning (he had to get up) an' [the Green Man] said _ what he have to do, he has..."Now" he said "I got a...a bar[n]" said "have a...uh...have astalled (ten head o' cows) for...for twenty year. An' you got to have it cleaned out...by sunrise...by sunset er...this evening." Well he got out an' he starts throwin manure out o' the barn an' (there's a tidy bit). By dinnertime he hadn't seen where he...where he started diggin yet. Well he (sits down anyway) he commenced to cry. An' the girl come, this girl _ Nan _ his...his girl Nan _ brought un his dinner an' /he/ said well he couldn't eat he said (Well)...(thy) father killin un. Said an' just as well for un to die...with empty stomach as (a full).   /she/
/he/

"No" she said "you eat." An' /she/ coaxed un an' coa[xed]...well she [said] "I carried ya over [the] glassen hill on...on the sly" she said "an' you...eat that dinner. That's (motherses best beef)."

An' when he [eat] (this meat) uh...the...the manure...commenced to fly out through the barn. By time he had his...his dinner eat by god the...(he'd) [the] barn cleaned out, clean (jinx). Well uh...that's alright, he left...(the barn) come home next morn(ing), brought his shovel an' come in, he said "How did ya get on in the morning...in th' evening?"

He said "Okay" he said. "Got the barn cleaned out."

"Oh" he said "you must thank my daughter for that."

"(By god)" he said "I'd like to see your daughters."

He said "You won't see 'em."

So next morning he had a...he had a bed /tick/ wi' a thousand   /tack/
yard...thousand uh...yard...uh...of uh...bed see _ a thousand yard tick into un.

"Now" he said "you got to have he full for...for sundown _ tonight 'cause I...I had your...ya have to have your head...have your head chopped off."

Well he (was there) an' ol' man...he went out an' he opened this big, big ba[g]...sack you know an' _ ONE little bird come along an' shake so many feathers in. At dinnertime he had a...couple o' feathers into...in the bag. Huh! [*laughs*] An' anyway _ the girl brought his dinner again.

"Now" (she) said uh..."now" she said "eat your dinner."

"No" he said he couldn't. He said how was he goin to full that bag, he said "I...been here _ ever since this...this morning" he said "an' I only got three feathers into un yet."

"Gar" she said "you eat your dinner." (She) said "You eat your dinner an' I cleaned the barn, you...got the barn cleaned out, you can eat that." Well coaxed un up a bit an' he started pickin. (By the time) he got it eaten by god _ by time he got it eat there...he had a...big sack right full o' feathers. (Full an' as...an'...I means a strong giant you know to carry it home). An' the ol' man (said) "Did ya do (it?)"

"(Oh) yes" he said "an' so much more if I had to do."

"Ah" he said "you must thank my daughter for that."

He said "I'd like to see your daughters."

"Well" he said "you've got...won't see my daughters."

Anyway -- he went home an' next mornin...they put un in...this...ol' woman put un in this...big pool o' water again. An' the girl got up an' put un in a nice...nice...feather bed. (Well) alright an' uh...next mornin just about daylight she...got him put un in the water.

And (he uh...) "One more job for ya to do."

He said what was that?

He said "Uh...(there's) a...a gold ring up on a...on a glassen pole _ fifty feet high. You got to go up an'...climb up on a...a grease...po[le]... grease pole. You got to climb up an' take that ring off."

Well he went up alongside an' he...(poor ol' feller), (his shoes 'd) go up an' DOWN he slips _ t' ol' gla...a...a glassen pole, greas[y pole]...well he'd never do it, he's tried it till he...now the girl (come out) [with] his dinner. (Said) "Eat dinner" she said

And he said "No that's unpossible. I CAN'T do that. Can't be done. Get /clung/ up that fifty feet" he said er..."on a glassen pole, /climb/ up there" he said "an'...an' get that ring off."

"Well" she said "you got to eat you...start to eat your dinner."

/she/ "No" (/he/ said) he couldn't eat. By...by an' by his...tears runnin over his eyes. He said "(Well)...the ol' man uh...your father['ll] kill me an' then uh...('tis [as] well for me to) die...wi' empty stomach as a full one."

/he/ "Well" /she/ said "are you eatin it? But" (she) said "you...go up the...the...go up" said _ "an' climb up _ an'...an' you take that a[xe]..." she /bought/ /brought/ a little axe wi' her. "Now" she said "when yous...(ready well) you hit me in the head an' knock me down" she said.

136

"Oh my god" he said he couldn't do that. He couldn't do that. He'd sooner die his own self than (he could do that [to] she).

"Well" (she) said "you won't hurt me. Whatever you do (they'll be a ladder) o' my bones" she said "go up on top o' that tree." An' (she) said "Whatever you do don't miss nar rung comin down. If you do you'll cripple me."

An' he went up...he went...wi' the...an' he just pat her _ just touched her _ an' she was out an' go the ladder up the tree. An' he runned to the tree an' got it...go...(the) gold ring. An' when he come down she land...to step clear _ an' she...uh he lost...he /stepped/ on that one, the last one he never stepped onto (it was)...(An' she stood up for a...) young girl again so far now. So /she/ said "You crippled me." Oh god, frightened un almost to death now, crippled her.

/zipped/

/he/

She said "That's nothing" she said. "It's only me little finger." The little finger was...was a little crooked. She said "Father 'll never notice that."

Went back an' she...an' he brought the ring in to un.

"Yes. You done it. Well now" he said "(Well now)" he said "you got the...you got the ring" he said "now" he said _ "you be me servant." And uh...by this time _ the girl got up in the night _ an' she put un in water again. An' the girl got up _ an' (she) said "Now we'll run away. We'll (beat it) _ to your country." So (?try with her again) she said Well uh...they had a lot o' horses in his stable. He went out an' he...they harnessed...she knowed the best horses they had. An' they picked out...the best horses...no I'm before me story there...the best horse they had anyway. An' she said "Now we'll bake three cakes. A...one hour cake _ an' a two hour cake an' a three hour cake. The one hour cake we'll put up...put it up an'...a talkin cake _ he could talk _ put un up _ an' he'll talk for a hour. (We)...we'll be packin up our...she picked up all her jewelry _ everything she had in jewelry. An' (it)...by an' by an' by th' ol' man sung out _ "No sleepin in my country. How's he gettin on in your place?" An' he put...she put up the...the two hour cake. An' by that time, time the two hour cake run down _ by god she had all of her...jewelry all...packed up, she had a lot o' jewelry _ packed up.

An' he said "We'll go (out) an'...an' saddle the best horse th' ol' man got." Put a*...a double saddle onto un _ side saddle an' a (straight) saddle. An' then when they [untrans.] up...when they...but they put un up then the...three hour cake. An' by that time...they had their horse all in order _ to go. They go[t] on the horse an' away she goes.

*rep. 4

He sung out (once the hour) was up. No answer. He jumped up to see what the trouble [was] _ an' they was gone. Went out in his barn an' his best horse was gone. So he took after un. He got a crowd o' men [an'] took after ['em]. He ride to a...he rode till he...come to a...a big forest o'

because of the misapprehension that the story is vulgar, but as the teller progresses he becomes more confident and we are able to move the microphone closer to where he is sitting and so obtain as good a recording as possible.

It is interesting to compare this version of the tale with those of the Bennetts (Nos. 8, 10, and 11). Although Thomas Walters does not offer a title for the story it is obviously very similar to those from St. Pauls and since the Bennett and Walters families were related by marriage this version demonstrates one way in which recensions are disseminated over time and space. This Rocky Harbour narrative differs from those of the more northerly communities, for example, in Thomas Walters' use of *the king's son* rather than *Jack* as the leading character. On the other hand, references to *the king's son* may well reflect older recensions of this and other stories (cf. for example Nos. 36 and 43).

Background noise and conversation make this tape unusually difficult to transcribe, especially in the initial stages, the opening words being lost, and this problem is exacerbated by the mispronunciation, slurring, and misencoding of words by the teller who had recently been ill. As the tale progresses, however, he becomes more coherent. Even so, the transcription is exceptional in the degree of reconstruction necessary, and large stretches of speech remain incomprehensible and defy interpretation. Material in parenthesis is therefore largely guesswork—a reconstruction of feasible, rather than probable, forms, helped on occasion by the formulaic repetitions which allow the transcriber to interpret, or at least guess, what the narrator intends. Phonemes, morphemes, and parts of morphemes are used incorrectly or omitted; the grammar is therefore very difficult to reconstruct as vital inflections are missing. Nevertheless, the main details of the plot are communicated to the audience, often aided by strong emphasis on individual words. The tape has to be changed near the end of the tale, and after a little prompting the teller immediately picks up the thread of the story again.

As with other versions of this tale, we have used an improvised spelling of *Eggum,* reflecting the pronunciations, in the absence of further evidence about the word. Apart from the frequent use of West Country English *un* (it, him), Thomas Walters pronounces *weasel* as /'wizl/, *fill(ed)* as /ful(d)/, elides the intermediate vowel in *th' ol, th' evening,* and uses the aphetic form *'cause;* he also uses *unpossible* for impossible, *puncheons* (barrels), and *time* (party, celebration), pick (peck; cf. *OED Pick* v.[1], I. 1b, Obs.), the possessive inflection *-es* in *motherses,* and the archaic weak inflection in *glassen.* An Anglo-Irish construction appears in *his own self,* while the typical Newfoundland *abroad* (apart) and *nar* (not any) in *nar rung* are also evident. Irregular present tense verb forms include *I knows,* [they] *is,* and there are also the past tense forms *meet, flied* (flew), *swimmed, runned, come, knowed, sung out,* and the past participles *aheard, astalled,* and *eat.*

Note also the rhetorical parallels in the cataloguing of the tools and receptacles used by the ogre to clear the obstacles during the pursuit: as he rushes to cut down the forest he takes "Saws an' axes an' chisels an' planes...." and when he tries to empty the ocean he uses "buckets an' barrels an' puncheons an'...shovels."

Type and Motifs:

AT313C. *The Girl as Helper in the Hero's Flight.*

N4.2. *Playing game of chance (or skill) with uncanny being.*

Cf. S221.2. *Youth sells himself to an ogre in settlement of a gambling debt.*

F150.1. *Way to otherworld hard to find.*

N825.3. *Old woman helper.*

F531.6.17.7. *Giants are wise.*

N812. *Giant or ogre as helper.*

H1235. *Succession of helpers on quest.*

F571.2. *Sending to the older.*

F751. *Glass mountain.*

Cf. D361.1. *Swan Maiden.*

K1335. *Seduction (or wooing) by stealing clothes of bathing girl (swan maiden).*

D531. *Transformation by putting on skin.*

B552. *Man carried by bird.*

G461. *Youth promised to ogre visits ogre's home.*

G465. *Ogre sets impossible tasks.*

Cf. F846.1. *Perilous bed [hero forced to sleep in pool of water].*

G530.2. *Help from ogre's daughter.*

H1102.2. *Task: emptying in one day a barn filled with manure.*

D1335.1. *Magic strength-giving food.*

H901. *Tasks imposed on pain of death.*

H1129.2. *Task: filling twelve bed-ticks with feathers.*

H1114.1. *Task: securing three eggs [gold ring] from top of glass tower.*

F848.3. *Ladder of bones.*

Cf. E33. *Resuscitation with missing member.*

K231.2. *Reward for accomplishment of task deceptively withheld.*

D1611.8. *Magic cakes answer for fugitive.*

D672. *Obstacle flight.*

D941.1. *Forest produced by magic.*

D921.1. *Lake (pond) produced by magic.*

C120. *Tabu: kissing.*

D2004.2.1. *Dog's licking of man produces forgetfulness.*

D2003. *Forgotten fiancée.*

Cf. D2006.1.3. *Forgotten fiancée reawakens husband's memory by having magic doves [hen and rooster] converse.*

K1911.3. *Reinstatement of true bride.*

T115. *Man marries ogre's daughter.*

Z10.2. *End formula.*

International Parallels: See No. 7.

10. THE GREEN MAN OF EGGUM

Clarence Bennett
St. Pauls, Great Northern Peninsula
25 July 1970

AT313A
TC978 71-50
Collector: HH

[*recorder off*] *** [there was a man] by the name o' the Green Man of Eggum one time. An' he visit this...person's house you know, there was only just the man an' the wife. An' Jack...an' Jack but he was only just a...small baby _ boy just ol' enough to talk. So really thought a lot o' Jack.

/goes/

And so he said to Jack he said "Now" he said "Jack" he said "when you /grows/ up" _ he said "to be a...a man" _ he said "or...ol' enough to travel" he said uh..."why don't you visit me?"

"Yes" Jack said, he would.

So anyhow Jack was uh...round seventeen, eighteen year old an'...well he was goina visit the Green Man of Eggum. Well they told un _ when he start on his journey well he'd never make it, no (he'll) never make the journey because he had to pass three...big giants _ an' they was wicked old men, they'd kill un anyhow. But he was goin regardless, he was goin...to visit the man.

So anyhow _ off Jack goes. He travelled all night. An' he...yeah he travelled all night. An' by an' by he come to a light just 'fore dark. So anyhow he said to hisself he'd see what 'twas anyhow. So anyhow he went up to this house an' this...what it was _ an ol' giant. But it wasn't one o' them anyhow, 'twasn't one of them ol'...ol' wicked ones. But anyhow there was...this ol' feller took un in for the night an' gave un a lunch an' _ he told un his story where he was goin an' visit the Green Man of Eggum

"Well" he said "just (as) well for ya to give it up Jack" he said "you'll never get there." He said "Because they'll kill ya" he said "they'll know you're comin" he said _ "along before you gets to th' house an' they be waitin for ya." He said "Now that is three mile apart." [*coughs*]

*noise of
children in
background

/rear/

So well Jack said he was goin regardless, whatever happened _ he had to go an' visit this man.*

Well when they was ready in the mornin to leave anyhow _ he said to Jack "Well" he said "I'll bake ya a cake now _ a little bun." He said "An' if then th' ol' giant comes out an' he'll be right **MAD**" he said "/ready/...ready to tear ya in pieces" he said "give un this little bun" he said "an' I think" he said "you'll get along."

"Yeah."

An' so Jack took his bun an' away to go. So 'fore he got to th' house anyhow he heard the ol' giant out oh right roarin mad.

"Hold on" Jack said "hold on now" he said "hold on" he says "a bit" he

142

said "don't go too far" he said. He said "I got something here for ya." So he took out this bun an' give it to th' ol' giant. So anyhow _ th' old giant took un in an' treat un o' the best. Now they were three brothers see.

But he said "Jack" he said "where's ya goin?" He's...told un he was goin to visit the Green Man of Eggum.

"Ah" he said "Jack uh...just useless" he said "you'll never get there." He said "Me other two brothers" he said "is.../worse/" he said "than I am" he said "an' they'll...oh" he said "you won't get through" he said "regardless."

/worked/

But anyhow he went to...bed that night an'...sleeped her up an'...next mornin "Well" he said "Jack" he said "you're goin."

"Yes" Jack said "I'm goin."

"Well" he said "I'll...do the same" he said "as you get...done for me" he said "I'll bake ya a bun."

So anyhow he bake Jack the bun an'...an' Jack took the bun in under his coat an' 'way to go.

Well he only had to go three mile. An' begar this...ol' giant come out right roarin mad again.

"Hold on" Jack said "hold on" he said. "You (got) lots o' time" he said "yet" he said "lots o' time yet" he said "I got somethin here" he said "'ll give ya" he said "might...might work out" he said "(alright)."

So anyhow _ Jack give un the bun an' _ sure enough, perfect. 'Way to go again.

So he took [un] in _ they had supper an' big chat "Well" he said "Jack" he said _ "what's your story?" He said "Where are you goin?"

"Oh" Jack said "I'm goin to visit the Green Man of Eggum." He said "He told me to visit him" he said "when I...get old enough to...travel" he said "so" he said "I'm goina visit un."

"Ah!" he said "Jack" he said "you can't make that trip. It...you...can't get there" he said "me...brother" he said "down the street" he said "from me now" he said "(they're)...worse than I am" he said "an' _ that's the end o' ya" he said "you won't get past him anyhow."

Oh well. Didn't make no difference, Jack was goin. So they sleeped her up that night, had a rest up an' next morning he got up

"Well" he said "Jack you're goina finish your trip?"

"Yes" Jack said. "I'm goina finish un."

"Oh well" he said "I'll...bake ya a bun now" he said. He said "That might help along" he said "but I hardly expect it will."

So anyhow he baked un a bun an' Jack thanked un an' _ 'way they go...'way he goes. When he got so far from th' house th' ol' feller come out again right...roarin mad the same as usual.

An' _ "Hold on" Jack said "hold on" he said "don't kill me now" he said "don't kill me" he said "till I talks to ya" he said "you got lots o' time yet." Said "Lots o' time" he said "yet" he said. "You're way bigger than I am" he

143

said "an' _ we'll…straighten this up between us." So Jack shoved a hand in under the coat an' hauled out the bun. Gave un, oh begar (he's) right **PLEASED** with the bun. Took Jack in an' gave un a big…feed an' oh everything.

So anyhow _ sleeped up that night. "Now Jack" he said _ "you're goina visit the Green Man of Eggum"

"Yes" he said

"Well" he said _ "you got a big problem ahead o' ya yet." An' this [*aside to Int:* could ya shut off for a sec.] [*recorder off*] He said "You got a…a big problem ahead o' ya yet." He said "You got a big pond" _ he said "an' you got a big glassen hill to go over." He said "If once you can get over that hill" he said "you got it made."

"Well" Jack said "I'll…I'll try it" he said. "Seems pretty difficult but" he said "I'm goina try it anyhow."

"Well" he said "Jack" he said "I'll tell ya what to do." He said "You go to the pond" he said "to the foot of the hill" he said "an' sit down." He said "An' wait a while" he said "an' bimby [i.e., *by and by*] you'll see three swans comin _ three white swans" he said "an' they're goina pitch [i.e., *land*] in the pond for a swim. Now" he said "this 'd be the…Green Man of Eggum's three daughters." He said "An' the youngest one" _ he said "you take her clothes an' hide it away." He said "An' don't give her back her clothes _ till she carries you over the hill."

Well very good. He had that worked out alright. So (anyway) he went to the hill, he sat down an' he waited an' by an' by sure enough _ here comes the three swans. All pitched in the pond. Pull off their clothes an' pitched in the pond, had their swim.

So Jack took _ the youngest one's clothes an' he hid it away. An' uh…they swimmed around in the pond, they got tired an' _ by an' by they came ashore to dress. An' the young one _ couldn't find her clothes.

"Well" she (said) "Jack" said "you got my clothes."

"No" Jack said "I ant got your clothes, I ant seen it." Said "I haven't /even/ touch your clothes."

/eveny/

"Oh yes you **SURE** as shot, you had i[t]…you…you got my clothes."

"No." He arged with her. Well she arg with un so much

"Well" Jack said last time "oh" he said "I'll make a bargain with ya." He said "You carry me over the hill" _ he said "an' I'll give you your clothes."

"Oh good enough." She'd do that. So anyhow he gave her back her clothes an' she carried un over the hill. [*aside to Int:* you just shut off again] [*recorder off*] So anyhow _ Jack stayed all night an' he _ got up next mornin

"Now" he said "Jack" he said "I got a job for ya to do." He said "I got a feather bed out there to fill." He said "An' you got to stand out

there by the door _ an' 'cordin as the birds flies _ you have to /fill/ un up   /pick/
with feathers _ out o' the birds 'cordin as they flies along before they's
dead."

"Oh well" Jack said _ "that's a job I'd never do" he said "just as
well for me to...die" he said "now" he said "as die later."

"Oh never mind" he said "Jack" he said "try" he said "anyhow."

So Jack went out an' the birds fled back an' forth an' he grabbed
an' he couldn't get a feather. Not a feather!

So this...girl now, Ann, Nan they used to call her _ come out "Well" she
said "Jack" she said "have your dinner."

"No" Jack said "I don't want no dinner." He said "Just as well for me to
die" he said "on empty belly" he said "as a full one" he said "no difference
into it" he said "I don't want no dinner anyhow."

"Oh well" she said "Jack" said "eat your dinner" she said uh..."you might
get along better after dinner."

"Oh no" 'twould be no different, he couldn't do that anyhow.

So he sat down, he eat his dinner an' _ she went on, anyhow after he
had his dinner an' _ he got up an' the birds was flyin an' he was grabbin
their feathers, no time at all he had his bed filled. Yeah he done
WONDERFUL.

So he went in, th' ol' feller said "How ya get on" he said "Jack?"

"Oh" Jack..."oh"...Jack said   "done perfect" he (said) "I got the bed
filled" he said "no time at all"

"Good enough. Well now Jack" he said "tomorrow morning" he said "I
got a barn out there" he said "with...so many head o' cattle been tied into
'em but...for a certain amount o' time" he said "he hadn't ever been cleaned
out" he said "anyhow. So" he said "you must clean he out tomorrow
morning."

Oh well Jack thought to hisself _ that was a big job too.

So he went out in the morning in the f...to the barn an' _ he shovelled
out one shovelful an' another one 'd come back. Shovel out one, 'nother one
come back. Well he couldn't get ahead.

"Oh well" Jack said "this is hopeless." He said "I'll never get through wi'
this anyhow."

By an' by come dinner time, same as usual an' _ Ann went out with his
dinner.

Ann said "Jack" said "sit down an' have your dinner"

"No" Jack said "I (don't) want no dinner. Just as well for me to die" he
said "on a full belly" said "emp[ty]...yeah...empty belly 'stead o' full one"
he s[aid] "don't make no difference." He said "I don't want none."

She coaxed un up...an' by an' by she got un round to eat his dinner.
Well he got up an' he...started at his work again an' oh no time at all he had
the barn all clean, perfect _ wonderful now.

do see 'em comin" she said "take this bottle o' water" she said "an' do the same thing." Said "There'll be a big ocean o' water" she said "an' a glassen hill spring up." Said "An' he **WON'T** get over that" she said "anyhow."

"Oh very good" Jack...[said] they had it all planned up. [*clears throat*] So they'd rode on, rode on.

By an' by "Yes" he said. "The cloud" he said "is risin again"

"Well" she said "Jack" she said "throw the bottle!"

Throw the bottle over an' here was the big hill, now they was on...the other side.

That's so far as I knows. I can't get the rest [*recorder off*] I don't know _ **ALL** the story, there's only just a few more words on the end o' the story. But on the end of it _ the two o' them got married an' was livin together contented.

[Int: You don't remember what was in the part that's missing?]
No I don't remember what was in the part no. No there's just a few more words.
[Int: So they...she threw...they threw seed an' it became a forest an' they threw _ wa[ter] bottle.]
Yeah. Bottle o' water. An' a...a glassen hill an' a pond sprang up. Well they couldn't get over the glassen hill, they had to go back from that. They continued on _ to his home town _ an' married.
[*recorder off*] Ol' man was tellin ya _ about uh...a while ago _ Uncle Charl Benoit.
[Int: Who...who _ was the one _]
Was the one I learned that story from.
[Int: How long ago _ Clarence?]
Oh sir I was uh...about ten or twelve years old.
[Int: Have you told it many times?]
I've atold it I allow a **DOZEN** times. Hundr[ed]...oh yes fifty times I guess. Round in camps you know an' _ people tellin stories and _ asked about certain stories you know, ol' people or oldish people an' meself and _ (have) atold 'em an' _ well they was uh...really interest[ed] in the story, but I knew un all. Knew the...works of that. I told 'em there one time in the winter but I couldn't remember the last part of un.

Duration: 15 min., 11 sec.
Source: Charles Benoit (great uncle), St. Pauls, Great Northern Peninsula, "I was about...ten or twelve years old."
Location: Sitting room of teller's house.
Audience: Interviewer.

Context, Style, and Language: This text provides a good example of careful reconstruction for the benefit of the collector in the full knowledge that it is being recorded. It is therefore self-conscious to a degree, for example in the various asides to the interviewer. Even so the narrative proceeds smoothly, undeterred by the voices of the teller's wife and children who are in the adjoining kitchen.

Like that of his father, Everett, and his uncle, Freeman, Clarence Bennett's speech is of the West Country English type and includes many of its typical features such as the frequent use of the pronoun *un* and various dialectal verb forms. His speech is very rapid and he rarely pauses between phrases and sentences, in strong contrast to such narrators as Allan Oake. The speed of delivery causes transcription problems, especially when it blurs the boundaries between words. His tales are characterized by very lively dialogue whose animation is achieved partly by many changes in pitch and stress patterns and which arouses and sustains the interest of the audience in spite of the very fast delivery. The dialogue, again like that of his father and uncle—and no doubt modeled on their style and that of another uncle, Charles Benoit, from whom he learned this story—is frequently punctuated by *he/she said,* which serves to mark off segments of speech as effectively, and in much the same way, as the conventions of written punctuation. He also uses *(So/But) anyhow, by an' by, (Well) very good,* and *good enough* to mark new phases in the narrative. He is quite at ease with the tape recorder and asks the interviewer to switch it off when he needs to pause to recollect the details of the next section of the story. There is considerable activity and background noise which hampers transcription and sometimes intrudes on the narration.

The name in the title of this story is consistently pronounced by all three of the Bennetts, the first syllable having the diphthong /ei/. Typical features of Clarence Bennett's speech here include the half-long central vowel in *far,* the short lowered close front vowel in the first syllable of *catches,* and the contracted form *bimby* (by and by), the diphthong /ou/ in *none,* the lowered close back round vowel in *crooked* /krukt/, the loss of final consonant in *of, old, with, have,* the problem of distinguishing between *the morrow* and *tomorrow,* frequent use of aphesis, e.g., in *'fore, 'way* (away), *'cordin as, 'stead,* the absence of initial vowel in *'twas(n't), 'twould,* the elision of schwa (often accompanied by loss of initial /h/) in *th' axe, th' hole, th' house,* dialectal inflections in *glassen, hisself,* plural inflection omitted in *year,* and the lexical items *lunch* (snack), *begar* (a borrowing of Anglo-Irish *begorrah* common in the Bennetts' narratives), *pitch(ed)* (land[ed]), *arg(ed)* (argue[d]), *perfect* (adverb), *ne'r* (no, any), *whe'r* (whether), *right* (intensifier), *allow* (reckon). Note also the use of *he* in the object case and of *it* with the plural referent *clothes,* the phrases *'way to go* and *the both of us,* the present tense forms *I talks/ant/knows, he do, you looks, they's, they comes,* the past tense forms *start, they was, give, sleeped, bake, come, fled* (flew), *climb, slip, keeped* (of which *bake, climb,* and *slip* might alternatively be construed as vivid present), the past participle *hide* (hidden), and the double negatives *didn't make no difference, don't want no dinner, don't know nothin,* and *don't miss ne'r step.* The passage of time is signaled by repetition of the verb phrase: "So they'd rode on, rode on," a stylistic device also used by the older narrators in the family.

Type and Motifs:

AT313A. *The Girl as Helper in the Hero's Flight.*

H1210. *Quest assigned.*

N812. *Giant or ogre as helper.*

F151.0.1. *Hospitable host entertains (guides, advises) adventurer on way to otherworld.*

H1235. *Succession of helpers on quest.*

D361.1. *Swan Maiden.*

K1335. *Seduction (or wooing) by stealing clothes of bathing girl (swan maiden).*

B552. *Man carried by bird.*

F751. *Glass mountain.*

Cf. G461. *Youth promised to ogre visits ogre's home.*

G465. *Ogre sets impossible tasks.*

H901. *Tasks imposed on pain of death.*

Cf. H1129.2. *Task: filling twelve bed-ticks with feathers.*

G530.2. *Help from ogre's daughter.*

D1335.1. *Magic strength-giving food.*

H1102.2. *Task: emptying in one day a barn filled with manure.*

H1114.1. *Task: securing three eggs [gold ring] from top of glass tower.*

F848.3. *Ladder of bones.*

Cf. E33. *Resuscitation with missing member.*

H331. *Suitor contests: bride offered as prize.*

Cf. H57.0.1. *Recognition of resuscitated person by missing member.*

D1611.8. *Magic cakes answer for fugitive.*

D672. *Obstacle flight.*

D941.1. *Forest produced by magic.*

D921.1. *Lake (pond) produced by magic.*

D932.0.1. *Mountain created by magic.*

T115. *Man marries ogre's daughter.*

International Parallels: See No. 7.

11. THE GLASSEN POLE

Everett Bennett   AT313C
St. Pauls, Great Northern Peninsula   TC251 66-24
24 August 1966   Collectors: HH and JW

[*recorder off*]*** dozens an' dozens of 'em an' I knowed 'em all, he learned all...(I) learned all his stories.
[Int: Did ya now.]

(I took 'em) I forgot 'em all. Don't know none of his now. No. [*recorder off*]*** old king you know had a _ you've heard he _ heard "Ship Jack?" "Ship Jack" an' er...well now Jack was to marry his daughter you see? [Teller's brother: Yeah.]

An' er...he er...told Jack that he had er...to _ a job for un tomorrow he said "Jack" he said "you got to do." He said "I'm goin to uh...there's a horse out there in the yard" he said "was never bridled or saddled." Said "You got to catch that horse tomorrow" he said "an' break un in."

Well Jack got out the next morning for to _ catch the horse Got out next morning (go) catch the horse he couldn't get handy to un. Couldn't get handy th' horse at all. At it all day till dinnertime. Now he [*the king*] had a daughter called Nan see. An' er...she come out, she said "Jack" (she) said "dinnertime."

"I don't [want] no dinner" Jack said. "What's good for me to go to get dinner?" he said "I can't catch this horse" he said "an' th' old man'll kill me when I comes this evening _ when he comes this evening."

"Never mind Jack" she said uh..."come in."

So Jack went in an' had his dinner an' _ went in an' had his dinner an' _ just the same after dinner he went out, the same thing _ couldn't catch th' horse. An' er...she come out with a old bridle and saddle "Here" she said "Jack" she said uh..."take this one." Give Jack th' old bridle an' Jack...[took] th' old bridle an' saddle an' Jack walked out to th' horse an' caught un an' put the bridle an' saddle on an' got on his back an' _ just about had the horse killed when th' old man come home. "Well Jack" /he/ said "how you get on?"   /she/

"Oh! That's no trouble" Jack said. "Not much trouble to catch a...horse I don't suppose an' break un in."

"Thank my daughter Nan" he said "for that."

"The hell with your daughter Nan" Jack said "I don't know nothing 'bout your daughter Nan."

"Ne'r mind Jack" he said "I got another job tomorrow for you to do."

So anyhow _ in the morning come "Now" he said "Jack" he said er..."my old grandmother" he said "there's a barn down there an' he hasn't been cleared out...cleaned out" he said "for a number o' years." He said "An' she lost a darn-needle in that" he said "an' you got to find that today _ have that found 'fore I comes back _ with the barn cleaned out an'...darn-needle found."

Well _ Jack got down the barn in the morning, 'cording as he'd heave up one forkful there'd be 'nother one come back. Worked at it till dinnertime an' _ girl come down, Nan come down again an' said _ "Never mind Jack, come up to dinner."

"Ah" Jack said "I'm going [to] dinner" he said "I'll never get this job done."

"Oh never mind Jack" she said "come up to dinner, (yous'll) have better luck after dinner." So anyhow Jack went up _ [to] dinner. After dinner he come down, the same darn thing. -- She took a _ old fork _ got an old rusty fork an' brought down, she said "Here Jack" she said "take this fork." Jack took the fork an' so fast as he could fork it out 'twas goin you know. Still no sign o' the darn-needle. When he took up the last forkful to heave out there was the darn-needle. (He's) alright now.

When the old man come "How you get on Jack?"

"Oh" Jack said "I got the barn cleaned out."

"Thank my daughter Nan for that Ja[ck]..." [he] said "Jack."

"Hell with your daughter Nan" Jack said "I know nothing about her. [She] haven't done nothing for me."

"Never mind" he said "Jack" he said "I got a _ harder job tomorrow for ya."

So in the morning when _ old man leaved there was a _ glassen pole _ up. An' right on the end o' the glassen pole there was a ring. "Now" he said "Jack" he said "you got to shin that pole" he said "an' get that ring off top o' that pole." Well Jack to his...thought to hisself "That's a job I'll NEVER do." So anyhow he got at it. He couldn't get up the pole, get up a little ways an' slip back.

She come out to dinner an' "Ah" Jack said _ "I'm not goin in" still he didn't stand much coaxing 'cause he had...thought he had a very good chance. -- So anyhow he went in to dinner. Come out after dinner an' same thing an' _ by an' by he seen her comin out with a hammer in her hand. An' uh..."Now" she said "Jack take that hammer _ an' knock me in head. An' when you do" she said "there'll be a ladder to the top of that pole. But" she said "whatever you does" she said "step on every step 'cording as you comes down. If you don't _ I'll be cripple."

So anyhow Jack knocked her in head an' when he did here was the ladder to the top o' the pole. Up Jack goes an' gets off the ring now. An' he stepped on every step till he come to the second last one. When he...step...second last step he stepped on the ground. Soon as Jack stepped on the ground up she jumped. She said "Look Jack" she said "my finger's crooked _ an' that's be...what you done." Well now Jack was _ was to marry her now he'd adone the three things.

So anyhow _ old king come home, he'd done the three jobs. Well he was goina marry her, goina marry her. But still he wasn't goina marry her, th' old thing...king thought he was goin to kill un [Jack] now.

Now she baked _ nine cakes _ an' every one o' them speak...cakes could speak. An' she put 'em on the steps o' the stairs. Now _ Jack an' the girl went to bed. Old king an' old queen went to bed. Stayed in bed so long an' he said "I wonder is he to sleep? -- 'Sleep Jack?"

"No sir." All night like that _ till the nine cakes was gone. Now Jack an' the girl was gone all this time. -- When the nine cakes was gone, no answer, he jumps up _ grabs his pistol an' went up. Bed empty, nobody in.

Old king had a dog she had nine pups. An' he...she took the ni[ne]...he took...she took the nine pups an' put /them/ 'board the vessel _ an' away to go. Now then this dog could /tow/...tow the ship _ faster stern foremost _ than she could take her 'head...she could go ahead with her sails on. /her/ /tur/

Away she goes. An' by an' by _ they seen the dog comin. She said "Jack" she said "look out" she said "an' throw over a pup." When the dog got so close _ throwed over the pup, dog went back with un. She follied like that _ till the nine pups was gone. An' they was just in sight o' land _ when she s...leaved to go back with the _ last pup.

"Now" she said "Jack" she said "be all ready" she said "an' get right out on the jibboom. An' when she strikes the land _ " she said "jump." An' they was all ready an' when she got out _ struck the land _ he jumped an' the dog took her [the ship] _ right on back.

So now he was home to his _ not to his right home no...but he was home on his own shore. Well he said to his uh...wife "I'd like to go home an' see some (o') me people."

"Well" she said "go home. But" she said uh..."I'll tell ya afore you goes _ don't let none of 'em kiss ya."

"No." Wouldn't allow that. An' when he got home to his _ people an' oh they was right overjoyed, they went to kiss Jack. No, no, nobody goin to kiss un. Now had a little dog when he was home. An' the dog knew un soon as he come in. He jumped up in his arms an' licked un on the face. Forgot all about his wife. Knowed no more about after (his) wife.

So he was gone for as...uh long a time, well she knowed what happened. She went. -- An' that night as she got there _ there was a big time on. An' she bought a golden cock an' a golden hen. -- An' she took it to the _ time.

Now Jack was there, she knowed Jack. Jack didn't know she. An' she throwed out the crumbs. An' the _ cock _ picked the hen. She said "Ah you naughty bird" she said "you can't remember when I gives ya the bridle an' saddle to catch the horse." Course Jack never thought nothing about that.

An' _ by an' by she throwed out some more _ an' [the cock] picked her again. "Ah you naughty bird" she said "you can't remember _ when you been...when I gived you the old fork to clean the barn out to find the darn-needle"

He thought to hisself "That happened to me ONE time."

153

such additional punctuation as is adopted in the texts presented here. This inevitably leaves a considerable degree of ambiguity in the representation of what was actually said, and demands that the conventions are strained to breaking point. In the absence of a transcription of the intonation, the reading audience is left to gather what it can of the vigor and usefulness of this unusual narrative technique which has an immediate impact within the context of oral storytelling but almost defies representation in print. A similar ambiguity is reflected in those nonstandard verb forms which might be interpreted as either present or past tense, again allowing for greater flexibility of reference than in standard usage, cf. "when I gives ya the bridle" in the dénouement of this tale when the past tense *gave* would be expected—itself often rendered as *give(d)* in Newfoundland speech.

Everett Bennett's speech is of the West Country English type and exhibits all the usual features of that usage found in Newfoundland, not least the frequent use of the pronoun *un* and typical dialectal forms of the verb. As with other speakers of this type in the province, however, there is an admixture of Anglo-Irish features, notably the asseveration *begar* and the idiomatic *Don't be talkin!*—a dismissive expression of wonder or disbelief (cf. *DNE talk* v. 2). Like his brother Freeman and his son Clarence he frequently punctuates dialogue with *he/she said* and uses *Alright, Very good,* and similar expressions to mark the end of a narrative segment, while *by an' by* signals the passage of time and/or a new step forward in the plot.

This story begins under the title "Ship Jack" but it is clear from its final words, spoken as a sign-off to complete the narrative, that it should be called "The Glassen Pole." It may be that this title came to mind when the *glassen pole* was mentioned in the story itself. Because of the exploratory nature of the interview and the difficult recording conditions, the tape recorder was switched on and off quite often and the first few words of the story were not recorded. The opening is hesitant but the narrative runs smoothly after that, and when it comes to Jack's final recognition of his wife his words "You're my wife" are said very movingly and convincingly, the teller's voice breaking with emotion. When the cakes are responding to the king's asking if Jack is asleep, both their voices and that of the king are imitated, the cakes replying in a low but resolute voice like that used to characterize Jack elsewhere in the tale. The reader, and certainly the listener, can gather that it is the cakes which are replying and not Jack himself, even though the teller does not make this clear. The mingling of direct and indirect speech is seen, for example, in Jack's response to the warning that no one must kiss him: "'No.' Wouldn't allow that," where *No* is in direct speech, and *Wouldn't allow that,* with its past tense form and ambiguous omission of subject pronoun, is in reported speech but with the vivid intonation of direct speech. There is formulaic repetition in the thanking of the old man's daughter and the girl's scolding of the "naughty bird." The simple but amusing end formula is similar to those used by several other storytellers on the northwest coast, and contrasts markedly with the elaborate endings used by Az McLean in the neighboring community of Payne's Cove and also found in several stories from the south coast and the Burin Peninsula.

The principal features of Everett Bennett's style and language are amply illustrated here. The narration is often elliptical or condensed, as seen for example in the frequent omission of function words such as the definite article before *girl, old king, old queen,* and in such expressions as *knock me in head.* Pronouns are also omitted, notably *he* and *she* before *said,* and others in the objective position, e.g., *brought down* for *brought it down.* Speed and urgency are suggested by such elliptical utterances as *Bed empty, nobody in* where two verbs are omitted as well as function words. Phonological features include the long close front vowel /i:/ in *shin;* variation between /i:/ and /e:/ in *leaved;* the diphthong in /dɐuz/; the half-open back unrounded vowel in *put* (well attested in West Country English dialects and elsewhere in Newfoundland); the reduction of /ou/ to the lowered close front vowel in the second syllable of *follied* (followed), the same vowel being found also in *hen* and *picked* (pecked); the typical omission of final /d/ in *old* and *crippled* and of final /t/ in *foremost;* syncopation of the second syllable of *darning* to produce *darn-needle;* loss of medial consonant in *ne'r* (never), elision of schwa in *th' old,* aphesis in *'bout, 'fore, 'cordin as, 'nother, 'Sleep,* and the absence of the initial vowel in *'twas.* At the morphological level we find the archaic weak inflection in *glassen,* and the dialectal *hisself.* Of lexical interest are: *handy* (near), *killed*—in the probable sense of "tired out, tamed," the nautical *jibboom, right* as an intensifier, and *time* (party, celebration). The pronoun *he* is used with the neuter referent *barn,* and *she* in objective position in *Jack didn't know she.* Present tense verb forms include *I/you comes/gives, you does/goes,* and in the past tense *give(d), knowed, come, leaved, seen, they was, throwed,* and the archaic past participle *adone.* Note also the typical phrase *away to go,* purposive *for to,* and the double negatives *don't know nothing, haven't done nothing,* and *never thought nothing.*

Type and Motifs:

AT313C. *The Girl as Helper in the Hero's Flight.*
Cf. H310. *Suitor tests.*
H1010. *Impossible tasks.*
H901. *Tasks imposed on pain of death.*
H1154.8. *Task: capturing magic horse.*
G530.2. *Help from ogre's daughter.*
D1209.2. *Magic saddle.*
H1102.2. *Task: emptying in one day a barn filled with manure.*
D1205. *Magic shovel [fork].*
H1114.1. *Task: securing three eggs [gold ring] from top of glass tower.*
F848.3. *Ladder of bones.*
Cf. E33. *Resuscitation with missing member.*
K231.2. *Reward for accomplishment of task deceptively withheld.*
D1611.8. *Magic cakes answer for fugitive.*
B541.4.1. *Boat towed by dog.*
Cf. D672. *Obstacle flight.*
C120. *Tabu: kissing.*

D2004.2.1. *Dog's licking of man produces forgetfulness.*
D2003. *Forgotten fiancée.*
Cf. D2006.1.3. *Forgotten fiancée reawakens husband's memory by having magic doves [cock and hen] converse.*
K1911.3. *Reinstatement of true bride.*
Z10.2. *End formula.*

International Parallels: See No. 7.

Allan Oake

12. THE HEAD CARD PLAYER OF THE WORLD

Allan Oake   AT313C
Beaumont, Green Bay, Notre Dame Bay   TC309 66-25
10 September 1966   Collectors: JW and Harold Paddock

[Int. A: That's what they call it is it?]
Yeah. That's the title of that story (yeah).
[Int. A: "The Head Card Player of the World?"]
"Head Card Player o' the World." Uh? **YOU** [i.e., *Int. B.*] heard un.
[*recorder off*] Now this uh...I just as well tell un. I think I...I think I can
manage to tell un alright.

[*clears throat*] He uh...there was a head card player o' the world you
know there was nobody could beat un but er...one day there was a young
man come...come there an'...well he asked un what he come for. He
uh...(to) have a game with un he said.

"Well" he said "what will ye play for?"

"A thousand dollars again a thousand" he said.

"Okay." Well this young /man/ wanted the best two out o' three. Well   lang/
he said...he told un he'd have another game with un, he'd give him another
chance. He put those two thousand...again his...property an'...an' land (you
know) so on _ the best two out o' three. So this young man he won it.
"(Yeah) I'll give 'ee one more chance." [Int. B: Mm.] He said "I'll put your
money...an' your...house an' land" he said "against your life _ the best two
out o' three." Well this young man he won it. Well now HE was head card
player o' the world.

"Now" he said "I'm leavin. An' in a hundred an' one year" _ he said "you
got to come to find me. If ya don't" he said "I'll come an' have your life."
Well this er...young man he travelled _ through the forest no one knows
where. So -- the time was ALMOST up you know when this uh...feller
thought about...th' other feller thought about (it). Well he said he suppose
he must start off to look for the head card player o' the world.

Well he didn't know where...where to start to or where to go. So he
started walkin, he was walkin all day to sundown. [The] once he seen a light
ahead. He [said] "Probably now that's where he lives to." Went an' knocked
to the castle door an'...an' ol' feller come out. He asked un if he knowed
anything about where the head card player o' the world was.

He told un he said "No sir" he said "I don't know anything about it" he
said "for I'm only one hundred years old" _ he said "an' I don't know much
about un. But" he said "I got a brother" he said "a day's walk from here _ two
hundred." He said "He might know _ something about un." Alright.

Stayed there all night an' the next mornin he start off in the dawn ya know an' walked away all day an' _ when it's sundown _ he began to see this light. Well he said to hisself "This is where his other brother must live." Knocked to the castle door an' this ol' feller come out. He asked un if he could tell un anything about the head card player o' the world an' he said "No." He said "I don't know ANYTHING about un." He said "I'm only two hundred year old. An'" he said "an' I don't know anything about the head card player o' the world. But" he said _ he..."I got a brother" he said "a day's walk from here _ three hundred." He said "Now if there's anybody KNOWS anything about th' head card player o' the world 'tis he."

Stayed there all night an' next morning started off in the dawn. Travelled all day. By an' by he seen this light an' he said uh "Mm." Asked un if he...thought to hisself "Well that's...that's where he lives." So he went an' knocked to the castle door an' this ol' feller come out. He asked un if he knowed anything about the head card player o' the world. "Well sir" he said "if I don't" he said "there's NOBODY knows." He said "I'm only three hundred year old" he said. He said "I got two brothers beside, one two an' th' other one one" He said "An' we're ALL witches." He said "There's a pond sir" he said..."two hours' walk from here." He said "You go there an' stay there...go there in the dawn an' stay there an' uh...to this pond an'" he said uh..."you'll s...an' you'll see, look away to the mountain tops you'll see a cloud" he said "a little cloud risin. The once" he said "you'll see three girls comin down for a bathing. An' now" he said "when the youngest girl gets her clothes off" he said "you can...go an' take it. An' not give it up until she tells you where the head card player o' the world is."

(Well) he stayed there all night an' started off next morn. Got to this pond. Stowed away an' looked away to the mountain tops. The once he seen this little cloud you know risin. Waited a bit an' he seen three girls comin down. [clears throat] Come down, he was stowed away in the tall grass. (The) once they got their clothes off he runned along an' catched this young girl's clothes an'...an' told her...asked her where the head card...player o' the world was. But wouldn't give her up her clothes.

"Well" she said uh...she said "th' head card player" she said "I'll do whatever lies in me power for ye" she [said] "th' head card player o' the world" she [said] "lives behind that mountain. But" she said "don't come with...wi' us _ 'cause he'll s...he'll say that we told 'ee."

So they went on back again an' after...they was gone long enough he started off. Went up an'...once he got around this mountain of course he seen the castle. Went an' knocked to the door an'...ol' feller come "Oh" he said "you've come. I was just...goina start off to look for YOU" he said. An' he said "If I had" he said "I'd had your life."

"Oh" he said uh…he said "the barn…hasn't been cleaned out for one hundred year. My wife she lo…lost her ring _ into that barn _ one hundred years ago _ an' you got to find that…ring" he said "before six o'clock _ or" he said "or else I'll have your life."

Well he was at it all day shovelling you know. An' uh…never found the ring. Quarter to six he sot down you know an' begin to cry. An' this young girl come along and she said "What are ya cryin about?" He told her. She (said) "I thought I told ya 's morn I'd do whatever lied in me **POWER** for ye" she said. "Here" she said "take this gold shovel. Heave un over /your/ shoulder" she said "in the devil's name _ turn around an' pick up the ring." Well that's what he done. An' by an' by th' ol' feller come down an' she _ took the shovel again of course.

/me/

He said um…"You got the…ring?"

"Yes sir" he said "but a lot of shovellin though."

"Well" he said uh…"tonight" he said "you sleeps wi' the pigs." So the girl come an' told un that er…to take the first food that come down because the pig…pig 'd eat the same as he.

Well next mornin "Now" he said "how do ya like…last night…sleepin with a pig?"

"Well" he said he could manage…he managed it alright.

"Well" he said "there's a…a…a /goat/" /he/ said "(now) in the…in the gard[en] that nobody never could catch. An'" he said "you got to catch her" he said "before…six o'clock this evenin _ an' put her in the barn. If you don't" he said "I'll have your life."

/coad/ /she/

Well he was after (her) all day you know. An' couldn't catch her. No more handier to her then we'll say than he was…in the mornin when he started. An' quarter to six he give it up you know an' started crying. Little girl come down _ before six o'clock an' uh…he said uh…she said "What are ya cryin about **NOW**?" Well he told her. She said "I (thought) I told ya yesterday I'd do whatever lied in me power for 'ee. Here" she said "(take) this gold saddle _ walk towards the /goat/ an' the /goat/ 'll walk towards you." So he's…took an' led her in the barn.

/coach/

When he…th' ol' feller come in "Well" he said "you **IS** smarter" he said "I didn't think" he said "you was…near so smart as that. [Int. B: Mm.] Well tonight" he said "you sleeps wi' the hens." So alright.

He uh…she come an' told un to take the first food that come down with the hens 'd eat the same as they did. Now _ next mornin when he comes out now "How 'ee's like to sleep wi' th' hens?"

"Well" he said "not bad."

"Well" he said "there's a…there's a glassen pole" he said "out there in the garden _ two hundred feet…high. An'" he said "there's birds" he said "breeds, there's a bird breeds on the top o' that pole. An' you got to get to

/only's/

the top o' that pole" he said "an' bring me the eggs _ before six o'clock" he said "/?or else/ I'll have your life."

/he/

Well ya knows what 'tis like climb a glassen pole. He was at it all day. He couldn't...was nowhere. So this girl come quarter to six she..."What are ya cryin about now?" /she/ said. He told her. "Well" she said uh..."I thought I told ya" she said "I'd do whatever lied in me power _ for ya. So here" she said "cut off four o' me fingers." An' he cut off four of her fingers. "Now" she (said) "wherever you touches the pole wi' that finger _ there'll be a branch spring off." Well he climbed the pole we'll say an' got the eggs. Brought 'em down. "Now" she said "stick 'em on again" she said "stick 'em on (in) a hurry _ 'cause" she said..."('cause)...time is gettin short." He stuck 'em on...up till it come to her little finger see. An' he stuck he on crooked. [*coughs*]

But ol' man come..."Well" he said "you is smart lad." He said "Tonight" he said "you can...have a woman to bed with ya." So alright next mornin _ when he come to bed "Now how ya like...wi' woman to bed wi' ya?"

"Not very good sir" he said. He said "I wasn't in bed very long after **SHE** got there."

/he/

"Well" he said "I'm goina give ya a choice today" he said "which one of me daughters" (said) "you wants to marry." So /she/ stuck...her hand...you know out through the...door _ each hand, well _ one we'll say with the crooked finger on he **SEED** un. Well that's the one he took.

/coach/

So -- they got married then. They got married right away an' he uh...alright. So she come to un after dark. "Now" she said "get that /goat/" she said "you caught th' other day an' put [un] in the barn um...an' be ready at midnight _ 'cause father see is goin to kill the two of us tonight."

So he got ready at midnight an' they started. An' they hadn't been gone long...[th]ey wasn't goin long before...they hear th' ol' man comin. And she said uh...she said "Father 's gainin on us."

An' he said "What's he comin on now then?"

/he/

"Comin on a pig's back" she said. So _ well /she/ (said) "Catch a egg out the basket an' (it's) heave over your shoulder" she said "an' there'll be a pond [to] cross." Well that's what he done. An' _ 'twasn't very long before he heard th' ol' man **CHOPPIN**.

"Oh" she said "he's...buildin a raft to come over on now." 'Twudden [i.e., *twasn't*] very long before we'll say he had his...raft made an' was across the river...across the pond. An' he was **GAININ** on 'em.

/he/

"Now" /she/ said "take another egg" she said "out o' the basket an' heave over your left shoulder in the devil's name" she said "an' there'll be a mountain rise up." Well he done so we'll say.

She [said] "We're safe now" she said "a pig got short legs he can't run uphill." Alright they're drivin on. By an' by they come to...[*clears *throat*] they was passin on by a house _ an' she said to un she [said] "(Ye) know who lives there?"

"No" he said.

"Well" she said "that's your mother an' father lives there." Well now of course he want to go in to see 'em you know. But she said "Don't let nobody kiss you" she said "whatever you do _ or you'll forget me." Well _ he wouldn't let nobody kiss un _ you know an' they had a little dog there see. Well he jumped up an' licked...an' licked his face. Well he never thought no more about this girl we'll say was outside.

So they had a servant girl _ an' he wanted to...they wanted he to uh...wanted un to hang on now an' marry this servant girl. On the last of it he decided he would. He'd stay there an' marry her. Well now of course when they...SHE was goin to get married they want another servant. So they picked up one out around somewhere they didn't know anything about an' HE didn't know.

So before they got married he wanted everybody to tell a story. Well they all told a story clear o' this new servant girl see? So -- by an' by it come to HER turn. Wanted she [to] tell a story, no she couldn't tell nar story. But he keeped on at her an' by an' by "Well" she (said) "i[f] you give me fifteen minutes to dress" _ she'd tell a story.

"Yes."

So she come down and she (said) "Once upon a time me an' me two sisters was down to a pond for a bathing." She (said) "There was a young man there caught me clothes an' wouldn't give 'em up until I told un where the head card player o' the world was. So I told un" she (said) "an' I done all in me power for un. An' now he has for...saken me." Well he dropped everything then you know _ an' grabbed she.

Well s...he an' she got married then in place o' the other one we'll say an'...I thought 'twas time for me to be...tryin to get home.

[*recorder off*]*** ...heard a story now _ you...you never hears two stories alike. Never hears one feller tell...one story the same.
[Int. B: No.]
Always a little different.
[Int. B: Yeah. Slight...]
[*recorder off*] [Int. A: How do these variations come about you think?]
I don't know I'm sure _ how they come about. You know somebody 'd probably say you know perhaps add a little more _ on what th' other feller's was. Probably we'll say he was /tryin/ to outdo the other feller or something /fyin/ you know he add on something. We'll say Harold uh...tell something here now an' I'd go out tomorrow we'll say an' tell...well he add in 'nother word [or] two see _ into un. Well that 'd made all the difference see _ lots o' times.

Duration: 12 min., 2 sec.
Source: "Fifty year ago."
Location: Store in garden of teller's house, afternoon.
Audience: Interviewers.

Context, Style, and Language: (For context see notes to No. 1). Note also that the early part of the story is addressed directly to Harold Paddock, the interviewer from the same community, who is well-known to the teller. This allows the second interviewer to assume the more passive role of recording technician, eavesdropping as it were on the event.

The two versions of this tale were recorded nine years apart and are very similar in form and structure, although the second (No. 13) is somewhat longer. It had already been told to the collector before the recording was made. This rehearsal, and the enforced leisure of the teller's convalescence in hospital, may account for the increased length, coupled with the fact that the version collected in 1966 was recalled from memory after a long period of inactivity. The early sections of each version differ only in minor details, but the same events are expressed sufficiently differently for each telling to be regarded as unique. It is noticeable that despite the many different ways of expressing the same ideas, certain constant elements recur in each version; for example, certain individual words like *sundown* and such longer segments as "(A) thousand dollars again a thousand," the dialogue of the three "ol' fellers," the words of the head card player when the young fellow arrives at the castle, the interdiction "Don't/don't let nobody kiss you/ya...whatever...or...you'll forget me," "On the last of it he decided he would," "i(f) you'll give me fifteen minutes to dress," and especially the almost identical wording of the recapitulation in the penultimate paragraph. As with other narrators who provided us with more than one version of a given story, Allan Oake evidently needs to retain reference points such as these in each version; they are essential to every performance. Some of these focal points are highlighted by strong stress, although not always on precisely the same word in each case; in No. 12, for instance, *witches* is stressed but in No. 13 the stress is on the preceding word: "An' we're ALL witches."

A comparison reveals certain differences between the two versions. For example, in the second the witches are introduced to the audience before the young man meets them, whereas in the first the "ol' fellers" are not revealed as witches until he meets the oldest. The earlier version includes the youngest daughter's agreeing that she will "do whatever lies in me power for ye" when the young fellow gives back her clothes, and again after the first task; this detail is lost in the later version. In No. 13, the allotment of the tasks is less clear than in No. 12, but the teller simply points out, as elsewhere, that he is "a little bit before me story," and casually explains how he will put this right. Even so the details of sleeping with the pigs, the hens, and the woman are linked with different tasks in the two versions. In No. 12 the two young people got married, and this is not explicitly stated in No. 13, but the former has the goat (consistently realized as *coach* by the speaker in both versions) put in the barn, presumably an error for the horse in the latter version, and notwithstanding his correct use of *goat(s)* in No. F10. The later retelling also omits to mention that the eggs are thrown "in the devil's name." The predominant impression, however, is of the remarkable similarity of the two versions, notwithstanding the countless minor differences of expression which make each telling unique. Immediately following the story the narrator has some interesting comments to make on the reasons for such variation when more than one person tells the same story; these comments might also be applied to his own storytelling.

In this version of the tale the hero is not named as "Jack," and the name appears only once in No. 13, almost as an afterthought in the closing lines. Indeed it is unclear in both versions whether the hero is the young man who challenges the Head Card Player, or is in fact the defeated Head Card Player himself. Obviously the traditional balance of sympathy lies with a young man, without status or possessions, against an older one in a position of entrenched power.

The girls at the pond are not swan maidens but merely bathing girls. There is nothing magical about the clothes which the hero steals, there is no glass mountain, and the hero merely follows the youngest girl to her father's castle; he is not carried there.

The matter of the unlikely bed parallels in a way the "sleeping in the pool of water" episode in Thomas Walters' version (No. 9). However in Allan Oake's versions the hero's accommodation improves each time he demonstrates his "smartness" by accomplishing the impossible task. From pigs, to chickens, to a woman, the bed partners are improved, but the hero ironically claims not to have slept well with the woman.

Apart from the linguistic matters noted under No. 1, Allan Oake uses the archaic West Country *'ee* (thee, ye), and the punctuating phrase *the once* (at once, now) (cf. *EDD THE*, 12, and *ONCE*, I. 19 [Devon] Thee mun goo to bed to onst. . . .) which marks a new stage in the progression of the narrative in the same way that *Alright* occasionally marks the end of a segment. Dialectal pronunciations include the half long lowered half-open front vowel in *bathing* (the *th* realized as /t/), the diphthong /au/ in the first syllable of *shoulder* (in which the /d/ is lost or falls together with the preceding /l/), the close or half-close front vowels /i/ and/e/ in *catch(ed)*, the /ei/ in *heave*, the elision of schwa in *th' other*, the absence of /n/ in *a egg*, the aphetic form *'cause*, and the lack of initial consonant in *'tis, 'twudden* ('twasn't, with typical alteration of medial /z/ to /d/). Morphologically we have the archaic double comparative *more handier, hisself,* and *glassen,* while at the lexical level we find *again* (against), the nautical *stowed away,* the pronouns *he* and *she* in the object case, and *nar* (no, not one). Note also the phrase *on the last of it* (finally), the present tense *you sleeps/touches,* the past tense *sot, lied* (lay), *done, give, seed, want, come, keeped,* and the double negatives *nobody never could catch, don't/wouldn't let nobody,* and *never thought no more.*

See also the notes to No. 1.

Type and Motifs:
   AT313C. *The Girl as Helper in the Hero's Flight.*
N2.5. *Whole kingdom (all property) as wager.*
Cf. S221.2. *Youth sells himself to an ogre in settlement of a gambling debt.*
F150.1. *Way to otherworld hard to find.*
N825.2. *Old man helper.*
F151.0.1. *Hospitable host entertains (guides, advises) adventurer on way to otherworld.*
F571.2. *Sending to the older.*

other feller lived. When he knocked to the castle door an' _ this feller opened un. Asked un if this was...witch.

"Yes."

Asked un could he tell un where the head card player o' the world was.

"No" he said. Couldn't tell him nothing about un. "But" he said "I got a brother" he said "a day's walk from this _ three hundred, now" he said "he may _ know _ all about it."

So he stayed there all night an' _ started off next morning just in the dawn. Travelled all day to sundown an' seen this other light, well this is where t'other brother must live. He went an' knocked to the castle door an' /Cast/ this old feller opened un. /Asked/ un about the...did he know where the head card player o' the world was.

"Well" he said _ "if I don't" he said "there's nobody knows." (For) he said "Come in sir" he said. He said "The head card player o' the world." He said "There's a pond two hours' walk from this." He [said] "You go down there" he said "just in the dawn an'...and stow away an' you'll see _ look away to the mountain tops" he said "you'll see a cloud a little cloud risin. By an' by" he said "you'll see three girls comin down _ to the pond for a bathing. Well" he said "when the youngest one...gets her clothes off you go an'...an'...grab it. An' _ don't give it up till she tells you where the head card player o' the world is."

So he stayed here all night an' the next morning just in the dawn he started off for this pond. Got down. Watched to this mountain like the old witch told un an' by an' by there was a cloud rose you know he could see _ like a...bank o' fog I suppose. Come on down an' by an' by he could see the three girls comin down, (from) when the youngest one _ got her clothes off, or he **THOUGHT** 'twas the youngest, course _ he...grabbed her clothes. [*clears throat*] An' wouldn't give it up till she'd tell un where the head card player o' the world was.

"Well" she said _ "if you'll...you'll give it me back then will you?"

"Yes" he said "I will."

"Well the head card player o' the world" she (says) "lives behind that mountain. But" she said "don't come with we _ when we goes _ because he...he'll know that you...one o' you fellers...one o' we told 'ee."

Well alright. She...he stayed there we'll say an' they had their bathing an' went on back home. Gone back again.

/he/ 'Twas after /they/ was gone about a couple o' hours or more _ he started off. Went up _ tearin up when he got up behind this mountain he come across a castle _ where the head card...knocked to the door an' this ol' feller "Oh" he said "you're come. I was just comin to look for ya" he said. "An' if I had" he said "I'd had your life." An' he said uh..."Now" he said "the uh...you sleeps tonight wi' the hens" he said.

And ＿ so the uh...alright. This girl come an' told un ＿ that uh...to take the first food that come down because the hens 'd eat the same as they EAT. So ＿ alright. So (as uh...?thought about it) 'twill be alright. Better go (an' do) that. I'm a little bit before me story there. Course he...uh...be gettin a job o' work to do. [Int: Mm.] But that'll come now. An' we'll have to give the...two jobs an' right after one another.

"Well" he said "now ＿ my wife ＿ lost a...a gold ring" he said "in the barn one hundred years ago. An' he haven't been cleaned out since. Now then" he said "you got to...find that...you got to find that ring." He give un a shovel an' he said "You got to find that ring now by six o'clock this even" he said "or otherwise I'll have your life."

So he was at it all day to quarter to six. So he gave it up. Sot down...sot down an' start to cry 'cause he was goin to lose his life now.

This young...girl come to un, she said "What are ya cryin about?"

"Can't find the ring" (he said). "Six o'clock" he said.

"Well" he...she said ＿ "you take this shovel." She had a gold shovel with her. "You take this shovel" she said "an' heave over your shoulder in devil's name" she said "an' ye'll pick up the ring." Alright this is what he done.

Course she was gone again then of course an' th' ol' feller come. "Oh" he said uh..."you got the ring."

"Yes" he said.

"Well boy" he said* "you...(you're) a pretty good ＿ smart hand" he said. "NOW" he said "you sleeps wi' the hens tonight." [aside to Int: I'll come back to that again now ＿ for to get it to come right.] Alright.

*bell ringing

Then she come an' told un to take the first food...that uh...come down for the hens to eat [a] (certain day).

The next mornin now when he come "How 'ee" he said "to like to sleep with hens last night?" [Int. laughs]

"Not too good" he said.

"Well" he said uh..."there's a /goat/ in the garden...no ＿ there's"...no ＿ "there's a glassen pole in the garden" he said, "two hundred feet high. An' there's birds" he said "breeds on the top of un. An' you've got to get to that pole" he said "before ＿ six o'clock an' get me them eggs ＿ or otherwise" he said "I'll have your life."

/coach/

He was at it all day you know he couldn't...he couldn't climb this glassen pole. 'Bout quarter to six now he gave it up an' start...sot down an' start cryin, the girl come ＿ this young ＿ girl come along you know

"What ya cryin about?" He told her.

"Oh, why" she said "I told 'ee...yesterday that I'd...do whatever lies in me power for ya. Here" she [said] "cut off one o' me fingers." Cut 'em off you know. "Now wherever you touches then...pole" she said "wi' them fingers, there'll be a branch spread ou[t]...spring out. An'" /she/ said "you'll

/he/

169

be able to (get)...go an' get the eggs." So he...got up an' got the eggs alright. Come down.

"Now" she said "stick 'em on again" had (to) stick 'em on...stick 'em on in a hurry. So he stuck 'em on until it come to her little finger you know an' he stuck he on crooked. Well _ to work...'twill come out alright [the] once of course.

Ol' man come. "Oh" he said "you got th' eggs. Boy" he said "you IS a smart guy after all _ (get on) that glassen pole" he said "an' get them eggs." Now he knowed all about what was happenin see. [Int: Yeah.]* (He used to know). "Oh" he said "you sleeps wi' the pigs tonight" he said. You know an' she...she come an' told un _ before he _ barred un in to take the first food that come down. The pigs 'd eat same as they.

So _ "How do ya...how do ya like" he said, the next morning the ol' man let un out "how you like sleepin with pigs last night?"

"Not too good" he said.

"Well" he said "there's a /goat/ in the garden" he said "that nobody could never catch. An'" he said "you got to catch her an' put her in the barn before six o'clock this even. Or otherwise" he said "I'll have your life."

So _ alright. At it all day an' he couldn't get handy to it.

So sh[e]...girl come along quarter to six _ around quarter to six an' she said "What's...cryin about?"

"Can't catch that /goat/" he said.

"Oh" /she/ said "here _ take this golden saddle _ heave over your shoulder an' 'ee will _ walk up an' take the horse." That's what /he/ done. So he...put her in the barn.

The ol' feller come over he said "You got th' horse. Well" he said "you IS some smart you is. Well" he said "alright" he said "now _ you can...have a woman to bed wi' ya tonight." Well he got in bed you know wi' this woman.

The next morning th' ol' feller come. "How did ya like wi' a woman in bed wi' 'ee" he said "last night?"

"Not very well sir" he said "I wasn't in bed long after she got in." 'Fore he got up! Alright.

Now then he was goin to uh...goin to...give him his...which one of his daughters he wanted you know _ (they'd be) married, marry _ goina let un marry one of his daughters.

So they stu[ck]...had their hands stuck out through the door you know all of 'em. So _ here was this crooked finger. An' he stopped an' this is the one he picked. So uh...alright.

She come to un then about quarter to twelve in the night

"Now" she (said) "you...get that horse you've (got), put in the barn _ tonight" said " _ and _ harness un. 'Cause father's goin' to kill the two of us tomorrow. An' be ready" she said "by twelve o'clock."

*noise in background

/coach/

/coach/
/he/
/she/

Well he went an' got th' horse an' got her ready _ an' (had un) /?fed/. /ferried/
Twelve o'clock they left.

Now /she/ said "Drive whatever you can drive!" By an' by uh...[*clears* /he/
throat] "(There)" she s[aid] "father's comin. He's goin to catch us."

An' he (said) "What's he comin on?"

"Comin on a pig's back." [Int: Mm.]

So she s[aid] "Take a egg out" she (said) "an' heave across an' there'll
be a pond _ there'll be a pond 'cross behind us." So he catched th' egg out
o' the basket an' hove un, there was a pond 'cross you know. So _ alright.

'Twasn't very long 'fore they hear un _ choppin. She said "He's
choppin an' he's buildin a wha[t]...a raft now to come over on. Well"
she said "he's landed _ on the other side, he's gettin pretty handy to us. Take
another egg" _ she said "out o'...out the basket _ throw over your left
shoulder an' there'll be a mountain rise." Well alright he...she said "We are
safe now for a pig got short legs, he can't run up the mountain see _ not
fast."

Alright they drove...drivin on you know an' _ so by an' by he
come...they was passin a house an' she [said] "You know" she said "who
lives there?"

"No" he said.

"Well" she said "that's your...where your father an' mother lives
there." Now then of course he wanted to get in to see 'em. "Well" she said
"don't let nobody kiss ya _ whatever _ or you...if you do you'll forget
me."

So _ alright. Went in you know an' _ everybody wanted to kiss un, he
wouldn't let 'em. An' they had a little dog there see. The once
he...(the)...this dog jumped up an' licked his face.

Well now they had a servant girl an' _ well they want him to stay
there an' marry the...their servant girl. On the last of it he decided he
would. Well now when he...in that case they had to get another servant girl
'cause uh...he was goin to marry this one. [Int: Yes.] [*clears throat*] So
they got a girl (runnin') round they didn't know we'll say _ an' he didn't
know (ne'r) about her THEN when they...

Well before they was ready he said "Now then" he said he wanted
everybody to tell a story _ before he'd get married. Well they all told stories
an' by an' by (it) come to this servant girl, new servant girl they had. Well
uh...wanted she [to] tell a story too. Well _ she wasn't fit to tell a story
_ she said.

On the last of it "Well" she said "if you'll give me fifteen minutes to
dress _ I'll tell a story." Okay. Gave her fifteen minutes.

So she went upstairs an' got...dressed we'll say an' come down.

She said "(Now) [*coughs*] once upon a time" she said _ "me an' me three
sisters" she said "went down to a pond for a bathing. [*coughs*] There was a

171

young man there" she said "caught me clothes _ an' wouldn't give it up until _ I told un where the head card player o' the world was. Well" she said "I told un where the head card...player o' the world was" she said "I've done all in me power for un. An' I sove his life an' now he's forsaken...forsaken me."

Oh he...got...brought un right back to his senses. So _ Jack took th' other one an' married THIS one. Well I _ just stopped long enough to get a cup o' tea. An' I left _ I left...I didn't...[?stay] [*laughter*]

Duration: 14 min., 45 sec.
Source: "Fifty year ago."
Location: Springdale Hospital.
Audience: Interviewer.

Context, Style, and Language: Allan Oake is spending some time in hospital and is interviewed during his convalescence. The student interviewer has already heard the tale once but presumably failed to record it. Allan Oake agrees to tell it again, encouraged by the interviewer's occasional responses and laughter. The narrative is not interrupted by the sound of a bell ringing, nor by other background noise, including the voice of a child, presumably visiting the hospital ward. Apart from some confusion over the order of some of the episodes, the storyteller has little difficulty in recounting this quite lengthy story, in spite of a persistent cough which is the only obvious sign of his physical condition.

The typical West Country English voicing of initial /s/ and /f/ is heard in *Sir, see, found* (final /d/ lost), and *feller*. Aphesis occurs in *'Bout* and *'cross;* we also find the present tense forms *you wants/touches, [they] breeds/lives,* the past tense *knowed* and *sove,* the purposive *for to,* and the double negative *didn't know nothing.*

See also the notes to Nos. 1 and **12.**

Type and Motifs:
AT313C. *The Girl as Helper in the Hero's Flight.*
N2.5. *Whole kingdom (all property) as wager.*
Cf. S221.2. *Youth sells himself to an ogre in settlement of a gambling debt.*
Cf. F150.1. *Way to otherworld hard to find.*
G207. *Male witch.*
N825.2. *Old Man helper.*
F151.0.1. *Hospitable host entertains (guides, advises) adventurer on way to otherworld.*
F571.2. *Sending to the older.*
H1235. *Succession of helpers on quest.*
K1335. *Seduction (or wooing) by stealing clothes of bathing girl (swan maiden).*
G530.2. *Help from ogre's daughter.*
F145. *Mountain at borders of otherworld.*
Cf. G461. *Youth promised to ogre visits ogre's home.*

172

G465. *Ogre sets impossible tasks.*

H901. *Tasks imposed on pain of death.*

H1102.2. *Task: emptying in one day a barn filled with manure.*

D1205. *Magic shovel.*

Cf. F846.1. *Perilous [obnoxious] bed [hero forced to sleep with animals].*

H1114.1. *Task: securing three eggs from top of glass tower.*

F848.2. *Ladder of fingers.*

Cf. E33. *Resuscitation with missing member.*

Cf. H1154.8. *Task: capturing magic horse.*

D1209.2. *Magic saddle.*

F868.1. *Golden saddle.*

Cf. H57.0.1. *Recognition of resuscitated person by missing member.*

Cf. B184.1.6. *Flight on magic horse.*

B557. *Unusual animal as riding horse.*

D672. *Obstacle flight.*

D921.1. *Lake (pond) produced by magic.*

D932.0.1. *Mountain created by magic.*

C120. *Tabu: kissing.*

D2004.2.1. *Dog's licking of man produces forgetfulness.*

D2003. *Forgotten fiancée.*

D2006.1. *Forgotten fiancée reawakens husband's memory.*

H11. *Recognition through story-telling.*

K1911.3. *Reinstatement of true bride.*

Z10.2. *End formula.*

International Parallels: See No. 7.

14. JACK AND THE MERMAID[†]

Dan McCarthy   Cf. AT315A
Bellevue, Trinity Bay   TC1175 72-51
25 November 1971   Collector: Helen Hoskins

There was a young man one time an' he was very fond of the gun. He [was] always goin away with the gun, he had three dogs. But whatever happened this is...one...the day /he/ was out the dogs frightened some birds on (un).   /we/

An' he says "You won't frighten 'em on me tomorrow because I'll bar ye in." Said "You won't (?keep) [frightening 'em]...on me."

So anyway he'd abarred in the dogs. There was Herald, one of 'em was Heral' _ the other was Swift _ the other was Maxim. But Maxim was a very ol' dog _ very feeble _ very strong _ too.

So he travelled away with his gun an' by an' by he come to the side [o'] the lake _ watchin some birds. An' up comes a sea monster. An' he come in of course. An' he was goin to take...Jack right off o' the bat. (Yeah). So -- thi[s]...this old sea monster or whatever they...the...the...they called him had a...mermaid or whatever, it was a...(thing)...a seahorse, she was...they were able to t...it was able to talk anyway.

He said uh...Jack said "Gi'..." he said "gi' me uh...will you gi' me uh...three whistles _ three hollies _ three whistles an' three coughs" _ he said. Now he had his dogs broke in to this you know uh...Jack did. Oh yes he'd give un that time alright.

/picked/   He said "Alright" so he coughed. Begar Heral' /pricked/ up her ears. Coughed again. Uh...she know Jack she know 'twas he _ (he said). So she got up an' started uh...scratchin the door, begar Jack coughed again. An' begar _ Swift heard un. Now they got up, they got out the door _ two dogs an' after a spell they got un down. So Jack coughed agai[n]...hollied again. And as well...so hard as they could go, course Swift could go pretty good but Heral' wasn't so good as she [*Swift*] was _ ('cause he's)...an' old Maxim an' he was lyin down the ol'...shack sleepin it off, snorin it off.

So -- anyway after a bit begar he [*Maxim*] heard un. But the racket their dogs had I suppose they woke un an'...that uh...he got up. An' the two dogs took off. This ol' _ mermaid used to have her hand out you know almost or almost gettin Jack _ almost gettin un. An' he'd back away _ back away, wi' prayin to god his dogs 'd come _ now. But by [an'] by begar _ Heral'

/she/   come. An' she got (out)...at th' ol'...mermaid. An' /he/ [*Herald*] just could
/'em/   do it to keep /her/ [*the mermaid*] off. Uh...by an' by begar Swift come an' the two of 'em got after un. An' the...they was gainin ground on the two dogs an' there was ol' Maxim he slavin along _ (just) take his time _ dodgin away.

Now Jack said "By the name o' god I suppose he won't get here at all!" Huh! Huh! [*laughs*] An' he'd ALMOST have un _ an' ALMOST have un. An' by an' by begar he seen old Maxim slavin along _ dodgin along takin his time _ worried about nobody. Anyway begar he got up. (When) he got up to her he slewed his backside (to it) he give her a flick with his backside an' beat un _ under the tout-piece! [i.e., *backside*] [*laughs*]

Duration: 3 min., 23 sec.
Location: Kitchen of teller's house, evening.
Audience: Fieldworker and several friends or relatives of both sexes.

Context, Style, and Language: Skipper Dan McCarthy, who is married to the fieldworker's grandmother, is sitting on the couch, smoking his pipe. Intermittent microphone noise suggests that the interviewer is unable to maintain a specific position during the narration.

Skipper Dan is very much aware of the tape recorder, but is much less nervous than in the first long story recorded at the same interview and the nervous laughter is much less evident (see notes to No. 3). His lively style is exemplified by considerable tonal variety, especially in the contrasting characterization of the three dogs.

Many of the linguistic features commented on in the notes to No. 3, "Daddy Redcap," are again in evidence here. On this occasion, however, the teller's style is more cryptic, so much so that it is at times difficult to follow the events of the story, especially as the motivation is not always explained, e.g., for the use of the whistles, hollies, and coughs which the audience is left to gather are signals to summon the dogs. The teller often pauses for several seconds before the final word or phrase of a sentence, adding these almost like an afterthought and thereby contributing to the suspense. In transcribing these final words it is often necessary to use the symbol _ rather than a full stop to indicate the pause, in order to preserve the continuity of the narrative, even though the intonation pattern may suggest that the sentence ends before the afterthought. This is one of many problems which beset the transcriber in attempting to render a narrator's speech in detail. This cryptic style is similar to that of Ron Murray (see No. 82) who also adds words in an undertone after completing a sentence. Both tellers use this device to reiterate a phrase which they have just said, or to act as a kind of continuity system which helps the audience to bridge the gap from one sentence to another.

Dan McCarthy again makes frequent use of the asseveration *begar*. He also uses *ye* in the objective case in the first sentence of the second paragraph, the archaic past participle *abarred*, and the form *holly* for *hollo* (cf. *folly* [follow]). The punch line depends on the final compound *tout-piece* [ˈtautˈplːs], (cf. *OED Toute* Obs. The buttocks, etc.; *EDD* TOUT sb.[3] The rump; the posterior), apparently hitherto unrecorded in Newfoundland. Note also the unusual construction of *frighten* + nominal + *on* + pronoun in the first two paragraphs.

See also the notes to No. 3.

Type and Motifs:
   Cf. AT315A. *The Cannibal Sister.*
B81. *Mermaid.*
G308.1. *Fight with sea (lake) monster.*
Cf. K551.3. *Respite from death until victim has blown on horn (three times).*
B524.1.2.1. *Dogs break bonds and kill master's attacker.*

International Parallels: In 1951 Halpert recorded a Kentucky cante fable, somewhat related to our Newfoundland recension, in which the names of the dogs were not only memorable in themselves, but became even more memorable because they were sung repeatedly throughout the tale. On a moonlit night a young man is walking on a mountain, having left his three hound-dogs behind, fastened in his cabin. When he finds himself pursued by three witches, he climbs up a large sycamore tree. As they chop at the tree with a hatchet, he sings out in a five-tone melody, calling his dogs by name to come to his assistance. The dogs howl in response in a two-tone chant. He repeats his song with increasing volume and urgency as the tree begins to sway; the dogs' response gets louder and louder as they race to his aid up the mountain. Just as the tree is about to fall, the dogs arrive and promptly eat up the witches.

Fascinated both by the dramatic cante-fable performance and by the unusual names of the dogs, Halpert began to assemble folktale parallels to this cante fable. He had a prior interest in some very different cante-fable patterns, including several discussed in this collection in the notes to Nos. 49, 65, 90, and 115. He also started to collect references to the different varieties of dog names found in folktales and other folklore genres as well as in literature.

Tale No. 14, given above, is obviously related to Halpert's 1951 Kentucky text. Therefore, when we decided to include the Newfoundland recension in this folktale collection, we had a large body of data available, assembled over some twenty years, upon which to draw for our preliminary annotation. The variations between the Kentucky and Newfoundland texts will be commented on later in this discussion.

Both the Kentucky tale and its congeners are closely parallel to Incident IV in AT315A, "The Cannibal Sister," with witches or other fearsome beings replacing the evil sister. Although the AT index refers only to versions from India for this Type, our notes add seven reports of the Type from southeastern Europe and the Near East. But the more important fact that our notes demonstrate is that tale versions resembling this Kentucky narrative have a vigorous independent existence in oral tradition, one that is quite apart from the Type in which Incident IV occurs. However, since this group of independent tales has not achieved recognition as a Type in the AT index, we have used the label "Cf. AT315A" to include both our Newfoundland recension and the analogues in our notes. Baughman lists two Kentucky versions of this tale under AT303, "The Twins or Blood-Brothers." To the best of our knowledge, no other versions are cited in his *Index*.

We soon realized that we had to reserve for a separate study the data on the use of dog names in literature, ranging from Acteon's dogs in Ovid's *Metamorphoses,* and the dogs in Chaucer and Shakespeare, to the named dogs in Robert Surtees' nineteenth-century English novel, *Handley Cross*. Similarly, despite the fact that a majority of the named animals in Cf. AT315A are hunting dogs, we cannot include here a survey of the use of dog names in the long, but still unwritten history of English hunting songs. We have left a few key references on these two topics in our "Studies and Notes" below.

Originally, in addition to the parallels to Cf. AT315A, we had intended to include in our annotations all tales in which dogs are named, but had to abandon the idea because the notes became too extensive and diffuse. It is obvious, however, that dogs (occasionally replaced by other animals) have an essential function in versions of both AT315A and Cf. AT315A. To put that function in proper focus, let us survey briefly several other Types in which dogs have important roles.

In some versions of AT300, "The Dragon-Slayer," the hero has secured three remarkable dogs. These dogs either help their master slay the dragon, or do the whole job by themselves.

In AT303, "The Twins or Blood-Brothers," each of the twins has one of twin horses and one of a pair of twin dogs. One brother meets a witch. Unwisely he ties his horse and his dog with hairs given to him by the witch, and the hairs magically prevent his animals from helping him. In consequence, all three are turned to stone. When the other twin also meets the witch, he only pretends to tie his animals with the proffered hairs, but instead puts the latter in the fire. Consequently, when the witch calls on the hairs to tighten, they are unable to do so. As a result the second twin's horse and dog help him to overcome the witch, and thus he is able to restore to life the captured brother and his two animals.

Extraordinary dogs have a very significant role in AT315, "The Faithless Sister." They break loose and save the hero when his life is in danger, and later, when his sister kills him with a poisoned bone, the dogs dig up his corpse and remove the bone, or lick out the poison, thus restoring him to life.

Not dogs but lions play a similar part in AT590, "The Prince and the Arm Bands." When his treacherous mother, who has a giant as her lover, sends her son on a quest to get magic apples that cause him to fall asleep, the lions protect him from the giant's brother. Then, when his mother steals his strength-giving belt and has him blinded and set adrift in a boat, the lions rescue him, learn how to restore his sight, and proceed to cure him.

For full analyses of these four Types and of some of their interrelationships, see the studies by Ranke, Espinosa, Dawkins, Delarue, and Christiansen listed under "Studies and Notes" below. They include comments on the roles of the dogs and some observations on the dog names. There are interesting dog names in many of those versions of AT300 in which dogs figure, and also in nearly all English-language texts of AT315. Sometimes the names describe the characteristics of the dogs: their strength, speed, ferocity, and so on; at other times the names are colorful, but any special meanings they may originally have had are no longer obvious. Both kinds of names are found in many versions of Cf. AT315A.

As a tentative generalization, in these four Types the dogs or other animals are obtained by the hero(es) either in supernatural fashion, as in AT303, or from a supernatural personage. In AT303, each of the twin brothers calls on his dog and his horse for assistance against the witch. In each of the other tales the dogs/animals obviously have supernatural knowledge and warn their master of various dangers or take action to help him when he is in danger without being called on, or initiate action on their own, e.g., to cure their master's blindness or to restore him to life.

In many North American examples of Cf. AT315A, as well as in versions from elsewhere, the dogs are apparently ones the hero has trained and they are devoted to him. They have been left fastened up at home when he is attacked by one or more personages or creatures with supernatural powers. He lets the dogs know he is in urgent need of their assistance by singing their names, or by whistling or calling to them, or by blowing on a whistle or flute—in short, by whatever signaling method the dogs have been trained to obey. When they hear his signal, the dogs break loose and rush off to aid him.

In other narratives instead of a direct oral signal to call the dogs, another more magical device is employed. As Bascom points out: "Sometimes he leaves behind a life token so that the dogs can be released when he is in danger; it is usually a liquid that turns red or turns to blood. . . ." Here again when the dogs are made aware that their master needs them, they respond eagerly. We should observe, however, that there are a number of versions in which we find both the life token and the calls to the dogs.

Before discussing the Newfoundland recension we shall summarize briefly our notes on the geographical distribution of this independent form of Cf. AT315A. The tale is well known in the United States in both the white and black traditions, but particularly

Parsons nor Thompson had cited any others. Our notes indicate that seven versions of Cf. AT315A have been reported from southeastern Europe and the Near East. We also have two examples of the independent form of this narrative, from Ireland and from the Bashkir A.S.S.R. Whether a knowledge of these additional versions might have caused Bascom to modify, however slightly, his theory of the African origin of this tale, is not a question that concerns us. We are interested in trying to determine the relationship of our Newfoundland recension to Cf. AT315A.

From Bascom's discussion, as well as from the title of his article, it is evident that he regards what he calls the "tree refuge" from which the dogs rescue their master as an essential element of this story. Since there is no "tree refuge" in our Newfoundland recension as we ourselves have pointed out, Bascom would probably have excluded it from his study. Nonetheless, despite the lack of the tree refuge, our recension, which we assume from the narrator's name is probably of Irish origin, in all other respects is extraordinarily close to many of the texts examined both by Bascom and by us.

Since it seems unlikely either that the Newfoundland tale is a local invention or that it was carried here from the United States or Africa, can we find anything to reinforce the assumption of Irish origin? There is a quite different story worth examining that is told as one of his adventures by the Black Thief in a County Galway version of AT953, "The Old Robber Relates Three Adventures"; see Dillon, *King,* pp. 28-30. The Black Thief has stolen a valuable sword from the house of three giant hags while they are sleeping, knowing that they will pursue him when they awake. Because it is snowing outside and his footprints would be easy to follow, he decides to hide from them on the side-wall of their house, hoping the snow will cover and conceal him. After the hags have searched in vain for footsteps, the snow melting from his body reveals his whereabouts to them. They set to work "at each wing of the house." From this predicament he is rescued by his hunting dogs (they are not named) to whom he calls by whistling. They come quickly and when they arrive they get rid of the hags.

Here again we have a tale with elements that parallel many examples of Cf. AT315A, except that here "hags" replace the more common "witches." As in the Newfoundland recension and many other versions, the man calls his dogs and they rescue him. Once again no "tree refuge" is present, though the house side-wall seems a reasonable substitute. At least it provides the barrier of distance lacking in the Newfoundland story.

It is the absence of the "tree refuge" in both the County Galway and the Newfoundland narratives that tempts us to suggest that there may be an Irish oikotype of Cf. AT315A in which the tree refuge is either missing or has been replaced by a substitute. However, two different versions of a tale hardly provide sufficient evidence for such a proposal, though there may be more examples in the Archives of the Department of Irish Folklore, University College, Dublin.

As we observed earlier, the "tree refuge" scene adds a fine dramatic touch to most versions of Cf. AT315A. The man in danger from witches or other supernatural personages is up in a tree calling to his dogs who are some distance away. The witches are chopping away at the tree and it is beginning to sway. Just as the tree is about to fall, the dogs arrive and save him. While the dogs also rescue their master in the two stories just discussed, neither tale has the "tree refuge," as we have reiterated.

We have already cited one story from an Irish version of AT953, "The Robber Relates Three Adventures." It was while we were analyzing and annotating the Newfoundland recensions of this Type, Nos. 62-64, that we were startled to discover excellent versions of the "tree refuge" scene in them, though in a very different context. Since we treat these in detail in the notes to No. 62, we shall only summarize our discussion here.

The story is one of the adventures of the Black Thief/Chief, which he tells to show how very close he had been to death and yet escaped. As we point out in the notes to No. 62, Irish versions of the narrative occur in the following: *The Royal Hibernian Tales,* pp. 156-57; Curtin, *Hero-Tales,* pp. 99-101; and MacManus, *Book,* pp. 169-70. Here is a summary.

The Black Thief had stolen some gold from under the heads of three sleeping witches. When they pursue him closely, he climbs a tree to escape from them. They promptly start to cut it down in order to catch and kill him. As their chopping proceeds, the tree sways back and forth and is almost ready to fall. However, the Thief is saved from death at the hands of the witches, not by his dogs, but because at cockcrow (sunlight, daybreak) the witches lose their supernatural powers, change back into normal human form, and then hurry away.

What is particularly interesting about this story is not merely the close parallel in the "tree refuge" scene, but also the powers of transformation these witches or hags possess: their ability to turn themselves into animals or tools, and then to return to the shape of blandly ordinary persons. There is a striking resemblance in this respect to the transformations that occur in connection with the "tree refuge" episode in many versions of Cf. AT315A.

In short, several important features of the widespread narrative that Bascom describes in "Dogs Rescue Master from Tree-Refuge" are present here and have been known in Ireland in the English-language tradition since before 1824; see the notes to No. 62 for a summary of Ó Duilearga's comments on the chapbook known as *The Royal Hibernian Tales.* The fact that in this narrative the man is not rescued from the "tree refuge" by his dogs is, of course, a very major difference from Bascom's outline.

As we have already shown there is a County Galway story in which dogs do rescue their master from supernaturally powerful hags, though it is from the top of a house side-wall rather than from a "tree refuge." It would be interesting to learn if any unpublished versions of Cf. AT315A have been collected in Ireland, versions that combine the witches, the "tree refuge," and the rescue of their master by his dogs.

We have found no published examples of Cf. AT315A in the Scottish sources available to us. However, we should call attention to the fact that an excellent cante-fable version of the tale from the United States, one that may have Scottish antecedents, has been published; see Wright, *JAF* 54 (1941), 197-99. The contributor, Estelle Wright, supplied the following background: "This story was told to me when I was a child by my mother. I later learned that my great grandmother, who came from the Scotch colony in North Carolina, had told it to my mother. And my great grandmother first heard it from her grandmother."

We have no information on where in North Carolina this "Scotch colony" was located, nor when it was settled, nor from what section or sections of Scotland its founders came. Nor for that matter can we be certain that the narrative was one actually learned in

Scotland. There is always the chance that the contributor's distant female progenitor could have heard it from someone in the United States. Nevertheless the unusually detailed chain of transmission in this family tradition deserves respectful attention and further investigation. Researchers might still locate versions of Cf. AT315A in Scotland.

Whether or not other versions of this story are found in Ireland or Scotland is, after all, a minor matter. What is more significant is that, working quite independently of each other, both Bascom's researches and ours demonstrate that Cf. AT315A is a widespread international folktale that has eluded the folktale indexers. A place for it and a Type number will have to be established in a future revision of the AT index.

Bascom's excellent discussion of many of the variant forms of the narrative (pp. 462-64) will be a convenient beginning for the future indexer who must write a description of the incidents found in the new Type, and who will undoubtedly also take advantage of Bascom's full summaries of 117 texts. Since the new Type will not be limited to African and American narratives, our citations of some European and Asian versions may be a useful starting point for a broader survey.

Since our references were assembled independently to supply parallels to our Newfoundland recension, they differ from Bascom's in one important respect. Because there is no "tree refuge" in our recension, our notes include some texts without this element, together with many that have it. Bascom's citations are limited to narratives that have the "tree refuge." To clarify the relationship between his notes and ours: where both of us deal with the same text, we refer the reader to the number of the full summary of the text in his article by noting in parentheses a "B" plus the relevant summary number, immediately after our citation. Some of our references supplement Bascom in that they are to texts that meet his criteria and have the "tree refuge," but were not included in his article. Each of these citations is followed by the indication: "(not in B)." If there is no citation of Bascom's article, either positive or negative, after one of our references, it usually indicates that the text noted is one without the "tree refuge" element.

At the start of this discussion we stressed our original interest in the kind of cante-fable performance exemplified in the Kentucky version summarized there, in which the dogs are called by name in a song and respond by howling in a melodic chant, both call and response being reiterated in the narrative with increasing urgency and volume. As our notes indicate, only a few published versions of the tale from the United States, the Caribbean, and Africa include the tunes of the songs the man sings.

That tunes are not given for the many other versions which state that the man sang to call his dogs may be due to any of a variety of reasons. If the text was secured by dictation, the collector may not have felt musically competent to note the tune. If it was recorded on disk or tape, he might not have known a music transcriber he could call upon. Or, either the collector or the publisher may have regarded the printing of the music as an unnecessary luxury. Last, the collector may have been interested only in the text, and quite unaware of the importance of including the tunes.

Some collectors, interested in presenting the tunes with the text, apparently do not realize that the howls of the dogs running to aid their master can quite frequently be transcribed as two-tone musical chants. A melody may even be involved in texts which say the man called to his dogs rather than that he sang to them. Calls to dogs, like the calls to many other domestic animals, commonly use a two- or three-tone chant. Other potential melodic elements may be found in versions which say the man whistled to his dogs or that he blew a flute or a whistle. In some versions of the tale the witch(es) or other being(s) cutting down the tree sing(s) a song. The only example that we have found for this pattern, in which the tunes sung both by the endangered boy and by the axmen are given, is the second Jamaica version in Tanna, *Folk Tales*, pp. 127-28.

Whether potential musical elements are actualized in a particular narration depends on whether the storyteller presents them dramatically or only reports the actions. In the Kentucky cante-fable recording described earlier, the narrator sings the songs with which the dogs are called, and reproduces the sounds of their answering howls. This contrasts with the recording of the Newfoundland recension. In the latter the narrator reports that the man coughed, whistled, and hollied to his dogs, but makes no attempt to illustrate these sounds dramatically.

Only a very few of the versions in our notes make it clear that the telling of this tale is a performance in which the songs and responses have an important dramatic function. An excellent example of such a performance is in a North Carolina text: Wright, *JAF* 54 (1941), 197-99. Since the narrative is not summarized in Bascom's article, we give one here. The story, apparently one frequently heard in childhood, is given in great detail. A little boy has two big dogs, named Sammy Lingo and Bobby Cuso, who wear bells around their necks which play a tune when they run; the tune is given. The boy is enticed away from home by two men and leaves his dogs behind, locked up in the smokehouse, but he also leaves a life token. His father is to release them if the water in a pan turns to blood. The boy carries six grains of corn with him. When the men try to grab and kill him, he flees. Each time he gets tired he drops a grain of corn, which produces in turn an obstacle: first, a huge cornfield, then a great river, and last a thick wood. His pursuers must traverse each of these. Too tired to run further, the boy climbs up a tall tree.

In the meanwhile the father sees the water has turned to blood, releases the dogs, and they race away. The men commence to chop the tree, and the boy starts calling his dogs by name in a song; the tune is given. In answer he hears, very faintly, the sound of the bells: onomatopoeic words are given, so it is apparent that this is sung, but the first time it is in a very soft voice. When the tree is nearly cut through, the boy drops a fourth grain of corn and the tree becomes twice as big. The alternation between the boy's singing and the increasingly louder song that represents the sound of the dogs' bells as they run, continues, with the boy dropping another grain of corn each time the tree is nearly cut through. The boy has dropped his sixth and last grain of corn, and the tree is nearly down, when the dogs rush up and kill the two men. Then the boy and his playmates go home.

A unique feature of this narrative is the use of a song that represents the dogs' bells and serves as a musical response to the boy's song. We know of no other version in which bells are featured. But what this text also demonstrates most convincingly is that a full cante-fable performance does not always require a sound recording that must be transcribed. Here the method of presentation, with its descriptions of the increasing volume of the song of the bells given alongside the repeated song text, is tellingly graphic. We must admit, however, that such well-presented versions are not common, either of dictated or transcribed texts.

The collection and study of the cante fable has suffered for years because few folktale collectors can handle the musical side, while the few musicians who have demonstrated interest in cante-fable melodies were usually unfamiliar with folktale scholarship. It is to be hoped that with the contemporary interest in folktale performance, there will be an increase in collaborative work in this fascinating area in which songs and prose are interspersed in narratives.

We mentioned earlier that the curious and varied names of the dogs in the different versions of this tale not only are intriguing in themselves but also represent a cultural practice of great antiquity that is found in various genres besides the tale. Of course, the best evidence that the naming of dogs is virtually a worldwide practice is found in the tales themselves, as Bascom's notes and ours demonstrate.

What needs to be stressed is that the individualizing of dogs by giving them names reflects the close relationship boys and men have with their dogs. Dogs require careful individual attention and training from puppyhood on. During that process the trainer develops an affection for the animals and a reliance on them which the dogs reciprocate. As these tales demonstrate, when the man calls his dogs, whether by singing or calling their names, or by any other audible signal to which they are accustomed, he feels confident that he can depend on their prompt and eager response.

It is interesting to find that both this pleasure in unusual dog names and an indication of a man's fondness for, and reliance upon his favorite dogs are not limited to western culture. We find both points noted in an excellent recording of an African version of cf. AT315A, collected from the Limba people of Sierra Leone by Finnegan (*Stories,* pp. 117-24). The text is a cante fable, and though Finnegan does not include the tunes, she supplies illuminating comments on several features of the performance in footnotes to specific sections of the text. In the tale the narrator has just explained that the hero, Sara, has trained three dogs and gives their names. Here is Finnegan's comment (p. 121, n. 2) on this statement: "Dogs often have names, sometimes with special meanings. Here Salialoho means 'jumping well' and was uttered here and later with lingering affection by Karanke [the storyteller], implying how rightly fond Sara was of him. The recurrence of these unusual and attractive names seemed to be one of the effective points about the story for the audience."

Such an insight into a performance feature can only be achieved by a thorough knowledge of the culture and of the storytelling style. Yet long before such knowledge is obtained, a collector's impressionistic observations on aspects of performance can enrich a text and vivify it for the reader.

Studies and Notes
Surtees, *Handley Cross,* pp. 1-13, chap. 1, "The Olden Times"; "Names of Dogs," *N & Q* 7th ser., 6 (25 Aug. 1888), 144-45, ibid. (6 Oct. 1888), 269-71, ibid. (10 Nov. 1888), 374, ibid. (15 Dec. 1888), 462-63; Boas, "Notes on Mexican Folk-Lore," *JAF* 25 (1912), 259 and n. 1; Kidson and Neal, pp. 70-71; Fortescue, "Sports and Pastimes: Hunting." In *Shakespeare's England,* 2, pp. 334-50, chap. 27, sec. 1; Parsons, "Die Flucht auf den Baum," *Zeitschrift für Ethnologie,* 54 (1922), 1-29; Beckwith, *Stories,* pp. 269-71, no. 82; Robinson, *Works,* p. 245, line 3383 (The Nun's Priest's Tale), and p. 861, note; Ranke, *Die Zwei Brüder, FFC* no. 114; Parsons, *Antilles,* 3, p. 167, no. 180, headnote; Espinosa, *CPE* 3, pp. 9-26; Dufton, *Hunters' Songs;* Dawkins, *Modern,* pp. 156-57, no. 28, headnote; Dean-Smith, *Guide;* Starnes, "Acteon's Dogs," *Names* 3, no. 1 (March, 1955), 19-25; Dorson, *Folktales,* pp. 232-33, note 163;

Delarue, *Catalogue,* 1, p. 269; Christiansen, *Studies,* pp. 34-35, 46-47; Finnegan, *Stories,* p. 121, note 2, p. 123, and notes 3 and 4; Bascom, "African Folktales in America: XII. Dogs Rescue Master in Tree Refuge," *RAL* 12 (1981), 460-519.

Canada

Cf. Teit, *Traditions,* pp. 34-36, no. 6 [2 dogs: Grizzly Bear and Rattlesnake], Thompson River Indian (British Columbia) (B61).

In a note to the editors, Dr. Margaret Low points out that in the Lacourcière-Low "Catalogue," "rescue by dogs is a frequent motif in T.[AT]315."

United States

Cf. Parsons, *Islands,* 1, pp. 121-25, no. 43 (with 313), cf. pp. 125-31, no. 44 (with 313, 780), cf. pp. 131-32, no. 45, cf. pp. 132-34, no. 46 (with 326), 4 versions [3 dogs: Flower, Hour, and Moment; 3 lions: Hours, Moment, and Wait; 1 dog: Little Lion; 4 lions: Jira, Mariano, Salamansa and Sojiroconjiro], English trans. of Portuguese texts, nos. 43 and 44 have tunes, Cape Verde Islands, black (Massachusetts) (B62, 63, 64).

Cf. Harris, *Friends,* pp. v-vi, mentions a MS. text similar to the version he gives on pp. 91-100, no. 12; his contributor learned it from his grandfather who had heard it from his old black nurse in British Guiana [2 dogs: Yarmearoo and Genga-maroto] (New Jersey) (B65).

Cf. Dorson, *Folktales,* pp. 198-99, and see pp. 232-33, note 163 [2 dogs: Dan and Rangtang; Dorson remarks, "The fantastic names of the dogs especially distinguish this plot" and he gives several groups of the names], black (Michigan) (B66), and rpt. in Dorson, *American,* pp. 249-50, no. 125.

Cf. Crimmins, *PTFS* 9 (1931), 165-66 [Mr. 'Possum and Mr. Coon instead of boy and witch; 4 dogs: Longie, Sonnie, Billie, and Buckena], learned in Virginia, black (Washington, D.C.) (B75).

Cf. Swanton, *Myths,* pp. 72-73, no. 79, from the W. O. Tuggle collection [3 dogs: Simursitty, Jeudawson, and Ben-boten], Creek Indian (Southeastern United States) (B74).

Cf. Parsons, *JAF* 30 (1917), 189-90, no. 39 [2 dogs: King Kilus and King Lovus; note says in one variant dog's name is Carlo], black (North Carolina) (B76).

Cf. Hendricks, *Bundle,* pp. 178-79 [5 dogs: Bark, Berry, Jupiter, Kerry, and Darker-in-de-mawnin'], literary reworking, black (North Carolina) (B77).

Cf. Wright, *JAF* 54 (1941), 197-99 (with 313, III) (has 2 tunes) [2 dogs: Sammy Lingo and Bobby Cuso], Scotch colony (North Carolina) (not in B).

Cf. Rodenbough, *NCF* 19 (1971), 180-81 [5 dogs: Bark, Berry, Jupiter, Kerry, and Dockery in the morning], black (North Carolina) (not in B) [cf. Hendricks, *Bundle*].

Cf. Parsons, *Sea Islands,* pp. 80-83, no. 73, 3 texts (first has tune), cf. pp. 83-88, no. 74 (with 327 and 300; has tune), 1 text, 4 versions [2 dogs: Jimmie Bingo and Jim Bolden; 2 dogs: Cut-Throat and Suck-Blood; 4 dogs: Cut-er-Throat, Suck-er-Blood, Crack-er-Bone, and Smash-er-Meat; 2 dogs: Cut-de-T'roat and Suck-de-Blood], black (South Carolina) (B78, 79, 80, 81).

Cf. [Penn School], *JAF* 38 (1925), 223-24 [3 dogs: Cut throat, Crack bone, and Drag it Away], black (South Carolina) (B82).

Cf. Parler, *JAF* 64 (1951), 422-23 (with 327B) (has tune) [2/3? dogs: Bah-manecker rody Kai-anger], Gullah dialect trans. into standard English, black (South Carolina) (not in B).

Cf. Harris, *Friends,* pp. 91-100, no. 12 [2 dogs: Minny-Minny Morack and Follamalinska], black (Georgia) (B84).

Mayer, *Guide,* pp. 114-15, no. 109 (315A) [2 falcons] (Japan) (not in B).

The Philippines
Santos, *JAF* 34 (1921), 393-95 (cf. 315A) [1 dog, not named] (Manila) (not in B).

Africa
Cf. Finnegan, *Stories,* pp. 117-24 [3 dogs: Kondengmukure, Sosongpeng, and Salialoho], cf. pp. 143-46 [3 dogs: Denifela, Sangsangso, and Tungkangbai], 2 versions, Limba tribe (Sierra Leone) (B6, 7).

Cf. Rattray, *Folk-Tales,* pp. 164-69, no. 43 [4 dogs: Sniff-sniff, Lick-lick, Tie-in-knots, and Gulp-down], Ashanti text and English trans., Ashanti tribe (Gold Coast) (B16).

Cf. Herskovits, *Narrative,* pp. 186-90, no. 27 [6 dogs, not named], cf. pp. 240-41, no. 51 [dogs, not named], cf. pp. 271-72, no. 63 [3 dogs, not named], cf. pp. 275-84, no. 65 [7 chief dogs of 41: Loka, Loke, Loki, Wesi, Wesa, Gbwlo, and Gbwloke], cf. pp. 284-87, no. 66 [dogs, not named], 5 versions (Dahomey) (B18, 19, 20, 21, 22).

Cf. Tremearne, *Superstitions,* p. 298, no. 51 [blows flute to call dogs, not named] (B24), cf. pp. 298-99, no. 51, variant, abstract only [calls his dogs, not named] (B24), cf. pp. 455-56, no. 100, variant, abstract only [calls his 3 dogs, not named] (not in B), 3 versions, Hausa people (Nigeria).

Cf. Vernon-Jackson, *Folk Tales,* 1, pp. 35-39 [dogs, not named], Angas people (Northern Nigeria) (B28).

Cf. Frobenius, *Nights,* pp. 182-87 [3 dogs: He Who Cuts, He Who Snaps, and He Who Cleans] Yoruba tribe (Nigeria) (B29).

Cf. Walker, *Folk Tales,* pp. 17-19 [3 dogs, not named], Yoruba tribe (Nigeria) (B30).

Cf. Fuja, *Cowries,* pp. 155-61 [plays magic flute to call his 3 dogs: Cut to Pieces, Swallow Up, and Clear the Remains], Yoruba tribe (Nigeria) (B31).

Cf. Dayrell, *Ikom,* pp. 11-13, no. 6 [5 dogs, not named], Ikom district (Nigeria) (B37).

Cf. Talbot, *Shadow,* pp. 247-54 (with 313, III, cf. 1115) [2 dogs: Oro Njaw and one not named], Ekoi people (Nigeria) (B36).

Cf. Tracey, *Lion,* pp. 15-24, no. 4 (with cf. 301A; has tune) [3 dogs: Madembo, Machena, and Puppy], Shona people (Rhodesia) (not in B).

Cf. Stayt, *Bavenda,* p. 348, no. 10 [shouts and whistles for dogs, not named], Ba Venda tribe (Northern Transvaal) (B54).

Cf. Brownlee, *Lion,* pp. 116-20 [hunters' dogs, not named], tribe not specified (South Africa) (not in B).

Cf. Theal, *Folk-Lore,* pp. 122-26 [3 dogs, not named], Kaffir people (Cape Colony) (B58).

Cf. Kidd, *Childhood,* pp. 224-30, no. 1 [1 dog: White], Kaffir people (South Africa) (B50).

Cf. Callaway, *Nursery,* pp. 47-52 [pack of dogs, not named], cf. pp. 53-54 [dogs, not named], cf. pp. 142-47 (with 313, III) [dogs, not named], 3 versions, Zulu texts and English trans., Zulu people (South Africa) (B55, 56, 57).

15. MASTER ARCH

Az McLean   AT325
Payne's Cove, Great Northern Peninsula   TC133 64-17
11 July 1964   Collector: M. M. Firestone

One time you know there was an old man walkin the seashore, well he saw Master Arch ['s son] playin ball 'while too. Well he was playin ball pretty good but not so well as Master Arch's. Well it vexed th' ol' man, the ball come ashore he went an' picked un up. Well Master Arch walks up to un aks un why he take that ball for.

"Well" he said "my son couldn't play so good as yours."

"Well there" he said "you couldn't expect un, mine full (trained?) your[s] a little but give me your son for twelvemonth he'll play as good as mine."

Well ol' man 'greed to give him his son for a twelvemonth anyway, he went home, the twelvemonth soon passed away.

Well this old man come walkin the seashore again. (He) [*his son*] could play ball pretty good today, not so well [as] Master Arch's. Anyway the ball come ashore, it vexed th' old man, he went an' picked un up again. Well Master Arch walks up an' (aks him) what he take that ball for.

"Well" he says "my son couldn't play so good as yours"

"Well there" he said "you couldn't expect un. Mine full (trained) [yours a] (little) but give me your son for twelvemonth he'll play so good as mine"

Well ol' man 'greed to give him his son for another twelvemonth anyway. Well th' ol' man went home, the twelvemonth soon passed away, he come walkin the seashore again.

Well he [*the old man's son*] could play ball ON the water today just as well as Master Arch's but he wouldn't play ball UNDER water so well, well [it] vexed th' ol' man (that way) the ball co...sh...come ashore he went an' picked un up again.

Well Master Arch walked up to un aks un what he take that ball for

"Well" he said "my son couldn't play so good as yours."

"Well there" he said "you couldn't expect un, mine full (trained an' yours a little) but give me your son he'll play so good as mine."

Well ol' man 'greed to give him his son _ anyway. Well he went home. Well he didn't know what to do now he (would) give away his son (didn't) know what to do anyway. Well he said he wouldn't eat two meals (off o') one table so he drinked three sups out of one cup 'fore he get his son so started out off to look for his son.

Well he comes to the ol' man

"Well" he said "you're in search of your son"

"Oh no" he said he couldn't sell the bridle anyway.

"Well father" he said "[there's] goin [to be] another race run here tomorrow" he said. "Well they're goin bettin a hundred on the horse, you bet two on me" he said "you'll gain un. Whatever you do" he said "don't sell the bridle, well if you sells the bridle" he said "I'm gone."

Well the next mornin they come an' bettin a hundred on the horse, th' ol' man bet two on his. Anyway (he) went in the ring once, he went around twice, anyway he gain the race. So they want to buy the horse so he sold the horse. They went to take the bridle off un "Oh no" he said

"Oh yes" they said

"Oh no" he said. So he sold th' horse.

"Well now father" he said "goin be another race run here tomorrow" he said "an' they're goin bettin a hundred...two hundred on th' horse, you bet four on me" he said "you'll gain un. Whatever you do" he said "don't sell the bridle, well if you sells the bridle" he said "I'm gone."

Well the next morning come bettin two hundred on th' horse, th' ol' man bet four on his. Anyway went (to) the ring once, they went round twice, anyway he gained the race. Well Master Arch be here today, he knowed the horse, knowed un well, anyway he want to buy un. So he sold un th' horse, well he went to take the bridle off un "Oh no" he said

"Oh yes" he said.

Well he said he'd give ya four hundred more for the bridle. Well he sold horse, bridle an' all, he's just as bad (however) his son was gone again.

An' Master Arch jumped on his back. Well I tell you he drilled un. Well as far as I can mind wh[en he] got home he'd mud from his ass to his nose anyway. Well she drove him in the stable while she went an' told her oldest daughter about un, well she want to go out an' see un so out she goes. Well the horse was dead, famished for a drink, you couldn't say much else. But nothing do she had take the whip an' cuttin him on the guts. My son! You tell (between) squeals the sport to see the shape she got into, well he got down [on] his knees an' everything.

Well she went back an' she told the second oldest, well the second oldest want to go out an' see un so out she goes. Well the horse was dead, famished for a drink, you couldn't say much else. But nothing do she had take the whip an' cuttin him on the guts. My son! You tell between squeals the sport to see the shape she got into, well he got down [on] his knees an' everything.

Well she went back an' she told the youngest about un, well she want to go out so out she goes, see the horse anyway. Well the horse was dead, famished for a drink, you couldn't say much else. But she never had heart enough to hit un, she goina give him a drink. Well he wouldn't have a drink till she drive him to the river

(She said) "Drives ya (to) the river ya run away"

No he wouldn't run away anyway so she drove him to the river. Well he wouldn't have a drink till she take the bridle off, she take the bridle off [he'd] run away, no he wouldn't run away anyway so she took the bridle off (un).

My son! So quick as the bridle pitched off he turned hisself in[to] a trout. An' if ever you seed [a] thing go up river that's where he went to. Well they missed un gone, well he turned /hisself/ in...into twelve otters an' /sez/ if ever you seen water fly now you see water fly to. Well they got so close on there he turn hisself to a mouse an' went in the grass. Well my son! (They was into) the twelve mowyers [i.e., *mowers*] now an' if ever you seen hay fly _ that's where they made hay fly to. Well they got so close on there he turned hisself (into) a pigeon an' flied in the air, gettin a long ways away when they seed un too. Well they turned theirself into twelve kites an' flied after un. Well there was a lady at her winder (but) he flied in through her winder.

"Oh my!" she said. "What a pretty bird!"

"Well" he said "I'm no bird" he said "I'm a man." Well she want to see what sort of a man he was. Anyway he's soon a man before (her), smart lad he was, some sich man as me, you knows he be smart anyway. [*laughter*]

"Well there's twelve men after me" he said "you could save me if you like."

Well she'd do ANYTHING to save such a smart man. "Well" /he/ said /she/ "I'll turn myself into [a] diamont ring (an') go on your finger, you chuck me in the furnace an' I'm clear."

Well the twelve men come in the house, well they aksed th' ol' man (did) he have a daughter.

"Well yes" they say

Well they said they want to see her. Well th' ol' man sung out, (she) didn't care much for comin, kind o' vexed th' ol' man, mind, anyway the next time he spoke he spoke cross. Anyway when he spoke she...when he spoke she come.

When she goin across th' house "Oh my!" he said. "What a pretty diamont ring!"

"Oh yes" she said "not yours."

When she goin along by the furnace she chucked un in the furnace. Well my son! (They's into) twelve pokers an' if ever seen ashes fly they made ashes fly to. Well they got so close on there he turned hisself as a worm, went in th' oat bag. My son! (They was into) twelve turkeys an' if ever you seen oats fly (it's made) oats fly to. Well they got so close on there he turned hisself to a fox. Well he took the heads off then in a blink o' your eye.

Well he frightened the old man till he fainted off. He rubbed the old man, he come to. He got married to th' ol' man's daughter. An' if he didn't

193

its abnormal features, is a constant reminder that the story is set in an unreal world. Although transcription from tape of such a style of narration poses many problems, the listener who is present at the storytelling event is able to pick up the essential intonational and paralinguistic cues which materially assist the understanding of the tale.

Sentences and breath-groups tend to be short and staccato, monosyllables predominate, and the narration is frequently punctuated with *anyway,* which usually occurs under strong stress at the end of a run of rapid speech, sometimes preceded by a brief pause. Its use marks the end of a narrative segment, allowing the teller to pause briefly for breath, and the listener to assimilate the flow of the plot. Strong stresses on individual words for antithetical and other rhetorical effects are also a feature of the style, and triple formulaic repetition occurs at several points, e.g., the identical recurrence of "Well the horse was dead, famished for a drink, you couldn't say much else."

As in Ron Murray's "The Heelstick[†]," No. 82, Az McLean presents himself as an eyewitness to the events narrated, the conventional "as far as I can mind" being used several times, indeed more than is necessary, to remind the audience that he supposedly witnessed the events and is now recalling them from memory. Like Ron Murray, he characterizes himself in a mock-egotistical vein, tempered by the humor through which he jocularly involves himself with the story. Both these storytellers thus play a dual role: as narrator and as participant in the plot, affording the audience the opportunity to hear an "eyewitness" account and at the same time to view the events with some sense of distance and objectivity as they know full well that the narrators' apparent involvement in the plot is only a pose. For further discussion of this narrative style, see the notes to No. 42.

The dialogue of Az McLean's tales is of particular interest. Quite apart from its quick-fire nature, there is an unusual degree of mixing of direct and reported speech. While giving added immediacy to indirect speech by presenting it directly, the switching from one to the other contravenes the normal rules of tense sequence, present and past tense forms being intermingled. A similar phenomenon is also to be found in many of the tales told by the Bennett family, where shifting of tenses from present to past and vice versa is common.

There are also a number of distinctive phonological and lexical features in Az McLean's speech, several of which are not found, or found very rarely, in that of other tellers. His consistent pronunciation of *such* with a close front vowel, *sunce* (since) with a half-open back central vowel, the central vowel in *for* and *far, his* with a long close front vowel, together with the metathesis in *aks* (ask) and *gert* (great) (in No. 16, "Brave Jack[†]"), the medial /j/-glide in *mowyers,* the frequent use of *un* (him, it), *mind* (remember), and numerous morphological points strongly suggest conservative West Country English usage, despite the lack of voicing of initial voiceless consonants. Aphesis is inevitable in such allegro speech, e.g., *'while* (awhile), *'greed* (agreed), *'fore* (before), *'gain* (again), *'bout* (about), and the initial vowel is lacking in *'twasn't.* He pronounces *does* as /duːz/, and the final syllable of *window* with the central vowel plus /r/, and devoices final /d/ in *diamont.* He uses *pitched* (landed), the nautical *sung out* (shouted), the typical Newfoundland exclamation *My son!,* the reflexives *hisself, theirself,* and the adjectival forms *good* and *cross* for the adverbs *well* and *crossly*. Dialectal present tense forms include *you does/sells, they flies,* and the past tense forms *flied* (flew), *begin, seed* (saw), *knowed, want, sung, seen,* and the past participles *runned* and *seen* also occur. At the syntactical level, the curiously cryptic *they missed un gone* is noteworthy too, and the end formula includes *nar one* (none)—a specific problem of transcription in that it follows final /n/ in *seen* and is transcribed as *ar one* in Nos. 16 and 31 but *nar one* in No. 42, the possibility of a double negative being obscured by the speed of the delivery and the syncopation of essential elements. An accurate detailed transcription of the whole of the end formula is virtually impossible, especially such phrases as *hove outdoors* which might well be *over doors,* and comparison with those of Nos. 16, 31, and 42 will indicate several minor variations of what is presumably the same basic run of speech.

Type and Motifs:

AT325. *The Magician and his Pupil.*

Cf. S212. *Child sold to magician.*

D1711.0.1. *Magician's apprentice.*

M151. *Vow not to eat until certain event is brought to pass.*

H1233.1.2. *Old man helps on quest.*

H1233.6.2. *Bird helper (adviser) on quest.*

B552. *Man carried by bird.*

D2153.1.1. *Island created by magic.*

Cf. F134.0.1. *Series of otherworld islands.*

H161. *Recognition of transformed person among identical companions. Prearranged signals.*

D166.3. *Transformation: man to turkey.*

H621. *Recognition of person transformed to animal.*

D250. *Transformation: man to manufactured object [cold chisel].*

D192. *Transformation: man to worm.*

D154.2. *Transformation: man to pigeon.*

D141. *Transformation: man to dog.*

D131. *Transformation: man to horse.*

D612. *Protean sale: man sells youth in successive transformations.*

C837. *Tabu: loosing bridle in selling man transformed to horse.*

L54. *Compassionate youngest daughter.*

D722. *Disenchantment by taking off bridle.*

D179.1. *Transformation: man to trout.*

D615.2. *Transformation contest between master and pupil.*

D127.2. *Transformation: man to otter.*

D117.1. *Transformation: man to mouse.*

Cf. F681.11. *Marvelous swift mower.*

D152.6. *Transformation: man to kite.*

Cf. D641.1. *Lover as bird visits mistress.*

D263.1. *Transformation: man to ring.*

choices: he claimed his son would always eat twice as fast, jump twice as high, and run twice as fast as anyone else.

Although the remainder of the story follows the standard pattern and needs no special comment, it has some vivid touches: Master Arch rides the boy transformed into a horse so roughly that he is "mud from his ass to his nose," and how brutally Master Arch's two eldest daughters beat the same worn out and thirsty horse. The kindhearted youngest daughter takes the horse to the river to drink, whereupon he promptly transforms himself into a trout and escapes, only to be pursued by Master Arch and his eleven assistants.

After various transformations the boy, or rather young man, flies in bird form into a lady's window. When he tells her he is a man, she wants to see what sort of man. He turns to his natural form and asks her help. The storyteller stresses that he is a "smart," i.e., personable, young man and the lady would do "ANYTHING to save such a smart man." This is a delightful touch. Not surprisingly, after the young man succeeds in getting rid of his opponents, he marries the girl.

Studies and Notes

Child, *Ballads,* 1, pp. 399-402, no. 44, headnote, 2, p. 506, no. 44, 3, pp. 506-7, no. 44, 4, p. 459, no. 44, 5, p. 216, no. 44, 5, pp. 290-91, no. 44; Clouston, *Popular Tales,* 1, pp. 413-60; MacCulloch, *Childhood,* pp. 164-66; Bolte and Polívka, 2, pp. 60-69, no. 68; Fansler, *Tales,* p. 149, notes; Penzer, *Ocean,* 3, pp. 203-5, note 2, "The 'Magical Conflict' Motif "; Kittredge, *Witchcraft,* pp. 183-84, and pp. 502-3, notes 91-103; Boggs, *Index,* Type 325, pp. 46-47; Thompson, *The Folktale,* pp. 69-70; Delarue, *Borzoi Book,* pp. 369-70, no. 15, notes; Dorson, *Folktales,* pp. 211-12, note 29; Delarue, *Catalogue,* 1, pp. 283-85, 291-92; Christiansen, *Studies,* pp. 164-73, 246-47; Jackson, *Popular Tale,* pp. 59-61, 115-17; Robe, *Index,* Type 325, pp. 58-59; El Shamy, *Folktales,* pp. 247-48, no. 6, notes.

Canada

Thomas, *Types,* cites 1 version of AT325 from Newfoundland French tradition.
Lacourcière-Low, "Catalogue," cites 8 Francophone versions of AT325 from Canada: 1 (Acadia), 6 (Quebec), 1 (Ontario).

United States

Parsons, *Islands,* 1, pp. 337-41, no. 114, English trans. of Portuguese text, Cape Verde Islands, black (Massachusetts).
Brendle and Troxell, pp. 18-22, Pennsylvania German tradition, in English (Pennsylvania).
Cf. Dorson, *Folktales,* pp. 59-60 (325, IV), black (Michigan), and pp. 211-12, note 29, and rpt. in Dorson, *American,* pp. 141-42, no. 45.
Cf. Saucier, *Folk Tales,* pp. 39-40, no. 8, French tradition, in English trans. (Louisiana).
M. Campbell, *Tales,* pp. 92-94, no. 7, pp. 243-44, no. 3 (325, IV), 2 versions (Kentucky).
Carrière, *Tales,* pp. 91-96, no. 18, French text with English summary (Missouri).
Brewer, *Dog Ghosts,* pp. 9-14 (325, IV), pp. 20-21 (325, IV), 2 versions, black (Texas).
Zunser, *JAF* 48 (1935), 167-68, no. 11 (325, IV), Spanish tradition, in English (New Mexico), and rpt. in Dorson, *Wind,* pp. 434-35.
Rael, *Cuentos,* pp. 732-33, no. 259, English summary of Spanish text (New Mexico).
Lacourcière-Low, "Catalogue," cites 3 Francophone versions of AT325 from the United States: 1 (New England), 1 (Louisiana), 1 (Missouri).

Mexico

Aiken, *PTFS* 32 (1964), 41-42 (Mexico), and rpt. in Aiken, *Folktales,* pp. 145-46.

Wheeler, *Tales,* pp. 358-62, no. 122, Spanish text with English summary (Jalisco).

See Robe, *Index,* Type 325, for other Mexican versions.

The Caribbean and South America

Beckwith, *Stories,* pp. 153-54, no. 120, black (Jamaica).

Parsons, *Antilles,* 3, pp. 255-57, no. 255, English abstracts of two French texts, black (Guadeloupe, Haiti).

See Hansen, *Types,* Type 325, for references to the Dominican Republic, Puerto Rico, and Argentina.

Wales

Guest, *The Mabinogion,* pp. 263-64, "Taliesin" (325, IV), literary, and rpt. in Rhŷs, *Folklore* 2, pp. 613-14.

Ford, *The Mabinogi,* pp. 162-64, "The Tale of Gwion Bach" (325, IV), literary.

Scotland

Cooke and Headlee, *Tocher,* no. 17 (1975), 16-18, Scottish traveller (Forfarshire).

Bødker, *European,* pp. 122-31, Scottish traveller (Glasgow).

Buchan, *Tales,* pp. 59-60 (Aberdeenshire), and rpt. in Briggs, *Dictionary,* A1, pp. 162-63.

Briggs, *Dictionary,* A1, pp. 347-50, condensed version of a transcription from School of Scottish Studies recording by Hamish Henderson, Scottish traveller (Perthshire), and rpt. in Briggs, *Sampler,* pp. 34-36.

Goldstein and Ben-Amos, *Tales,* pp. 31-43, Scottish traveller (Perthshire), and pp. 154-56, notes.

MacColl and Seeger, *Doomsday,* pp. 60-67, no. 2, Scottish traveller (Perthshire).

Douglas, *King,* pp. 14-19, Scottish traveller (Perthshire).

Mackay-Campbell, *Gillie,* pp. 12-31, Gaelic text and English trans. (Barra), same text source as in McKay-Campbell, *Tales,* 1, pp. 210-27, no. 16.

Cf. the magical transformation combat (325, IV) in the Fenian story in Campbell, *Popular Tales,* 2, pp. 422-23, no. 51, English trans. of Gaelic text (Barra).

Cf. Child, *Ballads,* 1, pp. 402-3, Child no. 44 (325, IV), 1 ballad text (Aberdeenshire).

Ireland

Curtin, *Myths,* pp. 139-56 (Ireland).

Cf. Curtin, *Folk-Tales,* pp. 59-63 (325, IV, with 753) (Ireland).

MacManus, *Book,* pp. 231-50 (Co. Donegal).

Cf. Gmelch and Kroup, *Road,* pp. 138-45 (325, IV, with 303, 329), Irish traveller (Co. Longford).

Jackson, *Béal.* 8 (1938), 85-86, no. 1 (with 753), English summary of Irish text (Co. Kerry).

Ó Duilearga, *Béal.* 30 (1962), 10-16 (Co. Clare).

Irish Types, Type 325, 221 versions.

Continental Europe and the Middle East

Grimm no. 68, "The Thief and his Master," Grimm-Hunt, 1, pp. 286-88, no. 68 (Germany), and see 1, pp. 431-32, no. 68, note, for summary of another version and additional references, and for other trans. see Grimm-Magoun, pp. 266-67, no. 68, and Grimm-Zipes, pp. 267-69, no. 68.

Dasent, *Popular Tales,* pp. 290-98, no. 41 (with 313, III) (Norway).

16. BRAVE JACK[†]

Az McLean   AT326A*
Payne's Cove, Great Northern Peninsula   TC133 64-17
11 July 1964   Collector: M. M. Firestone

One time there was a ol' king anyway had two sons _ by the name Jack an' Bill. Well they was great comrades right from be[ing] children up till they got growed up men. But when they got growed up men they said they go look for a job, anyway they went to look for a job. Well they come to a man he want [them] to sail away in the schooner anyway. Well he only want one, well they wouldn't go anyway, they was great comrades right from (their) children up, they wouldn't go 'fore they get chance for the two of 'em.

Well they walked along for another while (where he) want another man to go to sea in the schooner. Well it didn't suit 'em that way. They was great comrades right from their children up an' they wouldn't go 'fore they get a place for the two of 'em.

Well he walked on for another while while he come to a man, he want a man to go...two men to go to sea in a schooner, well now this...they was great comrades right from their children up, anyway they went.

Well they went to sea for a few months, well far as I can mind [they were] after makin a few dollars out of it anyway. They come back out of that and they went into alehouse. Well Jack never come to 'fore all of his money was gone an' begged Bill (?to take) all of his. Well after the money was gone certainly Jack he was sober again.

Well Jack said to Bill he said "We'll go to sea again"

"Ah" Bill said "nonsense! We'll never get nothing like this."

"Ah" Jack said "if I gets it again I'll know what to do with it!"

Anyway they went to sea for a few **MORE** months. Well they made a few dollars out of (it) far as I can mind but they come back out of that an' they went into a alehouse again. Well Jack's never come to 'fore all of his money was gone an' begged Bill (take) all of his. Well after the money was gone certainly Jack he was sober again.

Well Jack said to Bill "We'll go to sea again"

"Ah" Bill says "nonsense Jack. We never get (nothin) like this"

"Ah" Jack said "if I gets [it] again I'll know what to do with it!"

Anyway they went to sea for a few more months, anyway they made a few dollars out of it far as I can mind about anyway. Well they come back out o' that an' they went to alehouse again. Well Jack never come to 'fore all of his money was gone an' begged Bill (take) all of his as he thought. But he didn't, Bill had some kept back, mind, anyway. Well certainly after the money was gone certainly Jack he was sober again.

Well anyway they said they go look for another job. Well while they [were] walkin along they runned up again alehouse.

Jack said "What about goin in uh..." Bill said "What about going in here Jack" he said "an' get a grog?"

"What Bill" he said "A voice [*?advice*] from you here [or] voice from heaven?"

Bill says "It's a voice from me"

He didn't think Bill had any money, mind, anyway so they went in an' they got their grog. They walked on for awhile. An' Bill said to Jack "Why don't we go in HERE an' get a grog?"

"What Bill" he said "is [it] a voice from you" he said "or a voice from heaven?"

Bill said "'Tis a voice from me." An' they went in an' they went an' they got their grog.

They come out o' that an' they walked on 'long. When they...while they were walkin along they seen a beautiful gert buildin ahead of 'em. Nice lookin buildin he was too.

"Well" Jack said to Bill "if we could only get that beautiful buildin."

"Go on Jack" said Bill...Bill said "with your nonsense Jack, you know we never get the like o' that"

"Ah" Jack said "you never knows."

Well while they 's walkin along they run up again a young gentleman.

"Good morning Jack" he said.

"Good morning young gentleman" he said. "Know what I was just sayin to Bill?"

"What's that?" he said.

"I was just sayin to Bill 'If we could only get that beautiful buildin.'"

"Well now Jack" he said _ "you can have that buildin if you thinks you can live in [it]. No man can live in that for spirits" he said. "An' everything you could mention is in there" he said.

"There Bill" he said "I knowed I 's goin to get un." Anyway they walked around till dark an' they got in an' they got playing cards. Well they played cards so long an' Jack said to Bill "Take the jug an' go an' draw a jug o' rum."

Anyway Bill took the jug an' away (to) go down the cellar to draw a jug o' rum. But when he went down there was a UGLY ol' feller down there, mind, anyway Bill come back he never drawed the rum anyway.

Well Jack (picks) up the jug hisself an' 'way to go an' drawed the rum anyway. They come up an' they played cards till bedtime an' they went to bed.

Well they wasn't into bed very long _ 'fore in come three men in through the winder, two big feller[s] an' a little feller got playin ball. Two big fellers playin on a little feller, sacking [i.e., *beating*] him pretty bad too mind.

Well Jack said "Get out an' help him Bill."

"Go on Jack" he said "they'll kill us."

"No" he said "get out an' help him."

"Go on Jack" he said "they'll kill us."

Last goin' off [i.e., *finally*] Jack jumped out in his drawers an' went right to the little feller, anyway he sacked off the two big fellers. Well when he turned round to speak to him he went through the window [in] a ball o' fire.

"Well" Jack said "he's no man, he won't stop [to] speak to anybody." An' wi' that they went to bed.

Young gentleman walked around pretty late the next mornin...between nine _ like that. No smoke rose

He said "They're dead this mornin." But between nine an' half past nine the smoke rose, young gentleman walked in.

"Good mornin Jack" he said.

"Good mornin young gentleman" he said

"How you (get) on here LAST night?"

"Oh alright" Jack said "only a few rats knockin about the house."

Well they sport around all that day, certainly when it got dark they got in they got playing cards again. Well after they got playing cards so long Jack said to Bill "Go draw a jug o' rum" anyway Bill wouldn't go.

So Jack took the jug hisself, away to go. Well he went down, (now) if he [*the ugly ol' feller*] was ugly the night before he was THREE times as ugly tonight, sot across [the] cask. But Jack rammed th' ol' jug down between (his) legs an' drawed the rum anyway. They come back an' they played cards till bedtime an' they went to bed.

Well they wasn't into bed very long 'fore in come those three men in through the winder again, two big fellers an' a little feller, they got playin ball. Playin on the little feller, sacking him pretty bad too.

Well Jack said to Bill "Get out an' help him" he says "he might stop [an'] speak to you, he won't stop [an'] speak to me."

"Go on Jack" he said "they'll kill us."

"No" he said "get out an' help him, he might stop [an'] speak to you" he said "he won't stop [to] speak to me."

"Go on Jack" he said "they'll kill us."

Last goin off Jack jumped out in his drawers an' went right to the little feller, anyway he sacked off the two BIG fellers. When he turned around to speak to un he went out through the winder in a ball o' fire.

"Well" Jack said "he's no man, he won't stop [to] speak to anybody." An' wi' that they went to bed.

Young gentleman went walkin round pretty late next mornin between ten an' half past ten, no smoke rose

He said "They're dead this morning."

Between half past ten [an'] eleven the smoke rose. The young gentleman walked in "Good morning Jack" he said

"Good morning young gentleman" he said.

"How you (get) on here last night?"

"Oh alright" Jack said "only a few rats knockin about the house."

Well they sported around all that day, (well) certainly when it got dark certainly they got in they got playing cards again. They played cards so long. Anyway Bill said to Jack, well Jack said to Bill "We'll draw a jug o' rum."

Anyway Bill wouldn't go so Jack took the jug hisself an' 'way to go. If he 's ugly the night before he's FIVE times as ugly tonight, he sot across the cask. Jack went to ram the jug down 'tween his legs an' he wouldn't let un. He up fist an' knocked un off o' the cask an' drawed his rum anyway an' come back an' played cards.

Well when it come bedtime they went to bed. Well they wasn't into bed very long 'fore in come those three men in through the winder again, two big fellers an' a little feller. They got playin ball. Playin on the little feller an' sackin him pretty bad too mind.

Well Jack said to Bill "Get out an' help un, he might stop [to] speak to you, he won't stop [to] speak [to] me"

"Go on Jack" he said "They'll kill us."

"No" he said "get out an' help un" he said "he might stop [to] speak to you. He won't speak to me"

"Go on Jack" he said "they'll kill us."

Last goin off Jack jumped out in his drawers an' went right to the little feller, anyway he sacked off the two big fellers. Well when he turned round to speak to him the two big fellers was gone an' the little feller was stood before (un).

"Well now Jack" he said "'tis yous I was fighting for. If you've been like Bill" he said "yous 'd been killed." He said "I'm that young gentleman's father" he said. "An' them two men killed me" he said. "Now tell un where my bones 's at an' get un [to] bury 'em decent."

Well Jack said "Yes I'll tell un" he said "but I knows he won't believe me"

"Yes Jack" he said "believe every word you says." He hauled (out) a drawer of twelve crocks o' silver, (here's) six for ya...Jack an' six for the young gentleman, he hauled out (another) of twelve crocks o' gold, (here's) six for Jack an' six for [the] young gentleman.

Well Jack said "Yes I'll tell un" he said "but I knows he won't believe me"

"Yes Jack" he said "believe every word you says. And tell un" he said "of my wish for you to be married to his oldest daughter."

Well Jack said "Yes" he said "I'll tell un" he said "but I know he won't believe me."

"Well yes Jack" he said "he'll believe every word you says." An' with that they went to bed.

Well young gentleman walked round pretty late next morning between twelve o'clock an' half past twelve, no smoke rose.

He said "They're dead this morn."

Between half past twelve an' one the smoke rose. The young gentleman walked in "Good morning Jack" he said

"Good morning young gentleman" he said.

"How you get on here last night?"

"Alright" Jack said. "I seen your father here last night"

"Did ya?" he said

"Yes" he said. "He was tellin 'bout the two men killed un" he said. "An' tellin where his bones is at an' told me to tell you to get 'em [an'] bury 'em decent but I told un nonsense, you wouldn't believe me"

"Yes Jack" he said "I'll believe every word you says."

"He hauled out [a] drawer" he said "twelve crocks o' silver in, six for you an' six for me. Hauled another wi' twelve crocks o' gold in" he said "six for you an' six for me. I told un nonsense, you wouldn't believe me"

"Yes Jack" he said "believe every word you say."

"An' he told me" he said "how he's wished for me to be married to your oldest daughter but I told un nonsense, you wouldn't believe me."

"Well yes Jack" he said "I'll believe every word you says."

Well now anyway Jack was goin to marry to his oldest daughter. Well Jack an' Bill was great comrades right from their children up.

Well Jack said to Bill he said "Why couldn't you go for the other one?"

Well Bill said "I didn't see as I could get her."

Well Jack said "I noticed the other night [when] we were playin' cards *** [*recorder off; tape changed*] *** yeah I noticed they're playing cards you noticed her wink 'cross table at ya"

"Yes" Bill said "I noticed that too."

An' they got married an' if they didn't live happy I don't know...don't know who did. An' they had children in baskets _ hove outdoor in shelffuls _ sent to the sea to make sea pies an' the last time I seen 'em I wished 'em goodbye an' I haven't seen ar a one sunce.

Duration: 7 min., 41 sec.

Source: Andrew McLean (uncle), Shoal Harbour East, Great Northern Peninsula, "when I was eighteen or twenty."

Location: The home of Gilbert Parrell, teller's stepbrother, evening.

Audience: Teller's wife, people of the household, John Crane (a well-known traditional singer from Pines Cove), interviewer and his wife.

Context, Style, and Language: (For context see notes to No. 15). This tale is remarkable for its repetition of fixed phrases, e.g., "They was great comrades right from their children up. . . ." (used four times in the first three paragraphs). Neither is the teller shy of repeating episodes, though he makes subtle variations in them. Two examples are the increasing ugliness of the ol' feller astride the rum cask in the cellar, and the increasing lateness at which smoke appears from the chimney on the morning after each night's ordeal, signifying to the young gentleman that Jack and Bill have survived again.

The opening formula is vestigial and out of keeping with the characterization of Jack and Bill. Jack and Bill are portrayed like a couple of Newfoundland sailors, who like grog and play cards to pass away the evenings in the house. The closing formula is developed with more enjoyment and sureness of touch; it has a nice rhythmic rise into absurdity which the teller neatly disengages himself from at the last.

Jack is drawn as being inherently more recklessly brave than Bill; Jack knows his dangerousness to himself and seems to beg Bill to take his money for safekeeping when they go drinking at alehouses. As Lüthi says of the Märchen hero, ("Aspects of the

Märchen and the Legend," 168) he accepts relationships easily, and so takes on the challenges of the haunted house, the ugly ol' feller guarding the cask, and the fight between the revenants. Similarly, he suggests to Bill that he try to marry the gentleman's other daughter; Bill is too bashful, despite the girl's "wink 'cross table" at him, noticed by Jack, while they played cards. If the tale has a "moral" it supports Jack's goodhearted, reckless bravery; the ghost tells him, "'tis yous I was fighting for. If you've been like Bill" he said "yous 'd been killed." Thus Jack is more "manly, true, and brave" from his drinking, on the one hand, to his eye for his brother's chance with the other daughter, to his selfless jumping into the fight on the side of the beleaguered little fellow. In terms of masculine competitiveness it is also significant that in confronting the ugly ol' feller astride the cask Jack has to "ram the jug down 'tween his legs" which suggests a rather phallic challenge and assault.

The many features of allegro speech noted under No. 15, "Master Arch," are again in evidence here, though with even greater fluency and fewer pauses or hesitations. Similar formulaic repetition and emphatic utterance are also found. Aphesis is again common, e.g., *'tis, 'way* (away), *'tween* (between). At the lexical level we have *again* (against), *grog, sacking, sacked,* the verb evidently meaning to sock, hit, beat, whether literally or metaphorically (cf. *OED Sack* v.[1] 5b, *EDD SACK* v.[2]), the plural pronoun *yous,* and the demonstrative *them* (those). A specific problem of transcription is whether *a voice* (from Bill or from heaven) should be rendered as *advice,* the pronunciation being unclear, but on balance the former seems the more plausible. The use of *they were after makin,* and perhaps of *sacking, sacked,* illustrates the Anglo-Irish influence even on such West Country English type speakers as this who still retain, for example, the masculine pronoun *he* with inanimate reference to a building. Dialectal present tense forms include *you thinks/knows/says* and in the past tense we find *they was, come, runned, sot* (sat), *drawed,* and the past participle *growed.* The phrases *Last goin off* (finally) and *(a)way to go* are typical of Newfoundland usage, while the cryptic quality of the narration is enhanced by such economical expressions as *he up fist.*

See also the notes to No. 15.

Type and Motifs:

AT326A*. *Soul Released from Torment.*

P251.5.4. *Two brothers as contrasts.*

H1411. *Fear test: staying in haunted house.*

H1430. *Fearless traffic with ghosts.*

E577.1. *Dead persons play ball.*

E467. *Revenants fight each other.*

Cf. F407.1. *Spirit vanishes in smoke [ball of fire].*

E231. *Return from dead to reveal murder.*

E235.2. *Ghost returns to demand proper burial.*

Cf. E371. *Return from dead to reveal hidden treasure.*

E373.1. *Money received from ghosts as reward for bravery.*

Besides the hero's involvement in a football game or fight on the side of the weaker party, his general behavior is worthy of comment. He observes with calm or amusement many strange occurrences, occasionally dismissing them with some remark. When a coffined corpse is brought in, it may sit up in the coffin, but if the coffin does not open by itself, Jack may break it open and take the corpse out. As with Father Drumcap in No. 97, Jack invariably treats his strange guest with hospitality. He offers it food, drink, and often a pipe full of tobacco. If the ghost throws down the drink or the pipe, Jack warns it he will not put up with such discourtesy. Indeed sometimes he demands repayment for the waste before he allows his guest to leave. Jack may comment that his visitor is cold and take him close to the fire. Sometimes he may even take him to bed to help him get warmer. In bed the corpse usually crowds Jack, whereupon Jack may split the blankets in two, so that the corpse can have its own covers. When Jack is sitting on a bench two visitors may begin to press against him, or several of them begin to squeeze him into a corner, whereupon Jack protests against their behavior and they desist, sometimes with laughter. In short Jack ignores the fact that his supernatural visitors are not alive and behaves much as he would with ordinary human visitors.

What is essential, both in the legends and in the more elaborate folktales included under AT326A*, is that the person exposed to the strange experiences should display courage. In the legends the person may resolve the situation by addressing the revenant, usually with some version of the ritualistic query: "What in the name of the Lord troubles you?," a similar form of words being incidentally well known in the oral tradition in Newfoundland as we witnessed in our own fieldwork. This permits the ghost both to reply and make its wishes known and also to reward the inquirer with all or some part of the hidden treasure.

Curiously enough, in the folktales the ritualistic query is less frequent than a more direct one; but even the latter may not be required. It seems sufficient for the ghost to have observed Jack's unflinching behavior in the face of a series of potentially frightening experiences for it to be willing to speak to him, praise him for his courage, and explain why it cannot rest and what must be done for it to stop it from haunting the building.

To sum up: although ghost legends and the folktales under AT326A* may embody the same folk beliefs, the legends are more straightforward. In the legend, the hero/heroine faces a frightening supernatural being and by asking the proper ritual question learns what is troubling it and is able to satisfy it, thus causing the haunting to cease. In the folktale the hero usually faces a whole series of frightening episodes before he discovers the problem that has caused the haunting. These episodes are extremely variable.

What troubles the ghost is also variable since it may be any of the problems listed above that are found in different legends. We must therefore conclude that AT326A* can best be considered a framework in which both the cause that troubles the ghost(s), and the multiple events that take place in the haunted building, may occupy particular slots in the structure of the plot. These slots are filled differently in each recension.

The problem or problems that trouble the ghost differ in each recension, but are basically variations on a limited set of folk beliefs—those noted above. By contrast there is no similar limitation on the frightening experiences which the hero must undergo.

212

Widdowson has demonstrated *(If You Don't Be Good)* that the kinds of frightening figures used to threaten children are extraordinarily variable in world cultures. In theory at least the variety of frightening experiences in AT326A* might similarly be limited only by the scope of the human imagination. In practice, however, since our survey has only covered American, British, and Irish versions of the tale, there are cultural limitations. The sampling of frightening experiences we give above, while far from being comprehensive, suggests many of the themes which recur in varying combinations in the analogues.

Studies and Notes

Gardner, *Schoharie*, pp. 187-91, no. 18, notes, pp. 193-94, no. 19, notes; Roberts, *Greasybeard*, p. 187, no. 16, notes; Delarue, *Catalogue*, 1, pp. 296-97, 4, and p. 305; Christiansen, *Studies*, pp. 180-87, 247-48.

Canada

Cf. Creighton and Ives, *Folktales*, pp. 61-65, no. 8A (New Brunswick).

Fowke, *Folktales*, pp. 32-38, no. 5 (with 326), trans. from French text in Lanctôt, *JAF* 39 (1926), 383-87, [no. 117] (Quebec).

United States

Gardner, *Schoharie*, pp. 185-87, no. 18 (with 569) [2 redcaps fighting 1 whitecap; 2 to 1], pp. 187-91, notes (New York).

Gardner, *Schoharie*, pp. 191-93, no. 19 [2 whitecaps fighting a redcap; 2 to 1], pp. 193-94, notes (New York).

Cf. Brendle and Troxell, pp. 61-62, Pennsylvania German tradition, in English (Pennsylvania).

Bacon and Parsons, *JAF* 35 (1922), 290, no. 50, 290-91, no. 51, 2 versions, black (Virginia).

Wigginton, *Foxfire 2*, pp. 353-54 (Georgia).

Roberts, *South*, pp. 35-38, no. 9a (Kentucky).

Roberts, *Greasybeard*, pp. 72-75, no. 16 (Kentucky).

Roberts, *Settlers*, pp. 209-12, no. 103 (Kentucky).

Roberts, *Settlers*, pp. 298-301, no. 159 (Kentucky).

Carrière, *Tales*, pp. 259-66, no. 59 (with 326, 935), French text with English summary (Missouri).

Thomas, *Good*, pp. 178-80, no. 18 (with 326, 935), French text and English trans. (Missouri).

England

Cf. Campbell, *Popular Tales*, 1, p. xlvii (with 326) [little chap with red cap sitting on beer barrel], incomplete summary only, heard from a tinker (London), and 2, p. 285, note, and rpt. of summary in Groome, *Folk-Tales*, pp. 242-43, note, and again rpt. in Briggs, *Dictionary*, A1, pp. 200-201.

Briggs, *Dictionary*, A1, p. 404, summary from *Thompson Notebooks* [football match], Gypsy (Lancashire).

Cf. Leather, *Folk-Lore*, pp. 41-42 [devil with great big eyes sitting on cider hogshead; football game; "two to one's not fair"] (Herefordshire).

Wales

Groome, *Folk-Tales*, pp. 235-42, no. 57 (with cf. 327E), Gypsy (Wales), and rpt. from the same source in Yates, *Book*, pp. 182-89, no. 42, and rpt. in summary from Yates in Briggs, *Dictionary*, A1, pp. 140-41.

the night." So they went _ to the door. An' they knocked an' this old woman came out. So Peg ask her could she...keep 'em for the night.

And she said "I can keep two but I...can't keep three."

Well she said it...she didn't make no matter _ about herself. She said she didn't care _ where her was. So she got some place for her two sisters.

So she took the three of 'em in. But th' old woman had...two daughters. So she...takes these sisters [and they] had to go to bed. But Peg lay down on the floor.

So they went up _ an' they went to bed. But th' old woman put _ caps on her...daughters' heads. And she was goin to bed. So _ they all went to bed an' went to sleep an' some time in the night _ Peg got up an' went up. And she took the caps off o' their heads an' put 'em on her sisters' heads. An' then she went back _ away down again.

So th' ol' woman got up. She went over for to kill her [*Peg's*] two sisters. An' she went to the room where those two with no caps on [were]. So she killed them uh...but they were her own daughters.

So _ when the...when the LIGHT...daylight come _ uh...Peg got up an' got her two sister[s] to get out. They...she said they got to "Get out o' here so quick as we can." So they got out of it.

And...th' old woman got up in the morning, it was her two daughters she had killed.

So alright Peg...her two sisters got their jobs somewhere or another. But Peg I don't know what she was doin all the time.

But there was a king there an' he had three sons. So Peg went up an' minded she was goin to go to the king. So she went.

And she went to the gate an' the guard asked her...when...what did she want. And she said she wanted to see the king. So anyway he...was satisfied for her to come to see him whatever way it was. So she went in.

An' he said "Peg" he said "what can I do for you?"

She said "I...want to know" she said "if you'd be satisfied for your...oldest son to marry my...oldest sister?" And she said "I bring ya...a 'canter [i.e., *decanter*] that could never be empted."

Well he said "That would be a nice thing for a king." An' he said "What would you want to get that?"

And she said "I'd want a handful o' pepper."

So he gave her the handful o' pepper. And she went to the house an'...an' the ol' man...was /eatin/ his dinner. An' when he was finished his dinner he told th' old lady for to bring him out...the 'canter. So she brought it out an' she lay it on the table. An' he was...drinkin. So _ Peg went in and she threw the handful of pepper at him. So he begin to cough and sneeze an' all that but anyway _ Peg took the...'canter and went away with it. They brought it to the king. So the king...'s son...and her sister were married.

/beatin/

216

So after a while _ she went to the king again. An' he said "Peg what can I do for ya today?"

"Well" she said "I want to know if you'd be satisfied for your second youngest son to marry my second youngest sister. An' I'll bring you a lantern _ that can show a half-a-mile light."

"Well" he said "that WOULD be a handy thing for a king." So he gave consent. An' he said "Peg what would you want to get that?"

And she said "I'd want a handful of salt."

An' anyway...the...Peg's hand could hold a hogshead o' salt. So she went.

An' th' ol' lady was cookin soup. An'...Peg got on the roof. But she'd started the soup and it was too fresh [i.e., *not salty enough*]. So she...wanted some salt in it. So Peg used to (the)...let...the salt drop down in the soup. An' after a while she let it all down. So when she stirred it up it was TOO salty. So she told the girl to go to the well for water. So they took the lantern an' they went. And 'twas a mile to the well. So they could...go (a) half mile an' lay down the lantern an' then that 'd show 'em th' other half _ like th' other half.

So Peg followed her. And she took the lantern and she brought to the king. So -- the king's...second oldest son an' her second oldest sister got married.

So after a while she went back to the king again. An' the king said to her "What do you...what can I do for ya now Peg?"

"Well" she said "I come to see if you'd be satisfied for your youngest son to marry me." But he didn't like that one bit. [*laughter*] So after a while [*laughs*]...so after a while he said...he said "What would you want now" he said "for to uh...get that?" No. She said "I'd uh...I'd bring ya a horse" she said _ "that can go seven..." go...(before)...[*pauses to recollect*] she said "I'll bring ya a horse that can go ten times swifter than a cannonball. An'" she said "there's a golden bell from every hair on his mane."

"Well" he said "that would be a nice thing for a king." So after a while he gave consent. An' he said "Peg what do you want to...get that?"

Uh she said "I wants a...a saw _ and a knife." So they gave her the saw an' they gave her a knife. So she went to th' ol' witch's house.

"(Well)" she said "Peg you're come!" She said uh..."You were the cause of me killin me two daughters. You stole me 'canter" she said "that never could be empted and ya stole me lantern that could show a half-mile light." She said "Peg have a...Peg" she said "if I did that to you what would you do to me?"

Well Peg said "I'd take ye an' I'd put ye in a bag. And" she said "I'd take you away to the side o' the road. An' then I'd go" she said "an' I'd pick...hazel rods _ an' I'd beat ya _ till you'd miaow like a cat, bark like a dog _ an' your bones will rattle like crockeryware."

begins with the more conventional "Once upon a time" and the taped version with ". . .one time in OLDEN times," the strong emphasis on OLDEN being one of many features of oral style which are not noted in the manuscript and which may well be less prominent in the more constrained dictation. The manuscript version also ends with the highly conventional formula "So he married her. They lived happily ever after" which is entirely absent from the taped story.

At a rather more detailed level one might note the many similarities of plot, of the description of the three girls, and the introduction of the old man (presumably the old woman's husband, a figure otherwise not essential to the story) later in the tale. More significant are the virtually identical forms of expression which act as constant elements binding the two versions together, and appear to mark certain stages in the narrative, perhaps constituting foci for the teller's recalling of the plot: "they saw a little hut of a house"; "But there/There was a king there and/an' he had three sons"; Peg(g)'s dialogue when she first meets the king; her confrontation with the witch before the witch puts her in the bag (the dialogue being particularly lively, almost formulaic, again suggesting a focus for recall); "Peg(g) your word's come true," "So one day there was a knock came on the door," and "the beautiful(l)est lady that ever the sun shined on."

Differences, however minor, far outweigh similarities between the versions. The tape-recorded story, being the longer, includes many details omitted from the manuscript. For example, in the opening section it notes that the trees are "growing there in the garden"; there is some hesitation before the woman eats the prohibited fruit: "So she looked at th' other one for a little while"; "Nobody like[d] Peg" is made clear on the tape, but only implied in the manuscript; the taped version includes brief dialogue about the sisters' intention to go away, and the old woman explicitly goes to kill Peg's sisters, whereas in the manuscript she goes to look at them first and we are not told in advance of her intentions. Also it is made clear that she has killed her own daughters and this is re-emphasized when she gets up in the morning, whereas the reader is left to gather this from the manuscript.

On tape we are given fuller details of the two sisters leaving in the morning and of Peg following them—daylight is mentioned, and there is brief dialogue; also, Peg's second request to the king is for the "second youngest" son and sister, a mistake corrected shortly afterwards. The king's response to Peg's third request is much more negative than in the manuscript: "he didn't like that one bit" rather than the non-committal "he didn't know what to say." The order in which the cat and dog in the bag are hit is reversed in the two versions. Finally, Peg uses her full name in "You were married to Peg _ Bearskin," although the brief pause before the second name suggests this may be a clarifying afterthought in the tape recording.

The manuscript, on the other hand, incorporates details not on the tape. Several of these are clarificatory, perhaps the product of the more deliberate delivery and slower pace of the dictated narrative. For instance, the manuscript gives fuller information about which fruit is to be eaten and which is prohibited; it notes that the woman "goes out" in the morning before picking the fruit; there is iterative repetition of "went on," indicating passage of time and space, and the conventional narrative marker "(So) that was all right/So all right," used by other tellers in this collection, delimits stages in the progress of the plot, rather than the one perfunctory "So alright" on the tape. The manuscript plainly states and repeats that the old woman is a witch, but on the tape she is always simply "the old woman." Another formulaic element is the repeated reference to the size of Pegg's hands, the word *hogshead* (so typical of the salt-fish industry of Newfoundland) being sedulously glossed, while there is only one reference to *hogshead* on the tape (interestingly at a point in the narrative where it is omitted in the manuscript). The collector may have misheard "he gave consent" (as it appears in the manuscript version) when he wrote "he gets unset," this being further proof that the manuscript was written from dictation. In addition, details of the divided ring come out quite naturally in the manuscript, but there is a brief hiatus on the tape, during which the interviewer suggests in an undertone that Peg gives her husband "Half a ring"—a suggestion which Mrs. Brewer immediately accepts. Even so, there is a further pause when the narration resumes, indicating a degree of uncertainty on the part of the teller.

The manuscript euphemistically emphasizes Pegg's death: "Now that he have her done away with" and arouses our sympathy with the comment "he is real sad." This sympathy develops into a sense of expectation absent from the taped version when her husband realizes what he has done: "He don't know what is going to happen to him."

The manuscript version appears more conventional, pointed, direct, and clarificatory, whereas the longer version on tape shows evidence of some difficulty on the part of the narrator to put the final stages of the story together, as seen in the hesitations and lengthy pauses when she wishes to reassure herself about the ring. The lack of paragraphing and of much conventional punctuation in the manuscript tends to detract from the impact of the narrative in that the reader has to supply pauses, emphases, interrogative and exclamatory intonation contours, and other interpretative features. Nevertheless, the accuracy of the written version is verified by the close parallels with the taped story, and it succeeds in representing the flavor and vigor of vernacular speech.

Mrs. Brewer's language, as heard on the tape, includes many typical Anglo-Irish pronunciation features, notably the breathed quality of final retroflex /r/ and the centralized half-open back round vowel which precedes and is influenced by it in such words as *her, stirred* etc. On the other hand there are West Country English features too, e.g., the short close back vowel in *roof,* the word *empted,* and the use of the pronoun *her* in the subject position in *where her was.* Other items of note include the penultimate lateral in *chimley,* the stress on the final syllable in *cannonball,* the elision of schwa in *th' other, th' old,* and the aphetic *'twas* and *'canter* (decanter). At the lexical level we find the pronoun *ye* (with singular referent); *matter,* meaning "importance, cause for concern," in the double negative clause *she didn't make no matter; minded* used untypically to mean "decided" or "resolved" rather than "remembered" (see *EDD MIND* v. 7. To wish, have a mind to; to feel inclined or disposed to); the adjective *fresh* in the archaic sense of "insufficiently salty" (still well known as a noun in Newfoundland to designate unsalted meat), and *satisfied* used formally for "agreeable" or "consenting"—common in current usage in the province and found in similar formal contexts in other tales in this collection. Note also the present tense form *you gets,* the past tense forms *eat, shined, ask, begin, was stood,* the frequency of purposive *for to,* does not take place conveniently and pleasantly on her wedding day, but some time later, after a period of unhappy marriage. Indeed it requires some rather drastic action by her unfortunate husband, which he undertakes only after considerable goading by Peg. His reward for following her advice is a transformed wife so beautiful that he happily takes her to every party that winter.

But we must consider yet another point before deciding on the most appropriate classification of our text. In the *Irish Handbook,* pp. 611ff., Ó Súilleabháin summarizes a number of tales told in Ireland in which magic plays an important role and suggests that they appear to be Irish types, or "ecotypes." In his listing he includes one tale description (pp. 617-18, no. 29) that is very close to our "Peg Bearskin," even to the disenchantment of the hairy lady by throwing her into the fire. Bearing in mind not only the discrepancies noted above and the inclusion of elements of AT327B and AT328 in our recensions, but also Ó Súilleabháin's description and comment, we feel that on balance it is best at this point to classify our tale as a combination of AT327B and AT328 plus several key elements of AT711. It would be misleading, however, to include AT711 in the classification without some qualification. We have therefore labeled those elements of the tale as Cf. AT711. Among other advantages, such a classification draws attention to the existence of versions of AT327B and AT328 in which a female is the protagonist. This important fact may well have been overlooked if we had concentrated attention exclusively on the parallels with AT711. Nevertheless, because the tale begins with a succession of episodes which closely parallel the Type description of AT711, one might equally justify its classification under that number, plus the relevant elements from AT327B and AT328.

Commenting on AT711, Thompson (*The Folktale,* p. 96) remarks: "This story is popular in Norway and Iceland, and seems quite unknown elsewhere." Some fifteen years later in the AT index Thompson enlarged this distribution somewhat by adding a few Irish, Greek, and Turkish citations and one published English (actually Scottish) reference, as well as two Franco-American and one English-American reports. In our own search for analogues we can cite only one English translation of a Norwegian text. In short, while AT711 is an international folktale, it is not widely popular outside the Scandinavian area.

Studies and Notes

MacCulloch, *Childhood,* pp. 354-56 (327B, 328); *Irish Handbook,* pp. 617-18, no. 29; Thompson, *The Folktale,* p. 37 (327B), p. 38 (328), p. 96 (711); Dégh, *Society,* p. 293, no. 6 (328), notes.

Canada

Lacourcière, Index, cites 2 Francophone versions of AT711, with AT327B, from Canada: 2 (Quebec).

Lacourcière, Index, cites 1 Francophone version of AT711, without AT327B, from Canada: 1 (Ontario).

United States

Chase, *Grandfather,* pp. 40-50, no. 4 (327B, with 328), composite text [3 sisters; Mutsmag] (Virginia and North Carolina).

Roberts, *Settlers,* pp. 228-32, no. 108 (327B, with 328), [3 sisters; Muncimeg] (Kentucky).

Baughman, *Index*, Type 711, reports an unpublished version from New Mexico.

Scotland

Bannerman, *Tocher,* no. 18 (1975), 67-71 (328) [3 sisters; Kitty Ill-Pretts (Ill Pretts = nasty tricks)], originally learned in Fife (Edinburgh).

Gregor and Moir, *FLJ* 2 (1884), 68-71 (327B, with 328), [3 sisters; Mally Whuppie] (Aberdeenshire), and rpt. in Briggs, *Dictionary,* A1, pp. 400-402, and rpt. with dialect anglicized in Jacobs, *English,* pp. 125-30, no. 22.

Campbell, *Popular Tales,* 1, pp. 251-59, no. 17 (327B, with 328) [3 sisters; Maol a Chliobain], English trans. and Gaelic text (Islay), pp. 259-66, English summaries of 3 other Highland texts; in the 4th the youngest sister is called Maol a Mhoibean (Dunbartonshire).

Cf. Lang, *FL* 1 (1890), 299-301, no. 4 (cf. 711, with cf. 306) [2 half-sisters; Kate (Crackernuts)] (Orkneys), and rpt. in Briggs, *Dictionary,* A1, pp. 344-46, and rpt., but largely rewritten in Jacobs, *English,* pp. 198-202, no. 37. [We agree with the late Katharine Briggs that this story "bears no real resemblance" to AT711, even though Baughman so classifies it].

Ireland

Kennedy, *Stories,* pp. 3-9 (327B, with 328, cf. 711), [3 sisters; Hairy Rouchy] (Co Wexford).

Ó Tuathail, *Béal.* 7 (1937), 65-66 (327B, with 510A, cf. 711) [3 sisters; Hairy Rucky] (Co. Carlow).

Danaher, *Folktales,* pp. 102-7, no. 34 (327B, with 328, 1535, V, cf. 711) [3 sisters; Máirín Rua] (Co. Limerick).

Irish Handbook, pp. 617-18, no. 29.

Irish Types, Type 711, 5 versions.

Continental Europe

Dasent, *Popular Tales,* pp. 333-39, no. 48 (711) [2 sisters; Tatterhood] (Norway).

Hodne, *Types,* AT711, 6 versions (Norway).

Dégh, *Society,* p. 293, no. 6 (328), notes (Hungary); Dégh comments: "The international index does not indicate the female version of the tale which is very popular in Hungary."

18. PEGG BEARSKIN

Elizabeth Brewer   AT327B + AT328 + Cf. AT711
Freshwater, Placentia Bay   76-485/pp. 6-21
18 November 1976   Collector: Harold Healey

Once upon a time, in the old times, a man and woman were married for a long time and never had any children. So her husband was real nasty with her. So, ah, one day she was out in the door and there was an old man come along and he asked her what was her trouble. She told him she was married for a, a long while and never had no children. She said her husband was real nasty with her. So he said to her, he said, you see them trees, you see that tree there he said and he said when you gets up tomorrow morning, he said, there will be three berries growing on that tree. He said one berry will be as sweet as

225

molasses, the other as sweet as sugar and the other as bitter as gall. He said you eat the two sweet ones but don't eat that one, ah, the bitter one. So, ah, when she got up in the morning and went out, the three berries were there. She eat the one as sweet as molasses and the one as sweet as sugar and she, well she said she would eat the other one too. That one was as bitter as gall, so she eat it. That was all right.

In nine months she had three children, three girls. Two were as pretty as ever the sun shined on. The other one was big, ugly and hairy. [*laugh!*] So anyway, ah, she called her Pegg Bearskin. So they grew up to be girls. So the two said one day to their mother, we are going to go away on our own, we're not staying here any longer. They wanted to get away unknownst to Pegg. How they were going to do it, they didn't know. So anyway they started off and there were three roads to go. So they went one of the roads. So Pegg, she said she was going to go too, so she went. And she went on the road that they went on. So she followed them and followed them. After awhile they heard a noise. One said to the other, that's Pegg. The other one said no, no that can't be Pegg. The other one said yes that's her. So after awhile Pegg go up to them. They wanted her to go back so they threw stones and everything at her. No, she wouldn't go back, so they let her come on. So they went on and went on and went on and it was getting late. It was almost night. So they saw a little hut of a house. Pegg said we'll go there now for the night, so they went. 'Twas a old witch and she had two daughters. So all right. She invited them in. She said she couldn't,...she told Pegg she couldn't take her because she had no place for her to sleep. She would take her two sisters. Pegg said she didn't care where it was, she would lie on the floor or anywhere. So anyway the witch took the three of them in. The two girls, they went to bed and the witch's two daughters went to bed. The witch put night caps on her daughters. So all right they all went to bed and Pegg lay down on the floor. Some time in the night Pegg went up and took the caps off the two daughters and put them on her sisters' heads. So the old witch got up in the night and she went to the ones who had the caps on and then she went to the other ones who had no caps on, so she killed them. So the next morning Pegg took off, herself and her two sisters. So they went away and travelled away for...,I don't know how long anyway. So anyway Pegg got jobs for her two sisters. There was a king there and he had three sons. So Pegg went to the king. Now the old witch, she had a canter (decanter) that could never be emptied, a lantern that showed a half a mile light and she had a horse that could go ten times swifter than a cannon ball, and the horse had a golden bell on every hair on his mane. So anyway Pegg went to the king and she told the guard she wanted to see the king. So the king ordered for her to go in. He asked Pegg what he could do for her. Pegg said I wants to know if your oldest son could marry my oldest sister. I can bring you a canter that can never be empted. The king said, well he said that would be a nice thing for a king to have. So he agreed. And he said now what do you want to get that. She said I want a handful of pepper. So the full of one of Pegg's hands was a hogshead. (A hogshead is a large barrel that can hold from 50 to 120 gallons). So he gave her the pepper. Pegg went to the witch's house. When the old man was finished eating, he told the old woman to go in and bring out his canter. The old woman brought out the canter and laid it on the table. Pegg went in and threw the handful of pepper at them. They began to sneeze and everything. Pegg took the canter and brought it home to the king. So his oldest son and Pegg's oldest sister got married.

Another day Pegg went again. She went in and the king said what do you want today Pegg. Well, she said, I come to see if you'd be satisfied for your second oldest son to marry my second oldest sister. I'll bring you a lantern that will show a half a mile light. So he said that would be a nice thing for a king to have. He said, what do you want to get that. She said I wants a handful of salt. So she went to the witch's house. The old woman was cooking soup. So Pegg got up on the roof. Pegg let all the salt go down into the soup. And then the salt, I mean the soup was too salty. So the old woman sent her girls for water. They had to go to the well for water, so they took the lantern. Now it was a mile to the well. They brought the lantern and laid it down half-way. Pegg took after them and she took the lantern and brought it to the king. So then the second oldest son and Pegg's second oldest sister got married. So that was all right.

After awhile Pegg went back to the king. He said to her, what do you want today, Pegg. She said I want to know if you'd be satisfied for your youngest son to marry me. I'll bring you a horse that can go ten times swifter than a cannon ball and a golden bell to every hair on his mane. So he, he didn't know what to say. But after awhile he gets unset and he said that would be a nice thing for a king to have. So anyway he said, Pegg what do you want to get that. She said I want a saw and a knife. So he gave her the saw and the knife and she went on. So she went to the old witch's house. The old witch was very angry with her. She said, Pegg, she said you're the cause of me killing me (my) two daughters. You stole me (my) canter that could never be empted. You stole me lantern that showed a half a mile light. Pegg, she said, if I did that to you, what would you do to me. Well, Pegg said, I'd put you in a bag and I'd bring you to the side of the road and I'd get a rod and I'd beat you till you barked like a dog and meowed like a cat and your bones rattled like crockeryware. Pegg, she said, that's what I'll do with you. So she put Pegg in the bag and brought her to the side of the road. Then the witch had to go into the woods to look for a rod. While she was gone Pegg ripped open the bag. She went to the old witch's house and took her dog, cat and some of her crockeryware. She went and put it into the bag. Then she went back and took the horse. The old witch came back with the rod and she beat the bag. She hit the dog and the dog barked. Then she hit the cat and the cat meowed. Then she hit the crockeryware and that rattled. She said, Pegg, your words come true. The witch went back to her house and missed the dog, cat, and crockeryware. So she went to the stable to get the horse and that was gone. She had another horse that could go almost as fast. So she took after Pegg. There was a river with a big bridge across it. Pegg had the bridge sawed. When the old witch went to cross the bridge, it gave away and she went away in the river. Pegg took the horse back to the king. So the king couldn't break his promise. So the king's son and Pegg got married.

So they got married but he didn't want her. So he used to be crying, days he used to cry and everything like that. He was right sad. So she said, one day she said, you don't want me. He said no. Well she said, ah kill me. He said, no, I couldn't do that. So she said, put me in the fire and burn me. He said, no, he wouldn't do that. So after awhile, anyway, she got him to do it. Before he burned her, she took her ring and she broke it in two and she gave him half. She said if you ever meet another woman with this half to go with your half, she will be your wife. He put her in the fire and she went in a blaze up the chimney. Now that he have her done away with he is real sad. He don't know what is going to happen to him. So one day there was a knock come on the door. He was half afraid to go open the door. He went and opened the door. There was the beautifulest lady that ever the sun shined on. So he invited her in and she said to him, you were married to Pegg. He said, yes. She said, you burned her, and he said, yes. Then she said, did Pegg leave you anything before you burned her. And he said yes, a half ring. So she took out a half ring and put it against his half ring, and they went together. So he married her. They lived happily ever after.

Source: "When she was a young girl."
Location: Teller's house.
Audience: Fieldworker.

Context, Style, and Language: This version of the story was taken down at dictation speed by the fieldworker, along with several other tales. He notes that Mrs. Brewer learned the story when she was a young girl living in the small fishing community of Southwest Clattice Harbour, Placentia Bay, where she lived from 1902 until 1966 when she moved to Freshwater. As in most Newfoundland communities, visiting houses was a popular pastime: "At these gatherings stories would be told and songs would be sung. This provided a great source of entertainment since there were no radios, TV's or clubs at this time."

See also the notes to No. **17.**

Types and Motifs:
AT327B. *The Dwarf and the Giant* + AT328. *The Boy [Girl] Steals the Giant's Treasure* + Cf. AT711. *The Beautiful and the Ugly Twin.*
Z10.1. *Beginning formula.*
N825.2. *Old man helper.*
T548.2. *Magic rites for obtaining a child.*
T511.1.2. *Conception from eating berry.*
C225. *Tabu: eating certain fruit.*
T551.13. *Child born hairy.*
L145.1. *Ugly sister helps pretty one.*
G262. *Murderous witch.*
K1611. *Substituted caps cause ogre to kill own children.*
P251.6.1. *Three brothers.*
Cf. H310. *Suitor tests.*
D1652.5. *Inexhaustible vessel.*
G279.2. *Theft from witch.*

D1162.1. *Magic lamp.*
Cf. K337. *Oversalting food of giant so that he must go outside for water.*
Cf. H1151.9. *Task: stealing troll's golden horse.*
F989.17. *Marvelously swift horse.*
P651.2. *Bells on horse's mane.*
K526. *Captor's bag filled with animals or objects while captives escape.*
R235. *Fugitives cut support of bridge so that pursuer falls.*
L162. *Lowly heroine marries prince (king).*
D1860. *Magic beautification.*
D576. *Transformation by being burned.*
D1865. *Beautification by death and resuscitation.*
H94.5. *Identification through broken ring.*
Z10.2. *End formula.*

International Parallels: See No. 17.

19. JACK GETS INTO HEAVEN[†]

Daniel Hutchings   AT330*
Cow Head, Great Northern Peninsula   TC250 66-24
24 August 1966   Collectors: HH and JW

Well _ you…you've always heard self-brag was scandal? [*laughter*]
[Int: Self-brag scan…was scandal huh?]
Self-brag was scandal. [*recorder off*]*** three or four good drinks o' whiskey or something you _ what's in's got to come out then. [*laughter*] [*recorder off*]*** just the same as I'm doin now. Little better than I'm doin 'cause I'm past me singin days now. [*recorder off*]*** know some uh…I never known ever…
[Teller's wife: I was sayin there's a _ man, he's gone now I guess er…that's Nimmie _ Payne.]
[*recorder off*]*** two fellers an'…they were buddy all their lifetime an' _ an' one…Jack said he'd like to be goin to heaven. Well he watched _ by an' by he seen a clergyman go. (So) he crept up behind un an' St. Peter let the clergyman in. So finally he turned the door on Jack. An' he went back to his buddy he said er…"I don't know _ but if I'm not makin (a mistake)" he said "I'm goin to…to beat St. Peter."

So he went up to the gate again an' knocked and St. Peter come an' said "What have you got there?"

"Oh I got the parson's luggage" he says.

"Oh come on in with it come on in with it" he says. [*laughter*]

229

laughter and happiness of these few people. . .gathered around and talking of the good old days and how much everything is changed today." The stories were noted down by the collector during the evening.

This manuscript tale opens with the stock formula that it is true, qualified by "anyway he said 'twas true," and the use of named local people adds to the pretense of authenticity. The story relies on the understated humor of the events and the explication in the final paragraph. Note the attention-getters *see* and *Listen,* and the continuity marker *(So) anyway.* The language is straightforward at all levels, and includes such typical Newfoundland features as the absence of initial consonant in *'tis* and *'twas,* the verb *dodge* (to stroll, saunter; *DNE dodge* v. 1) and the past tense form *done.*

Type and Motifs:

Cf. AT330*. *Heaven Entered by Trick.*

A661.0.1.2. *Saint Peter as porter of heaven.*

Baughman *A661.0.1.2.1. *Are You Riding?* Slave and master go up to heaven. Master knocks at heaven's gate. St. Peter asks, 'Are you mounted?' Is told he must go back and get mounted. Tells this to slave and gets on latter's back. Returns, knocks on gate, and is told to tie his mount outside and come in.

Cf. K2371.1. *Heaven entered by a trick.*

International Parallels: In this attempt to get into heaven by a trick, the person carried is successful, but the carrier is left outside. This contrasts with the Irish version cited in the notes to No. 19, in which both the carrier and those carried are admitted. Some class distinction in heaven is implied in No. 19 in that either a gentleman or a clergyman is allowed to have his luggage with him. Although it is not stressed in No. 20, class distinction is even more marked in that admission to heaven is granted only to a mounted individual, i.e., usually someone from the upper classes. Both this tale and the previous one also display a typically male attitude toward religion: one of profound cynicism and scepticism. In No. 19 Jack, as a poor man, feels the only way he can sneak in is by pretending to be the parson's lackey.

Both class and racial discrimination are stressed in most North American versions of this tale, especially in those from the United States, nearly all of which were collected from black informants. Since symbolically the white man in America has been riding on the black man's back for several centuries, it is not surprising that in most texts the black man is induced to take the role of the horse and carry the white man on his back to Heaven's Gate. Once there, in all versions the white man is admitted to heaven but told to leave his mount outside.

That this symbolism is recognized by blacks is brought out by three similar versions of the story, one from Texas and two from Kentucky, each of which, like the Newfoundland tale, was told as a dream. A black man says he could not get into heaven because he was on foot; on his way back he meets a white politician—in one version two of them—explains the reason for his rejection, and in each case is induced to carry the white man or men on his back and return. At Heaven's Gate in all three dreams the whites got in but the black man was left outside. Since each of these dreams was told at a political rally in which the white politicians were running for office, the black speaker's meaning was obvious to his audience: the white wants to be on top, i.e., to get elected, entirely for his own benefit.

As Almqvist points out, in Ireland this story is used to express national antagonism. See Almqvist, *Béal.* 39-41 (1971-73), 43, for the translation of a published Irish language text in which an Irishman goes to heaven riding piggyback on an Englishman. St. Peter admits the Irishman, but says he must leave his donkey behind. Almqvist also refers to an unpublished Co. Sligo text about a Jew and a Catholic, so the story obviously can also be used to show religious antagonism. Surprisingly there is no reference to any older texts that might parallel the American form more closely by having an Englishman, the nationality which for several centuries was dominant in Ireland, riding to heaven on the back of an Irishman. Since the pattern of this story can be so easily adapted to fit any two antagonistic groups, whether nationalities, races, or religions, it seems likely that in the future we will learn that similar tales are known and told in other countries.

The Newfoundland story, however, appears unique in lacking the heavily charged racial or national antagonism evident in the American and Irish versions. Here the dream is only a device for telling a humorously improbable story without being accused either of sacrilege or of lying. Nonetheless, there are overtones of prejudice about women. That the woman gets in while the man does not also suggests the male view of religion as the domain of women, especially older ones, and has implications concerning their supposed overindulgence in religious matters.

Canada
Fauset, *Folklore,* pp. 52-53, no. 36, 2 versions [white man rides white; white man rides black], one white text about Pat and Mike, one black text about two named individuals (Nova Scotia).

United States
Sterling, *Laughing,* p. 135 [white man rides black] (Southern black).
Johnson, *Culture,* pp. 153-54, no. 17 [white man rides black], black (South Carolina).
Smiley, *JAF* 32 (1919), 373, no. 33 [white man rides black], black (Alabama).
Eddins, *PTFS* 9 (1931), 160-62, told as a dream [white man rides black; both are politicians] (Texas).
There is an English summary of a Spanish text in Rael, *Cuentos,* 2, p. 258, no. 290 (Colorado), in which a Spanish trickster gets a black man to serve as his horse.
For other versions in American collections of humor see:
Landon, *Kings,* pp. 558-59 [two white politicians ride a black man], story ascribed to the famous newspaper editor, Col. Henry Watterson, who said it was a black man's report of a dream (Kentucky), and rpt. in Botkin, *Anecdotes,* p. 44-45.
Kieffer, *Bone,* pp. 64-65, told as a dream [white politician rides black man], black (Kentucky).
In two other humor collections the source and locality are not given:
Lupton, *Book,* pp. 566-67, no. 1112 [pastor rides his parishioner to heaven's gate], a white version.
Meiers and Knapp, *Thesaurus,* p. 229, no. 2266, condensed to a brief joke; no skin color mentioned.
There is an unpublished text from a New Jersey white informant in the Halpert Folklore Collections; it is described in Baughman's motif.

our expenses 'll be" he said uh...* "'fore we gets to town" he said "if we ever gets there."

So uh...got the two [loads of] money _ an' the two of 'em started. And uh...this is where they got to. They got there _ an' hid away under this bridge. An' by an' by they all come. An' uh...the head fella was wonderin say he wondering to himself uh...what happened Jack, where was Jack to, they...he's not along 'fore this time.

Now all of 'em spoke up an' /one/ said "Begar" he said "you don't know" he said "if...you don't know" he said "perhaps" he said "you...you uh...trusted Jack too much" he said. "(Perhaps) you don't know" he said "but Jack is after bein...[to] the cave" he said "an' got a load o' money" he said "an'...an' left _ an' the lady too."

And she...an' they were listenin to 'em under the bridge. So uh...anyway he went back to the cave. They went back to the cave an' when they went back sure enough -- he was gone.* So when he got 'em gone he...they got out o' bi...out o'...out o' the bridge _ on the bridge an' 'twas a (fair)...uh...an ol' woman* _ half ways _ from that to...out to the...the ferry-boat _ where they'd...ferry across the...ferry across an'...an' then when they'd ferry across an' get over on that side _ uh...they'd meet the...be a crow[d]...a crowd there waitin for to...uh...get 'em out to town.

So uh...come over _ come in to this ol' woman an' she said uh..."Now" he said uh...he said "the robbers" he said "'s after us." An' he said uh...he said uh...he said "You got to sh...to...to hide me...hide us" he said "somewhere."

"Well now" she [said] "you can see" she said uh..."I got no place to hide ye." Took up the hatches, said "There's a...a hatch there" she said "in the floor, you can get down there" she said "yourself an' _ the lady if you wish" she said "that's th' only place I got."

Oh she rose up the hatch an'*...Jack got uh...Jack got down an' when he got down there were her husband _ an' her son _ was dead down there, corpse.

Jack said "I'm not goin to stop here" he said.

"Oh yes" she said "hush, hush" she said uh..."the robbers" she said "are right 'longside."

"Now" he said "you put 'em" he said uh..."on the longest road" he said "you (could) get...find." He said "You put 'em _ on that road" he said _ "to the ferry man." An' he said "When they goes" he said uh..."put us" he said uh..."on the shortest one."

So uh...alright _ they were there talkin to her a spell an' by an' by they left, she went out an' _ showed 'em the beach...the road to go on.

So uh...Jack got up an' Jack said uh..."Got ne'r bit o' board here?" he said.

"No" she said. Said...she said "What do you want the board for?"

"Oh" Jack said uh...he said "I'm goina make a coffin for them two poor...men now" he said "before I leaves this."

So gar she give him [the] table. An' he...he beat down [the] table _ an' made a...a square box. An' put the two corpse into it. Oh then he left. An' uh...an' he was uh...on the /road/ uh...out get aboard a ferry-boat _ when the robbers got there _ on the road they were there. An' uh...they come out an' they offered the ferryman uh...a FORTUNE for the rest of his life if he'd bring back the...Jack _ an' the prisoner. /row/

Jack said "You're not bringin the...not bringing him back" he s[aid] "not bringin us...takin them aboard" he said "till you lands us first." Says "You got to land us" he said "an' 'fore we takes them aboard."

So uh...begar _ he started. Row down to the end o' the lake uh...an' land uh...Jack _ an' the*...an' the lady, now he's goin to go right back for...the robbers. An' Jack _ got out an' jumped on the...jumped out on the sand.* Hauled (her) up [a] bit. Then uh...up foot an' give it to her [i.e., *kicked the boat*]. An' broke a hole into her.* An' uh...oh th' ol' man got m...mad, he said that was th' only way in the world he said he had to make a cent. "An' now" he said uh..."I got no way now" he said "I'm goin to starve." *loud background noises *loud background noises *loud background noises

Jack said "No" he said "you won't starve."

He took [the] /lady's/...money what he had in the...had in the bag. An' he give him all the money _ enough for to do _ for himself _ all a lifetime an' a generation after. So _ he was glad of his life. /leady's/

So he left an'...an' got out to the...to the...the town an' when they got out [to] town there sure enough the...the father's ship was there waitin for (her).

An' uh...she was so long gone _ that her father said uh..."Anyone 'd bring back the lady _ goin to have her in marriage."

So she wen[t]...went (right) out an' went aboard. An' begar he didn't want to take Jack.

"Well" she said "if you don't take Jack" she said "you won't get me." She says "I'll not go neither."

So begorrah after a spell uh...he took Jack aboard. An' he tried every way in the world to try to...make away with un _ an' he couldn't do it. An' one day she was up on the quarter deck _ sewin. Now when he got a chance he...he took her sewin basket _ an' hove it overboard. And uh...when it drove away a piece he's...sung out an' asked who'd volunteer _ to go after the lady's uh...sew...basket. No one o' the rest spoke an' Jack said "I will."

with it." He said "You be gone off the premises" said uh…"THIS is the man" he said "is goin to…to wed my daughter."

An' begar ˍ herself an'…Jack ˍ got married the next day. An' uh… that's what they were at now, well uh…I left about three o'clock.

Duration: 17 min., 48 sec.
Location: Kitchen of teller's house, early afternoon.
Audience: Teller's wife, interviewer.

Context, Style, and Language: Although the normal domestic chores are going on around him, children and adults come in and out of the kitchen, and various other noises are heard constantly throughout, the teller is largely unperturbed and quickly makes it clear to visitors that he is talking and does not want to be disturbed.

It is intriguing that the tale should begin with Jack as a boy in the ashes and concerns his rescue of and marriage to the King of Ashes' daughter. Yet the two "ashes" references seem unconnected. The name "King of Ashes" is itself enigmatic. Jack entirely shakes off any hint of laziness once he sets out on his quest and there is no further reference in his characterization to his ashy beginnings. Perhaps the "Ashes abode of unpromising hero" motif is simply suggested to the teller by his title, or it may be for him merely a standard opening formula.

Ambrose Reardon's speech manifests numerous Anglo-Irish features: the clear /l/, the substitution of /t/ for initial *th,* the breathed quality of final retroflex /r/, the use of *after* before a present participle, and the asseveration *begorrah* (often realized as *begar*), for example. Nevertheless, he also uses such West Country English pronunciations as the half-open back unround short vowel in *took* and *hove,* and occasionally the pronoun *un.* Transcription proved difficult at times because of distortion and poor sound quality on the archive tape copied from the original and there is frequent background noise; consequently some details are represented only tentatively. Although of advanced years, Uncle Am, as he was affectionately known in Croque, is able to sustain the lengthy narrative and greatly enjoys telling it, enlivening it with vigorous dialogue and a considerable range of vocal contrast, emphasizing certain key words for dramatic effect. Like the Bennett family from the opposite coast of the Great Northern Peninsula, he makes frequent use of *he/she said* to punctuate the dialogue. It is important to remember that these two coasts enjoy a degree of contact via road links and are not so unconnected as they may appear on a map. The speech is fairly slow, with frequent brief pauses. There are a number of misencodings but these do not impede the flow of the plot. Indeed, as this tale was recorded later in the interview than No. 43, when the teller had relaxed and got into his stride and external interference was considerably lessened, it is noticeably more fluent. There is an interruption towards the end when someone comes into the room but the teller resumes without undue difficulty.

Of linguistic interest are the pronunciation of *quay* as /kei/ and *does* as [duːz], the stressing of the third syllable in *separate* and *separated,* such aphetic forms as *'way* (away), *'bout, 'longside,* and *'fore,* the absence of initial vowel in *'twas, 'tis,* the verb *dodge* in the sense of "stroll casually, saunter," the use of *ye, They* (There), *e'r one* (any one), and *n'er* (no), the intensifier *wonderful,* the typically nautical *hatch* (trap door), and *breeze* (gale), *lanched* (launched), and *paddle* (oar). The highly idiomatic style of the storyteller is seen in such typical Newfoundland usages as the dismissive *Go 'way,* the unconcerned *no odds,* the ambiguous *was he any good to rob* (was he any good as a robber), and the economical *up foot an' give it to her* (raised his foot and kicked it); also *latter end* (finally), *he put her* (he hurried), *I leaves this* (I leave this place), *it drove away a piece* (it drifted some distance), *into her* (in her), *make away with* (kill), and the common proverbial comparison *as saucy as a black.*

There is no marker of plurality in *corpse* (corpses), present tense verb forms include *we gets/takes, I leaves/wants, they goes,* past tense forms are *bid, sot, confound* (confined), *come, rose* (raised), *knowed, sove, you done;* the auxiliary is omitted in *I going to* and the preposition in *what happened Jack,* while the double negative occurs in *I don't want no money.*

Type and Motifs:

AT506B. *The Princess Rescued from Robbers.*
P251.6.1. *Three brothers.*
L111.3. *Widow's son as hero.*
L131.1. *Ashes abode of unpromising hero.*
H1220. *Quests voluntarily undertaken.*
N765. *Meeting with robber band.*
R12.1. *Maiden abducted by pirates (robbers).*
R45.3. *Captivity in cave.*
R111.1.2. *Princess rescued from robbers.*
T68.1. *Princess offered as prize to rescuer.*
K2200. *Villains and traitors.*
S141. *Exposure in boat.*
E341.1.1. *Dead grateful for having been spared indignity to corpse.*
R163. *Rescue by grateful dead man.*
K1932. *Impostors claim reward (prize) earned by hero.*
N681. *Husband (lover) arrives home just as wife (mistress) is to marry another.*
H35.3.2. *Recognition by embroidery.*
L161. *Lowly hero marries princess.*
Z10.2. *End formula.*

International Parallels: Of the several folktale types in which the grateful dead play an important role (see Thompson, *The Folktale,* pp. 50-53), only one, AT506, "The Rescued Princess," is represented in this collection. Thompson comments that of the two related tales about a rescued princess included under this Type, one, AT506A, "The Princess Rescued from Slavery," is the more popular and is known in all parts of Europe as well as elsewhere, while the second, AT506B, "The Princess Rescued from Robbers," seems to

Let us compare the appearance and behavior of the dead in this tale Type with that in the only other Type in this collection in which the dead return: AT326A*, "Soul Released from Torment." As we point out in our discussion of No. 16, in AT326A* the dead appear in a variety of frightening forms: skeletons, animals, and so on. If they are in human form, their throats are cut. It is important to emphasize that the hero takes all of these strange appearances as calmly as if they were everyday occurrences. In many situations he acts as if the visitations were normal neighborly visits, and offers hospitality, food, drink, and warmth to his visitors. At the end his courageous calm is recognized by the returning dead and he is praised and rewarded.

There is a great contrast between the normal everyday human likeness of the returning dead in AT506B and the frightening guises in which they appear in AT326A*. Yet in both Types the returning dead reward the hero for his behavior. In AT506B it is for his earlier neighborly action in burying the dead. In AT326A* it is because of the courage he displays by calmly treating the dead as if they were ordinary neighbors on a normal visit.

Addendum

The motif in No. 96 of the three knots in a rope that provide increasingly stronger winds as each knot is unloosed is listed by Thompson in the *Motif-Index* as D2142.1.2., "Wind raised by loosing certain knots." Thompson gives only four citations for this interesting motif. Since two of the four are from Jutland and not easily available, it may be useful to supply additional English-language reports as well as a few in English translation.

That the motif is an old one in Europe is evident from Archer Taylor's remark (*The Black Ox,* p. 42) about "the medieval tradition which declared that Lapps sold knotted ropes to mariners. When the first knot was opened a gentle breeze sprang up, the second provided a stronger wind, and the third a hurricane." According to Rappoport, *Superstitions,* p. 86, the belief that the sorcerers of Lapland could sell a favorable wind to their clients still prevailed in the north of Sweden in the seventeenth century. The sorcerer tied three knots in a handkerchief and handed it to the wind purchaser. Baker, *Folklore of the Sea,* p. 154, reports but does not give her source that as late as 1861 there was a Cornishman who could provide winds. Each customer received a thrice-knotted cord. His trade apparently fell off about that date because the captains of steamers did not need to buy wind.

Some of the narratives that follow are told as legends, while others are reported as personal experiences. In all versions the wind purchaser is handed some material with three knots tied in it. This material may range from a strand of wool, a thread, a piece of string, twine, or rope, to a handkerchief or other piece of cloth. In nearly all versions the instructions are much like those in the Newfoundland text and in Taylor's description: untying one knot will provide a gentle breeze, undoing the second one will bring a stronger wind, but—and in most examples the warning is quite explicit—loosening the third knot will produce a hurricane. In some versions the first knot gives a fair wind, the second a storm or gale, and the third a hurricane.

In all but two of the remaining examples the wind-provider is a woman; sometimes she is called a sorcerer or witch, but frequently she is not labeled at all. The wind-purchaser, becalmed at a certain port or faced with contrary winds, applies to a recommended local woman for favorable winds so that he can return to his home port, and he is given an amulet with three knots. In all of these legends or personal experience stories, the emphasis is on the consequences of untying the third knot.

In all versions of the story loosening the first two knots works admirably. The wind speedily brings the ship to the harbor mouth or near to the landing; in some versions the vessel has even been berthed. Out of curiosity the third knot is untied, and then all hell breaks loose. If a fishing boat is drawn up on shore, it is capsized and smashed. If it is near the shore, the men may have to jump overboard to drag it in. Sometimes the captain is killed. If the ship is at sea, the hurricane may even drive her back to the place from which she started.

In a North German legend reprinted in Rappoport, *Superstitions,* pp. 83-84, some Schleswig herring fishers, who need an east wind to return home, receive a cloth with three knots from an old woman at Siseby on the Slei. Undoing the first knot gives them a fair wind from the east; undoing the second produces a storm that speeds them to their home city. Out of curiosity they untie the third knot and are assailed by a hurricane from the west so that they have to leap into the water to draw their vessel on shore.

Kvideland and Sehmsdorf, in *Scandinavian Folk Belief and Legend,* translate two versions of this legend. In the one from Finland (pp. 150-51, no. 32.1), a crew that had sailed to Sweden could not return home because of a head wind. A fellow came along who gave them a handkerchief tied into three knots. He told them not to untie the third one until they could see the shore at home. They followed his instructions, and the ship ran ashore at their home port. In a second story from Sweden (pp. 262-63, no. 52.6), a skipper who had carried a load of rye for a beautiful woman and, following her instructions, cast it into the sea at a certain point, was taken under water by her. He received from an old man a handkerchief that had three knots in it with the warning not to untie the third knot. Untying the first two knots worked admirably; "But he must have untied the third knot, too, because nobody ever saw him again."

All but two of our other reports are from northern and western Scotland. Rappoport, *Superstitions,* pp. 84-85, cites a version in which a skipper from Kintyre, Argyllshire, who made trading voyages to Ireland, secured two strings, each with three knots in it, from an old woman. The first string was to provide fair winds to take him to Ireland; the second was to secure them for the return voyage. On the outgoing voyage when near the Irish coast he untied the third knot and a hurricane destroyed some of the houses on shore. On his voyage back to Kintyre he was careful to unloosen only two knots. Securing two knotted strings is not reported in any other text we have found, but the fact that the ship and crew received no damage from the untying of the third knot is not too common.

Sutherland, *Gleanings,* pp. 60-62, tells about a skipper who wanted to go north to Lybster, Caithness, from Portmahomack in Ross and Cromarty. He secured a thread with three knots. Near the entrance to Lybster harbor he untied the third knot, and the gale swept his vessel back to Portmahomack. Polson, *Witchcraft,* p. 151, reports that a mariner bought a string with three knots from a Stornoway woman, on the Isle of Lewis in the Outer Hebrides, to get winds to take him south. Near his harbor he undid the third

Lacourcière-Low, "Catalogue," cites 15 Francophone versions of AT506B from Canada: 2 (Nova Scotia), 8 (New Brunswick), 2 (Quebec), 3 (Ontario).

United States

Cf. Parsons, *Islands,* 1, 344-48, no. 117 (lacks 506, II, the rescue of the princess), English trans. of Portuguese text, Cape Verde Islands, black (Massachusetts).

Cf. Espinosa, *Folk-Tales,* pp. 203-4, no. 42 (506A), English summary of Spanish text (New Mexico).

Cf. Weigle, *Two Guadalupes,* pp. 97-101 (506A), Spanish tradition, in English (New Mexico).

Cf. Rael, *Cuentos,* pp. 639-40, no. 98 (506A), cf. pp. 640-41, no. 99 (506A), 2 versions, English summaries of Spanish texts (Colorado).

See Robe, *Index,* Type 506, for references to other Hispanic American versions.

Cf. Thompson, *European,* pp. 404-9, no. 14, "The Marooned Rescuer," for analysis of Canadian and American Indian tales that have a helper (506, Ib), the marooning of the hero (506, III), and the recognition motif (506, IV), but lack "The Grateful Dead Man" (506, Ia).

There is a British broadside or verse garland version of AT506A found in oral tradition in the United States.

Cf. Ring, et al., *JAF* 66 (1953), 54-55, "The Turkish Bride," in verse and prose (New York).

Cf. Belden and Hudson, *Ballads,* pp. 220-22, no. 60, "The Turkish Factor" (North Carolina).

Cf. Dobie, *PTFS* 6 (1927), 56-65, no. IV, "The Turkish Factor," text and full discussion (Texas).

For other American versions from oral tradition and print, see Laws, *British Broadsides,* p. 292 (Q37, "The Factor's Garland") and consult Dobie's discussion for further American and British references.

Mexico

Cf. Wheeler, *Tales,* pp. 344-46, no. 117 (506A), Spanish text with English summary (Jalisco).

For references to other Mexican versions, see Robe, *Index,* Type 506.

The Caribbean and South America

Cf. Parsons, *Andros,* pp. 148-49, no. 100 (lacks 506, II, the rescue of the princess), black (Bahamas).

Beckwith, *Stories,* pp. 152-53, no. 119 (506B), and p. 184, no. 119, notes, black (Jamaica).

Cf. Parsons, *Antilles,* 3, pp. 259-61, no. 259, English summaries of 5 French texts containing many elements of AT506, but lacking the rescue of the princess, black (Martinique, Guadeloupe, Haiti).

See Hansen, *Types,* Type 506, for references to versions from the Dominican Republic, Puerto Rico, and Chile.

England

Although we have not found published versions of AT506 either in prose or verse from oral tradition in England, for a printed reference see

A Collection of Old Ballads, 3, pp. 221-28, "The Factor's Garland" (506A), in verse, with tune named. For other printed versions see the references in Dobie's notes (above: Texas) and in Gerould, *Grateful Dead,* pp. 24-25.

Scotland

MacDougall and Calder, *Folk Tales,* pp. 74-95 (506B, with cf. 2009), Gaelic text and English trans. (Argyllshire).

Cf. McKay, *Béal.* 4 (1933-34), 292-98 (506A, with cf. 611), Gaelic text from the J. F. Campbell MSS. and English trans. (Islay).

Cf. MacDonald and Bruford, *Tales,* pp. 14-17, no. 11 (506A) (North Uist).

Cf. Campbell, *Popular Tales,* 2, pp. 110-29, no. 32 (506A), Gaelic text and English trans. (Barra).

For a version in verse, cf. Greig, *Folk-Song of the North-East,* no. 120, "The Factor's Garland" (506A), tune mentioned (Aberdeenshire).

Ireland

Cf. Ó Duilearga, *Béal.* 15 (1945), 199, no. 2 (506A), English summary of Irish text (Co. Galway).

Irish Types, Type 506A & B, 54 versions.

Continental Europe and Asia

Cf. Grimm and Hansen, *Tales,* pp. 123-26 (506A) (Germany). This text, rejected and not published by the Grimms, was printed by Bolte and Polívka (3, pp. 490-92), and listed as Grimm no. 217.

Cf. Dasent, *Fjeld,* pp. 90-94 (506A) (Norway).

Hodne, *Types,* AT506, 12 versions (Norway).

Cf. Massignon, *Folktales,* pp. 44-48, no. 10 (506A) (France).

Cf. Andrews, *FLR* 3 (1880), 48-52 (506A) (France).

Cf. Webster, *Legends,* pp. 146-50 (506A) [angel helper instead of grateful dead man], cf. pp. 151-54 (506A) [fox helper], 2 versions (Basque).

Cf. Crane, *Popular Tales,* pp. 131-35 (506A), and pp. 350-51, n. 12 (Italy).

Cf. Calvino, *Folktales,* pp. 138-41, no. 45 (506A) (Italy).

Straparola, *Nights,* 2, pp. 214-21 (Night XI, Fable 2) (506B, I, II, IV, V), literary (Italy).

Cf. Wolf, *Fairy Tales,* pp. 204-10 (506A) (Germany).

Cf. Mijatovies, *Folk-Lore,* pp. 96-106 (506A) [angel helper instead of grateful dead man] (Serbia), and rpt. in Petrovitch, *Hero Tales,* pp. 291-99, no. 13.

Cf. Parker, *Village,* 2, pp. 130-36, no. 104 (506A) (Ceylon).

22. JACK AND THE PRINCESS[†]

William B. Hewitt   AT506B
Barr'd Islands, Notre Dame Bay   TC214 65-12
1 September 1965   Collector: L. Harris

[Int: Now you go on talk away about Jack.]
About Jack.
[Int: Yeah.]

Er...there once were a princess an' she got kidnapped. She got kidnapped by...by...by...the /pirates/ _ the...the robbers. An' they carried her away er...an' put her into a...into a cave _ into a cellar into the cave. An' at that time there was a schooner goin along and she got wracked _ and all the crew were lost clear o' Jack. An' they had a lot o' money on

/pilots/

delivery gives a sense of urgency to the telling. Transcription is also hampered by a lack of clarity in the recording itself which is probably due to the fact that in this and the other two stories he tells (Nos. 70 and 95) the speaker was some distance from the microphone. The tendency to omit monosyllabic words at times, or to de-emphasize them so much that they can hardly be heard, again causes problems for the transcriber although it is quite clear from the response of the audience that they had no difficulty in following and enjoying each of the tales to the fullest extent. This is also true of the ambiguities of reference in the use of the pronouns *her, his,* and *he,* which in one case result in the blend *hers* (her/his). These are more difficult for the reader to follow than they are for the listener, as is the substitution of *prince* for *princess* throughout most of the narrative.

Part of the final paragraph of the story is spoken in a very formulaic way, like the more structured "runs" and formulas in other tales in this collection, almost as if in verse:

> thát wăsn't thĕ mán thăt sŏve hĕrs lífe
> thĕ mán Ī márrĭed
> bŭt thís wăs thĕ mán thăt sóve hĭs lífe, Jáck

Even though in the original speech reproduced here the teller's expression lacks formal accuracy, his intended meaning is clear, and the formulaic delivery, consisting almost entirely of monosyllables, succeeds in communicating despite errors of reference. This illustrates the fact that in the actual storytelling situation the absence of formal accuracy does not constitute a barrier to understanding.

Mr. Hewitt's speech is a good example of conservative English West Country usage, notably in the pronunciation of the stressed vowels in *livyers* (inhabitants), *mornings, corpse,* etc., the typical semivowel /j/ in the second syllable of *livyers,* and the frequent use of the pronoun *un.* Metathesis of /k/ occurs habitually in *aksed* (asked), intrusive initial /h/ is found in *early* and *oar,* and aphesis in *'longed* (belonged). The typically local sharply rising intonation within a statement seeking confirmation from the audience is well illustrated in "pilot un in" in the dénouement. Also of interest is the passing reference to *cellar* in the opening lines of the tale as in Newfoundland this word usually refers to a "root cellar," i.e., an underground chamber where vegetables are stored, the use of *time* in the local sense of "party, celebration, dance," etc., of *make away with* (kill), and of *nar* (no, not any).

Regional forms of the past tense and past participle are especially common, e.g., *come* (came), *hod* (hid), *hove* (heaved), *sot* (set), *laid* [led] (lay), *knowed* (knew), *seen* (saw), and *sove* (saved). The lack of an audible past tense inflection in several occurrences of *aks(ed)* allows the possibility of their being construed as vivid present tense forms, and the same is true of *come.* The present tense marker *-s* is seen in *I wants,* while the plural morpheme is absent in *corpse.* Double negatives are also very much in evidence.

Type and Motifs:
AT506B. *The Princess Rescued from Robbers.*
R12.1. *Maiden abducted by pirates (robbers).*

R45.3. *Captivity in cave.*
N765. *Meeting with robber band.*
R111.1.2. *Princess rescued from robbers.*
K2200. *Villains and traitors.*
S141. *Exposure in boat.*
F341.1.1. *Dead grateful for having been spared indignity to corpse.*
R163. *Rescue by grateful dead man.*
Cf. T68.1. *Princess offered as prize to rescuer.*
Cf. K1932. *Impostors claim reward (prize) earned by hero.*
Cf. N681. *Husband (lover) arrives home just as wife (mistress) is to marry another.*
H35.3.2. *Recognition by embroidery.*
L161. *Lowly hero marries princess.*

International Parallels: See No. 21.

23. THE BLUE BULL

Allan Oake   AT511A + AT650A + Cf. AT300
Beaumont, Green Bay, Notre Dame Bay   TC309 66-25
10 September 1966   Collectors: JW and Harold Paddock

Yeah. (?may)...uh what they call "Blue Bull."
[Int. A: The what?]
"Blue Bull" _ was the title of un. [*recorder off*]*** threequarters who he...take an hour an' threequarters to tell he. [Int. B laughs] [*recorder off*]*** Oh yes Jack was into that one alright you know _ well they had to...[*clears throat*] it starts we'll say _ it starts with the...he was a king's son we'll say then _ an' there was two...three sons of 'em. Well their mother died, well you know they had a bull. He was a blue bull we'll say an'...when she died _ she to[ld]...said 'twas Jack's _ Jack's bull. Well alright.

Well the king went to another country see an' got married. Well now _ he had his sons come over there...his...his last wife (you) wanted to see their...his sons er...he had three sons out in th' other country, well [you] [k]now when Jack went we'll say he went with...when they went he went wi' his bull TOO.

Well now after he was there...after he was there for...a time you know the um...the ol' man...or th' ol' woman we'll say you know this...began to tell...her husband _ she had one daughter _ or was tellin her daughter _ you know what was goin to happen. These...this three sons was goin to have all her property an' she'd get NOTHING. Well

253

/Is/

"Five hundred pound" _ to make a walkin cane. So _ you know Jack used to get up this hammer you know an' let un fall down an' all of it an' _ by an' by the ol' blacksmith roared at un "/If/ you're goin to hit the iron" he said "hit it!" So he come down wi' this iron see an' struck it an' knocked the...old blacksmith out...out one side.

"Oh" he said "take your three hundred pound," first...first...first was three hundred pound see. "Take your three hundred pound iron" he said "get out."

"Oh no" he said he'd...he'd work uh...work _ a year an' one day for three hundred pound iron.

/?wires/

Well after the...the year an' one day was up he went to work an' /?welds/ all together you know. Took up on his little finger an' swung it round like that an' wasn't hardy enough...heavy enough (to play then). He think he'd have two more _ hundred on top o' that. Well he'd work another year an' one day _ for this two hundred pound iron.

Well the once he finally _ got it. Well he...got his five hundred pound iron walkin cane now an' he _ went off to look, he _ was FINISHED wi' that job.

He went off an' he knocked on a FARMER'S door. [clears throat] Ol' farmer told un he'd like...(to) be able to hire un on but he said he...he had no money to pay un. Oh he said he didn't want...he didn't want no money, he only wanted just grease enough to grease a bone.* [That's what] he wanted. Well _ in that case he said he'd...he'd hire un on he said if that's all he want.

*noise in
background

(Well) he had so many cows you know he had to drive off an' _ drove off the cows next day to a pasture, a piece o' pasture ground _ they feed all day an' in th' even when they come back _ their udders was SOLID full o' milk _ right chinched. Well the ol'...farmer he began to...to get...begin to like this Jack AWFUL well so _ he told missus an' he...he wanted to get up a LITTLE bit earlier next (mornin). He had further to go he said he...look for some more...pasture ground so _ went off that day an' _ found a pasture...piece o' pasture ground.

So [coughs] they feed all day an' in th' evenin when they'd er...an' their d...udders was draggin the ground when they come back. Oh they (was)...wonderful delighted (then).

So he told the missus he wante[d]...missus he wanted get up a hour earlier _ well he said he had further to go. But that day he FOUND _ this big strip of...pasture ground you know (where) he was...waitin for his cows to feed.

Well the next mornin he went off an' he made a beat [a] (hole) through this piece o' pasture, let 'em in. Wasn't in there very long you know before erm...he heard a little...a mutterin sound. So he...[clears throat] he looked up we'll say an' here was a...a giant comin down _ one headed giant _ down through. An' he come over with Jack you know an' started makin fun o' Jack 'cause he was only a little small feller again he. He reached down to pick (hold) Jack an' Jack struck un wi' his walkin cane see an' knocked un out. Took un up by the...slack o' the poll and...ass an' fired un out there into a ditch. So _ alright. Next _ he went back that even wi' his cows, oh was...everything was full o' milk.

He...went off again the next mornin. Let his cows in, there was thousands o' feed there for his cows. By an' by 'twasn't very long before he hear another...sound you know, looked up, here was a TWO headed giant comin down. Come down over where Jack was an'...begin to mutter about those cows an' Jack said "If you've anything to say" he said "say it to ME not to the cows." Over he come where Jack was, he hadn't seen Jack 'fore then. Reached down his hand you know for to pick hold [o'] Jack _ an' Jack struck un wi' the...this five hundred pound cane an' knocked un out. [*coughs*] So alright.

Now he knowed _ Jack begin to know we'll say that there was something around somewhere. Well he told his er...missus next even he'd...he'd like to get up a bit earlier...he had another piece o' land, he wanted to get a little further away _ (ground). But uh...he didn't have much...(an') uh...he uh...didn't have no (further) [to] go an' he thought perhaps he'd have a ramble _ around there. Drove his cows off next mornin an' he was sot down _ he was sot down in the grass an' the once he heard...looked up an' seen this...THREE headed giant comin down. Come over an' he started mutterin you know an' he hadn't aseen Jack. Took hold one [o'] the cow you know an' to heave her out of it an' Jack said "Don't touch that cow!" he said. "If you got anything to...say now" he said "come over an' say it to me!" Well all of a sudden he /seen/...he seen Jack you know he...he was goin to have a bit o' FUN for hisself. (Come) over to Jack you know an' before he knowed anything Jack struck un wi' this...walkin cane. Knocked un out. Well he said uh...he said "I got a bridge across this...this uh...ditch now" (?beside) him. "Got a bridge across here now" he said. Alright. /sons/

Went home that even, now NEXT day he was goin to have the ramble _ around. [*clears throat*] Told the miss[us]...his missus he wanted to get up _ at the CRACK o' light or before light he said _ because he had the LONG piece to drive his cows.

Well the next morning he started off an' put his cows in. 'Twas only a little bit you know before he heard this mutterin sound, looked up an' here was this...a WOMAN comin down. She was uh...(well) she was six mile...she was six mile TALL. An' her hair now was seven mile long see? She come down an' she never done nothing, come over an' reached down her hand an' picked up Jack you know. Hove un up there. Well Jack was into it now he didn't know what he was goina do but when she was goin to take un down you know he struck her wi' his cane _ an' knocked her out. Well Jack fell down in her hair. Never hurt hisself. Went off (down) to the...[*coughs*] went off an' found her barn you know the...an' uh...th' house an' everything (there were) that was all (of un).

So he come back now an' she...(now)...an' the missus was tellin about a GIRL was goin to be uh...burned to death _ five hundred mile _ across another country _ to a stake _ (well) laced down [?near] to the...water an' burned. [*coughs*] He wasn't interested. Wasn't interested he said [in] that at all. 'Twas...get a...feed for his cows _ all he was interested in. He went off drove off his cows next mornin, put 'em in an' went straight on to the barn an' goin dressed up in this one headed giant's suit. Jumped th' horse, on horseback _ (see) on their...on their horse. They had three horses there. [*coughs*] [*recorder off*]*** [He went] cross country _ down we'll say an' just as he got down there see the fire was just startin. But he douted the fire. Th' horse douted the fire. Alright.

So -- he come back again. So he _ she the...this woman the...the missus told un you know about uh..somebody savin this girl that day. Now he wasn't...didn't pay no attention to her. He wasn't interested in it at all. Alright.

Next mornin he started off again. He went over an'...had this uh...took this...uh...two headed giant's suit, dressed up in an' this uh...two headed...giant's horse. Started off over 'cross country. So uh...[*aside:* I got a little tangled up but don't let it go on like that. The first thing I said there in the fire you know'd be the LAST thing _ supposed to come.]

But uh...he got there in time, they had everything barred off you know, let un down through we'll say an' they had it all bound around like chain for to...for to...for to stop un. 'Twas a...'twas a dragon was comin out o' water then was goin to take the girl but uh...[*clears throat*] went down an' they started fightin. He got there just in time. So...by an' by th' hor[se]...hor[se]...the horse banished un.

Well this ol' feller said...then he said uh "Nothing 'll save her tomorrow. There'll be nothing save her in a fire. Fire is th' only thing...there's goin to be that much fire nothing 'd save her." (Well) he went up through the crowd an' bust...up everything 'cordin as he went. Crossed back home again.

(So) the next morning (he) went off there again. Took the three headed giant's horse an' uh...an' the three headed giant's...suit he dressed up. An' he went down an' he got to a pond. Well a...(an') 'twas a big pond he was six mile long an' four mile wide. Well th' horse got to this pond an' he drinked...started drinkin. He drinked an' drinked well J...Jack /went/ to un on his [*the horse's*] back, /but/ he got tired an' he got off an' he boiled his kettle an' he had a lunch. The other horse drinked away an' drinked away.

/walked/
/'cause/

258

He dried the pond out. Well Jack jumped on the back again an' give it to her [i.e., *urged the horse on*]. An' when he got there...he was just in time. This dragon come out o' water an' every time he'd come out (there) was a skir...a squirt of flame 'd come out (on) un you know onto the girl an' every time that a squirt o' flame come there'd be a gush o' water come [from] th' horse _ an' douty it. Well the once he'd finally finished it.

Well that was the last of it we'll say, he jumped on horseback an' put her [i.e., *urged the horse*] back home again. They...but they couldn't catch un. They bust up everything on their way (but)...up through the crowd. Went back home.

First thing there missus told un about this uh...feller savin this girl. He didn't know, he didn't want to hear it. He wasn't interested in (it). All he was...was interested in feed for his cows. Th' only thing he was...that he was interested in.

(So) they started they got up a big feast an' invited everybody there you know round _ every country. Tryin to find out who this feller was. (See) Jack was...well the next even his missus told un about it. Ah he wasn't interested in that at all. He wasn't interested in goin to the feast he said. He knowed he didn't save her that's all he (worried).

But uh...on the final...in the final rest of it he...they caught him on...an' 'twas he...he an' she got married...all (solved) on the last of it.

[*recorder off*] Oh my dear man 'tis a long time [since I heard the tale]. Now there's **PARTS** of un that I...I've really forgot. There's par[t]...I never finished un off _ you know 'cause there's parts o' un that I...I don't know (in other words).

[Int. B: The full thing used to take an hour an' threequarters?]

Yes full thing was to take an hour an' threequarters. [*laughs*]

[Int. A: He's a long story.]

(You know) then there was scattered bit I'd left out 'cause there's one place you know when he (went)...an' knocked to the farmer's door see when th' ol' woman come out. The uh...his walkin cane fell down an' /broke/ her foot. Now I...I...uh skipped that see I forgot all about that.   /brought/

[Int. A: What happened after that?]

Oh she had her foot...she got her foot...fixed up after that _ you know an'...she struck this walkin cane well _ anything five hundred found...pound fall on your foot. [*coughs*] [*recorder off*] But that...in that...that much was very good.

Duration: 17 min., 18 sec.
Source: "Fifty year ago."
Location: Store in garden of teller's house, afternoon.
Audience: Interviewers.

Context, Style, and Language: (For context see notes to No. 1). Although the opening of the tale characterizes Jack as the youngest of a king's three sons, this attribute is quickly forgotten: he becomes simply a poor boy seeking work. This is a ubiquitous trait in the collection as a whole. For the most part, Jack is no different whether he is a king's son, or a poor sailor, or orphan. The family and situation into which he is born are usually of little importance to the tale, or to his characterization, once circumstance forces him out into the world.

As with Nos. 12 and 13, this tale was recorded twice over a period of nine years and has many stylistic and linguistic features in common with those already discussed in the notes to those versions. A comparison of the two tellings again reveals close parallels in the plots and in certain focal points essential to the progress of the narrative, many of these being highlighted by strongly stressed individual words and phrases. The story as a whole is also characterized by the repeated use of the punctuating phrase *we'll say* and the markers *So alright/Alright* and *the once* to signal the completion of a stage in the plot and the commencement of a new one. The passage of time (and the horse's drinking capacity!) is indicated by the iterative "drinked away and drinked away."

The two tellings are expressed very similarly, e.g., such identical or near-identical segments of dialogue as "I'll have **three** eyes tomorrow" and "If you're...goin to hit the/that iron...hit it!" Apart from minor divergences in expression, the later version mirrors the earlier until it is unfortunately cut short at the point where Jack first takes the farmer's cows to pasture, thus losing the encounters with the giants, the rescue of the girl from the dragon, and her marriage to Jack. Even though the 1966 version is purportedly unfinished and omits the episode where the walking cane falls on the old woman's foot, it is nevertheless much fuller than the truncated 1975 retelling; it has a sense of completeness, and it would have been interesting to be able to compare the two versions in full. It seems likely that as the teller himself was apparently recording the second version during the temporary absence of the fieldworker, his unfamiliarity with the machine led to his not realizing that the tape had run out, or perhaps the machine was accidentally switched off for a time. As the Archive tape is a copy of the original it is not clear which of these explanations is the more probable. The tale which follows the 1975 version on the tape (No. 72) begins precipitately, the crucial opening words being lost, and this again suggests accidental failure to record the intervening section of the interview. Both versions are rather confusing with regard to the names of the animals which fight with the blue bull. Somehow the narrator fails to discriminate between the golden, silver, and copper bulls and the cliffs which they presumably inhabit or guard. Consequently, and especially in No. 24 when all semblance of correct reference is lost, it seems as if the cliffs themselves are fighting (cf. the teller's use of *coach* [*goat*] in Nos. 12 and 13). In the later version the collector questions this but singularly fails to obtain any clarification, and in fact the narrator compounds the difficulty their necks an'...'fore daylight next mornin they had the last one killed. Well now then he goes up for her now. "An' now" he said "John my son" he said...

"Now" Jack said "I'm clear this time ol' man. There's nothing else can be done."

"Well Jack" she said "my son" she said "I don't know what's (goina) become of (us)."

"Now" Jack says "you can do what you like" Jack said "I've adone all I can do. An' there's nothing else I'm goina do" he said "only take your...take your two heads an' go an' shove on a spear instead of ours." Well she was all bawls an' when th' ol' man _ they didn't...didn't bother th' old man but ol' woman had the most (trouble).

So anyhow they made away with th' ol' woman an' he's /cried/...cried for **GOD'S** sake not to kill he. So anyhow Jack said "Now where's your money? Deliver up your money." An' Jack said "All my boat" Jack said "is awful light on*...in ballast." So he went in, he opened his safe an' he took silver an' put in the after hold _ an' he took coppers in the middle an' gold forrard. "Now" Jack said "we'll trim her just like we want" Jack said "an' we'll sail on...home where our father 's to."

So 'fore he come away he said to hisself he had a mind to set afire to the works [i.e., *everything*] an' burn it but Jack said "I don't think I will" Jack said.

So -- Jack went on, Jack come on "Now" Jack said "four o'clock this evenin" Jack said "we got to go an' start for home. We got a long ways to go."

So anyhow they started off an' four o'clock that evenin he gave orders to (lighten...they had the anchor) up an' he loosened her jib an' she /wore/ on her anchors an' away she goes. Anyhow th' ol' woman was tired an' weary waitin for...Bill an' Tom was...I don't know whe'r [i.e., *whether*] they was goin to get married, 'twas somewhere handy to that. "Anyhow" she said "keep 'em on all the time, th' ol' man uh...poor old John" she said "the worst one in our family" she said "an' I suppose we'll never hear tell [o'] him again."

Bill an' Tom said "That's the best thing for that. That was never no good anyhow."

"Well" she said "no he's never no good, you said /he/ wasn't no good boy" he said "an' he's gone this time, we'll never year tell [o'] un no more." So anyhow Bill an' Tom was out in the...out 'gain the door one day. An' /they/ look up to the nor'west an' he said "There's something up there now" he said "Pa, comin look" he said.

"Oh" he said "that's John, my son. That's John comin." Anyhow oho come down [in] front o'..."Yes" he said "that's right (now)" he (says) "that's Jack comin now" he said. "He **HAVE** her aint (un)?"

/cree/

*rep. 5

/swore/

/they/

/you/

/he's/
/moh/

Anyhow Bill an' Tom went down the stage [i.e., *building on seashore where fish is processed and stored*] an' they hide away. An' I suppose /they 's/ down there yet. An' To[m]...an' John come down "Oh my god" she said "John my son" he said "you'll have all my.../?oh/ no" he said "you'll run the castle down."

An' Jack said "Never mind father" he said "I never run no castle down." So he put her down 'bout half a mile. He turned her up in a yard an' he smacked down the anchor, she went in far enough to put her bowsprit through one o' the glasses. Well the ol' woman come out with all kinds for un, Jack said "I don't want none of 'em, I got PLENTY meself." So when I come away Jack was married then an' had seven or eight children. An' I think she was goin to have six more. An' I come away an' had a five or ten (on my side), come all the ways home skatin on me ass, never sawed it. Now I cut un off there, I wasn't finished. That's the last (of it).

[Int: Was there more to it?]

Um-hm. Oh yeah, could put more on it but uh...that's all. I get tired in talkin. Yeah.

[Int: I wish you'd put some more on it.]

Yeah. Sure he would. That's half hour now or more.

[Int: Where did you learn that one?]

I got that here from a...old Quann, ol' Mr. Quann. Old Mr....Tommy Quann.

Duration: 26 min., 29 sec.
Source: Tommy Quann, Sagona Island, Fortune Bay.
Location: Sitting room of teller's house, afternoon.
Audience: Adult male visitor, young child sitting on teller's knee, interviewer.

Context, Style, and Language: (For context see notes to No. 7).

The interviewer here overcomes an initial problem of the level of the recording by asking the teller to begin again. This he does easily and naturally after a momentary hesitation. He speaks rapidly and there are occasional transcription problems as a result. As with No. 7, "Greensleeves," there is some confusion between the pronouns *he* and *she* in the dialogue and the opening formula is again spoken as a breathless run with only two very brief pauses. The articulation of the title and its subsequent repetition in the text are insufficiently clear for a definitive transcription. The clause is invariably spoken very quickly and sounds more like "ship sail down wind or water" than the postulated original "ship sailed on wind an' water." Again the problem of unclear word boundaries leaves considerable room for doubt in interpretation.

Jack frequently uses "Ah" /æː/ as a pejorative comment on the various fools he meets, an exclamation very common in Newfoundland usage. In addition to the notes on No. 7, one might mention here the pronunciation of *elm* as "hellum," the frequent use of the West by suggesting that it is a "Piece of...silver cliff" which is fighting. As noted earlier, he is content to leave such anomalies unexplained and indeed in this case seems unable to explain. This lack of precision and concern may well be symptomatic not only of the narrator's lack of practice in telling the tale, having few opportunities to do so, but also of the general decline of the Märchen tradition in Newfoundland as a whole. After a rather hesitant start, the story runs quite smoothly until the confusion over the golden, silver, and copper bulls, and then moves forward steadily again, apart from a slight juxtaposition of episodes in the rescuing of the girl, which the teller as usual passes off disarmingly with a brief explanatory aside. Needless to say, even this fuller version by no means extends to the fabled "hour and threequarters" claimed in the preamble and closing discussion.

There is again some slurring and mispronunciation of words which hampers transcription, sometimes leaving the transcriber with two equally valid interpretations. It is in such ambiguous contexts that this narrator is especially prone to misencode, perhaps a further indication of his uncertainty over the details of a rarely told story. A similar problem which has more plausible dialectal origins is the interpretation of "used to" which is often indistinguishable from "was to" in his speech. In addition to such West Country English features as the voicing of initial consonants in *fall, full,* and *further,* Allan Oake's pronunciation of the lateral consonant in final position is very dark, especially in the word *bull;* he alternates the short open back round and the long half-open back round vowels in *rode,* and uses the diphthong /ei/ in *beat,* the half-long half-open front vowel in *grease,* offglide /t/ in *clifft,* and /f/ as substitute for final *th* in *blacksmith,* while /n/ is typically omitted in *a eye* and the initial vowel is lost in *'twasn't.* There are several instances of a steeply rising final intonation contour, seeking assurance from the audience that they are following the story, notably when "a mutterin sound" betrays the presence of the first giant, and also when Jack shows an apparent lack of interest in the "feller savin this girl." Note also the dialectal forms *pitched* (landed), the nautical *right chinched* (absolutely stuffed full) (see *DNE chinse,* and cf. *OED Chinse* V. 2, to caulk, of which this represents a semantic transfer), the intensives *awful* and *wonderful, thousands* (a great deal, plenty), *dout(y)* (put out (a fire)), and *lunch* (snack). These contrast with the rather formal and literary word *bestraddled* (perhaps an isolated hint of a printed source), and with such vernacular phrases as *little small* (very small), *slack of the poll* (scruff of the neck), *he give it to her/put her* (urged on (a horse)), and *Jack was into it,* i.e., in trouble. Plural inflections are lacking in *mile, foot,* and *cow,* past tense forms include *drinked* and *sove,* and double negatives are *he didn't want no money* and *she never done nothing.*

See also the notes to Nos. 1, 12, and 13.

Types and Motifs:

AT511A. *The Little Red Ox* + AT650A. *Strong John* + Cf. AT300. *The Dragon Slayer.*
P251.6.1. *Three brothers.*
S31. *Cruel stepmother.*
G207. *Male witch.*
Cf. K929.1. *Murder by leaving poisoned wine [soup].*

respectively the guardians of a copper, a silver, and a golden forest. The Newfoundland tale is confusing at this point, but the bulls appear to be the guardians not of forests but of cliffs. As in many other versions, Jack's bull wins the first two fights, but in the third he is killed by the golden bull.

It is at this point in the action of the Newfoundland tale that we find the greatest discrepancy from other versions of the Type. In most of these the bull, knowing that he will be killed in one of his battles, has instructed his protégé in advance on what he must do. Most commonly he is to cut a long strip of hide from along the dead bull's backbone and take it and one horn to serve as weapons. Usually the strip or strap can be ordered to tie an opponent while the horn beats him. This resembles the obedient strap and stick found in some analogues of AT563; for these again see the notes to No. 34. In some versions the strap can be ordered to act as a whip, one powerful enough to cut off the legs of an opponent or to cut through an iron chain. In still other versions the bull's-hide strap when used as a belt gives the wearer enormous strength which makes him unconquerable, while the horn, or a stick from the horn, becomes an invincible sword. In short, at this point our hero is well equipped to battle successfully against giants, dragons, or any other opponents, no matter how powerful they are.

In our Newfoundland tale these useful pieces of equipment made from the bull's body have been lost. Our hero has acquired, how is not explained, enormous strength—the strength of all the bulls—but he has been left without more tangible weapons. Perhaps some earlier storyteller, who had in mind continuing the plot by having the hero overcome giants and other opponents, felt the need to have him secure a weapon fitting for someone of his great strength. It may be that such a version is what Allan Oake is striving to recall here.

Maybe this presumed earlier storyteller knew a version of AT650A, "Strong John," and, remembering in that story the strong man's interest in acquiring a huge iron walking cane, decided to use that element of the tale as a transition to the later action. Certainly a five-hundred-pound iron cane wielded jauntily by a strong man would serve admirably for clobbering giants and other monsters—and this, of course, is exactly what happens in our Newfoundland tale.

We seem to have here an excellent illustration of the creative ability of an earlier storyteller. To supply an element he must have felt was lacking in his tale, he drew on a different tale to fill that lack. The hearer or reader finds a logical progression in the plot which he can accept readily. It is a seamless join, not an arbitrary or artificial combination.

The transition works so successfully in this story that it is only by comparing other non-Newfoundland analogues that we can see how Allan Oake's tale differs from the standard form. The magical straps and sticks typical of many versions of AT511A are replaced in these two recensions by the heavy iron walking cane characteristic of Incident II of AT650A. Nearly all other versions of the tale have some combination of the strap and horn weapons and do not need the iron walking cane. To put it another way, this is the only version of AT511A we know which uses AT650A as a transition to versions of AT300.

In reading this tale we get the impression that either the narrator or whoever first put the story together in its present form utilizes the magical elements as his framework, but could not resist adding humorous embellishments. In other versions of the tale, the bull with the boy on his back successfully jumps over all barriers when they first escape. Here the storyteller improves on the scene: the bull jumps five hundred miles.

We are told that the hero is only four feet and five inches tall, so small that the giants do not even notice him. In No. 23, Allan Oake clearly wishes to emphasize Jack's smallness, and does so with a rare ironical reinforcing comment: "Well you knows he wasn't very...very big." We are therefore left in no doubt about the hero's absurd smallness in comparison with the height of the giants. Although we are not told how tall the first three giants are, their mother is six miles high and her hair is seven miles long. Furthermore the storyteller is not interested in describing heroic combats. With no fuss Jack disposes of the giants and their mother. He merely taps each in turn with his five-hundred-pound iron walking cane, then casually picks up the body and tosses it into a ditch. His only comment is that he now has a bridge.

Before our hero sets off on each of his rescue missions, we are told that he puts on the clothing of one of the giants and rides the giant's horse. Did he magically grow larger or did the clothes shrink to fit him? The storyteller ignores the problem. We do, however, get the clear impression that the giants' horses are large!

When a hero fights dragons in other Märchen, his mighty horse with its flying hoofs frequently is nearly as important a helper as the hero's sword. In the Newfoundland tale when the hero rides the three-headed giant's horse to fight the fiery dragon, the horse stops to drink all the water in a big pond six miles long and four miles wide. Jack gets tired of waiting and gets down to boil his kettle and have a lunch, a standard Newfoundland practice. Of course this large reservoir of water is extremely useful in the ensuing battle. Each time the dragon squirts flames, a gush of water from the horse puts them out. This is obviously helpful; it is, however, more of a comic than a heroic scene.

In fact, if one rereads the tale with the suspicion that the original storyteller was a humorist, one wonders whether the whole tale might perhaps be a quiet spoofing of the magical and heroic elements in Märchen. The king's two elder sons are killed with poison in their soup, but the court is not disturbed. (Incidentally, soup is not only a staple part of outport Newfoundland diet, but is also a substantial dish, usually including salt meat, a variety of vegetables, and whatever other ingredients are available at the time. Its taste therefore varies considerably, and it would be relatively easy for an additional poisonous ingredient to be masked by these differing flavors). Daughters with varying numbers of eyes may be plausible in a Märchen, even if faintly absurd, but a witch who can add a third eye and then half an eye is a comic absurdity. The bull's three battles with other bulls are handled in summary fashion; they are not emphasized, any more than Jack's fights with the giants, or Jack's battles with the dragons.

From this viewpoint we can see why In No. 23 Allan Oake was unhappy that he had forgotten the quietly absurd business of Jack's iron walking cane falling and breaking the farmer's wife's foot. Perhaps he felt that this additional comic touch was an essential part of the story as he had originally heard it. In keeping with his characteristically laconic style (see linguistic notes to No. 1) Allan Oake does not indulge in elaboration or ornamentation. He is apparently unconcerned about details of plot and motivation and

Ortutay, *Folk Tales,* pp. 192-99, no. 7 (Hungary).
Cf. Khatchatrianz, *Folk Tales,* pp. 83-90 (511A, I, II, with 510) (Armenia).

Indian Subcontinent
Cf. O'Connor, *Folk-Tales,* pp. 68-75, no. 12 (Tibet).
Dracott, *Village,* pp. 83-87 (Simla).
Devi, *Pearls,* pp. 84-96 (Bengal).
Elwin, *Folk-Tales,* pp. 127-28, no. 8 (Mahakoshal, Central India).
See Thompson and Roberts, *Types,* Type 511A, for other analyzed references.

Africa
Cf. Hurreiz, *Folktales,* p. 117, no. 46 (511A, I, II) (Sudan).
Cf. Macdonald, *FL* 3 (1892), 353, Bantu people (South Africa).
Cf. Klipple, *Folk Tales,* pp. 459-60 (with cf. 563), English summary of tale from Held, *Märchen und Sagen der afrikanischen Neger,* Hottentot people (South Africa).
Cf. Theal, *Folk-Lore,* pp. 169-71, Kaffir people (Cape Colony), also summarized in Cox, *Cinderella,* p. 460, no. 339.
Cf. Brownlee, *Lion,* pp. 106-10, 111-15, 2 versions (South Africa).

AT650A. Strong John.
International Parallels: In *The Folktale* (pp. 32-33, 85-86, 279) Thompson presents a useful survey of various folk narratives associated with the supernaturally strong man. He stresses that in most of these stories the hero's strength comes either from his marvelous birth, or his unusual nurture, or a combination of the two. In our tale, however, the hero acquires the strength of a series of fighting bulls. How he does this is not explained, but his acquisition of strength from this source appears to be unique to Newfoundland.

In the majority of the analogues we give below, AT650A is seen as the normal preliminary to AT301B, which is itself a form of AT301, "The Stolen Princesses." AT650A, which Thompson describes as "a very definite entity," primarily Scandinavian, but also known in nearly every European country, is found in the English-language tradition only occasionally, and does not appear in its complete form in this Newfoundland collection. In our recension, Jack's working for a blacksmith to acquire a large iron walking cane and then setting off on his adventures resemble the elements in Incident II of AT650A. At this point, however, our storyteller abandons the remaining Incidents of AT650A and shifts to adventures typical of AT300.

Although AT650A is cited by Thompson as the introduction for AT301B, he points out that the two forms of AT650A diverge. We have already noted the comparative scarcity, in the English language tradition, of folktales such as AT650A about supernatural strong men. Nevertheless, both in North America and England there are numerous legends and personal experience narratives concerning people with extraordinary strength. Since the AT index focuses on fictional tales, however, it obviously gives no hint about other forms of traditional narrative which often treat this topic in a more realistic way. While acknowledging that such narratives are beyond the scope of the AT index, it is surprising that the more broadly based Motif-Index also fails to take due account of them. These more realistic tales cannot be classified under the Motif-Index series that begins with F610, "Remarkably strong men," because the individuals and their feats are not supernatural. Neither, since many of them are told as if true, can they justifiably be classified in the series of motifs in the Baughman Index that begins with X940, "Lie: person of remarkable strength."

In their New England anthologies both Dorson (*Jonathan,* pp. 121-26) and Botkin (*New England,* pp. 222-32) reprint reports of strong men who performed extraordinary feats of lifting and sometimes of carrying such objects as sacks full of grain or potatoes, full barrels or hogsheads, and even anvils or anchors. Stories of this kind are widespread elsewhere in the United States and in England. Some of these accounts are probably fictional, but others are more credible and may originate in accounts of real-life events, albeit structured and/or exaggerated in transmission.

We should bear in mind that many communities had contests in lifting heavy weights long before "weightlifting" became an official athletic event with special rules and equipment. Unquestionably there have been and still are many individuals and even families notable for their extraordinary strength. Their feats of strength are reported by individuals who had witnessed them and the stories may then be passed on in local tradition. Before the advent of machines, skills acquired by men working at specific tasks of course included the lifting or moving of very heavy weights. The accomplishment of such tasks usually involved a combination of strength and know-how. Today, even verified reports of such feats would be regarded with scepticism. In former times, however, many such reports would be accepted at face value, and the feats of strength would be admired and talked about. Originally factual and straightforward accounts, passed on repeatedly by word of mouth, would lend themselves very readily to the kind of embellishment and exaggeration which eventually removes them from a factual to a fictional plane. Indeed one might view all narratives about such feats of strength as a cline or continuum, ranging from fact to fiction, where reported facts actually witnessed, and/or believed in oral transmission, become structured and exaggerated over time; what was originally true is first transmitted as credible, but may then shift towards improbability, and ultimately develop into a lying tale and/or a total fiction. While the various indexes are instrumental in classifying the latter two genres, they become progressively less useful as one approaches the more realistic end of the continuum where it is more difficult to distinguish between the probable and the improbable.

The difficulty of making such distinctions is part of the more general problems of classification. The various indexes of folk narrative tend to be so specifically focused that they make little or no allowance for a given story to be told in a variety of ways, ranging across the whole spectrum of categories from personal experience to total fiction. Indeed the tendency towards perceiving these categories as sacrosanct militates against the development of a more flexible and comprehensive system of classification.

We are quite prepared to believe that in the stories of powerful men who threw their opponents over a fence such events may actually have occurred and that these narratives were not necessarily tall tales. Stories of feats that combine both strength and skill, like a single man mowing a wheat field with a scythe, or a woodchopper cutting quantities of cordwood far greater than what could be accomplished by the average chopper, have been reported from various areas, frequently by individuals who were present. In other

Cf. Kennedy, *Fictions,* pp. 21-28 (cf. 650A, with 571) (Co. Wexford), and rpt. in Graves, *Fairy Book,* pp. 79-90.

Cf. Curtin, *Hero,* pp. 140-62 (cf. 650A) (Co. Kerry).

Ó Duilearga, *Béal.* 30 (1962), 2-10, no. 1 (650A, with 300) (Co. Clare).

Gmelch and Kroup, *Road,* pp. 112-23, Irish traveller (Co. Roscommon).

Irish Types, Type 650, 475 versions.

Continental Europe and Asia

Grimm no. 90, "The Young Giant," Grimm-Hunt, 2, pp. 16-23, no. 90 (Germany), and see Grimm-Hunt, 2, pp. 383-87, no. 90, for discussion and other references, and for other trans. see Grimm-Magoun, pp. 326-32, no. 90, and Grimm-Zipes, pp. 328-34, no. 90.

Hodne, *Types,* AT650A, 57 versions (Norway).

Cf. Delarue, *Borzoi Book,* pp. 45-64, no. 6 (with 301B) (France).

Do Douro, *FLR* 4 (1881), 142-51 (with 301B, 313A) (Portugal).

Jegerlehner, *Legends,* pp. 47-53 (Switzerland).

Zobarskas, *Folk Tales,* pp. 79-88 (with 301B) (Lithuania).

Fillmore, *Apron,* pp. 57-88 (with 590) (Czechoslovakia).

Jones and Kropf, *Folk-Tales,* pp. 244-49, no. 46 (with 301B, 513A, cf. 300) (Hungary).

Dégh, *Folktales,* pp. 3-15, no. 1 (650A, with cf. 511A, I, II, III [in part], cf. 301B) (Hungary).

Creangă, *Folk Tales,* pp. 67-81 (with 301B) (Romania).

Sturdza, *Fairy Tales,* pp. 113-25 (with 301B) (Romania).

Groome, *Folk-Tales,* pp. 74-80, no. 20 (with 301B), Gypsy (Bukovina).

Mijatovies, *Folk-Lore,* pp. 24-31, pp. 123-45 (with 301B), 2 versions (Serbia).

Nicoloff, *Folktales,* pp. 78-83, no. 25 (with 301B) (Bulgaria).

Kent, *Fairy Tales,* pp. 23-30 (Turkey).

Afanas'ev, *Fairy Tales,* pp. 221-23 (with 1009, 1063, etc.) (Russia).

Afanas'ev, *Fairy Tales,* pp. 262-68 (with 301B) (Russia).

Zheleznova, *Mountain,* pp. 48-64 (with 301B) (Ukraine).

Bilenko, *Folk Tales,* pp. 20-31 (with 301B) (Ukraine).

Wardrop, *Folk Tales,* pp. 68-83, no. 12 (with 301B, cf. 300) (Georgian S.S.R.).

Cf. Papashvily, *Yes,* pp. 81-103, no. 9 (cf. 650A, with 301B, 516) (Georgian S.S.R.).

Cf. Busk, *Sagas,* pp. 36-53, Tale 3 (cf. 650A, with 301B, cf. 300) [no rescue of princess], Kalmuck people, literary (Kalmuck S.S.R.), also trans. in Coxwell, *Folk-Tales,* pp. 188-92, no. 5.

Devi, *Pearls,* pp. 151-57 (with 301B, 302B) (Bengal, India).

Seki, *Folktales,* pp. 43-47, no. 18 (650A, with 513A, cf. 300) (Japan).

Mayer, *Guide,* p. 5, no. 2 (650A, with cf. 300) (Japan).

The Philippines

Fansler, *Tales,* pp. 17-23, no. 3 (with 301B).

Africa

In several of the African versions the unborn child in the womb sings to his mother asking her to swallow a knife. She does so and he cuts his way out, later healing his mother with a touch. The child grows to full height and strength in a few days.

Rattray, *Folk-Lore,* 1, pp. 210-31, no. 12, Hausa text and English trans., Hausa people (Nigeria).

Chatelain, *Folk-Tales,* pp. 84-97, no. 5 (with 301B, cf. 300, 303), Ki-mbundu text and English trans., Mbamba tribe (Angola).

Klipple, *Folk Tales,* pp. 487-89, and p. 489, 2 versions, English summaries of 2 tales from Tenel, *Contes de Madagascar* (Madagascar).

24. THE BLUE BULL

Allan Oake   AT511A + AT650A + Cf. AT300
Springdale, Notre Dame Bay   TC1827 75-287
15 June 1975   Collector: Christina Pynn

I'll tell 'ee this one now "The Blue Bull."
[Int: Okay. Don't turn (the knob) don't an...turn (that). [O]kay.]
[Male listener: Eh?]
[Int: Alright. Go ahead.]

Uh...there was the king, an ol' king you know he was married an' _ an' he had three sons. There was Tom, Bill an'...an' Jack _ we'll say. Jack was the youngest of course. [Int: Yeah] Well his wife died. An' the ol' king now he still lived there you know on the uh...on his own place _ or boys did.

Th' ol' king he went to ano[ther] [*coughs*] _ the ol' king he went to another place see? An' he come up wi' another woman. Well by an' by he will he said he fell in love wi' her _ an' uh...got married. Well they only had one...she only had one girl (we'll say) _ when he's married her.

Now then after a time he told her he had three uh...[*aside:* 'kyou] [*has a drink*] he told her he had three sons out in th' other country where...where he was fi[rst]...where he was first married, well she'd...like to see 'em you know. So he send for 'em. An' uh...they all...they all come of course. Well she was delighted to see 'em you know come. [Int: Mm.]

By an' by you know there was ol'...there was ol' WITCH there in the place _ too. An' he told this uh...girl _ her daughter _ that uh...ol' feller was goin to...we'll say, goin...when his wife (you know) 'd pass out _ the ol' feller would...the ol' king 'd give all o' the land, everything to his boys. She wouldn't get none.

So she went an' told her mother _ [*clears throat*] about it. And uh...then th' ol' witch seen the old woman too an' he told her the best thing to do was get clear o' 'em _ put poison in their food an' _ give...make away wi' 'em. Well this is what she done.

An' now...Jack we'll say uh...his...his mother _ they had a blue...a bull see. She called un the blue bull. [Int: Mm.] Well when she...'twas always...she always give un to Jack. 'Twas Jack's bull. [*coughs*] Well they had their bull (?their own).

273

/cliff/

They rode on, the next one was…bigger you know every one was bigger an' bigger, well the golden cliff he was a real **BIG** /bull/ ya know. He come out. An' they start in fightin _ again. An'…the golden cliff [bull] conquered that time an' beat…beat out the blue bull. Here was Jack now he was leaved singlehanded. Nobody only hisself.

Well he had no money. Well he didn't know what he was goin to do. So passin along he seen a blacksmith _ marked up over a place _ iron _ stuff we'll say an' went in there. He asked if he…there was any chance o' getting a job o' work.

"Yes." Told un he wanted uh…for a spell uh…or…he wanted a _ feller to help un. So alright. Jack said he'd _ take on the job. He didn't want no money. He wanted…only he wanted enough iron now to make a _ walkin cane. Three hundred pound (o') iron _ he wanted to make a…a walkin cane. That's all he wanted.

So 'twas only a…he…you know he took up an'…he took up the sledge you know, poundin this iron an' 'twas all…he wasn't only _ like he wasn't able to lift un and so on an' _ by an' by the old feller…roared at un.

"Hey!" he said. "If you're _ goin to hit that iron hit it!"

So he come down wi' his blow you know hard blow _ knocked the ol' blacksmith out one side an' the…fire (led) all over the place.

"Ar" he said "take your three hundred pound iron an' get out!"

"No" he said. "You don't work a year in one day _ (right)?"

Worked away an' by an' by when he got his iron _ you know _ took un up on his little…finger like this _ you know. Swung un around. It wasn't hardly heavy enough (for he). He'd have another two hundred pound he said to put on it you know. That'd be five hundred pound. Alright then. (That's) what he done.

Worked away another you (know) _ year an' one day _ for that. So _ [*clears throat*] got his two…two hundred pound iron an' put that on uh…well he was alright he's…he could still swing it around on his little finger _ but he [*the iron*] was heavy enough.

Well he was finished wi' that job he _ think he'd like to have another job. So he…when he (was) dodgin along he seen you know where there was a kind of a farmer marked up an' he went up an'…knocked to the door an' there was a ol'…lady come out. He wondered whe'r [i.e., *whether*] there was any uh…any chance to…to get…get a job o' work to his likin.

"Well" she said "we wants a helper but" she said "we got no…money to pay"

"Oh" he said "I don't want _ as long as I gets grease enough" he said "to grease me bones." An' when he did you know his uh…he had his (iron)…walkin cane stuck up there again the side o' th' house an' _ he [*the cane*] fell down an' broke her foot. Fell down [on] her foot (broke her foot). So he uh...so alright. They took un in an' _ he has ever so many cows now, that's all he had to do was just look after his cows an' lead 'em off to some uh...some feedin ground you know an' _ then in the evenins have 'em back again. [*recorder off*]

Duration: 11 min., 22 sec.
Source: "Fifty year ago."
Location: Springdale Hospital.
Audience: Interviewer.

Context, Style, and Language: (For context see notes to No. 13.)

A similar confusion is apparent in this version to that in No. 23 when the cliffs, which are presumably each supposed to have a champion bull, are actually personified and fight each other. Even the fieldworker's direct question about the silver cliff singularly fails to resolve the difficulty, the teller covering up the confusion by maintaining that it is a piece of the silver cliff which is fighting. Unfortunately the dénouement remains unrecorded in this otherwise more elaborated version.

The punctuating phrase *we'll say* is again very much in evidence, and *By an' by* signals a new phase in the narrative. Additional language points include the typical West Country English voicing of initial /f/ in *find* and *fell*, the diphthong /ei/ in *beat*, the short back open rounded vowel in *rode*, aphesis in *'fore*, and the elision of schwa in *th' ol'; went to work* (set about), *tormented* (annoyed/upset), *to* rather than *at* in *knocked to the door*, and *whe'r* (whether); the present tense forms *they cooks, you'm, you is, I catches*, and the past participle *leaved*; and the double negatives *she wouldn't get none, don't eat no more, he wouldn't never, you can't eat nothing, nobody is not goin to, didn't want no money.*

See also the notes to Nos. 1, 12, 13, and **23.**

Types and Motifs:

AT511A. *The Little Red Ox* + AT650A. *Strong John* + Cf. AT300. *The Dragon-Slayer.*
P251.6.1. *Three brothers.*
G207. *Male witch.*
Cf. S34. *Cruel stepsister.*
S31. *Cruel stepmother.*
K929.1. *Murder by leaving poisoned wine [food].*
B184.2. *Magic bull.*
B411.1. *Helpful bull.*
Cf. B2111.1.5.1. *Speaking ox.*
B521.1. *Animal warns against poison.*
B115. *Animal with horn of plenty.*

*children talk-
ing

*noise in
background

So anyhow Jack _ only took a few buns, that's all Jack took. He wasn't…he was goina have the dirtiest (line) anyhow.* [*aside: [untrans.*] an' them out there? [Male ?relative: Yeah] Well…is Joe out there? [Male ?relative: Yeah] (You) tell un he got to wait.] [*aside to child:* (no sir…I'll collar ya now)]* [*aside to Int:* just fooled her up then.]

An' uh _ anyhow Jack went on. Jack went on an' walked on an' walked on an' walked on. An' Jack come across a little…a house with a _ with seven spears hung up over the door _ an' they've seven heads onto 'em. Well Jack says soon as Bill an' Tom did come back Jack says "I suppose if I goes in here I'll never hear tell of I no more." Anyhow Jack says "Well knock the door." Well anyhow he knocked to the door an' _ out he come an' "Good day" he said "John."

(So) Jack said "You knows me."

"Yes" he said "I knows 'ee."

He said "I wants uh…I wants service."

"Oh well" he says "you can" he said "boy" he said "we want a boy" he said. "We wants a cowboy now" he said "an' uh…we'll give 'ee forty pound…a day."

(Well) _ Jack said "That's good money (anyhow)." So anyow Jack went in an'…sot down. "Now" he said "Jack" he said _ he said "when I ships you" he said "John" he said "my son" he said "there 'll be no terms on nar side now. You can't frounge [i.e., *complain*] ('gain) me" he said "an' I won't be able to frounge 'gain you."

Well Jack said "Alright." An' Jack said "What have I got to do?"

"Well" he said "my son" he said "we got a lot o'…ground to mow" he said "down there" he said. Said "We got seventy or eighty acres o' land an' we can't…[get] nobody to do it."

Well Jack said "That's a devil to mow."

So anyhow "Now" he said "John" he said "go to bed my son, have a good night's rest an' tomorrow mornin you get up an' go to work." So very well.

Well Jack got up next morn(in) an' had his breakfast. Never stopped to put on any clothes. Come out with his pants hangin down over his ass like a (woods hand).

"An' now" he said "John" he said "go out an' pick out the best scythe we got out there" he says "and see what you can do in mowin."

"Well" Jack said "I don't want the best one _ 'cause if I had the best one I mow TOO much but uh…give me the WORST one you got."

So anyhow Jack went out an' he [*the scythe*] was rusty, he's uh…all shapes. "No" Jack said "I wants (that one) there. I'll take that rusty one there look."

"My son" he says "[if] you can mow ever so well you'll (never) mow (wi') that."

Well Jack said "I'm goin to take her." So he took her an' he give un the dagger [i.e., *whetstone*] an' away they goes down the field. Jack went down an' mowed away an' mowed away. An' Jack said uh…"Twelve o'clock. No sign [o'] no dinner." [*aside to Int:* You'll be tired holdin up (that) [*microphone*]] I…a uh…"Well" Jack said uh…"I can't say nothing" Jack said "'cause when I shipped with un yesterday" he said "I shipped on no terms on nar side" he said "an' if I goes havin uh…say anything to him next thing you know my head 's goin on a spear like they 's up there now." So Jack said "I'd like to see somebody come" Jack said "an' what I mows 'fore dinner I'll give away for me dinner." (Well) words were no sooner out of his mouth 'fore a little man come up, an inch…a little feller 'bout that long I suppose ‗ 'bout two inches. [*gestures with thumb and forefinger to indicate size*]

"Hello" Jack said "me son" he said "where you goin?"

"Oh" he said "John you've got a lot o' hay mowed."

Jack said "Yes" Jack said "an' I'd had more mowed if I'd had me dinner."

"Oh" he said "had no dinner?"

"No" he said he got no dinner yet. "An'" /he/ said "an' I can't go up where the uh…boss is to" he said "where th' old grand /vizier 's/ to ‗ 'cause if I did" he said "my head got to go on a spear like they put up there." /I/ /vizer 's/

"Oh" he said "Jack my son I tell you what I do, you give me what hay you got mowed 'fore dinner I'll give ya your dinner."

An' Jack said "I'd be only too glad (to) do it old man."

So anyway he took a little tablecloth out of his pocket 'bout…two inches wide I suppose.

An' Jack said "What in the name o' god you (goina) put on that?"

Anyhow he took [un] out. "Now" he said "what do 'ee want?"

Jack said "I want some steak" Jack said uh…"anything what 've you got."

"Oh" he said "I can give 'ee whatever you want."

So anyhow Jack finished up (hisself) an' he put out…(well) he…he couldn't touch half of it. An' Jack said he never had time to thank un 'fore he was gone just so quick as the…just so quick as that.

Very well. Well Jack said "That's a queer feller." Jack said "An' I suppose it's goin be LAST o' me this time. Bill an' Tom DID return home but I won't I don't think."

So alright. So Jack mowed…started to get up again, had a smoke ‗ an' mowed away again, six o'clock come, no supper.

"Hm" Jack said "now that's a good one!" Well Jack said "I can't say nothin to him" Jack said "when I goes up" Jack said "'cause if I do" Jack said "I suppose they'd say no my head got to go on a spear. So I won't say nothin anyhow."

The words were no sooner out of his /mouth/ 'fore little ol' man come again, the same feller. /out/

281

"Oh" he said "John" he said "you come…you got your lo(t) o' hay mowed."

Jack said "Yes an' how much would I ha' mowed if I'd had my supper! I got no supper yet!"

"Woh" he said "John" he said "you give me what hay you got mowed" he said "an' I'll give 'ee all the supper you want."

"(Well)" Jack said "I don't want a big lot" Jack said "I can't eat too much 'cause I got a nice bit to walk."

So anyhow there (was)…took out his little tablecloth same as he done before an' spread un down an' Jack had his supper, the best kind.

"Now" Jack said "I'm goin home." The words were no sooner out of [his] mouth 'fore he was gone [in] (air) again.

Well sir, very well. Jack (went) up.

He said "How you get on" he said "John?"

"Well" he says "my son" he said _ "I got on alright" he said "but 'tis poor terms" he said "I never had no dinner an' never had no supper."

"Now" he said "John _ you know what I done yesterday, I ship(ped) you on…no terms on nar side"

Jack said "I know that sir."

"Now" he says uh…"you can have (your) supper now. An' I'll go out an' have a look at (it)." So he had his supper an' he went out. Well [*tone of amazement*] when the ol' man (an') th' ol' woman went out an' look at what…th' hay he had mowed _ so many acres mowed an' NEVER a bit on the ground, everything cleaned away _ well certainly where she was savage before she was nine times savager that time. She was tearin lumps o' hair off her head so big as my hand.

"Well" she says [to] th' ol' man she says "[If] you don't tell me the way to make away wi' Jack" she said _ uh…"your head got to go on a spear."

Well Jack said…(well) the ol' man said "I tell you one thing we can do." He said "Send un away…send un…send un away to build ship sail down wind or water which I know can't be done" /he/ says "an' that's th' only way we can get clear wi' Jack."

/she/

So anyway _ he went 'longside o' Jack an' he said uh…"Jack my son" he said "you got to have another (trial) tomorrow morn" he said "you got to go offs an' build ship sail down wind or water" he said "an'…if you don't" he said "your head got to go on a spear."

(So) Jack said "That's what I'm comin for" Jack said "for…th' ol' father send me out for that" Jack said. "An' I don't 'pose ever I'll do it."

"Oh yes" he (says). "You might."

So anyhow Jack got up next mornin an'…had his breakfast an'…went on.

"Now" he said "John" he said "my son _ take all kinds o' tools, I got all kinds o' tools" Jack said "I want **NO** tools."

So she baked un up a sack of flour into a big...one big cake an' 'way he goes. Anyhow Jack was walkin all that day _ an' till nine o'clock in the night, Jack said "By god" Jack says "there's a big stick there! A fine stick, a hellum [i.e., *elm*] stick." Jack said "Good keel for her anyhow" Jack said "if I can get he down." Anyhow Jack smacked his hatchet into...underpart of un. ('Fore) he meant to (take) the first chip out, the little ol' man come up 'bout that long I suppose. [*gestures with thumb and forefinger to indicate size*]

"Oh" he said "John my son" he said "what are ya doin?"

Well Jack said "I'm tryin to bui[ld]...get...cut down some stuff now" he said "to build a ship (to) sail down winds or water" he said "which I don't suppose is goin to be done."

"Oh my son" he said "yes, ey" he said "you go home" he said "an' whatever lies in me power for 'ee I'll do for 'ee." But he said "You aint got nothin to eat have 'ee John?"

"Oh" Jack said "I got plenty (grub)."

"Well" he said "I be only too glad" he said "'cause I been this twelvemonth" he said "an' I aint had a bit." Little ol' man he was only 'bout _ that long. [*gestures with thumb and forefinger to indicate size*]

So very well Jack said "My dear man" Jack said "I can give 'ee all you...all you wants." So anyhow Jack...give him all the grub he had there an' put it down...put it...put it down for him an' 'way he goes _ went on home.

"Well" /he/ said "John how you come on?"   /she/

"Well" Jack said "now you knows how 'll I come on" Jack says "I been walkin all day" Jack said "I just got where her keel is to. That's where I got now _ just to her keel."

"Alright" he said "John my son" he said "go to work an' uh...go to work an' have your...have your...have your tea now an' go to bed" he said "an' tomorrow mornin" s[aid] "bright an' early" he said "ya got to go again."

So anyhow Jack said "I know that."

So anyhow Jack...next mornin she had the grub (an') all packed up for Jack. 'Fore daylight next mornin Jack got up, had break[fast] an' 'way he go 'fore ol' man got up.

Anyhow Jack went up an'...('fore) he got up to the...where he had it...was goina build the ship to _ he heard a crackin an' tearin into the woods. An' Jack said "By god 'tis ghostes here I suppose." Anyhow when he went in this was the little ol' man, the sweat was comin off him...sweat come off 'bout size o' hen's egg. Goin right to it. He had her keel laid _ he had the timbers in her _ an' he had the last board to put on her stern, all night now at it.

"Well" Jack said "(?planks is) in the water" Jack said. "Well" Jack said "now _ there's one little bit there look that he never had...in un." Never see no sign [o'] nobody. Jack said "No wonder he hadn't put that plank a little closer than that" he took the hammer an' just tou[ched]...

"Oh" he said "John" he said "my son sit down." [*high-pitched urgent tone suggests that the little man does not want Jack to touch the boat*] Very minute he's touched the plank...uh...he was up 'longside of him again.

"Now" he said "Jack" he said "lie down an' have a good nap now" he said "an'...this evenin" he said "four o'clock" he said "I'll have her finished."

/do/

"Phooh well!" Jack said. "He might be (able to say)...you can see you can do work" he said "fast as /?you/ work. But" he says "you'll never do that."

"Oh yes" he said "John my son" he said. "An' tomorrow evenin" he said...said "you'll ha[ve]...you'll (have un at) four o' clock."

Alright. Anyhow Jack said "Now" he said "John my son you can go on home again."

/he/
/he/

So Jack went on home again an' went in to th' ol' woman, /she/ said "How did you get on" /she/ said "John my son? Seem like you 's doin well with it."

"Well" Jack said "I got...the keel cut down" Jack said "an' I got some of the timbers in un uh...it's uh...hard work" he said "(to cut I tell 'ee)."

"No" he said "there's nobody (yet)..."

Jack said "I don't want no one. I wouldn't have (nobody)." [*coughs and clears throat*]

So "Very well Jack" [she] said. "Now" she said "John my son you got to get up again tomorrow morning."

Jack said "I know that ma'm."

He had his breakfast...uh...had his supper that night an' went to bed an'...next morning he get up again an' Jack went on. My gee whiz when Jack got up next morning he was puttin the LAST bit o' plank onto her. Had her all finished.

"Well now" he said "John my son" he says "I got the rails an' that to put on yet an' I got the two masts of the ship. Now" he said "you got to go off now" he says "and ship six fools nine times bigger fool than you can tell _ for to go in that boat _ besides yourself. You'll be the skipper."

Well Jack says "That's no odds." [*coughs*] [*aside to child:* (will 'ee) set down [on the] chair (will 'ee)]

And anyhow Jack said "Now" he said "Jack" he said "I'll give you a...a paper now _ what to do."

Anyhow Jack said "Alright."

So he wrote it down. "Now" he said "John _ you got to ship nine...uh...six fools nine times bigger fool than (you can tell)."

An' Jack says "That's very well." Jack said "I might get 'em."

284

So anyhow Jack...he...give Jack the road an' he said "There's three roads here now" he said "there's one mud, an' sand" he said "an' clay."

"Well" Jack said "now I'm takin the worst one is there an' that's the one I'm takin." So Jack went on stuck to his ass in mud when he was goin, the worst one Jack had to take anyhow.

So Jack was walkin somewhere round two or three hours when he uh...when he seen a man with his year [i.e., *ear*] to the ground hold up his hand "Stop!" he said. "For GOD'S sake stop!"

An' Jack said "What am I goina stop for you bloody old fool!"

"Oh" he said "I was listening to a preacher" he said "down the other world" he says "preachin hymns" he said "I got every bit of it" he said "(if) you hadn't spoke."

"Ah!" [*dismissive tone*] Jack said "you gert fool" Jack said "leave that off." He said "An' ship...er...an' go with I now" he said "I'm goin in a ship sail down wind or water. (Give) ya forty pound a month."

"My god" he said "I'd be only too glad."

An'...uh..."Now" Jack said "I got to name you."

"Yes" he said "I don't care, anything 'll do for me master." Called un "master" right straight see?

"Well" Jack said "I name you Year [i.e., *Hear*] Well."

"(Well)" he said "anything's good enough for me"

"Now" Jack said "I'm got to go on again, now you got to go on the same road I go now" he said "an' get aboard me ship _ an' wait till I come. An'" he said "I 'spect the old man" he said "is goina put you to work when yous get there _ pickin whittle rods an' make sails." So anyhow _ Year Well went on.

So anyhow Jack walked away again an' walked away again somewhere round half a mile from that _ when Jack seen a man comin with a gun to his face.

An' Jack said "You gert fool" Jack said "don't fire" Jack said "'cause you'll kill me!" [*spoken quickly in loud apprehensive tone*]

"Oh well _ now" he said "my son" he said "Jack" he said "my son if you hadn't spoke when you did I'd have...I 's goina have a shot at a...a shot o' black ducks in other world."

"Well" Jack said "ya gert fool" Jack said "I got o[ne]...I got ONE fool" Jack said "an' I better get you" Jack said "that 'll be TWO. An' the ol' man told me (to) ship six fools an' I'm damned if you isn't (a) bigger fool."

"Well" he said "old man I was just uh...aimin at a black shot o'...shot o' ducks" he says "in th' other world."

"Well" Jack said "now" Jack said "leave that (off)" Jack said "/fling/ 'way th' ol' gun, boy" he said "an' go...ship with uh...go with me now" he sai[d] "in ship sail down wind or water, (give you) forty pound a month." /cling/

"Indeed I will captain" he said.

285

way to dryin 'em an' she was out tryin...carryin some sun into a basket an' see if she could dry the pe[as]...dry the peas in th' house. So...(she) was pretty sensible too! So anyhow Jack..."Oh" she said "ol' man" she said "my!" (to) th' ol' grand /vizier/ she said "I believe Jack is comin" she said "there's a black cloud up there (to) nor'west comin down to, something is comin whatever it is."

/vize/

"Ah" /he/ said "we won't know no (trouble) wi' Jack no more" /he/ said. "Jack an' his crowd is gone."

/she/ /she/

Anyhow Jack slewed her down, slews her down an' by an' by they was /hollerin/ "For **GOD'S** sake don't run the castle down!"

/haulin/

Jack said "Uh...never mind 'bout runnin the castle down." So Jack put her down 'bout half a mile, let her come up an' _ shoot up in the yard an' her bowsprit went in broke a (pane) o' glass right in th' ol' man's house. Well...down anchor right in the yard. Stopped her.

Now then, very well. [*aside to children:* go. Go (on). Go. Go on (out). Go on. Go on. Go on out] So _ that was very well now, he said uh..."Now" he said (to) th' ol' /grand vizier/ he said uh..."well" she said "if you don't tell me the way /to make away/ wi' Jack an' his crowd" she said "your head got to go on a spear."

/garner vizer/
/way/

"Now" he said "you've send un off sail a ship...sail down wind or water an' he got **THAT** done. An'" she said "there's nothing else we can do with un."

"Well" she says.../she/ said "there's one thing I can do." /She/ said "You send Jack an' his crew now tomorrow morn" she said "to th' eastern end of world" /she/ said "an' get a bottle of leaden beauty water will cure your stomach. I knows that can't be got" /she/ said "an' uh...an'" she said "that's th' only way we 'll make away with un." Very well.

/he/ /He/

/he/
/he/

So he went an' had to get up a ladder, side the boat, (they got out o' there the same time). Had (to) take a ladder an' get up aboard the side of his ship. An' he got up an' the first man he meet with was Run Well. "Hi" he says "skipper what's...all cleared?"

"No" he said. "We 's up against something now" he said "that I don't expect is goina be done. I've adone all in my power" he said "to do everything an' whatever I does" he said "I can get it...get through it alright. But this is one hard thing that I can't...I'm not goina get."

He said "What's that?"

"We got to go th' eastern end the world" he said "an' the footman is goin with us" his footman is goin what he got in there. "Go to eastern end the world" he said "an' get a bottle o' leaden beauty water cure the old woman 'cause she been sick this twenty year."

"Hoh!" Run Well said "That's not two steps for I." Well he had...the men all aboard to do it see?

"Oh anyhow we'll start over" he said "start at eight o'clock tomorrow morn" the footman got...went out an' took way for to go th' eastern end the world. Well anyhow the footman left an' he [*Run Well*] made one step an' he was gone miles an' miles from his footman. He [*the footman*] was somewhere round half a mile from the house when /Run Well/ _ was down in th' other world _ an' got the bottle of uh.../leaden/ beauty water an' on his way back again when uh...when he meet un [*the footman*].   /the footman/ /dippin/

"Well!" he said. "You'll be home" he said "before I gets HALFWAYS there" he said. "You still...you been eastern end o' world now an' back." He said "What about sittin down now" he said "an' have a little chat." He said "An' have a look at your water you got there."

"No" he said "I 's not goin to look at it" he said "because I knows that's goina cure her." So as he did...when he sat down now this footman...catched away the bottle from un see. An' Year Well...was aboard a ship somewhere round ten twelve mile from un. Now he yeard un...sit down on...see he heard un take this bottle away from un. An' he jumps on...on deck with his gun. An' he fires a sleepy pin, he put un under his year-lap [i.e., *ear lobe*] _ an' never cut un an' down falled the footman see. So Jack got up an' he give him a /?whang/ on top o' that an' he put un down   /whine/ with his...just his two years [i.e., *ears*] in the mud. Anyhow Jack said "Now you can stop there."

So very well. So Jack went on an' come on overboard "Now" Jack said "sonny I knows we're clear now. We got that now" he said "which I knows" he said..."that...nobody else 'll never get it _ only we got it. Well now" he said _ "go in there." Well sonny when he...went into the ol' woman that time...th' ol' /woman/ _ where she was savage before she was nine times   /man/ savager that time. She was takin lumps o' hair off her head 'bout size...'bout size o' my hand I suppose.

"Well" she said "if you don't tell me the way to make away wi' Jack" she said "then your head got to go on a spear."

"Well" she said...he said "there's /only/...only one more thing" /he/ said   /nonly/ /she/ "I knows we can do" /he/ said. "Put Jack an' his crowd out in our stable" he   /she/ said "tonight" _ he said "where there's forty puncheons" he said "o' yeastins o' rum an' one drop is good enough for any man" /he/ said "an' make un   /she/ drink that tomorrow mornin" he said "an' then all the crowd 'll be all fixed off."

So anyhow Jack lo...[J]ack goes out an' gets up the ladder again. First man he meet was uh...Dip Cup.

"(Well)" he says "captain" he said "what's the trouble now?"

"Well" he said "we're up again it this time." He said "We got to go out in" (he said) "th' ol' man's store now" he said "where...there's forty mile wi[de]...forty mile wide, no one knew how wide he is an' he got forty puncheons o' eastins o' rum out there, one drop is enough for any man."

289

"Hoo!" he said. "That's not a taste [i.e., *hardly a drop*] for I."

"Well (now)" he said "I know you been **DIPPIN** all...all your lifetime
_ you **SAYS** you have. Well now" he said "you're up again it. An'" he said
"an' he's uh...four steel /?spears/" he said "as he can hold one [i.e., *?one of
which is enough to keep us out*]." He said "How*...we goina get in there?"

/spheres/
*rep. 4

"Phooh well" Hard Ass is right to the end see? Hard Ass said "My dear
man" he said "that's only a ju[mp]...[th]at's only a s...couple o' (?gambols)
about for I" he said "to take that down."

So anyhow they went in. The butler come round with a big key an' they
had to take un...carry it on a bar [i.e., *barrow*]. You know (why) that was
the key! Wonderful store. They unlocked the door an' here they was shinin
_ everything right (glistenin). An' over yere the forty puncheons o' rum
_ what they had to drink. Anyhow Hard Ass went in first. So Hard Ass went
in first an' very well. He goes in first an' he...whips around with his naked
ass only...half an hour into it he had a[s] good a steel dust bed ever you
wished to si[t]...ever you wish to...lie on. An' Dip Cup gone in took the
hatchet an' he beat in one o' drums, he start at it.

Very well. Next morn th' ol' man went outside for...thinking 'bout Jack
an' all his crowd 'd be all gone. So when he went out next mornin -- Dip
Cup was suckin the last stave, had (it) **ALL** gone _ suckin the staves now,
never had a taste yet! Well sonny he...he went in. Where /she/ was savage
before /she/ was nine times savager that time. [*aside to Int:* I'll have [to] cut
un off Jack 'cause the only...'ll never get (an ending).] So anyhow th' ol'
man says "Well there's one...there's one more thing" he said "I suppose I
can do. That's all I knows" he said "an' only for that" he says "we all got to
finish." (So) he said "You carry un out in the...in that...field now" she said
"where there was a hundred an' some odd wild savage pigs, nobody can't
feed 'em." An' she said "Put he an' his crowd in there tomorrow mornin,
won't be none left (of 'em)." Alright.

/he/
/he/

So anyhow Jack goes out. Jack said "I thought I were clear that time but
this time I suppose I **WON'T** be clear." An' the very first man he meet when
he got up on the deck was Feed The Pigs.

He said to..."Captain" he said "what's trouble?"

"Well" he said "an'...an'...done it all" he said "for the ol' man" he said
"yere." He said "(Well) I suppose we got to be all straight after all." He said
"I an' the crowd now" he said "got to go in that field tonight where the
hundred an' odd pigs is to _ savage pigs, nobody can't get handy to 'em an'
feed 'em." He said "An' we got to /feed them/ 'fore daylight."

/eat/

"Ah" Feed The Pigs says "well I be the first one to get in, I'll show you
what to do with the pigs."

So anyhow that was the first thing, they went out they opened the yard
an' sent him in. Feed The Pigs got over alongside of 'em an' he start twistin

290

Country English metathesized form *gert* (great), and the short vowel in *spoon*. Aphetic forms such as *'longside, 'fore, 'pose* are also common. At the lexical level one finds *thousands* to mean "a great deal," *ships, shipped* (hire[d], employ[ed]), *frounge 'gain* (to have cause to complain against), (cf. *EDD FRANGE, FRANZE, FRUNSH), dagger* (whetstone), *out* (took out), *dip* (bail, ladle), *crowd* (crew), *leaden* (cf. *OED Lead sb¹* 12, *lead-water,* dilute solution of acetate of lead; for *-en* suffix cf. *DNE glassen, tinnen* etc.), *stage* (covered platform where fish is processed and stored). Local color is also provided in *woods hand* (man who works in the [lumber] woods), and the frequent use of *my son* as a form of address. Of further interest are the past tense forms *heared* and *falled,* and the rhetorical repetition of verbs to indicate the passage of time, e.g., "walked away again an' walked away again," "walked on again an' walked on." For the use of *black* as an intensifier see *EDD BLACK* adj. and adv.I.7, and *DNE black* a 2,3.

Both in its language and the details of the plot, this is the classic example of the immanence of the Newfoundland background in many of these stories. For instance, we see reflected here the importance of women in Newfoundland culture, controlling, as it were, from behind the scenes. The boatbuilding episodes of course are especially relevant to the local context, and we also have here the juxtaposition of the "stage set" of literary Märchen and the real vernacular architecture of a Newfoundland outport, e.g., the bowsprit through the window, and the fact that Bill and Tom go down to the stage to hide. In these ways the world of the folktale is brought much closer to reality and to the everyday lives of the audience.

See also the notes to No. 7.

Types and Motifs:

AT513B. *The Land and Water Ship* + AT1000. *Bargain Not to Become Angry* + AT1002. *Dissipation of the Ogre's Property* + AT1245. *Sunlight Carried in a Bag into the Windowless House.*
Z10.1. *Beginning formula.*
P251.6.1. *Three brothers.*
H900. *Tasks imposed.*
D1533.1.1. *Magic land and water ship.*
H901.1. *Heads placed on stakes for failure in performance of task.*
F613.3. *Strong man's labor contract: anger bargain.*
L210. *Modest choice best.*
N810. *Supernatural helper.*
D1472.1.8. *Magic table-cloth supplies food and drink.*
K1400. *Dupe's property destroyed.*
H931. *Tasks assigned in order to get rid of hero.*
N821. *Help from little man.*
Q40. *Kindness rewarded.*
H1312. *Quest for the greatest of fools.*
F601. *Extraordinary companions.*
F641. *Person of remarkable hearing.*

F661. *Skillful marksman.*
J1967. *Numskull bales out the stream.*
F681.1. *Marvelous runner keeps leg tied up.*
F680. *Other marvelous powers.*
Cf. F626.1. *Strong man flattens hill.*
J2123. *Sunlight carried into windowless house in baskets.*
H1321.2. *Quest for healing water.*
F681. *Marvelous runner.*
Q261.1. *Intended treachery punished.*
H1142.1. *Task: drinking wine-cellar empty.*
F625. *Strong-man: breaker of iron.*
F633. *Mighty drinker.*
Cf. H1155.3. *Task: feeding dangerous man-eating sow.*
G500. *Ogre defeated.*
G512. *Ogre [ogre's wife] killed.*
Cf. Q421.1. *Heads on stakes.*
G610. *Theft from ogre.*
Cf. K2211.0.1. *Treacherous elder brothers.*
H1242. *Youngest alone succeeds on quest.*
Z10.2. *End formula.*

International Parallels: When we consider the extraordinary difficulties of travel by land in the long period between the days when the Romans built superb roads for their armies and our modern roadbuilding for automobiles, it is not surprising that magic transportation is so important in Märchen. The tales include seven-league boots, obliging eagles, and remarkable horses or other animals which can carry a person long distances at great speed.

By contrast with the plodding nature of land travel, transportation by water, whether by boats on rivers or ships on the sea, was relatively speedy. Vessels could carry a number of people in addition to those required to row them or to work the sails. The first imaginative leap forward is to have a self-propelled ship. From that to a ship that can fly over land is a comparatively easy step.

It is interesting to observe that AT513B with its central motif of magical transportation is found only in Europe and in areas like the Cape Verde Islands and the western hemisphere to which it was carried by European settlers. A flying ship was apparently not of interest to narrators in the East; for speedy travel in their stories they could utilize the magical flying carpet best known to us from the *Arabian Nights.*

Since No. 25 is an unusual version of AT513B because it is combined with AT1000, in comparing the Newfoundland versions of the tale we shall first discuss No. 26 and No. 27, two recensions by the same narrator. In their overall structure both these tales are close to the AT analysis of Types 513, 514. The two elder brothers in turn go out to try to build a ship that can sail over land and water; whoever succeeds in doing this will win the king's daughter as his prize. Each has some buns for his lunch. In No. 26, after Bill cuts down a tree, an old man appears and asks what he is doing. Bill replies that the more he chops the more the wood turns into a pig trough, and the old man says that is what it will be. When Tom tells him it just turns into a ten-pound tub, the old man says again that that is what it will be.

When Jack, the youngest brother, in his turn is asked what he is doing, he says what he cuts is turning into a ship and the old man predicts that that is what it will be. We get the impression that the elder brothers spoke ruefully to the old man rather than rudely, but that they were punished for their lack of vision.

However in No. 27, which has more details, there is no question about their rudeness. When the old man asks to share Bill's lunch, Bill refuses. When Bill goes to the pond to get a drink, a little bird flies around and shakes its tail and the water turns to blood. Similarly when Tom refuses to share his lunch with the old man, the bird turns the water to blood. After Bill's efforts produce only a pig's trough and Tom's a ten-pound tub, Jack wants to try his hand, but his mother disparagingly calls him an "ashy cat," i.e., a male Cinderella, to use Thompson's term, but finally gives him a lunch. When the old man appears Jack optimistically tells him he is making progress on building a ship and freely shares his lunch with him. When Jack goes for a drink, the bird turns the pond to honey.

Here we are closer to the AT analysis than in No. 26, since the older brothers have been unkind to the old man while Jack has been kind and thus gets his help. The theme of the bird changing the water unfavorably for the older brothers but positively for the youngest is one we also find in Nos. 29 and 30 (AT551). The old man works with Jack all afternoon, shares another meal with him, and they finish building the ship.

In No. 26 the old man tells Jack to hire a crew; in No. 27, he is more specific about whom Jack is to hire. In both Jack employs four men, each of whom has characteristics described by their names: Eat All, Run Fast, Clear All, and Hard Ass. When Jack and his crew bring the ship to the king to claim his daughter, the king sets Jack a series of tasks: a race with a witch, clearing trees from a large plot of ground, eating a large amount of food, and sitting on a chair which has many knife blades protruding from the seat. In No. 26 the first three are accomplished by Run Fast, Clear All, and Eat All, and Hard Ass sits on the chair and flattens the knives. Jack marries the princess. In No. 27 only Eat All's feat is described; the remainder of the tale was unfortunately unrecorded.

No. 28 is a very brief tale lacking many of the elements of the full Type. It simply tells about Jack's building of a punt, with the aid of an old witch, as distinct from the building of a full-rigged ship that flies over land and water. When his two older brothers in turn go out to build a quite ordinary punt, each rudely refuses to share his lunch with an old witch who appears and asks for some. The same two incidents occur in No. 27, except of course that in this case they are trying to build a larger vessel. The witch ominously tells each of them, "You will get your reward." After lunch, when the first brother tries to cut trees, he finds they have turned to glass. When it is the second brother's turn, the trees have turned to iron. When Jack goes to try his luck, he shares his lunch generously with the old witch and is told that he too will get his reward. That afternoon the witch tells him what to cut and as soon as he cuts the keel, the witch has the boat timbered out; when he returns from cutting a tree for making planks, the punt is already planked.

When Jack asks how he is going to paint the punt, the witch hands Jack a paintbrush and tells him to brush a stroke on each side of the punt. The punt then is immediately beautifully painted in seven colors. As an added bonus Jack learns the punt will fly at one simple command and land again at another.

Unlike the standard form of AT513B, Jack does not need to acquire helpers, but flies the punt to the king's court. There the princess falls in love with him, and the king has no objection to her marrying a man who owns such a wonderful boat. But before the wedding our hero feels it is his duty to return home to tell his two brothers. When he arrives, his brothers are envious at his luck, but are eager to try out the punt. Jack tells them the magical command which makes the punt fly and they jump on board and fly off before he can tell them the second command that would tell it to land. Like the punt with the brothers in it, the story ends in mid-air.

The version of AT513B found in No. 25 is our longest recension and is full of vivid humorous details. What is quite unexpected is that in it the plot has been combined with part of AT1000, "Bargain Not to Become Angry." This is a combination that, so far as we know, has not been reported from oral tradition in the English language except in a version of AT513B from Placentia Bay, Newfoundland (see Lannon and McCarthy in *Studies and Notes* below), which includes AT1000 in an attenuated form. In analyzing No. 25, we shall point out which elements are drawn from AT1000, and which belong to the standard form of AT513B.

The tale starts with the three brothers usually found in both AT513B and AT1000. Three sons of wealthy parents are set the task of building a land and water ship; the successful one will get the parents' money. Bill's effort is derisively called a scoop by his father, while Tom's is called a wheelbarrow. This resembles Bill's pig trough and Tom's ten-pound tub in Nos. 26 and 27; however, neither Bill nor Tom was involved with any witch; their results are merely the product of their own ineptness.

Unlike the usual sequence in AT513B, Jack, the youngest son, does not go out to attempt to build such a ship. Instead he sets out and reaches the house of the Grand Vizier. At the house he finds seven heads stuck on seven spears. All through the tale, Jack is constantly warned that if he fails in any task, his head will go on a spear. We have had the same threat similarly reiterated in an earlier story, No. 7 (AT313), told by the same narrator. Although this beheading and impaling threat is known in folk narrative tradition elsewhere (cf. Motif Q421.1. "Heads on Stakes"), in our Newfoundland collection it is only found in these two stories. It is also reported, however, in the Placentia Bay, Newfoundland, version of AT513B with cf. AT1000, referred to above.

At this point our story suddenly takes on the pattern of AT1000, for Jack is employed by the Grand Vizier with the agreement that neither the employer nor the employee can complain about the bargain. We should note, however, that unlike other versions of AT1000, Jack's two brothers did not precede him in this employment.

Jack's first task is to mow an eighty-acre field. He is offered a choice of two scythes and chooses the rusty one. Folklorists call such an action an unpromising choice. Martin Lovelace points out, however, that English harvesters preferred blades on which rust had formed, believing that the iron had been rusted out of them and that a sharper edge would then be secured from the steel blade. At noon Jack gets no dinner, a standard practice in other versions of AT1000. Jack trades the hay he has mowed to a little man, two inches high, in return for a dinner provided on a magic tablecloth. (Food-providing tablecloths are common, of course, in AT563; see the notes to No. 34). Then the man and the cut grass disappear. The same occurs at supper. This episode of trading the hay is classified as AT1002, "Dissipation of the Ogre's Property," frequently found with AT1000. When Jack returns to the house, he starts to complain about getting no meals, but is reminded of the agreement. He is then given a supper. When the Vizier and his wife go to inspect the mowed field, they find that the hay is no longer there, but they too cannot complain because of the agreement.

The second task assigned to Jack is to build a ship that will "sail down wind or water." This, of course, is the very same task that Jack did not attempt earlier in the story when his brothers had tried to do it and failed. Even though this is not normally one of the tasks typical of AT1000, Jack is obliged to undertake it at this point in this recension. In most versions of AT513B, the reward offered for building such a ship is marriage to the king's daughter. A reward of this kind, however, is not even hinted at in our version.

Jack refuses all tools (does he suspect that his employer may have bewitched them?), but does accept one big cake for his meals. With his own hatchet he starts to cut an elm tree for the keel of the vessel. The little man reappears and offers to help him, and Jack gives him the big cake. Jack goes to the castle on that night and the succeeding one. The little man refuses to let Jack even touch the work. The ship is almost finished in three days.

At this point the little man sends Jack off to collect a crew of six fools. Although the storyteller gets a little mixed up at one point in the search, Jack obtains his extraordinary crew, each of whom he names individually for his chief characteristic activity: Hear Well, Shoot Well, Dip Cup, Run Well, Feed the Pigs, and Hard Ass. When he returns with them to the ship, it is ready to sail. The little man who has built the ship tells Jack he will not appear again unless called on. Collecting the extraordinary companions for the flying ship is a standard element in AT513B.

With his crew aboard Jack flies his ship back to the Grand Vizier's castle in proper nautical style. He berths the ship in the yard so precisely that the bowsprit breaks a window in the castle. We should observe here that before the days of engines, berthing his ship precisely at its dock was one of the acknowledged tests of a sailing skipper's skill. We must assume that Jack's breaking the castle window is a humorous touch of bravado, one that is repeated later in the story.

The Vizier's wife is presented as a termagant. She had even threatened to put her husband's head on a spear if he did not assign a task that would enable them to kill Jack. It is therefore an unexpected touch of foolishness in her aggressive character that when Jack sails the ship into the yard she is busy carrying sunshine in a basket into a hen house to dry peas she has in there. This is a version of AT1245, "Sunlight Carried in a Bag into the Windowless House," a tale Type which is only occasionally found with versions of AT1000. We can only speculate that this humorous touch was introduced to hint at the weakness of an otherwise strong character.

Jack is then assigned in succession three further tasks. Setting such tasks is here treated as part of AT1000, but we must observe that similar tasks are a normal feature of versions of AT513B. It is also quite usual in AT513B for the tasks to be accomplished, as here, by the extraordinary companions. The first task, to secure a bottle of living beauty water from the eastern end of the world, is accomplished by a combination of the skills of Run Well, Hear Well, and Shoot Well. The next task, to drink in one night forty puncheons of extra strong rum which are barricaded by four steel spears, is taken care of by two of the crew: Hard Ass breaks down the spears, while Dip Cup has no difficulty in disposing of the rum.

The job of feeding a hundred savage pigs before daylight is turned over to Feed the Pigs who has experience in such matters. His rather unexpected handling of the task is to twist their necks and kill all of them.

Having successfully accomplished all the tasks assigned, Jack feels it is now his turn to act. He kills the Vizier's wife, takes the Vizier's money, and sails for home. His brothers are dismayed since ironically he has the ship that sails down wind and water, even though he originally had not set out to build one. However, since he is now wealthy, he does not want his parents' money. Apart from the sailing for home, this conclusion combines an element often found in AT513B, the taking of the Vizier's wealth, along with the punishment of the task-setter, in this case the Vizier's wife, which usually terminates versions of AT1000. Was the Vizier's punishment of losing his wealth regarded as sufficient punishment because he too had suffered from his ferocious wife? We cannot say.

Before summing up, perhaps a word is due on the extraordinary companions. Four of them, the great runner, the remarkable hearer, the expert shot, and the great drinker, are commonly found in versions of AT513B, often joined by others, such as a great eater, a great blower, or a great withstander of heat, where the story requires them. Hard Ass, often euphemized in different versions as Hard Haunches, or Hardback, Hard Shins, or even Hard Head, appears as Hard Ass only in a recently published (1991) text from Newfoundland and in a version of AT513A from the Bahamas. We have found no parallel to the man who uses his tool (penis) to feed the pigs. (See, however, the motifs cited under *membrum virile* in the index to Thompson, *Motif-Index,* vol. 6). Neither that character nor the hard man appears in the list of companions in the AT analysis. Were folktale versions with these two characters not known to folktale indexers or were they omitted because of Victorian scruples? A healthy folk tradition has no hesitation about including such characters, for humor concerning the bodily parts and bodily functions is long-established and universally recognized.

To summarize, in this tale we have a unique combination of two Types, neither of which completely follows the AT analysis of the Type. When each of the two brothers attempts to build a flying ship it is not in order to secure a princess as a bride, only to inherit their parents' wealth. When their building efforts come to grief, it is due not to any unkindness to an old man, as described in the AT analysis, but only to their own ineptness. Jack, the youngest brother, does not immediately go out to build such a ship, but seeks other work. His employment, with its curious bargain that neither he nor his employer can complain about each other, is clearly a form of AT1000, except that it is usual in the latter Type for his two older brothers to precede him and be unsuccessful in such employment.

Jack's first task, to mow a field, is the stock opening task in AT1000. Equally conventional are the failure of his employer to provide him with food, and Jack's disposing of the product of his work to a stranger in return for meals. This combination of incidents is classified as AT1002, which, as we observed earlier, is a Type frequently found in versions of AT1000.

Jack's other tasks are not the ones ordinarily found with AT1000, but instead follow very closely the normal pattern of AT513B. Jack is ordered to build a flying ship and succeeds in doing so because of his kindness to a supernatural helper, usually an old man, but here a little man two inches high. What is ironical is that, as noted above, this is the very task he had not attempted to do earlier when his brothers had tried to build such a ship but failed. His collecting a crew of extraordinary helpers is a standard procedure in AT513B.

The series of additional tasks assigned by his employer and successfully accomplished by his helpers again follows the standard pattern of AT513B. Even his carrying off the Vizier's wealth is frequently found in versions of that Type. Only the punishment of the task-setter, the Vizier's wife, can properly be classified as part of AT1000.

There is a nice irony, as we said earlier, in that Jack then returns home with the flying ship, demonstrating that he had succeeded in accomplishing the task at which his brothers had failed, but that he has no need for the reward of his parents' wealth, the promise of which had motivated his two brothers.

Examining this tale from the point of view of the AT index, we could describe it as an incomplete version of AT513B since there is no princess given as a reward. On the other hand, it does not fit the pattern of AT1000 completely, since few of the large number of Types usually associated with AT1000 are present. But in practice, when we consider the tale as performance rather than simply from the point of view of classification, such comments are largely irrelevant. What we have here is a well-told story that holds our interest completely with its effective combination of dramatic action and humorous details. It is a superb illustration of the artistic qualities of a good story told by a fine and creative storyteller.

Studies and Notes

Bolte and Polívka, 2, pp. 86-95, 3, pp. 272-73; Chase, *Jack,* p. 194, no. 11, notes; Thompson, *The Folktale,* pp. 53-55; Delarue and Tenèze, *Catalogue,* 2, pp. 289-91, 297-98; Baughman, *Index,* Type 513B, p. 13; Robe, *Index,* Type 513B, p. 91.

Canada

Lannon and McCarthy, *Fables,* pp. 17-28 (513B, with cf. 1000, 1640, II) (Lawn, Placentia Bay, Newfoundland).

MacDonell and Shaw, *Collection,* pp. 19-34, no. 3, Gaelic text with English trans. (Nova Scotia).

Lacourcière-Low, "Catalogue," cites 19 Francophone versions of AT513B from Canada: 2 (Nova Scotia), 2 (New Brunswick), 10 (Quebec), 5 (Ontario).

United States

Parsons, *Islands,* 1, pp. 244-48, no. 82, pp. 248-51, no. 82a, 2 versions, English trans. of Portuguese texts, Cape Verde Islands, black (Massachusetts).

Fauset, *JAF* 41 (1928), 537-39, no. 19, "fly-boat," informant born in Virginia, black (Pennsylvania).

Cf. Perdue, *Devil,* pp. 62-65, no. 14 (571, with 513A, cf. 513B) (Virginia).

Carter, *JAF* 38 (1925), 346-49, no. 3 (North Carolina).

Chase, *Jack,* pp. 96-105, no. 11, and p. 194, notes (North Carolina).

Saucier, *Folk Tales,* pp. 41-43, no. 9, French tradition, in English (Louisiana).

M. Campbell, *Tales,* pp. 143-47, no. 3 (Kentucky).

Carrière, *Tales,* pp. 144-48, no. 30, French text with English summary (Missouri).

Thomas, *Good,* pp. 83-90, no. 8, French text and English trans. (Missouri).

Lacourcière-Low, "Catalogue," cites 2 Francophone versions of AT513B from the United States: 1 (Louisiana), 1 (Missouri).

The Caribbean and Central America

Parsons, *Andros,* pp. 32-33, no. 20, Version I, black (Bahamas).

See Robe, *Index,* Type 513B, for a Panama reference.

Wales

Cf. Sampson and Yates, *Folk Tales,* pp. 55-57 (513A, with cf. 513B), English trans. from Romany, Gypsy (Wales), and rpt. in Yates, *Book,* pp. 18-20, no. 3.

Scotland

Campbell, *Popular Tales,* 1, pp. 236-50, no. 16 (with cf. 301A), Gaelic text and English trans. (Argyllshire).

McKay-Campbell, *Tales,* 1, pp. 48-61, no. 3, Gaelic text and English trans. (Argyllshire).

Ireland

Curtin, *Hero-Tales,* pp. 182-97 (Co. Donegal).

MacManus, *Heroes,* pp. 86-102 (Co. Donegal).

Irish Types, Type 513B, 67 versions.

Continental Europe

Dasent, *Fjeld,* pp. 341-52 (Norway).

Cf. Dasent, *Popular Tales,* pp. 180-94, no. 20 (cf. 513B, with 300) (Norway).

Hodne, *Types,* AT513, 37 versions (Norway).

Pourrat, *Treasury,* pp. 175-85 (France).

Cf. Delarue, *Borzoi Book,* pp. 157-63, no. 18 [Instead of the land and water ship, which Delarue says is found in nearly all of the 30 French versions, here we have a self-propelled carriage, "the first automobile."] (France).

Crane, *Popular Tales,* p. 364 (Italy).

Withers, *World,* pp. 9-17, and note, pp. 109-10 (Italy).

Calvino, *Folktales,* pp. 362-65, no. 99 (Italy).

Cox, *Cinderella,* p. 525, note 76, brief summary (Finland).

Bowman and Bianco, *Tales,* pp. 1-11 (Finland).

Zobarskas, *Folk Tales,* pp. 119-26 (Lithuania).

Strickland, *Legends,* pp. 69-72, Kasubian (Northwest Slav).

Bain, *Fairy Tales,* pp. 22-29 (Russia).

Coxwell, *Folk-Tales,* pp. 981-85, no. 1, from Afanasief's *Russian Popular Tales,* no. 83 (Ukrainian S.S.R.).

The Philippines

Fansler, *Tales,* pp. 92-97, no. 11b, cf. pp. 89-92, no. 11a [carriage of gold instead of flying ship], 2 versions, and cf. pp. 98-114, no. 11c (513B, with 621, 506), paraphrase of a Pampango metrical romance, and see pp. 114-19, for comparative notes.

For international notes to AT1000, see No. 68.

Stephen P. Snook

26. THE SHIP THAT SAILED WITHOUT WIND OR WATER

Allan Oake
Beaumont, Green Bay, Notre Dame Bay
10 September 1966

AT513B
TC309 66-25
Collectors: JW and Harold Paddock

[*recorder off*]*** Hear the one about the ship that sailed without wind or water? Jack's in that. Well Jack would **BE** in all that kind o' stuff. [*recorder off*] (All) 'bout a ship (that) sailed /without/ wind or water, there was three brothers of 'em see? Or Bill an' Tom. Now the king now was offerin a big...big job. An' was offering a sack [of money]...an' he's offerin his daughter _ to a feller that could build a ship that sailed without wind or water. So Bill...said to his mother one day he said uhm...he said..."Bake a few buns for me mother" he said "I'm goin up now" he said "and see if I can't build (this)...goin out now an' see if I can s...um can't build a ship to sail without wind or water _ to get the king's daughter." Okay she baked the buns and...[he] started off...[*clears throat*]

/about/

Went in to chop down a tree you know an' started choppin. There was a...[*clears throat*] old man come along an' he...he s[aid] "What ya doin uh...what ya doin Bill?" He said he's tryin to...to build a ship would sail without wind or water but he said the more he chop the more (it) turned into pig's trow. Well he said "A pig's trow you shall have." When he's finished that's what he had. Alright. There was nothing to that we'll say.

By an' by...this Tom you know he...he said to his mother one day _ he said "Build me a...bake a few buns" he said he'd go off to...see if he could...build a ship that sail without wind or water. So she baked the buns.

So -- [*coughs*] he went...cut down a tree. An' started choppin, this ol' feller come out again. He said "What are ya doin...Bi[ll]...Tom?" He said he's tryin to...to build a ship he said to sail without wind or water, more he chopped more 'twould turn into...a ten pound tub. "Oh" he said "a ten pound tub you shall have."

Well two or three days after that Jack went in th' house _ one day. "Mother" he said "bake a few buns" he said he...

"What 'ee want buns for _ Jack?" [*coughs*] [*recorder off*]*** "(build) [a] ship" he said "that sailed without wind or water."

"You ya ashy cat" she (said) "you get in under the stove an' lie down (yous). You aint goin to do nothing" she said "th' other boys never done nothing."

"Oh" he'd..."bake a few buns" he said "never mind." So _ alright.

She baked the few buns, he...went off cut down the tree. Bad job an' this ol' feller come along again.

"What ya doin Jack?" He said he...he was tryin to...to build a ship he said that sailed without wind or water, the more he'd chop the more she'd turn into a ship. "A ship you shall have Jack" he said. Now he started in. The once you know come LUNCH time.

"Jack" he said uh...um Jack was goin to have a lunch, this ol' feller come again, he said..."Havin a lunch Jack?"

"Uh _ yeah" Jack said. "Do ('ee) want one?"

Yes he said he'd have a lunch. Well _ cat away you know. Well...by this time we'll say they had uh (pretty)...he's chipped in then an' help Jack. But he had the ship _ builded.

So _ he told Jack then now to ship his...an' uh...how to hire all his crew. Every man he'd see you know they'd be the right man. So Jack went out town, the first feller he seen you know was a feller _ oh he was runnin _ runnin an'...like the mischief. Runnin away from a ol' witch, there was ol' witch there. Runnin away from this ol' witch. Jack [said] to hisself "Now that's a...that's the man for me." So hired un on.

By an' by he seen another feller _ was eatin. Oh he was eatin anything you mind to come across. He said "There's another feller for me." And uh [coughs]...er...I don't know. [pauses to recollect]* Oh yes he find where he come 'cross another feller clearin ground. There was two of 'em there clearin, th' ol' witch you know an' this other feller. An' he could clear so many trees again as th' ol' witch could. Clearin an'...he said to hisself now Jack said "That's...(the) feller I wants."

*pause: 4 sec. approx.

So _ he wanted one more feller. By an' by he come 'cross a feller whatever he'd sit down on (you know) was flatten it all down on the ground. "Ah" he said "now that's the feller for me." So he called one Eat All _ an' he calls th' other one Run Fast _ an' then th' other feller he called Clear All _ an' this last feller was Hard Ass _ called un.

So they got (her in) s...went in port we'll say an' hove down the anchor an' _ went ashore now _ to look for the king. Well now he had...there was so many JOBS you know _ that he had to do before he get his daughter. There was a...ol' witch there an' he had a feller to runned...he wanted a feller to run wi' th' ol' witch, well this...he got out this Run Fast. Ol' witch couldn't get ar bit handy into un at all.

An' then we'll say 'twas uh...[clears throat] clearin ground. Got th' ol'...got this...Clear All _ (out) wi' th' ol' witch. An' then we'll say uh... cooked up a big feas[t]...feast in the field, had uh...got 'em all round, they had s...so many cows you know _ an' everything. Had the real big...feast for 'em. Now it had to be all eat. Well they (eat)...eat we'll say, Jack he eat ya know till he couldn't eat no uh...hurt hisself. An' all the rest of 'em, well this Eat All he eat an' eat an' by an' by he eat the /?rest/...eat all was on the table an' eat the table -- an' he looked an' he..."Goddamn it" he said "gi' me a meal!" He hadn't a...hadn't had a meal yet! [laughter] Alright. [Male listener: (Tell 'em that he was finished)] That was the last of (it). He can go in now to get the ki[ng']s daughter. An' you

/(?fifth)/

/sittin un
down in/

know they put out two...they put out two chairs. Jack was takin another feller in with un _ an' _ one chair they had stuck full of penknives see who...for Jack to sit down in. Instead o' Jack /sittin down in un/ Hard Ass sat down in 't _ an' squat everything down on the floor. So they _ he got to the daughter an' got married an'...I got a cup o' tea out of it an' let's be headin for home! [*laughter*] [*recorder off*]

[Int. A: An' you learned that one...again, how long ago did you learn most of these _ now?]
Oh my dear man _ fifty year ago probably. Yeah I knows I wasn't no more than twenty when I learned...when I...learned all they.
[Int. A: I daren't ask you how old you are now!]
[*recorder off*]*** fifty year now. 'Twas...'bout fifty year I been tellin 'em.
[Int. B: And how old are you now Allan?]
I'm s...I'll be seventy-one now sir. [*recorder off*] Yeah. Uh...[if] I lives now an'...if I lives to see the twelfth of April comin I'll be seventy-one.
[*recorder off*] [Int. B: You were still tellin a lot o' stories I think _ when I was a boy.]
Oh yes. Well now 'tis only this last _ well there's an odd one now uh...sometimes _ feller come in (he was)...first thing he'll say _ "Tell me a story." Now there's scattered feller comes in **NOW** _ wants me to tell un a story right away _ you know.
[Int. B: Who...who would be still interested in hearin a story?]
Well there's a lot of young fellers. Oh my (son there's) maybe all the young fellers around here they be interested now _ for hear...hear **ME** tell a story.
[*recorder off*]*** I don't know, I'd say...thirty year probably...probably _ oh twenty-five...twenty-five year ago probably _ that most died out. [*coughs*] [*recorder off*]*** there's lots o' times you know we've set down (to) tell stories.

Duration: 5 min., 52 sec.
Source: "Fifty year ago."
Location: Store in garden of teller's house, afternoon.
Audience: Interviewers, adult male neighbor.

Context, Style, and Language: (For context see notes to No. 1). A neighbor who is passing by stays for a while to listen to the story.

As with Nos. 12 and 13, 23 and 24, the two versions of this tale were recorded nine years apart and although they are substantially similar they differ in a number of ways. In this, the first version, Allan Oake is recalling the tale after several years and asks the collectors if they have heard the story, adding that Jack is in it and that "Jack would **BE** in all that kind o' stuff." The recorder is then switched off while the collectors explain that that is the kind of tale they would like to hear and encourage the teller to recall it. The openings of the two versions are very much alike, although in this the king offers a sack of money in addition to his daughter, the mother bakes buns for her sons rather than packing a lunch for them, and there is no mention of the pond when Bill goes to chop down the tree. Bill's dialogue with the "ol' feller" ("old man" in this version) is partly in indirect speech whereas that in No. 27 is entirely in direct speech, only the tense of the verb differing in the "ol' feller's" final words to Bill. There is no mention of the little bird in this encounter and in No. 27 the bird is merely rather carelessly implied in the pronoun *he,* the listener being left to guess what it is that "flew around" until the bird is introduced a little later. Indeed the pond, the little bird, and its effects on the water in the pond are entirely absent here, but introduced in some detail in the later version, providing interesting parallels with the identical motifs in Nos. 29 and 30, "The Queen of Paradise' Garden." Further, Bill and Tom do not have a lunch in version one, thus removing the motivation for the "ol' feller's" response to their denial of food. The elaboration in No. 27 suggests that the teller recalled the tale in more detail during the years which separated the two recordings.

In this first version Jack is called an "ashy cat" by his mother, reminiscent of his characterization in No. 21, "The King of Ashes' Daughter," where the unpromising hero is also depicted as an indolent good-for-nothing lying near the stove, like his counterparts Aschenputtel and Ivan in German and Russian folktales. It is also notable that in No. 27 the teller strongly emphasizes the present participles *runnin, eatin, squattin,* and *clearin,* which gives a much clearer impression of tighter structuring than appears in the first version. However, version one includes references to Run Fast and Clear All competing with old witches both when first encountered by Jack and also in some of the subsequent tasks—details lost in No. 27 as is also the proverbial comparison "like the mischief" in describing Run Fast's speed. The crew appear and perform their tasks in a different order in each version—again evidently of no consequence to the teller whose attitude to such matters remains casual, as noted earlier. Version one has Jack himself naming each of his helpers whereas version two implies that the "ol' feller" had already told him their names. The reference to the ship going into port and anchoring is omitted in No. 27. However, the details of the "feed" which Eat All consumes are much more elaborated in No. 27, again suggesting that Allan Oake has reconstructed the story more completely in the intervening years, as does the addition of the important point that Jack was unaware of the additional task of sitting on the chair "stuffed full o' penknives." The end formulas also differ slightly.

The overall impression gained from a comparison of the two versions is that they run parallel but differ in detail, none of the differences being very significant except for the omission of the pond and bird motifs in this version and of the witches in No. 27. The narrative in the earlier version, however, tends to be much more hesitant, with frequent pauses, including a lengthy one for recollection as the teller pieces the story together. It also includes a great deal of useful contextual information.

As in his other tales, Allan Oake pays little attention to consistency in his narration, often mispronouncing words without apparent regard, leaving the audience to adjust and interpret what is said. He again employs his favorite punctuating *Alright* and *we'll say*, the latter being in itself an excuse for minor inaccuracies, encouraging the listener not to be too concerned about details. Central pillars of the plot, however, remain constant in the two versions, e.g., the "ol' feller's" comments to the brothers, and certain segments terminate in clauses such as "There was nothing to that...," "That was the last of (it)," while new phases of the plot are signaled with *By an' by*.

Apart from the linguistic points noted under Nos. 1, 12, 13, 23, and 24, one might mention the pronunciation of *trough* as /trou/, the aphesis in *'twould*, the lexical items *squat* (squash/flatten), *scattered* (occasional), and the phrase *ar bit handy to* (anywhere near to), the past tense forms *builded, have*, and *eat*, and the double negative *aint goin to do nothin*.

See also the notes to Nos. 1, 12, 13, 23, and 24.

Type and Motifs:

AT513B. *The Land and Water Ship*.

P251.6.1. *Three brothers*.

H331. *Suitor contests: bride offered as prize*.

D1533.1.1. *Magic land and water ship*.

L131. *Hearth abode of unpromising hero*.

L13. *Compassionate youngest son*.

Q40. *Kindness rewarded*.

N825.2. *Old man helper*.

H1242. *Youngest alone succeeds on quest*.

F601. *Extraordinary companions*.

F681. *Marvelous runner*.

G267. *Man pursued by witches*.

F632. *Mighty eater*.

F614.9. *Strong man clears plain*.

F621. *Strong man: tree puller*.

G221.3. *Witch has extraordinary bodily strength*.

H335. *Tasks assigned suitors*.

H331.5. *Suitor contest: race*.

H1129.6. *Task: building causeway, clearing land, etc.*

H1141. *Task: eating enormous amount*.

F639. *Extraordinary powers—miscellaneous*.

F786. *Extraordinary chair*.

L161. *Lowly hero marries princess*.

Z10.2. *End formula*.

International Parallels: For international parallels to AT513B see No. 25.

27. THE SHIP THAT SAILED WITHOUT WIND OR WATER

Allan Oake   AT513B
Springdale, Notre Dame Bay   TC1827, 1828 75-287
15 June 1975   Collector: Christina Pynn

[*recorder off*]*** where he build a ship without...sailed without wind or water?
[Int: Yeah okay.]

Well there was uh...three brothers. There was Jack now ‿ Bill an' uh...an' Tom. Well king was offerin ‿ his...his daughter ‿ to whoever could build a ship that sail without wind or water.

Well now Bill said to his mother one day he said he...he..."Pack up a lunch for me, mother" he said "I'm goin off now to...get the ship that sailed without wind or water."

(Well) he come uh...he come to a pond you know, got there at lunch time where he...cut down this piece o' timber we'll say an' started choppin. By an' by /little/ ol' feller come out an' he said "What are ya doin Bill?"   /?a bit o'/

He said "I'm tryin to...to make a ship" he said "that sailed without wind or water. But the more I chops" he said "the more it turns into a pig's trow."

"Well" he said "a pig's trow you should have."

Then he [*a little bird*] flew around...then 'twas uh...lunch time.

An' "Jack" he said "now what...or uh...Bill" he said "what about a lunch?"

"No" he said he'd...only had...just enough for hisself. He didn't know whe'r [i.e., *whether*] he did or no. So then there was a little bird fled around the pond and shook his tail an' turned...all the water into mud. Well Jack couldn't get nar...or Bill couldn't get nar drink. Well that finished that.

So one day at after that Tom said "Mother" he said uh...[*clears throat*] "pack us up a lunch now" he said. "I goes off an' try to get the ship ‿ that sailed without wind or water." Well she packed up a lunch for un. Started off.

Come to this pond we'll say an' chopped down this...piece o' timber. Started choppin.

Ol' feller come out an'..."What are ya doin" he said uh..."Tom?"

He said "I'm tryin to build a ship" he said "without...sail without wind or water but the more I chop the more it'd turn into ‿ a pig's...or uh...ten pound tub."

"Well" he said "a pig's...ten pound tub" he said "you'll...shall have."

Now 'twas lunch time.

"What about a lunch Tom?" he said.

"Only just got enough for meself" he said.

307

(Well) this little bird come out then an' fled around the pond and shook his tail an' turned...turned all the water into blood. He was finished.

So -- some time after Jack...uh some time after that Jack said "Mother" he said _ "pack up a lunch for me" he said.

"What do you want (a) lunch _ for?" she said "ya ashy cat" she said "best place for you is up behind the stove."

No he wanted a lunch, he was goin to...to build a ship now that sailed without wind or water. So he kept on an' the once she _ got a lunch for un. Started off (an') got to this pond. Chopped down...uh...this timber we'll say an' started choppin.

This ol' man come out an' he said "What 'ee doin Jack?"

He said "I'm tryin to build a ship now" he said "without sail...'ll sail without wind or water an' the more I chops" he said "the more she _ turns into a ship."

"Well" he said "ship you shall have."

This time _ he said _ was lunch time. He said "What about a lunch Jack?"

"Yes sir" he said "you can have a lunch. Eat all you wants."

Out...out come this little bird, flew around again an' shook...shook his tail an' turned the...all the water into honey. Well now they ate away an' the once it come _ lunch time again an' they had their ship nearly done.

Th' ol' man said "What about it Jack?"

"Yes sir" he said "eat away. There be...there'll be plenty left after you'm finished." They eat away and uh...finished the ship.

Now the ol' man told un, this old feller told un that he'd know his crew when he'd get in port an'...an' take..."An' every one" he said "if you knows _ now" he said "you'll _ hire 'em on. You'll see a feller" he said "by the name" he said "a hard feller he's...clearin [a] bit o' land. Another feller" he said "RUNNIN fast. An' another feller EATIN all" he said "eatin everything he sees. An' then" he said "another feller sittin down on everything an' SQUATTIN it down to the ground. Now that's the crew that you want to order" he said.

Alright. Went in port now an' told un no...(told un to) heave down his anchor. As...when he went ashore we'll say (if he must)...there was a...he seen this feller you know _ sittin down on everything _ you know an' squat it all down to the ground an' he said to hisself "Well this must be Hard Ass th' ol' feller told me about." He said "What about comin...comin wi' me, one o' me crew?"

"Yes" he said. "I'll come wi' ya."

Then by an' by he seen another feller RUNNIN you know so hard there was nothing it seemed like could catch un.

He said "Well this must be _ th' har[d]...Run Fast this old feller talked about. Well" he said "now" _ (said) "I wants ya...you for...you for one o' me crew."

"Yes sir" he said "I'll come wi' ye."

An' by an' by he...come across another feller **CLEARIN** land, the trees was flyin away from him 'cordin as he'd cull you know an'...

"Well" he said "this must be Clear All th' ol' feller's..." He said "I wants for you" he said "wants (for)...you for you for one o' me crew."

"Yes sir" he said.

Now then _ the next feller was a...[Male listener: Was it...?] what was the next feller? /Eat All/ did I say _ Don? No. Run...'twas Run Fast wasn't it? Feller eatin. Oh _ eatin everything he'd see.

/Eat Out/

He said "Well (now) this one must be Eat All (that) th' ol' feller told (me about)." Asked he _ he want him for a crew. That was five of 'em I suppose. (So) he's...five an' [there] be hisself. That was four of 'em: Eat All, Run Fast, Hard Ass an' Clear All. Alright. They're up to the...they went up to the king now for this...for his daughter. He had this uh...ship now that come in with...sailed without wind or water.

Well now they had to have a big feast _ feed now. Well they cooked a hundred an' fifty cows. (There's) four...five...five hundred sacks o' potatoes an' turnips. Had the big...out...the big...table out in the field.

Well now they start in. Jack he eat all...eat all he could eat. 'Twas goin to hurt un you knows he eat that much 'cause he [Int: Mm.] they wanted to...he had to clean it all up. Well they **ALL** done the same. Well Eat All he was the last one left. [*recorder off; tape changed*] Eat away _ eat away _ eat away. Eat all was on the table _ or...yes _ eat all was on the table _ slewed around an' eat the table. [Int: Hm!] An' he said "Damn it, gi' me a meal!" Alright. That was all of it.

Now then we'll say _ he was goin...king he...had another task for Jack but Jack didn't know it _ you know 'fore he'd get his daughter. [*clears throat*] When he went in to get his daughter now _ Hard Ass went in with un see? An' the chair he had put out now for Jack to sit in was stuffed full o'...penknives. But this is the one the...that Hard Ass sot down in _ an' squat un right down to the floor see?

Well the other one now well there you are. He got the daughter an'...[Int: Mm-hm.] I thought 'twas time for me to get home 'fore dark. [*laughter*]

Duration: 7 min., 32 sec.
Source: "Fifty year ago."
Location: Springdale Hospital.
Audience: Adult male visitor, interviewer.

Context, Style, and Language: (For context see notes to No. 13).

This tale proved difficult to transcribe as the recording quality is not good, there is a great deal of background noise from the hospital ward in which it was recorded, and the speaker's voice is not always clear, probably due in part to his illness which may also account for the frequent pauses and comparatively short sentences. Once again the typical punctuating *Alright* is in evidence, while *by an' by* and *the once* mark new stages in the narrative. Note that the feast included potatoes and turnips—typical fare in Newfoundland, while *Clear All* is said to *cull* trees—a transferred sense from the normal local meaning of sorting and grading dried codfish (see *DNE cull*). Other local usages are the aphetic *'cordin as,* the present tense form *I chops,* the past tense forms *build, fled* (flew), *seen,* and the double negative *couldn't get nar drink.*

See also the notes to Nos. 1, 12, 13, 23, 24, and **26.**

Type and Motifs:

AT513B. *The Land and Water Ship.*

P251.6.1. *Three brothers.*

H331. *Suitor contests: bride offered as prize.*

D1533.1.1. *Magic land and water ship.*

Q2. *Kind and unkind.*

B172. *Magic bird.*

D478.4. *Transformation: water becomes bloody.*

L131. *Hearth abode of unpromising hero.*

L13. *Compassionate youngest son.*

Q40. *Kindness rewarded.*

D478.5. *Transformation: water to honey.*

N825.2. *Old man helper.*

H1242. *Youngest alone succeeds on quest.*

F601. *Extraordinary companions.*

F610. *Remarkably strong man.*

F614.9. *Strong man clears plain.*

F621. *Strong man: tree-puller.*

F681. *Marvelous runner.*

F632. *Mighty eater.*

F639. *Extraordinary powers—miscellaneous.*

H335. *Tasks assigned suitors.*

H1141. *Task: eating enormous amount.*

F786. *Extraordinary chair.*

L161. *Lowly hero marries princess.*

Z10.2. *End formula.*

International Parallels: For international parallels to AT513B see No. 25.

28. JACK, TOM AND BILL
(Jack and the Beautiful Punt[†])

William Pittman
Sop's Arm, White Bay
28 November 1967

AT513B + AT2250 + Cf. AT2280
68-10/pp. 58-63
Collector: Claude Hamlyn

When I was just a kid about age ten (1949), I used to enjoy hearing my step-grandfather, Bill Pittman, tell stories about "Jack, and Tom, and Bill." Sometimes he would tell these stories to visitors while my brother and I listened in, or he might tell them to us alone. He was then in his late fifties. Many of these stories I have forgotten, but there is one in particular that I recall which was quite long but nevertheless very interesting. I will try here to tell the story in his language as I recall it.

Jack and Tom and Bill were three brothers. One Spring they decided to go fishing, but they never had nar punt. So Tom said to his mudder one day, "Mudder, bake me up some molasses buns 'cause I'm goin in the country the mar to cut some timbers fer a boat." So his mudder baked up the buns fer him.

Next morning, Tom went off into the woods. When he reached the place where he thought was a good place to cut the timbers, he was tired and hungry, so he boiled his kettle and had lunch. While he was eating, an old witch came out of the woods and in a nice way asked Tom fer a bun.

"You'll get nar bun here," said Tom, "I only have enough fer meself."

"Alright," said the old witch, "you will get your reward," and she went back into the woods again.

After Tom had finished his lunch, he started to cut some timbers. But every time he hit the tree, shards of glass went everywhere. The trees were all glass. When he went home he told Jack and Bill that he had met an old witch and that she had put a spell on him.

"Ah," said Bill, "I'll go tomorrow. I bet you I'll get some timbers."

So next morning Bill went off into the woods. As he was havin his lunch the old witch came along and asked him fer a bun.

"You'll get nar bun here," said Bill.

"Alright," said the old witch, "you will have your reward."

Bill finished his lunch and began to cut some timbers, but when he struck the tree with his axe, he found that each tree was solid iron. Like Tom, he went home with no timbers.

Jack laughed when he heard his story. Now it was his turn to go and try his luck. So next morning he set out with his axe and lunch bag with the buns. While he was having his lunch, along comes the old witch and asks Jack fer a bun.

"Sure," said Jack, "you can have two if you want 'em"

So the old witch sat down and had lunch with Jack. She asked Jack what he had come into the woods fer.

"To cut timbers for a punt," said Jack.

"I will take care of that fer you," said the old witch. "Go and cut me a timber, and when you gets back here, I'll have the boat all timbered out fer you."

Sure enough, when Jack got back, the punt was timbered out.

"Now," said the old witch, "cut me a plank stick." Jack went off to cut a plank stick. When he got back, she was all planked.

"How am I goin to paint her?" asked Jack.

"Well," said the old witch, taking a brush out of her pocket, "take this brush an' give one smear on each side and the punt will be seven different colours."

Sure enough, when Jack had made two smears with the brush, the punt was seven pretty colours. It was the prettiest punt he ever saw.

"How will I get the punt out of this place?" asked Jack. "That's easy," said the old witch; "first get into her and I'll tell you the magic words." Jack got in. "Now," said the old witch, "tell her to fly, and the punt will go wherever you want it; say 'Pitch' and she will land jes where you want her."

"Fly," said Jack, and away he sails into the air. Soon he landed in England where he met the king's daughter. She took a liking to Jack and they decided to get married. The king too was proud of Jack fer having such a punt.

"Before I can get married," said Jack to the princess, "I've got to go home to see me brothers, 'cause I know they must be uneasy about me by now." In a few minutes he was home. His brothers could hardly believe it when they saw the beautiful punt and heard Jack's plans about marrying the king's daughter. They envied him very much. If they could only get Jack's punt, they would be able to go away and perhaps get married to some rich lady too.

They decided they would ask Jack if they could have his punt, "just to try her out." Jack consented and Tom and Bill jumped aboard.

"How do she work?" they asked.

"Just tell her to fly," said Jack. They were so eager to get going that they both shouted, "Fly!" before Jack could tell them the magic work 'Pitch.' So away they sailed up into the air and out of sight. And I guess they're flying yet.

My step-grandfather would always say, at the end of his story, "Then I had a cup of tea and went home," or "I had me lunch and went home." This would help to bring an extra burst of laughter from the listeners.

Audience: Collector and his brother, visitors.

Context, Style, and Language: This manuscript story from White Bay provides interesting parallels not only with Nos. 25, 26, and 27, but also in that its end formula is very similar to that used in most of the stories told by Allan Oake who comes from neighboring Green Bay on the opposite side of the Baie Verte Peninsula. There is some evidence of the mingling of direct and indirect speech, a stylistic device used often by the Bennetts and other narrators in this collection, in "They decided they would ask Jack if they could have his punt, 'just to try her out.'" Although recalled at second hand the narrative captures several important features of Newfoundland dialect, e.g., the loss of the final velar nasal in words ending with *-ing,* the medial /d/ in *mudder,* the reduction of *my* to *me* in *meself* and of the vowel in *fer* (far) and *just* (which also loses its final /t/); *tomorrow* is rendered as *the mar* indicating the ambiguity of *to-* and *the* (cf. *tonight/the night* elsewhere in this collection) and the preservation of West Country English /ar/; aphesis occurs in *'cause*. At the lexical level we find *nar* (no, [not] any), *punt* in its local sense of an undecked fishing boat (see *DNE punt* n.), *plank stick* (length of timber for planking a boat; see *DNE stick,* n.), *Pitch* (Land/Alight), while in the grammar there are such examples of present tense forms as *you gets, do she,* and the double negative *never had nar punt*. Incidentally, the use of the word *punt* throughout this narrative represents the localizing of *ship* (cf. Nos. 25, 26, and 27) within the Newfoundland context. In contrast with naval parlance, *ship* is comparatively rare in local speech, such words as *boat, punt, dory* etc. being substituted for it. The noun is reserved for ocean-going vessels as distinct from inshore craft, although *ship* remains in common use as a verb.

Types and Motifs:
AT513B. *The Land and Water Ship* + AT2250. *Unfinished Tales* + Cf. AT2280. *Old Woman's Dogs Run Away.*
P251.6.1. *Three brothers.*
Cf. G265.10. *Witches bewitch trees.*
Cf. F811.1.6. *Glass (crystal) tree in otherworld.*
F811.1.9. *Iron tree.*
Q2. *Kind and unkind.*
Q40. *Kindness rewarded.*
G284. *Witch as helper.*
Cf. D1273. *Magic formula (charm).*
D1533.1.1. *Magic land and water ship.*
T91.6.4. *Princess falls in love with lowly boy.*
K2211. *Treacherous brother.*
D861.3. *Magic object stolen by brothers.*
Q212. *Theft punished.*
Z12. *Unfinished tales.*
Z10.2. *End formula.*

International Parallels: For international parallels to AT513B see No. 25.
This story is unusual in that it appears to have a double ending. The two brothers hastily jump into the punt, having learned how to command it to fly but not how to order it to land. As a result they sail up into the air and out of sight. At this point the storyteller closes the narrative with the mildly humorous remark, "And I guess they're flying yet."
The recorder of the story, who apparently had heard it told by the same narrator on different occasions, implied that the listeners laughed at this first inconclusive ending. After this the storyteller would always add one of two stock Newfoundland end formulas, the kind often employed at the end of a Märchen or other tale of wonder—and the sudden realism of the formula would again draw laughter.

313

Besides playing for the expected laugh, why did the storyteller use this end formula device? We can suggest one possible reason. Perhaps, as an experienced narrator, he realized that the unfinished ending might leave some listeners feeling dissatisfied. Rather than have the mood of the story broken by having some literal-minded person ask, "But what *happened* to them?", he introduced a stock end formula. This would effectively prevent a possible question by signaling that the narrative was over.

We have found a similar double ending in another unfinished story, an American tale from Georgia. The storyteller concludes his tale with a scared man running down the road from an invisible ghost. Then he introduces an amusing end formula. Unlike the close of the Newfoundland tale, however, the teller then adds a variation on his previous ending with: "So, I suppose he's running yet."

Another Newfoundland story, No. 126, again about a scared man, has an unfinished ending resembling the Georgia one, but with no use of a stock end formula. The storyteller concluded his yarn by saying: "If the devil didn't catch him, he's still running yet." We have listed below the few other published examples of similar tale endings that we have found. We realize that we may have overlooked other examples in our reading, but we hope that by drawing the attention of folklorists to this ending, other examples will soon be forthcoming.

Where the closing remark is "still flying" or "still running," or the like, such endings are classified under the general category of AT2250, "Unfinished Tales." This group of endings is one not clearly distinguished either in Thompson's remarks on unfinished tales in *The Folktale,* pp. 229-30, or in the AT index. There might be some justification for classifying the group with AT2280, "Old Woman's Dogs Run Away," which ends: "She starts to weep—and she is still weeping." We feel, however, that our group is sufficiently distinct from the latter to be given a separate number in the AT index.

See No. 136 for a different version of AT2250, one that fits the description in the AT index.

Canada

Desplanques, *Folktales,* pp. 19-21 (with 304), French tradition, in English (Newfoundland), which ends: "They got married and if they're not dead, they're living yet."

Cf. Fowke, *Folktales,* p. 73, no. 22, trans. from French text in Lambert and Lanctôt, *JAF* 44 (1931), 261, no. 153 (2) (Quebec), which ends: "and if they haven't gone they live there still."

Thomas, *Types,* cites 1 version of AT2250 from Newfoundland French tradition.

Lacourcière, Index, cites 6 Francophone versions of AT2250 from Canada: 3 (New Brunswick), 1 (Prince Edward Island), 2 (Quebec).

United States

Goldstein and Ben-Amos, *Tales,* pp. 45-51 (301A, with cf. 327E), from Irish family tradition (New York), which ends: "And as for the brothers I don't know whether they ever did get away from that stick. The last I heard they were still running."

McDermitt, *NCFJ* 31 (1983), 16-19 (with 401, 402) (North Carolina), which ends: "An so the last time that I seed Jack, he was still there runnin that ranch."

McDermitt, *NCFJ* 31 (1983), 19-22 (with 1000, 1007, 1011, 1563) (North Carolina), which ends: "An so far as I know Lucky Jack is a-cuttin shoe strings yet."

Hartsfield, *Betsy,* pp. 55-57, no. 1 (Georgia; discussed above), which ends: ". . .both going down the road. Of course I couldn't hang around, because I had on paper clothes, and I was afraid the wind might blow or it might rain. So, I suppose that he's running yet."

Hartsfield, *Betsy,* pp. 96-97, no. 26 (Georgia), which ends: "And the last time I saw them, they were still going down the road."

Cf. Robe-Jameson, *Folktales,* pp. 206-7, no. 188 (with 1888*), Spanish tradition, in English (New Mexico), which ends: "So they went sailing like a kite and its tail. And for all I know they may be going still."

Robe, *Index,* Type 2250, cites 2 Hispanic American texts. The Parsons version from Puebla, Mexico, resembles the form described here, but adds a punning catch.

Scotland

Douglas, *King,* pp. 93-97 (with 301A), Scottish traveller (Dunbartonshire), which ends: "The auld man an his wife disappeared an if they went tae that valley, they're still in that valley yet!"

Williamson, *Thorn,* pp. 36-61 (with 461), Scottish traveller (Argyllshire), which ends: ". . .as the story says, *he's still rowin yet!* An that is the end o my story!"

For yet another unfinished tale form that differs from those above, see Gardner, *Schoharie,* pp. 185-87, no. 18 (with 326A*, 569) (New York), which ends: "But I didn't stay to see how they made it. I left them." Cf. however the similar ending of No. 33, AT551, below.

29. THE QUEEN OF PARADISE' GARDEN

Albert Heber Keeping	AT551
Grand Bank, Fortune Bay	TC149 65-16
29 July 1965	Collectors: HH and Ronald G. Noseworthy

Well this is a true story that I heard er...way back in er...fifty years ago _ on a fishin voyage in...in Connaigre Bay. I was a boy o' twelve _ an' I was cook. An' after the day's work was finished those old _ men would tell up some old yarns, ghost stories _ an' so forth _ and one I kind o' remember _ more distinctly than others. It wasn['t]...it was two old people they had three sons, Jack, Bill an' Tom. An' they'd aheard about the Queen of Paradise' Garden _ an' a fruit that was growin there _ uh...

[Int: Yeah _ right. An' this was about...an' this was on a ship _ that you heard it?]

Yeah on the ship yeah.

[Int: Yeah. An' ah...now how did the. how did the old man start the story?]

Well he...he started off with uh...with uh...(with) once upon a time (ye see)...yeah.

315

[Int: Yeah let's hear that. Say that _ the way he...you said it before.]

[*coughs*] An'...an' uh...I heard _ the story starts off _ once upon a time an' a very good /time/ it was _ not in your time _ 'deed [i.e., *indeed*] in my time _ in olden times. (When) quart bottles hold half a gallon an' house paper[ed] with pancakes _ an' pigs run about, forks stuck in their ass _ see who wanted to buy pork [*laughter*].

/trime/

There was two...there was two old people they had three sons Jack, Bill an' Tom an' uh _ they've heard about the Queen o' Paradise' Garden if you could...get there _ there's a fruit growin there that er...would make their father (an') mother young again. So they started off _ an' they come to three cross roads. And here they were goin to take different roads so _ they all stoops down to get a drink o' water and uh...a little bird flipped her tail an' tu...turned it into blood and he couldn't drink. An' Tom done the same but when Jack went to drink _ the little bird flipped her tail and turned it into wine. So _ that's how the story went an' they started off an' _ he met an old man _ that was...on the way _ an' he had...he asked Jack _ what he was lookin for. An' he told him and he said "I'll do all I can to help ya." So he give him the pipe "Now" he said "when you think you're lost you _ take three draws o' that pipe an' whichever way the smoke blows that's the way you go."

An' after a few more days on the road he come across another old woman. Sh(e)...she asked him the same story an' uh...she said she would help him on his way. She heard about it _ an' she give him an apple. "Now" she said "when you gets up on that hill over there ya...you'll see another hill. Well you cut a piece out of the apple an' 'bout the time you put it in your mouth you'll wish you was on th' other hill _ an' you'll be there. An' when you gets on that hill an' lookin down you'd seen the Queen of Paradise' _ castles an' everything down there. An' cut another piece out of the apple an'...an' wish that all...everybody would fall asleep." So he no sooner had the apple in his mouth 'fore everybody was asleep an' he goes down an' he finds the fruit _ that would make his father an' mother young again an' he _ he's lookin around he _ went in one room an' he...he seen the _ Queen of Paradise lyin on the bed an' she look(ed)...very beautiful. An' there was a piece o' music there that would play anything you'd tell it to play _ and a loaf of bread that if you cut a slice off he was just as big as ever an' a...a bottle of wine if you took a drink out of her he was just as full as ever so _ Jack takes off (a) slice o' bread an' he had some wine an' _ an' he went...he thought a...slice off a cut loaf is never missed so he goes in to see the Queen o' Paradise 'gain [*laughs*].

An' uh...after he had _ finished with everything he started on his journey again an' when he got back on that hill again he cut another piece out o' the apple an' he wish everything woke up. So everything come to life again an' everything went on as usual but the Queen o' Paradise was worried a bit, she knowed somebody'd been there so she...she started out to look for the **MAN** that uh...that's been there. So...Jack on...hi(s) on his...goin back home visit the...some old farmers on the way an' he give away the piece o' music that _ he got at the Queen o' Paradise' Garden an' _ and further on the road he met another _ old farmer an' he gave away the loaf o' bread an' _ an' another old farmer he give away the bottle o' wine before he gets back home an' the Queen o' Paradise _ on her route she visit the same places an' she had the same story to ask _ what kind of a man he was an' so forth, she said "I know he must (have) been some man or otherwise he wouldn't done what he have done!" [*laughs*].

An' after arrival...when Jack arrived home his parents disowned un they thought he was...dead an' _ they just hired him on as a pantry boy. Well Bill an' Tom was the s...the sons an' _ well when the Queen o' Paradise arrived she*...she questioned the...the...the two _ Bill an' Tom an' uh...   *rep. 7
she...she found out that they'd never been to the Queen o' Paradise' Garden but uh...she knew there was somebody in that _ house that **WAS** there so _ she got after th' old woman an'...an' old woman said "Well we got a pantry boy here, I don't think he's ever been anywheres uh..."

"Well" she said "bring un out." An' when Jack marches out with the big grin onto un, all kinds o' dough over his hands (why) _ she said "Have you been [to] Queen o' Paradise' Garden?"

"Yes" he said _ "I've been there."

"(Well)" she said "what did you see there?"

"I see" he said "I seen **YOU**."

"Well yes" she said "I knows you did!" [*laughter*]. An'...an' she touched cr...Jack with her magic /wand/ an' he...he turned out to be a   /wen/
beautiful prince an' _ they got married. An' they were havin babies in basketfuls when I left and all the(y)...all they give me is a slipper an' a glass. I come all the way slidin on me ass [*laughs*].

There you got the most of it didn't ya Halpert? [*laughter*] I never thought ever I'd repeat that much of it.

Duration: 5 min., 3 sec.
Source: Billy Quann (Sagona Island, Fortune Bay), Connaigre Bay, Fortune Bay (fishing voyage), fifty years ago.
Location: Sitting room of teller's house, afternoon.
Audience: Elderly male visitor (neighbor), interviewers.

Context, Style, and Language: Mr. Keeping prefers to rehearse his stories aloud and in full before allowing them to be recorded. Unfortunately, the rehearsed version was longer and much more dramatic than the recorded one presented here. Having just told the rehearsed version he perhaps felt that a more economical one would be adequate. On the other hand he may have been inhibited to some extent by the tape recording, and he refused to allow the taping of a vivid and dramatic personal experience narrative of a hazardous Mediterranean voyage on the grounds that it was not worth recording. His comment at the end of the tale that he never thought he'd be able to remember so much of it indicates that he has probably not told it for a long time, and is further evidence of a declining tradition.

The title of this tale is ambiguous in that the word *Paradise* functions as a possessive but lacks the usual inflection /s/ after the final syllable. We have attempted to resolve this ambiguity by adding an apostrophe, as, for example, in "for conscience' sake," (cf. Partridge, *You Have a Point There,* p. 158, IV), in order better to convey the notion "The garden of the Queen of Paradise." Mr. Keeping's prior rehearsal of the tale results in a shorter retelling here. At first he seems about to begin the narrative without giving the opening formula in full but is encouraged by the interviewer to say it. It proves to be quite elaborate and is spoken in a formulaic patterned manner with strong stresses and insistent rhythm in each phrase, and minimal pauses between segments (cf. the similar openings to Nos. 25, 30, 44, and 89).

The pattern of strong stresses can be represented as follows:

once upon a tíme an' a véry good tíme it wás _ not in your tíme _ 'deed in mý tíme _ in ólden times _ (when) quárt bóttles hóld half a gállon an' hoúse páper with páncakes _ an' pígs run abóut, fórks stuck in their áss _ see who wánted to búy pórk

The speed of the delivery makes transcription difficult in places and, as is often the case with such runs of speech, neither the articulation nor the transcription is precise in every detail. For example, although the word preceding *pancakes* sounds like *with* both here and in No. 30, the later retelling of this tale, the teller may have intended *were*. Even so, as there is no final morpheme in *paper* which might indicate whether it is a verb or part of a compound noun (*house[s] paper[ed] with* or *house paper/papers was/were*) the phrase defies exact resolution. Similar problems surround the verb *hold* (?present or past tense), and the omission of *(?)with* before *forks* and *(?)to* before *see* which is typical of the economy of such patterned spoken runs. The teller obviously enjoys saying the formula and laughs at the end of it in the same way as he does when Jack goes in to see the Queen of Paradise later in the story. At that point, and also near the end of the tale when the Queen recognizes Jack, the teller chuckles and extracts the maximum from the situation by skillful and meaningful use of stresses and other intonational features in the dialogue:

"Have you been [to] Queen o' Paradise' Garden?"
"Yes" he said _ "I've been there."
"(Well)" she said "what did you see there?"
"I see" he said "I seen YOU."

"Well yes" she said "I knows you did!" [*laughter*]

All this byplay and innuendo, however, is kept in a low key and managed with great propriety and decorum which is an essential part of the charm of this particular narrative.

Another interesting feature of the teller's style is the tendency not to pause at the end of a clause or sentence but to run on, often using a conjunction such as *and* immediately after the sentence might be expected to end, and only then to pause briefly after the linking word. This has the effect of giving a sense of flow and continuity to the narration, as the listeners are already primed by the linking word to expect the sentence to continue.

Mr. Keeping's speech tends towards the West Country English type, as in his pronunciation of *been* as /bin/ and his use of *un* (it, him). However, the initial /t/ in *thought,* for example, is reminiscent of Anglo-Irish. In addition to the omission of initial /h/ common in Newfoundland, we find the aspirate added before stressed vowels, often for emphasis, in *apple, ask, everything, disowned;* other pronunciations of note are *route* /raut/, *dead* /di:d/, and *wand* /wen/, the latter perhaps indicating unfamiliarity with the original word. In *cross roads* the second element has the strong stress, and aphesis is found in *'deed* (indeed), *'fore, 'gain* (again). At the morphological level we find *anywheres* and the first and second person singular and third person plural tense verb forms *stoops, gets, knows.* The past tense forms include *done, come, give, you was, knowed, visit;* we also find the past participle *aheard* and the cryptic *he wouldn't done.*

Type and Motifs:

AT551. *The Sons on a Quest for a Wonderful Remedy for their Father.*

Z10.1. *Beginning formula.*

P251.6.1. *Three brothers.*

H1333.3.0.1. *Quest for rejuvenating fruit.*

N772. *Parting at crossroads to go on adventures.*

B172. *Magic bird.*

D478.4. *Transformation: water becomes bloody.*

N825.2. *Old man helper.*

N822. *Magic object received from old man.*

D1313. *Magic object points out road.*

H1235. *Succession of helpers on quest.*

N825.3. *Old woman helper.*

D1470.1.5. *Magic wishing-apple.*

Cf. D1520.4. *Magic transportation by golden apple.*

D1364.4.1. *Apple causes magic sleep.*

D849.4.1. *Magic object found in garden.*

N711.2. *Hero finds maiden in (magic) castle.*

D1210. *Magic musical instrument.*

D1652.1.1. *Inexhaustible bread.*

D1472.1.17. *Magic bottle supplies drink.*

T475.2. *Hero lies by princess in magic sleep and begets child.*

K1815.1. *Return home in humble disguise.*
H1381.2.1. *Woman seeks unknown father of her child.*
H480. *Father tests. Tests as to who is unknown father of child.*
D572.4. *Transformation by wand.*
H1242. *Youngest alone succeeds on quest.*
L161. *Lowly hero marries princess.*
Z10.2. *End formula.*

International Parallels: The story of "The Sons on a Quest for a Wonderful Remedy for their Father" (AT551) is known across Europe and Asia. Both in its overall structure and in many of its episodes it closely resembles versions of AT550, "Search for the Golden Bird." The two Types are analyzed together in the AT index, and Thompson attempts to differentiate them by enumerating the characteristic elements of each. In practice, however, the distinction between them is not so clear-cut; various elements in a given recension may shift from one Type to the other and it is often difficult to decide which Type is dominant. So far as we know there is no comprehensive study of either AT550 or AT551 in English, so their interrelationships have not been explored in detail.

Some of the stories in which the search for the water of life is an important element are discussed in Gerould, *Grateful Dead,* and in MacCulloch, *Childhood of Fiction.* Bolte and Polívka provide extensive parallels to both Types of the story in their annotations to Grimm no. 57, "The Golden Bird," and Grimm no. 97, "The Water of Life." (See references in the *Studies and Notes* below.)

AT551 is well known in Ireland and also among the Gypsies and travellers in Wales and Scotland. However, there are no reports of this tale from England. Although it is well known in the Franco-American tradition in North America, we have located only one English-language version from the United States. Since the story has been so rarely reported in the English language, it is surprising to find no fewer than five versions collected from three narrators in widely separated communities in Newfoundland. All these versions share certain episodes which are more typical of AT551 than of AT550, including the magic garden, the hero's lying with the sleeping princess, and the princess' seeking and finding the father of her child. Several of the other episodes in these recensions are listed in the AT index as being characteristic of AT550, and it therefore appears that they may be recombined in various ways under either Type, their classification as one or the other depending on the predominance of typical elements.

Since the AT types are inevitably somewhat hypothetical constructs, classifications such as AT550 and AT551 with their fluid and largely interchangeable form offer unusual opportunities for utilizing a variety of episodes, elements, and "floating" motifs in different combinations to arrive at the dénouement appropriate for each. As the five recensions presented here demonstrate, such tale types are an ideal vehicle through which Newfoundland storytellers can give free rein to the creativity which characterizes many of their narratives.

Perhaps the clearest way to show how this creativity operates is to compare the recensions told by the three narrators, checking them against the outline of the Type. In each of the five recensions there are three sons, Jack, Tom, and Bill. In each tale all three go on a quest. In Nos. 29 and 30, they seek the Queen of Paradise' Garden which has a fruit that will make their parents young again. In Nos. 32 and 33 the quest is for a bottle of World's End Water to cure their sick father. In No. 31, the somewhat ambiguous quest for the Flower of the World is not for their parents' benefit, nor, unlike the other two quests, is it one included in the AT analysis of Types 550 and 551. Nonetheless the quest has their father's approval since he equips in turn each of the two older sons with good, well-supplied vessels. Jack, the youngest son, is not equally favored since he gets only an old schooner even though it is also well supplied.

The three sons go on the quest, apparently in succession since Incident II of the AT analysis says the first two fail because of their unkindness to animals or people that they meet. Let us see how our Newfoundland stories handle this theme. In Nos. 29 and 30 the three brothers start on the quest for the Queen of Paradise' Garden not in succession but together. At a crossroads near a stream each of the three goes in a separate direction and we hear no more about Tom and Bill till much later in the story. The crossroads as a device to have characters separate, usually in order for them to have individual adventures, is a stock feature of several tale types, for example, AT303, "The Twins or Blood-Brothers." It should be noted that this crossroads separation of the brothers is not a theme included in the AT analysis.

Before the brothers part, each in turn wants to take a drink from the stream. When Bill and Tom try, a little bird whips its tail in the stream and turns the water to blood; when Jack tries, the bird again whips its tail in the water, turning it to wine in No. 29, but just back to water in No. 30. What is curious about this little episode is that none of the brothers has done anything to motivate the bird's actions, unlike the similar motif in No. 27 (AT513B) where the bird's actions reflect the unkindness of the two elder brothers as against the kindness of Jack.

In No. 29 Jack starts off and meets an old man who offers to help him. The old man gives him a pipe on which he is to draw three times and then follow the direction of the smoke. We have had the motif of the pipe with the smoke that serves as a guide in No. 7 (AT313). The smoke leads him to an old woman, who, like the old man, volunteers to help Jack. She gives him a magical apple and instructs him in how to use it. He is to cut a piece out and wish and he will be in the place where he wants to be. In No. 30, he is told his wish will bring him to a hill from which he can see the Queen of Paradise' Garden. Then he is to cut another piece from the apple and wish that all there should fall asleep. In No. 30 the storyteller confuses the order of the incidents, but then realizes he has done so and gives them in the proper sequence. In this telling we have the added information that the piece cut from the apple should go into Jack's mouth before he makes his wish. In neither recension has Jack done anything in particular to earn the assistance of these two helpers.

In No. 31, the brothers set out in succession on the quest for the Flower of the World. Each in turn comes to an old man's house, but Bill and Tom act ungraciously and get no help. Jack, however, acts courteously, insists on the old man joining him at table and sharing his meal. While the old man goes out to do some work, Jack takes a shave. When the old man returns, he admires Jack's shave so Jack shaves him and he looks smart. The old man comments that Jack's two brothers weren't like him, then lends him a pair of two-league boots and sends him to his brother. At the second brother's house Jack repeats his previous actions, insisting that the old man eat with him, shaves himself, and then shaves the old man. The latter lends him five-mile boots and sends him to a third brother. At the third brother's house, the identical series of actions occurs: the sharing of the meal and the two shaves. The third brother lends him a swift white mare, and gives him precise instructions about what he must do. We have had much the same sequence of going to three brothers, shaving each one, and getting their help in No. 7 (AT313).

In Nos. 32 and 33, the three brothers leave in succession by ship to secure a bottle of World's End Water to cure their father. Each in turn gets to the same port and each goes on horseback till he meets an old lady. Bill is told to tie his horse and, after he does so, the woman strikes him with her magic stick and turns him and his schooner to marble. The same happens to Tom. When Jack gets to the woman's door he refuses to tie his horse. When she tries to hit him with the magic stick, Jack jumps aside, then grabs the stick from her and turns her to marble. This curious sequence, certainly not mentioned in the AT analysis, apparently derives from AT303, but in that Type the untied horse (and dog) help the hero to defeat the old woman. In No. 33 there is a different handling of the scene with the witch. When she hits Jack with the magic stick, it just does not work, though we are not told why. At that point Jack leaves without taking any action against the witch. He has not recognized that the marble men are his brothers.

In No. 32 Jack rides on and meets another old witch, a male one, but he is helpful. He tells Jack he must cross a body of water, but that a crow will carry him across. He also gives Jack a spoon to drop when the crow tires and this will create an island on which they can rest. In No. 33 there is no second witch. Jack meets a crow which offers to take him across the water and tells him to take two spoons to create islands on which they can rest. In fact when they travel one spoon is used twice so that they have rest breaks on three islands. In No. 15 (AT325) we have had a similar series of islands on which the eagle rests while it is carrying the boy's father, but they are created from three apples. The crow also instructs Jack on what to do when they reach the other side.

Let us now compare Jack's actions after he nears his goal. In Nos. 29 and 30 he is in complete control of the situation since with his wishing apple he has put everyone to sleep at the court of the Queen of Paradise. In the garden he takes a piece of the fruit that will make his parents young again. He finds the Queen of Paradise lying asleep on a bed inside the castle. Beside her is a piece of music, i.e., a musical instrument, that would play anything, a loaf of bread that does not diminish if a piece is sliced off, and an inexhaustible bottle of wine. He tests the music, the loaf of bread, and the bottle of wine, and then lies with the Queen. Then on the principle that a slice off a cut loaf is never missed, he lies with the Queen again. Afterwards, taking with him the three portable objects, he leaves, pausing at the top of the hill to wish that everything in the garden and palace wake up again. On the way home he gives away to different old farmers the piece of music, the loaf of bread, and the bottle of wine.

In No. 30, he finds and takes the magic fruit, and tests the bottle of wine and loaf of bread on a table and learns of their special qualities. Then in another room he sees the Queen of Paradise lying on a bed, lies with her, and then on the principle that a slice off a cut loaf is never missed, lies with her again. For the proverbial saying "A slice off a cut loaf is never missed" see the North Carolina version "A slice from a cut loaf is never missed" in Whiting, "Proverbs and Proverbial Sayings," p. 477, *Slice,* which gives many references. In checking these references we found only one that even mentioned the saying's use in connection with sexual matters. However, both of the editors, one from New York, the other from northern England, recall that only slightly varied versions of the saying always referred to sexual activities. Again we have the distinct suspicion that such usage is widespread and that the comparative lack of comment on this aspect reflects genteel avoidance of such a topic by most proverb collectors and editors.

To continue with No. 30, when Jack leaves he takes with him not only the loaf and the bottle of wine, but also the piece of music which would play whatever you told it. After cutting another slice of the apple and wishing everything to wake, Jack travels on. In this version the narrator gives more details about the leaving of the three objects with farmers. At one place the farmer regrets that he has no wine to give Jack. Jack produces the inexhaustible bottle; they make merry that night and Jack leaves the bottle with the farmer. Another farmer host regrets that he has no bread for his guest. Jack produces the remarkable loaf, from which they cut all the bread they need, and next morning he leaves the loaf with his host. At a third farmhouse, the owner wishes they could have music, and the piece of music entertains them and is also left behind the next morning. It will be observed that neither in No. 29 nor in No. 30 does Jack use his magic apple to wish himself home. As we will observe later, leaving these objects serves a useful function in the next section of the story.

Very curiously, when Jack gets home nothing is said either in No. 29 or 30 about the magic fruit he had obtained that would make his parents young. Jack is not recognized and does not identify himself. He is hired as a pantry boy.

In No. 31, when Jack arrives at his destination he is aware that the door opens promptly at twelve o'clock but that he must be gone by one. In that hour he finds the Flower of the World asleep, lies with her, and then escapes from the castle by one o'clock. He then returns home with the successive help of the white mare and then the three brothers, each in turn but in reverse order.

In No. 32, Jack has been warned he must pass through a lane of savage beasts just at midnight when they are asleep in order to get to the room of the girl who has the bottle of World's End Water under her pillow. He does this, and sleeps with the girl, staying with her till 4 A.M. when she warns him to leave before the beasts awake. He gets through the lane just in time. The crow takes him back to the port from which they had started. At the first witch's house he finds the magic stick and disenchants his two brothers and their ships. They persuade him to return with them on one of their ships. In order to steal the bottle of World's End Water, they throw him overboard. The crow saves him and flies him home before the brothers arrive.

In No. 33 there are a number of variations from the preceding story, including fuller details at many points. The crow who carries Jack across the body of water advises him to take the horse that is there and travel till he reaches a lane full of savage beasts. Since they only sleep between midnight and one, Jack must go up the lane at midnight and be back out of the lane by one. Jack goes up the lane and comes to a room in which a sleeping girl has the bottle of World's End Water under her pillow. (In neither tale is there any explanation of how the girl obtained the bottle of World's End Water, nor why she sleeps with the bottle under her pillow). She is so pretty that he stays with her till almost one o'clock, but he gets out of the lane just as the animals awake. He again rides the horse to the water's edge and the crow carries him back over the water. At the witch's house he again tells the witch he has not tied his horse, but this time he takes her magic stick from her and turns her into marble. He disenchants his brothers, Bill and Tom, and takes them back with him in his ship. In order to steal the bottle of World's End Water, his brothers throw Jack overboard. In No. 32 he was rescued by the crow. In No. 33 he falls on a lumpfish's back and it carries him to land. In neither case has Jack done anything to make these creatures feel grateful to him; this lack of motivation for their kindness contrasts with the explanation for the helpfulness of the animals in the AT analysis.

The motif of the two treacherous brothers who try to destroy their heroic younger brother and steal what he has obtained is also found in No. 3 (AT301A), while there is a parallel to throwing Jack overboard in No. 96 (AT506B) and in No. 53 (AT888A*). In these two stories Jack is cut adrift in a small boat without oars, and in both, through the aid of supernatural helpers, he is enabled to get ashore at home before the arrival of the treacherous captain who had tried to get rid of him. In these last two stories Jack is recognized and the treacherous captain is punished. Although Jack gets home before his brothers in both No. 32 and No. 33, he becomes a chimney sweeper and is not recognized. It is his brothers who cure their father with the stolen bottle of World's End Water.

Jack's making love to a sleeping lady, which occurs in all the Newfoundland recensions, is paralleled in many versions of AT304; see the notes to No. 4. As is frequently the situation in many versions of AT304, in all of the Newfoundland recensions of AT551, Jack's lovemaking has inevitable consequences. To find her unknown lover, in AT304 the lady sets up an inn where meals are given free in return for each recipient's telling his adventures. By this means the lover is discovered. In our recensions of AT551, the lady takes more vigorous action and goes in search of the unknown man. This might have been an easier task for her if he had written down his name and left it near her on his departure, an action described in the AT analysis, but no such scruple is evidenced in the Newfoundland tales.

In No. 29 and No. 30 when the pregnant Queen of Paradise sets out to find the man responsible for her condition she stops in turn at the houses of the three old farmers, each of whom has received from Jack one of the Queen's possessions, the piece of music, the loaf of bread, and the unfailing bottle of wine. She realizes that the man she is seeking has been there and asks each of them to describe the man. Each describes Jack as the finest kind of a man, thus predisposing her favorably toward him even before she finds him. When she gets to his home, she asks Bill and Tom if either of them has been to her palace. Each claims he has, but she soon finds they are lying and insists on seeing the pantry boy. When she asks Jack if he has been there and what he has seen, he replies he has seen *her*. She replies, "I know you did!" In No. 29 she touches him with a magic wand and he becomes a beautiful prince. They marry. In No. 30 after the Queen finds Bill and Tom were lying, she threatens to smash the place to matchwood unless the man who *has* been to the garden is brought out. Jack is brought from the pantry, and when he says he has been to the garden she knows he is the man. They marry. Nothing is said of a magic wand.

In No. 31, the Flower of the World takes her young son and goes in search of the child's father. She soon finds that neither Bill nor Tom had been there. When Jack appears, the baby promptly greets him with "Dad Dad da." The couple marry.

In Nos. 32 and 33 it is not till seven years later that the lady arrives with her young son to find the man who had brought the bottle of World's End Water to the king. The king produces Bill. Bill claims he had taken the bottle, but the lady puts an electric tape around his neck and warns him that if he lies, his head will come off. When Bill again claims he was the man, his head comes off. The same thing happens to Tom. The young child exclaims when it sees Bill and Tom: "That's not Dadda, Mamma." When the lady asks if there is another son, the king admits that there is Jack, but he is only a chimney sweep and has never been anywhere. When Jack is brought in, the child says, *"That's Dadda, Mamma."* Jack triumphantly passes the lie detector test and retains his head, proving that he was indeed the father of the child. He and the girl marry.

As already noted in the Introduction to this collection, certain tale types are particularly susceptible to change and variation in their structure. Judging by the Newfoundland recensions discussed above, AT551 is clearly one such type. In our five stories few elements remain constant: three brothers, a quest in which only the youngest brother succeeds, and a concluding marriage. The inclusion and ordering of the other episodes and elements vary not only among the three narrators, but even in different tellings by a single narrator.

Studies and Notes

MacCulloch, *Childhood,* pp. 52-79, 353-54; Gerould, *Grateful Dead,* pp. 119-52; Bolte and Polívka, 1, pp. 510-15, no. 57, 2, pp. 394-401, no. 97; Thompson, *The Folktale,* pp. 107-8; Espinosa, *CPE,* 3, pp. 43-51; Delarue and Tenèze, *Catalogue,* 2, pp. 348-51, 363-64; Baughman, *Index,* Type 551, p. 14; Robe, *Index,* Type 551, pp. 98-99.

Canada

Thomas, *Types,* cites 1 version of AT551 from Newfoundland French tradition.
Lacourcière-Low, "Catalogue", cites 43 Francophone versions of AT551 from Canada: 2 (Nova Scotia), 13 (New Brunswick), 26 (Quebec), 2 (Ontario).

United States

M. Campbell, *Tales,* pp. 183-85, no. 1 (Kentucky).
Carrière, *Tales,* pp. 167-72, no. 34, French text with English summary (Missouri).
Thomas, *Oral,* pp. 108-15, no. 10, French text and English trans. (Missouri).
Lea, *Literary,* pp. 186-89, Spanish tradition, in English (New Mexico).
Robe-Jameson, *Folktales,* pp. 95-98, no. 57, reduced version, Spanish tradition, in English (New Mexico).

Lacourcière-Low, "Catalogue," cites 1 Francophone version of AT551 from the United States: 1 (Missouri).

Mexico
Wheeler, *Tales,* pp. 346-50, no. 118 (with cf. 505), Spanish text with English summary (Jalisco).
See Robe, *Index,* Type 551, for other Mexican references.

The Caribbean and South America
Parsons, *Antilles,* 3, p. 281, no. 282F, English summary of French text (Marie Galante, West Indies).
See Hansen, *Types,* Type 551, for references to versions from the Dominican Republic, Puerto Rico, Uruguay, Argentina, and Chile.

Wales
Groome, *Tents,* pp. 299-317, Gypsy (Wales), and rpt. in Groome, *Folk-Tales,* pp. 220-32, no. 55, with notes, pp. 232-34, and rpt. with changes in Jacobs, *More English,* pp. 132-45, no. 71, and rpt. in Briggs, *Dictionary,* A1, pp. 355-63.

Scotland
Cf. Briggs, *Dictionary,* A1, pp. 560-61, from School of Scottish Studies recording, incomplete version, Scottish traveller (Banff-shire).
Campbell, *Popular Tales,* 1, pp. 164-75, no. 9, Gaelic text and English trans., travelling tinker (Scottish Highlands), and trans. rpt. in Groome, *Folk-Tales,* pp. 272-78, no. 73.
Cf. Douglas, *Tocher,* no. 31 (Summer 1979), 36-46, Scottish traveller (Perthshire), and see Douglas, *King,* pp. 20-25, for a slightly varied version from the same narrator.

Ireland
Cf. Curtin, *Myths,* pp. 93-113 (Ireland).
MacManus, *Well,* pp. 1-20, pp. 164-89, 2 versions (Co. Donegal).
Kennedy, *Stories,* pp. 87-91 (Co. Wexford).
An Seabhac, *Béal.* 2 (1929-30), 223-24, no. 4, English summary of Irish text (Co. Kerry).
Ó Duilearga, *Béal.* 30 (1962), 39-46, no. 7 (with 550) (Co. Clare).
Gregory, *Wonder Book,* pp. 180-83 (Co. Galway).
Dillon, *King,* pp. 37-51 (Co. Galway).
Gmelch and Kroup, *Road,* pp. 79-81 (with cf. 301A), Irish traveller (Co. Roscommon).
Hyde, *Fire,* pp. 129-41 (Co. Mayo).
Irish Types, Type 551, 90 versions.

Continental Europe and the Middle East
See Grimm no. 97, "The Water of Life," in Grimm-Hunt, 2, pp. 50-55, no. 97, composite text, and 2, pp. 399-401, no. 97, notes (Germany); for other trans. see Grimm-Magoun, pp. 356-61, no. 97, and Grimm-Zipes, pp. 356-61, no. 97.
Dasent, *Fjeld,* pp. 289-311 (Norway).
Hodne, *Types,* AT551, 9 versions (Norway).
Webster, *Legends,* pp. 182-87 (Basque).
Cf. Webster, *Legends,* pp. 111-20 (cf. 551, with 313, III, 314) (Basque).
Calvino, *Folktales,* pp. 207-13, no. 61 (Italy).
Wolf, *Fairy Tales,* pp. 50-60 (Germany).
Cf. Curtin, *Myths and Folk-Tales,* pp. 273-94 (with cf. 301A) (Czech).

Jones and Kropf, *Folk-Tales*, pp. 288-98, no. 51 (Hungary).

Curtin, *Fairy Tales*, pp. 61-78, pp. 175-94, 2 versions (Hungary).

Dégh, *Society*, pp. 307-8, no. 29 (with 550), notes (Hungary).

Sturdza, *Fairy Tales*, pp. 245-83, literary (Romania).

Cf. Cooper, *Tricks*, pp. 159-73 (with 550) (Albania).

Megas, *Folktales*, pp. 25-37, no. 20 (Greece).

Cf. Walker and Uysal, *Tales*, pp. 10-24, no. 1 (551, I, III, IV, with cf. 301A, cf. 300) (Turkey).

Bain, *Fairy Tales*, pp. 96-111 (with 301, V) (Russia).

Curtin, *Myths and Folk-Tales*, pp. 72-81 (Russia).

Cf. Coxwell, *Folk-Tales*, pp. 763-67, no. 23 (in verse) (Russia).

Cf. Afanas'ev, *Fairy Tales*, pp. 314-20 (with 300, 301A) (Russia).

Cortes, *Folk Tales*, pp. 74-78 (with 613) (White Russia).

Dirr, *Folk-Tales*, pp. 86-91, no. 14, Avarian people (Caucasus).

Cf. Downing, *Folk-Tales*, pp. 46-50 (cf. 551, with 550) (Turkish Armenia).

Schwartz, *Violin*, pp. 133-37, Jewish tradition (Iraqi Kurdistan).

Asia

Davidson and Phelps, *JAF* 50 (1937), 4-8, no. 1, Portuguese text and English trans. (New Goa, Bombay, India).

Cf. Bompas, *Folklore*, pp. 244-47, no. 81, Santal Parganas (Central India).

Elwin, *Folk-Tales*, pp. 3-13, no. 1 (with 301A, 1061) (Mahakoshal, Central India).

Parker, *Village*, 1, pp. 57-66, no. 4, pp. 173-78, no. 22, 2, pp. 356-60, no. 152, 3 versions (Ceylon).

Clouston, *Romances*, pp. 240-88, literary, and notes, pp. 519-40 (Persia).

See Thompson and Roberts, *Types*, Type 551, for additional Indian references and analysis.

Cf. Mayer, *Guide*, pp. 92-93, no. 88 [youngest son secures Nara pears to cure father's blindness, and rescues his 2 brothers swallowed by monster] (Japan).

Africa

African versions of AT551 differ considerably from the European form. A tribal chief is very ill and can only be cured if someone will bring to him the great doctor: a huge python or other big snake. Various people (the king's sons/the men of the tribe) attempt this but are frightened by the great snake. When they fail, only a daughter (or the youngest son, or all the king's young children) has the courage to carry the python to cure the king and then carry it back to its cave.

Cf. Posselt, *Fables*, pp. 39-41 [daughter], Bantu people, Barozwi tribe (Rhodesia).

Cf. Tracey, *Lion*, pp. 10-14, no. 3 [children; magic song given with tune], Shona people (Rhodesia).

Cf. Stayt, *Bavenda*, pp. 330-33, no. 1 [youngest son; song given with tune], BaVenda tribe (Northern Transvaal, South Africa).

Cf. Junod, *Life*, 2, pp. 248-51 [little boy], Thonga tribe (Mozambique).

Cf. Klipple, *Folk Tales*, pp. 430-31 [youngest son], English summary of tale from Berthoud, "Weitere Thonga-Märchen," Thonga tribe (Mozambique).

Albert Heber Keeping with one of his grandchildren

30. THE QUEEN OF PARADISE' GARDEN

Albert Heber Keeping   AT551
Grand Bank, Fortune Bay   TC432 65-16
27 August 1967   Collector: HH

[Int: What do you call it?]
Uh Jack, Bill an' Tom, a story about uh...if you could find the Queen o'
Paradise' Garden you see you'd uh...you'd find a fruit growin there that 'd
make your father an' mo(ther)...young again. So the...three brothers started
out on the road _ to...look for the Queen o' Paradise' Garden an' uh...they
stopped at the crossroads uh...where they were goin to take separate roads
ya know an' uh...there's a...little stream runnin there so _ they stooped down
to have a drink you see so _ Bill an' Tom stooped down to have a drink and
a little bird was there, she whipped her tail into it an' she turned it into blood
an' they couldn't drink it you see so (when) Jack stooped down she turned
it back to water again an' he enjoyed the drink see so they...they started off
anyway so uh*...on the...on the way along uh...Jack meets (this) old woman   *phone rings
he sa[id]...he said uh...she asked him where he was goin, well he said he
was lookin for the Queen o' Paradise' Garden. Well she had a apple. An'
she _ takes out the apple an' she gives him [it]

"Now" she said "you see that hill over there? When you get over there
you cut a piece out o' the apple an' you wish you was on the OTHER hill."
And sure enough that's...that's...that's what /he/ did see. An'...and then he   /she/
meets another old one an' uh...he asked* un where he was goin an' he told   *phone rings
un an' _ he had a pipe an' he...he took a draw* o' the pipe an' said "Which   *phone rings
way was...smoke goes that's [the] way you go."*   *phone rings

So he went on like that till he...uh...he...he come to the last one that he
met an' uh...that's...uh...that's where er...she give him a...after, before me
story I think, that's where she give him a piece of apple.

"Now" she said "when you gets on to the hill over there you look down
an' you'll see the Queen o' Paradise' Garden. An' you cut a piece out the
apple an' just as you're puttin it in your mouth you wish everything fall
asleep." And so -- sure enough when he got on the hill he looked down an'
seen the Quee[n] o' Paradise' Garden you know and...he cut a piece o' th'
apple an' put [it] in his mouth an' everything fell asleep, the blacksmiths fell
asleep at the anvil an' everybody fell asleep like they was, so he walked
down an' he...he FOUND the fruit _ that _ is growin there to make his father
an'...mother young again so he took that an'...he's havin a look around an'
there was a bottle o' wine on the table an' he had a drink out o' the bottle so
the bottle...was just as full as ever. [Male listener: Yeah.] Never missed at
all. So there's a loaf of bread there, he cut off a slice of bread an' the loaf

329

of bread was just as big as ever (see)...so ‿ he['] lookin around, he went into different rooms an' he seen the Queen o' Paradise lyin on the bed you know so uh...he went in with her you see an' uh...he comes out again, well he thought to hisself "Bugger. A slice off a cut loaf is never missed so here goes in again." So he went in again see [*laughs*] so ‿ when he left it, when he got up on the hill he cut another piece out o' the apple an' he put (it) in his mouth, he wished everything wake up. (No)...I['m] before me story with that because he found something there, he found a piece o' music, whatever you tell it 'twould **PLAY.** An' then...the loaf o' bread an' the bottle o' wine he took that.

On his way back home he stopped at the...some old farmer's you know an' the old man said "We aint got very much here."

"Well" Jack said "I got a bottle o' wine here, the more you drinks out of he, he's just as full as ever." So they had a...**GRAND** night see.

Then the next place he put up to the old farmer said "We aint got no bread."

Anyway Jack said "I got a loaf here...the more you cuts off him he's just as big as ever" so -- the next place he put up, the next old farmer er...this piece o' music, th' old man said "[If] we had some music now well we'd have a good time."

So Jack said "I got a piece here [which plays] whenever you tells it to play."

So ‿ finally -- he passes along that way an' he arrives back home, well he's gone so long that uh...nobody don't recognise him when he gets home, even his people don't...recognise him but Bill (an') Tom is home. An' they rejoined but Jack had to go stay with some of (his) relatives I suppose they didn't [recognise him]...you know and ‿ finally uh...his mother an' father they...they wanted a servant see, they wanted a boy to work in the pantry so uh...they hires Jack on, they didn't know 'twas his so[n]...their son see so they hired un on for to do the job an' uh ‿ finally the Queen o' Paradise uh...there's uh...there's somethin wrong with her so she got (to) start out to find the man that...that done it you see so she starts on the same route that Jack did and she puts up ‿ to the same houses that uh...Jack put up, the first...house she put up [was] where the...where the bottle o' wine was to an'..."Yes" she said. "I knows somethin 'bout that" she said. "What kind of a man was he?"

"Well" he [*the man at the house*] said "he [*Jack*] was the finest kind of a man just (the) same he...the very best."

"Yes" she said "he must have been or he wouldn't have done what he **HAVE** done."

So the next time she...put up [with] the same old farmer with the loaf of bread you see. On the way along (an') she put up with the same (place /new beauty/   where the /piece of music/ is) she said "That's the man."

330

An' she arrives at Jack's home town an' uh...she interviewed uh...Bill an' Tom you know. She had 'em before the court you know see. An' uh...she said to uh..."Was you to Queen o' Paradise' Garden?"

"Yes" he said.

/She/ said "What d' you see there?" Well he seen this an' that an' the other thing an'...he never named up nothin that was there you see, well she said "You haven't been there." So they...they have the other feller up _ Bill or Tom whichever one 'twas now come up next and she questioned him about what he seen (in) the Queen o' Paradise' Garden, he named up [a] lot of stuff that wasn't there at all so _ she said "YOU haven't been there. But" she said "there's somebody in this house have BEEN there" she said "an' if you don't...bring him out" she said "I'll have this...big [pla]ce [smashed like] matchwood to the ground see." /He/

Well th' ol' woman says "We got a boy that works in the pantry" she says "I knows HE /aint/ been there" so Jack comes out an' he got his hands all dough where he's mixin up something on 'em, she said "(There's)...were you to Queen [o'] Paradise' Garden?" /(have)/

"Yes" he said "I was there."

(Said) "What you see there?"

"I seen YOU!"

"Yes" she said "well I knows you seen me too!" [*laughs loudly*]

So they got married an' they lived happy ever afterwards. An' all they give me 's (a) slipper an' a glass. I come all the way slidin on me ass.

Old Billy Quann belong to Sagona. Yeah.
[Int. What was his name?]
Billy Quann.
[Int: And where was he from?]
Sagony. Yeah Sagony.

Duration: 5 min., 31 sec.
Source: Billy Quann (Sagona Island, Fortune Bay), Connaigre Bay, Fortune Bay (fishing voyage), fifty years ago.
Location: Sitting room of teller's house, afternoon.
Audience: Elderly male visitor (neighbor), interviewer.

Context, Style, and Language: The teller is undeterred by the persistent ringing of the telephone in the early stages of the narrative. His neighbor responds with a quiet "Yeah" to the fact that the bottle of wine remains full after Jack drinks from it, reminding us again of the restrained but positive way in which the listeners frequently reassure the teller that they are following and appreciating what he says.

331

This later version of the story, by the same narrator as No. 29, is rather longer and more elaborate in some respects. It lacks the opening formula of the earlier version and although the plots are parallel there are many minor points of difference. These extend to the language in that the later version, for example, uses *whipped* rather than *flicked* with reference to the bird's tail, *the crossroads* for *three cross roads,* it is an *old woman* not an *old man* who gives Jack the magical pipe, there are hints of an original list of people such as blacksmiths who fall asleep after Jack wishes them to do so which are lacking in No. 29, the humorous use of the proverb "a slice off a cut loaf is never missed" is given added weight by being preceded by a jocular curse, and the praise of Jack as "the finest kind of a man" is part of the greater elaboration of the Queen of Paradise's quest to find Jack which is described much more briefly in the earlier version. Strong stresses are also more in evidence, e.g., *other, found, play, grand, have, you, been, he,* revealing a more animated style of narration.

In addition to the linguistic notes on No. 29, it will be seen that many commas have been used to indicate sense-breaks in the transcription as the teller pauses so rarely at such points. The initial sound is lost in *'twould* and *'twas,* the objective pronoun is omitted in *she gives him,* and grammatical gender survives in the use of *him* for *it* with reference to the loaf of bread; *named up* is used in the sense of "listed by name" and we also find the reflexive pronoun *hisself.* Second person and third person plural present tense verb forms include *drinks, cuts,* and *hires,* and the negative *aint* occurs too, while in the past tense we have *he seen* and *somebody. . .have been,* and the double negatives *nobody don't recognise* and *never named up nothing.*

See also the notes to No. **29.**

Type and Motifs:

AT551. *The Sons on a Quest for a Wonderful Remedy for their Father.*

H1333.3.0.1. *Quest for rejuvenating fruit.*

P251.6.1. *Three brothers.*

N772. *Parting at crossroads to go on adventures.*

B172. *Magic bird.*

D478.4. *Transformation: water becomes bloody.*

N825.3. *Old woman helper.*

D821. *Magic object received from old woman.*

D1470.1.5. *Magic wishing-apple.*

Cf. D1520.4. *Magic transportation by golden apple.*

H1235. *Succession of helpers on quest.*

N825.2. *Old man helper.*

D822. *Magic object received from old man.*

D1313. *Magic object points out road.*

D1364.4.1. *Apple causes magic sleep.*

D849.4.1. *Magic object found in garden.*

D1472.1.17. *Magic bottle supplies drink.*

D1652.1.1. *Inexhaustible bread.*

N711.2. *Hero finds maiden in (magic) castle.*

T475.2. *Hero lies by princess in magic sleep and begets child.*

D1210. *Magic musical instrument.*

K1815.1. *Return home in humble disguise.*

H1381.2.1. *Woman seeks unknown father of her child.*

H480. *Father tests. Test as to who is unknown father of child.*

H1242. *Youngest alone succeeds on quest.*

L161. *Lowly hero marries princess.*

Z10.2. *End formula.*

International Parallels: See No. 29.

31. THE FLOWER OF THE WORLD[†]

Az McLean   AT551
Payne's Cove, Great Northern Peninsula   TC133 64-17
11 July 1964   Collector: M. M. Firestone

Well one time there was a ol' king anyway have three sons _ by the name Jack, Tom an' Bill. Well when they got growed up men they said to go seek for the Flower o' the World.

Well...Bill said he'd go an' seek for the Flower o' the World, well th' ol' king he fit un out with a new schooner, cert[ainly] the best to eat an' drink. He sailed away so far as he could stay on his schooner an' he got out an' walked. Anyway he come to a halfway house. Well he aks th' ol' man for a boardin house.

"Well yes" he said "never a man here yet but I give him a boardin house anyway."

Well after he got in, mind _ Bill he had the best to eat an' drink an' they were very poor off, mind, like lots of us. Anyway Bill eat it back by hisself anyway.

"Well now Bill" he said "you're seekin for the Flower o' the World"

Well Bill said "Yes"

"Well" he said "you're goina have a poor chance."

Well Bill got out next day an' he walked an' walked till he seed no light. Anyway he turned round to go back. Well far as I can mind when he got back to his schooner he [was just] about ragged an' tore up anyway. He got in his schooner an' sailed for home, flags hoist, gun firin, "Welcome Bill wi' the Flower o' the World." But you've been a lot handier to gettin [it than] what Bill had, mind.

333

Well...Tom said he'd go and seek for the Flower o' the World. Well certain[ly] the ol' king he fit un out with a new schooner, certain[ly] the best to eat an' drink. He sailed away so far as he could sail _ in his schooner, he got out an' he walked. Anyway he come to a halfway house. Well he aks th' ol' man for a boardin house

"Well yes" he said "never a man (here) yet but I give him a boardin house anyway."

Well mind now...Tom he had the best to eat an' drink an' th' ol' man he were very poor off (like) lots of us is, mind, anyway. Well certainly Tom eat it back by hisself

"Well now Tom" he said "you're seeking for the Flower o' the World"
Well Tom said "Yes."

"Well" he said "you're goina have a poor chance."

Well the next day he got out an' he walked an' walks till he seed no light, anyway he turned around to go back. Well far as I can mind about when he got back to his schooner _ well he was just about ragged an' tore up. Well he got in his schooner an' sailed for home, flags hoist, gun firin _ "Welcome Tom wi' the Flower o' the World" but you been a lot handier to gettin [it than] what Tom had.

Well Jack said he'd go an' seek for the Flower o' the World. Well ol' king he thought nothing o' Jack anyway. Well he give him a ol' schooner. Sure the best to eat an' drink, he had to give him that, he never had no worse than that to give un.

Well he sailed away so far as he could sail in his schooner, he got out an' walked, anyway he come to a halfway house. Well he ash...aks th' ol' man for a...aks th' ol' man for a boardin house.

"Why yes" he said. "There was never a man yet but I give him a boardin house anyway."

Well after he got in certainly Jack _ mind now he had the best to eat an' drink an' th' ol' man they were...poor off mind like lots of us is.

"Well now" Jack said to th' ol' man "you got to come an' eat [wi'] me"
"Oh no" he said.

"Oh yes" he said. So he come an' eat wi' Jack.

Well th' ol' man said to Jack _ Jack's beard was pretty long today, mine too, well th' ol' man said to Jack "I got to do me work, don't mind me."

"Oh" Jack said "I got to have a bit of a clean up. I'll have that when you're gone"

"Alright sure" he said.

Well after th' ol' man was gone certainly Jack he had a shave an' that, well when th' ol' man come back he hardly knowed Jack. He was such a smart man.

"Oh my! Jack" he said "could you do that [to] me?"
"Yes" Jack said "sure."

So Jack shaved up he too, yes he was a smart lad now, he's somethin worth lookin at.

"Well now Jack" he said "you're seekin for the Flower o' the World"

Well Jack said "Yes."

"Well" he said "you're goina have a chance."

He said "Your brothers was here" he said "an' they wasn't a bit like you"

Jack said "No."

"Well now" he said "I got some two-mile boots here" he said "every step they go two mile. At sunset ya see my brother's house, turn the boots an' boots 'll come home."

Anyway he took the two-mile boots an' every step they went two mile, sunset he seen the house ahead of him, he turned round the boots an' the boots went home.

Well he went up th' ol' man's house an' he aksed for a boardin house.

"Why yes" he said. "Never a man (come) yet but I give him a boardin house anyway."

Well after they got in certainly Jack he had the best to eat an' drink. Mind th' ol' man he were very poor off like lots of us is anyway.

Well now Jack said to th' old man "You got to come an' eat [wi'] me."

"Oh no" he said

"Oh yes" he said.

So he come an' eat wi' Jack. Well Jack's beard used to grow pretty fast mind. He was just so long today as he was the day before.

Well ol' man said to Jack "I got to do my work, don't mind me."

"Oh" Jack said "I had...got have a bit of a clean up. I have that when you're gone"

"Alright sure" he said.

Well after /the old man/ was gone certainly he had a shave and that an' clean up an' when /Jack/ come back...th' ol' man come back he hardly knowed Jack. He was such a smart man. /Jack/ /Jay/

"Oh my! Jack" he said "could you [do] that [to] me?"

"Yes" Jack said "sure."

So Jack shaved up he too, I tell ya [he was] a smart lad. Now he's somethin worth lookin at.

"Well now Jack" he said "you're seekin for the Flower o' the World"

Well Jack said "Yes."

"Well" he says "you're goina have a chance."

He said "You were to my brother's house last night."

"Well" Jack said "I don't know" he said "but I was to a man's house."

"Well yes" he said "an' he help [ya] along"

"Yes" he said.

"Well" he said "I'll help ya along today." He says "I got some five-mile boots here" he said "every step they go five mile. Sunset you seen my brother's house, turn the boots an' boots 'll come home."

Anyway he took the five-mile boots an' every step they went five mile. Sunset he seen th' house ahead of him, he turned the boots an' boots went home.

Well he went up th' ol' man's house an' he aksed for a boardin house.

"Why yes" he said. "There's never a man come yet but I give him a boardin house anyway."

Well after they got in certainly Jack mind he had the best to eat an' drink, well ol' man were very poor off _ like lots of us is.

"Well now" Jack said "you got to come an' eat [wi'] me"

"Oh no" he said

"Oh yes" he says

(So) he come an' eat wi' Jack.

Well Jack's beard used to grow pretty fast too mind. He was just so long today as he was the day before.

Well th' ol' man...said to Jack "I got to do my work, don't mind me."

"Oh" Jack said "I got to have a bit of a clean up. I have that when you're gone"

"Alright sure" he said.

Well after he was gone Jack had a shave an' that, well when th' ol' man come back he hardly knowed Jack, such a smart man.

"Oh my! Jack" he said "could you [do] that [to] me?"

"Yes" Jack said "sure."

So Jack shaved up he too, I tell you he was a smart lad now, he's something worth lookin at anyway.

"Well now Jack" he said "you're seekin for the Flower o' the World"

Well Jack said "Yes."

"Well" he said "you're goina have a chance. Well" he said "you was to my brother's house last night."

"Well" Jack said "I don't know" he said "but I was to a man's house."

"Well yes" he said "an' he helped [ya] along"

"Yes" he said.

"Well" he said "I'll help ya along today." He said "I got a white mare here she's swifter than the wind. At twelve o'clock you be there" he said "all doors open. But whatever [ya] do" he said "be gone again at one" he said "[or] you'll be shot."

So Jack took the white mare swifter than the wind, at twelve o'clock he got there, he hove his reins on over the post an' went to search for the Flower o' the World. Well five minutes to one he found the Flower o' the World. At one o'clock the gun fired, they just got the glimpse o' Jack goin out of sight so he never had very long with her, mind, anyway.

Well he worked back by help the same as he got there an' he got back to his schooner. Well he sailed for home. Perhaps there was a flag hoist, perhaps there was a gun fired. "Welcome Jack wi' the Flower o' the World" didn't think he seen her anyway.

Well certainly after Jack was home nine months the Flower o' the World she had a young son. Well certainly after the young son was old enough certainly she had to go an' look for the father o' the son. Well she comes to the old king's house, she aksed un didn't he have a son

"Why yes" he said.

Well he called in Tom. My son when he come in dressed he...uh...come in he was dressed up, he was worth lookin at when he come through the door I tell ya.

Well she said that wasn't he.

When he turned around an' called in Bill, my son if Tom was dressed up I tell ya he was past dressed up, well he were worth lookin at when he come through the door.

Well she said that wasn't he.

"Well haven't ya got another one?" /she/ said.   /he/

"No" he said he never had nar son, he had a something out there he said.

Well she said she want to see un.

Well he called in Jack. Well he wasn't dressed up half like Tom an' Bill. Perhaps a little better than a man be goin in the woods anyway. But when Jack come through the door the little child three months old said "Dad Dad da" so that must ha' been he.

An' they got married an' if they didn't live happy I don't know who did. They had children in baskets _ (hove outdoors) [in] shelffuls _ sent to the sea to make sea pies an' the last time I seen 'em I wished 'em goodbye an' I haven't seen ar one sunce.

Duration: 6 min., 42 sec.

Source: Andrew McLean (uncle), Shoal Harbour East, Great Northern Peninsula, "when I was eighteen or twenty."

Location: The house of Gilbert Parrell, teller's stepbrother, evening.

Audience: Teller's wife, people of the household, John Crane (a well-known traditional singer from Pines Cove), interviewer and his wife.

Context, Style, and Language: (For context see notes to No. 15).

For the main linguistic features of this teller's style, see the notes to Nos. 15 and 16. The typical allegro speech again poses the problems previously discussed, but the gist of the story is communicated nevertheless. We also again find the formula "[as] far as I can mind" which suggests that the events in the tale are actually remembered by the teller. This is an important aspect of the interaction between performer and audience, and serves as a kind of mock self-deprecation, implying that the speaker cannot quite remember accurately, as if, like any ordinary person, he claims no special powers of memory, while at the same time amply demonstrating such powers in the actual storytelling. The teller also amusingly involves himself in the narration, by proxy as it were, by remarking in a humorous aside to the audience that his beard is long, like Jack's. The description of the dress of a man going into the woods and the reference to poverty: "they were...poor off mind like lots of us is," add local color for the Newfoundland audience and contribute to the humor underlying the performance to which the listeners readily respond. Repeated formulaic utterance is also very much in evidence, spoken at the breathless pace for which this speaker is noted. These formulas, repeated with almost monotonous rapidity, contrast strongly with the versions of this tale Type by other tellers, as does also the cryptic, staccato, and frequently monosyllabic narration.

Although *nar* (no, not any) and *ar one* (any) are used in this tale, the teller also repeats the formulaic "never a man here," illustrating how these constructions exist side by side in current Newfoundland usage. Also common in local speech are *handier* (nearer), the use of *he* with reference to beard, the subject form of the third person pronoun in *that wasn't he*, the reflexive *hisself*, the present tense forms *[he] have, us is,* the past tense forms *fit, aks* (asked), *hove, come, your brothers was, they wasn't, he were,* the past participle *tore*, and the double negative *never had no worse*.

See also the notes to Nos. 15 and 16.

Type and Motifs:
AT551. *The Sons on a Quest for a Wonderful Remedy for their Father.*
P251.6.1. *Three brothers.*
Cf. H1333.5. *Quest for marvelous flower.*
Cf. H1301. *Quest for the most beautiful of women.*
N825.2. *Old man helper.*
F151.0.1. *Hospitable host entertains (guides, advises) adventurer on way to otherworld.*
L101. *Unpromising hero (male Cinderella).*
Q2. *Kind and unkind.*
D817.2. *Magic object received in return for being shaved.*
Cf. D1521.1. *Seven-league boots.*
H1235. *Succession of helpers on quest.*
B184.1.1. *Horse with magic speed.*
Cf. R121.6.2. *Locks marvelously open for person.*
C761.4. *Tabu: staying too long in certain place.*
Cf. N711.2. *Hero finds maiden in (magic) castle.*
Cf. T475.2. *Hero lies by princess in magic sleep and begets child.*
H1381.2.1. *Woman seeks unknown father of her child.*
H480. *Father tests.*

H481. *Infant picks out his unknown father.*
L161. *Lowly hero marries princess.*
Z10.2. *End formula.*

International Parallels: See No. 29.

32. THE BOTTLE OF WORLD'S END WATER[†]

Allan Oake
Beaumont, Green Bay, Notre Dame Bay
10 September 1966

AT551
TC308, 309 66-24
Collectors: JW and Harold Paddock

[*recorder off*]*** now Jack. There was a...had un t...an' Jack we'll say was
an ol' king's son, there was three of 'em see, there was Jack, Tom an'...an'
Bill. Well th' ol' king was sick. Got sick, well there was nothing can cure
un _ unless he could get a...a bottle o' water from the...the...a bottle o'
WORLD'S end water _ [we'll] call [un]. Well that couldn't be got only to the
world's end. Well Bill told un if he'd uh...buy un a ship _ that he'd go an'
get this bottle o' world's end water. So alright.

  Went an'...he bought the ship an' he got his crew you know an'
went uh...went so far as they could in port. An' uh...anchored we'll
say they couldn't get no further. Well they went ashore an' there was
an ol'...there was an ol' lady there you know she...she had a **MAGIC**
stick (of) course. An' uh...[*sighs*] they went there then...on horses and
horseback they arrived...rode there. And she...she told un to tie on
his horse outside. (Well) he tied on his horse an' he went in. An' he
was askin her about you know goin to the...gettin to the world's end.
But the once she slewed around wi' this stick an'...an' struck un see an'
turned un into a **MARBLE** stone _ schooner an' the works out there in the
harbour.

  Well _ years passed we'll say an' there was no sound...[o'] no type from
Bill. So this Tom he told un...come in one day an'*...an' told un that
uh...he uh...if he'd...have a ship for un...get a ship for un he'd...he'd go
an' get this...bottle o' world's end water.

  So he got a ship for un. Started off. (An') he...anchored in the same port
passin along wi' this big marble stone out there in the...an' anchored we'll
say an' went ashore an' he done the same **THING**. Got a horse then for to
ride on you know miles away _ course _ to the next place for...where he had
_ to go.

*listener
coughs

339

Well he went in, she called un in we'll say an' he had his horse tied outside. [*clears throat*] And she started lookin around wi' this...her...this stick we'll say an' struck HE an'...turned he into marble stone an'...an' ship as well.

Well years pass you know there was no talk of he. So Jack went in the house one day an' he said um _ "Father" he said _ "'ee buy me a ship" he said.

"Well my son" he said --

"I'm goin to the world's end" he said "(to get) a bottle o' world's end...water to cure you."

"Well" he said "Bill nor d...nor Tom hant adone it" he said "an' YOU won't do it."

He said "You buy me a ship an' see."

/allrest/ Well /alright/ he decided _ to buy a ship. So _ started off.

Come to this place you know where he had...port he had to go in. Went in there an' anchored, went...say (went) ashore there an' he got his horse _ went up to this old woman's door an' she come out an' opened the door.

"Tie your horse first" she said.

"No ma'm" he said "he...he don't NEED to be tied." So he went in, by an' by she...he seen her gettin this magic stick you know. [*clears throat*] When she hit at un he jump one side an' he grabbed the stick an' he...hit at SHE. Well turned SHE into a marble stone.

Well he's...he got on his horse back an' he rode on. So far as he could ride. An' he...he runned up again an ol' witch _ on that...on that route. Th' ol' witch told un an'...you know _ what he had to do. He [*the witch*] told un that uh...he had to...cross water the next mornin. An' there'd be a...there'd be a CROW _ take un across water. An' he told Jack to take a...take spoon _ so _ you know when he'd get tired _ drop this spoon and there'd be island rise for un to pitch [i.e., *land*] on. An' he done so. When he got tired you know he...he dropped this spoon. [*sighs*] Island rose up an' the crow rested you know and...Jack arest...('fore) he started off again.

By an' by he finally rested. The world's end you know an' he had to go up a lane now. This er...bottle o' world's end water was under...was under a girl's pillow. An' he had to go up through a lane now with all kinds o' sava[ge]...savage beastes _ into this lane. But the hour they got there you know, the hour he got there they was all asleep, twelve o'clock. Well he went up we'll say an' went into her room _ where she was to and...well she was...she was that pretty of course he had to hang on a while. [*clears throat*] He _ hung on to four o'clock. She told un he'd have to get out because the beast'd soon be woke. So he left. Alright.

Come back _ just as he got through the...close the gate they all woke, was right savage. He come back (waited) until this crow we'll say that

340

wa[s]...it was waitin for un, he got on this crow back an' fled to this island. Pitched there an' had a spell an' he come back. He come back we'll say an' took his horse. An' come on to this uh...this place where he went in. Now he went in there we'll say an' uh...wi' this stick he started lookin around. By an' by he hooked out Tom an' Bill see. An' he had it all changed now, they was all come to life and their ships out in the port too _ was all come back but this old woman she was still _ she was still _ a marble stone.

So they wanted Jack to get aboard with /THEY/. They'd take un home. On the last of it he decided he would. But they knowed he had the bottle o' world's near...world's end water. Alright.　　　　　　　　　　　　/HE/

Got aboard wi' Jack. [clears throat] An' on the way home see they hove him overboard _ once they had the bottle of world's end now. But when he pitched _ he pitched...he pitched in a...on...a...pitched in the water. An' there was...this...c...crow that brought un from those islands come an' picked un up. An' he had...he was in port three days ahead of uh...Bill an' they. Well he gained uh...he uh...joined uh...as a s...tim...chimley sweeper after he got back in port. An' they...never let nobody know see that he was back.

Well by an' by Tom an' they come an'...well they had...Bill had uh...the bottle o'...world's end water. Alright. [clears throat] Well that cured un. There was nothing about Jack _ you know he was still there but THEY didn't know un. (You know) his old ragged clothes an' all of it there an'...was chimley sweeper.

An' by an' by this girl...seven year from that see this girl arrived _ with a young son wi' her _ lookin for...king's son. Well he...he...she arrived in ship. You know the first one went DOWN was Bill an' she told Bill now...an' she had a electric tape see _ if he'd tell a lie _ [clears throat] she'd put this electric tape around un 'cause he told her 'twas HE you know that uh...got the world's...bottle o' world's end water. If 'twas a lie _ his head 'd come off. Well _ he done so.

She put the tape around an'...an' he...still told her 'twas he an' uh...his head come off. She asked the king if he had ar 'nother son. Yes. He had another son so...TOM come down. Said the same thing. An' she told un now not to tell no lies 'cause if 'twa[s]...'twas uh really a lie _ [coughs] 'cause every time this Bill's comin down see her...her son said..."That's not Dadda, Mamma." An' the same when Tom come down see _ comin down the wharf "That's not Dadda, Mamma" _ he'd say. So -- his head come off.

She asked the king _ if he...didn't he have another son? He HAD one he said but he...he'd went away, he been gone for years. And she said _ "Isn't he in town now?"

"No. He's not in town" he said _ not for he to know anything about un.

By an' by there was a feller come in an' said "Jack? Jack's in town" he said "I seed un a couple o' days ago." He said "I can tell 'ee where he's at. He's a chimley sweeper."

"Well" she said "go an' bring un." So he went off an' got Jack. Well Jack wouldn't go you know because he was all rags an' (somethin) you know, can't get un a suit o' clothes an'...dressed up. Goin down the wharf now an'...the young feller [said] "THAT'S Dadda, Mamma!" he said "that's ***[*recorder off; tape changed*]

[*teller recaps*]

/Jack/   Well _ when this feller come down an' told...the king Jack was still in town _ he was uh...he was a chimney-sweeper. Well /the king/ send for un. Well he wouldn't come an' he...had no clothes on he said _ all tore up an' well he _ got a suit o' clothes for un. Goin down the wharf now the young feller said "That's Dadda, Mamma" he said "that's Dadda." Went down there an' she asked un _ Jack if he was the feller that (had)...got the bottle o' world's end water under her pillow an' he said "Yes."

/he/   "Well" she said "I'm puttin this tape on your...neck now" she said "an' if 'tis a lie you'll fall off...your neck...head 'll fall off _ but if 'tis true" /she/ said "the tape 'll fall off."

So he said "Yes" he said "I'm the same lad." (So) the tape fell (off)...fell off.

Well now then -- the ol' king got ready you know for a big feast for 'em. Had a big time an' big wedding an' so on an' _ so _ I was there an' seen part o' the wedding an' _ got a cup o' tea an' left for home. [Int. B. laughs]

[Int. A: Where did you learn these from uh...Allan?]

/He/   I don't know s[ir]...[*laughs*] I don't know. You know _ the way it was uh...when I was pickin up them _ if I heard un _ that was all. /If I/ only heard un once I could tell un the next time.

[Int. A: An' where would people be telling them that you would hear them in the old days?]

Oh they'd be all dead see an' them all dead now all them...ol' people.

[Int. A: They were people from round here?]

Oh yes. People from round here yes.

[Int. A: Who used to tell them?]

[Int. B: Who were the best storytellers around?]

Uh...well I don't know _ who the best one...I don't know who the BEST storyteller is. Well ol' S[mith]...now Eli Smith _ he's up there to Port Anson. I think he was about so good a feller _ as ever I...heard (could) tell stories _ you know.

[Int. A: He used to tell these about Jack as well did he?]

Oh yes. He used to tell 'em...(right) 'bout Jack as well.

[Int. A: An' you've picked them up when you heard people in the woods and...elsewhere have you?]
Oh yes. When I...whenever...whenever I hear a story told see that I pick un up _ I'd knowed un. I could tell un then...right on _ after he was finished.
[Int. A: How lo(ng)...how...how many times would you have to hear un told?]
I only wanted to heard un once. [Int. B. laughs] All I done sir. Tell un to...you tell me a story once an' I'd tell un the next time. But I'm not so GOOD on that now you know uh...I might want to hear un two or three times now.

Duration: 9 min., 25 sec.
Source: "Fifty year ago."
Location: Store in garden of teller's house, afternoon.
Audience: Interviewers, adult male neighbor.

Context, Style, and Language: (For context see notes to No. 1). A neighbor who is passing by stays for a while to listen to the story.

As with most of Allan Oake's stories already discussed, this was recorded twice, with an interval of nine years between the recordings. The two versions presented here are typical of his quiet, undemonstrative style, enlivened by strong emphasis on individual words which provides rare stylistic contrast. They also demonstrate his ability to tell the same story in substantially similar ways on two widely separated occasions in different contexts and with different audiences. Each of the two versions includes the same basic motifs and each differs only in minor ways. For example, there is variation in the sequence of events in the plot—Jack recovers Tom and Bill earlier in this version, and he turns the old woman to stone later than in No. 33. The first version omits such details as the doctor in the opening lines and there is some confusion as to whether Bill ties on his horse in the second version. As elsewhere, Allan Oake pays scant attention to such matters, and leaves the listener to understand what is going on. Version two is more forthright in denigrating Jack before he sets out on his journey, but omits the witch who tells him about the crow. No. 33 also has more elaboration of the motifs of dropping the spoons, there being only one spoon and one "spell" in version one, but two spoons (one of which is retrieved and dropped again) to provide for three spells in the later version—an ingenious way of achieving Olrik's Law of Three. It is the crow which rescues Jack in version one when he is thrown overboard, whereas in No. 33 there is a local touch in his rescue by a "lump"—a fish well known in Newfoundland waters. In version one, towards the end of the tale, a "feller" reveals that Jack is in town, whereas in version two it is evidently Jack's father who reluctantly brings him before the lady. It was necessary to change the tape on the recorder before the end of version one, and the teller recaps with apparent ease before finishing the story. The end formulas also differ slightly, but for the most part the two versions are fully comparable, and they share numerous focal points including the child's insistent recognition of his father and rejection of the other two

343

brothers in the dénouement, and the motif of the "electric tape" (presumably an alteration of "magic tape" or a similar phrase). Version two is less hesitant and more elaborate than that recorded in 1966, indicating that the teller polished this item in his repertoire, as was also the case with several of his other tales, in the interval between the two recordings. This is also suggested by the use of the word *damsel* rather than *girl* in No. 33.

The typical markers *we'll say, Alright,* and *By an' by* are again evident in both versions. Points of linguistic interest include the voicing of initial /f/ and the reduction of the vowel to schwa in *far,* the occurrence of /l/ rather than /n/ in *chimley,* aphesis in *'nother,* the archaic plural inflection in *beastes* (medial /t/ also being lost), the past tense form *arest* (rested), the lexical items *the works* (everything), *again* (against), *spell* (rest), *ar* (any), the past participle *woke* (awake), the past tense *knowed,* the loss of the definite article in *in ship,* and the double negatives *couldn't get no further, never let nobody know,* and *not to tell no lies.*

See also the notes to Nos. 1, 12, 13, 23, 24, 26, and 27.

Type and Motifs:
AT551. *The Sons on a Quest for a Wonderful Remedy for their Father.*
P251.6.1. *Three brothers.*
H1321.2. *Quest for healing water.*
D1500.1.18. *Magic healing water.*
D1254.1. *Magic wand.*
G263.2.1. *Witch transforms to stone.*
D231. *Transformation: man to stone.*
D572.4. *Transformation by wand.*
L101. *Unpromising hero.*
G207. *Male witch.*
N825.2. *Old man helper.*
B451.4. *Helpful crow.*
B552. *Man carried by bird.*
F0. *Journey to other world.*
F141. *Water barrier to otherworld.*
D2153.1.1. *Island created by magic.*
D1177. *Magic spoon.*
F150.2. *Entrance to otherworld guarded by monsters (or animals).*
H1236.2. *Quest over path guarded by dangerous animals.*
T475.2. *Hero lies by princess in magic sleep and begets child.*
C761.4. *Tabu: staying too long in certain places.*
G270. *Witch overcome or escaped.*
D700. *Person disenchanted.*
K2211. *Treacherous brother.*
D861.3. *Magic object stolen by brothers.*
K1931.1. *Impostors throw hero overboard into sea.*
B541.3. *Bird rescues man from sea.*
K1816. *Disguise as menial.*

K1932. *Impostors claim reward (prize) earned by hero.*
H1381.2.1. *Woman seeks unknown father of her child.*
H480. *Father tests. Test as to who is unknown father of child.*
H251. *Test of truth by magic object.*
Q263.1. *Death as punishment for perjury.*
D1402. *Magic object kills.*
H481. *Infant picks out his unknown father.*
L10. *Victorious youngest son.*
L161. *Lowly hero marries princess.*
Z10.2. *End formula.*

International Parallels: See No. 29.

33. THE BOTTLE OF WORLD'S END WATER [†]

Allan Oake   AT551
Springdale, Notre Dame Bay   TC1827 75-287
15 June 1975   Collector: Christina Pynn

[*recorder off*]*** 'bout an ol' king see. He's uh...got sick. Well the doctor...went an' visit an' there was no cure for un without uh...he'd get a bottle o' world's end water. An' that couldn't be got only INTO the worldes end.

So ‗ there was three brothers of 'em ‗ there was Bill now an'...there was Bill an' Tom an'...an' Jack. Jack was only young fell[er]...the youngest feller o' 'em course. Well Bill said to un...one day he said uh..."Get a ship for me...father" he said "an' I'll go an'...get the...bottle o' world's end water." Alright he got a ship for un, he...sailed off.

Well now ‗ [*clears throat*] he went into a port. They went into a port then an' they...he took horse...took a horse ‗ went on horseback. An' he come to...he come to a place ‗ there was a ol'...there was ol' woman lived there. He uh...wanted a lunch.

"Yes" she said "you can have a lunch." So uh...he went in an' he had /tied/.../tied/ his horse see? The once he uh...   /never tied/
                                                                               /never tied/
"Horse not tied?" she said.

"/Yes/" he said. An' she had a cane you know and she wheeled un   /No/
around a time or two ‗ an' turned un into a MARBLE ‗ man. Turned the ship out there in...in the harbour we'll say ‗ to a...a marble ‗ knob. Well that was finished.

Sometime after that Tom said...he'd uh...go to look for un, he said Bill must be lost _ somewhere. [If] he had a ship now he'd go an'...look for /a/ land [pause] where ('twas with) the bottle o' world's end water. Yes. Could have un.

/un/

He got the ship ready for Tom an' he sailed off. Well he come to this _ port where he...where this schooner was turned into a marble an' he went ashore we'll say an'...took a horse an' he ride till...he got to this...ol' woman's shack. He /tied/ _ /tied/ his horse.

/never tied/
/never tied/

"I want a lunch."

"Yes" she said. She wheeled around wi' this stick a few times an' turned HE into a marble...marble man an' turned the ship into a marble stone. Well that finished uh...all that.

Sometime afterward Jack said "Father" he said uh..."build me a ship" he said "I'll get the bottle o' world's end water for 'ee." He said "Th' other fellers is all lost or something happened to 'em."

(So) _ "You isn't goina get nothing" he said "'cause you isn't nothing... nobody."

"Well" he said "you gi' me a ship. You'll find out I'm somebody!" Well _ alright he got a ship for un.

Well he sailed...got aboard this ship an' he sailed her till he got to this port now where those two...marble...ships was _ marble stones an' (well) he...he uh...he anchored there an' went ashore an' took a horse we'll say an'...ride on till he got [to] this shack. Now he never tied his horse. (You) know got off her, he asked for a lunch.

"Yes." An' she [said] "Horse tied?" An' she wheeled un round _ "Horse tied?" she said.

Jack said "No not tied." Well her...her marble stick wasn['t]...marble stick she had was no good.

So he...[coughs] he leaved that then by horse an' went on. He seen those two marble MEN there but nuh...well he didn't...he...he never thought nothing about it. He went on we'll say an' then he meet a crow _ come to _ the water. An' this crow _ was goin to take un now an' fly across this water. So he told Jack he said to take _ "Two spoons with ya" he said. "(For)" he said "'tis a long stretch" he said "an' we'll want a spell [i.e., *rest*]."

So he got on...a crow's back an' away they goes. Well by an' by he said to Jack he said "Drop a spoon" he said. An' there'd be a island rise up. So he dropped a spoon, there was a island...rose up an' he...pitched [i.e., *landed*] we'll say an' they had a spell. An' uh...started off again _ (fled) on. By an' by 'twas spell time again.

"Drop your other spoon Jack" he said. So he dropped th' other spoon. An'* made a is[land]...island out of it. They had to stop an' had a spell.

*tape noise

346

"Now Jack" he said "you better take that spoon again. 'Cause" he said "we'm goin to need un _ before you gets to the world's end." Alright, Jack took this spoon, they fled on, fled on _ till by an' by they come to _ another /place/. He dropped the spoon an'...had another spell. But this time Jack uh...the.../the/ crow landed un.

"Now" he told Jack he said "now you travel" he said "take that horse there" he said. "An' travel...travel" he said "till you comes to a lane" he said. "But DON'T" he said "go up that lane before twelve o'clock in the night. 'Cause if...if you do" he said _ "that lane is full o' wild animals _ savage. An' they're asleep" he said "one hour" crow told un. "Enter there" he said "twelve o'clock. An' be sure" he said "you comes out of it before one. Or" he said "you won't get out." Alright.

Jack went up then...went up an' went to this room...went into this room where this li...where the /damsel/ was we'll say an' this bottle o'...of uh...world's end water was under her pillow. Well Jack got...Jack got the...bottle o' world's end water, now of course she looked that...she looked that nice an' pretty in bed, well he had to stay...stay wi' her a bit! [*laughter*]

'Bout FIVE minutes uh...to one he leaved. [*coughs*] An' he's just got soon had the gate...shut when...they all woke. (But)...oh they was right...savage. Come on, he got on this crow's back again. An' he come back till he got back to the...to where he took th' horse to. [*coughs*] Got on this horse again an' come on _ till he got back to this lake you know where those two islands was. He had a spell there. Come on again an' got off _ on this other...island. Has another spell there an' they come on then. He come back to this shallow...shack where this old woman was. But he never tied his horse /up/.

"Horse tied?" she said.

"No" he said "horse not tied." So he GRABBED the...this uh...marble stick out of her you know _ out of her hand, made a...wheel or two we'll say an' struck her an' knocked SHE into a marble.

Now then he was root...he rooted it out those two...marble men was there an' this was uh...Bill an' Tom. Well he...he rooted they out. Well he had a ship anchored out in port.

"Well" he said "you can come home wi' me now an' wa...in...in...MY ship. Leave your uh...two ship out there." Alright they decide they would, they got aboard Jack's ship an'...started to come home you know. Now they knowed Jack we'll say...they...had the bottle o' this...world's end water. Alright.

On their way home we'll say they...fire Jack overboard _ you know an' get this...come on wi' this bottle...bottle o' world's end water _ to their father. Well 'twas THEY had the bottle, they wouldn't know where JACK was to. [Int: Mm.] But when they fired un overboard he...he pitched

/plake/
/they/

/zamzel/

/nup/

347

fair on a lump's [i.e., *lumpfish's*] back. Well this lump we'll say come on with un an' land un _ on the land.

Well he come we'll say _ [*coughs*] he come into this city where...where they was _ where they lived. Now he didn't go home. He joined _ a chimley sweeper. That's what he joined in then _ when he got in port he...nobody'd know un. You know _ cleanin out chimleys, you knows what kind of*...what his clothes was like we'll say when he was...when he was uh...in por[t]...in port and.../cleanin/...cleanin chimleys.

Well Bill an' they come you know wi' this bottle o' world's end water an' _ th' old man cured up, well Bill _ 'twas Bill had the bottle o' world's end water.

Well seven year after that [*clears throat*] there was a lady come there. Had a little boy with her. An' she asked the king if he had...who brought un the bottle o' world's end water?

"Bill" he said.

An' uh...the little boy said _ "That's not Dadda, Mammy" he said "that's not Dadda."

Well she'd...find out, she'd put it out, she said "Now" she said _ "I'm goin to know whe'r [i.e., *whether*] 'tis a lie or whe'r 'tis true." She had a 'lectric tape _ [*coughs*] put around his neck we'll say an' if the...if 'twas a lie _ /his/ head 'd come off. But if...if 'twas true we'll say the neck...the 'lec...the tape break.

"(Well)" she says "not HE. Have you got ar 'nother one?"

"Yes" he said. "Got another one." Called in this Tom. He told her 'twas HE 'd...got the bottle o' world's end water.

Little boy said "No Mamma. Not Dadda. That's not Dadda, Mamma" he said.

Put this 'lectric tape around you know an' _ took his head off.

"Have 'ee got ar 'nother son?" she said.

"No" he said. "Well" he said "I have got a...son he...but" he said "'tisn't...Jack. Jack" he said "his name is."

When the young boy said "That's Dadda, Mammy" he said. "That's Dadda."

So uh...but he said "He's...just...he's...he isn't uh...he aint been nowhere" he said "he's a /chimley/...a s...a chimley sweeper."

Well he wasn't fit to come up.

"Well" she said "you'd better get un" she said "an' bring un here...before me. That I knows whe'r [i.e., *whether*] 'tis he or no."

Well he...got Jack we'll say an' got a suit...gid un a suit o' clothes an' he went down. When he's goin down on the wharf _ little boy said "Mamma that's Dadda! That's Dadda! That's Dadda comin down there."

*tape noise

/chowin/

/her/

/swimley/

An' she come down 'longside her an' she said "You'd...is you the boy" she said "that...the man" she said "(that) sove my...got this bottle o' world's end water?"

Jack said "Yes" he said "I am." [coughs]

"Well" she said "I soon goin to know. I'll soon know" she said "whe'r [i.e., whether] 'tis you or no." Put this electric tape around his neck. An' the 'lectric tape broke _ comed off.

"Ah m..." his little boy said to her. "I knowed that was Dadda, Mamma." Well all r...alright. Now then he...they was goin to get married. Tuh...they got ready we'll say and...ol' king was...ol'...ol' king was...was sayin...tellin 'em something...you know about gettin married. [clears throat] An' we'll say I leaved an' come home, I didn't stop there. I didn't stop there to get none o' the weddin.

Duration: 11 min., 9 sec.
Source: "Fifty year ago."
Location: Springdale Hospital.
Audience: Interviewer, other patients or visitors.

Context, Style, and Language: (For context see notes to No. 13). It appears that the patients in the ward are having a meal, as the sound of crockery is heard, along with subdued conversation in the background during much of the story.

Allan Oake launches very quickly into the narrative and the opening words were unrecorded. Features of language and style in this version are very similar to those of the preceding version, No. 32. Additional points are: aphesis in 'lectric, 'longside, loss of initial vowel in 'tisn't, the archaic possessive inflection in worldes, without (unless), the present tense we'm, the past tense he ride, comed, and the double negative aint been nowhere.

See also the notes to Nos. 2, 12, 13, 23, 24, 26, 27, and **32.**

Type and Motifs:
AT551. *The Sons on a Quest for a Wonderful Remedy for their Father.*
H1321.2. *Quest for healing water.*
D1500.1.18. *Magic healing water.*
P251.6.1. *Three brothers.*
D1254.1. *Magic wand.*
G263.2.1. *Witch transforms to stone.*
D231. *Transformation: man to stone.*
D572.4. *Transformation by wand.*
L101. *Unpromising hero.*
B451.4. *Helpful crow.*
B552. *Man carried by bird.*

F0. *Journey to otherworld.*

F141. *Water barrier to otherworld.*

D2153.1.1. *Island created by magic.*

D1177. *Magic spoon.*

C756. *Tabu: doing thing before certain time.*

F150.2. *Entrance to otherworld guarded by monsters (or animals).*

H1236.2. *Quest over path guarded by dangerous animals.*

C761.4. *Tabu: staying too long in certain place.*

T475.2. *Hero lies by princess in magic sleep and begets child.*

G270. *Witch overcome or escaped.*

D700. *Person disenchanted.*

K2211. *Treacherous brother.*

D861.3. *Magic object stolen by brothers.*

K1931.1. *Impostors throw hero overboard into sea.*

B541.1. *Escape from sea on fish's back.*

K1816. *Disguise as menial.*

K1932. *Impostors claim reward (prize) earned by hero.*

H1381.2.1. *Woman seeks unknown father of her child.*

H480. *Father tests. Test as to who is unknown father of child.*

H251. *Test of truth by magic object.*

Q263.1. *Death as punishment for perjury.*

D1402. *Magic object kills.*

H481. *Infant picks out his unknown father.*

L10. *Victorious youngest son.*

L161. *Lowly hero marries princess.*

Z10.2. *End formula.*

International Parallels: See No. 29.

34. DUNG, ASS, DUNG†

John Myrick   AT563
St. Shotts, St. Mary's Bay   TC528 68-43
21 July 1968   Collector: HH

[Int: Uh...I was asking you...you...I think [it] was yesterday _ about the _ what Mr....Dr. McGrath called the shanachies, the old...time storytellers. What were you telling me that...were there any of those around when you were young?]

Yes there was two old gentlemen ‿ two Molloys. Well ‿ they were gone before my time but ‿ oh one of 'em was but Pat Molloy here in St. Shotts ‿ he used to tell the old Irish stories. An' Bill Molloy from Trepassey. He was even better than Pat.

[Int: An' did...did you...you heard one of them?]

Well old Pat Molloy here belong St. Shotts had the old s...story called "Mick an' the Liar." Uh...it runs something like this.

[Int: Did he tell it in English or in Irish?]

He told it in English. [Int: Mm.]

That uh...he was walkin one night and he stopped at an inn ‿ this ol' fella. An' ‿ he had a donkey ‿ an' he asked could they put the donkey in the barn an' th' old man an' old woman said yes. An' he had a little box with him. An' he asked could he take that in the house an' they said yes.

So when he was goin to bed that night ‿ he said "If you goes in the barn ‿ whatever you do don't say 'Dung, ass, dung.' Or" he said "don't say 'Slap in the bang an' bang (him)'" ‿ he said "here in the house."

An' they'd...looked at one another an' wondered why but ‿ when the ol' man went to bed ‿ th' old woman said "We'll go out and see what he's talkin about."

They went out an' th' ass was up in the stall. And uh...th' ol' man said "Dung, ass, dung." Up comes the ol' ‿ ass's tail an' ‿ guineas started to pour all around the barn everywhere an' th' old woman runned with her apron ‿ she got it full. An' when 'twas stopped she lugged 'em into the house ‿ an' hid 'em.

"An' now" she said...th' ol' man said "I wonder what's in the box? He told us not to say 'Slap in the bang an' bang him.'" So he said "I'll slap in the bang an' bang him out o' that."

Ah the next thing there was...the box...there was a fella come out o' the box an' he knocked down the pictures on the wall, he broke the lookin glasses, he knocked th' old woman upside down an' th' ol' fella ‿ heard the noise an' he came down over the stairs ‿ put him back in the box again, he had like to kill 'em. But all the guineas was over the floor when he come down, he knew they were after bein out in the barn [*laughs*] "Dung, Ass, Dung." [*laughs*]

(Now) these...these old stories they used to tell like that, I don't know if they're true or not but he had a lot of old ghost stories too.

[Int: This is Pat?]

Pat Molloy yes.

[Int: Mm-hm. When would he tell stories like this, Mr. ‿ Myrick?]

Well he used to come out to Cape Freel where he live ‿ we were only young you know. We'd get him out an' then ‿ when he'd come out we get th' oh..."Skipper Pat" we used to call un "tell us a story" an' he'd sit down an' he'd tell us th' old story o' Micky the liar.

Duration: 1 min., 45 sec.
Source: Pat Molloy, Cape Freel[s], St. Mary's Bay, who learned the tale from his grandmother.
Location: Sitting room of teller's house.
Audience: Interviewer.

Context, Style, and Language: Like other speakers from St. Shotts in this collection, John Myrick has a pronounced Anglo-Irish accent which is evident, for example, in the raising of the short vowel /i/, the breathed quality of voiceless plosives, especially in word-final position, and the use of the "clear" lateral consonant. These Irish qualities are also seen in the syntax, e.g., in the construction "they were after bein." However, in common with other Irish Newfoundland speakers, he uses the typical West Country English pronoun *un,* and other features which occur frequently in the province's dialects, including *'twas, th' ol(d),* present tense *you goes,* past tense *runned, come,* and *live,* the omission of the preposition in *belong St. Shotts,* and the constructions *he came down over the stairs* and *he had like to kill 'em.*

The title of the story (and the generic name of what seems originally to have been a whole cycle of tales) has become "Mick an' the Liar," perhaps an alteration of the more plausible "Mickel [Michael] the Liar" to be found in Gus Molloy's version of "Jack Wins the King's Daughter"[†] (No. 44). Indeed, John Myrick later refers to "Micky the liar" in the discussion which follows the tale. His version of the story also seems to be the same as the fragment Gus Molloy himself recalled in "Dung, Horse, Dung"[†] (No. F5), and both versions retain the archaic *guineas.* Incidentally, the amusing catchphrase "Slap in the bang and bang him" in No. 34 makes little sense as it stands. Perhaps the speaker (or the original) intended "Slap in the *bag* and bang him," the pronunciation of both words being similar, the transcription of final /g/ and *-ng* being problematical after the preceding diphthong /ei/, possibly resulting in the apparent alteration of *bag* to *bang.*

Type and Motifs:
AT563. *The Table, the Ass, and the Stick.*
B103.1.1. *Gold-producing ass. Droppings of gold.*
D861.1. *Magic object stolen by host (at inn).*
Cf. D1401.2. *Magic sack furnishes mannikin who cudgels owner's enemies.*

International Parallels: In the standard pattern of AT563, a man receives two successive magical gifts, a food-providing table (tablecloth, napkin), and a gold-dropping ass (or other animal), each of which is stolen, often being replaced by an object or animal similar in appearance. The third gift, the stick that beats on command (or a container with a manikin who beats on command), punishes the thief, forcing him to return the original gifts to their owner. All three of the objects or animals and the gifts or punishments they provide may vary from one tradition to another, but whatever variations occur in these details their functions are the same.

This Newfoundland text differs from the standard pattern in that there are only two magic objects: the gold-dropping ass and a box with a manikin who bangs vigorously. It also differs in that both are introduced into a household at the same time, so that the attempt by the householders to steal the first object (or at least the guineas the ass deposits) is foiled when the power of the second one comes into play. Having the two magic objects introduced simultaneously rather than in succession makes a plausible and effective story here, but so far as we know this breaking of the serial pattern is rare; we have not found it in other versions. This, of course, does not preclude the possibility that it is a subtype which occurs elsewhere.

As Thompson observes (*The Folktale,* pp. 72-73), AT563 is widely distributed. It is found in almost every collection of stories from Europe and Asia, is well known in Africa, and has been carried to both North and South America. "A tale with its essentials was current at least as early as the sixth century [A.D.]. . .in a collection of Chinese Buddhistic legends." Thompson summarizes the 1911 examination of the folktale by Antti Aarne (a study not otherwise available to us except in the digest by Kaarle Krohn, *FFC* 96). Aarne relates AT563 to a folktale in which there are only two magic objects: AT564, "The Magic Providing Purse and 'Out, Boy, out of the Sack!'" Thompson apparently agrees with Aarne that AT564 may well be nothing more than an abbreviated form of AT563 adding, "this particular form appears in a very limited area around the eastern end of the Baltic Sea." In a third story also discussed by Aarne there is only one magic object: AT565, "The Magic Mill." The mill grinds out one product: in different versions it may be meal, salt, or porridge; but, as the thief learns to his sorrow, the mill can only be stopped by its owner.

Our observations in the following discussion refer primarily to the group of analogues we have assembled. This group consists of English-language folktale texts, and of such tales in other languages as were available to us either in English translations or had accompanying English summaries or abstracts. Many though not all of our references postdate Aarne's early study.

A survey of these analogues confirms Thompson's remarks about the very wide distribution of the tale form with three (sometimes four) magic objects. The magical stick or cudgel may be replaced by other objects that punish, or by some creature such as a bee, or, as the AT index description suggests, by a container holding a man or men wielding sticks or whips. But other analogues below contradict the suggestion that tales with two magic objects are limited to the Baltic region. Nor, for that matter, do many of the versions we have assembled fit the pattern of AT564. Lastly, none of our small group of tales with a single magic object includes Aarne's magic mill. These variations from the patterns described in Aarne's survey and thence carried over into the AT index deserve further attention. We have therefore described them in some detail.

The analogues referred to in our notes demonstrate that the form of the tale in which two magic objects are found occurs, admittedly sparsely, in several areas of Europe as well as in India: in Ireland, Italy, Germany, Russia, and Bengal. In North America it occurs in American Indian tradition, in the Ukrainian tradition in Canada, in the English-language tradition in Kentucky, and in the Spanish-language tradition both in Colorado and in Jalisco, Mexico. In black tradition in the Americas it has been reported from

Alabama, from Cape Verde Islanders in Massachusetts, and also from Surinam in South America; it is quite common in the black tradition of the Caribbean Islands. In Africa the two magic objects form of the tale is the predominant pattern. In the analogues listed below, stories with fewer than three magic objects are marked *cf.*

The versions with only two magic objects can be divided into two categories, each determined by what the first magical object supplies. In the first group it is gold (silver/money); in the second it is food. In only one of the analogues for the first group below, a story from Germany, do we find a "magic providing purse," to cite part of the title for AT564. Instead, as in the standard versions of AT563, the gold is usually supplied by an animal that has an everyday familiarity to the listeners, more rarely by an object, e.g., in one Kentucky text a marble rolls out money. We find this gold-providing pattern in North American Indian tales, in a few of the black tales from the Antilles, and in one African text from the Akamba tribe in Kenya.

The tale form in which food is provided by the magic object is much better known. Only in a few examples, however, is the food-providing object a table, or napkin, or tablecloth, as in standard versions of AT563. At other times it may be a common household implement associated with food: a spoon, a ladle, or a dipper, and in one instance a knife and fork; but more often it is an implement or utensil associated with the cooking or serving of food: a pot, wooden dish, cup, or calabash. We shall discuss below analogues in which other kinds of containers are involved.

We have stressed that, apart from the magical elements, in both forms of the tale the animal that provides gold, or the object that provides food are alike in being drawn from the common stock of everyday animals or of normal household implements or equipment. This is also true of the second magic object, which is introduced to punish either the theft or the misuse of the first. Here again the objects themselves are of the everyday kind that might normally be used to punish wrongdoers by striking, beating, or whipping them: a stick or sticks, a cane, a whip, a club, or a skin or mat that might be used for hitting. What makes them magical is that, like the standard magic animals and objects which give the Type its name, they work by themselves when properly activated by the human voice. Among the analogues we have been describing, only in a couple of versions, besides the Newfoundland text, are there containers which hold a figure or figures that do the punishing.

So far as we can see, the tales with only two magic objects are so close to the standard pattern of the three magic objects form, in every other respect except number, that they should be classified merely as a subdivision of AT563, rather than requiring a separate AT number for the group. The classification of another dozen or so of the analogues in our notes, however, is less certain even though we have inserted *(cf. 564)*, in our descriptions of each tale. In this group only two magic objects are received in succession, but the objects are usually two identical containers. Only two of the pairs of containers are specifically food related: calabashes (Jamaica) and cups (Bengal). The other pairs are: chests (Ukrainian-Canadian), bags (Kentucky), bottles (Ireland), boxes (Italy), wallets (Germany), sacks (Russia). In Africa the pairs of objects may include calabashes, horns, or drums. We have noted the geographical areas from which these tales have come so as to indicate that they are not limited to black tradition, but are also found in several countries in Europe, and, though sparsely, in white tradition in North America.

In all but one of these analogues which feature two containers, food is the main product supplied by the first container or object, sometimes by way of a food-providing table, a couple of times by men called up from the container, but more often without such intermediaries. The second container or object may supply whips that punish, but more commonly provides men with sticks, cudgels, clubs, or whips to do the punishing. There are, of course, a few minor variations, e.g., in two African versions in which the first of a pair of horns supplies food, the second horn does the beating.

The last analogue to be considered in this group is Ranke's tale from Germany. Here at last we seem to have a clear-cut version of AT564, "The Magic Providing Purse and 'Out, Boy, out of the Sack!'" In the story two small wallets are received in succession. Three men can be ordered out of the first to provide either food or money, while the three men ordered out of the second wallet provide only beatings. Ranke, who mentions in his notes (see Ranke, *Folktales,* p. 215, no. 41) the early Aarne study and Krohn's summary of it, adds: "Our version of this tale plainly shows its origin from the Baltic-White Russian area." This is obviously a reference to Aarne's study, which Thompson had cited in his discussion of the distribution of AT564 (see above). Yet Ranke, an extremely knowledgeable folk-narrative scholar, and thoroughly familiar with the AT index, does not mention AT564 in his notes, but classifies the tale merely as one of the 54 versions of AT563 found in Germany. He does not indicate whether or not he has discussed the problem of classifying variants of AT563 elsewhere, so we can only guess at his reasoning on this matter.

Leaving this problem in abeyance for the moment, let us examine briefly the few analogues we have located that have only one magic object. Four of the five are from black tradition. In a text collected by Herskovits from Surinam, a whip first provides food, then beatings; in Dayrell's story from Nigeria, a drum first produces food, then Egbo men with whips, which they use; in Knappert's Swahili tale, a stick first provides silver, then delivers a beating. Last, in Doke's Lamba text, a calabash first gives food and drink, but then cuts off fingers.

We have discussed above the analogues in which the first of two identical magic containers or objects provides gifts, while the second gives punishments. In these four versions, all from black tradition, the same ends are achieved efficiently by doubling the functions of the single magic object—first by providing, then by punishing—a simple and logical variation of the pattern.

Quite unlike any of these single object stories are Bodding's three texts from the Santal Parganas of Central India. Jackals give a boy a magical cow which produces anything requested, and later swallows what is not needed. In each text the cow is stolen from the boy but eventually, usually after some form of judicial trial, he recovers his property.

As our survey has shown, even the limited group of tales we have assembled indicates that Aarne's early study of AT563 and related tales was incomplete. Since our discussion has been based only on tales available to us in English, our conclusions must be regarded as tentative. Obviously the entire group of tales, including the texts in other languages that we have not drawn upon, deserves a full study.

Studies and Notes

Clouston, *Popular Fictions*, 1, pp. 87-93, 102-4; Cox, *Cinderella*, p. 510, note 54; MacCulloch, *Childhood*, pp. 214-16, 219-21; Bolte and Polívka, 1, pp. 346-61, no. 36; Thompson, *European*, pp. 413-14, no. 16; Krohn, *Übersicht, FFC* no. 96, pp. 48-53; Chase, *Jack*, p. 191, no. 5, notes; Parsons, *Antilles*, 3, p. 223, no. 237, headnote; Thompson, *The Folktale*, pp. 72-73; Espinosa, *CPE*, 3, pp. 75-83; Roberts, *South*, pp. 232-33, no. 23, notes; Delarue and Tenèze, *Catalogue*, 2, pp. 419-20, 430-33; Baughman, *Index*, Type 563, p. 14; Ranke, *Folktales*, p. 215, no. 41, notes; Robe, *Index*, Type 563, pp. 102-3.

Canada

Fauset, *Folklore*, pp. 33-35, no. 16, cf. pp. 41-43, no. 18, variant (cf. 564, with 300), 2 versions [wind gives boy food-providing tablecloth, mare that shakes gold and silver, and stump that smashes things; fairy gives boy tablecloth, and belt and stick that clinch and beat] (Nova Scotia).

Leach, "Celtic Tales," pp. 48-49, no. vii [duck drops gold, mill grinds gold, and sod wraps up everything], English trans. of tale told in Gaelic (Nova Scotia), and rpt. in Fowke, *Folklore*, p. 129.

MacDonell and Shaw, *Collection*, pp. 11-18, no. 2 [filly shakes gold and silver, quern mills flour and meal, and bludgeon binds people], Gaelic text with English trans. (Nova Scotia).

Cf. Mechling, *JAF* 26 (1913), 219-24, no. 1 [mare defecates gold, sticks beat], Maliseet Indian (New Brunswick).

Cf. Radin and Reagan, *JAF* 41 (1928), 125-26, no. 29 (with 1642) [goat defecates gold, cane fights], Ojibwa Indian (Ontario).

Cf. Klymasz, *Narrative*, pp. 39-44, no. 5 (cf. 564) [2 chests: 1 with food, clothing, etc.; 2d with Cossacks that whip], Ukrainian tradition, in English (Manitoba), and rpt. in Fowke, *Tales*, pp. 28-34, no. 11.

Teit, *JAF* 50 (1937), 177-82, no. 4 (with 313) [white tablecloth mat provides food, donkey drops gold, rod of iron beats], Thompson Indian (British Columbia).

For early references to North American Indian parallels, see Thompson, *European*, pp. 413-14, no. 16.

Thomas, *Types*, cites 2 versions of AT563 from Newfoundland French tradition.

Lacourcière-Low, "Catalogue," cites 43 Francophone versions of AT563 from Canada: 11 (New Brunswick), 30 (Quebec), 2 (Ontario).

United States

Cf. Speck, *JAF* 26 (1913), 81-83, no. 1 [old white horse defecates gold, pair of sticks carved like man and woman beat], Penobscot Indian (Maine).

Parsons, *Islands*, 1, pp. 99-100, no. 35, pp. 100-101, no. 35a, cf. pp. 101-3, no. 35b, 3 versions, wolf and king [dish, donkey, and sticks; dish provides food, plate produces gold and silver, club beats; wooden dish provides food, club beats], English trans. of Portuguese texts, Cape Verde Islands, black (Massachusetts).

Parsons, *JAF* 30 (1917), 210-12, no. 3 [tablecloth, donkey shakes out gold and silver, club], black (Maryland).

Carter, *JAF* 38 (1925), 363-65, no. 12 [rooster lays gold eggs, sword cuts trees or heads, club beats] (North Carolina).

Chase, *Jack,* pp. 47-57, no. 5, and p. 191, notes [tablecloth, rooster that lays golden eggs, club] (North Carolina).

Cf. Fauset, *JAF* 40 (1927), 214-16, no. 1, terrapin and king [food-providing dipper, cowhide that beats], informant born in Dahomey, West Africa, black (Alabama).

Musick, *Hills,* pp. 145-47, no. 34 [switch produces soldiers, tablecloth provides food, harmonica plays compulsive music], Italian tradition, in English trans. (West Virginia).

Cf. Roberts, *South,* pp. 84-86, no. 23a (cf. 564) [2 bags: one produces food-providing table; the second 2 men who beat], a similar second version is summarized on p. 232, note 23 (Kentucky).

Cf. Roberts, *Greasybeard,* pp. 99-105, no. 23 (with 302, 313A) [marble that rolls out money, club], pp. 105-9, no. 24 [tablecloth, horse, stick], 2 versions (Kentucky).

Carrière, *Tales,* pp. 204-6, no. 40, and cf. pp. 130-34, no. 26, with animal characters, 2 versions [napkin, horse, and bumblebee; napkin, horse, and stick] French texts with English summaries (Missouri).

Thomas, *Good,* pp. 127-32, no. 12 [napkin, horse, and bumblebee], French text and English trans. (Missouri).

Dobie, *PTFS* 6 (1927), 45-47 [Nor'west Wind gives colt that will shake out anything wanted, napkin, and pot that thumps] (Texas).

Espinosa, *Folk-Tales,* p. 202, no. 38 [table, gold-dropping ass, a sack with a black dwarf who whips], English summary of Spanish text (New Mexico).

Weigle, *Two Guadalupes,* pp. 115-18 [donkey, and then sack, produce whatever is requested, cane beats], Spanish tradition, in English (New Mexico).

Rael, *Cuentos,* 2, pp. 708-9, no. 217, cf. 2, pp. 709-10, no. 219 (with 592), 2 versions [tablecloth, donkey that drops money, stick; tablecloth, and violin that plays compulsive music], English summaries of Spanish texts (Colorado).

See Robe, *Index,* Type 563, for references to additional New Mexican and Mexican texts.

Lacourcière-Low, "Catalogue," cites 2 Francophone versions of AT563 from the United States: 2 (Missouri).

Mexico

Wheeler, *Tales,* pp. 87-88, no. 42, cf. pp. 503-4, no. 182, 2 versions [tablecloth provides food, table provides wine, and stick beats; tablecloth and stick], Spanish texts with English summaries (Jalisco).

The Caribbean and South America

Cf. Parsons, *Andros,* p. 141, no. 92 [food-providing pot and whip], 2 versions, 2d fragmentary, black (Bahamas).

Hurston, *JAF* 43 (1930), 307-9, no. 13 (with 212) [2 brothers in turn lose food-providing table and gold-dropping donkey; 3rd brother gets their return with his gift, a stick in a sack] (Bahamas).

Cf. Beckwith, *Stories,* pp. 31-32, no. 25a (cf. 564), Anansi and family [one calabash produces a table with food, the other a cow-whip that whips], cf. pp. 32-33, no. 25b, Anansi and people [knife and fork provide food, a horse-whip whips], 2 versions, black (Jamaica).

Cf. Tanna, *Folk Tales,* pp. 93-94, Anansi and family [talking pot provides food, talking cowkin (cowskin) beats], black (Jamaica).

Cf. Parsons, *Antilles,* 1, pp. 109-11, no. 9 [food-providing napkin and bottle of carbins (fairies) who beat], black (St. Vincent, Windward Islands).

Cf. Parsons, *Antilles,* 2, pp. 366-67, no. 13, Brer Nancy, the spider, and his brother [food-providing pot, skin that beats], black (St. Kitts), cf. 2, pp. 441-42, no. 32, Anancy and his wife [food-providing pot; loses power when misused], black (St. Croix, Lesser Antilles).

Cf. Parsons, *Antilles,* 3, pp. 223-25, no. 237, summaries of 3 English texts listed above, and of 5 French texts, all black: A, [donkey, table, and whip] (Trinidad), C, [donkey and stick] (Dominica), D, [whip to make vegetables grow, and donkey] (Guadeloupe), E, [donkey and whip] (Guadeloupe), H, [napkin and club] (Haiti). See headnote to no. 237 for additional references: Apache Indian, Santo Domingo, Jamaica, 13 African sources, the Philippines, and several for Europe.

See Hansen, *Types,* Type 563, for references to versions from the Dominican Republic, Puerto Rico, and Chile.

Cf. Herskovits, *Folk-Lore,* pp. 222-25, no. 41, Anansi and his family [pot and whip], pp. 224-25, no. 42, Anansi and his family [whip: first provides food, then beatings], 2 versions, "Taki-taki" texts with English trans., black (Surinam).

England

Baring-Gould, *Household,* pp. 327-29, no. 7 [ass drops money from mouth, table, stick] (Yorkshire, West Riding), and rpt. in Jacobs, *English,* pp. 206-10, no. 39, and again rpt. in Briggs, *Dictionary,* A1, pp. 141-44.

Baring-Gould, *Household,* pp. 329-31, version 2 [2 brothers in turn lose purse that always has one coin, round food-providing table; 3rd gets them returned with his gift: a stick that bangs people] (Yorkshire, East Riding).

Blakeborough, *Wit,* pp. 265-68 [gold-dropping ass, food-providing hamper, stick] (Yorkshire, North Riding), and rpt. in Briggs, *Dictionary,* A1, pp. 169-71.

Wales

Briggs, *Dictionary,* A1, pp. 478-81, rpt. from article in *Journal of the Gypsy Lore Society* [each of 2 brothers loses his gift: gold-dropping horse, food-providing table; Irishman gets gifts returned with his gift: clogs which dance or kick], Gypsy (Wales).

Scotland

McKay-Campbell, *Tales,* 2, pp. 78-82, no. 51 [quern that grinds meal, filly that shakes out gold and silver, thong that binds, and bludgeon that strikes], Gaelic text and English trans. (Islay).

Ireland

O'Connor, *Stories,* pp. 77-84 [sieve shakes out gold, pepperbox provides food, blackthorn stick beats rogue] (Ireland).

Cf. MacManus, *Corners,* pp. 69-82 (613, with cf. 563, 569) [napkin for food, wishing cap for travel, inexhaustible purse] (Co. Donegal).

Kennedy, *Stories,* pp. 25-30 [hen lays golden eggs, tablecloth, stick] (Co. Wexford).

Cf. Croker and Wright, *Legends,* pp. 41-51 (cf. 564) [2 identical bottles: first provides food, second, men with cudgels] (Munster), and rpt. in O'Faolain, *Children,* pp. 58-68.

Cf. Ó Cróinín, *Béal.* 35-36 (1967-68), 360, no. 17 [food-providing table-cloth and box of soldiers], 360, no. 18 [mare shakes money from its ear, food-providing table-cloth, yellow stick that beats], 2 versions, English summaries of Irish texts (Co. Cork).

Ó Duilearga, *Book,* pp. 108-12, no. 21 [white cloth, gold-dropping horse, rod] (Co. Kerry).

Cf. Gregory, *Poets,* pp. 187-89 (cf. 564) [2 identical bottles: first has 2 men who provide food, second 2 men who beat with blackthorns] (Co. Galway).

Hyde, *Stories,* pp. 23-67 (with 1541, 1386) [food-providing pot, cow that shakes out money, stick], Irish text and English trans. (Co. Mayo).

Irish Types, Type 563, 298 versions.

Continental Europe and Asia

Grimm no. 36, "Table-Be-Set, the Gold-Donkey, and Cudgel-Come-out-of-the-Bag," in Grimm-Hunt 1, pp. 143-53, no. 36 (with 212) [2 brothers in turn lose food-providing table and ass that drops gold from its mouth; 3rd brother gets their return with his gift: a sack with a cudgel that beats] (Germany), see Grimm-Hunt 1, pp. 386-87, no. 36, notes, for a trans. of a variant text and other references, and for other English trans. see Grimm-Magoun, pp. 131-40, no. 36, and Grimm-Zipes, pp. 134-42, no. 36.

Thorpe, *Yule-Tide,* pp. 326-28 [food-providing cloth, goat that makes gold ducats, cudgel that beats] (Norway).

Hodne, *Types,* AT563, 29 versions (Norway).

Dasent, *Popular Tales,* pp. 250-53, no. 34 [cloth, ram, stick] (Norway).

Delarue, *Borzoi Book,* pp. 204-16, no. 26, with notes [napkin, duck that lays silver or gold, and a walking stick that beats], mentions there are 80 French versions (France).

Cf. Massignon, *Folktales,* pp. 175-76, no. 51 [gifts stolen by foster parents] (France).

Darnton, *Massacre,* p. 38, summary [tablecloth, (gold-dropping ass), staff that beats] (Brittany).

Cabellero, *Bird,* pp. 174-80 [purse, food-providing cloak, cudgel] (Spain).

Coote, *FLR* 1 (1878), 202-4 [gold-spitting donkey, tablecloth, cudgel], cf. 204-6 (cf. 564) [2 boxes: one provides food, the other man or men with sticks], 2 versions (Italy).

Crane, *Popular Tales,* pp. 123-27, and p. 347, n. 10 [ass, tablecloth, club] (Italy).

Calvino, *Folktales,* pp. 437-41, no. 127 [gold-dropping donkey, food-providing napkin, club that beats] (Italy).

Cf. Calvino, *Folktales,* pp. 301-4, no. 83 (cf. 564) [2 boxes: one provides food, the other men who beat with clubs] (Italy).

Basile, *Pentamerone,* 1, pp. 17-24 (Day I, Diversion 7) [ass that defecates jewels, napkin that provides treasures, stick that beats], literary (Italy).

Cf. Ranke, *Folktales,* pp. 104-6, no. 41 (cf. 564) [two wallets: one has men who provide food or money on request, the other men who beat], notes there are 54 versions of cf. AT563 in Germany (Germany).

Bowman and Bianco, *Tales,* pp. 12-24 [mill grinds flour, tablecloth provides any food, wallet has men who do bidding] (Finland).

Wratislaw, *60,* pp. 101-6, no. 16 [lamb that shakes out gold, food-providing tablecloth, and cudgel that produces 2 men who beat], trans. from K. J. Erben, Kashubian people (Pomerania), for another English trans. from Erben see Strickland, *Legends,* pp. 73-76.

Yates, *Book,* pp. 49-53, no. 9 [4 gifts: tablecloth, loaf of bread that stays whole, lamb that shakes out money, 2 cudgels that strike], Gypsy (Poland).

Fillmore, *Apron,* pp. 207-24 [tablecloth, gold-crowing rooster, clubs] (Czechoslovakia).

Jones and Kropf, *Folk-Tales,* pp. 161-63, no. 34 [tablecloth, gold-producing lamb, club], and p. 394, notes (Hungary).

Nicoloff, *Folktales,* pp. 46-48, no. 18 [kerchief, goat, stick] (Bulgaria).

Bain, *Folk-Tales,* pp. 42-52 (563, with 1030*, cf. 1681B, 1653B, 1000, 1002, 1120) [table, mill that grinds gold or silver, 2 sticks] (Turkey).

Kúnos, *44,* pp. 98-101 [table, mill that grinds gold or silver, cudgels] (Turkey).

Dawkins, *MGAM,* pp. 374-79, no. 10 (with cf. 433), pp. 544-49, no. 24 (with 314), Greek dialect texts and English trans., 2 versions [gold-dropping donkey, food-providing dish, club produces negro with gun; table, gold-dropping donkey, gourd produces 2 negroes with clubs], and pp. 224-25, notes (Turkey).

Cf. Afanas'ev, *Fairy Tales,* pp. 321-24 (cf. 564) [2 sacks: 2 men who provide food come from one, 2 who beat people come from the other] (Russia).

Cf. Bain, *Fairy Tales,* pp. 235-40 (cf. 564) [2 sacks], same as Afanas'ev (Russia).

Dirr, *Folk-Tales,* pp. 124-25, no. 25 [horse provides food, goat spits gold, stick beats], Kabardian people (Kabardine-Balkar A.S.S.R.).

Cf. Papashvily, *Yes,* pp. 159-69, no. 15 (563, I, with 325) [gold-dropping donkey, food-providing tablecloth; both sold] (Georgian S.S.R.).

Cf. Khatchatrianz, *Folk Tales,* pp. 19-26 (with 325) [tablecloth, pumpkin out of which come armed horsemen] (Armenia).

Coxwell, *Folk-Tales,* pp. 1028-32, no. 1 [cup provides food and clothing, ass passes gold, billet of wood and piece of rock strike], Darvash people, Bokhara (Uzbek S.S.R.).

Noy, *Folktales,* pp. 47-50, no. 21 [food-providing coffeemill, money tray, stick], from Tunisia (Israel).

Indian Subcontinent

Stokes, *Fairy Tales,* pp. 27-34, no. 7 (with 1600) [pot provides food, box provides clothes, rope and stick bind and beat on command] (Punjab).

Day, *Folk-Tales,* pp. 53-63, no. 3 [3 pots: 2 provide food, 3rd punishing demons] (Bengal).

Cf. Devi, *Pearls,* pp. 1-12 (cf. 564) [2 cups: one provides food, the other beating fists] (Bengal).

Cf. Shankar, *Wit,* p. 118, note (cf. 564) [2 pots: one supplies sweets, second has rope and hammer] (Bengal?).

Shakespear, *Clans,* pp. 100-101 [stirring rod provides cooked rice, goat passes amber and cornelian beads, piece of cane and mallet tie and beat] (Assam Hills).

Barkataki, *Folk-Tales,* pp. 37-38, no. 22 [same as in Shakespear] (Assam Hills).

Elwin, *Folk-Tales,* pp. 124-26, no. 6 [cow defecates gold, pot and spoon produce rice, golden rope and bar of wood tie and beat] (Mahakoshal).

Cf. Bodding, *Folk Tales,* 1, pp. 33-39, no. 4, pp. 39-59, no. 5, pp. 59-91, no. 6, 3 versions [jackals give boy cow which produces anything requested, and swallows what is not needed; it is stolen; various ways of recovering cow] Santal texts and English trans., Santal Parganas (Central India).

Cf. Bompas, *Folklore,* pp. 81-88, no. 21, from the Bodding collection, Santal Parganas (Central India).

Frere, *Days,* pp. 120-32, no. 12 [jackal gives a melon which produces precious stones, a food-producing pot, and a rope and stick that tie and beat] (Mysore).

Parker, *Village,* 2, pp. 101-6, no. 97, with notes [food-providing plate, ring that returns when sold, cudgel] (Ceylon).

See Thompson and Roberts, *Types,* Type 563, for additional references and analysis.

Eastern Asia

Cf. Mayer, *Guide,* pp. 99-100, no. 88 [mallet provides one man with anything desired; for greedy second man mallet produces little men who kill him] (Japan).

The Philippines

Fansler, *Tales,* pp. 231-37, no. 27, with notes [purse that gives money, goat that gives money, food-providing table, cane that beats wrongdoers].

Gardner, *JAF* 20 (1907), 106-7, no. 6 [tree gives boy a goat that shakes money from its whiskers, net which catches fish even on dry ground or in a tree-top, pot always full of rice, and spoon with vegetables, stick that beats], Tagalog tribe.

Africa

Cf. Finnegan, *Stories,* pp. 299-301, Spider and his wife [food-providing pot, mat that whips], Limba tribe (Sierra Leone).

Cf. Klipple, *Folk Tales,* pp. 470-71 (cf. 564), spider and old woman [2 horns: first produces food, second beatings], English summary of tale from Tauxier, *Nègres Gouro et Gagou,* Gouro tribe (Ivory Coast).

Cf. Rattray, *Folk-Tales,* pp. 62-67, no. 19, Father Ananse, the spider, and his wife and children [food-providing dish, whip], Ashanti text and English trans., Ashanti tribe (Gold Coast).

Cf. Herskovits, *JAF* 50 (1937), 75-76, no. 12, Ananse's son and his father [food-providing pot, stick], Ashanti tribe (Gold Coast).

Cf. Barker and Sinclair, *Folk-Tales,* pp. 39-44, no. 4, Anansi, the spider, and his wife and son [food-providing pot, stick] (Gold Coast).

Cf. Rattray, *Folk-Lore,* 1, pp. 80-107, no. 5 [food-providing spoon, whip], Hausa text and English trans., Hausa people (Gold Coast).

Cf. Dayrell, *Stories,* pp. 20-28, no. 4 [drum first provides food, then Egbo men with whips] (Nigeria).

Cf. Lomax, *JAF* 26 (1913), 10-12, no. 15, Spider and his family [2 food-providing pots, whip], Yoruba tribe (Nigeria).

Cf. Itayemi and Gurrey, *Folk-Tales,* pp. 81-85, no. 27, Tortoise and king [food-providing ladle, whip], Yoruba tribe (Nigeria).

Cf. Fuja, *Cowries,* pp. 125-28, man and tortoise [wooden spoon provides food, whip flogs], Yoruba tribe (Nigeria).

Cf. Talbot, *Shadow,* pp. 46-48 (cf. 564), animal characters [2 drums: one provides food, the other Egbo images with whips], Ekoi tribe (Nigeria).

Cf. Klipple, *Folk Tales,* p. 465 (cf. 564), animal characters [2 drums: first produces food, second 5 men with horse whips], English summary of tale from Mansfeld, *Urwald-Dokumente vier Jahre unter den crossflussnegern Kameruns* (Cameroon).

Cf. Klipple, *Folk Tales,* pp. 465-66 (cf. 564) [2 horns: first cooks food, second beats], English summary of tale from Sieber, "Märchen und Fabeln der Wute," Wute tribe (Cameroon).

Cf. Nassau, *Animals,* pp. 113-20, no. 11 (cf. 564), animals and king [2 drums: one provides food, the other whips], Benga tribe (Gabon).

Cf. Mbiti, *Stories,* pp. 64-65, no. 11 [lamb drops money, club dances and beats], Akamba tribe (Kenya).

Cf. Knappert, *Myths,* p. 151, no. 10 [stick first provides silver, then beating], Swahili people (East Coast of Africa).

Klipple, *Folk Tales,* pp. 462-64 [bag produces food, goat drops gold from mouth, stick beats], English summary of tale from Dempwolff, "Beiträge zur Kenntnis der Sprachen in Deutsch-Östafrika" (Tanganyika Territory).

Cf. Doke, *Folk-Lore,* pp. 32-35, no. 15 [calabash provides food and drink, also cuts off fingers], Uwulamba text and English trans., Lamba people (Rhodesia).

See Klipple, *Folk Tales,* Type 563, for several other versions not included in these notes.

35. JACK THE APPLE SELLER[†]

Allan Oake
Springdale, Notre Dame Bay
15 June 1975

AT566
TC1827 75-287
Collector: Christina Pynn

Uh...Jack, Bill an' Tom now. Jac[k]...(Jill)...er...not Jack but _ whatever we'll call him Jack anyhow. (There's) _ don't make a matter _ as I know for. [Int: (No) right]

*background
noise

Just as well (for) it be Jack*
[Int: Yeah.] (as) anything else.

*pause: 3 sec.
approx.

[Int: Sure]*

Well Jack he had uh...he...he...he was (the) main John you know he was boss over 'em. Well Bill an' Tom now they was...they'd only...get what Jack 'd give 'em.

Well now the...king's daughter was there you know. [*coughs*] They used to go playin cards, Tom went off playin' cards wi' her. An' he'd lose every bit o' money that uh...he'd take, she'd win all the money from un. So uh...Pat he...Tom had to give up we'll say, he couldn't get no further, he...he had all the money spend _ that Jack 'd give un. Well he wouldn't

/Pat/

give un no more. But /Bill/ he started. Started an' _ went an'...an' he...he was just the same. He lost all the money.

Of...Jack said to un "Alright" he said _ "I'll give 'ee...I'll give ya a chance tonight" he said "an' (?least g...) I'll give ya the purse that was never emptied. An' for sure she won't be able to get all that."

Well he went over an' he said "You won't beat me...you won't take it all tonight" he said "I got the purse what was never emptied." [*coughs*] (Well) on that you know she SNATCHED the purse out of his hand. Leaved un without ar copper.

So he come back an' he tol' [*coughs*]...Jack about it

"Alright" he said "that's alright" he said "tomorrow night" he said "when you goes over" he said "I'll give ya the horn _ that blow through one end" he said "an' there'd be a thousand soldiers right there." He said uh..."Make her give...give up the purse was never emptied."

Alright. He went over, he said uh..."I'm goin to have me purse back."
And she...said "You won't get un back."

"Well" he said "I..." he took out this horn, he said uh...up. He blowed through an end, out comes a thousand soldiers. "Now" he said "(I) wants me purse" and whe[n]...[*coughs*] when he did she GRABBED the horn from un

/he/

/she/...blowed through the other end an' they all disappeared. Very well, he went home without ar [copper] again. Went back an' tol' _ Jack ('bout) it.

362

Well Jack said "Alright" he said _ "tomorrow night" he said "I'll give ya
the coat _ overcoat an' uh…when you gets where she's to" he said "heave un
around you an' she an' wish the two o' you was in the country. An'" he said
"you'll be there."

Well this is what he done. He (would) uh…make her he said then give
up the purse an' eh…an' the horn. Well alright this is what /he/ done. Went   /she/
over an' /hove/ the coat around he an' she an' _ they was in the country.   /hold/
Well she **GRABBED** the coat from un an' hove un around she an' he
again an' wished they was back in town. Well alright. They was back in
town.

Now then they was uh…[*coughs*] they was all broke up now there was
no more money, the…they were…they couldn't play no more. Well
they…they went on their own way, Bill an'…Pat…er Bill an' Tom er…Bill
an' Tom went on their own way, Jack he bid in town. He started uh…sellin
apples. Now th' other fellers gone off now to see /if/ they could _ earn some   /it/
money. But Jack he didn't go, he stayed in town an' _ got some apples. The
big ones, there was two…size (o') apples there you know. The big ones was
seventy dollars apiece. Now the small ones you'd get **TWO** for seventy
dollars.

One evening a servant girl…the uh…king's daughter send…send a
servant down to get _ two apples. She wanted **TWO** _ for seventy dollar. No
he wouldn't sell un two.

So he told…he said uh…to the daugh[ter]…hus…to the servant "I'll tell
ya what I'll do" he said. "I'll give you…I'll give **YOU** one" he said "an'…an'
take seventy dollars for th' other one fr…for the…for the uh…daughter."
Alright. Went home you know. [*coughs*] Well 'twas bedtime now an'…an'
uh…*   *pause: 4 sec.
                                                                                    approx.
[Int: Yeah, go ahead.]   noise nearby
she took a bite* _ she…she…took a bite out o' the apple [*aside:* hoh might   *noise in back-
as well tell all I suppose.]* An' the…daughter done the same thing. She took   ground
a…bite. (But after) she have had one night in bed _ an' there was a apple   *talking in
tre[e]…sprung out of her head. An' the same by [i.e., *with*] the servant girl.   background
But he [*Jack*] /?chose/ some small apples _ for the servant. He give her one
when the…old king started…talk about it _ Jack _ an' he [*Jack*]…he (cure   /made/
her).

Now then uh…a servant girl, he wasn't goin to [let the king into the
room]…I…ol' king he said…he [*Jack*] let the…servant girl out, well _ she
was alright, she was good enough.

Well he [*Jack*] started down _ he wouldn't…let /the king/ go in, told   /her/
the king no he wasn't comin in _ (to) where the servant girl was to, he…wi'
his daugh[ter]…where his daughter was to, he [*Jack*] had to go in there
alone.

363

/sick/

So — went in _ "Now then" he said "I wants the uh...before you're cured _ I wants /?thick/ [i.e., *the*] purse what never emptied an' the...an' the horn an' the coat."

/pens/

"Well" she said "you won't get that unless you.../pins/...puts some...a

/pen/   /pen/

/pin/ _ stabs my...my finger on the joint with a...with a /pin/." So that's what he done. So he gave her a small apple and she eat un an' she was cured. So the ol' king you know he was delighted and uh 'cause he seen _ she come back alright.

So then they started goin in the country. An' there was a...a golden bed in there and a silver bed _ an' a ol' manogany [i.e., *mahogany*] [*coughs*] bed. Pat he took er...or Bill he took the golden bed _ [*coughs*] Tom he took _ the silver bed _ an' Jack said "I'll take the ol' manogany bed, the one I was always used to."

/his/

So they was only there a little bit 'fore a girl apiece come an' got in bed wi' 'em. [*coughs*] An' the same one got in...bed wi' Jack now who had this mark on...on /her/ finger, this king's daughter. He seen the mark. But um...some time they went back again out an'...out in the city [Int: Go ahead.]* +uh...uh well they went out in town. Some time afterwards _ they went into town again _ in country. They took same...took the same beds they had before. Jack he took this ol' manogany one. So he...he got the uh...bed an' in comes this same girl an' got in bed with un. One got in /bed/...bed wi' Tom an'...an' [one wi'] Bill.

*pause: 65
 sec. approx.
+talking in
 background
/bes/

So they went out _ they was there all night an' my s...next mornin they leaved an' went out an'...out in...town again. [*coughs*] Jack he started sellin (those) apples. An' uh...few days afterwards he went back _ went back again. They went in town. So -- goin to get married to those girls now. So they had their hands stickin out through the door. An' he went to work an' Tom...and Jack he picked out this one, he had this one marked. [*coughs*] Well he got married then _ settled down an' I had a lunch an' I come home. [*laughs*]

Duration: 10 min., 34 sec.
Source: "Fifty year ago."
Location: Springdale Hospital.
Audience: Fieldworker, visitors.

Context, Style, and Language: (For context see notes to No. 13).

This is one of the few Jack tales recorded only on the second visit to Allan Oake and it may have come to mind in the intervening years. It begins very unsurely, the teller deciding to call the hero "Jack," and, with a casualness typical of him, justifying this by saying it might as well be this name as any other. The tale itself is also very confused, e.g., the frequent use of the name *Pat* rather than *Bill,* probably influenced by the names in stories of

Pat and Mike. The confusion is made worse by considerable background noise in the hospital ward where it was recorded, and also by numerous interruptions including two very long and unexplained pauses. The narrator's speech is often slurred, probably because of his illness, and transcription is difficult, especially in the first section of the tale. Consequently it is necessary for the listener to make an even greater effort than usual with this narration to follow the gist of the story. Although the basic elements of the plot are there in the motifs, it demands considerable patience and powers of interpretation to make sense of the confused and jerky narrative. It is all the more surprising, in view of the difficulties which Allan Oake has in piecing the story together, that he does not make use of his favorite phrase "we'll say" which so often helps to gloss over confusion and inaccuracy in his other stories. The only hint of such a usage is in the opening lines when he is excusing himself for not being positive about the hero's name. He does, however, use the marker *Alright* several times to signal a stage in the progress of the narrative.

Linguistic points include the consistent mispronunciation of "mahogany" as *manogany*—probably a malapropism, the omission of final /d/ in *tol'* (told), the possible use of the West Country English demonstrative *thick* (this), the present tense form *I wants,* the past tense forms *blowed, bid* (stayed), the past participle *spend,* and the double negatives *couldn't get no further* and *wouldn't give un no more.*

See also the notes to Nos. 1, 12, 13, 23, 24, 26, 27, 32, and 33.

Type and Motifs:
   AT566. *The Three Magic Objects and the Wonderful Fruits (Fortunatus).*
Cf. P251.6.1. *Three brothers.*
D1451. *Inexhaustible purse furnishes money.*
D861.6. *Magic object stolen in card game.*
D1475.1. *Magic soldier-producing horn.*
D1520. *Magic object affords miraculous transportation.*
D1470.1. *Magic wishing-object. Object causes wishes to be fulfilled.*
Cf. D1375.1.1.1. *Magic apples cause horns to grow on person.*
Cf. D881.1. *Recovery of magic object by use of magic apples. These apples cause horns to grow.*
Cf. D895. *Magic object returned in payment for removal of magic horns.*
Cf. D1375.2.1.1. *Magic apple removes horns from person.*
L210. *Modest choice best.*
T475. *Unknown (clandestine) paramour.*
H51. *Recognition by scar.*
Cf. H324. *Suitor test: choosing princess from others identically clad.*
L161. *Lowly hero marries princess.*
Z10.2. *End formula.*

International Parallels: The specific objects in this narrative about the stealing of certain magic objects and their recovery by utilizing the effects of other magic objects are all to be found in AT566, "The Three Magic Objects and the Wonderful Fruits (Fortunatus)." In reading this Newfoundland text, however, we feel as if the perspective of the tale has been foreshortened. For example, although versions of all of the magic objects noted in Incident I of the AT Type description are present, unlike the Type description there is no explanation of how they were secured or how they got into Jack's possession.

In Incident II there are other differences from the Type description. All the objects are stolen by the princess from the two brothers who play cards with her, not from the hero, Jack. When the princess is carried away to a distant place by one of the brothers by the use of a magical traveling overcoat, a plausible substitution for the traveling-cap of the Type description, she promptly uses the coat to bring the two of them back rather than, as in the Type description, leaving her abductor stranded. Therefore, since no one is stranded, Incident III, which describes how the stranded hero found the magical apples, is completely omitted from the tale. So once again, in Incident IV as in Incident I, we have no explanation of how the apples got into Jack's possession.

Of the four incidents in the Type description only IV is intact: Jack uses the magic apples to secure the return of the stolen objects. Even in this section, however, there is an interpolation not found in the Type description, nor in any other versions of the tale that we have read. Before the princess will return the magic objects she insists that Jack stab her finger on the joint. Why she makes this demand is never explained though it does serve a useful identificatory function in later sections of the narrative.

The next section of the tale is extremely curious. The three brothers go to a house in the country. There they find three beds, and we are carefully told which of the beds, the mahogany one, the hero, Jack, chooses while one of his two brothers takes the golden bed and the other the silver one. There is not the slightest hint that the beds have any strange powers or other qualities. However, when the young men get into their respective beds, each one is suddenly joined by a young woman. How the young women got there is never explained. We suggest the storyteller implies that the beds have a magically compulsive power that transports the women there. This pleasant experience also happens to them on two other occasions. All we do learn is that from the mark on her finger Jack realizes that it is the princess who is his bed companion.

So far as we know this unusual episode is not found in other versions of AT566, nor is it in any other folktale that we have read. Apparently Thompson's *Motif-Index* does not include any motif that fits this theme. There may be a distant relationship to a Scottish legend which Halpert recalls reading in which young men out hunting are unexpectedly joined in their beds at night by women, but in that story, unlike ours, the results were fatal to most of the men.

In the final episode, which is told very briefly, the three brothers are to choose their marriage partners by each selecting one of the girls' hands protruding through a door opening. Jack picks out his girl, the princess, by the mark on her finger. There is a similar method of recognition in some of our versions of AT313; see Nos. 8, 10, and 12. In these the hero selects the hand of the girl who had assisted him by the crooked finger she got when she helped him.

In the following notes we have indicated in parentheses what other types are combined with AT566 in a particular version or if AT566 is incomplete. In brackets we show what deformity or transformation occurs to the person(s) eating the magical fruit.

Studies and Notes

Herford, *Studies,* pp. 203-19, 405-7 (Fortunatus); Clouston, *Popular Tales,* 1, pp. 72-122; MacCulloch, *Childhood,* pp. 158-60; Aarne, *Vergleichende Märchenforschungen,* pp. 83-142; Bolte and Polívka, 1, pp. 470-85, no. 54, 3, pp. 3-9, no. 122; Thompson, *European,* pp. 399-401, no. 12; Kittredge, *Witchcraft,* pp. 183-84, 502-3, notes 91-103; Krohn, *Übersicht, FFC* no. 96, pp. 100-101; Thompson, *The Folktale,* pp. 73-74; Espinosa, *CPE,* 3, pp. 75-83; Delarue and Tenèze, *Catalogue,* 2, pp. 438-39, 442-43; Hoogasian-Villa, *Tales,* pp. 458-60, no. 13, notes; Robe, *Index,* Type 566, p. 103.

Canada

Barbeau and Hornyansky, *Phoenix,* pp. 23-40 [long nose], English trans. adapted from French text in Barbeau, *JAF* 32 (1919), 112-16, no. 84 (Quebec).

Honigmann, *JAF* 66 (1953), 314-16, no. 2 [horns], Woods Cree Indian (British Columbia).

Lacourcière-Low, "Catalogue," cites 18 Francophone versions of AT566 from Canada: 2 (New Brunswick), 12 (Quebec), 4 (Ontario).

United States

Speck, *JAF* 28 (1915), 56-58 [apples; tree grows from head], Penobscot Indian (Maine), and rpt. in Thompson, *Tales,* pp. 238-41, no. 85.

Parsons, *Islands,* 1, pp. 238-41, no. 80 [horns], English trans. of Portuguese text, Cape Verde Islands, black (Massachusetts).

Cf. Brendle and Troxell, pp. 28-30 (566, I), Pennsylvania German tradition, in English (Pennsylvania).

Hoogasian-Villa, *Tales,* pp. 145-53, no. 13 [buffalo], Armenian tradition, in English trans. (Michigan).

Saucier, *Folk Tales,* pp. 43-45, no. 10 (with 505) [long nose], French tradition, in English (Louisiana).

Cf. M. Campbell, *Tales,* pp. 195-96, no. 8 (with 567) [horns; horse] (Kentucky).

Cf. Rael, *Cuentos,* pp. 710-11, no. 221 (566, I, II), English summary of Spanish text (New Mexico).

See Thompson, *European,* pp. 399-401, no. 12 (566) [tree].

Lacourcière-Low, "Catalogue," cites 1 Francophone version of AT566 from the United States: 1 (Louisiana).

Mexico

Wheeler, *Tales,* pp. 388-90, no. 128 [tail], pp. 390-92, no. 129 [horns], 2 versions, Spanish texts with English summaries (Jalisco).

For other Hispanic-American and Mexican references see Robe, *Index,* Type 566.

The Caribbean, Central and South America

Parsons, *Antilles,* 3, p. 296, no. 296 [horse], English summary of French text, with notes, black (St. Lucia, West Indies).

See Robe, *Index,* Type 566, for reference to a text from Costa Rica.

See Hansen, *Types,* Type 566, for references to texts from Puerto Rico and Chile.

England

So far as we know, no oral versions of AT566 have been reported from England. For literary ones, see:

Thomas Dekker, *Old Fortunatus,* literary (England) [horns], see pp. x-xv for discussion of the play and its sources.

Cf. "The History of Fortunatus," in Ashton, *Chap-Books,* pp. 124-37, literary (England).

See Briggs, *Dictionary,* A1, pp. 245-49, for a summary of a literary adaptation of a prose chapbook version of *Fortunatus* [horns].

For discussion of the history of the various versions of *Fortunatus,* see Herford, *Studies,* pp. 203-19, 405-7.

Scotland

Campbell, *Popular Tales,* 1, pp. 176-88, no. 10 [rack of deer antlers], Gaelic text and English trans. (Islay), pp. 188-93, discussion and English summaries of three other Gaelic versions: no. 2, pp. 188-89 [a wood like a thatch grew on head] (Ross-shire), no. 3, pp. 189-91 [deer's horns] (Barra), no. 4, pp. 191-93, no clear summary (Ross-shire).

McKay, *Béal.* 4 (1933-34), 398-99, 401-2, no. 2 [thick forest on head], Gaelic text from J. F. Campbell's MSS. and English summary (Ross-shire).

MacDougall, *Tales,* pp. 222-57, no. 10 (566, with hero tale) [apple makes flesh fall from bones], pp. 299-304, notes, Gaelic text and English trans. (Argyllshire).

Ireland

Wilde, *Legends,* pp. 12-17 [horns] (Ireland).

MacManus, *Heroes,* pp. 167-80 (with 567) [horns] (Co. Donegal).

Murphy, *Talking,* pp. 75-85, no. 68 (with 326A*) [horns] (Co. Cavan).

Kennedy, *Stories,* pp. 67-74 [long nose] (Co. Wexford).

Gmelch and Kroup, *Road,* pp. 41-51 (with 567A) [horns], Irish traveller (Co. Roscommon).

Irish Types, Type 566, 107 versions.

Continental Europe and the Middle East

Grimm-Hunt, 2, pp. 420-22 (566) [long nose], summary in note to Grimm no. 122, "Donkey Cabbages" (Germany); see also 2, pp. 422-23 for further references. For another trans. see Grimm-Zipes, pp. 691-95, no. 234.

Swan, *Gesta Romanorum,* pp. 216-20, no. 120 [one fruit causes leprosy, other cures it], trans. from medieval Latin, literary.

Hodne, *Types,* AT566, 9 versions (Norway).

Cf. Thorpe, *Yule-Tide,* pp. 336-55 [long nose], literary reworking (Denmark).

Massignon, *Folktales,* pp. 217-28, no. 65 [long nose] (France).

Busk, *Legends,* pp. 129-36 [long nose], pp. 136-41 [long nose], pp. 146-55 (with 567) [donkey], 3 versions (Italy).

Crane, *Popular Tales,* pp. 119-22 (with cf. 559/571) [horns], cf. pp. 122-23, summaries, and p. 347, n. 8 (Italy).

Calvino, *Folktales,* pp. 675-79, no. 189 [figs grow horns on head, face, and nose] (Italy).

Bowman and Bianco, *Tales,* pp. 42-52 [pair of horns] (Finland).

Curtin, *Myths and Folk-Tales,* pp. 356-69 [horns] (Czech).

Dégh, *Society,* p. 309, no. 31 (with 567), notes (Hungary).

Baudiš, *Folk Tales,* pp. 170-75 (with 330) [horns] (Czech).

Cf. Groome, *Folk-Tales,* pp. 85-90, no. 23 (cf. 566, with 301A) [apples; horns on head; 2 streams of water, leprosy and cure], Gypsy (Bukovina).

Cf. Dawkins, *Modern,* pp. 117-20, no. 22 (cf. 566, with 567) [horns] (Greece).

Cf. Dawkins, *MGAM*, pp. 410-19, no. 1 (cf. 566, with 567) [horns; ass], Greek dialect text and
    English trans., and p. 263, notes (Turkey).
Kent, *Fairy Tales*, pp. 170-82 [horns; ass] (Turkey).
Walker and Uysal, *Tales*, pp. 24-34, no. 2 [horns] (Turkey).
Schwartz, *Violin*, pp. 82-87 [pair of horns], Jewish tradition (Persian Kurdistan).

India
Knowles, *Folk-Tales*, pp. 75-97 (with 518, 567) [ass] (Kashmir).
McCulloch, *Household*, pp. 255-82, no. 26 (with 1152, 300, 567) [monkey] (Bengal).
For analysis of other references see Thompson and Roberts, *Types*, Type 566.

The Philippines
Fansler, *Tales*, pp. 10-15, no. 2 [horns], pp. 15-17 [horns, fangs, tail], summary of a second Tagalog
    version with discussion.

36. THE KING'S SON

John Roberts
Sally's Cove, Great Northern Peninsula
12 September 1971

Cf. AT611 [Irish by-form]
TC1052 72-4
Collectors: HH and Z. Sacrey

[Int: Can you tell a story about a fellow named Jack?]
Yes I could tell you one. I could tell you "The King's Son" but takes me
too long.
[Int: Oh come on there. They'd like to hear it, wouldn't you like to hear
it?]
[Listeners: Sure, sure.]
[Int: I'd...I think they'd ALL like to hear that, that's the real old-
fashioned]

The King of England _ [Male listener: I love to hear stories like that] an'
the King o' Germany _ well they was allowed to marry. An' [*coughs*]*
so _ the King of England went to Germany. An' _ they had a little...the
King of Germany's woman had a little girl. An' they [*the boy and girl*]
was the one age. An' they made it up they'd marry the two of 'em 'bout
we'll say _ February _ /?just/ _ four or five year old, five year old they
were. But* _ King of England married (her). (That) _ they took it...the
cerstificate an' _ when he come home _ he put it in his big trunk. They
have three trunks _ an' this big one he put it in.* Well -- by an' by his
father died.

*whispering in
background

/(church)/
*loud microphone
noise

*background noise

/truck/

They'd aseen the...so one day _ Mrs. Brown said to un _ she said uh..."Why don't you look in the big /trunk/? You haven't opened the big trunk since your father died." Well -- he opened the big trunk. An' what should he see there was the envelope sealed up. He tore it open _ an' when he tore it open this is what it was. He was married when he was five year ol' _ to the King o' Germany's daughter. [aside: will I finish the story? Heh! [laughs] He's a long one!]

[Int: Oh yeah!]

Huh!

[Int: Yeah.]

Well -- she was married to the...he was married to King of Germany's daughter. An' he had _ his cerstificate. Well -- he went to sea. An' he was gone a few months an' when he come back _ he...he barried [i.e., *talking and noise in background* borrowed]* (he had) a ol' pair o' pants with knees out of 'em. An' a ol' cap. (Out) _ (here) shirt sleeves uh...sleeves out of his shirt, he was dressed up in that kind of a way. An' he went to King o' Germany _ for to _ ask un would he give him a job o' work.

talking and noise in background

Well -- an' his daughter said to her father _ "Well now father" she said _ "you can give that poor...young fellow his job _ so he'd have a little better clothes to wear than what he got." Huh! [laughs] So he give un a job. There _ wasn't (allowed in). So _ he wasn't...he wasn't there very long _ before uh...the...this girl an' he _ when she [the king's daughter] come out of school* 'd go where he was to. And uh...an' one *talking in background* day they was in an'* the first thing she [the girl] seen her _ kiss *background noise* this man _ this young feller. So she witness _ an' she told her father. /pritting/ Now _ er...his daughter an' this feller must get out _ /?putting/ /his father/ people _ together _ she [the girl] seen /?this feller/ kiss her. Well _ she was listenin to it.

talking in background *background noise*

/pritting/

/his father/

So they come..."Now" she says "you go to father _ an' ask him for your (clearance) _ because he'll fire ya." Well -- he went an' asked. Well that was...that was all very good.

While he was there...for a few months _ he had no learning _ so _ she said to her father, s[h]e said "Father why don't you send this young man *child talking in background* to s...to school?"*

child talking in background

So _ he went to the lower school, she was goin to the high school. An' _ he [the teacher] used to say "A"

[Jack said] "A"

"B"

"B"

"C"

"C"

"What's this one here?"

370

"E." This was A. An' that's like it was for a week. An' they all...[laughs] all called un Hard Hea[d] [laughs] So _ she was goin to the high school an' he bes in the lower school, even little youngsters used to call un Hard Hea[d].

So one...one evening he was comin from school _ they had a little place to sit down to have a little rest _ talkin goin along.

An' _ "Well" she said "I got a terrible sum to do. An' I don't know if I'll be able to do it or not."

He said "Give ME your book."

"WHAT'S the good to give you the book when you don't know A B C?"

"Well" he said "no harm for me _ [to] take your book."

So he took the book an' he said "Gi' me a pencil now"*   *background noise

She said "What are you goina do?"

"I will make un up" he said.

"Now Hard Head" she said "you haven't got learning enough _ here for that sum I know ('bout)." So she watched him.

"Now tomorrow" he said* _ "when you goes to school" he said _ "he'll   *background noise
ask you who done this sum, your father or your mother. You say 'Neither one of 'em. 'Twas Hard Head.'"

Well _ the next mornin they went to school and _ down he was...'longside the little youngsters _ in A B C. An' _ he give her another sum _ HARD one. An' goin home where they used to set down an' have a little talk _ she showed Hard Head uh...THIS sum.

"Well now" the Hard Head said _ "I'll do un for you in a quick time."

"Well well well" she said "Hard Head. The little youngsters _ all laughed at you 'cause you didn't know ABC." Heh! [laughs] "You knows un...twice as much as I do."

So he took the pencil an' _ then he made up her sum. "Now" he said "I'll give ya one _ for to give to the teacher. Give to your teachers to make up."

So _ the next day when they went to school _ she had her lessons, everything done. "Now" she said "there's a sum there for YOU to do for you to make up."

Well the teacher looked at it. "(Well I j...) can't do it my girl" he said. "I can't do it. Well what...who done this sum, your father [or] your mother?"

"Neither one of 'em" she said. "'Twas Hard Head. An' he put down this sum for you to do."

So _ they sond after Hard Head _ down to the lower school. An' he come up. Well Hard Head showed un how to do the sum.

Now _ they leaved school. Now he said to the girl _ he said _ "I'm goin away. I'm goina leave this place altogether. An' if I had the money* _ " (he said) an' /she/ had plenty o' money _ "if I had the money _ I'd buy a vessel _ an' I'd go to sea." Well -- she give him the money an' he bought a vessel _ now. An' _ it come a...breeze o' wind _ an' tore his mainsail _ nice bit. So they went in this harbour an' _ went to the wharf.

An' he said to the crew "I'm goin ashore to this boarding house." So he went up [to] the boarding house an'...and* _ the ol' woman _ well _ asked lots o' questions.

"Well" she said "you better stay here an' sleep tonight."

So anyhow when they was goin to bed _ she said "You can sleep with my daughter." So when they 's goin to bed she _ put her hand up on the shelf an' she took down a bottle.

She said "Have a drink 'fore you goes to bed then." Well it taste so good a rum _ as he thought that ever he drinked. An' he was[n't] into bed five minutes 'fore he fell off to sleep. Well the girl...he didn't know whe'r [i.e., *whether*] she sleeped with un or whe'r she didn't.

So the next morning [he] got up. An' he leaved his men there. An' _ after a time he got home. Well when he got home _ he seen his girl an' she give him money enough to buy another vessel. Well he bought another vessel. An' his...other one was to the wharf. Well he went up to this house this night _ an' _ this evening _ for...if he could get his mainsail _ fixed the next day. [*coughs*] Well -- she asked [him] to stop all night. So he stayed all night.

[*clears throat*] When they [was] goin to bed she says "You goina have a drink o' rum 'fore you goes?"
[Int: Uncle John, isn't there a part that she makes a bet with him?] Eh?
[Int: Doesn't she make a bet with him _ that he won't sleep with her daughter? Doesn't...is there a bet about it so he loses the vessel?]

Yes. But uh...'twas the king's daughter see.* I'll finish...I'll finish un after a while. So _ she took down this bottle again (said) _ "Have another drink o' rum" said "before you goes to bed." So they had a drink. An' he wasn't in bed not...three minutes 'fore he was asleep. Well the girl come an' got in bed with him so far as he know an' sleep with un. Well the next morning he...he...that was two vessels he'd alost.*

Well now then he...after a while he got home. He got home again _ told the girl that _ he'd lost his vessel. Well she give un enough money (to) buy another one. So he went.* An' put...uh.../sailed her/ to this spot _ he had his mainsail tore. An' 'cording however* _ there was a boat _ with a ol' man aboard of her. An' he hold up his hand _ for...the other feller [to] take un in tow. So -- but he kept away an' stopped _ his vessel an' _ took this man on board.

He [*the man*] said "This is not* the first time you've been here."
"No" he said "I've alost two vessels there."

"Yes" he said "an' you'll...you'd lose another one tonight. But
you won't lose un. You'll gain what you've alost."* He said
"That...that's sleepy drops she gives you. Puts it ('stead) o' rum.
Now" he said "here's a bottle just like hers _ exactly. An' _ you make
ev...everything...pretty straight an' leave it on the...table _ an' goin
upstairs _ you say 'I forgot my account. I got to go back an' give un un.'
Well she'll run back an' get the 'count _ you whip out her bottle an' hide
un away an' put in this one in...in his place."

Well _ she come back. Said w..."Is you goina have a drink 'fore you
goes to bed?"

"Oh yes" he said.

So he had a drink an' _ [*laughs*] she took the bottle an' put un away
an' _ went to bed. Up come her daughter. [*laughs*]*

"Well" she said "Mother" she said "I wonder is he asleep?"

"'Sleep my dear" she said "I guess he is asleep." Heh! [*laughs*] "He
had another drink _ just now."

Well -- she stripped off an' got in bed with un. An' he hauled up
her...nightdress an' give her a slap on the backside.

"Now old woman" he said "I guess I'll sleep with her tonight alright!"
[*laughs*] Went to sleep with her. [*coughs*]

Well -- he...he start _ a few days afterwards when he got his mainsail
an' that fixed on his vessel. An' he...took one of his vessels an' leaved
for home _ an' leaved the other two to the wharf.

Well when he got home _ to London bridge _ 'twas marked up
everywhere _ in the town _ that uh...the /mayor/ _ was goin [to] be
married to the king's daughter three o'clock in the evening.

Well he got on this big bridge an' it's all _ marked up an' _ by an' by
he seen un [*the mayor*] comin. [*coughs*] An' he begin goin over lookin
on this side an' on that side an' on this side.*

He said "What are ya lookin for?"

He said "I sot a lobster trap here" he said "five year ago. But now I'll
have so good fresh lobster into her tomorrow morning _ as ever you
seen."

So -- oh he was in a wonderful hurry.* He says..."Stop long enough
to tell me your name."

"Well my name" he said "is Poverty _ Part _ an' Good Company."
[*said slowly, loudly, and emphatically*]

So he took out his pocketbook.* "Well" he said "say your name over
again"

*loud noise in background

*child talking in background

*child talking in background

/governor/

*noise in background

*loud noises in background

*loud noises in background

373

"Poverty Part an' Good Company." So he put [it] on his pocketbook.

So when he come to the...king's house _ his girl come an' sot down on his knee.

An' _ "Well" he said "I meet the queer fellow this evening. He was on London bridge. An' he was goin back an' forth, back an' forth. I asked un what he was lookin for. He said he sot a lobster trap nine year ago _ an' he'd have so good a fresh lobster into un _ as ever I seen."

She said "You didn't ask him his name?"

"I got (he)" he said "on me pocketbook. His name is Poverty _ Part an' Good Company."* Well she knowed just who it was.

Well now then _ she was goin down to the Browns'* _ an' she said to her girl _ they were goina [be] married three o'clock in the evening* _ but the...mayor o' the town told un he was goina [be] married three o'clock.

"Damn fine wife" he say "if you gets her."

"Oh well" [laughing tone] he said "I'll get her 'cause I'm goina be married three o'clock."

So _ he went on down to Mrs. /Brown's/ again _ and uh*...he began to tell her about the fe...the feller he seen goin back an' forth the bridge lookin for a...a lobster trap he sot [laughing tone] nine year ago there.

"Well" she said "did ya ask him his name?"

He said "I got it in on me pocketbook. Poverty Part an' Good Company."

Well few minutes afterwards she said to her girl _ she said "Let's go down [to] Mrs. /Brown's/" _ 'cause they were goin to be married three o'clock. An' _ they went down.

Well when /?she/ got down _ home _ she seen who it was. Well _ 'tis seems like in regard...[?they was married] when they was...little children _ five year old. So anyhow /she/ got Mrs. Brown's nightdress. She stripped off an' put it on. An' _ [?he] took the cerstificate what he had an' _ put up over door an' tacked it up (now). An' _ an' she got her nightdress an' put on. An' _ they went to bed.

So _ by an' by the king said to...to the [servant] girl _ "Where's your missus?"

"She's down to Mrs. Brown's _ in bed with a man."

"Now my girl" [loud tones] he said "you tell me a lie _ you won't live to see two hours longer. I'll hang [you]...an' you'll be hung. Well _ " he said to the other feller "let's go down."

So when they went down an' opened the door* _ the first thing (out) was _ tacked on...on inside part of door. An' (did she have un) _ come

---

Margin notes (left):

*child making noise in background
*child talking in background
*loud noises in background

/(Colman's)/
*coughing and loud noises in background

/(Colman's)/

/he/

/he/

*loud background noise

right along an' she was in bed _ with Mrs. Brown's nightdress on. [*laughs*] Well when he seen who it was _ he was tickled to death [to] think it was the king's son _ what married his daughter* when she was five year old. Well his father and mother did.*

Well – while he was...lookin at it _ "Well well well" he said "'tis I'M SOME PROUD. I've afound the man _ that married my daughter when she was _ five year old." So -- 'twas marked up. He [*Jack*] hauled up his...wife's nightdress _ she had on Mrs. Brown's _ an' give her a slap on the backside.

"Didn't I tell ye" he said "I'd have so good a fresh lobster as ever...[*laughs*] ever you seen!" [*laughs*] Well. Oh my good gracious!

*listener sneezes
*child making noise in background

Duration: 16 min., 41 sec.
Location: Teller's son's house, sitting room, late morning.
Audience: Teller's daughter-in-law, people of the household, several visitors (approximately a dozen adults) and children, interviewers.

Context, Style, and Language: The context in which this story was collected is of a kind often encountered by the fieldworkers. The recording takes place in a room which opens directly onto the kitchen where several women in the household are busy preparing a late Sunday breakfast for the assembled company following earlier birthday celebrations for the baby. They can be clearly heard scouring pans and scrubbing surfaces, peeling and chopping vegetables, and moving crockery and utensils about. Doors are continually heard opening and closing as people come in and out of the room, and various individuals come in to listen to the story. A very young child is playing nearby, several other children are present, including a small baby which first gurgles happily but becomes increasingly fractious and eventually begins to cry. Those actually listening to the tale remain mostly quiet and attentive throughout, occasionally whispering to each other. John Roberts' daughter-in-law acts as an interpreter when interviewer A asks questions because her father-in-law is extremely deaf, and he fails either to hear or understand the question about Jack making the bet. Nevertheless, actively encouraged by the interviewers and the audience, the teller is quite unperturbed by all the noise and activity around him. His daughter-in-law suggests that he should move to a quieter room but this helpful suggestion unfortunately comes too late in the interview for it to be acted upon.

The considerable difficulties in the recording of this story are exacerbated by a great deal of talking and background noise throughout. The recording quality is poor and there is a constant hum on the tape. Consequently the transcription is less full and less reliable than most, and all material in parentheses should be regarded as a reasonable attempt to decipher the hearable speech, rather than as definitive. John Roberts obviously enjoys telling the story and laughs quite frequently at the events in the plot. He often pauses deliberately for dramatic effect and to heighten suspense, and makes use of strongly marked stress on individual words, especially in the dialogue. The name of the hero is rarely pronounced clearly or fully here,

375

the final /d/ being usually omitted and the name sounding more like *Hardy* than *Hardhead*. However, the latter form has been used in the transcription throughout to facilitate the narrative.

John Roberts' speech leans towards the West Country English type, as seen, for example, in *bes* /biz/ in the third person singular present tense of the verb *be* and in the frequent use of *un* (it, him). Other dialectal pronunciations include *cerstificate, barried* /barid/ (borrowed), and such aphetic forms as *'longside, 'fore, 'stead* (instead), *'count* (account), *'sleep* (asleep), *'twas*. Archaic past tense forms include *sond* (sent), *drinked, leaved, meet, sot* (sat), and the past participles *aseen, alost, afound*. Note also the purposive *for to give* and the typical Newfoundland use of *evening* for afternoon in *three o'clock in the evening*.

Type and Motifs:
Cf. AT611. *The Gifts of the Dwarfs* [Irish by-form].
Cf. T69.2. *Parents affiance children without their knowledge.*
K1816. *Disguise as menial.*
T91.6.4. *Princess falls in love with lowly boy.*
L142. *Pupil surpasses master.*
N831. *Girl as helper.*
K675. *Sleeping potion given to man who is to pass night with a girl.*
Cf. N15. *Chastity wager.*
Cf. N2.5. *Whole kingdom (all property) as wager.*
Cf. K92. *Gambling contest won by deception.*
N825.2. *Old man helper.*
K1865. *Deception by pretending sleep.*
N681. *Husband (lover) returns home just as wife (mistress) is to marry another.*
Cf. H586.2.2. *Traveler says he must look after his net to see if it has taken fish.*
H151. *Attention drawn and recognition follows.*
Cf. K1831.0.1. *Disguise by changing name.*
T102. *Hero returns and marries first love.*

International Parallels: This group of Newfoundland tales, all recorded on the west coast of the province, does not belong to a standard type but rather to a by-form found primarily in the Irish and Scottish Gaelic traditions. While the Newfoundland recensions share many elements of this by-form with the Irish and Scottish Gaelic versions available to us in English, English translation, or English abstracts, there are some interesting differences. The major difference is that in all of the Newfoundland recensions there are two sea voyages financed by the girl. On these the hero loses his ships and their cargoes not by disasters at sea, which is a pattern found in some of the Irish versions, but by losing a most unusual bet. He regains all of his lost property on his third voyage by winning the same bet, thanks to the assistance of a mysteriously knowledgeable stranger. He then returns home just in time to claim his girl before she can be married to someone else.

This bet, which is found in all of our Newfoundland texts, is not known in the Irish or Scottish versions of the tale. This section of the narrative apparently derives from an Italian novella which scholars regard as the chief source of Shakespeare's *Merchant of Venice.* We will examine the novella version and compare it with its Newfoundland congeners later in this discussion.

There are brief outlines of the plot of the by-form in *Irish Handbook,* p. 569, no. 611, and in *Irish Types,* p. 131, in the note accompanying Type 611. A much fuller description is given with references in McKay-Campbell, *Tales,* 1, pp. 390-92. Both as a convenience to the reader and for the purposes of our discussion, we present here a description of the plot in which we have drawn on all three of the references, but with several changes and additions.

Two wealthy men, usually close friends and sometimes partners, marry or betroth the son of one of them to the other's daughter when both are infants or young children. Both men keep the marriage or betrothal agreement a secret, but retain records of it in their private papers. In some versions the record is the original marriage certificate.

The father of the boy is killed or dies from natural causes and creditors leave the wife and child penniless; the girl's father either does not help the widow, or only pretends to do so in order to defraud his late partner's wife of her share of the property. In a few versions where the families live in different countries, the widow lives too far away to ask his help. As the girl grows up, she is attracted to the boy; occasionally she helps him get educated. Frequently she is the one who discovers that they had been married, or that they were betrothed. Since he is very poor, she subsidizes him in business ventures, sometimes repeatedly. In the Newfoundland versions it is the young man who knows of their marriage in infancy.

In some versions the way the girl subsidizes her lover (husband) is by enabling him to purchase a ship and merchandise and go to sea; sometimes she does this several times. In other versions it is the father who sends the young man on a dangerous sea voyage hoping it will lead to his death. The father wants to get rid of the young man so that he might then marry his daughter to some wealthy person. The sea voyage is an opportunity for storytellers to introduce other plots, such as AT1651, "Whittington's Cat," and AT505, "Dead Man as Helper." The Newfoundland handling of the sea voyage sequence will be discussed separately below.

In nearly all versions of this narrative the hero becomes wealthy from his sea voyage and returns home. Here many narrators take the opportunity to introduce a well-known tale Type, AT974, "The Homecoming Husband," in which the husband or lover arrives home just as his wife is to marry another. This Type is occasionally combined with elements belonging to AT875D, Incident II, but these elements appear with varying degrees of fullness in different versions.

We know, of course, that the heroine and hero were married in childhood, and that this has been a well-kept secret. Because of the hero's long absence, we must presume that the girl's father believes that the hero is safely out of the way, and that the daughter is now in a position to make a fitting marriage.

Sometimes when he is nearing home the returning husband meets a gentleman who reveals he is on his way to marry the heroine of the story that very day. It is at this point that some versions differ. Larminie's County Donegal text has the most complete form of

AT875D, II. The hero, who has sent ahead a rich store of merchandise in the enigmatic name of "The Servant of Poverty," tells the gentleman he meets that he is looking for the herring net he set years ago. When a heavy rain comes down, he shares his plaid with the gentleman; he rescues the latter from being drowned when they are crossing a river; he also shares his food with him. He tells the gentleman he should have carried his house with him, should always take a bridge with him, and should never travel without his mother. The gentleman regards these statements and the one about the herring net as extremely foolish, and so reports them when he arrives at the king's home. The king interprets two of these enigmatic remarks correctly, saying that undoubtedly the man wore a good topcoat and rode a good horse.

In the Latin *Gesta Romanorum,* all of these statements, about the house, the bridge, the (father and) mother, and the net, are made by a knight who is returning from the Holy Land to marry the emperor of Rome's daughter, who had promised to wait for him seven years. He is speaking to the King of Hungary who is also on his way to marry the emperor's daughter. The emperor interprets the first three of the supposedly foolish enigmatic statements correctly, but when the net is mentioned he deduces that his daughter is the net and hastily sends for her. They find that the knight has run off with her (Swan, *Gesta Romanorum,* pp. xxxvii-xxxviii).

The enigmatic statement about a net or a cage is also found in Child's headnote to the ballad "Hind Horn" (Child, *Ballads* 1, pp. 189-91). In a footnote (p. 191) Child cites not only the story from the *Gesta Romanorum* (see above) and other references, but also J. F. Campbell's folktale "Bailie Lunain" (Campbell, *Popular Tales,* 1, 289-96, no. 17b).

In the Campbell tale we have again the enigmatic statements about the net, and about traveling with your mother, your house, and your own bridge, remarks the Saxon to whom they are made regards as foolish, but which are correctly interpreted by the Bailie, the girl's father, who tells the Saxon he was the fool and the other a smart lad. This tale is not a version of the by-form, but both Larminie, *Folk-Tales,* p. 256, and McKay (McKay-Campbell, *Tales* 1, p. 392) recognize that many incidents in it parallel the by-form.

The only other Scottish-Gaelic tale that needs comment is the one in McKay-Campbell, *Tales*, 2, pp. 38-52. In this the hero helps his rival get across a river in his carriage by tying his own horse's tail to the two horses drawing the carriage. He does not, however, make any enigmatic statements about this. When asked his name, he says it is, "I am the good that was and that went to waste." Since his rival is unable to write the strange name down, the hero borrows his pocket-book and writes it for him. In this version, as in most of the Newfoundland ones, the name in the pocket-book is the clue to the girl that her lover has returned. The other Scottish and Irish versions we have listed in our analogues lack both the enigmatic names and the series of enigmatic statements.

It is useful at this point to survey the endings of the Newfoundland recensions. In all of them we have the hero returning home just as his wife is supposed to be married to a rival (AT974). In all of them he meets his rival on a bridge. The enigmatic statements which the rival regards as foolish have been reduced to one statement and to our hero consciously playing the part of a fool. In all of the Newfoundland recensions we have the substitution of that very maritime device, a lobster trap, for the fishing net. The supposedly foolish hero tells his rival that if he finds the trap which he left some years before, he will have a fine fresh lobster for breakfast. When the rival asks the foolish fellow his name, he is told some variant of the old English proverb: "Poverty Parts Good Company," which, in all but one recension, the rival writes in his pocket-book. For an historical survey of this proverb see Smith and Harvey, *English Proverbs,* p. 514, "Poverty Parteth Fellowship (Friends, Good Company)."

At the home of the lady he expects to marry, the rival tells the assembled company of the foolish behavior of the man he met on the bridge, and when asked if he knows the latter's name, reads it from his pocket-book. This is the clue to the girl that her husband has returned, and she goes to find him. When they are together, in most versions her husband pins their childhood marriage certificate over the door, and takes her to bed. When the indignant father and the lover go to verify the report that she is in bed with a man, the marriage certificate is pointed out to them. The husband then lifts his wife's nightgown, slaps her on her bare backside, and tells the rival that here is the fine fresh lobster he said he would have. This earthy humorous scene is limited to the Newfoundland recensions.

One curious difference between a few of the Irish and Scottish versions and all of the Newfoundland ones is on the question of the hero's education or lack of it. Only in two of the Scottish and one of the Irish versions does this topic receive any attention. In Larminie's Co. Donegal version and in the Barra text translated in McKay-Campbell, *Tales,* 1, pp. 372-89, the boy gets his education slowly and painfully over a period of time. In the London text translated in McKay-Campbell, *Tales,* 2, pp. 38-52, when the boy's mother is forced to withdraw her son from the expensive school he has been attending, he is able to return there when the girl underwrites the cost of his education. Only in the Larminie story is there any "test" of the young man's acquired scholarship. When two clerks in Dublin after working three days are unable to settle the accounts between the king and a merchant from London, the girl suggests to the king, her father, that they try the shopman (our hero) with the remark, "They say he has good learning." The shopman is invited to try and in very short order settles the account. "Good learning" in this instance seems to be skill in bookkeeping or perhaps as a public accountant.

Schooling plays a dramatic role in all of the Newfoundland recensions, but its treatment is very different from its handling in the versions just described. In each of the Newfoundland texts the king's daughter persuades her father to send the poor boy, Jack, to the school she is attending. In a couple she is in high school and Jack in the lower school. The storytellers have great fun illustrating how thick-headed and uneducable Jack appears to be. He even seems unable to learn the alphabet and as a result is given the sobriquet "Hard Head" or "Hard Un."

In each of the Newfoundland versions, the king's daughter is returning from school one afternoon crying or half crying because of the difficult sum the teacher has set for her. She does not want to show it to Hard Head because he is notoriously ignorant, but after some persuasion she allows him to see it, and he quickly "makes it up." Sometimes on the next day the teacher sets an even harder sum and Hard Head easily makes it up as well. In all but one of the recensions, after having done the sum, Hard Head turns over the slate or the "scribbler," and sets a sum for the teacher to do. The teacher is unable to do it and in No.

37 says that Hard Head has better education than he has. In No. 40 the king's daughter tells her father that Jack has more learning than the teacher.

The whole scene, with its realistic touches of doing sums on an individual slate, or in a "scribbler," a small notebook made of cheap paper, is reminiscent of pre-Confederation schooling in Newfoundland. The teacher, baffled by Hard Head's sum, sounds like one who had only passed his Grade 11 examination before being sent out by a Church School Board to take charge of an outport school. It is curious to observe that the "making up" (solving) of difficult arithmetical sums [possibly "arithmetical problems" is meant?] is accepted as a proof of superior education.

Jack has obviously been well-educated before he comes to the girl's school. Since he is the son of the King of England in No. 36, and the son of the King of France in No. 43, we can assume that he had excellent tutoring in his youth. But in Nos. 37, 40, and 42 there is insufficient information on his earlier background for us to determine how he got such "good learning." Nonetheless because of his skillful role-playing, he has acquired from it his unforgettable nickname.

In only one of the non-Newfoundland versions do we have a description of the boy as a risk taker. In Larminie, *Folk-Tales,* pp. 117-18, he takes the money the girl lends him to buy hardware for peddling and loses it twice, once by betting on a fighting-cock, the second time by betting on a racehorse. When he tells her he lost her five pounds a second time, the girl calmly remarks: "Well. . .unless there was venture in you, you would not have lost them," and her third loan to him is spent properly. In all of the Newfoundland versions the young man is very much a risk taker and not with such small amounts as five pound bets. Twice he loses a ship and cargo by losing a rigged bet, and only regains them when he makes the same bet for a third time and, with outside help, manages to win.

It is now time for us to examine the voyage-and-bet sequences found in all Newfoundland versions of Cf. AT611. Hardhead persuades his girl to send him to sea as skipper of a well-stocked vessel purchased with her money. In all versions, whether he is going around the Cape of Good Hope or passing by Naples or by some unnamed harbor, invariably a sudden violent storm wrecks his canvas and the ship must limp into port. The skipper goes ashore and looks for a boarding house in which to stay while the ship's gear is mended or replaced.

The boarding-house keeper offers to bet her property against his ship and cargo that her daughter (two daughters in No. 42) can spend the night in bed with him and that the next morning he will not know whether she is man or woman. Hard Head takes the bet. When he is going to bed, she pulls out a bottle and offers him a drink. He accepts and promptly falls into a heavy sleep. When he awakes or is awakened next morning, he has lost his ship and cargo.

After a long period Hard Head returns home and tells his girl he lost his ship but, of course, does not explain how. She equips him with a second ship, and we get a repeat of the first trip: the storm, getting into harbor, the boarding house, the bet, the drink, and next morning the second ship is lost.

Once again he gets back home eventually and his girl outfits him for the third and last time. In some recensions she tells him that if he loses this ship, he need not return. On this third voyage the same kind of storm strikes. But this time, either while he is still at sea or after the ship is tied up at the wharf, he gets advice. The variations in who his adviser is and the help he gives will be discussed later. To summarize the episode here, he is told that the drink he gets is drugged: it is "sleepy drops." He is given a bottle to substitute for the landlady's bottle, and by this means stays awake when the girl(s) come to bed; by next morning he has regained his lost vessels and won the boarding-house keeper's property, so that he is able to return home a wealthy man.

We wondered if this unusual voyage-and-bed sequence, which we had not located in any published versions of Cf. AT611, might perhaps be found in unpublished archival recordings or manuscripts. Dr. Séamas Ó Catháin, archivist of the Department of Irish Folklore, University College, Dublin, replied to our inquiry that the Newfoundland combination of this subplot with the Irish by-form of AT611 had not been reported from Ireland. Similarly, both Dr. Alan Bruford, Archivist of the School of Scottish Studies, University of Edinburgh, and his colleague, Dr. Donald Archie Macdonald, told us that they do not know any Scottish versions of the by-form that also have the Newfoundland subplot.

For that matter, so far as we can determine, not only is this Newfoundland voyage-and-bet sequence absent from other versions of the by-form of AT611, but it is rarely found in oral tradition in connection with any folktale type. The single published example we have located can best be discussed after we examine the literary background of the theme.

The only older parallel we have found for the three voyages and the bet is in an Italian novella which Shakespeare used for the main plot of *The Merchant of Venice*. "The Story of Gianetto of Venice and the Lady of Belmont," to use the title given in Spencer's translation of the Italian text (Spencer, *Stories*, pp. 177-96) "is found in a collection of fifty stories called *Il Pecorone* ('the big sheep,' that is, dunce—an ironical title) and attributed to a certain Ser Giovanni of Florence. Although written in the fourteenth century it was not printed until 1558." (Spencer, *Stories*, p. 28).

In the story in *Il Pecorone* (IV, I), Gianetto and several friends go cruising together, each in his own vessel; the others are going to Alexandria on a trading expedition, he is going mainly to see the world and enjoy himself. These were his instructions from his godfather, Signor Ansaldo, who had given him a richly supplied ship. When they were passing a fine harbor, the captain of the ship tells Gianetto it belongs to a beautiful widow who has made a law that every man who arrives there (captains or owners of ships are implied) must sleep with her. If he succeeds in enjoying her, he must marry her and become Lord of the country; if he fails, he loses his ship and its contents. Despite the captain's warning that many gentlemen who had gone there had lost all their possessions, Gianetto is intrigued and orders the captain to slip away from the other ships and head into that port.

Gianetto is well received by the Lady of Belmont and the day is spent in courtly entertainments in which he takes an active part. In the evening the Lady takes him into her room and two maidservants come in with wine and sweetmeats. The Lady says she knows he must be thirsty and suggests he take something to drink. He drinks some of the wine, which is drugged, and as soon as he goes to bed falls asleep. Although the Lady lies next to him, he never notices anything; next morning she arises. When he is awakened later, he is told he must leave; he has lost his ship and its contents.

The Lady gives him a horse and money for traveling expenses and he finally returns to Venice. Ashamed to admit his fault, he says he has been shipwrecked. His godfather consoles him and next spring outfits another ship very richly for him in which he sails, accompanied by his friends in their own ships. But Gianetto once more deserts them and sails to Belmont where he is well received. However, that evening he once again drinks the wine offered to him and falls asleep, completely ignoring the Lady next to him, and next morning finds he has lost his second vessel.

When he reaches Venice, he again claims he has lost his ship in a natural disaster. His godfather, who has spent the bulk of his fortune in buying and furnishing the first two ships, urges his godson to stay quietly at home. But Gianetto is so miserable that his godfather allows him to go on a third voyage. This time to buy and equip the ship his godfather has to sell off most of his remaining property. To get the final ten thousand ducats needed, Signor Ansaldo has to borrow it from a Jewish moneylender, who insists as security that he sign a bond that if the money is not returned by the agreed date the lender can cut a pound of flesh from any part of Ansaldo's body that he chooses.

Gianetto, who has fallen in love with the Lady, again manages to elude his friends and reach Belmont. On his two previous visits, he has made such a good impression on the lords and ladies of the court by his charm, good manners, and skill in dancing, jousting, and other gentlemanly activities that he is warmly received. Fortunately for him this liking and goodwill towards him is shared by one of the Lady's maidservants. Before he goes to bed with the Lady for the third time, this maidservant quietly warns him to pretend to drink the wine when it is offered to him before going to bed, but not to drink it. Gianetto is quick-witted enough to understand this advice. Therefore when the wine is proffered, he only acts as if he were drinking it, but throws it into his bosom instead. As a result he stays wide awake and consummates his love for the lady in a fashion most satisfactory to both of them. Next day he is knighted, proclaimed Lord of the country, and then weds the Lady with full pomp and ceremony.

Gianetto is so involved first with celebration and then with his new duties that he forgets Ansaldo's deadline for repaying his debt until the day it is due. When he recalls it and tells his wife, she speeds him off to Venice by land with a large sum of money. She follows, disguised as a gentleman-lawyer, who, when he arrives in Venice, proclaims his readiness to judge any legal questions brought before him.

Since Ansaldo has defaulted on his debt repayment, the Jew demands forfeiture of the bond and refuses to accept proffers of many times the original sum to cancel the bond. The case is presented to the lawyer. After reading the bond he first advises acceptance of the offer of ten times the debt in place of the forfeit. When this is refused the lawyer states the forfeit may be collected. Before the Jew can use his razor, the lawyer warns him that if the amount of flesh cut off is either less or more than the exact pound, the Jew will be executed; likewise if he sheds a single drop of his victim's blood. When the Jew in despair offers to accept in its place the large sum originally offered to him, he is told that he is too late and can collect nothing but the forfeit. In fury he tears up the bond and Ansaldo is then released from custody.

The lawyer, who is ready to depart, refuses all payment, but says he would like Gianetto's ring. The latter explains that his wife has given it to him and she asked that he always wear it for love of her. The lawyer finally persuades him to part with it, but advises him to hurry back to his wife.

His wife gets home before him and changes into woman's garb. When Gianetto returns bringing his friends and Ansaldo with him, she pretends to be indignant that he no longer has her ring, rejects his explanation, and accuses him of wenching in Venice. He is so upset that he begins to weep. His wife then shows him the ring and tells him that she herself was the lawyer. The maidservant who had given him the warning not to drink is rewarded by being married to Signor Ansaldo.

Let us now compare Ser Giovanni's tale with the Newfoundland recensions. In the Newfoundland treatments of the "bed test" we are in a completely different world from that in the novella. Unlike Gianetto, Hard Head does not go voluntarily to the port where he makes the bet, but is storm-driven there three separate times. We get the impression that either evil magic or fate is involved. Far from going to the court of a reigning princess, Hard Head goes to a boarding house. It sounds remarkably like one of the familiar boarding houses on Brazil Square in St. John's, which many outport visitors to the city frequently patronized. Instead of a law that he must sleep with the ruling princess, we have a straightforward bet with the boarding-house mistress which Hard Head, apparently a compulsive risk taker, accepts. The attractive Lady of Belmont with whom Gianetto is deeply in love is replaced here by the daughter of the boarding-house mistress. The girl herself is of such little importance as an individual that she is not even described.

Gone is any mention of courtly pleasure in which the hero's manners and skills attract and charm all beholders, and particularly the lady's helpful maidservant. Instead the helpful advice to avoid drinking the "sleepy drops" comes from a character who has not appeared before in the story, indeed has not even been mentioned. This character gives him a bottle that is an exact duplicate of the one with "sleepy drops" which the boarding-house mistress has twice before tricked him into drinking. Thanks to having a drink of good rum from his own bottle instead of the sleeping potion, Hard Head stays awake when the girl comes to bed, and next morning, having won the bet, takes over both his own lost property and the possessions of the boarding-house mistress. There is none of the pomp, ceremony, and celebrations such as ensued when Gianetto was proclaimed winner of the bet, and which delayed his return to Venice. Hard Head settles his affairs with businesslike promptness and heads back to where his own lady lives.

In the Newfoundland recensions there is considerable variety in the ways of presenting the helpful character who serves the same role in these tales as the helpful maidservant in the story from *Il Pecorone*. The helper appears only in the third voyage. In No. 36, it is an old man in a boat, who holds up his hand requesting that he be towed by Hard Head's vessel as it limps into port, but instead is taken on board. In No. 38, an old man in a small boat comes alongside Jack's vessel and the hero invites him on board. In No. 40, during the storm off the Cape of Good Hope, Jack sees an old man whose boat is in a dangerous situation, a tiderip; Jack respectfully calls him grandfather, and asks him to come aboard or he will be drowned. In No. 42, when Hard Un's vessel has drifted into the harbor, a man from another schooner comes on board. In No. 43, Jack is already in port in Naples and on the way to the boarding house, when he meets a man on two crutches who greets him as "the king's son of France," and introduces himself to Jack as his godfather.

In all the recensions, whether the old man comes on board from a small boat, or from another schooner, or is met on land, he turns out to be extremely knowledgeable, indeed supernaturally so. He is always aware that this is the third time Jack's vessel had been in a storm and had been forced into the same port. He always knows that Jack had twice before lost both the bet at the boarding house and his vessel. In every version he tells our hero that the drink he was given by the boarding-house mistress on the two previous occasions was from a bottle doctored with "sleepy drops."

In all of the Newfoundland recensions except No. 43, Jack's helper gives him a bottle identical to the one the woman offers him, and advises, though with varying amounts of detail, that this time Jack should draw up a legal formalization of the terms of the bet and have the woman sign it. Jack is to leave the papers downstairs, and after he has gone to bed he is to insist on going downstairs to get them. The idea is that the old woman will herself go down for them instead, and while she is gone Jack is to substitute his new bottle for hers. All of this occurs and Jack is able to stay awake and do what is necessary for him to win the bet.

The version in No. 43 is far more elaborate. Jack's godfather knows about the sleepy drops, but tells his godson not only that the boarding-house keeper is a witch, but also that her basement is full of the dead bodies of others who had made similar wagers; they were supposed to be in a drugged sleep but had flinched when tested with a red hot poker and had been stabbed to death and thrown into the basement. The godfather gives full instructions about formalizing the terms of the bet but also insists that the first and second mates from Jack's vessel are to sleep in an adjoining room. Before going to bed he is to ask for a private room so that he can write a letter home. When in the room, he is to strip and grease his entire body with the contents of a bottle his godfather gives him. This coating will not only protect him from feeling the hot poker, but keep him from being affected by the "sleepy drops." However, just in case the woman's witchcraft is stronger than the godfather's and his godson begins to feel sleepy, his godfather gives him a pin with which to prick himself and keep awake.

Although the storyteller gives no details, obviously this time Jack wins the bet, because next morning he sends for the police, and now owns not only his three ships but also the woman's whole estate. He sells the estate back to her relatively cheaply for five hundred pounds, puts captains in his other two ships, and all three head back to England. The business of the hot poker and the dead bodies has apparently been introduced into this story from a migratory legend. What we find extremely curious is that even though the police are brought to the boarding house, they are not told about the bodies in the basement. The narrator ignores the whole affair in order to concentrate on the main story.

It is only in this version that the hero's helper admits to having witchcraft, i.e., supernatural power. Yet, as we suggested above, unquestionably each helper in the different versions has extensive supernatural knowledge. In this last recension we may assume that a proper godfather would do everything in his power to help his godson, but we have no clue to explain how the little old men in boats acquired their knowledge, nor why they bother to intervene in the story to help our hero. These supernatural elements in all versions of the story stand out in strong contrast with the realistic treatment of the rest of the tale.

Turning again to the Ser Giovanni story, we can easily see why scholars agree that it provided the main plot of *The Merchant of Venice*. Shakespeare tightened the structure by having only one courting voyage to Belmont. Antonio is a close friend of Bassanio, not his godfather. Bassanio, for whose use of 3000 ducats (not 10,000) Antonio signed the bond, was not responsible for Antonio's lack of funds. That was occasioned by Antonio's putting all his wealth into many vessels sent off on trading ventures, but which were either wrecked or not heard from and therefore presumed lost. The lady's home in Belmont, her disguise as a lawyer whose exact interpretation of the bond rescues Antonio from losing the pound of flesh, and the wheedling from Bassanio of the ring from which he had sworn to his wife he would never be parted, all replicate the Ser Giovanni story.

The main difference between the Ser Giovanni story and *The Merchant of Venice* is in the subplot. We have already suggested that having one courting voyage rather than three helps to tighten the structure of the play. But Spencer (*Stories,* p. 28) proposes a plausible explanation for the chief reason that Shakespeare substituted another subplot for the one in his original source: "The 'testing' of Gianetto in bed by the Lady of Belmont is obviously unsuitable for dramatic presentation and strains credulity. In its place Shakespeare inserted another story of the 'testing' of a lover: the choosing of one among three caskets (gold, silver, and lead)." Spencer then discusses briefly (pp. 28-29) Shakespeare's probable source for the three caskets story. For a full comparative discussion of that story see Lee, *Sources,* pp. 294-311 (Day X, Novel I).

The Rotunda *Motif-Index* has three motifs to describe the subplot apparently rejected by Shakespeare: H347, "'Suitor test: to consort with princess.' Suitors are given sleeping potion "; K675, "Sleeping potion given to man who is to pass night with girl "; P616, "'Newcomers forced to pass night with ruling princess.' Given sleeping potion. Goods confiscated for failure to consummate marriage." For all three motifs Rotunda's only citation is the *Il Pecorone* story. In other words Rotunda found no other parallels in the large body of Italian novelle.

Stith Thompson, who incorporated Rotunda's motifs in his worldwide *Motif-Index,* has no other references to add, either printed or oral. However, in the years since the *Motif-Index* appeared, a Chilean folktale that has this subplot has been published in an English translation. A summary of the story from Pino-Saavedra, *Folktales,* pp. 194-98, no. 38, is relevant to our discussion. "White Onion" is the name of a wealthy princess who lives on an island in the middle of the sea. She makes a vow that she will give a ship full of gold and silver to whoever can go to bed with her and turn toward her side of the bed. He who turns is to marry her, he who does not is to give her a ship full of treasure. Four millionaires take the bet, are given a bedtime drink, and sleep soundly all night. Each loses his treasure ship.

The orphaned son of a rich man hears of her, sells his possessions to load a ship with gold and silver, takes the bet, accepts the drink, sleeps, and fails. He promptly goes to his very wealthy godfather to borrow a ship loaded with gold and silver. The godfather agrees to lend him such a ship provided that if it is not returned in three days, he can claim a pound of flesh from his godson's rump. The boy agrees. On his way through the garden near White Onion's house he hears a ragged old woman saying, "If only someone would tell him what it is White Onion gives him." He asks the old woman what makes him fall so sound asleep when he is with the lady. The old woman tells him to throw away secretly the drink he is given at bedtime. When it is time to go to bed, he does this. About midnight he rolls over to White Onion's side of the bed. Next morning they are married.

Because of the celebrations that follow the wedding, he forgets about returning his godfather's ship on time. When he finally sails the ship back, his godfather refuses to accept it, demanding instead his pound of flesh. When the boy refuses, he is thrown in jail. He writes to his wife, who promptly dresses herself as a viceroy and heads for the godfather's house, first notifying him to expect a viceregal visit. She goes ashore with true viceregal pomp, goes to the jail and begins to take declarations from the prisoners and set them free one at a time. In the last cell is her husband. When she gets his declaration, she asks the godfather if this testimony is true. When he says it is, she authorizes him to take his pound of flesh, but says it has to be all in one piece. She warns him he will have to pay if he cuts either too much or too little. The godfather's protest is rejected, so he gives up his claim. The viceroy takes the prisoner on board her ship and has him cleaned up and dressed. Then, having changed to woman's garb, she greets him, but has to prove to him that she is his wife.

Despite certain variations—the lady's strange name; the unnamed island rather than a named (if imaginary) seaport; there are two voyages, not three; the advice about the drugged drink comes from an old woman in the garden (how did she know?) rather than from a maidservant in the household, and so on—the tale is clearly parallel to the story in Ser Giovanni. The most curious difference is that here the godfather, instead of being the one willing to sign the dangerous bond to help his godson, is the one who wants to take the pound of flesh from him. The wife's disguise as a male vice-regent replaces the Ser Giovanni disguise as a gentleman lawyer, but her reasoning that the forfeited pound must be cut in one piece is the same as that in Ser Giovanni; it lacks, however, the touch about not shedding a drop of blood. Also missing in this tale is the farcical business of wangling his wife's ring from the hero and then accusing him for giving it away. Shakespeare apparently liked that touch so well that he doubled it in his play, but the folktale narrator found it unnecessary.

We offer two theories to explain how the novella story got into Chilean oral tradition. First, the story may have been in oral tradition in Europe. After all no one has any idea how Ser Giovanni acquired it or if it was his own invention. If it was in oral tradition in both Italy and Spain, a Spanish storyteller could have brought it to the Western Hemisphere. The fact that there are no other published citations in the Thompson *Motif-Index* is no proof that the story was not known. A somewhat better case might be made for a second theory which is that some storyteller, whether in Europe or in Chile, had heard the Ser Giovanni story read aloud, retained the basic elements of the tale in his memory, and then retold it, adapting it to the Chilean milieu. It must be admitted, however, that plausible as these theories may be we have no evidence to support either of them.

Although we can make some reasonable suggestions on how the complete plot of the Ser Giovanni story was transferred to Chile, we have more difficulty with our Newfoundland recensions of the Irish by-form of AT611. It is not with the basic plot itself. We have demonstrated above that, despite variations, our tale belongs to the same tradition as that found in both Ireland and Gaelic-speaking Scotland. What is harder to explain is how the subplot got here.

We have also shown that the only other versions of the subplot, which Spencer designates as the "bed test," are those connected with the AT890, "A Pound of Flesh" story in Ser Giovanni's *Il Pecorone* and also in the Chilean folktale discussed above. This latter story also includes Incident IV of the Type, the episode in which the hero's wife assumes male disguise and frees her husband from his obligation to pay his creditor a pound of flesh. Although the "bed test" subplot is found on the west coast of Newfoundland as part of all the recorded versions of the by-form of AT611, we have the assurances of two knowledgeable archivists, the one in Dublin, the other in Edinburgh, that it has never been found combined with the by-form in either the Irish or the Scottish-Gaelic tradition. This oikotype is apparently unique to Newfoundland.

It is reasonable to assume that all the Newfoundland versions derive from a single storyteller, presumably a Newfoundlander. The question of whether this storyteller was the first to combine the subplot with the main plot, or whether he had previously heard it with this combination either in the province or abroad, cannot be answered. Fortunately, however, such scholarly frustration will not interfere with the pleasure of hearing or reading such a fascinating group of stories.

Studies and Notes

Swan, *Gesta Romanorum*, pp. xxxvii-xxxviii, chap. 18; Child, *Ballads*, 1, pp. 187-201, no. 17, "Hind Horn," headnote; Giovanni, *Pecorone*, pp. 44-60 (Day IV, Novel 1) [Waters trans.]; Larminie, *Folk-Tales*, p. 256, notes; Lee, *Sources*, pp. 294-311 (Day X, Novel 1); McKay-Campbell, *Tales*, 1, pp. 390-92, notes; *Irish Handbook*, p. 569, no. 611; Smith and Harvey, *English Proverbs*, p. 514, "Poverty parteth fellowship (friends, good company)"; Pino-Saavedra, *Folktales*, pp. 194-98, no. 38, and pp. 273-74, no. 38, notes; Spencer, *Stories*, pp. 28-29, discussion, pp. 177-96, trans. of Ser Giovanni, *Il Pecorone* (IV, 1).

England

McKay-Campbell, *Tales*, 2, pp. 38-52, no. 47 (with 1651, 974), Gaelic text and English trans. (London?; see McKay's notes, pp. 50-51).

Scotland

Cf. Campbell, *Popular Tales*, 1, pp. 289-96, no. 17b (cf. 875D, II, with 974) (Argyllshire).
McKay-Campbell, *Tales*, 2, pp. 316-23, no. 70 (with 505, 974), Gaelic text and English trans. (Berneray, Outer Hebrides).
McKay-Campbell, *Tales*, 1, pp. 372-92, no. 23 (with 1651, 505), Gaelic text and English trans. (Barra).

Ireland

Larminie, *Folk-Tales*, pp. 115-26 (with 875D, II, 974, 882), and p. 256, note (Co. Donegal).
Ó Duilearga, *Béal.* 15 (1945), 200, no. 3 (with 1651), English summary of Irish text (Co. Galway).
Ó Cillín, *Béal.* 3 (1931-32), 42-43, no. 2, English summary of Irish text (Co. Mayo).

Irish Types, 68 versions ["In addition to the standard type, versions are included here of a by-form, which tells how the hero loses all he has by disasters at sea (or by gambling). . . ."]

Africa
Cf. Hurreiz, *Folktales,* pp. 127-28, no. 87 (Sudan).

37. HARD HEAD

Freeman Bennett
St. Pauls, Great Northern Peninsula
31 August 1966

Cf. AT611 [Irish by-form]
TC284 66-24
Collectors: HH and JW

[*recorder off*]*** Hard Head they called un. [*recorder off*]*** in the story, Hard Head. Yes. That's "Hard Head." That's uh...let me see. No I don't believe I knows that story now. [*recorder off*]*** I daresay I'll pick un up alright. I daresay I'll pick un up alright. [*recorder off*]*** (oh) that's uh...the same thing as I told ya there see, that's uh...back in olden times, that was uh...two fellers well they had a...a daugh[ter]...a daughter an' a son. Well now soon as they was borned see they married...the...they married 'em.

Well now they growed up. An' uh...they got...he got good education _ Jack did, his name was Jack. But they used to call un...the teachers used to call un Hard Head _ 'cause he was...hard to learn see? But he...he got good education just the same. An' uh...they growed up _ an' they used to be gettin around together. Now uh...the girl's father was see...he had...he was a well-to-do man see, he had a lot o' money but now the...the boy's father, well he...he never had much money, he had a little farm but uh...he wasn't gettin on very good with it.

(So) very good uh...they was gettin around together, well now the ol' man didn't want her to...to have him see? Well now Jack _ he had this certificate see? He had their marriage certificate. Well he...he didn't want 'em...the...their ol' man didn't want un to have her anyhow an' he...

There was a king _ lived alongside. An' uh...this girl...the king's daughter said to the king _ he said uh...she said uh...his father died see _ (that's) 'fore he got growed up but he had good education, he was a well educated...boy.

She said to the king, she said uh..."I got a mind" she said uh...she said "that little boy is over there" she said _ "why don't ya take un" she said "an' uh...give un some education?" She said "The poor little boy" she said "he got no education" she said "an' _ his father an' mother is dead" _ she said "an' uh...he got no education."

"Well" the king said uh..."yes" he said uh..."we could take un" he said "an' give un some education."

O' course, very good, the king took un. Now an'...he...send un to school, well now he had good education. But anyhow he'd make out like he didn't know nothing see? Make out like he was foolish _ didn't know nothing. And _ he couldn't learn nothing an' teacher couldn't learn un nothing at all an' _ he bid goin so long. An' the king's daughter _ she fell in love with un see. An' uh...now they was married see? Those two was married but uh...the...the...the kin[g]...uh the king knowed it _ but she didn't want un...(he) didn't want her to have un see _ because he was a poor boy.

An' _ [*coughs*] very good, he...he couldn't make un learn _ couldn't get un to learn an' uh...the king said "Well" he said "just as well take un out o' school" he said "it's no good to leave un there" he said "he won't learn nothing." Said "He's can't learn nothing, he's still uh..." he said "he's too hard headed to learn anything." Well they called un Hard Head.

So one day they was uh...comin from school. An' uh...he uh...king's daughter she was comin. An' she was uh...half on a cry see? And _ he said uh...Hard Head he said "What's wrong?"

"Oh" she said "I've got a sum here" she said "the teacher gi' me to do" she said "an' I can't do it." She said "I can't do that sum" she said "'tis too hard for me."

He said "Let me have a look at un."

"Hah!" she said "What's the good to show un to you" she said "Hard Head?" She said "No good to show un to you" /she/ said "you knows **YOU** can't do un."　　　　　　　　　　　　　　　　　　　　　　　　　　　　/he/

"Well" he said "there's no harm for me to lo[ok]...**SEE** un I don't suppose."

"Oh no" she said "I can show un to ya" (she) said "but that's no good" she said "for **YOU** to look at un."

He took the book an' he...looked at the sum an' _ he said "Gi' me your pencil."

She give un the pencil an' _ in (it's) couple o' minutes he had the sum done see? And _ he said "There you go."

"Well" [*surprised tone*] she said "Hard Head" she said "you got better learning" she said "than the teacher."

He said "Yes" said "I don't know" he said "if I [got] better learnin than teacher or no" he said "but I can do that sum. Now" he said [*sudden change to fast, excited, aggressive tone*] "when you carries that sum home" _ now he turned the book over _ after he had the sum done _ he turned the book over _ an' he made he...marked down another sum. "Now" he said "when you goes to...school tomorrow" he said "you'll give that one to the teacher. Let's see can he do **THAT** one."

/He/ /His/

/She/ carried the book home. An' uh...an' carried the book home. /Her/ father said to un _ he said "Who done that sum for ya?"

An' he...she said "Teacher never done un."

An' said "No" he said "I...I know the teacher hadn't done un" an' he said _ "I knows" he said uh..."Hard Head never done un" he said "'cause _ he couldn't do un."

Said "No" she said "Hard Head never done (un)."

(So) very good. She went to school the next morning. An' teacher said to un _ said "Who done that sum for ya?" He said "Your father or your mother?"

"No" she said "nar one of 'em."

"Well" she said "who done un?" She said uh...uh...he said "I knows Hard Head never done un."

She said "Yes" she said "Hard Head done un." He said uh...she said "Turn over the book."

/ya/

Turned the book over "There's one" she said "there Hard Head give /me/ for you." Huh! [*laughing tone*]

"Sure" he said "he got more education" he said "than I got." He said "Yes. Think he got more than I got."

She says "I didn't know it."

(So) she went to school that day an' when she went home _ she said uh..."Father" she said "you know" she said "Hard Head?"

He said "Yes."

/He/

/She/ said "He got more education than teacher got."

"Go on with you!" he said. "He got no education."

/He/ /he/
/he/ /He/
/he/

"Yes" she said "he have." She said "He got more education than teacher got." /She/ said "An' he put one down" /she/ says "on the scribbler" _ /she/ said "for the teacher." /She/ said "An' I carried un to the teacher" /she/ said "an' teacher couldn't do un."

"Oh well" he said "'cordin to that" he said "I guess" he said uh..."I guess" he said "we'll put un in th' **OFFICE**."

She said "Yes" she said "you can put un in th' office."

Very good, that's what he done with un. He put him in th' office. Now when Jack was in th' office he was the...big shot now.

So now _ every evening a girl is...she uh...his daughter come from school well she'd be out in th' office see with un. Well now he uh...that went on for a couple or three months 'fore the...the king got hold to it, well now she was goin with un, well uh...he didn't want **THAT** see _ for the...his daughter to be goin with a poor man. Well _ he decided he'd pay un off. An'

/unt/

get clear of /un/.

An' ‿ she said "Now" she said "Jack" ‿ she went down this night, she said "now" she said "Jack" she said "father" she said "is goina pay you off tomorrow." She said "You got...an' ('ee) got to leave."

Said "Now" she said "I'm goina give ya a ship" ‿ she said "I'm goina give ya a ship" ‿ she said "an'...an' you go" she said "an' uh...around" she said "the Cape o' Good Hope. An'" she said uh..."when you comes back" she said ‿ "I'll marry ya" she said "carry ya...carry...you...you take me away" she said "an' I'll have ya." Alright.

So she give Jack the ship, fit un out wi' the ship an' ‿ away Jack goes. "Now" ‿ she said ‿ "we're...we're leaving now" she said "an' ‿ you change your name." She said "I...I'll call ya" she said "Poverty Parts From Good Company." She said "That's the name you'll go by now" ‿ she said "Poverty Parts From Good Company." Alright. Away Jack goes.

When he got to the...uh...the...to the Cape of Good Hope ‿ he struck a storm. Oh a ‿ wonderful storm. He blowed the spars out of her. An' ‿ anyhow he got in. He got in to the pier. An' when he got in to the pier there was a feller comin down towards un. There was uh...no he didn't. He went...he got in to the pier an' he ‿ went up to a ol' woman's house ‿ an' he ask her could she put un up for the night.

And she said "Yes." Put un up for the night.

An' ‿ he had his supper. An' she said "Now" she said ‿ "I'll bet ya" she said ‿ "your ship an' cargo" ‿ she said "against ALL my property" she said "if you...you go sleep with my daughter tonight ‿ an' you won't know nothing about her."

"Alright" Jack says. "I'll bet ya." So by god she bet un.

An' ‿ when she went to...when he went to go to bed ‿ she went up with un, ol' woman went up with un. An' uh...when he went to go to bed she hauled out this bottle out of her pocket. An' uh...she said uh...(had it out) from under her piller. She said uh..."Jack" she said "HAVE a drink." She said uh...said "I don't know" she said "what your name is"

He said "My name" he said "is Poverty Parts From Good Company."

Said "You got a queer name" she said "I never heard a name like that afore."

"No" he said "I guess you didn't" he said uh..."I guess" he said "I'm about th' only one got a name like that."

"Well" she said "have a drink."

He said "Yes." Said "I'll have a drink." So here he took the big drink. Well this was uh...what they...what they calls the...put un to sleep see, what they used to call...they used to call at them times sleepy drops. He took the big drink an' he falled back in the bed an' he went right off dead to sleep an' course the.../her/ daughter come up an' got in bed with un an' he sleeped all night an' she got up the next morning an' ‿ when she got up he

/his/

391

was still to sleep. By an' by he got up an' _ well uh…she'd abeen in bed with un all night, well he didn't know nothing about it, well he'd alost his…uh…his ship. Very good. Now he had to get home somehow.

Well anyhow after a twelvemonth he got back home again. An' he went…now he used to stay to his aunt's see? An' went down to his aunt's and _ /ʔan'/ she [*the king's daughter*] found out he was down there. An' she went down.

/I/

"Ah" she said uh…"Jack" _ she used to call un Jack. She said "How you get on?"

"Oh" he said "don't be talkin" he said "I lost" he said "everything I had. Lost ship" /he/ said "an' everything I had."

/she/

"Uh now" she said "Jack" she said "I'll give ya another one." Said "I'll give ya another one" she said "try it again."

"Alright" Jack said.

So she give him another one, Jack started again. An' when he got [to] the Cape o' Good Hope _ he struck the same storm again. An' he lost everything again, blowed out…an' /blowed/ the spars out of her, well he got her in after a spell. An' when he got in his yuther [i.e., *other*] ship what he was in was still tied up to the pier see?

/drewed/

Ah _ up he goes to the ol' woman's house again.

"Hah hello!" she said "You got back!"

"Oh yes" he said "I got back again."

She said "Now" she said uh…"what about havin a bet again tonight?"

"Yes" he said "I'll bet ya again (to)night."

Well now he…he done the same thing see? He went upstairs an' she hauled out this bottle from in under the…the piller an' give un the big drink. Well he falled right back in the bed an' off he goes snorin again. Didn't know nothing till the next morning when he got up she was up an' -- he lost it all AGAIN.

Well now 'twas another twelvemonth 'fore he got back. (When) he got back again he went to his aunt's an' she [*the king's daughter*] found out he was there, well she went down. She went down an' uh…said "How ya get on?"

"Oh" he said "don't be talkin" he said "I lost it all again."

"Well now" she said "Jack" she said "I'm goina try ya once more." She said "An' this is all" she said "I can give ya." She said "If you can't get through this time" she said "I won't be able to give ya no more."

"Alright" he said, he'd try it again.

So he got the ship an' he started again. An' _ when he got to the Cape o' Good Hope he struck the same storm. An' when he was…comin in _ gettin in the harbour _ he seen a little boat comin. An' _ there was feller come alongside of un he said _

/How/

"/ʔNow/" he said "uncle" he said uh…"come aboard." He went aboard.

392

He was talkin to un, he said "Now" he said uh…"this is two ships" he said "you've alost…three ships" he said "you've alost here."

"Yes" he said.

"You've alost two of 'em" he said. "Th' ol' woman got two of 'em"

He said "Yes."

"Now" he said "look." He said "That…what she gives you" /he/ said "that's sleepy drops." She sai[d]…he said "Now" he said…he shoved his hand in his pocket "now" she s…he said "here's a bottle _ " he said "I'm goin to give you." /He/ said "Now" /he/ said "when he…when she takes ya up to go to bed" _ /he/ said "you slip her bottle" /he/ said "out from in under the piller _ an' shove yours in" _ /he/ says "now" /he/ said "'cause she's goina give ya another drink" /he/ said "that sleepy drops."
  /she/

  /She/ /she/
  /she/ /she/
  /she/ /she/
  /she/

So very good. He went in. "Hi sir" she said "hello" she said "you got back again?"

"Oh yes" he said "I got back again."

(Well) she said "I suppose" she said "you're goina have another bet tonight?"

"Yes" he said "I'm goina have another bet tonight." Well (he) eats his supper an' (well) now _ they had their bet. An' he went upstairs. An'…he said uh…"Now" he said uh…"we got to sign papers" he said "on this"

/She/ said "Well yes" she said "why" she said "are ya goin to sign papers on this?" She said "You ant signed papers on none of 'em."
  /He/

"No" he said "I ant" he said "but" _ he said "I've alost two" _ he said "an' it's time" he said "for me to get strict now" he said uh…"I've alost two" he said "an' this (is) the last one I got. Well if uh…" said uh…"if I come to loss this one" he said _ "I might win it" he said "well" he said "we got no papers signed onto it" he said "well" he said _ "I mightn't GET it."

"Alright" she said "we'll sign it up." Signed up the papers. Now he leaved this papers down on the table an' he went on upstairs see? An' when he got upstairs _ "Oh" he said "I've aleaved me papers" he said "down on (the) table" he said "I got to go down after 'em."

"Oh" she said "no" she said "I'll go down an' get 'em for ya." Now then she goes downstair(s) _ /he/ hauled her bottle out an'…an' shoved his in under an' shoved her bottle in his pocket see? When she come up _ she hauled out the bottle from under the pillow "An'" she said "have a drink."
  /she/

"Oh yes" he said "I'll have a drink." So he took a big drink now 'cause this is a drink o' RUM. Took a BIG drink. An' hung up his clothes _ lied down an' he lie…uh…falled back on his back an' starts snorin ya know. An' uh…the daughter went up. An' she looked at un. She come back an' she said "Mother" she said "I don't believe" she said "he's to sleep."

"Yes!" she said "He's to sleep" she said "the drink that he drinked" /she/ said "he won't wake till 'bout twelve o'clock tomorrow" she said "go on up an' get in bed" she said "he's alright."

Well she went up an' she hauled off her clothes an' she jumped in bed. Blowed out the light an' jumped in bed. An' soon as she did, well he turned over to her an' he whacked his arms around her an' _ course she...had the best kind of a time that night!

Got up next mornin "Ah!" he said _ "I knows what she is this morning!" (Well) _ th' ol' woman he...well _ he had it all, he had his two ships back an' he had all the ol' woman's place, he turned her outdoors. An' he sold it an' he got all the money an' he _ fitted up his two ships an' away he goes _ back home.

An' _ when he got uh...he never...[he] went to his aunt's house. 'Fore he got to his aunt's house _ now this night she was goin he...the king's daughter was goin to be married _ to the duke _ see? Now he had uh...Hard Head they calls un, he had the 'stificate in his pocket see? An' _ very good. He start to...to go home to his aunt's. Now he heard she [*the king's daughter*] was goin to be married. An' when he did _ when he was goin across this bridge _ he seen the duke comin see, well there's no such thing as cars them times, 'twas horse an' carriage see? Seen the duke comin on his horse an' carriage. An' he was on the bridge an' he start...makin out like he was foolish see, goin around from one side o' the bridge to the other an' lookin around. Well he was foolish now an' _ the duke went up to un, well now he was goin to get a good joke off on un, this foolish **MAN**.

An' uh...he said "Hello" he said uh..."what's ya lookin for?"

An' he uh...kind...makin kind o' stutterin to...like he couldn't get it out an' he said uh...he said "I...uh...I uh...sot a lobster trap there" he said "ten year ago" he said _ "an'" he said "if I can find un" he said "I'll show ye" he said "the best fresh lobster ever you seen in your life!"

An' he had the big laugh at un you know 'cause he was foolish see? An' he said uh...he said "What's your name?"

He said "Nuh nuh nurn" uh...[*stuttering*] he said "Po _ overty P _ arts From Good Company." An' he put it down (in) his pocketbook. An' away he goes, the duke went on. An'...Jack went on.

He went to his aunt's house an' _ (when) he got in there he _ hauled off his clothes an' he dressed up an' he put on the best kind of a suit o' clothes _ 'cause he had a lot o' money now, he sold the ol' woman's place an' he had _ three ships sailin down in the harbour an' _ put on a big suit o' clothes an' had a shave an' dressed up an' _ by an' by the duke come now an' he was...come into the king's house, they was goin to be married.

"An'" he said "well" he said _ "don't be talkin!" He said "I seen a man down there" he said "an' he was right foolish." He said "I meet un on the bridge" an' he said uh...

An' she said "Yes." Now when he...when she...when he spoke, she had a thought see? An' he said "Yes" he said uh...she said "yes" she said uh..."where ya see un to?"

"Down there on the bridge" he said "an' he told me" he said "he sot a lobster trap there" he said "ten year ago an' if he could find un he'd show me the best fresh lobster _ ever I seen!"

She said "(Well) then"

He said "He used to stutter."

An' she said "Yes" she said uh..."ya know his name?"

An' he said uh..."Well" he said "I...I got his name here in me pocketbook" he said "'cause I put it down." Took out his pocketbook (an') he said "Yes" he said _ "Poverty Parts From Good Company."

Well she knowed who 'twas. An' _ she stopped an' she said "I...I got to go out here" she said "a minute." An' she went out an' soon as she got out o' doors this is where she made off for, down...down to /his/ aunt's see? /her/
An' uh...when she went in, course sure enough this was he an' she said "How ya get on?"

"Oh" he said "don't be talkin!" He said "I got me three ships" he said "an' _ I got plenty o' money now."

She said "You have!"

Said "Yes. Got plenty o' money, now" he said _ "come on wi' me" he said "come in the room" /he/ said uh..."come in the room" he said "an' /she/ we'll go to bed."

"Oh my!" she said "I can't."

"Yes" /he/ said "come on. Come in the room" he said "an' we'll /she/ go to bed."

Got her in the room an' -- he shoved his hand in his pocket _ an' he took out the...the...birth cerstificate see? An' he pinned un right over the door. An' _ shoved his hand in his pocket an' uh...an' took out 'stificate an' pinned un over the door an' he jumped into bed with her. Two of 'em was in the bed.

An' by an' by _ she was gone so long _ the king sent up one of his servants see, to see where she was to. [Int. clears throat] An' /he/ come /she/ up. Now she [*the king's daughter*] was in the bed with uh...Hard Head as they called un. An' _ he [*the servant*] went back an' he said uh...she said uh...she [*the king's daughter*] was in the bed...she...in the bed she said with a MAN up there.

Oh well the king got in a wonderful passion to kind o' think...[when the servant] come back, his daughter was in bed with a man [when she was] goin to be married. An'...he was goin to kill un right away "Oh well" he [*the servant*] said uh..."go up" he said "an' see."

Any _ by an' by _ up comes the KING an' _ no _ the DUKE _ up comes the DUKE. And _ come in, opened the room door an' soon as he did he [*Jack*] hauled the clothes up an' he slapped his hand on her _ [*slaps hand on leg*] backside there he said "I told ye" he said "I was goina show ya the best fresh lobster ever you seen in your life" he said "there he is!" [*laughs*]

By an' by up comes the king. Up comes the king.

He [*Jack*] said "Ya see what's over the door?" Birth certificate. Well now (there's) nothing he could do about it see, they was married. Nothing he could do about it, well (I tell 'ee) _ when I leaved they had three s...three children. [*laughs*]

[Int: That's one you hadn't...hadn't uh...thought of!]
Yes. Yes.
[Int: Uh..."Hard Head" eh?]
That's "Hard Head."
[Int: Whose...whose story was that?]
I learned that one from me uncle.
[Int: This (Uncle) Charl?]
Learned that one from Uncle Charl _ yes. [*recorder off*] An' he'd be...if (he) was livin now he'd be uh...he'd be a hundred an' ten year old.
[Int: How o[ld]...how old***] [*recorder off*]
He was uh...he was seventy-nine when he died. [*recorder off*]*** this is his place what I'm livin on here see.
[Int: Oh?]
Yeah. I too[k]...we took un, he had no...'twas no one only his own self, his woman was dead an' he had no children an' _ we took un an' looked out to un, well...[*recorder off*]
*** "(King Whales)," I used to know that one. I used to know that one "The King o' Whales." Yes. I used to...I used to know that story but I don't know un now. I don't know how he goes. I used to know "The King o' Whales," I learned he from me uncle too.
[Int: Mm-hm.]
A long time ago. But I don't know un now.
[Int: Something about uh...] [*recorder off*]
Yeah.
[Int: I (mean) he had a soul _ outside of his body?]
[Int: Mm-hm.]
That's "The Man wi' Ne'r Soul" we used to call un.
[Int: Oh. Oh I see.]
Yeah. That's "The Man wi' Ne'r Soul" an' he...he had his soul on a island see?

[Int: Mm-hm.]
But uh...I can't tell ya them 'cause I don't know 'em.
[Int: Mm-hm.]
I forgot 'em.
[Int: Mm-hm.]
Forgot them stories. [*recorder off*]*** I used to know a lot o' stories, pile
of 'em one time but uh...so long ago an' I suppose I'm gettin older, I forgets
'em ya know an'...[*laughs*]

Duration: 19 min., 44 sec.
Source: Charles Benoit (uncle), St. Pauls, Great Northern Peninsula.
Location: The darkening sitting room of the teller's house in the late evening.
Audience: Mrs. Rebecca Bennett (teller's wife), male visitor, several children, interviewers.

Context, Style, and Language: (For context see notes to No. 4).

In common with Nos. 4, 5, and 6 this tale is unusual in that it was recorded three times from Freeman Bennett over a period of five years. It therefore gives us a further opportunity to study the style, presentation, and language of a single story and to observe which aspects remain constant and which are subject to variation over time. A comparison again reveals that this narrator makes few substantial changes in his telling and retelling of this story, as is true of other items from his repertoire which appear more than once in this collection. Yet what differences there are serve to distinguish each performance as unique, comparatively minor details shifting and recombining in subtle permutations at the whim of the speaker as he skillfully manipulates the many strands of plot, characterization, style, and linguistic form.

A full comparison of these three recensions is unfortunately precluded by the fact that the third and most recently recorded version is incomplete, lacking most of the dénouement. However, it is otherwise of comparable length and structure to versions one and three, as the following table shows:

	A (No. 37)	B (No. 38)	C (No. 39)
1.		teller's biographical details	
2.	family has two children	no reference to children apart from Jack	family has three or four children
3.	boy and girl married soon after birth	(added as afterthought after Jack wins third bet)	(added as afterthought when Jack gets office job)
4.	children grow up		

397

5. details about fathers of boy and girl		
6. explanation of why Jack is called Hard Head		
7. some confusion of exactly who girl's father is (king and daughter suddenly introduced; girl and king's daughter coalesce)		
8. (father and mother said to be dead—somewhat later in narration)	Jack's father and mother die	Jack's father dies
9.	fuller detail and dialogue about Jack at school	
10. king knows of infant marriage but does not want daughter to marry Jack		
11. further explanation of the name *Hard Head*		
12.	Jack works outdoors for king after leaving school	
13.		fuller details of girl's crying
14. Jack makes up sum for teacher	Jack makes up sum for teacher	
15.	further detail and dialogue about what girl must say to teacher	
16.	Jack is aged sixteen when put in office	
17. girl agrees to marry Jack on his return		girl agrees to marry Jack on his return
18. girl gives Jack his new name before first voyage	(new name appears only in dénouement)	(new name appears only in dénouement)

19. Jack goes up to old woman's house	Jack goes up to old woman's house	old woman first comes aboard Jack's ship
20. old woman asks Jack his name and comments on it		
21. Jack returns after a twelvemonth		Jack returns after a spell
22. Jack stays with aunt	Jack stays with grandmother	Jack stays with aunt
23. Jack returns after another twelvemonth		
24. man who comes aboard says Jack has lost two ships	man who comes aboard says Jack has lost two ships	
25. Jack given bottle (later revealed to contain rum)	Jack given bottle (later revealed to contain hard liquor)	Jack given bottle of rum
26.	Jack told to sign an agreement and leave it on old woman's table	Jack told to sign an agreement and leave it on old woman's table
27. explains why Jack leaves papers on table		
28.	needle test to see Jack is asleep	
29. fuller and more humorous description of girl getting into bed on third occasion		
30.	price of old woman's property given	
31. king's daughter to marry duke	king's daughter to marry mayor	king's daughter to marry mayor
32. duke travels in horse and carriage		
33.	Jack dressed in old clothes when on bridge	

34. Jack stutters	(perhaps a vestige of this in repetition of name)
35. Jack gets shaved and dressed up at his aunt's	
36. unclear whether the king sends a male or a female servant	king's servant is a "little feller"
37.	king sends second servant
38.	king builds palace for couple

Virtually all the differences listed here have little effect on the total plot. The same is true of interesting minor differences in the language, as for instance Jack's dismissal of the girl's questions about the first two voyages with "don't be talkin" in versions one (No. 37) and two (No. 38), but with the more mundane "Oh the same thing" after the second voyage in version three (No. 39); the use in version one of the word *uncle*—a common term of familiar and respectful address for an older man in Newfoundland—reveals that the man who comes aboard is not young; and Jack's response to the old woman after he wins the third bet is appropriately expressed with "I knows what she is" in version one, "I got ya this time" in version three, and simply with "you've alost your bet" in version two. When one compares these three versions with the two versions of this story told by Freeman's brother Everett (Nos. 40 and 41), it is possible to resolve the ambiguity in Everett's versions over who is threatened with beheading in the dénouement. Freeman's versions make it clear that it is the servant who brings back the news about Jack being in bed with the girl.

Apart from the general similarities which these three versions share, there are also several instances in which they all demonstrate their close kinship by having certain specific details in common, at times almost identical in their wording. For example, Jack asks the girl "Gi' me your pencil" in each version; the episodes of taking the drink at the old woman's house are very similar; all include references to the fact that the ships lost in the bet are tied to the pier; and all have the humorous account of Jack snoring when pretending to be asleep on the night of the third bet—a description made even more amusing by the teller's lying back in his chair to demonstrate Jack's posture and appearance. Note also that the passage of time is marked by the eating of supper and the hint that it will soon be bedtime in the account of Jack's first visit to the old woman's house. Versions one and two also mention Jack having supper on the second and third visits. Similarly, breakfast is mentioned as a time-marker on the morning after Jack wins the bet in versions two and three.

In the first version presented here Freeman Bennett is unsure about remembering the story and begins with some hesitancy, adding the revealing remark "I daresay I'll pick un up alright" which shows his confidence in his own ability to weave together what threads of the story he remembers as he goes along. This may also be the reason why Jack's name is introduced so casually, almost like an afterthought, but on the other hand this suits well with the typically understated way in which Jack is usually presented in these tales. The dialogue is again very lively and varied, as seen for example in the girl's response to Jack's offer of help with the sum and the sudden shift of tone when he gives her the sum for the teacher; the teller also amusingly imitates Jack's stuttering. The narrative includes several short sentences, many of them elliptical, which provide contrast with the longer utterances, and there is also the familiar mingling of direct and indirect speech, e.g., "'Yes.' Put un up for the night," which begins in direct speech and shifts to reported speech, with ambiguous tense form and typical absence of pronoun subject. The dialogue markers *he/she said* are excessively used, the pronouns and their referents also being confused on several occasions. Individual words are emphasized by strong stress throughout the narrative for clarity and for rhetorical effect, while pronouns and function words tend to be lost because of the elliptical style. The narrative markers *(So) very good, Alright, anyhow,* and *by an' by* are again in evidence, and the tag question *see* at the end of sentences occurs frequently, especially near the beginning of the tale where the teller is making sure that the listeners understand what is being said. One might also bear in mind that the lobster motif, if not exclusive to Newfoundland, is obviously very appropriate in the local context and is immediately appreciated by the audience. In No. 37 it is unclear at the outset that the girl is a king's daughter, and the audience has to assume that this is the case as the story proceeds. Note also the realistic touches in the reference to the Cape of Good Hope, the description of Jack as "big shot" in the office, and the details of signing papers.

A number of linguistic items are worthy of comment. At the phonological level, the title of the story and the first nickname of the hero are invariably pronounced without initial aspirates, as is usual in Newfoundland speech. The rather literary word *passion* has the diphthong /ei/ in the first syllable, with one exception *cerstificate* has an intrusive /s/ before /t/ at the beginning of its second syllable, *fitted* is pronounced as one syllable, the glottalized /t/ being articulated synchronically with the following /d/, and the final syllable of *pillow* is pronounced with schwa plus /r/. Aphesis occurs in *'stificate* and the schwa of *the* is lost in *th' office.* Note also *loss* (lose). Among the lexical items one might single out *learn* (teach), *bid* (stayed/remained), *nar one* (neither), *scribbler* (notebook; see *DNE scribbler* n.), *afore, them* as a demonstrative in *them times,* and *foolish* (simple-minded; see *DNE foolish* a), along with *hard to learn* (difficult to teach, or who found it hard to learn), and the Irish *don't be talkin* perhaps in the more literal sense "don't ask me" used effectively here to dismiss the girl's questions about Jack's voyages (cf. *DNE talk* v. 2). Dialectal present tense verbs include *you comes/goes, he have, I ant,* past tense forms are *growed, ask, lied* (lay), *drinked, Blowed,* and there are the past participles *growed, alost,* and *aleaved.* Double negatives feature strongly in Freeman Bennett's speech, and here we have *couldn't learn un nothing,* and the euphemistic *won't know nothing.*

See also the notes to Nos. 4, 5, 6, and 8.

Type and Motifs:

Cf. AT611. *The Gifts of the Dwarfs* [Irish by-form].
Z10.1. *Beginning formula.*

Cf. T61.5.1. *Betrothal of hero to princess while both are still in cradle.*
L101. *Unpromising hero.*
T91.6.4. *Princess falls in love with lowly boy.*
T97. *Father opposed to daughter's marriage.*
L111.4. *Orphan hero.*
L142. *Pupil surpasses master.*
Cf. K1831.0.1. *Disguise by changing name.*
Cf. N15. *Chastity wager.*
N2.6.5. *Daughter as wager.*
N2.5. *Whole kingdom (all property) as wager.*
K675. *Sleeping potion given to man who is to pass night with a girl.*
K92. *Gambling contest won by deception.*
Cf. N825.2. *Old man helper.*
K1865. *Deception by pretending sleep.*
N681. *Husband (lover) returns home just as wife (mistress) is to marry another.*
Cf. H586.2.2. *Traveler says he must look after his net to see if it has taken fish.*
H151. *Attention drawn and recognition follows.*
Cf. L161. *Lowly hero marries princess.*
Z10.2. *End formula.*

International Parallels: See No. 36.

38. HARD HEAD

Freeman Bennett   Cf. AT611 [Irish by-form]
St. Pauls, Great Northern Peninsula   TC1063 72-4
14 September 1971   Collector: HH

> [*recorder off*]*** once upon a time ‿ in olden times ya know ‿ [Teller's wife:
> (Well) Freeman my son.] [*recorder off*]*** [Int: just...] time an' a day
> uh...an' a date. Well I was born ‿ uh...Fre...I...Isaac Freeman is me name.
> Isaac F. I always puts. Isaac F. Bennett.
> [Int: And everybody calls you Freeman.]
> Yes. [Int: Uh huh.] Isaac Freeman ‿ Bennett.
> [Int: Right. When were you born Mr. F...][*recorder off*]
> I was borned in uh...in eighteen an' ninety-six.
> [Int: Mm-hm. Okay.]
> [Teller's wife: [Now he's] seven...at the age o' seventy-five.]

[Int: Now _ this is September 14, 1971 an' we're here in the...in the kitchen _ in your home in St. Pauls.]

Yes.

[Int: An' you're goin to tell us one of the old stories]

Yes.

[Int: Alright you...you go ahead.]

Yeah.

[Teller's wife: Go ahead.]

Eh?

[Teller's wife: Go ahead _ with your story.]

Well once upon a time in olden times _ there was a feller uh...his name was Jack see. An' uh...he was a poor man an' his uh...father was a poor man. But he had good education. He had good education _ wonderful education. Well he went uh...to see could he get any work. An' uh...no _ I'm before me story.

[Teller's wife: Ah! I thought so.]

His father an' mother died. And while he was off on the strand he had nowhere to go see. An' the king uh...king was livin in the...uh...close 'longside. An' his daughter _ king's daughter was comin from school one day _ an' she seen this little feller _ young feller he was about uh...twelve or fourteen year old. An' uh...she spoke to un. An' she ask un uh...his father's [and] mother's name.

He said uh..."I got no father" he said "or no mother." He said "They're dead" he said "an' I...got no place" he said "to go."

An' she said "Well" she said uh..."I'll see about that."

Well when she went home she told the king. An' _ he said "Well" he said uh..."we'll take un." He said "An' uh...send un to school" he said "an' give un some education, well" he said uh..."he might get education enough" he said "he could work in my office."

An' she said "Yes" she says "father" she said _ "'tis a pity" she said "to see that little boy" she said "with nowhere to go."

"Well" he said "now" he said _ "you go an' uh...get un" he said "an' uh...we'll take un."

Well went out _ an' _ she got un an' uh...he come in. An' now they was goin to send un to school.

Next morning they got un ready the next morning to send un to school. * Well _ he went in the lower school (lower) class school see. Now he had big education. He went in the lower /class/ school an' uh...well the...teacher was uh...tryin to learn un his letters, at THEM times you had to learn your letters see. And _ he had to ask him what this was. 'Twas a B. He'd say well 'twasn't a B at all 'twas a A. He made out like he didn't know the letters see? And uh...the teacher was at un _ for...for uh...two weeks _ and she couldn't le...he couldn't learn un the A an' the B.

*coughing in background /staff/

/he/
/he/
*microphone
noise

An' uh...this night when she went home she said uh..."Father" she said uh..."'tis not much good" she said "to send that uh...boy to school" /she/ said "'cause he been two weeks" /she/ "an' he...he don't know th' A from the B.*

"Oh well" he said uh..."we'll take un out o' school" _ he said "an' uh...so long as he's like that" he said "an'...I'll put un around" he said "just workin around outdoors" he said "an' uh...we'll keep un here" he said "to feed un" he said "anyhow."

Well that's what they done, they took un out o' school. An' uh...he was workin out around out uh...doors sort o' cleanin the...stuff away from the king's palace an' _ he walked out on the road one day an' he sot down an'...in the evening _ when uh...the uh...when his uh...king's daughter was comin home from school see? An' he was sot down an' when she uh...she come along _ she was cryin see?

An' he said _ "What's wrong?"

"Oh" she said "I got a sum" she said "the teacher gi' me" she said "to do" she said _ "an' I can't do it" she said "I'll never get un done."

An' uh...now the king...they...they...they named un over, Hard Head see. An' uh...she said "'Tis no (real) g...good to give un to you" she said "Hard Head." She said "You knows" she said "you...you don't know."

"Oh well" he said "'tis no harm" he said "for me to have a look at un I don't suppose."

An' she said "Oh no" she said "you can look at un" she said "but you knows **YOU** can't do it" she said "when you don't know a A from the B."

An' _ he dee...took the...she...he took the book _ an' he opened the book an' he looked at the sum. He said "Gi' me your pencil."

An' uh...she give un the...the...uh...pencil _ an' he made up the sum for her. An' he turned over the leaf _ again _ an' he put down another sum. "Now" he said _ "when you goes home the night _ when you goes to school tomorrow" _ he said "or the teacher askes you who done that sum for ya _ 'Was it your father?' An' you say 'No.' An' he said 'Well was it your mother?' An' you say 'No.' An' well he'll say 'Well for sure 'tis not Hard Head.' An' she...you say 'Yes 'tis Hard Head. Turn over the leaf.'" Turned the leaf over "Now" she said "there's a sum" she said "for you to do."

An' he took the sum. An' he couldn't do un. Th' high grade teacher. "Well" he said "he got more education" he said "than I got." He said "That's the feller" he said "was goin to school here?"

He said "Yes" _ she said "yes."

He said "He got more education than I got." He said "I can't do that sum" he said "what he got down (there)...what he got put down there."

An' _ she went home _ next evening an' she said "Father" she said uh..."that little feller" she said "what we got out there" she said "got more education" said "than the teacher got."

"Go on!" he said "You knows he ant."

"Yes" she said "he have." She said "He made up the sum for me" /she/ said "what I couldn't make up." She said "An' he put down another one" she said "for the teacher." /She/ said "An' the TEACHER couldn't make un up. An' the teacher said he had more education than HE had."

"Oh well" he said uh…"'cordin to that then" he said "I'll put un in the…in th' office."

So he took the…little feller, well now he was uh…sixteen year old now. He took (un) an' he put un in his office.

Well uh…he was in his office, king's office an' uh…every evening his daughter 'd come home _ she'd go out in office see _ where he was to. Well now she fell in love with un. An' uh…well the king _ he got hold to it see _ that his…daughter was uh…goin around with this uh…this feller, well uh…he couldn't marry un anyhow _ 'cau[se]…because he wasn't _ high enough see, he never had money enough _ rich man enough. Well -- if he ci…decided _ he'd /turn un/ away. He turn un off altogether. Well he turned un out. He laid un off. He paid un all his money an' he laid un off.*

"Well now" she said "Hard Head" she said "you got to go."

An' he said "Yes" _ he said "I got to go."

"Well" she said "I'll tell ya what I'll do."* She said "I'll fit ya out" she said "with a ship."* She said "An' uh…an' grub" she said "an' a crew." She said "An' I'll give it to ya."

"Alright!"

So that's what she done. She fit un out with a ship _ an' give un a ship an' a crew o' men an' _ 'way he goes.

An' he _ was s…sailin for…three or four days 'cause THEM times 'twas th' ol' fashioned ships with the…sails on 'em see. An' _ in the evening, gettin late awards the evening he come to the Cape o' Good Hope. Well when he come to the Cape o' Good Hope to go around the Cape o' Good Hope _ he struck the big storm. An' he blowed everything right off of her. Well he managed to get her in…in th' harbour see? An' he got her in an' he tied her up to the pier. An' uh…well now _ he was in there, he had everything blowed off of her an' he couldn't get out of it, well he didn't know what to do.

Well anyhow he decided he'd go an' try to get a…place for the night. An' _ he went up to this old woman's house _ an' he knocked to the door an' he…she ask un _ he ask her could she put un up for the night.

An' she said "Oh yes" she said "I can put ya up for the night."

An' uh…well anyhow _ he went in _ an' he had his supper. An' uh…well bedtime come.

An' she said "I'll bet you" she said _ "five (the)…I'll bet ya" she said "all my property _ against…'gainst your ship" _ she said "that you 'll sleep

/he/

/He/

/turned/
*teller's wife speaks in background

*noise in background
*banging noise in background

with my daughter all night" _ she said "an' won't know nothing about her in the morning."

"Come on" he said "I'll bet ya."

"Alright."

Well he put up his ship an' cargo. An' she put up all her...house an' place _ against it. Well _ very good, he went up to go to bed an' uh...th' ol' woman went up an' uh...shoved her hand in under the piller an' she said "Ya like to have a drink" she said "'fore ya go to bed?"

He said "I wouldn't mind" he said "if I would."

Well he...she took the stopper off an' he took the big drink. Now this is what they call...used to call _ th' ol' people used to call **SLEEPY DROPS** one time see. Well now....now they don't call it that now. An' uh...he falled back on the piller an' he went right off * (to) sound asleep. Well uh...her daughter come in an' lied down in the bed 'longside of un, next morning _ she got up. An' _ when he woke _ she was up an' downstairs, well he didn't know no more about her than he uh.../did/ when he went to bed. Well he lost it all.

Well now he had to get back home again _ somehow. Well anyhow, anyhow _ he managed to get back again. An' uh...he used to stay with his grandmother see. An' he got back home an' he went down to his grandmother's. An' uh...anyhow the king's daughter heard he was there see. An' uh...she went down. An' she said "Hello" she said "Hard Head" she said "how you get on?"

"Oh" he said "don't be talkin!" He said "Don't be talkin!" he said "I lost everything." He said "When I got to the Cape o' Good Hope" he said "I struck the storm" he said "an' blowed everything off her" he said "an' I lost everything."

"Well now" she said _ "I'll fit ya out again." She said "An' try it again."

He said "Alright."

So /she/ fit un out again an' _ he start out again. An' when he got to the Cape o' Good Hope _ he struck the big storm again. An' blowed everything off of her again, well he managed to get in th' harbour. Well when he got in th' harbour his ship was there still uh...tied up to the pier. An' uh...he tied the other one up 'longside of her. An' _ he went up to th' ol' woman's house again. An' _ he knocked to the door.

"Hello" she said uh..."Hard Head" she said "you're back again."

An' he said "Oh yes" he said "I'm back again." He had his supper.

"Well now" she said _ "you're goin to have another bet with me tonight?"

/He/ said "Oh yes." He said "I'll have a bet with ya tonight."

Well now he put up **THIS** ship against her...her property see. Well he went up to go to bed an' uh...ol' woman she went up too an' she shoved her hand in under the piller she said "Goina have a drink" she said "'fore you goes to bed?"

*microphone noise

/nid/

/he/

/She/

"Oh yes" he said "I'll have a drink." Well he took the big drink an' he fall back on the piller an' he went right off to sleep again * an' she [*the daughter*] come in an' _ she lied down 'longside of un an' she sleeped all night. An' uh…when he woke the next morning she was up an' _ he got up, well he…he had everything gone again.

*microphone noise

Well now _ he didn't know what to do. He had to get back home, well to go back an' tell the king's daughter what had happened again, he didn't…he didn't know how he was goina do it but anyhow he got back _ an' he went to his grandmother's an' uh…by an' by she heard he was there. An' she went down.

"Hello" she said "Hard Head, how you get on this time?"

"Oh" he said "don't be talkin!" he said "I lost* everything again." He said "I lost it all."

*noise of something falling onto floor

"Well now" she said "I'll fit ya out once more." She said "An' if you losses it this time" she said "that's all I can do for ya."

Well she fit un out again. An' next morning he start again. An' _ when he got to the…Cape o' Good Hope _ he struck the same storm again.

Well now gettin in the harbour _ when he was comin in the harbour _ he seen this little boat comin see? An' uh…he [*the man from the boat*] come up 'longside of un an' he…and he got aboard. An' uh…he said "This is uh…you've alost two ships" he said "here ant ya?"

He says "Yes" he said "I've alost two."

"Well now" he said _ "I'll tell ya." He said "You goes to that old woman's house. That's where you stays"

He said "Yes."

"Well now" /he/ said _ "that bottle _ that…drink what she gives you" /he/ said "that's uh…that dopes ya." She said "You…you falls to sleep" _ /he/ said "an' you don't know nothing" /he/ said "'fore" he said "'fore the next morning." He shoved his hand in his pocket _ an' he hauled out a little bottle "Now" he said "here's a little bottle" he said "the same size _ an' the same colour o' her bottle. Now" she said _ "now" he said _ "when you signs this agreement" he said "for the…the…gets…takes the bet _ goes up to her house an' haves the bet" _ he said "you sign a 'greement" he said "this time." He said "Well now" he said _ "go upstairs" he said "when you goes up to go to bed _ leave it on the table." He said "An' when you gets upstairs to go to bed" /he/ said "you say 'I forgot me papers down on the table. I got to go down an' get 'em.' An' _ she'll say 'No. I'LL go down an' get 'em.' Well now" she say…he said "when you go…when she goes down _ you haul out her bottle _ an' shove yours in." /He/ said "An' uh…when she hauls out the bottle to give you the drink, well" he said uh…"this is alright" he said "this is strong liquor."

/she/ /she/
/she/
/she/

/she/

/She/

407

/he/

Uh…very good. He got in _ an' he tied up, his two ships was still there. Tied up an' he went up to th' ol' woman's house, she "Hello" she said uh…"Hard Head" /she/ said "you're back again."

Uh…she said uh…"I suppose you're goina have another bet?"

He said "Oh yes" he said "I goina have another bet with ya tonight."

An' uh…very good, they had their supper.

And…"Now" he said _ "I'm goin to sign uh…papers" he said "on this."

He said…she said "Why are you goin to do that?"

"Well" he said _ "I tell ya why" she said "I've alost two ships" he said "at this." He said uh…"[We]ll I wants to sign an agreement" he said "I wants to sign all this agreement" he said uh…"that those two ships _ those three ships" he said "is again…both against your property." *

*sound of water run-ning in back-ground

An' she said "Yes."

"Well" he said "I wants to sig[n]…I have this all signed up" _ he said "to know" he said "what I'm doin."

Very good, he signed it all up an' _ he went upstairs to go to bed. An' when he got upstairs _ "Oh" he said "I laid me papers" he said "down on the table." He said "I got to go down after ['em]."

"Oh no" she said "'tis no difference" she said "I'LL go down an' get 'em." Well now -- she went down _ when she went down after un _ he hauled out her bottle out from in under the piller _ an' he shoved his in see. An' _ she come up _ an' she said "You goin to have a drink" said "'fore ya lies down?"

"Oh yes" he said "I'm goin to have a drink."

She hauled out this bottle an' [of] course _ Jack took the **BIG DRINK** _ 'cause this was hard liquor. Took the big drink an' he falled back on the piller an' he start snorin like that [*demonstrates by leaning back in chair as if asleep*] you know an' _ by an' by uh…she [*the daughter*] come up to go to bed. An' she went down an' she said "Mother" she said "I don't believe that man is 'sleep."

"Yes" she said "he's asleep" she said "he won't wake no more 'fore twelve o'clock tomorrow _ " she said "'cordin to the drink he've atook tonight."

She said "I don't know."

She [*the old woman*] said "I'll go up" she said "an' have a look at un." Anyhow she took a needle along with her. An' he was lied back _ sound asleep like this [*demonstrates by leaning back in chair as if asleep*] snorin (of) it off _ an' she stuck a needle into un. An' he never moved. Lied down with his eyes shut, snorin away an'* "Oh yes" she said "he's alright" she said _ "he won't wake before twelve o'clock tomorrow."

*sound of object falling on table

Very good, she [*the daughter*] come up. She undressed an' got in the bed an' soon as…soon as she got in the bed he turned over an' he put his arms right around her _ see. Well now he had her in the bed now an' _ they sleept there all night an' uh...next morning _ Hard Head got up. Ol'...th' ol' woman come up.

"Hello" she said.

"Hello" Jack said "how are ya gettin on" he said "this morning?" He said "Now" he saids _ "now" he said _ "you've alost your bet."

She shook her head. She said "Yes." She said "I've alost un."

Very good. Got up an' he had his breakfast "Now" he said _ "I owns all this property" he said "is here." He said "This is all mine. Now" he said "you got to get out." He said "You got to get out" he said "an' I goin to SELL this" he said "'fore I goes away." He said "I'm goina sell all this."

Well now _ she turned him out _ he turned un out, well now the...he sold his property _ sold all her property _ for three thousand dollars. Well that was a lot o' money them times see. An' uh...very good, he fitted up his...two ships _ his three ships, he fitted up his three ships _ an' got some men an' he started an' _ he went back.

Now _ in them times see _ there w...there was uh...uh...a couple of men livin here _ an' 'nother one livin here _ when the...when they was borned _ if uh...they...you had a...a boy _ an' this man had a girl _ well they 'd marry 'em see right away. Well now _ they was married see the king's daughter and he was. Well now he had the cerstificate see.

Uh...very good. He uh...fitted out his ships an' he went home an' uh*...he got home an' he went to his...grandmother's _ with his three ships out tied up to the pier you know an' _ by an' by she [*the king's daughter*] heard he was there. An' she said uh..."How you get on" she said "Hard Head" she said "this time?"* *footsteps in background

"Oh" he said "don't be talkin!" He said "I got money enough." *crockery rattling in background

She said "You have?"

He said "Yes" he said "I got enough." Said "I got money enough now."

Said "Good."

Now she was goina be married _ that night she was goina be married to the mayor o' the town see. Well now _ "Now" he [*Jack*] said _ "I tell ya"* he said "what I'll do." He said "I'm goin _ across" he said "goin down" he said "to me ships" he said "an' I'm comin back" _ he said "on the...the boat uh...* on the (bridge)" now he had to cross a bridge see. An' _ he said uh...uh..."The...mayor o' the town" she told un she was goin to be married* "comes down" he said "an' uh...I sees un, well" he said "I'll uh...fix it up with un." *teller's wife speaks in background *teller's wife speaks in background *talking and crockery rattling in background

Well anyhow he went down to his ships _ an' when he was comin across the bridge _ he meet the mayor o' the town what was goin to be married to the king's daughter. An' uh...he [*the mayor*] seen this

man comin, he haves on ol' clothes, he was dressed up in ol' clothes an'
_ "Hello" he said uh..."where are you goin?"

He [*Jack*] was...he was up on the bridge an' he was lookin all round
on this side the bridge [*demonstrating how Jack was looking from side to
side*] an' around on that side an' around on this side. An' he said "Where
are you goin?"

He said "I'm look...I put a...a trap here" he said _ "twenty-five year
ago" he said "an' if I can find un" he said "I'll show ya...show ya the best
lobster" he said "ever you seen in your life."

He said "What's your name?"

He said "Poverty Part From Good Company. Poverty Part From
Good Company." Now that's...that's what she named un
when...when...when he leaved there the last time see. Well he marked it
all down on his book see. An' when he went home to the king's daughter
_ when he went home to the king's house _ well he was tellin the king's
daughter about the...the foolish man he'd seen. He said "I...well" he said
"don't be talkin!" he said "I seen a foolish man" he said "when I was
crossin the bridge there." He said "He was up" he said "lookin around" he
said _ * "on this side the bridge" he said "an' on that side. An' he told me
he sot a lobster trap there" he said _ "tuh...twenty year ago. An' if he
could find un he'd show me the best lobster ever I seed in me life."

An' he said...she said "Ya know his name?"

An' he said "Yes" he said "I...I knows it" he said "but I can't mind" he
said "I got his name here in me pocketbook." Took out his book an' he
looked at un, he...he said "Poverty Part From Good Company."

Course when /he/ said that she knowed who he was. Well uh...she said
"I got to go out here" she said "for a minute." An' uh...she went out an' this
is where she went, down...down where Jack was to. "Hello" she said
uh..."Hard Head" she said "how you get on?"

"Oh" he said "don't be talkin!" He said "I got money enough." He
said "I got money enough now."

She said "You have?"

"Yes. Now" he said _ "we'll go to bed." He said "We'll go to bed."

"Oh" she said "I can't go to bed not now"

"Yes" he said "we'll go to bed." Went in the room "Now" he said "I
got cerstificate here." Shoved his hand in his pocket an' he hauled out
certificate, he said "We're married." He said "You see that?"

An' she said "Yes. Yes" she said "I sees it"

He said "We're married." Said "Now" he said "I'll pin that up over
the door." They went in the room an' they went to bed.

An' uh...by an' by she was gone so long _ the king send a...a little
feller down to see where she was to. An' when she wen[t]...when he
went down _ this is where he went to an' she was in the bed with uh...with

*footsteps in
background

/she/

410

Hard Head as he called un. An' ＿ he come up an' he told the king. Oh well the king got in a wonderful passion, he was goin to kill un ＿ to think his daughter was in the bed with another man an' goina be married.

"Well uh.../your/ honour" /he/ [*the little feller*] say...he said "she is."　　　/me/　/she/

"Well" he said "we got to prove it out." So he ＿ he send down someone else. Uh...they went down [and the answer was] yes.

Well now the king went down hisself. The king went the...the... mayor...the mayor o' the town went down hisself. When he went down ＿ he [*Jack*] had the room door open. An' uh...he said "I told ya" he said "I was goin to show you the best lobster" he said "ever you seen in your life." An' he hauled up her clothes an' he give her a smack on the backside. "Now" he said "that's the best lobster" he said "ever you seen (in) your life! Now" he said "you see that up over the door?"

He looked out, he said "Yes" he said "I sees it."

He said "We're married."

An' he went back, he told the king an' the king went down. An'... looked up over door "Yes" he said ＿ "right." He said "They're married." An' now he said ＿ now they...they got married uh...the an' the king build 'em a palace an' they went an' lived /with/ the king an' when they...when I left　　　/the/ they had three children.

[Int: Where did ya get that story Freeman?]

I...I learned that story from Jack...Jack Roberts.

[Int: How long ago?]

Ja...Jack Roberts up the...

[Teller's wife: How long ago?]

How long ago? Oh that's about uh...

[Int: How old were you?]

Oh I guess that's about uh...thirty year ago.

[Int: How old were you then?]

How old was I then?

[Int: Yeah]

Oh I was about uh...

[Teller's wife: [*whispers*] forty]

Uh...about forty year old I guess.

[Int: Is that right?]

Yeah.

[Int: Where...where was it that you learned it from him? Where were you when you heard it?]

I was do[wn]...I was up there. I was up there uh...come out o' the woods see? I come out the woods ＿ an' we was (havin) [a] little time [i.e., *party*] there...(havin) [a] little time there drinkin wine. Well now ＿ [Int. coughs] I want un to tell me a story 'cause he was wonderful man on stories. Well now this i[s]...this is the one he tol' me see? This is the story he tol' me.

[Int: How many times did you hear it?]

Only heard it once.

[Int: An' you...an' you've been tellin it...]

Yes. Only hear...only hear it once, I only want to hear a story once an' I knowed un all then.

[Int: Mm-hm. When did you first start to tell it?]

When did I first start [to] tell un? Oh uh...oh a long spell ago uh...(I started)...first start to tell un. Long spell ago, must be thirty-five year ago I say...start to tell un. Now I've aknowed that story ever since I was about...about forty year old. An' I can still remember un.

[Int: You certainly can!]

Yes.

Duration: 23 min., 11 sec.

Source: Charles Benoit (uncle), St. Pauls, Great Northern Peninsula, John Roberts, Sally's Cove, Great Northern Peninsula.

Location: Sitting room of teller's house, afternoon.

Audience: Mrs. Rebecca Bennett (teller's wife), other members of the family, interviewer.

Context, Style, and Language: Freeman Bennett's increasing deafness makes it difficult for him to hear the interviewer. His wife, who has obviously heard the story many times before, helps the interview along by interpreting the questions and encouraging him generally. In effect she monitors much of the storytelling and is aware that in the opening sentences Freeman momentarily "gets ahead of his story." There is a good deal of background noise throughout, as people move around in the sitting room and kitchen, making cups of tea and doing other domestic chores. The interviewer has to shift position several times and this causes some additional microphone noise. On this occasion, however, the interviewer takes particular notice of the gestural and postural features of Freeman's storytelling style—features commented upon individually elsewhere in the notes accompanying this narrator's tales. He observes that when telling stories Freeman sits leaning forward in his chair, his elbows resting on his knees—reaching out, as it were, to bridge the space between himself and his audience. In telling this story, as in others, he becomes very dramatic, both in vocal quality and gesture. When Jack writes down the sum for the teacher, Freeman uses the fingers of one hand to simulate writing, using the palm of the other hand to represent the book. When Jack has drunk the sleepy drops Freeman throws up his hands on either side of his head and jerks his head and upper body back in the chair to indicate Jack's drugged state. When the man from the boat gives Jack the substitute bottle, Freeman stands up and puts his hand in his own pocket to extract an imaginary bottle. Later, when Jack exchanges the two bottles, Freeman deftly switches imaginary bottles from one hand to the other, and then again leans back in the chair, eyes closed, to show Jack pretending to be asleep. Finally, Freeman gets to his feet and peers downward this way and that way to demonstrate how Jack looks over each side of the bridge, searching for the lobster trap. Such a wealth of effective kinesic, proxemic, and gestural features amply demonstrates the considerable degree of dramatization in these performances. Although often echoed in the variations and contrasts of vocal tone, such features are virtually lost in a mere sound recording. Videotaping would, of course, have captured much of the essential dramaturgy of the storytelling event, but we had no access to this technology in our fieldwork. In this collection we therefore have no alternative but to fall back on brief field notes, some of which, as in this case, reveal something of the vibrancy and immediacy of the performance tradition.

This second version of the tale was the latest to be recorded of the three but is presented second here as it is complete whereas No. 39 lacks most of the dénouement. Freeman Bennett seems rather less sure of himself here than in the two earlier versions and his wife plays a more supportive role in the interview. Even so, as the comparative table in the notes to No. 37 indicates, this is a lively version which includes some new material. There is a running together of Jack's instructions to the girl about what to say to the teacher and the actual situation when the teacher is given the sum to do, but this conflation does not materially affect the narrative flow and the audience is able to adjust to the change.

We again find here the hallmarks of Freeman Bennett's style, including the vivid dialogue, occasional short sentences, ellipsis (especially of function words and pronoun subjects), stress on individual words for clarity and dramatic effect, the use of *An'* followed by a pause and/or hesitation form at the beginning of sentences, and the punctuation of the narrative with *(Well) anyhow, very good, by an' by,* and *he/she said.* Notice also the use of the tag question *see* which is closely linked with explanations said half-aside to the audience, e.g., "'cause THEM times 'twas th' ol' fashioned ships with the...sails on 'em see," "th' ol' people used to call SLEEPY DROPS one time see," "Well that was a lot o' money them times see," and "Now _ in them times see _ there...was" etc. These explanations help to maintain the teller's rapport with his audience, remind them that the story is set in "olden times," and give a semblance of plausibility to the events described notwithstanding the "Once upon a time" opening formula. Another means of sustaining the audience's attention is through gesture and demonstration, seen especially in this version of the story when the teller twice imitates Jack lying asleep and snoring, and also when he demonstrates how Jack looks from side to side on the bridge.

The pace of the narration causes some confusion of pronouns and their referents, but otherwise this version is smooth and even in its texture, enlivened from time to time by a sudden change of vocal tone in the dialogue, e.g., after Jack wins the bet his speech reflects a significant change in his behavior: the quiet acceptance of his earlier losses is suddenly replaced by a confident decisiveness when he is seen to take full advantage of his newly won rights. In authoritative and unequivocal terms he tells the old woman that he now owns all the property and that she must leave. This dramatic reversal of their two roles is most effectively conveyed by the vocal quality used for Jack's speech at this point.

In addition to the word *passion* there is a hint of formal or literary language in the word *strand* which may have one of several related meanings here, whether generally for "coast, shore" (*OED Strand* sb.[1] 1, *EDD STRAND* sb[1]), or vaguely for "country, region" *OED Strand* sb.[1] 1.e), or more specifically for a "quay, wharf, landing-place" (*OED Strand* sb.[1] 1.c). There is, of course, an archaic and literary ring to the name *Poverty Parts From Good Company,* which incidentally appears in this version only in the dénouement. There may also be a clue in this recension to solving the name *Hard Head Hover* which appears in No. 43, *Poverty Parting With Good Company.* In explaining how Jack acquired the name *Hard Head* Freeman Bennett says: "they named un over, Hard Head see" which presumably means they gave him an additional name—i.e., over and above his own. It therefore seems possible that the addition of *(H)over* to Hard Head's name in No. 43 could be an alteration of an expression like "they named un over."

Other linguistic items include the West Country English /ar/ in *'cordin, awards,* the short lowered close back vowel in *foolish,* the typical Newfoundland pronunciation of the letter *A* as /æ:/, aphesis in *'greement,* and the problem of discriminating between *the night* and *tonight* which depends on whether the initial consonant is voiced or unvoiced. The word *grub* is used in an appropriately nautical context in the fitting out of the ship, and the neuter relative *what* is used with a masculine referent *mayor.* Present tense verb forms are *he askes, you losses/stays/falls, he haves;* past tense forms include *fit, seed, send* (the latter also being interpretable as a vivid present), along with the past participle *atook* and the double negative *won't wake no more.*

See also the notes to Nos. 4, 5, 6, 8, and **37.**

Type and Motifs:

Cf. AT611. *The Gifts of the Dwarfs* [Irish by-form].

Z10.1. *Beginning formula.*

L111.4. *Orphan hero.*

L101. *Unpromising hero.*

L142. *Pupil surpasses master.*

T91.6.4. *Princess falls in love with lowly boy.*

T97. *Father opposed to daughter's marriage.*

N831. *Girl as helper.*

N15. *Chastity wager.*

N2.6.5. *Daughter as wager.*

N2.5. *Whole kingdom (all property) as wager.*

K675. *Sleeping potion given to man who is to pass night with a girl.*

K92. *Gambling contest won by deception.*

Cf. N825.2. *Old man helper.*

K1865. *Deception by pretending sleep.*

Cf. H248.3. *Sham dead [sleeper] tested by pricking.*

Cf. T61.5.1. *Betrothal of hero to princess while both are still in cradle.*

N681. *Husband (lover) returns home just as wife (mistress) is to marry another.*

Cf. H586.2.2. *Traveler says he must look after his net to see if it has taken fish.*

H151. *Attention drawn and recognition follows.*
Cf. K1831.0.1. *Disguise by changing name.*
L161. *Lowly hero marries princess.*
Z10.2. *End formula.*

International Parallels: See No. 36.

39. HARD HEAD

Freeman Bennett
St. Pauls, Great Northern Peninsula
18 July 1970

Cf. AT611 [Irish by-form]
TC966 71-50
Collectors: HH and Helen Halpert

[Teller's wife: "Hard Head" uh…that's a story. He tol'…he told you that
when you was here before last time.]
[Int: Well tell it again.]

"Hard Head" yes. Well one time ‿ in olden times ‿ there was a man an'
he had uh…three or four children see. An' one's name was…was Jack. Well
now ‿ the ol' man ‿ he died. Now let's say he…Jack was the youngest one,
now the other ones could look out to their own self. Ol' man died, well now
‿ Jack ‿ he didn't know ‿ w(hat)…they didn't know WHAT they was goin to
do wi' Jack. Well the…the queen's daughter ‿ she uh…he was…he was goin
to school ‿ he was old enough, he was goin to school an' he had big
education. He had big education Jack did.

Now – the queen's daughter said to the king she said to her father she
said "I got a mind" she said "we'd take that li(ttle)…that…young feller." She
said "He got no one to look out to un" she said "I got a mind" she said "we'd
take un."

An' ‿ he said "Yes, well" he said "/'twill/ be alright" he said uh…   /to/
"Take un" she said "an' give un some education."
"Yes" king said "we could do that."

Well they took un. An' ‿ he used to go to school. Well now ‿ he
couldn't learn nothing see. He made out like he couldn't learn nothing but
still for all ‿ he had big education. (He) made out like he couldn't learn
nothing, he couldn't learn nothing at all. He didn't…he didn't know his
letters.

Well very good. He was goin home one night an' uh…she went
home one night an' uh…teacher said uh…she said to her father she said "I
don't know what you're goin to do with un" she said "he…he can't

learn nothing" she said "he won't learn nothing, he don't even know his letters."

Well the king said _ "We'll send un" he said "little bit longer" he said "see what _ he can do." He said "An' if he can't learn, well" he said uh…"we'll have to take un out o' school."

So very good. He went to school, now she…he was goin to one school an' she was goin to the other see, she was goin to the high school an' he was goin to the lower school. But still for all he had…he had more education than the king's daughter. An' _ well he (got) into school that…that evening. An' he was on his way home. An' he…he sot down on his way home an' /when/ he sot down on his way home _ the king's daughter she came out of school an' she was…comin along. An' she had uh…her handkercher in her hand like this [*uses hand to indicate wiping of eyes*] an' she was…wipin her eyes.

/well/

An' he said "Hello" he said "what's wrong?" Now they called un Hard Head see, the king did, the…the teachers did, they called un Hard Head. She said wha[t]…he said "What's wrong?"

"Well" she said "the teachers have gi' me a sum here today" she said _ "an' I can't do un." She said "I can't do un" she said uh…"there's no way" she said "for me to do un."

An' uh…Jack said, he said "Let me have a look at un."

"Huh! [*laughing, dismissive tone*] Let YOU have a look at un!" she said "What's the good for YOU to look at un _ " she said "when you don't know your letters?"

"Oh well" he said "I supposed" he said "there's no harm" he said "to show un to me."

"Oh no" she said "there's no harm" she said "Jack" she said "but you knows" she said "YOU can't do un."

"Well" Jack said "let me have a look at un."

So -- she opened the book an' uh..sot down 'longside o' Jack an' _ Jack…took the book an' he opened un like that [*demonstrates*] an' he said "Gi'me your pencil."

"Huh!" [*laughing, dismissive tone*] she said "Jack" she said "what's you goin to do?"

So -- she gives uh…Jack the pencil _ an' Jack _ started in uh…an' he made the sum up. "There you go" Jack said. "The sum is right. Now" Jack said "when you goes home" _ he said "if the…your father asks ya who made the sum _ an' who ma[de]…who done the sum -- you tell un _ 'Not the teacher.' An' well he'll say 'For sure 'tis not Hard Head.' 'No. Not Hard Head.'"

/he/ /she/

So when /she/ went home _ she said uh…king said to her _ /he/ said uh…"You've had a hard sum there."

She said "Yes." She said "A hard sum"

He said "Who done it for ya?" -- He said "Not the teacher."
"No."
"Well" he said "for sure" he said _ "'twasn't Hard Head."
"Yes" she said "'twas Hard Head."
He said "You don't mean to tell me" /he/ said "he done /she/
that sum?"
She said "Yes" she said "he done that sum."
"Well" he said "he got more education [than] you got."
"Well" he say...she said "yes" she said "I guess he have."
"Well" he said "I'll take un out o' school" he said "altogether" he said
"I'll put un in the office."
"Yes." She said "You can do that."

Well that's what he done. He took him out o' school altogether
an' he put un in his office. Well now _ he was in his office _ doin work, well
he was doin pretty good work, well now the king's daughter she fell in love
with un see.

Now them times when a...when a...of...two families was living
together see _ livin close together _ /if/ uh...you had a son _ an' I had a /of/
daughter _ well soon as they...they was born _ we'd marry 'em see? We'd
marry 'em an' get their bir[th]...get their marriage cerstificate see. Well
now Jack _ had the marriage cerstificate see down the...they was married
see? An' Jack had the marriage cerstificate.

Well now _ she fell in...Jack fuh...she fell in love wi' Jack, well
now the...the king got hold to it that they was gettin around together
an' uh...well he was goina turn un away. He wasn't goin to keep un
'cause he...he couldn't let uh...couldn't let un have his daughter _ not
a poor man like that _ have his daughter. Well _ he turned un away.
Goin turn un away.

"Well" she said _ "Jack" she said _ "I'll fit ya out" she said "I'll give
ya...I'll give ya a ship" _ she said "an' I'll fit ya out" she said "an' you
can...go sailin." She said "An' when you comes back" she said "well" she
said uh..."we might _ be able to get married."

"Alright" Jack said.

Well uh...she fit Jack out with a ship. An' _ he got a crew o' men
an' he started. An' when he got _ to the Cape o' Good /Hope/ _ he /struck/ /Oke/ /truck/
a suh...struck a storm. An' he blowed everything off of her. Well he got
in...port after a spell. An' got her tied up to the pier. Well now there was
a ol' woman come down aboard of un.

An' uh...she said uh..."You had a wrackin" she said.

"Yes" Jack said. He said "I had a wrackin."

She said uh..."Come up" she said "to the house" she said "an' stay the
night." "Yes" Jack said uh..."I think I will."

417

Well Jack went up _ up to the house an' he had his supper. She said "Now" she said "Jack" _ she said "you got a ship down there." She said "An' a...a lot o' stuff aboard of her." She said "I'll put up...my property" she said "against your ship" _ she said "that you'll sleep with my daughter tonight" _ she said "an' won't know no more about her" she said "than you did when you gets up in the morning _ [than you] did when you went to bed."

"Oh no" Jack said "I won't."

He's...she said "Will you bet?"

Jack said "Yes" he said "I'll bet." Well he bet...Jack bet with her.

Very good, bedtime come an' they went to bed an' _ ol' woman went up. Now she had a...a bottle o'...sleepy drops they used to call it them times see.

"Well" _ she said "Jack" she said uh..."ya have a drink" she said "'fore you goes to bed?"

Jack said "Yes" he said "I think I will." Uh...used to haul out this bottle. An' Jack took the big drink. An' he fall back in the bed an' soon as he was back in the bed he was sound asleep see. Course uh...she come up she got in bed wi' Jack an' she sleeped all night with un an' she got up in the morning uh...dressed herself an' went down an' _ when Jack woke _ she was out o' bed an' gone. Well now Jack had lost it all.

Well now very good he had [to] try to get hi[s]...work his way back home. Well after a spell he got back. Now he had a aunt there. An' that's where he used to stay to. He stayed to his aunt's. An' she found out, the /she/ king's daughter found out /he/ was there. An' she went over.

An'...she said "How you get on?"

/she/ "Oh" [*disappointed tone*] Jack said "I had bad luck" /he/ said "I lost everything I had."

She [said] "You lost it all. Well" she said "Jack" she said "I'll fit you out again."

/he/ An' /she/ fit Jack out again, give un another ship. An' when he got to the Cape o' Good Hope _ he struck the same kind of a storm. An' he blowed everything off of her. Well he got her in _ to the pier, well when he got her in _ his yuther [i.e., *other*] ship was still there tied up to the pier.

Well now this ol' woman come down again. "(Hallo)" she said "Jack" said "you're back again."

"Yes." Jack said "I'm back again" he said "everything gone."

"(Well) now" she said "Jack, you comin up?"

"Yes" Jack said "I'm goin up." An' _ Jack went up.

"Now" she said "Jack" _ she said uh..."what about havin a bet again tonight?"

"Yes" Jack said "I'll have a bet with you again tonight."

Well _ very good, Jack went up to go to bed, well she took out this bottle. Same thing an' she give Jack the big drink, well soon as she did Jack falled right back in the bed sound asleep. An' _ didn't know nothing till the next morning when he got up, 'twas uh…the girl that's got up an' dressed an' down in the house an' (down) to her breakfast an' Jack got up _ well he'd lost that one.

Well now he had to work his way back home again. [Teller's wife talks in background: (?Lost his luck)] He worked his way back home again an' he got home to his aunt's an' he went there, well she [*the king's daughter*] found out he was there. An' _ she went over.

S[aid] "How you get on this time Jack?"

"Oh" he said "the same thing" he said "I lost it all."

"Well now" she said "Jack, I'm goina fit ye out once more." She said "An' if you losses all this, well" she said uh…"I can't do it no more."

Well she fit Jack out again. Now well when…very good, when Jack got…to the Cape o' Good Hope _ he struck the same kind of a storm. Well now _ when he was gettin in _ gettin in to the pier _ 'fore he got to the pier _ he seen a little boat comin.

An' _ he come an' _ come up 'longside an' uh…Jack said "Come 'board."

/He/ went aboard. An' [*coughs*] "Now" he said "Jack" _ he said "you   /They/
stays to…the…th' ol' woman's house there don't ya?"

An' uh…Jack said "Yes."

"Well now" she say…he said _ "Do you know what she gives you every night 'fore you goes to bed?"

An' Jack said "No."

/He/ said "You…she gives ya sleepy drops" /he/ said "an' puts ya to   /She/ /she/
sleep." /He/ said "Now" he said _ "I got a bottle full here." He said uh…"I   /She/
got a bottle full o' rum here." He said "You take the bottle full o' rum." He
said "And _ when you go…when sh…you…you…she goes up" /he/ said "to   /she/
go to bed" _ /he/ said "now" he said "tonight" he said "you sign a 'greement"   /she/
_ he said "on this." He said "An' when you goes up to go to bed" he said
"leave it on the table." He said "When you get uh…(goes) to…gets upstairs"
_ he said "you say _ 'Oh. I've aleaved me uh…agreement down on the
table, I got to go down an' get it.'" An' uh "Well" he said "she'll go
down after it." /He/ said "An' you haul out her bottle out from in under the   /She/
piller" _ /he/ said "an' shove yours in." Well very good.   /she/
     /he/

Jack went up to the ol' woman's house. An' /she/ said "Jack" s[aid]
"you're back again."

"Yes" Jack said. "Back again."

She said "You're goin to have the bet tonight?"

"Yes" Jack said "I'm goina have un again tonight." Alright. Well they bet.

Well -- Jack…said "Now" he said _ "we got to sign a 'greement" he said "on this."

He said "Well" he said...she said "Jack" she said "how is that?" She said "We've had _ two bets" she said "an' we ant signed no 'greement onto un"

"No" Jack said. "I know we ant" he said "but I've alost everything I got" he said "'tis time" he said "for me to get down to business now" he said "an' do something." He said "I've alost everything I got."

Well _ very good, they signed the 'greement. Jack went upstairs an' she...she went up with un. An' uh...Jack said "Oh" he said "I've aleaved it" he said "all down on the table." He said "You'll have to go down" he said "an' get it for me."

"Yes" she said "I'll go down."

She went down, when she went down Jack hauled the...this bottle out from in under her piller an' shoved his in see. And _ when she come up _ (she) hauled the bottle out from under her piller "Now" she said "Jack" she said "you goin to have a drink" she said "'fore you go uh...goes to bed?"

"Yes" Jack said "I think I will." So Jack took the bottle an' he...tipped down an' had the big drink o' rum. Jack falled back in the bed buh...starts snorin you know an' _ by an' by she [*the daughter*] come up. An' uh...she looked at un _ an' _ she went down, she said "Mother" she said "I don't believe" she said "that man is (to) sleep."

"Yes" [*convinced tone*] she said "he's to sleep" she said "he won't wake up for about twelve o'clock tomorrow" she said "'cordin to what he've adrinked."

Well she went up an' she got in bed with un. Well soon as she got in bed with un well he _ turned over an' he put his two arms around her, he said "I got ya this time!" So -- he got...Jack got up next morning _ got up the next mornin "Now" he said _ "I got ya this time."

She said "Yes" she said "you got me alright."

"Well now" Jack said "I got it all" he said "I got me three ships" _ he said "an' I got...everything you got here." He said "I owns it all, now" he said "you got to get out."

Well Jack turned her out of her house an' he sold her house _ an' he fitted up his three ships. An' he started _ for home. An' _ he _ on his way home he anchored, he...he...he had to...to go in the harbour an' he had to walk so far see 'fore he could to get...'fore he could get home to his aunt's. Well now on his way home _ he meet the mayor o' the town see? Now the mayor o' the town an' the king's daughter was goina be married that night see. An' _ Jack seen un comin, now Jack heared that they was goin to be married. An' course Jack knowed un. An' Jack _ was on er...had to cross a bridge. An' he was walkin along on the bridge like this [*gets to his feet to demonstrate Jack's walk*] Jack was an' uh...walkin along like this an' lookin all around like this [*mimes Jack's peering from side to side*].

[L]ookin all around then he...he said uh...he said "Hello" he said uh..."what's you lookin for?"

An' he start to laugh at un, Jack said _ "I sot a lobster trap here" he said "about uh...ten or fifteen year ago" he said "an' if I could find it" he said "I'd show you the best fresh lobster" he said "ever you seen in your life." An' _ he start to laugh at Jack 'cause he thought he was foolish see. An' uh...Jack said "Well" he said ***[*recorder off*]

Duration: 15 min., 4 sec.
Source: Charles Benoit (uncle), St. Pauls, Great Northern Peninsula.
Location: Sitting room of teller's house, afternoon.
Audience: Mrs. Rebecca Bennett (teller's wife), interviewers.

Context, Style, and Language: (For context see notes to No. 5).

This version has been relegated to third place of the three told by Freeman Bennett as it is incomplete, the final section of the dénouement being unrecorded. The teller is reminded of the story by his wife, and he develops it well although with rather less detail and elaboration than in Nos. 37 and 38. The typical features of his style already commented on in the notes to previous tales are again evident here. Of particular interest is the skillful variation of tone quality in the dialogue which contributes greatly to the characterization. One might take, for instance, the dialogue between Jack and the girl concerning the sum she has been given. The hopelessness of the task is first suggested in the tone of voice used in her repeated statements that she cannot do the sum. We are already prepared to sympathize as we know she has been crying—the storyteller even imitating the wiping of her eyes. Jack then asks to see the sum and she responds in tones of friendly and amused dismissal of his being able to help, especially noticeable in such subtle nuances of pronunciation as those in the exclamatory "Huh!" and the strong stress on *you* in the ensuing sentence. The tone of Jack's reply is noncommittal, implying, as he says, that there is no harm in his looking at the sum. The girl agrees, but her tone again suggests her belief that he cannot do it. Both here and elsewhere in his tales, Freeman Bennett uses dialogue in a masterly way which cannot be transferred to paper, but which adds depth and fuller dimension to his characters. At the same time, dialogue of this kind increases the audience's interest in the plot by the creation of suspense—a quality essential to folktales, which tend to proceed by the posing and resolution of a succession of problems and dilemmas. The audience perceives that the characters are facing a problem and becomes interested in how it is to be resolved. The same kind of banter continues when Jack asks the girl for her pencil, and when he has done the sum with remarkable speed he returns it to her with quiet confidence, and does not display the truculence which so often surfaces in his encounters with giants and other adversaries; the storyteller relies on vocal tone and color to keep these two sides of Jack's persona apart.

In this version too we have an interesting example of the successful mixture of direct and indirect speech when Jack is heard rehearsing in advance the dialogue which will take place between the king and his daughter about who did the sum. The storyteller again conveys by tone of voice that the king does not believe Hard Head has done the sum, and also that his daughter strongly agrees with her father's appraisal of the situation. As before, the audience is therefore prepared for events yet to come and so participation in the plot is intensified; a sense of anticipation is created, and the audience is let into the secret of how the king's daughter will handle her father's questions.

Further points of linguistic interest are the absence of transitional /n/ in *a aunt*, aphesis in *'board* (aboard), the archaic *handkercher* and *wrackin* (wreck; cf. OED *Wrack* sb.^{2} 2), the omission of the object pronoun in *tipped [it] down,* the present tense *I owns*, past tense *heared,* past participles *gi'* and *adrinked,* and the double negative *can't/won't learn nothing, can't do it no more.*

See also the notes to Nos. 4, 5, 6, 8, **37,** and **38.**

Type and Motifs:
>Cf. AT611. *The Gifts of the Dwarfs* [Irish by-form].

Z10.1. *Beginning formula.*

L111.4. *Orphan hero.*

L101. *Unpromising hero.*

L142. *Pupil surpasses master.*

T91.6.4. *Princess falls in love with lowly boy.*

Cf. T61.5.1. *Betrothal of hero to princess while both are still in cradle.*

T97. *Father opposed to daughter's marriage.*

N831. *Girl as helper.*

N15. *Chastity wager.*

N2.6.5. *Daughter as wager.*

N2.5. *Whole kingdom (all property) as wager.*

K675. *Sleeping potion given to man who is to pass night with a girl.*

K92. *Gambling contest won by deception.*

Cf. N825.2. *Old man helper.*

K1865. *Deception by pretending sleep.*

N681. *Husband (lover) returns home just as wife (mistress) is to marry another.*

Cf. H586.2.2. *Traveler says he must look after his net to see if it has taken fish.*

H151. *Attention drawn and recognition follows.*

International Parallels: See No. 36.

40. HARD HEAD

Everett Bennett
St. Pauls, Great Northern Peninsula
24 August 1966

Cf. AT611 [Irish by-form]
TC251 66-24
Collectors: HH and JW

I knows a couple o' very good stories. [*recorder off*]*** livin by hisself you
see [*recorder off*] [*coughs*]*** the king's castle. The king had a _ a daughter
an' course she _ said to her father 'twas a pity to let un _ stay you know.
[*aside to Int. B:* you're turned on aint ya?]
[Int. A: Well, may we?]
[*aside to Int. B:* got un on have ya?]
[Int. A: May he have...may he (do it?)]
Oh my! I can't tell (ya). [*recorder off*]*** er...she said 'twas a pity she said
for un to stay there _ an' get no education you see. An' she er..."Well" he
said "we'll take un up an' send un to school." They took un up an' they sont
un to school an'...well his name was Jack. An' he...he never learned his
letters all day. But they took un...went home in the night. Next day he went
to school, the same thing. Still couldn't learn. Now she fell in love with Jack
_ an' on their way home that night _ teacher give her a hard sum _ to do.
They set down to have a chat an' _ she said "Well" she said "Jack" she said
 "I got a hard sum to do tonight" she said uh..."I don't know how I'm goina
do un."

"Show" he said "let ME see un."

"Well" she said "Hard Head" she said "'tis no good for you to...look at
un." She said "An' I can't do the sum" she says "you're sure you're not goina
do it."

"Well" he said "there's no harm for me to look at un anyhow."

Well he looked at the sum an' he _ finished...done the sum for her an'
he turned over the _ slates at that time, turned over the slate and (he) done
one on the other side. "Now" he said "you give that to the teacher
tomorrow."

Now when he went to school the next day he said er...she passed in her
slate

He said "Who done this sum?" he said "Your father or mother?"

"Neither one of 'em" she said "but Jack done that sum an' there's one
on that side for you to do."

So anyhow he was uh...he was all day...the teacher was all day at the
sum an' never finished un. – Well now 'twas no good to send un _ to the
teacher 'cause he had more learning than teacher. When he went home that
night er...she said "Father" she said "'tis no good to send _ Jack" she said "to
the _ school" she said "he got more learning that the teacher got."

"Well" he said "I'll put un in a office." So he put un in his office. Shift un in his office. Well she fell right in love with Jack. An' every day _ when she come home _ when she get chance she go in to have a yarn with Jack _ chat to Jack an' _ old king took notice of it. Finally he was goin to _ fire Jack anyhow. She found out. She found it out and she said er…"Now Jack" she said er…"father is goin to fire ya" she said "the best thing you can do" she said "is go an' ask for yer time." (So) he went in the castle for /his/ time.

/her/

He said "Why" he said "Jack" he said "you goina leave?"

"Yes" he said "I'm goina leave." Anyhow he aks for the time.

"Now" she said "Jack" she said er…"I'm goina fit you out with a ship _ ship an' cargo." So she fit Jack out with a ship an' cargo _ an' he leaved. An' when he got to the Cape o' Good Hope _ he struck a breeze _ storm. Took…blowed away all his canvas. Just get enough for to get in port.

Well Jack was a pretty _ big feller now _ have ships. He couldn't stay aboard either one of 'em, took a boarding house. A man an' a old woman an' her daughter there. Well when bedtime come showed Jack to his room. She pulled a bottle out from in under the _ no _ before me story.

She said "Jack" she said "I'll bet you" she said uh…"your ship an' cargo _ again my house an' land _ you'll sleep with my daughter all night tonight an' not know what she is in the morning."

"Yes" Jack said, he bet. So they left. When they got up _ to go to bed _ she had Jack up to the room _ she pulled a bottle out from in under the pillow an' asked him would he have a drink.

"Oh yes" _ he'd have a drink sure. So he haves a drink an' what should this be but a big _ dose o' sleepy drops now. Jack went off to sleep. Girl come an' got in bed an' sleeped all night with Jack an' _ gone the next morning 'fore Jack woke.

An' Jack come down in the morning "Well Jack" she said "you alost your ship"

"Yes" Jack said "I lost me ship."

An' a twelvemonth an' a day from that he was back where the queen's daughter was…king's daughter was to again.

"Now" he said er…"I lost me ship."

"Well" she said "Jack" she said "that's too bad."

"But" he said "I'm goina change my name now." He said "I'm goina change my name, 'Poverty Parts from Good Company.' When I was in **YOUR** company I was in good company, now I'm part from it" he said "that's poverty parts from good company."

/he/

"Now" /she/ said "Jack" she said "I'll fit you out again." So she fit Jack out the certain…second ship. When he got to the Cape o' Good Hope he struck the same kind of a storm. Lost everything. Just got in port. Well now he's goin up to _ the boarding house again to try to get his yuther [i.e., *other*] ship back.

424

"Well Jack" she said "you're come again"

"Yes" Jack said "I'm come again. What's goina be the bet tonight?"

"Well" she said...Jack said uh..."I wants me other ship up again this one." Alright. So they bet an' when bedtime come to go to bed away they goes an' _ she pulled out this bottle again to give Jack another drink an' _ off Jack goes _ to sleep again. Girl come an' sleeped all night an' _ gone in the morning.

An' twelve months from that he got back again.

"Well Jack" she said "what luck this time?"

"Same thing" Jack said. "Lost everything."

"Well Jack" she said "I'm goin to fit ya out once more" she said "for the LAST time."

Well /she/ fit Jack out again an' by god he leaved an' when he got to the   /he/
Cape o' Good Hope he struck the same kind of a storm. An' he seen a old _ man out in a boat, 'twas er...more of a tiderip like you know _ bad place _ tryin to get up to the ship. "No grandfather" Jack said "come aboard you'll be drowneded." So he got un aboard.

An' he said er..."This is three year follyin now" he said "a ship acome here" he said "an' _ struck a storm like this."

"Yes" Jack said "that's mine. That's...I been in three of them ships."

He said "An'...an' you lost two of 'em."

"Yes" he said "I lost two of 'em."

"Well" he said "the boarding house that you goes to" he said _ "that drink that she gives you in the night _ that's sleepy drops. Now" he said "here's a bottle here" he said "just like the one she got. You get the chance an' slip that bottle out an' put this one in under." Alright.

Anyhow they got in port an' Jack _ went up. Went to the boarding house. "Well Jack you're back again"

"Yeah."

"Well I'll put up ya two ships 'gain this one now."

"Yeah." That's what he want. But Jack said "We got to have it stricter this time [than] we've had it before" he said "there got to be papers" he said _ "drawed on this."

"Oh Jack" she said "that's nonsense."

"Oh ne'r mind" Jack said "it's time for me be get strict now" he said "that's two ships I've lost" /he/ said "an' likely lost third one."   /she/

So he made out all his papers on the table an' he lodged 'em on the table. Well _ he'd go to bed. -- "Oh" he said "I got to go back again. Had to go back get me papers all leaved on the table."

"No odds Jack" she said "I'll go an' get 'em." While she was gone Jack slipped her bottle out an' put his in under you see. When she come an' got in bed Jack was in bed when she comed. Asked Jack would he have a drink

"Oh yes" have a drink. Took a big drink Jack did _ fell to sleep.

425

By an' by the girl come up. -- She looked at un _ an' went down to her mother an' she said "Mom" she said "he's not to sleep."

"Yes" she said. She said "He won't wake 'fore ten o'clock tomorrow."

Anyhow she goes up an' gets in bed. -- But she found out Jack wasn't asleep that night! She knowed Jack wasn't asleep!

(Anyhow) they start _ got his three ships back. Next morning "Well Jack" she said "you got your three ships."

"Yes" Jack said.

Now he start back for home now, had _ three ships an' three cargo, sold it, course he was a _ pretty rich man now. -- So anyhow now the...the day that he got home his girl _ was goina be married to the mayor o' the town. An' Jack found out. An' he was walkin along an' he seen 'em comin...Jack knowed un. Seen 'em comin along on the street an' _ Jack was runnin lookin over one of the st...come to a bridge, lookin over one side the bridge an' runnin lookin over the other side an' _ ah he was havin great sport off o' Jack.

"What are ya lookin for?"

"Oh I don't know what I'm lookin for" said Jack "I don't know what I'm lookin for. I sot a lobster trap here" he said er..."three year ago. An' if I can find un I'll show you the best...best fresh lobster ever you seen."

Oh he went off in the big laugh. An' he said "What's your name?"

"Oh" he said "I got ne'r name. I got no name" he said "I don't know what my name is."

"Oh you got a name."

"Yes my name is Poverty Parts from Good Company." Took out his pocketbook an' he wrote it down you see.

So any[how]...he start back now to his _ bride (the) one he was goina be married to. Went in and _ got tellin of her about it. "Oh I seen the funny man _ today."

"Yeah, where to?"

"Over on the bridge."

"What's his name?"

"I don't know. I got it there on me pocketbook." Took out the pocketbook an' [read out] "Poverty Parts from Good Company." An' she knowed 'twas Jack you see.

Now Jack _ an' the queen's daughter...king's daughter was married when they was infants _ an' Jack had his cerstificate. -- So anyhow away she goes. She knew where Jack was to. Jack was over to his aunt's house. Away she goes over. Waiting maids _ went over. She was gone so long, went over an' _ come back _ she was in bed now she an' Jack. Jacky had his cerstificate put up over the door. Where was...where was the girl? Over in there...over in bed with another man. Oh now they was goin to

426

_ behead 'em right away to think the king's daughter was in bed with another man an' she goina be married today.

"Oh well _ you can kill me if you like. Go an' see for yourself that's where she's to."

Went over. Come in through the door _ start to go in the room.

"Don't come in here" Jack said "don't you see that up over the door?" He patted his hand on his wife's ass like that he said "Here's the fresh lobster I was tellin of ya about today." [*laughter*] [*recorder off*]

That's "Hard Head."
[Int. A: "Hard Head?"]
"Hard Head" yes.
[Int. A: "Hard Head." Mm. He has a pretty good head an'…on un after all.]
Pretty good head after all, he wasn't too hard was he?

Duration: 10 min., 51 sec.
Source: John Roberts, Sally's Cove, Great Northern Peninsula.
Location: Kitchen of John Edward Bennett's house, evening.
Audience: John Edward Bennett (teller's brother) and his wife, Clarence and Barbara Bennett (teller's son and daughter-in-law), Clyde Bennett and his wife, John Edward's daughter-in-law and her two children, Anthony Bryan (teller's son-in-law), interviewers.

Context, Style, and Language: (For context see notes to No. 11).

Two full versions of this tale were told by Everett Bennett. The one presented here was recorded on the second day of our first visit to St. Pauls in 1966, while No. 41 was recorded some four years later. A brief sketch of the beginning of the tale was also recorded on the first day and is presented as No. F6. The tale was learned from John Roberts whose version "The King's Son" (No. 36) differs from it only in minor details, except for one very significant and surprising omission. The opening of the Roberts story, which is of crucial importance to the motivation of the plot and to the dénouement, explains that the children of the Kings of England and Germany were married when they were four or five years old and that the King of England's son kept his *cerstificate* of the marriage. This opening motif is entirely absent from the two versions told by Everett Bennett, but is found in modified form without reference to the royal families in the brief summary of the beginning of the tale in No. F6. As this summary was recorded on 23 August 1966, it is strange that the opening motif was unaccountably omitted not only from the fuller version of the story recorded on the following day but also from that recorded in 1970. It is interesting to speculate on this omission since its importance to the story cannot be denied. In his attempts to recall the tale on the first day of our initial visit this motif of the marriage of the hero and heroine comes immediately into the teller's mind, yet his fuller retellings ignore it. This suggests that both the recall and the retelling of elements in a given tale are to some extent selective, if not capricious. It may be that Everett Bennett simply forgot this motivating explanation when he retold the story on the following day and in 1970. On the other hand he may have chosen to omit it, perhaps for reasons of brevity or merely because he regarded it as unimportant. Either way, the narrative as he tells it has to compensate for the loss and appear complete in itself. This makes considerable demands on both storyteller and audience who have to adjust the narrative and the response to take account of the change. Thus each telling is seen to be the unique creation of the narrator at a given point in time and may lose or add motifs and other elements or recombine them in a different way on each occasion.

Both full versions told by Everett Bennett are somewhat shorter and less elaborate than those of his brother Freeman, but the plots are substantially the same, although Freeman included the motif of the infant marriage at the beginning of two versions he tells, and as an afterthought before the dénouement of the third. Nos. 40 and 41 are also closely parallel although the latter is smoother and more polished; for example, it has a full and detailed opening, giving important contextual information in an economical and effective summary, whereas the opening of No. 40 was unrecorded; it gives more details of Jack and the king's daughter going to the high and low schools respectively, explains why Jack is called Hard Head, shows the king's daughter's surprise at Jack's cleverness, has her suggest that Jack is put in the office, explains the changing of his name at the appropriate point, and is uncertain of its chronology in that the bottle motif appears rather too early when the teller gets "before his story." On the other hand the first version includes the account of Jack going to the king to "ask for his time," that is, to be paid off before leaving the job—a practice of course well known to working men, the mention of which would immediately appeal to a Newfoundland audience—Jack is described as going into the castle to ask for his time as casually as if he was going to see the foreman on a construction site or in a lumber camp. This version also gives details about the servant girl in the dénouement which are omitted in No. 41. The third storm in version one includes a tiderip while in version two its vehemence is communicated by very strong emphasis on the word *fierce.*

Like that of No. 11, the style in this version is very elliptical at times which is typical of this narrator, e.g., *Still couldn't learn, Lost everything, Just got in port, Went over, Come in through the door _ start to go in the room.* This stylistic device, coupled with a number of short sentences such as *She found out, So they left,* gives a crispness to the narrative and an impression of businesslike forward motion in the plot. Other features typical of the style are the breaking up of the narrative into fairly short utterances, punctuated by frequent pauses and the occasional markers *(So) anyhow, By an' by, Alright.* Note however that on at least two occasions the word *Alright* could also be interpreted as being a spoken response from one of the participants in the dialogue. Direct and indirect speech are mingled, e.g., "'Oh yes' _ he'd have a drink sure" in which the first two words and the last are said with all the intonation features of actual speech, while the central section of the utterance, with its third person pronoun and past tense, is apparently reported speech. Three similar examples are found towards the end of the tale. The first is the imperious urgency of the question "where was the girl?", spoken as if by the king and with the intonation of direct speech. The second is the long sentence "Oh now they was goin to _ behead 'em right away to think the king's daughter was in bed with another man an' she goina be married today," where the intonation pattern, the tone of threatening displeasure, and especially the tense of *she goina* and the use of *today* rather than *that day,* strongly suggest direct speech in spite of the dominant reported speech forms in the surface structure of the sentence. The third is the servant's response to this threat of beheading—and it is unclear whether Jack is to be beheaded for his audacity or the servant is to be beheaded for bringing back such incredible news—which is spoken in a matter-of-fact way implying that the report is true and that if the king does not believe it he should go and verify it himself. The forcefulness of the vocal tone is such that the ambiguity of reference carries with it the possibility that both Jack and the servant are threatened with beheading, although the underlying plot structure perhaps intends the threat to apply to Jack alone. The punctuation in such passages is therefore necessarily arbitrary. There is also some further confusion in this final section of the narrative as it is not clear who brings the news that Jack is in bed with the king's daughter, and the difficulty of discriminating between the pronouns *him* and *'em* compounds the problem. It is probable, for example, that in the lengthy sentence just quoted above the teller intended to say "behead him," but appears to say "behead 'em" which adds to the confusion. Such details are usually immaterial to the audience in the storytelling context and are easily overlooked as the listeners concentrate attention on the main thrust of the plot.

Another distinctive feature of Everett Bennett's style is the vivid use of dialogue, especially for characterization, which is very much in evidence here. Jack is presented as a laconic character, very understated in his own speech and apparently resigned to his fate. When asked about losing his ships he simply confirms their loss. This understating of his personality makes his ultimate triumph all the more effective by contrast. The king's daughter is also restrained and uneffusive in her speech, responding to the loss of the first ship merely with "that's too bad" and calmly fitting Jack out with another one. When he finally wins the bet and the girl's mother tells him he has got his three ships back, he simply replies "Yes" and no further details are given: Jack is presented as a character who does not vaunt his triumph but who takes it as phlegmatically as he accepts misfortune. There is much subtle tone coloring elsewhere in the dialogue as for instance Jack's firmly spoken demand for papers to be drawn to make the third bet official, in response to which the woman's tone is one of scornful dismissal, suggesting that there is absolutely no need for such a formality. A similar dismissive tone is used when she reassures her daughter that Jack is asleep, while the girl's doubts are very clearly transmitted to the audience by the teller's voice quality.

Humor is conveyed in several ways throughout the tale, again largely through the subtle variation of vocal tone. It is seen to good effect, for example, in the decorously expressed implications of "But she found out Jack wasn't asleep that night! She knowed Jack wasn't asleep!" on the night he wins the bet; a similar decorum is incidentally observed in the euphemistic "not know what she is in the morning," with its biblical echoes of carnal knowledge. There is obvious humor in the comical description of Jack running from one side of the bridge to the other, and in the behavior of the mayor, especially in such descriptions as "Oh he went off in the big laugh" in which the tone of voice exactly captures not only the sound of the laughter but also the mayor's pompous nature and his contempt for Jack. This of course makes Jack's having the last laugh all the more appreciated by the audience at the end of the story.

Although Everett Bennett had already outlined the beginning of the story briefly (see No. F6) he was very hesitant about telling it in full as he thought he might not be able to remember it. As the tape recorder was being switched on and off to record the salient points of this exploratory interview he only became aware that it was recording shortly after he began the narration. One of the interviewers then asks more formal permission to record the story, as distinct from the previous general conversation. The teller readily agrees, checks with the other interviewer that the machine is on, but is then immediately overcome by nervous uncertainty and says he cannot tell the story. The machine is then switched off again while the collectors reassure him and explain their reasons for hearing the tale. As is often the case on such occasions, he then launches into the narrative so quickly that there is insufficient warning for the fieldworker to switch on the machine again and the opening words are consequently unrecorded. Once begun, the narrative proceeds smoothly and without interruption.

Everett Bennett highlights certain individual words with strong stress, e.g., on *your* in his explanation of why Jack is taking on his new name: "When I was in **YOUR** company I was in good company," which emphasizes the couple's close relationship, and on the word *last* when the king's daughter fits Jack out for his third voyage. The use of the pet name or familiar form *Jacky* towards the end of the tale helps the audience to identify more closely with the hero as it implies friendship and affection. All these little touches contribute to the success of this storyteller's artistry and are crucial in engaging the listeners' attention and prompting their response. The speed and economy of the narration are also seen in the omission of function words, e.g., of the definite article before *teacher, girl, third one,* etc. Certain set expressions, often articulated with care, act as important pillars in the narrative. These include the name *Poverty Parts from Good Company,* with its formal literary flavor, the equally formulaic *a twelvemonth an' a day* and *what luck this time?,* and the somewhat poetic *sleepy drops* which is reminiscent of the names of children's medicine or of a magical potion, and sounds more innocent and innocuous than it really is.

There are several interesting pronunciations: /starm/ *storm,* /sliːpt/ *sleeped,* metathesis of /k/ in *aks* (ask), the initial onglide /j/ in *yuther,* reduction of /ou/ to /i/ in the second syllable of *follyin,* intrusive /t/ before /f/ in *infants,* the consistent pronunciation of *cerstificate* with intrusive /s/ after /r/, the lack of transitional /n/ in *a office, a old,* and the emphatic initial /h/ in *aunt's* while initial /h/ is typically lost in the following word *house* and virtually all other words which would normally have it in standard English. Aphetic forms include *'cause, 'gain* (against), and the initial vowel is lost in *'tis.* Apart from the frequent use of West Country English *un,* common in all this teller's stories, at the lexical level we have *set* (sat), *lodge* (put, place; cf. *DNE lodge* v.), *breeze* used in the nautical and Newfoundland sense of "storm" and glossed with this word in the story, perhaps for the benefit of the collectors, and *either* (any). The phrase *take un up* appears to have the sense of "sponsor, adopt," and the preposition *to* has the sense "at," and is in fact superfluous in "where the queen's daughter…king's daughter was to again". Rather than taking a room in a boarding house Jack *took a boarding house, again* (against, i.e., put up as a wager), *asleep* is expressed as the archaic *to sleep.* The tautological prepositional group *off o'* is also found, while *of* is twice omitted from the phrase *of course.* Note also the common Newfoundland exclamation *Oh my*, used here to express dismay, the use of *an'* in "an' I can't do the sum" in a way very much akin to the seventeenth-century conditional *an* (if), and the lack of plural inflection in *three year*. Dialectal present tense forms include *I knows/wants, aint, he haves*, while past tense forms are *sont, he done, fit* (fitted), *blowed, past, want, comed, start*, and *sot*. An archaic but effective vivid past tense verb phrase is found in *you're come again*, while the ambiguous *I been* could be taken as a simple past tense form or an abbreviation of *I have been*. The past participle *drowneded* is more straightforward in its form than *alost* and *acome*, which could be construed in their contexts as reduced forms of *have lost, have come*. However, as Jack responds to "you alost ya ship" with "I lost me ship" the simple past tense is evidently the more likely. Finally one might note the unorthodox syntax of *I was tellin of ya about today*.

See also the notes to No. 11.

Type and Motifs:

Cf. AT611. *The Gifts of the Dwarfs* [Irish by-form].

L101. *Unpromising hero.*

T91.6.4. *Princess falls in love with lowly boy.*

L142. *Pupil surpasses master.*

Cf. T97. *Father opposed to daughter's marriage.*

N831. *Girl as helper.*

N15. *Chastity wager.*

N2.6.5. *Daughter as wager.*

N2.5. *Whole kingdom (all property) as wager.*

K675. *Sleeping potion given to man who is to pass night with a girl.*

K92. *Gambling contest won by deception.*

Cf. K1831.0.1. *Disguise by changing name.*

Cf. R138. *Rescue from shipwreck.*

N825.2. *Old man helper.*

K1865. *Deception by pretending sleep.*

N681. *Husband (lover) returns home just as wife (mistress) is to marry another.*

Cf. H586.2.2. *Traveler says he must look after his net to see if it has taken fish.*

H151. *Attention drawn and recognition follows.*

Cf. T61.5.1. *Betrothal of hero to princess while both are still in cradle.*

L161. *Lowly hero marries princess.*

International Parallels: See No. 36.

41. HARD HEAD

Everett Bennett
St. Pauls, Great Northern Peninsula
22 July 1970

Cf. AT611 [Irish by-form]
TC970 71-50
Collector: HH

Well once upon a time there was a…old king. An' ‿ his woman's ‿ mother lived with un. An' there was a feller down across the street ‿ by the name o' Jack ‿ livin all alone. An' he [*the king*] had a nice daughter.

So she said to her father one day s…"Father" she said "why don't you get that man up" she said "an' ‿ give un education? He got no ‿ education an' ‿ pity for such a nice young man to be there ‿ [with] no education."

"Well" he said uh…"ask him to come up."

So she asked un to come up and ‿ he said "Yes" he said he'd be glad to. Well ‿ goina send un to school. Alright.

Well now ‿ his daughter had ‿ pretty good education. Well Jack went to the ‿ lower school. She went to the high. (Now) every day ‿ on their way home they sit down an' have a little chat. [*coughs*] An' ‿ Jack said uh…Jack couldn't learn. Oh ‿ all the time couldn't learn his letters, didn't know…didn't know a letter. So ‿ through the school he went by the name…he went by the name of Hard Head. Couldn't learn nothing, they thought (see).

So this night comin from ho…comin from school they sot down an' she said "Well Jack" she said ‿ "I got a wonderful sum ‿ wonderful sum" she said "I got to l…to learn tonight" she said. "I don't know how I'm goina get through it."

"Yeah" Jack said "let's have a look at un."

"Well now" she said "Hard Head 'tis no good for you to look at the sum" she said. "If I can't do the sum" /she/ said "it's no good to give un to you."

"Oh well" he said "there's no harm" he said "for me to see un."

So he took the slate an' the…pencil ‿ done the sum in a short while.

"Well is it ever possible" she said ‿ "Hard Head you got more…learning than I have?"

"Well" he said uh…"if you can't do that sum" he said ‿ "I guess I have."

He turned her slate on th' other side an' he done…done a sum on th' other side. "Now tomorrow" he said "when you goes to school ‿ the teacher askes you ‿ who did this sum ‿ your father or mother ‿ say 'The neither one of 'em. The Hard Head done that sum ‿ an' there's one on th' other side for you to do.'" So very (good) he went on. Went home.

Next morning goin to school. Passed in her slate. Sum was finished.

"Who done this sum for you, your father or mother?"

/he/

"Neither one of 'em" she said. "Hard Head done that sum an' there's one on th' other side for you to do."

Well the teacher was the whole day at this sum an' couldn't...couldn't look at it at all.

Well they went home that evening. An' uh...she said uh..."Father" she said "'tis no good to send...that man to school, Jack" she said "to school" she said. "He got more learning than teacher got." She said "Why don't you put un in your office?"

"Well" he said "if he got good...education like that I'll put un in th' office."

Well _ put un in th' office. Now she was right in love wi' Jack (you see) _ right in love wi' Jack and _ Jack said uh...she used to come to see Jack _ every...day she come to dinner _ have a chat with un an' _ so by god th' ol' king got on to it. Ol' king got onto it. An' he...he uh...didn't want Jack at all. Goina turn un out.

"Well now" she said "Jack" _ /she/ said "I tell ya what I'm goina do."   /he/
Said "I'm goin to fit you out with a ship an' cargo _ and _ send ya off."

"Well very good" Jack said "I'll change me name. I goes in the name o' Jack." He said "Now _ I'll be Poverty Parts from Good Company. When I was in **YOUR** company I was in **GOOD** company. Now I'm partin from it that's poverty parts from good company. When you hears that name" he said "you'll know who I is."

"Yeah."

Oh away he goes. When he got to the Cape o' Good Hope _ struck a storm. Oh wonderful storm. An' there was a...he had...he just had...canvas enough to get in port. Got in port an' _ well Jack was a pretty wealthy man now, he wasn't goina stay aboard he was goin aboard...ashore an' take a boarding house. (Well) he went ashore an' went up to a house there. Ask 'em to put un up. "Oh yes."

So anyhow _ bedtime come.

"Now" he said...she [*the boarding-house mistress*] said "Jack" she said _ "I'll bet you" she said "your ship an' cargo _ again my house an' land _ that you can sleep...you'll sleep with my daughter all night tonight an' won't know what she is in the morning."

"Alright" Jack said. "I'll bet."

Oh well _ bedtime come, go to bed now. She went upstairs wi' Jack.

Jack got in bed an' _ [she] said "Will ya have a drink?"

"Yes" Jack said "'ll have a drink." Pulled a bottle out from in under the pillow _ give un the drink. 'Way he goes _ sleep now, sleepy drops this was. Put un to sleep.

Sleeped all night an' in the morning /when he/ got up the girl was gone.   /we/
That's all Jack knowed about it.

433

Come down. "Well Jack. Lost your ship."

"Yeah. Lost me ship."

Start back home. Twelve months from that he _ arrived home. Hard way to get around at them times.

"Well Jack what luck?"

"Oh! Poor. Lost everything."

"Never mind Jack. I'll fit ya out again."

Fit un out again. Started it again. When he got to the Cape o' Good Ho...Good Hope he struck the storm again. Struck the storm again. And _ just got canavas enough to get in port. Went up to the same house.

"Well Jack! Back again!"

"Yeah _ back again."

"Well we goin to bet again this time?"

"Yeah. Another one" Jack said. "I lost another one." Put up THAT

/his/ ship up again this one now. He slept with /her/ daughter all night an' _ wouldn't know what she was in the morning.

Ah _ goes to bed an' up she goes an' _ pulled this bottle out. "Have a drink?"

"Oh yes. Have a drink."

Took the big drink an' away he goes again. Slept all night and when he got up (in) the morning girl was gone.

"Well Jack _ you lost your ship."

"Yeah. Two gone" Jack said.

/bats/ Twelve months from that he got /back/ where the king was to again. Got back to where king uh...king's daughter was to and _

"Well Jack what luck?"

"Same thing. All gone."

"Well Jack" she said "I can fit you out once more" she said "but that's all" she said "I can't fit ya out any longer."

So he started back. When he got to the Cape o' Goo[d]...Good Hope he struck the storm again, oh FIERCE. An' he seen a ol' feller out in boat.

"Ah! Come aboard, come aboard grandfather, come aboard you're goina be...lost." Took un aboard.

An' he said "That's uh...three years follying" he said "a ship have come here" he said "an' struck those storms."

"Yes" Jack said "an' I'm the man."

He said "You've alost two."

"Yes" Jack said "I've alost two."

"Well now" he said uh..."that house you goes to" he said "that...drink that she gives you" he said "that's sleepy drops. Now" he said _ "here's a bottle here" he said "just like the one she got in under her pillow." He said _ "The night" he said _ "you slip that bottle out an' put this one in under."

"Yeah."

Anyhow _ back he goes up to th' house again.

"Well Jack, back again."

"Oh yes. Back again. Try to get them ships back."

"Alright" she said "Jack I'll put the two again this one."

"Yeah. Alright." Jack said "It got to be a little stricter this time. I'm goin to have papers drawed on this this time."

"Hoh no need o' that Jack."

"Oh" Jack said "'tis time for me to get strict now. After lossin two...ship _ cargo an' all" he said "'tis time for me to get strict. An' uh..."

"Yeah. Well alright." Drawed the papers now. Lies 'em on the table. Well _ he'd go to bed.

After he got uh...go to bed _ "Oh" he said "I got to go down th' house _ again" he said uh..."leaved me papers on the table."

"No difference" she said "Jack" she said "I'll go an' get your papers for ya."

While she was gone _ slipped out this bottle. Put this one in under. Now she give him the BIG dose now. Girl went up. Looked at un in the bed.

Went down, she said _ to her mother she said "He's not to sleep."

"Oh yes. Sleep" said "he won't...won't wake in the least afore ten o'clock" she says "in the morn." An' up goes the girl an' gets in bed with un.

When the morning come the two of 'em come down th' house together. "Well Jack" she said _ "you got your ships back."

"Yes" Jack said "I got it back."

Now he start back for home _ start back for home now. /Now/ he got   /How/
home an' the night...the day he got home _ this girl now was goina be
married to the mayor of the town _ his girl. He were goin alo[ng]...along on
a bridge, Jack was. An' _ he seen /un/ comin, he knowed the mayor o' the   /her/
town. An' he got lookin over each side o' the bridge an' back an' forth
an' _

"What ya lookin for?"

"Oh I don't know, I don't know." Ask him several times an' _ "I sot a lobster trap here" he said _ "three years ago _ an' if I can find un I'll show you the best fresh lobster ever I se...ever you seen." [coughs]

And uh...he asked _ went off in the big laugh "What's your name?"

"Oh I got nar name. I don't know. I got no name at all."

"Oh you got a name."

"Yeah. My name is Poverty Parts from Good Company."

Took out his pocketbook. Wrote it down. Home to his girl now. 'Way he goes. 'Way he goes to his girl and _ come in sot down on his leg an' he was...laughin at this feller

"I found a...seen the funny man!" [coughs]

"Yes. What's his name?"

"I don't know" he said "I got it in me pocketbook." Took out his pocketbook _ "Poverty Parts from Good Company." She knowed un right away.

They were there in the house a while and _ said "I got to go over to me aunt's." Now she knowed this is where Jack was to. Went over.

"Well" _ Jack said "you've come _ come. I guess now 'tis time for us to go to bed."

"Oh no Jack" she said "I can't" she said. [*coughs*] "I'm goina be married today."

"Married!" Jack said "You're married now!"

So in they goes in the room. Now her waiting maids was 'long with her. In they goes in room, got into bed an' he...leaved his room door open, he took his...marriage cerstificate an' he pinned un up over the door.

They wait so long and she never...come. Well _ went back home. The mayor ask her [*the servant girl*] where _ she was at.

"Over there in bed with another man" she said. Oh they was goin to behead her right away now 'cause she was in bed with another man.

"Oh well" she [*the servant girl*] said "you can do that. But" she said "that's right."

Over they marches to th' house. Soon as they did, faced...right facin the room door -- Jack said "Don't come in here!" He said "See that up over the door?" [*coughs*] Couldn't go in.

He smacked his wife on th' ass like that, he s[aid], "There's the fresh lobster I was tellin of ye about today!" [*laughs*]

[*aside to Int:* now see how he is now.]

[Int: Uh...let me ask you something, where did you learn that one?]

I learned that from me ol' uncle. That ol' feller that I was...no I didn't no. I'm tellin ya wrong. I learned that from John Charles Roberts, Sally's Cove. John Charles Roberts, Sally's Cove.

[Int: You left out a little piece when you were talking about the third time that...the third time at...at...the Cape o' Good Hope _ where the...the girl _ uh...gets in bed with him. You left out what he said to her _ there.]

There's nothing there...n...never...n...nothing. Just got in bed an' that was all. That's all there is to that yeah.

Duration: 13 min., 3 sec.
Source: John Roberts, Sally's Cove, Great Northern Peninsula.
Location: Kitchen of teller's house.
Audience: Interviewer.

Context, Style, and Language: This recording is unhindered by the background noise and activity which accompany most other recordings of Everett Bennett's stories. For once he is interviewed alone and perhaps this is why he asks for the tape to be played back after he has finished so that he can hear what it sounds like.

This second full version of the story told by Everett Bennett was recorded some four years after No. 40. It is a smooth, even, and well-constructed tale incorporating all the stylistic features commented on in the notes to Nos. 11 and 40 but lacks some of the tonal virtuosity, notably in the dialogue, and omits some of the details of when Jack is in bed with the girl and wins the bet. The teller seems to have forgotten these, as his answers to the questions following the tale indicate. The story begins with the "once upon a time" formula which is rare in this collection, and quickly sets the scene very economically in a few words. Elliptical sentences such as *Went home, Sum was finished, Goina turn un out,* and the punctuating expressions *he/she said, (So) very good, (So) anyhow* are again in evidence. Pronouns and function words are frequently omitted in the terse style. The urgency and concern in Jack's invitation to the *ol' feller* to come aboard are expressed in the triple repetition of *Come aboard,* a device used by other tellers when characters are heartily welcoming a stranger in their stories. A similar ambiguity of reference occurs in the threats of beheading at the end of the story as is found in No. 40, and on this occasion it is either the king's daughter or the servant girl who is threatened—apparently the former.

This version substitutes the disyllabic *askes* (with schwa in the second syllable and final /s/) for the metathesized *aks* of No. 40, and inserts schwa between the two syllables of *canvas* to form *canavas.* As elsewhere, *morning* is pronounced *marning/marnin* and on one occasion is syncopated to *morn,* pronounced *marn.* The aphesis so common in the speech of many Newfoundlanders is found here in *'Way* (away) and *'long* (along), and schwa is elided in *th' office, th' house.* We also have *woman* in the sense of "wife" (contrast the many dialects of English in which the reverse is the norm), the intensifier *wonderful* modifying *sum* and *storm,* with the sense of "awful, terrible," *house* in the local sense of "kitchen, 'house place,'" *nar* (no), *lossin* (losing), *lies* (lay), and the archaic *afore.* Note also the present tense forms *I is, they goes/marches,* and the double negative *couldn't learn nothing.*

See also the notes to Nos. 11 and **40.**

Type and Motifs:

Cf. AT611. *The Gifts of the Dwarfs* [Irish by-form].

Z10.1. *Beginning formula.*

L101. *Unpromising hero.*

L142. *Pupil surpasses master.*

T91.6.4. *Princess falls in love with lowly boy.*

T97. *Father opposed to daughter's marriage.*

Cf. K1831.0.1. *Disguise by changing name.*

N15. *Chastity wager.*

N2.5. *Whole kingdom (all property) as wager.*

K675. *Sleeping potion given to man who is to pass night with a girl.*

K92. *Gambling contest won by deception.*

Cf. R138. *Rescue from shipwreck.*

N825.2. *Old man helper.*

K1865. *Deception by pretending sleep.*

N681. *Husband (lover) returns home just as wife (mistress) is to marry another.*
Cf. H586.2.2. *Traveler says he must look after his net to see if it has taken fish.*
H151. *Attention drawn and recognition follows.*
Cf. T61.5.1. *Betrothal of hero to princess while both are still in cradle.*
L161. *Lowly hero marries princess.*

International Parallels: See No. 36.

Everett Bennett

42. HARD UN[†]

Az McLean   Cf. AT611 [Irish by-form]
Payne's Cove, Great Northern Peninsula   TC133 64-17
11 July 1964   Collector: M. M. Firestone

Well in olden times ya know it wasn't like it is now. Because now they waits till they get men an' women to get married. But in olden times they didn't. They'd be married when they is children an' wait to get men an' women an' go together. So those two was married when they were children, one day this boy he went to the ol' king, asked for a job. Well he didn't see as he had ar job for un so he turned un away. Well the girl said to her father "Why [didn't] ya took that poor boy for a job?"

Well he said he didn't see as he had a job for un, now he'd take un for a knife cleaner. Anyway he called un back an' took un for a knife cleaner. Pretty good job mind anyway.

Well he was at that for a little while, well he put un to school wi' his daughter, well now this was just the place he wanted to get anyway. So he went to school, this teacher says "Say THIS!"

"Say this" he said.

The teacher says "Say what I says!"

"Say what I says" he said.

The teacher said "Say THIS."

"Say this" he said.

The teacher says "Say what I says!"

"Say what I says" he said.

Well they couldn't beat nothing in /?to un/ uh...in his (head) he...he   /(horn)/
called un "Hard Un," he couldn't learn anyway.

So he [*the teacher*] give un...give the girl a sum that he didn't think she could do. Well on her way home by the road she sot down, she begin to cry, she couldn't do her sum.

Well Hard Un said "Give un to me"

"Well dear Hard Un 'tis no...'tis no good to give un to you."

"Well dear" he says "(nothing like) lettin me try."

Anyway she give Hard [Un] the sum, he soon done the sum.

"Now when you go to school tomorrow morning" he said "[if] the teacher aks you who done the sum you say 'Me ownself surely' (Well) he'll say you didn't, well you say 'You know 'twasn't Hard Un' well he say he know 'twasn't."

Anyway she went to school next morn teacher [asked her] "Who done the sum?"

"Me ownself surely" [she] said.

"Oh no" he said "you didn't."

"Well" she said "you know it wasn't Hard Un"

WELL he said he know it wasn't.

Well he give her one tonight he didn't think she could do _ anyway. On her way home by the road she sot down, she begin to cry, she couldn't do her sum.

Well Hard Un said "Give un to me."

"Well now Hard [Un]" (she said) "no good to give him to you."

"Dear" he said "(nothing like) lettin me try."

/he/ Anyway /she/ give Hard Un the sum, he soon done the sum.

"Now when you go to school tomorrow morn" he said "[if] the teacher aks you who done the sum you say 'Me ownself surely' well he'll say you didn't. Well you say 'You know 'twasn't Hard Un' he say he know 'twasn't."

Well she went to school the next morning, the teacher [said] "Who done the sum?"

"Me ownself surely" [she] said.

"Oh no" he said "you didn't."

"Well" she said "you know 'twasn't Hard Un."

Well he says he know 'twasn't.

Well he give her one tonight he knowed for sure she couldn't do anyway. On her way home by the road she sot down, she begin to cry, she couldn't do her sum.

"Well" Hard Un said "give un to me."

"Well dear" she says "no good to give him to you"

"Well dear heart" he said "nothing (like) lettin me try."

/Wany/ /?Well anyway/ she give Hard Un the sum, he soon done the sum. Now when he done the sum he turned over slate an' put one on the other side for the teacher.

"Now when you go to school tomorrow morn" he said "[if] the teacher aks you who done the sum you say 'Me ownself surely.' Well he'll say 'You didn't.' Well you say 'You know 'twasn't Hard Un' he say he know 'twasn't. Well when he do" he said "turn over slate" (he said) "'here's one Hard Un give to you.'"

Well next morning she went to school, teacher [said] "Who done the sum?"

"Me ownself surely" [she] said.

"Oh no" he said "you didn't."

/he/ "Well" /she/ said "you know 'twasn't Hard Un"

Well he said he know 'twasn't.

Well she turned over slate, said "Here's one Hard Un give to you." (Mister man) the teacher wasn't able [to] do un.

My son 'fore they got home the news was home to th' ol' king. Well /'stead/ of a knife cleaner he put [him to work as] a bookkeeper (that he) had a job out of her anyway.

/seed/

Well he's at that for a little while, well th' ol' king caught un at...some bad deed with his daughter, well you (can) imagine what 'twas, anyway he was going to turn un away. Well the girl she found out, well she told her boy about it, well he went an' aks th' ol' king for his time

"Well" he said "you want to leave?"

"Yes." So he give him his time.

Well after he leave certainly she...fit un out for sea with a new schooner. An' comin' round the Cape it come a big breeze o' wind, blowed every stitch of canvas off of her, she drift away for a long time, well she drift into a harbour. Well he went to a woman's home to take a boardin house so as lots of young men do anyway, asked her for a boardin house.

"Why yes" she said "there's never a man (here but I) give him a boardin house anyway."

Well after they got in, had their supper an' sot back talkin she said "I'll bet the price o' your ship again one" she said "[if] my two daughters sleep wi' ya an' you won't know it"

He said "I'll bet they won't."

Anyway wi' that he went to bed.

Well she said "Care for a drink?"

"Well no" he said he wouldn't mind a drink any time so he took a drink. Well he was soon asleep. Well the next morning the ship was gone.

Well he beat around for a long time, far as I can mind when he got arou[nd]...when he got home again he was just (as) ragged an' tore up again.

Anyway he run up again his girl _ again.

Well she said "I'll fit ya out for sea again" so she fit un out for sea again.

Well comin around the Cape it come big breeze o' wind, blowed every stitch o' canvas off her again. Well she drift away for a long time, well she drift into a harbour. Well when he went in the harbour he went up to ol' woman's house sort o' ask for a boardin house like lots of young men do anyway

"Well yes" she said. "Never a man here [but] we I give him a boardin house anyway."

Well after they got in an' had their supper an' sot back talking she [said] "I bet me the price o' your ship again one" she (said) "my two daughters /sleep with you/ an' ya won't know it"

/sleepin/

He said "I bet they won't."

An' with that they went to bed anyway. She [said] "Care for a drink?"

441

No he wouldn't mind a drink anyway so he took a drink, well he was soon asleep. Well the two girls sleep with un an' he knowed nothing at all about it anyway.

Well the next morning he [was] just as bad as ever, (his) ship was gone again. Well he beatin round an' round for a long time, far as I can mind, when he got uh...back home again just 'bout ragged an' tore up anyway why he run up again his girl again.

"Well" she said "I'll fit ye out for sea again" says "I got a ol' schooner here" said "an' I can't do any more. Well" she said "how would I know ye if I run up again (ye) again?"

"Well tell ya what I'll do" he said. "I'll put a nickname on meself, Public (Word) Good Company." Pretty good name mind anyway.

Well he sailed away, he come around the Cape the same as the year afore, come big breeze o' wind, blowed every stitch o' canvas off her again. Well she drift away for a long time, well she drift into a harbour. Well when she drift into harbour today there was ANOTHER schooner there. Well he [*the man from the schooner*] come aboard.

Well he said "'Tis three years (follyin that) a schooner drift in this harbour."

"Yes" he said "well" he said "that was me."

"Well" he said "you lost your schooner on a bet"

"Well yes" he said.

"Well now" he said "I'll tell ya what to do tonight" (said) "when you bets that for price o' two of 'em" he said. "An' have papers drawed on her" he said. "An' leave your papers on table" he said "an' I'll give ya a bottle just like hers. An' when you gets in the be[d] (you'll) say 'I got to go for me papers' she's sure to say she'll go" he said "well shove her [*the bottle*] in (under) your ass an' drink out o' this one" he said.

Well he went up th' ol' woman's house to take a boardin house like lots o' young men do anyway. He asked her for a boardin house

"Why yes" she said. "Never a man (here yet) but I give him a boardin house anyway."

Well after they got in an' had their supper an' sot back talkin like anybody would _ "Well" she said "I'll bet the price o' your ship again one" she said "[if] my two daughters sleep with ya an' they won't know it."

He said "I'll bet there are two of 'em they won't." Well he want paper drawed on it, well she was satisfied with that anyway, she drawed the papers on it.

Well they went to bed "Well" she (said) "care for a drink?"

"No" he said he wouldn't mind a drink any time so she give him the bottle. "Oh" he said "I got to go for me papers"

/he/   "Oh" she says "I'll go." While /she/ gone he shoved the bottle (in under) his ass an' he drinked out of his own. He had one just like hers

anyway. When /she/ come back well /he/ was soon asleep. Well she sent un   /he/   /she/
the two girls up (an') _

"Ah" he said "I knows they here tonight" he said.

Well he had the ship back again.

Well he sailed away for home, well when he got home _ he heard that the mayor o' the town was goina be married to this girl that he [*Hard Un*] was married to when he was a child. Well now he didn't know what to do anyway. But he knowed he had to cross a bridge the next mornin. Well this is where he went to this bridge, runnin round like a little foolish feller.

When mayor [o'] (the) town come the next mornin he said "What are you lookin for?"

"I" he said -- "I" he said "sot lobster pots here"

"What?" he said.

"I" he said -- "I" he said "sot lobster pots here, 'spects to have fresh lobster for my breakfast."

"What?" he said.

"I" he said _ "I" he said "sot lobster pots here, 'spects to have fresh lobster for my breakfast."

Well he was gettin great sport out o' this anyway. He hauled out his book, he said "What's your name?"

"Public (Word) Good Company" he said.

Put his name (down) in his book an' went on to the girl certainly that he was going to marry to. When he got there he was tellin the girl about the funny feller he see.

"Well" she said "what was his name?"

He hauled out his book, he said "Public (Word) an' Good Company."

My gosh! She knowed un better than he did. She went straight to look for un.

Well certainly when they come back he'd went...he went an' told th' ol' king there was another man in the bed with the girl that he was goina marry to. Well now th' ol' king felt vexed a mite at un anyway. Well he went to see about it. But as soon as he went through the door there was a 'stificate over the door _ where they was married when they was children. Well th' ol' king felt bad about it certainly, he had to go back an' tell the mayor o' the town anyway. Well he went back so the mayor o' the town went to the door he [*Hard Un*] hauled up her clothes, smacked the naked ass

"Ah!" he said "I told ya I have fresh lobster for my breakfast!"

An' if they didn't live happy I don't know who did! They had children in baskets, (hove outdoor) in shelffuls _ sent to the sea to make sea pies an' the last time I seen them I wished 'em goodbye an' (seen) nar one sunce.

443

Duration: 7 min., 43 sec.
Source: Andrew McLean (uncle), Shoal Harbour East, Great Northern Peninsula, "when I was eighteen or twenty."
Location: The home of Gilbert Parrell (teller's stepbrother), evening.
Audience: Teller's wife, people of the household, John Crane (a well-known traditional singer from Pines Cove), interviewer, and his wife.

Context, Style, and Language: (For context see notes to No. 15).

The allegro speech and other features noted in Nos. 15, 16, and 31 are also to be found here, there being very few pauses within individual utterances, hence the need for more punctuating commas than usual in the transcription. The speed of delivery results in whole phrases being syncopated on occasion, and such crucial words as the verb *said* are frequently lost. The limitations of the breathless pace are clearly in evidence in that there is a danger that the outsider or uninitiated listener may be confused or even excluded by the rapidity of the delivery and the blurring and omission of important linguistic cues. Such a style could act as a means of deliberately excluding the outsider, while at the same time arousing the admiration of the in-group by virtue of its verbal dexterity. Nevertheless, because there is so much redundancy in ordinary speech, a tale delivered as rapidly as this one does not lose a great deal of meaning when listened to in the context of performance. When one attempts to transfer such fractured language to paper, however, much of the structure essential for the comprehension of normal written usage is lost. Each segment or run of speech has an internal rhythm, punctuated, as already noted under No. 15, by certain strongly stressed words, especially *anyway,* the end-marker of a segment. Such words would not normally be stressed in everyday speech but here they contribute to the unique rhythmic quality of the style, the reiterated formulas also having a similar effect to that of the repeated phrases and rhyming words found in tongue twisters and analogous forms. The patterning in this and other tales by this teller is not so obvious or predictable in its structure as to assist the listener, and especially the reader, to apprehend the ways in which the narrative flows. Like the other stories Az McLean tells, this version is extremely condensed, as a comparison with the other variants of AT611 in this collection will amply demonstrate. The plot is reduced to its essential basic incidents.

Certain segments of the story create an impression of similarity by the repetition of almost identical wording, and by rhythmic phrasing which acts like the "paragraphing" of normal utterance. The narrative moves forward from incident to incident almost like verse paragraphs, linked only by the tenuous story line which is comparatively unobtrusive. Each incident is rhythmically almost self-contained, a rhetorical device not dissimilar from the "leaping and lingering" structural pattern of some ballads. The segments are short enough to be terminally marked by intakes of breath, and indeed this physical limitation may be one of the constraints governing the length of each segment. What few brief pauses there are usually occur at the end of narrative sections and before a new piece of dialogue, and once again there are virtually no hesitations in the headlong pace of the narration. A notable exception is the deliberate repetition of the pronoun *I* in Hard Un's responses to the mayor's questions.

These repeated forms are obviously intended to suggest stammering, cf. the same incident in one of Freeman Bennett's versions of the tale (No. 37).

In addition to the linguistic points commented on in the notes to Nos. 15, 16, and 31, the speed of delivery unfortunately makes Hard Un's nickname very difficult to transcribe. It lacks the essential conjunction or preposition between the two noun phrases, and the tentative transcription *Public (Word) Good Company* is unsatisfactory on several counts. The second word is perhaps intended to be *Work,* but even so the apparent alteration of *Poverty Part(s) an'/Poverty Partin* found in the other versions of this tale means the virtual loss of an interesting element of the plot and characterization.

Aphesis occurs in *'spects* (expects) and *'stificate* (certificate). The typical West Country English of this speaker, with its metathesized *perty* (pretty), nevertheless admits the Anglo-Irish *me ownself* (cf. *they were after makin* in No. 16), while *breeze* is used with reference to a gale. Dialectal present tense forms include *[he] aks* (asks), *they waits, you wants/gets,* and past tense forms are *give, done, drift, leave,* and *drinked.*

See also the notes to Nos. 15, 16, and 31.

Type and Motifs:

Cf. AT611. *The Gifts of the Dwarfs* [Irish by-form].

Cf. T61.5.1. *Betrothal of hero to princess while both are still in cradle.*

L101. *Unpromising hero.*

L142. *Pupil surpasses master.*

T91.6.4. *Princess falls in love with lowly boy.*

T97. *Father opposed to daughter's marriage.*

N831. *Girl as helper.*

N15. *Chastity wager.*

N2.6.5. *Daughter as wager.*

N2.5. *Whole kingdom (all property) as wager.*

K675. *Sleeping potion given to man who is to pass night with a girl.*

K92. *Gambling contest won by deception.*

Cf. K1831.0.1. *Disguise by changing name.*

N820. *Human helper [sea captain].*

N681. *Husband (lover) returns home just as wife (mistress) is to marry another.*

Cf. H586.2.2. *Traveler says he must look after his net to see if it has taken fish.*

H151. *Attention drawn and recognition follows.*

L161. *Lowly hero marries princess.*

Z10.2. *End formula.*

International Parallels: See No. 36.

43. POVERTY PARTING WITH GOOD COMPANY

Ambrose Reardon   Cf. AT611 [Irish by-form]
Croque, White Bay   TC543, 544 68-40
5 August 1968   Collector: G. J. Casey

[Int: What was the name of it?]
"Poverty Partin wud [i.e., *with*] Good Company."
[Int: (Now ya)…]

/it'll/

Now what? That's a long story ol' man I don't know whether /ī can/ tell
it to ya ya know
[Int: Try it anyway.]

    [*clears throat*] It starts this way. Now we ALL knows _ ourselves that
uh…we'll say uh…'twas all Roman Catholics one time in the world
wasn't it? [Int: Mm.] Well now the _ the King of England _ an' the
Queen of England _ went over to pay a visit _ to the King [and] Queen
o' France. Well the king _ the King of France then _ had a…a son seven

*noise of engine in
background

/squaw/

years of age.* King Edward _ was his name. An' uh…begar while they
were over in France uh…the Queen of England _ gave birth _ to a…a
young daughter. An' after the /four/ uh…everything was over _ the four
peop[le]…four…people as long as he uh…belong to the royal family
_ he said he'd have the two children _ married _ before they go home
_ home. Now Prince Edward…uhm…King Edward _ was seven years
of age _ an' uh…the young princess _ was only a month. So uh…the
bishop was brought an' the two children was married. An' uh…they
took a locket _ of each of 'em an' put one of 'em on one another's neck.
[Int: Locket of…] Eh? [Int: A locket of…?] A lock…uh yes uh…their
_ photo [Int: Oh yes, yeah.] likeness.

    An' uh…after it was all over _ they went home. For years an' years
after that uh…begar _ English and French _ went to war. Whatever 'twas
about I don't know but uh s…perhaps it be about uh…some o' this
lands _ down here that time because there is…there was hundreds an'
hundreds o'…o' gallons o' blood spilt over this island (once)…
before 'twas…'twas all taken. But anyway uh…she was still there. An'
uh…one evening after 'twas all over _ an' the…ships was all in lyin to

/prince/

the quay -- this young /princess/ she was seventeen years of age. When
she come out o' school she said to her…father she asked her father
_ could she go down an' view his ships.

    She said…he said "Yes" he said uh…"take your waitin maid with ye"
he said uh…"an' go down" he said uh…"an' whichever commander you
goes to" he said uh…"tell him" he said uh…"on MY orders _ that he got
to show you through the ship."

446

An' where d' she go _ only went down _ aboard the one uh...Jack was (aboard o'). [*aside:* (boys I forgot).] As I told ye before they went to war about France [or] something, France an' England. An' the English uh...won the battle.* An' the government said _ an' the people _ 'twas the way the king _ ordered the war _ that's how they come to lose the victory. So uh...he was brought up _ on trial _ [before] the government an'...an' the people. An' begar _ his crown was took away from [him] _ an' he was beheaded. An' this young fella _ was a hardy boy then. An' they were lookin for him an' they couldn't find [him]. So after 'twas for a spell when 'twas all gone _ he left uh...Engla[nd]...left France _ an' went across _ over to England. An' shipped aboard of an English man-o'-war. Give up all his uh...all his name an' called himself uh...plain Jack.

*noises in back-ground, children crying

So uh...(see) I told ye before _ she ask him...ask the...her father could she go down an' view his ships an' he said "Yes" he said uh..."take" he said uh..."a waitin maid with ye" he said "an' _ whatever ship" he said "you goes ove[r]...goes down aboard" he said "tell him" he said uh..."by MY orders _ " he said "you got to be showed through the ship."

An' where d' she go only down aboard o' one Jack was in. An' she caught his name _ he was scrubbin down the deck. An' she caught his name uh...by the...the...the commander _ callin him Jack. This how she come to get his name.

So uh...after it was all over _ she went up _ home. An' she said "Pap" she said uh...she said "there's people" she said "i[n]...in England" she said uh..."not HALF so well" she said "able to afford _ a valet" she said "as I am." An' she said uh..."He got uh...one" she said "an' I got no one." [*aside to Int:* Now you know what a valet is?] [Int: Yeah. No. Uh...] [A valet is a...the person that'll take your schoolbag _ to school _ an' take it back in th' evening.] [Int: Oh uh...] [That's what they calls a valet.]

An' he said "Well" he said "that was your...that's your own fault" he said uh..."because" he said uh...he said "you could have one" he said "for LONG ago" he said uh..."if you had to tell me." He said "Go out" he said uh..."in the street now" he said "an' whatever _ nice uh...sensible lookin boy" he said uh..."you sees" he said _ he said uh..."tell (un) to come in" he said "I wants him."

An' where did she go down uh...only down aboard this...this vessel _ the ship that Jack was into.

An' she said uh..."Jack" she said uh..."go up" she said "me father wants ya."

An' he got startled, frightened to death first. He thought that the...the commander was after him for givin in uh...puttin in t...false

447

reports again un. An' uh…that he was goin be uh…er*…gullentined [i.e., *guillotined*]. But after a time he _ dressed…dressed himself up an' he brushed his buttons _ an' he went up an' fell on his knees _ [to] the king.

An' the king said "Oh" he said uh…"rise young man" he said uh…"I got uh…nothing" he said "again you. But" he said um…"I suppose" he said _ "you're the one" he said "the boy" he said "that…that my daughter" he says "is after choosin" he said "for a valet. If so" he said uh…"I'll buy your discharge now" he said "from the navy." An' he said "I'll give ye" he said uh…"twice as much money" he said "as you're gettin there." An' he said uh…"You stay in the palace" he said "with us. Only four of us here" he said. An' he said uh…"All ya got to do" he says "is get up every morning" he said _ "an' take my daughter's bookbag" he said "an' bring it to school _ an' wait till it's over" he said uh…"an' then" he said "bring it back again." He said "Will you 'gree…will you uh…agree to it?"

Jack said uh…"Yes your honour" he said "I will so." So Jack got hired on. Now that…that's all he had to do.

So uh…he was bringin this back an' forth. An' by an' by _ when he come…at evenings when he come _ for to get the schoolbag to bring it back _ he wouldn't be fit to look at. But uh…there's as many of 'em there waitin around, those valets. Uh…(ask) I don't say Jack was a good (hand) himself too. (Now) Jack'd be mud an' gutter*…[Int: *aside to child:* hello] [Child: Hello. How is you?] [*recorder off*]*. [*clears throat*] /She/ come home to her father an' she said uh "Pap" she said uh…"Jack" she said "is a stranger here. An'" she said uh…"the boys" she says "is pickin on him." She said "If you give me consent" she said uh…"I'd have Jack" she said uh…"take un in school" /she/ said "with me _ tomorrow morning."

"Alright" /he/ said uh…"when ye goes [to] school to _ morrow morning" he said uh…"tell the teacher" he said "by MY orders _ that uh…Jack have to be taken in school."

Well the next morning when Jack went an'…passed in the schoolbag _ the mistress says "Oh" she said "come in." Well Jack went in _ an' she sot down Jack uh…in a little low schooled…a low stool _ in the corner of the school. An' she give him an ABC card _ paste on a shingle. I had 'em one time, I used it one time. An' uh…she'd be lookin at Jack sh…an' Jack didn't seem like he…he was any interested in it at all. She'd look at un by an' by uh…perhaps he'd have the card upside down.

Well when the card…cle…/classes/ was all over she c…call up Jack. An' when she'd point to A _ Jack'd say M. An' when she'd point to M _ Jack 'd say Q. An' when she find Q _ Jack 'd say W. An' she was at

Jack _ for a **LONG** time an' couldn't get no uh...no good of un. An'
by an' by she got out of uh...patience. An' she said "Jack" she said _ she
said "where do you come from?" _ she said "Or who reared ya?" She
said uh..."There's no harm to call you" she said uh..."Hard Head
Hoverd."

So begar uh...this...word got out around. An' when Jack 'd be goin
wi' the tea...wi' the...bag in the evening _ they'd be...hollyin out after
un "There goes Hard Head Hover! There goes Hard Head Hover!"

So _ begar _ the winter passed away. An' uh...the /daughter/ she   /teacher/
come out o'...she come out o' school one evening _ an' she was cryin.

An' Jack said, he said uh..."What are you cryin 'bout!"

"Well" she said uh..."there's no good" she said "in tellin you" she
said uh..."you can't (help) me."

"Oh well" Jack said uh...he said "it's no odds" he said uh..."I'd like
to know" he said "what you're cryin about all the...all the same."

"Well" she said uh..."the nurse...the...teacher" she said "give me a
sum _ this evening" she said "an' if I can have the sum right _ rightified"
she said uh..."the morrow morning" she said "when I goes to school"
_ she said uh..."me education is over. An' if not" she said uh..."I got to
spend a...whole uh...'nother twelve month in school."

"Oh" Jack said "accordin to that" he said uh...he said "if the sum is
right" he said uh...he said "my work'd be over too." An' Jack said
uh..."There's lots of...I'm here now" he said "all the winter." An' he
said uh..."There's lot o' things in England" he said uh..."I'd like to see."
An' he said uh.../You've/ never /once/" he said uh.../taken/ me   /You'll/   /the one/
uh...through town" he said uh..."since uh...since I come here last fall."   /that took/

"Oh well Jack" she said uh..."there's not much" she said "I can show
ya."* [Woman: Good evening.] [*aside to Int:* it's all over.]+   *loud noise, door
                                                                         opening etc.
[*recorder off*]*** uh...show Jack the places in England.* An'   +noise
uh...she's wa[lkin]...Jack had the schoolbag...on his back an' she was   *woman in back-
walkin behind.* An' they were passin along by a big church.   ground: Finished
                                                                            there Jimmy?
An' she said uh..."I suppose" she said "'tis not used to walkin _ but"   *woman talking in
she said uh..."I'm gettin tired."   background

"Oh well" Jack said uh..."we'll go up there" he said "an' sit down"
said "an' take a rest."

Well they went up an' sat down on the s...stone steps o' the...o' the   *pounding sound,
church.* An' uh...Jack come in wi' the...(got hold to) the schoolbag   ?footsteps
uh...but he hove it down as careless.

She said uh..."Jack" she said "mind what you're doin" she said "wi'
that sum." She said uh..."If you blots that sum" she said uh..."an' I can't
uh..." she said "see the figures tomorrow" she said uh..."I'm sure" she
said "I'll have to spend _ another twelvemonth _ in school."

Jack said "'Tis no harm" he said "to look at it I suppose."

"Oh no" she said uh...said "whatever you do" she said uh..."be as careful as you can wi' it" she said "don't blot out the figures."

So Jack took out the sum an' _ was lookin over un. By an' by he spit on it. He rubbed it all out. An' she...she was cryin before she was cryin ten times worst then. But after a spell anyway uh...Jack got her pacified. And Jack said uh...he said "Gi' me your pencil."

She give Jack the pencil an' Jack put down the same sum -- an' made it up for her _ and showed her _ how to make it up.

An' uh... _ when he had it finished _ he said uh..."Jack" she said _ "Who are you?"

Jack said "I'm the king's son o' France" he said. An' he said "I got a locket" he said uh..."on my neck" he said uh..."puts me of a mind of you."

"Yes" she said "an' I got one on my neck" she said. An' she said uh..."I often asked me father" she said uh..."who was the...th' owner o' that locket." An' he said...she said "He...he'd never give me no satisfaction _ who owned it."

An' Jack said "We're both married." He said "We're both man an' wife" he said. An' Jack said "You're a young princess" he said "an'" he said "I'm only a poor boy." He said "You got to do something for me."

"Yes Jack" said uh..."(Whatever)...yes" she said "Jack" she said "whatever ye wants."

"Well" Jack said "I love to be a sailor."

"Alright" she said "come down on the quay."

Went down on the quay an' she bought a...a ship for Jack _ an' load her up full o' merchandise.

An' she said "Now Jack" she said uh..."go away" /she/ said "an' when you get your...if you can...sell that one" /she/ said uh..."an' her...her cargo" /she/ said uh..."come back" he...she said "to me" she said uh..."an' with what money I got" she said uh..."'ll do us" she said "the rest of our life."*

So Jack took the...she load up the...vessel full o' merchandise an' Jack sot sail. An' he was sailin along by a...place called Naples. (It) was blowin hard uh...an' _ begar he put in _ for shelter for the night. Himself and his first mate uh...goes walkin up the street. An' they seed a notice on the door: "A Game o' Cards or a Lunch at /any/ Hour."

So Jack said "We'll go in here now."

So he went in an' sot down _ an' opened a...pack o' cards an' uh...hove out one game an' when he had the ga[me] when he had the p...hand hove out uh...he rung the bell. When he rung the bell uh...in comes a...a nice a lady as ever he...he's...put his eyes on.

/he/
/he/
/he/

*noises in background

/an/

450

An' Jack said uh…"Is there anything" he said "goes with this game o' cards?"

"Yes" she said "whatever you want."

Well Jack called for…a bottle o' whisky. An' they were playin there until nine o'clock.

Jack said "I think" he said "we'll go down aboard now" he said.

An' uh…before they left to go down aboard uh…down comes this hypocrite [i.e., *cripple*] on two critches [i.e., *crutches*]. Come downstairs uh…she said uh…"Jack" she said "what about a bet?"

"A bet on what?" Jack said.

She said "I'll bet you" she said uh…"for your load o' merchandise" she said uh…"and your vessel" /she/ said "ye got to the warf [*aside to audience:* no harm I suppose] _ that my daughter" she said uh…"she sleep with you the night" /she/ said uh…"an' you won't know her _ man from a woman in the morning." [*recorder off; tape changed*]

***(those) he could _ come down and she'd bet un. [*aside to Int:* I told you that sure.] [Int: Yeah you can (lead in) from there.]

But then uh…I couldn't say whether she…the daughter slept with un all night or no but uh…anyway he had a job to wake her in the morning. An' uh*…he got up an' they give him his breakfast an' _ he went out to his uh…down aboard his crow[d] s…crew…his ship the…ship an' he said "Well now boys" he said uh…he says "I got some money to pay ye." An' he said uh…"Everyone for theirselves" he said "an' god for us all." But he said uh…"I'm goin home to me wife."

(Went) home an' she was uh…she was stood in the same place where she told un _ if he come back in twenty years time _ she'd be s…stood in this place _ 'gain the palace. An' when he come back he met her an' he said…she says uh…"How d' ya do Jack?" she say.

Jack said he…"I lost her" he say. An' he never told un how he lost her. An' he says "You're a young uh…/princess/" he said "wi' plenty o' money." An' he said "You got to give me another chance."

"Yes" she said. She give Jack another chance.

An' he went away an' he done the same thing. An' he came back again.

[Int: Lost the ship.]

Lost the ship. He lost un by them bets. An' uh…he come back again. An' this was (the) third one now.

She said "Jack" she said "how d'ya do?"*

Jack said "I lost her." An' Jack said "You're a young princess" he said "an'…an' I'm only a poor _ boy" he said "you got to give me another chance."

/he/

/he/

*pause: 4 sec. approx.

/prince/

*women talking in background

"Yes" she said "I'll give ya one more chance now" says "Jack" she said. "And we loses this one" she said uh…"never come back to me any more." An' she said "If you gain" she said uh…"come back" she said uh…"in the name" she said "of Poverty Partin _ Wud Good Company."

So she loaded up Jack uh…an' Jack sot sail again. An' god bless if it didn't come [a] storm, he had to put in to…to Naples again. An' 'twas all up to mother's then for a…used to call her mother.* [untrans.] [laughs] (Haul) up there for a drink. [Woman aside: yeah he got that [the tape recorder] on. I didn't know.] An' uh*…when he was goin up the wharf _ he met an ol' man _ comin down _ with a…uh…with a critch _ two critches.

An' he said uh…"Hullo" he said uh…"the king's son o' France."

Jack said "How do you know" he said "I'm the king's son o' France?"

"Oh" he said "I knows all about ya boy" he said uh…"I'm your godfather." An' he said "You got two up there now" he said uh…"an' you're goin up" he said uh…"the night" he said "you're goin to lose…(the) third one _ if you don't beware. Don't you know" he said "she's the biggest witch in town?" He said "Her basement" he said "is full as…o' nothing else" he said uh…"only dead bodies" he said uh…"that she gains" he said "by those bets. 'Cause when she bets ya" he said "she'll always go up" /he/ said "an' try ya first. Well uh…she got a red hot poker* _ in one hand _ an' a…a dagger in th' other." An' /he/ says "If he fliniches at all" /he/ said uh…"they take the dagger" /he/ said uh…"an' run it through ya. Then" /he/ said "heave ye down the basement." But /he/ said uh…/he/ said uh…"I'll fit ye out tonight" /he/ said…he said "if you listen to me."* He said "You goes up the night" he said "she'll be bettin (still)." An' he said "If she bets" he said uh…"you better _ say yes. (An') put your whole three ships" he said uh…"again her uh…her whole estate." He said "She'll bet with ya." An' /he/ said uh*…"Here's a little bottle o' stuff." He said "Call this" he said…he said "for a…a private room an' say" he said "that you wants uh…to write a letter" he said "home to your wife." An' he said "Grease…strip off start naked" he said "an' grease yourself all over" he said uh…"wi' the contents o' this little bottle." An' he said "Here's a pin. Perhaps" he said "her pin" he said "her…witchcraft" he said uh…"might be [a] little stronger than mine. If you see…finds yourself" he said uh…"goin off [i.e., feeling sleepy]" he said "stick that pin" he said "into* your _ self" he said uh…"an' that'll spite her." [aside to wife: (anybody) goin to get a lunch Breen? Wished I'm…I'm hungry.] [Teller's wife: Yes have ya got that the…[aside to Int: got that shut off have ya?]] [Int: uh…yes. He's goin to finish this…]***[recorder off.] So uh…begar

---

Margin notes (left column):

*noise of door opening; woman speaking
*noise of door closing

/she/
*noise of door opening
/she/ /she/ /she/ /she/
/she/ /she/ /she/
*loud noise in background

/she/

*continued loud noise

*loud noise

/Jack did what the old man told him/. An' before he left to go /?home/ down she comes.

/he done what Jack ...did/   /whole/

Jack said "Look here" he said "you're after havin all the bettin now" he said "an' I had none." He said "'Tis my turn now" he said uh…"I'll put my three ships" he said "again your _ castle an' your whole estate."

"Yes" she said "alright."

So uh…"Now" Jack said "I wants a private room _ for to uh…write a letter home" he said "to me wife."

"Yes" she said "you can have that."

So Jack _ called for a room an' done uh…what she t…what he [*his godfather*] told him to do. An' then he _ then he uh…said "Now" he said "me two uh*…me s…first mate an' second mate" he said uh…"I wants them" he said "to sleep in this uh…castle" he said "with me tonight" he said uh…"in the next room to me."

*noise in background

"Yes" she said "you can have that."

So uh…the next morn uh…when she got…he sent for the…sent out for the police. An' when he sent out for the police _ begar here 'twas. He oweded the three ships _ back again _ an' _ her castle _ an' her wholed estate.

Jack said "I won't be too hard on ye" he said uh…he said "pay me" he said "five hundred pound. An'" he said "gi' me me three ships _ back again" he said uh…an' he said uh…"for the castle" he said "an' your whole estate" he said uh…"I don't want it" he said.*

*listener coughs

But she give Jack…pay Jack the five hundred pound _ an' give him his three ships back again. An' he got a…a captain _ an' put [one] in each of 'em. An' uh…he got aboard the last one himself. An' he said when uh…when he…when they sot sail _ he told the other two _ when they'd get in port be _ fore him _ for to fire uh…two s…salutes for England _ an' uh…three for France.

An' when they were goin along by uh…by Fra[nce]…by uh…England _ told 'em to land. An' he's down alongside o' London Bridge _ [Male listener: Hm! [*exclamation of amusement*]] soakin a cake o' hard bread. An' when he had it coaked…suh…cake o' hard bread soaked _ put it up to eat it. Told them to come an'…told all to come down an' be drinkin. He looked up an' there was a big uh…a whole…crowd of cars _ comin across the bridge.

He looked up an' he said "Well" he said uh…"it's just as well" he said uh…"to kill a man" he said "as frighten un to death."

And he say when he went to…eat a piece o' loaf he said uh…"Come down an' be drinkin." He said "That's what we calls eatin in our country." An' the same time _ when he was goin to drink _ "Come down an' be _ eatin."

453

An' he said "Well..." this fella said "well" he said uh..."I can't have much (good) time" he said "with ya _ tonight" he said uh...he said "I'm goina be married tonight" he said "to the king's daughter."

"Is THAT so?" Jack (said). "Well" Jack said "I hope" he said uh..."you'll have a good time."* He said uh..."I'm just as liable" he said "have just as...fresh a lobster" he said uh..."for my breakfast tomorrow morning as you will."

*banging noise

An' he give the ha-ha of a laugh. He said "I haven't got no time to fool with you" he said uh...be he said uh..."What would your name be?"

Well Jack said "My name" he said uh..."is Poverty Partin Wud Good Company."

An' he was _ repeatin it over in his mind uh...all the time _ far as he could hear _ "Poverty Partin [Wud] Good Company, Poverty Partin Wud Good Com(pany)."

/leathered/
/be married/

An' they were all /gathered/ in uh...waitin for the priest _ for the bishop _ come to /marry them/ _ the...the wedding crowd they'd...an' uh...an' she was sot between her father _ an' _ her intended, the fella she was goina be married [to].

An' uh...the father said "Well" he said "in olden times _ in oldeny times" he said "when we'd be waitin for this" he said uh..."there'd be always" he said "someone 'd sing a song" he said uh..."or tell a story." An' he said uh..."It used to always fall" he said uh..."on the bri.../bridegroom/."

/bridedress/

He excused himself an' said "Well" he said uhn..."I never sung a song (in) me life" he said uh..."nor I never told a story. But" he said "I'll tell ya something" he said uh..."that happened today" he said "when I was comin...comin over here" he said uh...he said "now it might be just as interest...interestin" he said uh..."(as) the best story" he said "ever you hear." He said "When I come down _ eatin" he said "this feller _ an old tarry sailor" he said "down there _ soakin a cake o' hard bread." An' he said "When he put the cake o' hard bread" he said "up to his mouth" _ he...said uh..."he asked me to come down an' be drinkin." "I told him" he said "'twas...'twas EAT in our country. An' he said 'Well' he said uh...''cordin to that' he said 'I'm away back.'" An' he said "When he went to...went to drink" he said "he told me to come down an' be eatin. I told him" he said "I didn't have much uh...time to fool with un, that I was goin be married. I asked him his name" he said "an' he told me" he said uh..."his name was Poverty Partin _ Wud Good Company. As far as /?ye/ could hear him _ this is what he was singin out."

/she/

So the...wedding crowd all come in _ waitin for the priest. Th' ol' feller said he said "Well" he said uh..."time" he said uh..."olden times" he said "we'd have a song" he said uh...[*aside to Int:* I told you

454

that didn't I?] An' he excused himself an' said "Well" he said uh…"I never told…sung a song an' learned a song [in] me life" he said "or I never…told a story." Up an' tell 'em this little yuh…interest[in] story _ little yarn comin across the bridge. An' when she said…when he said uh…"Poverty Partin (Wud) Good Company" _ she got up an' went out. An' when she went out uh…she went to the f…first porter she went to.

She told un _ he said…she said "If they come to look for me" she said uh…"me father comes" she said "an' ask (for) me" she said uh…"tell him" she said "you never see me." An' when she went to the second one _ she said "If me father comes" she said "an' /askes/ for me" /she/ said uh…"tell him" she said uh…"ye saw me goin to me room." /astes/ /he/

So when they all come in _ all gathered round* (to) be married _ well there's no sign of (find) the lady. So [it] got on the old man's uh…nerves an' he went lookin himself. And uh…when he went to the…the last por…uh…porter told un he said uh…"Yes" he said uh…"I saw her goin to her room."* *listener sneezes

They went in, knocked to the door. Callin her by name an' he said "Is ya there?" *child crying in background

"Yes" she said.

"Come out" /he/ [the king] said "an' be marr[ied]…come out" he said "an' be married." /she/

"No Pap" she said "I can't get married" she sa[id]…"(I) can't be married" she sai[d] "only once" she said "in the Catholic Church." An' she said uh…"I'm married" she said uh…"an' got me husband in with me."

An' he thought she was insane. (He said) "Don't be as foolish" he said "come out" he said "an' be married."

"No" she said "I told you" she said uh…"I'm married" she said "an' got me husband in with me."

An' he broke open [the] door. When he broken up the door she passed out the lockets. "Here" she said "look!" She said uh…"That locket there" she said "was the lo[cket]"* [she] said uh…"that you never…never give me /any/ /?direction/" she said "who owns it." Said "I'd find out meself now" he said "an' I got un uh…[laughs] in bed" she said "with me." *microphone noise /anty/ /the rest uh/

So uh…they had to go _ an' tell the…th' other feller [the man she was to marry] _ the story.* An' uh…he [the king] started uh…the wedding over again an' the wedding started uh*…well that…lasted for _ three days an' three nights. An' uh…that's was about when I left ol' man uh…the four of 'em were out* dancin at a…a three-handed *footsteps and sound of door opening *background noise *background noise

455

reel...four-handed reel. That they were when I left, that was three o'clock in the evening, (four o'clock then when I left).

[Int: Very good story. Uh...where d'ya hear that Uncle Am?]
Uh?
[Int: Where d'ya hear that?]
My dear son! The man that told me uh*...knowed a lot o' them stories. An' that was uh...ol' uncle Maurice _ uh...fella was in uh...Mickel uh... Mick...Maurice McDonald (fella wa[s]) _
[Int: Yeah]
Peter's father over there
[Int: Yeah. (After) heard him telling ya?]
Eh?
[Int: You heard him?]
Yes that's who told me a story.

*footsteps in back-ground

Duration: 31 min., 46 sec.
Source: Maurice McDonald, Goose Cove, Hare Bay, Great Northern Peninsula.
Location: Kitchen of teller's house, early afternoon.
Audience: Teller's wife, interviewer.

Context, Style, and Language: (For context see notes to No. 21). Ambrose Reardon takes pains to involve the interviewer in the details of the story. He first asks a semi-rhetorical question in the opening sentence; he speaks aside to the audience when he forgets or repeats a point; he asks if the listeners know what a valet is, and offers his own explanation of the word. For his part, the interviewer asks for clarification about the locket and receives an immediate response. However, none of these conversational interactions between teller and audience results in any loss of momentum in the storytelling, nor does the teller's urgent request for a lunch when he feels hungry about halfway through the narration, his appetite no doubt whetted by the aroma of bread which is being baked in the same room while the recording is going on.

Unfortunately the recording quality of this story, like that of No. 21, is not very good. In the opening section the teller's voice is distorted, probably by too high a level on the input volume control. There is constant background noise, perhaps from an engine or generator in the distance, and also perhaps from the motor of the recorder; voices are heard in the background, including those of neighbors' children playing outside, and there are also the loud ticking of a clock and the frequent creaking of a door. These noises cause serious transcription problems, especially by the further masking of otherwise unclear segments of speech. The final section of the tale is especially difficult to decipher, and here the transcription is to be regarded as tentative, although based on the collector's own transcript which served to corroborate the version presented here.

The narrative suffers a major interruption when the tape has to be changed, and on two further occasions when a child and later a woman come into the room. This latter disruption threatens to be final, as may be gathered from the teller's aside to the collector that "It's all over," i.e., the storytelling has to stop. Nevertheless, in spite of these interruptions, Mr. Reardon manages to resume the narration with no damaging omissions or noticeable change in style and delivery. However, the change of tape may be a reason why this tale includes no details of the three attempts to regain the ship or whether the teller knows the "sleepy drops" motif found in the Bennetts' versions. The hiatus may have given Mr. Reardon an opportunity to omit further details of Jack's sexual adventures. He had hinted just before the tape was changed, in his aside to the audience, "no harm I suppose," that he was somewhat diffident about telling this part of the story. His reluctance may well have been prompted by a female relative who was present and who objected to his telling these stories. She demonstrated her feelings by rattling the pots on the stove and making other loud noises. The editors have themselves encountered a parallel situation during fieldwork in Bonavista Bay when an irritated wife did her best to disrupt the recording session by similar means.

Although the opening description sets the story in France and England, the teller immediately brings it nearer to Newfoundland by suggesting that one reason why England and France went to war was the French Shore question in the province. However farfetched the suggestion, this links the tale with Newfoundland, a link later strengthened by more specific local references. For example, the comment that there are only four people in the place where the king lives is an endearingly "rural" view of the lifestyle of royalty and suggests a very homely scene. Even so, it would be common knowledge to teller and audience that the Newfoundland outport merchant, representing the local powerful and wealthy classes, would have until recently a number of servants "living in," so perhaps the narrator discounts servants in his enumeration of the inhabitants in the king's home. His comments on his own use of an ABC card like the one used in the tale also extend the localizing references by authenticating the article and making it relevant to the Newfoundland context. This helps to implicate the teller directly in specific elements of the plot and at the same time reassures the audience of the plausibility of certain events and details depicted. Note also the reference to "soakin a cake of hard bread"—a distinctively local touch in that such an activity was a normal everyday matter for Newfoundlanders until very recently, and is still common today in making the dish "fish and brewis," consisting of salt codfish cooked with "hard tack" or ship's biscuit. Furthermore, the notion of having to spend another year at school if one fails the relevant test is another localizing feature as it was certainly not remote from the education system of the province, children frequently repeating a year.

In addition to those present for all or part of the story who do not form part of the audience there is at least one other male listener apart from the collector. He responds with an amused "Hm!" to the mention of Jack being down alongside London Bridge. His response is restrained but significant; he otherwise sits in silence, participating only as a listener except for this one vocal contribution to the storytelling context.

The title of this tale itself poses a linguistic problem which is completely obscured by the normal spelling of the otherwise insignificant word *With*. In the title, and also when first said by the princess as the name Jack is to use when he returns from his third voyage, and again when Jack tells his story at the end of the tale, the word *With* is clearly pronounced /wud/ on the tape. For the sake of clarity we have rendered this as *With* in the title, but have offered a more representative phonemic spelling *(Wud)* in the story itself. On each occasion the teller articulates this phrase there is a clear break in the intonation pattern between the words *Partin* and *Wud*. Indeed, in three of the seven instances the break is sufficiently long for it to be signified by the pause symbol in the transcript, the breaks in two of the remaining four instances being less noticeable as the "fella" is rapidly repeating the words "over in his mind" so as to remember them. On every occasion the whole phrase is spoken formulaically in two almost equal segments, the first having five syllables and the second having four (the word *Company* being syncopated to two). *Partin* has a sentence-final contour and the intonation pattern may be represented as *Pôvĕrtў Pârtĭn* ↘ ‖ *Wúd Gŏod Cŏmpăny* ↘. The articulation strongly suggests that the teller is uncertain of the precise meaning of the phrase and fails to identify *Wud* as *with*. Probably partly under the influence of the vowel in *Good*, the original *with* thus shifts to *wud* and the intonation contour suggests that the teller may understand it as a verb, i.e., *would*, having learned the phrase by rote in two separate but balanced segments without fully apprehending its meaning as a whole. Similar misapprehensions occur in other versions of this story, for example the garbled *Public (Word) Good Company* of No. 42. The clear and deliberate pronunciation of *Wud* in the title with a close back vowel makes it questionable to transcribe it as *With,* which normally has a close front or close front centralized vowel in Newfoundland speech, notwithstanding the strong historical evidence of the interchangeability of /i/ and /u/ in English dialects. That the /u/ of *With* in the title is not simply a misencoding of /i/ in anticipation of the vowel in *Good* also remains doubtful. When the phrase is used in the story itself it is pronounced variously as /wud/ (three instances) and as /wul/ (two instances, one ending in dark /l/ and one in clear /l/ and even in one instance as /wil/ (the close front vowel being lowered and centralized). We therefore conclude that the teller himself is very uncertain of the word and we have chosen to represent it as *Wud* to reflect this uncertainty and ambiguity and as a compromise between the pronunciation in the title and those with final laterals in the body of the narrative.

Another tantalizing linguistic puzzle is that of the nickname with which the princess dubs Jack when he is at school. This is first articulated as *Hard Head Hoverd,* the third word with its final offglide /d/ being modified shortly after to *Hover,* pronounced like (and presumably meaning) *over,* with the emphatic initial intrusive aspirate common in Newfoundland speech and in many other regional dialects of English. The precise meaning of *Hover* remains enigmatic, a possible gloss of the whole phrase being "person with a thick head on (i.e., over) his shoulders," in contradistinction to such sayings as "a wise head on young shoulders." More intriguing, however, is the probability that this phrase, or whatever phrase it has come to replace, is the origin of the *Hard Head* in the Bennetts' versions of the tale. Indeed, Ambrose Reardon's version gives the impression of being older, and better motivated as regards its purported historical authenticity, than the others presented in this collection. The nickname is thus a direct link between the versions (see especially the notes to No. 38).

The preamble to the tale is somewhat garbled, the teller being unsure whether or not he can tell it. With the interviewer's encouragement he starts out, rather hesitantly at first. He does not introduce Jack at the beginning but soon gives a purportedly authentic account of Jack's origins and parentage, and of the young Prince Edward giving up his rightful name and calling himself "plain Jack." This is the only tale in this collection which seeks to give Jack some plausible origins and puts him in such a full historical setting. This may perhaps indicate the influence of a literary source, a possibility further suggested by the careful, assured, and deliberate articulation of the opening sentences. They are said as if the teller was relating accepted historical facts, and are strongly reminiscent of some literary recension in the background. This is corroborated by such words as *valet* (spoken as if rhyming with *pallet*), a spelling pronunciation which is so narrowly and amusingly glossed as "the person that'll take your schoolbag _ to school _ an' take it back in th' evening." Another pronunciation possibly influenced by a misrepresentation of a printed source is the malapropistic *gullentined* (guillotined, with /iː/ as the vowel of the strongly stressed last syllable). More positive evidence of possible literary influence is found in the aphorism "Everyone for theirselves...an' god for us all" and such formal constructions as "If you give me consent." Furthermore, "the king's son o' France" is a construction already archaic in Shakespeare's day.

The comparatively slow speech with frequent brief pauses and distinct Anglo-Irish characteristics noted under No. 21 is again in evidence here, as are also the punctuating device *he/she said* in the dialogue and the highlighting of individual words by strong emphasis, e.g., the repeated authoritative demands of the king that things be done "on MY orders." Other points of linguistic interest not already discussed are as follows: the alternation of /eː/ and /iː/ in *quay* (cf. No. 21); the pronunciation of the first letter of the alphabet as /aː/ rather than /ei/, the former being common in Newfoundland; the medial /i/ in *hollyin;* the short close back round vowel in *hove;* the close front vowel in *critches* (crutches; cf. *EDD CRITCH* sb³, with supporting quotations from the West Country); the trisyllabic *fliniches,* with /e/ in the first syllable; the same typical confusion between /i/ and /e/ in local pronunciations of *pin* and *pen;* the diphthongs /ou/ in *none,* and /ei/ in the first syllable of *pacified* and *lasted;* the Anglo-Irish close front vowel in *Mickel;* the offglide /d/ in *wholed* (whole); and the stress on the third syllable of *interestin* and the first syllable of *insane;* aphesis is found in *'gree, 'nother, 'gain, 'cordin.* Lexical items include *ol' man* as a term of familiar address to the (much younger) collector; the use of *un* with a feminine referent; *again* (against); *hardy* in the sense of "adult, mature" (cf. *OED Hardy* a. 4. Capable of enduring fatigue, hardship, rigour of the weather etc; physically robust, vigorous); *bring* meaning "take"; *gutter* in the set phrase *mud and gutter,* probably Anglo-Irish (see *EDD GUTTER* sb. and v.¹ 9. Mud, mire; the dirt of the street [supported by numerous quotations from Scots and Irish sources]); *rightified* (see *EDD RIGHTIFY* [identified exclusively from Irish sources]); *lunch* in the Newfoundland sense of a snack eaten at any time; *hypocrite* (see *EDD HYPOCRITE* 2. A lame person [reported from Sussex]); the archaic use of *no* in *all right or no,* and of *start naked,* of which historically *stark naked* is a later alteration: *start naked* is not recorded in *OED* between 1325 and 1892 when it surfaces in North Carolina, and is also reported from Warwickshire in

1896; *goin off* (feeling sleepy); the curious adjectival form *oldeny*, uttered with clarity and precision as if to add weight to the preceding phrase *in olden times;* and the nautical *singin out*. Non-standard forms are seen in the inflections of *askes* and *Pierce'* (possessive), in the present tense *I knows, Is ya* (interrogative), the conditional present *And we loses* (in the absence of *it*, this is an interesting example of the possible survival of earlier *an* as conditional marker), the past tense *[they] was, give, load, seed, hove, spit, rung, was stood, owneded*, and the past participle *paste*. The object pronoun is omitted in *an' put [one] in each of 'em*, and there is also a typical double negative, *haven't got no time*.

As a footnote it is interesting that in his hesitant preamble the narrator uses *we'll say*, an expression employed frequently by Allan Oake to mark stages in the progress of a narrative, and perhaps indicative of a common stylistic tradition among storytellers on the northeast coast of the province.

See also the notes to No. 21.

Type and Motifs:
Cf. AT611. *The Gifts of the Dwarfs* [Irish by-form].
Cf. T61.5.1. *Betrothal of hero to princess while both are still in cradle.*
Cf. T69.2. *Parents affiance children without their knowledge.*
Cf. H82.3. *Tokens between lovers.*
Cf. T91.6.4. *Princess falls in love with lowly boy.*
N831. *Girl as helper.*
N15. *Chastity wager.*
N2.6.5. *Daughter as wager.*
N2.5. *Whole kingdom (all property) as wager.*
Cf. K1831.0.1. *Disguise by changing name.*
N825.2. *Old man helper.*
G262. *Murderous witch.*
Cf. H248.3. *Sham dead [sleeper] tested by pricking [hot poker].*
D822. *Magic object received from old man.*
Cf. H1484. *Continual pricking with pin in order to remain awake.*
N681. *Husband (lover) returns home just as wife (mistress) is to marry another.*
H151. *Attention drawn and recognition follows.*
Cf. H11. *Recognition through story-telling.*
Cf. L161. *Lowly hero marries princess.*
Z10.2. *End formula.*

International Parallels: See No. 36.

44. JACK WINS THE KING'S DAUGHTER†

Jack A. Teller
St. Shotts, St. Mary's Bay
21 July 1968

AT852 + AT1960L + AT1920E*
+ AT1960D + AT1950 + AT1920E
+ AT1960M₃ + AT1911A + AT1960G
+ AT1882 + Cf. AT1886
TC529 68-43
Collector: HH

Well once upon a time an' that very good time it was _ 'twas neither in
MY time or YOUR time _ the time that birds used to go round buildin nests in
old men's whiskers _ an' pigs goin around with forks stuck in their...quarters
singin out who'd buy pork. But there was an old man an' he had uh...one
son, the son died. So uh...after a while _ there was a young fella. He picked
up with a young fella an' he asked him if he'd go a servant with him. An'
all he wanted the young fella [for] was _ uh...to go around day after day to
bring uh...him back...the news in the evening.

So begob the young fella said he'd ship with him. So he agreed to ship
with this...man. So he went home an' he told his mother _ he was after
getting a berth for the...the year. So he _ packed up his duds the next
morning an' _ no he said to his mother he said "I shipped" he said "with
Micky the /liar/."   /lord/

"Ah foolish woman...foolish boy" says the mother "to go ship with
Micky the liar."

So he _ packed up his duds the next mornin an' he _ started off for
Mickel. So Mickel had him goin around _ from place to place pickin up _ the
news for him. So begob /anyway/ he's...this day he was goin along _ the   /an' way/
street an'...[aside: what way do we go now then?] [recorder off]*** "Now"
he said there was a bird flew over his head _ an' dropped an egg on the
middle o' the street. An' 'twas in everybody's way _ they had to get
crowbars an' hand spikes an' pickaxes to roll it an' it bursted an' it
drowneded half the street.

So he went back that evenin with the...news to Mickel. So -- he said
"I'll go to the king's palace tomorrow" he says "an' I'm goina tell him" he
said "the lie." An' whoever tell now...the biggest lie _ was supposed to get
the king's daughter in marriage. "But" he said "you'll have to come" he says
uh..."a short while after" he said "to confirm the lie for me."

"Well alright" says Mickel "I'll confirm the lie for ya."

So this young fella started, JACK was his name _ the next morning and
he went to the king's palace an' he rapped on the door. So the king c...come
out.

An' he said "Well me boy" he said "what's the news of you this
morning?"

461

"POOR news _ your honour" says...Jack. "Comin along this morning" he said "there was a bird flew over me head" he said "an' he dropped an egg on the middle o' the street. An' 'twas in everybody's way" he said "we had to get crowbars an' hand spikes an' pickaxes to roll her an' bursted it an' drowneded half the street."

"Clap that man in irons" says the king "he's tellin me a lie."

So begob he was clapped in irons. He wasn't long clapped in irons when along come Mickel. Mickel went up to the door an' he _ raps an' the king come out.

"Well me man" he says "what's...your request this morning?"

"I have poor news this morning _ your honour" says _ Mickel. "Comin along meself...this mornin, meself an' a little boy" he said _ "there was a bird flew over our heads on the middle o' the street" he said "he dropped an egg. An' 'twas in EVERYBODY'S way, we had to get crowbars an' hand spikes an' pickaxes to roll un" he says "an' it drowneded half the street. Is uh...at the same time" he said "I don't know but the little boy was drowneded _ because I was wet meself" he said "from the sole o' me foot to the crown o' me head. Only for that" he said "I'd...might be here a little sooner."

"I have a man in irons...for...for that" said the king. "An' ye can release that man" he said "that's no lie."

So they let him out o'...jail _ an' he brought him along uh...out through a garden. An' he showed him a field o' cabbage.

So the young fella said, he said "That's nothing to cabbage me father reared."

"An' how big must your father's cabbage be!" he said.

"Well now" he said "we had a hundred men to work an' meself an' me father one day" he said "an'...an' it come (for) a big shower o' rain" he says "an' we cut off" he said "one o' the leaves [o'] the cabbage. An' we shored it up" he said "with our shovels. An' it 'd cover" he said "the hundred men _ an' meself [an'] me father" he said "from the shower o' rain."

"My cabbage is not as big as that" says the king.

Why he brought him alon[g]...'long another...short distance, he said _ "Are them large turnips?" says the king.

"Well them are nothing to turnips me father reared" says Jack.

"An' how big must your father's turnips be!" says the king.

"Well" he said "we had a sow pig home" he said _ "one time" he said "and she was goina get a...litter o' bonnifs [i.e., *piglets*]. So" he said _ "we missed the pig one day. An'" he said "we're huntin for the pig" he said "for a whole week. An' when we come at the pig" he said "she had a hole scooped in one o' the turnips. An' she had six bonnifs in the turnip...besides herself. So" he said "we took the...six bonnifs _ an' we took the pig an' we brought her home. An' we took up the turnip" he said "an' we _ cut the turnip up" he said "and it fed twelve bullocks" he said "for six months more."

"(Well) my turnip is not as big as that" says the king.

So he brought him along another bit. An' he said "Isn't that a...a lazy boy?" he said.

"Well that's a nothing to me brother I had" said Jack.

"An' how lazy must your brother be!" says the king.

"Well" he said "I often see him" he said "lyin on the street" he said "an' horses an' cars _ goin along" he said "an' _ he'd wouldn't...he be that lazy he wouldn't get out o' the way" he said "for the horses an' cars."

"Well my b...boy is not as lazy as that" says _ the king.

He brought him along another small bit. An' he said "Is that a lazy boy?"

"Well that's a nothing to a brother I had" says Jack.

"An' how lazy must your father...your brother be!" says the king.

"Well" he said "he was that lazy" he said "if he was in bed" he said "with a woman" he said "he would...he was too lazy" he said "to turn his head" uh...he said "to look at her."

"Well my boy is not a lazy as THAT" said the king.

So he brought him along another bit an' he says "Isn't that a small boy?" he said.

"Well that's nothing to a brother I had" said Jack.

"An' how small must your brother be!" he said.

"Well he was that small" he said "I often see me mother" he said "gettin...or sweepin the floor" he said "in the mornings _ an' then gettin down on her hands an' knees" he said "with a pin _ an' pickin him out of the seam o' the floor."

"Well my boy is not as small as that" said the king. [Male listener: Huh! That's a good one! Huh!] [listener laughs]

So he brought him along another...piece. "Are them large beans?" he said.

"Well them are nothing to beans me father reared" says Jack.

"An' how large must your father's beans be!" says the king.

"Well" he said "we had a bee home one time" he said "your honour" he said "an'...an' we missed him. An' we put our ear to the ground" he said "an' we heard him buildin a cage in London. So" he said "we sot off" he said "with a box _ and hunted for our _ bee...our bee. An'" he said "we filled up our pockets" he said "with...those beans. An' we used to drop one here an' there" he said "accordin as we were goin" he said _ "in the way we'd find our way back" he said "by the beans" he said "(when) we get to where our bee was.

Well" he said _ "we got to London" he said _ "our bee" he said "had two sacks o' honey made. So" he said "we took the two sacks o' honey an' we

463

took our bee an' we put the bee into the box an' we took the two sacks o' honey" he said "a sack on each of our back. An' we came along _ your honour" he said "till we met up with an old horse. So we caught the horse" he said "an' we hove the two sacks o' honey" he said "across the horse's back. But" he said "the horse was very old an' feeble" he said. "He hardly could...get along with the two sacks o' honey. But we came along your honour" he said "to where we came to where those hazel nut trees grew. So" he said "we got our knife an' we cut off one of 'em" he said "an' we pared it out" he said "very smooth. An' we shoved one...end of it" he said "up in his ass" he said "an' out in his mouth" he said "an' it strengthened the horse's back" he said "very good. So" he said [*laughing*] "I got along [*laughs*]...I got along" he said " _ me two sacks o' honey" he said _ "complete. But we were comin' along" he said "your honour" he said "an' we met (a place) where we were after droppin our beans. An'" he said "they're after growin that tall" he said _ he said "you hardly could see the height of 'em. So" he said "I took to climb your honour" he said "on one" he said "I went uh...went out o' sight o' theirs. An' if I did that me head got giddy an' I'd slip an' I'd...come down" he said "I went to me two shoulders in a solid rock.

So" he said "I plunged a lot" he said "an' I couldn't get uh...get clear o' the...rock" he said "I was after...gettin jammed in. So" he said "I thought of...of a plan your honour" he said "an' a very good plan I thought 'twas. I cut off me head" he said "an' I sent it home for the pickaxe. So..." he said "that was the day" he said "the fox an' the hounds was out" he said "an'

/head/   they...caught my head" he said "an' they gave it a /?hell/ of a...of a tearin up. So" he said "when I see...me head comin back in such scords [i.e., *?gashes*] o' blood" _ he said "I made three or four plunges an' I bursted the rock" he said "in several pieces. An' at the same time" he said "when I got clear o' the rock" he said uh..."fox was passin by. So" he uh...s...I...he said "I'd seized the...fox by the two hind legs. An' I gave him three bangs" he said "against the rock. An' every bang" he said "he let a fart. An' every fart"

/as/   he said "was as good /a/ king as what you were."

"You lie" says the king.

"Thank you sir" says Jack, he said _ "I got your daughter in marriage."

"Begar ya did Jack!" he said. "Ya got me daughter."

/Lord/   Well tha...that's the "Mickel the /Liar/" for ya now. Well now there's uh...scattered word left out of it, I don't say...I haven't got it all correct. [*laughs*] Excuse th' expression of [it]. [recorder off]

[Int: Would...your father would tell that story very often?]

Oh god he'd tell that story _ [teller's wife laughs] just...just the same now er...if we sat down an' start talkin yes an' no. He had it _ hand packed.

[Int: Did he have many other stories like that?]

Yes he had a lot o' stories.

Duration: 10 min., 12 sec.
Source: Father, St. Shotts, St. Mary's Bay.
Location: Kitchen of teller's house, afternoon.
Audience: Teller's wife and son, interviewer.

Context, Style, and Language: The teller is hesitant about his ability to remember the story and warns before he begins that he may have to pause to recollect. This he does briefly in the early stages of the narrative but quickly picks up the story again and continues it at a rapid pace. The audience readily responds to the humor of many of the episodes in which Jack outwits the king. Note that Jack's name is not introduced at the beginning of the story and it seems to come suddenly into the teller's mind as if he could not remember it initially.

The elaborate opening formula is enunciated more slowly and clearly than the similar ones in Nos. 25, 30, and 89. The teller hesitates momentarily before the word *quarters,* perhaps trying to remember this comparatively unusual word, but perhaps using it euphemistically for *arses* which appears in the toned-down singular form *ass* in the opening formula of No. 89 from the community of Grand Bank, over a hundred miles to the west in Fortune Bay.

There are many Anglo-Irish features in the language of the tale. Quite apart from the general pronunciation, individual forms such as *Mickel* (Michael) and the asseveration *begob* illustrate this, together with such lexical items as *bonnifs* (piglets; see *DNE bonnive*), *scords* (?gashes), and the repeated use of *meself.* Note also the typical Irish construction of *after gettin* and *after droppin,* the archaic colloquialism *duds* (clothes), the past tense forms *drowneded, bursted, come, sot,* and *hove,* the West Country English *un,* and the common Newfoundland usage of *young fella* (young man—stressed on the first word) (young man), and *ship* (accept a berth on a ship). The deliberately exaggerated intonation patterns of the king's exclamations in response to each lie function as repeated structural formulas and contribute to the humor of this amusing tale which the narrator himself thoroughly enjoys telling.

Types and Motifs:
AT852. *The Hero Forces the Princess [King] to say, "That's a lie"* + AT1960L. *The Great Egg* + AT1920E. *Greatest Liar Gets his Supper Free* + AT1960D. *The Great Vegetable* + AT1950. *The Three Lazy Ones* + AT1920E*. *Lie: Seeing (Hearing) Enormous Distance* + AT1960M₃. *Large Bumblebee* + AT1911A. *Horse's New Backbone* + AT1960G. *The Great Tree* + AT1882. *The Man Who Fell out of a Balloon* + Cf. AT1886. *Man Drinks from own Skull.*
Z10.1. *Beginning formula.*
X1813. *Lie: the great egg.*
H331. *Suitor contests: bride offered as prize.*
T68. *Princess offered as prize.*
X905. *Lying contests.*
X907.1. *The second liar corroborates the lie of the first.*
X1423.1. *Lie: the great cabbage.*
X1431.1. *Lies about big turnips.*

X1401.1. *Lie: animals live inside great vegetable, usually feeding from it.*

Cf. W111.1. *Contest in laziness.*

Cf. F535.1. *Thumbling.*

X1282. *Lies about bees.*

F641. *Person of remarkable hearing.*

Cf. R135.0.2. *Train of grain (seeds) [beans].*

X1721.1. *New backbone for a horse made from a stick.*

X1402. *Lie about the fast-growing plants.*

Cf. F54.2. *Plant grows to sky.*

Cf. X1731.2. *Man falls from height, goes into solid rock up to knees.*

Cf. X1731.2.1. *Man falls and is buried in earth: goes for spade and digs self out.*

X1726. *Man cuts off own head.*

H342.1. *Suitor test: forcing princess [king] to say "That is a lie."*

L161. *Lowly hero marries princess.*

International Parallels: In his discussion of AT852, Stith Thompson comments (*The Folktale,* p. 156): "The interest of the story is primarily in these 'tall tales.'" After describing some of the varieties of such stories, he adds: "Though this tale appears to have no literary history, it is scattered rather evenly over Europe as an oral story and it is found in single versions in Indonesia, North and Central Africa, and in the British tradition of Virginia and the French of Missouri." A careful search of the available references, however, suggests that the Virginia reference is erroneous, a fact confirmed by the absence of the tale from both the AT and Baughman indexes.

Up to March 1989, when the completed manuscript of this collection was sent to a publisher, there had been no report of AT852 from North America. [See, however, Supplementary References, p. 1061 below]. Since the popularity of tall tales in the United States is well-recognized, the absence of this mega-tall tale cluster is striking. Because AT852 is fairly well known in Ireland, we suggest that systematic collecting of folk narratives in some of the areas settled by the American Irish might yield versions of this as well as of other infrequently reported tales.

A surprising number of the individual tall tale types in our Newfoundland recension of AT852 are found not only in Scottish, Irish, and European versions of our tale, but also occur, often singly, in North America and elsewhere. It is also of interest to note that many of them appear as well in other tall tale complexes that have been reported from Europe and the Near East.

For clarity we have arranged the analogues below into three groups. Group 1 includes international references on AT852 as a whole. Group 2 has a few comparative references on some of the component tall tales found in our Newfoundland recension of AT852. In Group 3 we have included notes to several other tall tale cycles that seem closely related to AT852 both in structure and content. With each version cited under Groups 1 and 3, we include in parentheses all the individual AT types found in that text which we could identify.

Worth stressing in our version of AT852 and in most of the analogues presented in our first group of notes is the method of achieving the climax of the tale by introducing a surprise element. The princess, or the king, as in ours and many other versions, shows a bland willingness to accept the possible truth of a whole series of highly improbable tales. In desperation the person telling them suddenly makes a startling statement, frequently vulgar, that casts aspersions on the dignity of the princess or king or of some other member of the royal family. Stung by this the king/princess calls him a liar, whereupon, of course, he gains the prize: the princess.

A surprise element is also introduced in the climax of several of the related tale cycles for which we give analogues in Group 3. In three of the cycles the character who is listening to the stories is startled into calling the yarn-spinner a liar, thus giving the latter the prize. In the fourth the climax is often a coarse statement about the person listening, along with the claim that the yarn-spinner has won the prize.

Group 1
AT852. *The Hero Forces the Princess [King] to say, "That's a lie."*

Studies and Notes
  Bolte and Polívka, 2, pp. 506-16, no. 112; Thompson, *The Folktale,* pp. 156-57.

Canada
Lacourcière, Index, cites 14 Francophone versions of AT852 from Canada: 4 (New Brunswick), 7 (Quebec), 3 (Ontario).

United States
Carrière, *Tales,* pp. 248-50, no. 55 (with 1960G, cf. 1889K), French text with English summary (Missouri).
Cf. Rael, *Cuentos,* pp. 755-56, no. 313 (cf. 852, with 1960M, 1960J, cf. 1889K, cf. 1960D), English summary of Spanish text (New Mexico).
Robe, *Index,* Type 852, cites Rael, Wheeler (Mexico), and one unpublished text from the Spanish southwest.

Mexico
Cf. Wheeler, *Tales,* pp. 475-77, no. 169 (cf. 852, with 1960M, 1960J, cf. 1882), Spanish text and English abstract (Jalisco).

The Caribbean
Hansen, *Types,* Type 852, cites one version from the Dominican Republic.

Scotland
Briggs, *Dictionary,* A2, pp. 424-32 (with cf. 1892, 1960M, 1881, cf. 1882, cf. 1886), transcription of School of Scottish Studies recording by Hamish Henderson, Scottish traveller (Perthshire), and rpt. in Briggs, *Sampler,* pp. 77-86.
MacColl and Seeger, *Doomsday,* pp. 108-11, no. 18 (with 1960M$_3$, 1881, cf. 1882), Scottish traveller (Perthshire).
Douglas, *King,* pp. 30-32 (with cf. 1960M$_3$, 1881, cf. 1882, cf. 1886), Scottish traveller (Perthshire).

Ireland

O'Faolain, *Children,* pp. 87-90 (with 1960M₃, 1911A, 1960G, 1889E, cf. 1881), trans. from Irish (Ireland).

MacManus, *Corners,* pp. 241-56 (with 1960A, 1960M₃, 1960D, cf. 1882, cf. 1886) (Co. Donegal).

Cf. O'Sullivan, *Folktales,* pp. 249-52, no. 53 (with 1960D, cf. 1911A, cf. 1892, cf. 1889D) (Co. Donegal).

Murphy, *Talking,* p. 43, no. 44 (with 1960D) (Co. Down).

MacAirt, *Béal.* 19 (1949), 43-48, no. 4 (with cf. 1950, 1960Z [cheese], 1911A, cf. 1889D, 1960M) (Co. Tyrone).

Ó Cróinín, *Béal.* 35-36 (1967-68), 364-65, no. 29 (with 1960D, 1960M₃, 1911A, 1960Z [manure heap], 1889E, cf. 1882), English summary of Irish text (Co. Cork).

Ó Tiomanáidhe, *Béal.* 1 (1927-28), 197-98 (with 1960D), English summary of Irish text (Co. Mayo).

Duncan, *FL* 4 (1893), 188-90 (with 1960D, 1960G, 1960M₃, cf. 1882, cf. 1886) (Co. Leitrim), and rpt. in Briggs, *Dictionary,* A2, pp. 411-12.

Irish Types, Type 852, 255 versions.

Continental Europe

See Grimm-Hunt, 2, p. 413, note to no. 112 (with 1960D, cf. 1960G, cf. 1889K, cf. 1882) (Germany), and another English trans. in Grimm and Hansen, *Tales,* p. 145.

Dasent, *Popular Tales,* pp. 122-23, no. 7 (with 1960E, 1960A, cf. 1960K, 1911A, 1960G, cf. 1889E) (Norway).

Hodne, *Types,* AT852, 20 versions (Norway).

Withers, *World,* pp. 90-100, slightly altered (with 1960D, 1960M₃, cf. 1920G, 1960L, 1960E, 1911A, 1960G, 1889E), p. 117, notes (Denmark).

Orczy, *Fairy Tales,* pp. 93-95 (Hungary).

Ortutay, *Folk Tales,* pp. 465-67, no. 41 (Hungary).

India

Cf. Swynnerton, *Tales and Entertainments,* pp. 442-57, no. 91 (cf. 852, with 888A, 217, cf. 945) (Punjab).

Group 2

Under Group 2 we had intended to offer a few comparative notes for the various individual AT types found in our version of AT852 in the order in which they appear in our narrative. For one Type, however, AT1950, our notes grew to such length that we decided it would be less confusing to the reader to treat that story first. Apart from that tale the other Types are given in the sequence in which they occur in the Newfoundland tale.

We give AT1950 in considerable detail, because it has not received full scholarly attention for a number of years. Our other notes in Group 2 are only preliminary. Many of the tales will also be found in the references under Groups 1 and 3.

AT1950. *The Three Lazy Ones.*

Stories of contests in laziness are recounted, as Thompson (*The Folktale,* p. 210) points out, "in the [medieval] *Gesta Romanorum* and in nearly all later books of anecdotes. . .and in folktale collections from nearly all parts of Europe. . . ." We should note, however, that the number of persons involved in such contests is not stable but usually varies from one to three, and even twelve in one version. Two individuals, as in this Newfoundland recension, are found in many versions, but the proofs of their laziness may differ widely. So far as we know, however, the only other examples of the Newfoundland theme of the man in bed with a beautiful woman who was too lazy to turn to face her are found in Irish tradition.

Studies and Notes
Swan, *Gesta Romanorum,* pp. 163-64, no. 91; Bolte and Polívka, 3, pp. 207-13, no. 151, and cf. p. 213, no. 151a; Pauli and Bolte, 2, p. 322, no. 261, notes; Thompson, *The Folktale,* pp. 210-11; Randolph, *Hot Springs,* p. 253, no. 345, notes; Perry, *Babrius and Phaedrus,* pp. 597-99, no. 703; Baughman, *Index,* Type 1950, p. 62; Tubach, *Index, FFC* no. 204, p. 227, no. 2896, p. 236, no. 3005.

Canada
Lacourcière, Index, cites 5 Francophone versions of AT1950 from Canada: 1 (New Brunswick), 4 (Quebec).

United States
Randolph, *Hot Springs,* p. 123, no. 345 (Missouri), and see p. 253, no. 345, notes, for extensive American references.
Abrahams, *Afro-American,* pp. 283-84, no. 96, black (Texas).

The Caribbean
See Hansen, *Types,* Type **823A,B, for citations from the Dominican Republic and Puerto Rico.

England
Williams, *Villages,* pp. 249-50 (Berkshire), and rpt. in summary in Briggs, *Dictionary,* A2, p. 299.
Gutch, *East Riding,* p. 167, cited from T. Edmondson, *History of Fimber,* 1857 (Yorkshire), and rpt. in Briggs, *Dictionary,* A2, p. 86.

Wales
Jones, *Folklore,* p. 228, brief mention only.

Ireland
Douglas, *Book,* pp. 281-85 (with Irish Type 1950*), trans. from Irish by "An Seabhac" (Ireland).
Jarrell, *JAF* 77 (1964), 105, from Irish Folklore Commission MSS., told of Dean Swift (Ireland).
MacManus, *Stories,* pp. 61-74 (with Irish Type 1950*, 1920E*) (Co. Donegal).
Dillon, *King,* pp. 104-6 (with Irish Type 1950*) (Co. Galway).
Irish Types, Type 1950, 149 versions.

Continental Europe
Grimm no. 151, "The Three Sluggards," Grimm-Hunt, 2, pp. 219-20, no. 151, and see 2, pp. 445-47, no. 151, for other references. For other trans. see Grimm-Magoun, pp. 514-15, no. 151, and Grimm-Zipes, pp. 505-6, no. 151.
Cf. Grimm no. 151*, "The Twelve Idle Servants," Grimm-Hunt, 2, pp. 220-22, no. 151*. For other trans. see Grimm-Magoun, pp. 515-17, no. 151*, and Grimm-Zipes, pp. 506-8, no. 151a.
Hodne, *Types,* AT1950, 2 versions (Norway).
Straparola, *Nights,* 2, pp. 78-86 (Night VIII, Fable 1) (with 1351), literary (Italy).

Sachs, *Merry Tales,* pp. 76-78 (with 822), literary (Germany).
Rausmaa, *Catalogue,* Type 1950, 51 versions (Finland).
　　For some older references see:
Swan, *Gesta Romanorum,* pp. 163-64, no. 91.
Perry, *Babrius and Phaedrus,* pp. 597-99, no. 703.
Tubach, *Index,* no. 3005.

India
Shankar, *Wit,* pp. 105-6, no. 1, p. 106, no. 2, 2 versions (India).
Jethabhai, *Folklore,* pp. 25-28, no. 8, pp. 28-30, no. 9, 2 versions (Gujarat, Bombay).
Mohanti, *Village,* p. 51 (Orissa, Central India).
See Thompson and Roberts, *Types,* Type 1950, for other analyzed references.

Eastern Asia
Mayer, *Guide,* p. 227, no. 224 (Japan).

Africa
El-Shamy, *Folk-Tales,* pp. 226-27, no. 62 (Egypt).

AT1960L. *The Great Egg.*
Dobie, *PTFS* 19 (1944), 36-41 (with 1920E, 1920A, 1960J), Spanish tradition, in English (Texas).
Hansen, *Types,* 1960Z (Puerto Rico).

AT1920E. *Greatest Liar Gets His Supper Free. . . .* Each lie is corroborated by a confederate, who poses as a stranger.
Dobie, *PTFS* 19 (1944), 36-41 (with 1920A, 1960J, 1960L), Spanish tradition, in English (Texas).
Aiken, *PTFS* 12 (1935), 55-57 (with 1920A, 1920D), Spanish tradition, in English (Texas-Mexican border), and rpt. in Aiken, *Folktales,* pp. 61-63.
Withers, *World,* pp. 7-8 (France).

AT1960D. *The Great Vegetable.*
Thomas, *Types,* cites 2 versions of AT1960D from Newfoundland French tradition.
See Baughman motif X1401, "Lie: the great vegetable," and especially the subdivisions under X1401.1., for many American references.
See Toor, *Treasury,* pp. 494-95, Yaqui Indian (Mexico).
For some English versions see Briggs, *Dictionary,* A2, pp. 103, 104, 109.
For Ireland add: *Irish Types,* Type 1960D, 80 versions.
Hodne, *Types,* AT1960D, 3 versions (Norway).
Rausmaa, *Catalogue,* Type 1960D, 177 versions (Finland).

AT1960G. *The Great Tree.*
Thomas, *Types,* cites 6 versions of AT1960G from Newfoundland French tradition.
Lacourcière, Index, cites 1 Francophone version of AT1960G from Canada: 1 (Quebec).
Baughman, *Index,* Type 1960G, refers to American versions under several motifs.
Irish Types, Type 1960G, 72 versions (Ireland).
Cf. Hodne, *Types,* AT1960G, 2 versions (Norway).
Rausmaa, *Catalogue,* Type 1960G, 84 versions (Finland).

AT1911A. *Horse's New Backbone.*

Baughman, *Index,* Type 1911A, cites versions from Indiana and Kentucky, then lists tales in which a flayed horse is covered with a sheepskin and grows wool.

Irish Types, Type 1911A, lists 108 versions, which include the same two stories as Baughman, but does not distinguish between the two forms in the references.

We have not attempted to assemble additional references for the other Types found in the Newfoundland versions of AT852: AT1960M$_3$, "Large Bumblebee," AT1882, "The Man who Fell out of a Balloon," and cf. AT1886, "Man Drinks from own Skull." Versions of several of them will be found either in the references in Group 1 or in the notes to the related tale complexes cited in Group 3, especially in the tale of the lying contest between the boy and the beardless miller.

Group 3

We next offer some references for several tales or tale complexes that seem related to AT852: cf. AT1920C, cf. 1920F, 1920H, and a special version of AT1920.

Cf. AT1920C. *The Master and the Peasant: The Great Ox.*

The master brought to say "You Lie." Cf. AT852.

In these stories there is usually a lying contest between a farm owner and a peasant for a prize, which is often the entire harvested crop. The farm owner either says his opponent lies or admits that he has lost the contest.

Continental Europe

Massignon, *Folktales,* pp. 161-62, no. 47 (cf. 852, with cf. 1920C, 1960G, 1889E, cf. 1882) (France).

Wolf, *Fairy Tales,* pp. 334-35 (cf. 852, with cf. 1920C, cf. 1960G) (Germany).

Rausmaa, *Catalogue,* Type 1920C, 43 versions (Finland).

Cortes, *Folk Tales,* pp. 123-24 (cf. 852, with 1920C, cf. 1882, cf. 1960G, cf. 1889E) (White Russia).

Africa

Cf. Posselt, *Fables,* pp. 83-85 (cf. 852, with cf. 1920C), Jindwe tribe, pp. 116-17 (cf. 852, with cf. 1920C), Chikunda tribe, 2 versions (Southern Rhodesia).

Cf. AT1920F. *He Who Says "That's a Lie" Must Pay a Fine.*

In most of the versions given below a royal personage offers a reward as a prize to anyone who can get him to say that a story he is told is a lie. As in AT852, he listens blandly to a series of tall-story tellers. Finally a man comes with a huge pot and claims that years ago his father had lent the king's father that pot full of gold pieces and he now requests repayment of the loan. Since the sum involved would be far greater than the promised reward, the king says it is a lie and gives the claimant the prize. In the Korean version repayment of a large sum is requested, but the prize is the Minister's daughter.

Continental Europe and Asia

Wardrop, *Folk Tales,* pp. 160-62, no. 4, Gurian tradition (Georgian S.S.R.).

Downing, *Folk-Tales,* p. 56 (Armenia).

Surmelian, *Apples,* p. 287, no. 35 (Armenia).

Noy, *Folktales,* pp. 106-8, no. 44, storyteller born in Iraq (Israel).

Campbell, *Told,* pp. 83-87, Arab storyteller (with cf. 1960D, 1960M, cf. 1960A) (Iraq).

See Thompson and Roberts, *Types,* Type 1920F, for four Indian references.

Zŏng, *Folk Tales,* p. 195, no. 94 (cf. 852, with cf. 1920F) (Korea).

Miyake, *Folktales,* pp. 71-73, no. 17 (Okayama, Japan).

AT1920H. *Buying Fire by Story-telling.*

As in AT852, we have here a series of tall tales told to a man, climaxed when the listener interrupts to call some statement a lie. For this interruption he is punished or killed.

Continental Europe

Rausmaa, *Catalogue,* Type 1920H, 6 versions (Finland).

Berindei and Brown, *FL* 26 (1915), 310-11 (1920H, with cf. 852, 1962, 1960G, cf. 1886) (Romania).

Hodgetts, *Tales,* pp. 315-19 (1920H, with cf. 852, 1889P, cf. 1889K, cf. 1900) (Russia).

Afanas'ev, *Fairy Tales,* pp. 345-48 (1920H, with cf. 852, 1889P, cf. 1889K, cf. 1900) (Russia).

AT1920. *Contest in Lying.* Cf. AT852.

Stories of a lying contest between a boy and a beardless miller (in the Balkans and the Middle East beardless men have a reputation for trickery) are popular from Yugoslavia through the Near East. The prize is usually all the flour the miller has ground for the boy, which sometimes has been made into a large loaf of bread. The boy's tall tales, which are superior to the miller's in their extravagance, end unexpectedly with his statement about a letter dropped or kicked out of a fox. The letter says that the boy is to have the bread or flour and that the miller should eat dung, or endure some other insult. The boy then snatches up the prize and runs off.

Continental Europe and the Near East

Ćurčija-Prodanović, *Folk-Tales,* pp. 37-41, no. 6 (with cf. 1960J, 1960M₃, 1962, 1960G, cf. 1889K, cf. 1882, 1960A, cf. 1886) (Yugoslavia).

Mijatovies, *Folk-Lore,* pp. 107-12 (with cf. 1960J, 1960M₃, 1962, 1960G, cf. 1889K, cf. 1882, 1960A, cf. 1886) (Serbia), and rpt. in Petrovitch, *Hero-Tales,* pp. 283-87.

Nicoloff, *Folk-Tales,* pp. 186-87, no. 74 (with cf. 1960D, 1960M₃, cf. 1889D), pp. 187-92, no. 75 (with cf. 1889D, 1960D, cf. 1241, cf. 1250, cf. 1200, 1960G, cf. 1889K, cf. 1882), 2 versions (Bulgaria).

Dawkins, *Modern,* pp. 408-9, no. 68 (with 1960G, 1962, cf. 1886) (Greece).

Megas, *Folktales,* pp. 191-92, no. 69 (with 1960M₃, cf. 1962, 1960G, cf. 1889K, 1886) (Greece).

Dawkins, *MGAM,* pp. 534-35, no. 21 (with cf. 1960D, cf. 1960J, cf. 1892), Greek dialect text and English trans., and p. 234, notes (Turkey).

Walker and Uysal, *Tales,* pp. 165-71, no. 13 (with 1960M₃, cf. 1892, 1960D, 1960F) (Turkey).

Noy, *Folktales,* pp. 56-58, no. 24 (with cf. 1960D, 1960M, cf. 1892), learned from a Turk (Israel).

45. JACK AND THE SLAVE ISLANDS†

John Roberts   AT882
Sally's Cove, Great Northern Peninsula   TC258 66-24
26 August 1966   Collectors: HH and JW

When he [Int. B] gets aboard [i.e., *into the car*] I'll start un. [Int. A: Go ahead. You just go right ahead.]

One time there was uh...Jack an' Tom. Well they lived in one place together. An' _ when they got big enough they _ got aboard of a vessel together. Well Tom ha...had very good education. Well he got a chance to go mate. Well Jack went...[as] a hand aboard an'...well they worked away like that _ an' be...sometime be four an' five months 'fore they get home. Well -- by an' by _ Tom said to Jack _ "Now Jack" he said "if you was so willin as me" he said "we got a bit o' money" he said "we'd buy a vessel of our own _ and go tradin."

Well Jack said he was willin. Whatever Tom 'd say he was willin. Well Tom was skipper an' Jack was mate, he was a step ahead of un yet. Well now they was sail[in] together like that for four or five more years an'...an' when they go home _ they most generally have _ a week home or a fortnight _ sometimes a month 'fore they see 'em. So THIS time _ when they got out _ they was out for a couple o' months _ well Tom...well Jack said "Tom boy I got something to tell ya."

"What's that?" says Tom.

He said "I'm goin be married when I gets back this trip."

"Well Jack boy" he said "I been goin to tell you that" he said "this last week. I intended to get married this time _ when we gets home." So they was home an' they stayed home for two months 'fore they leaved again. So anyhow they 's gone. An'...they was gone a...a twelvemonth an'...an' ten days _ away from home. An' when they got back Tom's wife had a...a little girl _ an' Jack's wife had a boy. So uh...anyhow -- /Tom's/ wife...had the little girl...called Mary _ an' uh...Tom's wife _ an' Jack's wife had uh...her first boy _ called after his father, John.   /Jack's/

So uh...they sailed together an' sailed together -- oh for four or five year. The...two children was five year ol'. An'...they was out to sea an' in THEM times captain was allowed to marry. You've read that _ (now). Well anyhow -- Tom said...to Jack "Jack boy" he said "we was boys together an' we been sailin together all of our lifetime" he said _ "an' we got married together an' we kept up our wedding together." He said "What about me marrying your boy to my girl?" Well Jack was well satisfied. They was five year ol' um...well Tom says "I'll keep the...cerstificate."

473

Well anyhow -- they got married. Well -- that was th' only child Tom's wife had was this one little girl. But Jack's wife had two more boys. She had three boys _ Tom an' Bill. There's nothing about them, only Jack. So -- by an' by they got...big enough to go to school _ old enough to go to school an' /they/ went to school together an' _ so -- after they was goin to school _ Tom said "Jack boy" he said "look! Ever since we been young fellers together we been goin to sea. What about sellin our vessel _ an' live home with our wives? There's no comfort, gone like this all the time."

/we/

"No" Jack said "Tom boy. And I'd be only too glad _ so I could...stay home."

Well _ Tom said "Now then" he said "we'll sell the vessel _ an' we'll...half the money. You take one half an' I'll take the other. You can set up a little business ye own _ and I'll do the same thing."

Well now...there was five o' the...Jack's in family. But there was only four in Tom's. Well now then _ every year _ from...say time this little girl was born _ till she was _ goina school _ he was givin her so much every year of her life to put away for...time she's old enough to get married. But little...she thought she WAS married. So anyhow -- it went on an' it went on like this an' by an' by _ they start goin to th' high school, Jack an' the girl. An' _ well by an' by Jack's father took sick. An' _ 'twasn't very long 'fore he died. Well Jack said to his mother "Mother" he said _ "I'll go this quarter _ an' I'll give up goin _ to high school _ an'" he said "an' I'll go to Dublin. An' /Bill/ an' Tom _ an' you, you can manage the little business. I'll make a bit o' money for meself."

/Billem/

Well -- anyhow the girl come over in the morning _ as the...school was out _ an' she said to Jack she said uh _ "Is you ready to go to school?"

He said "I'm...I'm goina give up" he said "Mary at school now an'...go away."

"Oh no" she said. "DO come to school for another quarter." She says "I'LL pay your way."

"No" Jack said "I don't want a woman...a girl to pay my way. I can pay me own way to school."

"Well" she said "for MY sake" she said _ "we're always together" she said _ "come to school for another quarter."

Well after the quarter was out _ she come over in the morning she said "Jack...you're not goina school this morning?"

"No" Jack said "I'm NOT goina school."

"Well now" she said "I'm seventeen year ol' an' so is you too." She said "You ask father for me the night in marriage." She said "An' let you an' me get married."

Well -- Jack went over an'...his father was buried an' everything stowed away an'...and uh...got then _ Uncle Tom to...got tellin him some places where they'd abeen an'...by an' by Jack said uh..."Uncle Tom do you know what I come over for tonight?"

"I don't know boy" he said _ "what you come for."

"I come over to see if you'd give Mary _ your daughter to...for a wife for me."

"**NO**" he said "I will not." Well _ Jack got up an' went home.

The next morning the girl come over an' she said "What did father say?"

"He said no."

"Well now" she said "you ask un for...you (can)...ask...ask father for me again the night. Ask un three night follying" she said. "See what he'll say." She said "'Tis only a mouth speech anyhow." So anyhow -- next night Jack went over again an' talked a little while. "Uncle Joh[n]...Uncle Tom" he said "have you made up um...your mind for me to marry your daughter?"

"**NO**" he said "I haven't."

So the girl said to un next morning _ "And what did father say last night?"

"He said no."

"Well" she said "ask un for /me/ tonight _ whether he says yes or no.   /her/
An' don't ask no more." So anyhow -- Jack went over the next night, talked to un (a) little spell. "Well Uncle s...Tom" he said "I come over to see if you've made up your mind for me to marry your daughter?"

"**NO**!" [*shouts*] he said "I...I told (you) in the first time."

"Well" Jack said "I...you won't...catch me askin you no more. 'Cause" he said "I'm leavin this place altogether."

So _ over come the girl the next morning. She said "What did father say?"

"He said no."

"Well that's good enough" she said. "You...didn't you tell father you was goin away?"

"Yes" he said.

"Where you goin to?"

"I'm goin to Dublin."

"Now Jack" she said _ "if you're goina Dublin _ ever since" she said "that I was...month old _ my father has aput away so much money for **ME**. An' when I got seventeen years of age he gave it over...over to me for me own. He's still givin me money _ to spend. Now" she said "I'm givin you some money. An' I wants you...for you to buy a place _ an' set up a business for yourself"

Well anyhow Jack started for Dublin. He went to a boarding house where a woman had three daughters an' _ uh he used to be talkin to the youngest one _ a nice bit.

An' she [*Mary*] said "In a twelvemonth an' a day" she said "I'll be there. I'll be to Dublin twelve...in a month...in...a m...twelvemonth an' a day."

Well sir the twelvemonth an' a day...she come. An' she went to this boarding house _ where Jack stayed an' _ she asked where he was to. She said "He's down to his store" she said _ the boardin mistress said. She said "He's goin with my youngest daughter."

"'Twon't make no difference" she said "who the...who he's goin with" she said "I'd like to...I want to see un." So anyhow _ she was dressed in disguise, Jack didn't know her. She come in, she asked for a piece o' goods. Jack took down piece o' goods. That didn't suit her. Took down another piece an' that didn't suit her. Took down another piece. That didn't suit her. Well she went on like that for about twenty minutes. Well Jack said "Nothing I takes down don't suit...'ll...'ll suit ya. What about meself? Will...will I suit ya?" [*laughs*]

"Yes" she said "Jack" an' she slung back her veil. Well well well!...So this...ol' girl [*Mary*] come.

Well three days after that they were married in the church.

Well -- she bought a house -- for 'em to live in. An' _ there was a vessel going to sail to the...to uh...not Slave Islands but uh...ah to the...ah...[*coughs*] [*teller tries hard to remember*] you'll hear it over the radio every night _ to China. Uh...the merchants used to have the...vessels goina China tradin. [*rising intonation seeking agreement from listeners*] Well uh _ anyhow this feller _ had a store an' a vessel of his own an' _ well _ he was gone while Jack was married. So _ anyhow when he come back _ Jack an' he was pretty good friends. Jack went down aboard (an') _ he said "Jack" he said "you're married since I was here last."

"Yes" Jack said "I'm married boy. An' got a...nice little home too."

"Well" he said "I'd bet my ship _ an' cargo _ an' my house an' stores _ an' all the goods is into her _ that I could go up _ an' do what I like with your woman, while she's (asleeping)."

"Well" Jack said "I'll go ya. Everything I'm th' owner of."

Well anyhow the agreement was drawed up an' signed pres[ently]...an' Jack said "I'll stay here till you comes."

Well anyhow away he goes. He goes up an' knockses at Jackses door an' servant girl come an' _ he said "Where's your mistress?"

She said "She's upstairs." She said "What do you want?"

He said "I'll give ya...a big handful o' money _ if you'll show me where that _ woman _ 'll unstrip to go to bed."

"I will" she said "if you don't go handy to her or harm her of...in no kind of way."

"No" he said "I'll promise you that."

"Come upstairs" [*urgent semi-whispered tone*] she says. 'Twas all glass, you could see from one room to the other. Well when she...when he went up ⌐ she gave him a chair to sit down on an' ⌐ Mary was sat down readin ⌐ an' by an' by ten o'clock come.

"Well" she said "I wonder where's John to tonight? He's not home. But he must be with some company. I'll read till half past ten an' I'll go to bed."

So when half past ten come ⌐ she got up an' put up her book an' ⌐ had a look out through the window an' ⌐ went to a chest o' drawers an' took out a...a big nightdress. Well he put down on his pocketbook what kind o' slippers she had on ⌐ what kind of a...dress she had on ⌐ how she had her ⌐ hair done up and ⌐ everything on his pocketbook an' ⌐ and by an' by when she was...when she just start...took out this big ⌐ nightgown ⌐ well she was face towards him. She never had no dress. But anyhow when she went to put on this big nightgown ⌐ here is a big mole ⌐ about a inch from her left breast. An' uh...he see un. He put that on his pocketbook an' ⌐ come downstairs an' the girl let un out an' 'way to go.

"Well" he said "you're married to the commonest thing that ever growed" ⌐ he said. "I never thought a...woman could be so common" he said "as what she is."

Well Jack lost all. Well ⌐ when he lost all ⌐ when he went out...to vessel where they bet to ⌐ here was a vessel goin to Slave Islands. He jumped aboard this vessel an' went in the slavery.

Up comes this feller the next morning an' turned this lady out of her house an' bought up th' house ⌐ 'twas all his. Jack was gone ⌐ didn't know where he was to, she couldn't find out. Well the poor thing she didn't know what to do. So -- she went to work an' she took the road to go in the country. She walked an' walked an' by an' by she come to a farmer's yar[d]...farmer's farm. So she sat down an' had a spell cryin an' ⌐ she got up...an' a hour from that she come to another one. Well she done the same thing. By an' by she come to the third one, gettin late in the evening. Nothing to eat. Frit to death. Ol' farmer was there workin. An' he come around where she stood to the fence, he said um..."Where are you goin?"

"I don't know" she said "I'm lookin for a job. I don't suppose you'll gi' me a job" she said "on your farm?"

"Yes" he said. "But it's better for me" he said "by the look o' ya ⌐ come to YOU to look for a job" he said "than you come to me."

She said "What I got I...I'm stood up in."

"Yes" he said "I'll give ya a...a job carryin the...the rocks" he said "off my field an' put 'em in piles." So..."Come in the house." So he...went in an' said to his wife ⌐ "I got somebody now to carry the rocks off my field. Give her a pan now tomorrow morning an' let her go carryin rocks."

So the poor little girl ⌐ she was carryin rocks next morning and ⌐ an' the next day an' ⌐ dinner time come. An' ⌐ his wife said to her husband she said

…"Isn't you ashamed o' yourself" she said "to see that poor little woman" she said "or girl whatever she might be _ carrying rocks?" she said. "I don't suppose ever she done a stroke o' work in her life."

"Well" he said "you can have her in…in here with you if you wants her _ 'bout the milk an' butter an' _ cheese an' one thing an' the other."

So -- she come out o' the room where she was havin her dinner. "My dear" she said "don't go out in the field no more carryin rocks. Stay in with me." Well she was a mother to her.

Well she worked away an' worked away an' worked away an' her _ dress an' that got so…dirty an' bad onto her she had to take it off an' wash it. An' her shoes is _ broke an' everything else. Never asked un for a dollar, never asked what he was givin.

So by an' by one night _ after she was there so long _ he said to her he said "Mary" he said uh _ "you been here now" he said _ "well up for twelve month" he said "an' you haven't asked me yet for a dollar. Your boots is off o' ya feet."

/many/ "Well now" she said _ "when you thinks _ that I got enough /money/… money made _ to buy a sailor suit from top to bottom _ to go to sea" she said "that's what I wants."

"Well [if] that's the case" he said "I'll go to town an' buy it…buy it for you this evening. I knows what you wants." Took the measure of her, her heighth an' _ size of her foot an' everything, away he goes. Well she went to the barber an' got her hair trimmed _ like a boy an' _ so she went to the…the office _ to get a chance cook _ into a vessel. Well the owner said "I got a vessel" he said "goin to uh…China" he said "an' I'm havin a new one built for un [*the captain*] _ the other one is gettin old. An' his cook _ they don't know what time he got to go to hospital but he been with him this couple times. He might have to stop in this time." He said "What's your name?" So she told un her name. Her name was Bill White. An' uh _ anyhow _ she went up an' she…to this boarding house. An' there's where she stopped. He told her…he said uh…so th' ol' feller [*the owner*] give her s[ome]…bit o' money for pay her board.

So anyhow by an' by the vessel come in. An' the cook had to go to th' hospital. So _ when the captain come up to the owners _ before he went to customs he said "How is the cook?"

"Oh" he said "our cook is (sick) he's…he'll never sail with me again. He's too sick."

"Well" he said "I got a young man" he said "cook now _ waitin for ya." Anyhow sont after un. Down he comes an' gets aboard the vessel, cook. Well anyhow she cooked away an' cooked away an' by an' by the day come for her to sail. Well they sailed an' they went to…to uh…Spain. An' _ well _ everybody's…the cook seemed such a nice little man they all took

wonderful fancy to un. But anyhow this /time/...this time _ when they got
back th' old [*untrans.*]...th' /owner/ says "Now" he said "captain _ the next
trip _ we'll have the new vessel _ ready for you to sail in."

    Well -- away they goes _ to Spain again. An' 'tis a LOVELY fine
day...twelve o'clock, sh[e]...she was only one on...on the deck at twelve
o'clock see. Well she had all the navigation that woman t...could get. So she
went down an' to...got the navigatin gear and _ come out an' took the sun
an' took what depth the water was in under her an' _ where they was to an'
everything an' put [it] on a big paper an' left there _ on the cabin. So
_ when the...uh the...captain come back _ the first man come to take the
wheel _ course she went on _ down the forecastle again _ dry up the dishes
an' have her dinner.

    So anyhow -- when the captain come back he seen this paper an' he took
it up an' _ sung out to the mate to come. "Well mate" he said "'tis a lot better
for you to be captain _ than 'tis mate." He said "I never knowed you had
uh...the navigation you got."

    "Well captain" he said "that's not me. I wish I could do it."

    Well now the captain said "I thought I had very good navigation. But
there's a man aboard of her he got better...got better education" he said
"than me." He said _ "Look! The depth o' water where we're to! [*laughs*]
What part o' worl[d]...world we're in!" Huh! [*laughs*] "Everything" he said.
"Well" he said "'tis wonderful."

    "Well we don't know what our crew can do."

    So they called up one an' "No sir 'twasn't me."

    "No sir 'twasn't me."

    "No sir 'twasn't me."

    So the mate said..."Captain the only one was on the deck _ at twelve
o'clock" he said "was our cook." And he.../he/ said "We don't...we don't
know what kind of a man our cook is. He's a nice little man anyhow." So
uh...anyhow begar -- he sont after the...the cook [to] come back aft, he want
un. Cook went back an' _ he said "Cook" he said "was it you picked out the
vessel twelve o'clock?"

    "Yes" he said "Captain but I didn't do no offence did I?"

    "Oh no" he said "my man!" he said. "'Stead on you COOK" he said "you
should be uh...the captain of one of the biggest ones sails. A man with the
navigation you got. They havin a new...vessel built for ME" he said _ "this
time when we gets back. But" he said "I'll tell...the owners to give that
vessel to you. An' I'll still keep th' ol' one."

    Well -- that's what he done. Well when the...he went _ up to
the...owners _ they told un they had the vessel all ready an' _ crew an'
all for her. "Well now" /he/ says "give that vessel _ the...to ah...my...our
cook _ for he's a wonderful man." Says "I don't suppose there's a man in the
world got any better...navigation" he said "[than] what he got." So he told

/tads/
/ol' captain/

/she/

/they/

479

/he/
/you/

th' owners what he done an' _ "Well" /they/ said "that's up to you. If you're willin for him to take the...new vessel _ /he/ can take un."

So -- when he got to...captain come after him an' there's...they went down to the new vessel an' the two crowds [i.e., *crews*] was stuck up together an'...and uh...mate said to un "Captain" _ he says "you goina give him a chance to pick his crew?"

"Well now" he [*the new captain*] said "it...I'm 'cquainted with our own ship's crew" he said. "But any man like to go with me hold up their hand" all th' ol' ship's crew [*laughs*] hold up their [*laughs*] hand. "Oh no" he said. "Uh we'll divide 'em, you...I'll take half an' yous...th' ol' captain take the other half."

So -- when he got aboard o' the vessel that night this...a man come aboard. An' he said uh..."Captain" [*laughs*] he said "you got a new vessel."

"Yes" he said.

"Well now" he said "when you comes in the next time" he said "I'm goina tell you a story. I'm goina tell you a story" he said "how I trick[ed] [*laughs*] a feller...what come here an' got married to a girl. A twelvemonth...afterwards she come. An'...he bet everything he was th' owner of an' so did I" _ he said. "An' when I...an' when you comes in next time" he said "I'll come down your cabin, tell ya the whole yarn. An'" he said "I...I've served un that bad" he said "he jumped aboard of a vessel, went to Slave Islands." Well THEN she knowed where Jack was gone an' wind was northeast _ fair wind to Slave Islands.

So -- stuck up his sails an' _ an' away he goes for s...for uh...Slave Islands. Went up to chief o' the slavery an' _ they ask what he want, he say he want to buy a man. Said "What slave do you want to buy?" Now the...Jack's hair was all down...round his neck an' his shirt was tore up an' _ oh uh...[*laughs*] a eye-sight to look at. So _ he said "I'll have that one there."

"I'll give him you...I'll give you that man" he said "for two hundred dollars." So she paid two hundred dollars for the slave and...and uh...went aboard. She went to the stateroom _ opened the door, she said "Go in there. An' DON'T come out no more" she said "'fore I tells ya." [*commanding tone*] She said "Your food 'll be brought to ya" she said. "An' water be brought for ya to wash. But don't [let] me see ya in this cabin." Poor Jack was frightened to death.

So -- when they got in...uh the...Dublin _ not Dublin but uh...China _ she said to ol' captain she said "Captain this one sails almost twice as fast as th' ol' one. Suppose I got to keep...keep me mainsail down all the time _ I wants for you to get in the harbour to...when I gets _ 'cause I'm goina have a story told to me _ an' I wants for you to be there to listen to un."

"Alright" says the captain. So anyhow that's what they done.

480

So — when they got in harbour ‒ she opened the stateroom door. Jack's hair an' whiskers, oh he was a awful sight. She said "Set down there ‒ on that locker. An' here's a revolver" she said "an' when I says 'Fire!' you fire. Suppose you [i.e., *however*] don't aim to kill. If you don't" she says "**I'LL** aim to kill with this...this one that I got in **MY**...hand" she said. Poor Jack was frightened almost to death. Didn't know what was to become of un.

So after supper down comes this...this captain ‒ what had all the stuff. "Well captain" he said "I'm comin to tell you the story." He said "There was a feller come here to...an sot up business" he said "an' ‒ after a while" he said ‒ "his wife come ‒ 'bout a...twelvemonth afterwards ‒ twelvemonth an' a day or something like that. So" he said ‒ "but after they were married a little spell I went down aboard an' I offered to bet my ship an' cargo ‒ an'...house an' store an' goods an' everything that I got ‒ again his store ‒ an' house what his wife had abought ‒ that I'd go up an' do ‒ what I like with her ‒ an' bring...back witness that I done it." So Jack now was listenin to this. But he didn't know who the captain was. He'd only hear this...this one...feller tellin it.

So — he said "I give the girl" he said "a handful o'...o' gold ‒ an' she showed me her [*Mary's*] room ‒ an' she was settin down readin. And" he said uh..."he was settin down readin...she was settin down readin" she said "an' ten o' clock come. So she got up an' she looked out she says she supposed John was...with...company that night. But she'd read till half past ten an' go to bed." So as...she said...he said uh..."When half past ten come she...got up an' ‒ took out a big nightdress out of a chest of drawers an' ‒ she was standin right awards me" he said. "An' when she p[ut]...went to put un on ‒ I...here I spies a mole" he said "in under her left breast 'bout ‒ half inch or a inch from un. I leaved. But when I told her husband 'bout that...mole on her left breast ‒ '**DAMN** the women!' [*laughs*] You uh... [*laughs*] you...couldn't trust one!"

"**FIRE!**" she said. So he fired an' he broke his [*the other captain's*] leg. "Now gentlemen" she said um...to the captain an' all what was there "I'm not a man at all, I'm a woman. Now that's my husband. Now you see how I was served? Just be[cause] o' that man's dirt."

So ‒ anyhow ‒ Jack got...[*laughs*] he lost everything he had an' Jack got it all an' they ‒ come back an' lived in their own house an' after I left ‒ I had to come an'...call Miss Mary Polly Kenny an' ‒ here I'm tellin you the yarn.

[Int: Where did you get that story?]
Hey?
[Int: Where did you get that story?]
Uh...oh uh...fellers tellin stories out of a book see, readin it out of a book.
[Int: Hm-hm.]

481

I just heard it read, that's all I done.
[Int: Hm-hm. Where was [*recorder off*]*** do you know?]
Hey?
[*recorder off*]*** long ago?
[Int: Yeah.]
Oh...I could have been married an' I may not be married.
[Int: Where were you living then?]
I was livin to Woody Point, Bonne Bay.
[Int: Woody Point, Bonne Bay. Mm-hm. Do you...you...'member the name of the fellow who was readin the story?]
Ah...yes. I knows his name if I...he's a Frenchman. Uh...John...Deluney.
[*recorder off*] [Int: ***was readin it.]
Oh yes.
[Int: Mm-hm.]
Well he could read...you could understand un readin.
[Int: Mm-hm.]

Duration: 27 min., 45 sec.
Source: John Deluney, Woody Point, Bonne Bay, Great Northern Peninsula.
Location: Interviewers' car, en route from Sally's Cove to St. Pauls.
Audience: Interviewers.

Context, Style, and Language: John Roberts told us stories at his son's house during the morning but when it became obvious that the midday meal was almost ready we made our excuses, and arranged to return in the afternoon to record him again. When we got back, however, he came in carrying his jacket and said he was ready to go with us to St. Pauls. We had made no arrangements to do this but agreed to take him. It later turned out that, among other things, he wanted to attend a funeral at St. Pauls. As soon as he was in the car he began to tell a long and involved romantic story and as we had time to spare we stopped for a while so we could listen to the story and see if he knew others. We asked if he knew any other tales about Jack and he immediately launched into this narrative even though he had not finished the rambling love story which he had been telling before we stopped the car.

John Roberts' response to our inquiries about the source of the story are not entirely convincing. Perhaps under the pressure of questioning, he seems to be casting around for the name of the man from whom he learned it. However, when the name comes into his mind he seems reasonably sure of it, and this surname, a variant of the French *Delaunay,* is known in the neighboring Humber West electoral district (E. R. Seary, *Family Names of the Island of Newfoundland*).

It is interesting to note that Jack is portrayed here for the most part as a patient, unaggressive, uncontentious fellow, although he insists on paying his way to school and later firmly refuses to go there after he is seventeen. Even so it is clearly Mary who plays the dominant role in the decision-making before Jack leaves for Dublin.

Although this tale was recorded in the interviewers' car, the recording quality is quite good. Transcription, however, was difficult at times because of the noise of vehicles passing by. There are also a number of misencodings, as for example when the teller confuses pronouns and their referents, but these do not detract from the narrative which is animated and compelling. The delivery is mostly fluent and clear, and the untranscribed material largely consists of single words or short phrases where misencodings occur. In the narration Mr. Roberts skillfully employs contrasting tones of voice, especially in the dialogue, ranging from an urgent whisper to loud commands, with many subtle variations in between. For instance, he conveys a sense of great admiration in the comments on the achievements of the disguised Mary when she is the cook on board the vessel: "He's a wonderful man," etc., and registers a strong feeling of shock and dismay in the disapprobatory pharyngeal tones of "Jack's hair an' whiskers, oh he was a awful sight." There is excitement and urgency in the half-whispered invitation to the captain to "Come upstairs," and Jack's quiet resignation and patience are clearly shown in the tone of the few words he says when he decides to go to Dublin after Mary's father refuses to allow him to marry her. Thus the skillful manipulation of vocal contrast contributes significantly to characterization and to influencing the audience's response. Individual words are also strongly stressed for rhetorical effect, and a sharply rising sentence final intonation contour in *vessels goina China tradin* (vessels going to China, trading), solicits the audience's assurance that they are following what is being said.

The passage of time, as in several other tales in this collection, is suggested by the repetition of a verb, e.g., *they sailed together an' sailed together, She walked an' walked, she worked away an' worked away an' worked away, she cooked away and cooked away*. The impression of time passing is often heightened by the phrase *by an' by* immediately following, which suggests that a considerable time has elapsed. More formulaic triple repetition is found, for example, in Jack's taking down of three pieces of goods in his store at Mary's request, implying that he took down many more over a period of some twenty minutes. A similar formula is to be found in the repetition of the crewmen's denials when asked if they had *picked out the vessel* (plotted the position of the ship): "No sir 'twasn't me," again said three times but implying a much greater number. The end formula, by contrast, is spoken as a continuous run, punctuated only by very brief pauses.

In addition to the forms commented on under No. 34, "The King's Son," dialectal pronunciations include *follyin* (following) and the short front vowel in *keep* /kip/; as in much Newfoundland speech *tonight* is pronounced *the night,* and *(?)into slavery* is pronounced here as *in the slavery*—a basic problem of transcription. The vowel of the definite article is elided in *th' only, th' owner, th' ol',* final /n/ of the indefinite article is omitted in *a awful sight,* aphesis occurs in *'fore, 'Cause, 'way* (away), *'bout, 'stead on* (instead of), *'cquainted* (acquainted), and the initial vowel is lost in *'Twon't, 'Twas.* Of lexical interest are the nautical expressions *gets aboard* (gets into [the car]), *stowed away* (arranged, taken care of, put away), and *sung out* (called, shouted), along with dialectal *boy* as a term of familiar address, *mouth speech* ([?superficial] speech, [?as

483

distinct from heartfelt speech]; cf. *EDD MOUTH*, 14, and *OED Mouth*, sb., 20a), *I'll go ya* (I'll bet you), *unstrip* (strip; cf. *OED Unstrip*), the archaic *heighth* (height), *put up* (put down, put away [a book]), *'way to go* (off he went), *went to work* (set to work, began), the combination *off of* in *off o' ya feet*, *picked out* (plotted [the position of the ship]), *crowds* (crews), the verb *want* plus *for* in *I wants for*, *eye-sight* ([unpleasant] sight; cf. *EDD EYE* 2, 20), *set[tin]* (sit[ting]), *again* (against), *awards* (towards). Archaic inflections include *knockses* (knocks), *Jackses* (Jack's), the present tense first and second verb forms *gets, comes, thinks, wants, is(n't)*, the third person plural present/?past tense form *they's gone*, the past tense forms *you/they was, been, leaved, come, growed, done, sont* (sent), *sung out, knowed, want, sot* (set), the present participle *asleeping* and the past participles *abeen, aput, frit* (frightened), *broke, abought*. Note also the past participle form in *was sat down*, and the double negatives *'Twon't make no difference, never had no dress, don't go out in the field no more*, and *didn't do no offence*.

See also the notes to No. 36.

Type and Motifs:

AT882. *The Wager on the Wife's Chastity.*
T69.2. *Parents affiance children without their knowledge.*
T97. *Father opposed to daughter's marriage.*
N831. *Girl as helper.*
K1821.3. *Disguise by veiling face.*
Cf. K1814. *Woman in disguise wooed by her faithless husband.*
N15. *Chastity wager.*
N2.5. *Whole kingdom (all property) as wager.*
K2252. *Treacherous maidservant.*
K2112.1. *False tokens of woman's unfaithfulness.*
K92. *Gambling contest won by deception.*
Cf. R61. *Person sold into slavery.*
K1837. *Disguise of woman in man's clothes.*
F679. *Remarkable skill—miscellaneous [woman skilled as navigator].*
R152. *Wife rescues husband.*
Cf. J1141. *Confession obtained by a ruse.*
Q261. *Treachery punished.*
Z10.2. *End formula.*

International Parallels: Scholarly interest in the sources of both Boccaccio's *Decameron* and Shakespeare's *Cymbeline* has provided information on many earlier literary analogues to the bet on the wife's chastity as well as to the wide distribution of the theme in folk narrative.

What has interested us in our examination of the folk narrative parallels to our Newfoundland tales in English or English translation (we have not found any published English language versions from North America) is to learn what kinds of evidence the villain produces which convince the husband that his wife was unfaithful. The evidence may be a description of the bedroom; production of such articles as the wife's personal jewelry and/or intimate garments such as her garter or nightgown; or even one or more of her husband's possessions which are in her keeping, such as his signet ring. More telling, however, is the villain's knowledge about some distinctive and uniquely personal physical feature such as gold hairs on her navel, or a mole on some part of her body, which modesty would normally conceal from all except her husband.

We also investigated how the incriminating objects and personal information were secured. In Hispanic American and also in some European versions, the villain bribes some old woman (witch, sorceress, hag) to devise a way of getting into the house to steal the objects and to learn of the wife's secret physical features. In other tales the villain, usually with the help of an old woman or a suborned maid, gets himself taken into the house, frequently in some container, and steals the objects and/or observes the undressed wife.

In Synge's Aran Islands version the villain bribes the old hag who sleeps in a big box in the wife's room to let him occupy the box, and he watches the wife through a hole in the box. In the English Gypsy version in Briggs, he is taken into the wife's room in a chest of drawers. In Groome's Bukovina Gypsy version, at the old woman's suggestion he has a chest made with a window in it, through which he sees the mole under the wife's right breast. This version is closest to the "showcase" of the Newfoundland recensions.

When the husband accepts the false evidence that he has lost his bet, he either tries to kill his wife and thinks he has succeeded, or orders that she be killed. He usually has to give up his property and work as a laborer, or else he becomes a tramp. We have found no parallels to the Newfoundland versions of his becoming a slave. There are, however, widespread parallels to the rescued wife's putting on male clothes and becoming a resounding success either as a male warrior or in any other masculine occupation she undertakes. Her intelligence, courage, and general superiority to most men are stressed in nearly all versions of the tale.

There are many different ways in which she obtains the proof that the trickster used false evidence to win the bet with her husband. Frequently the admission of guilt is made in a court of law with the husband present to hear the revelation. Occasionally the wife in her male garb gets the trickster to confess. In the Irish version in Larminie the admission is made before witnesses; in Campbell's Scottish version the husband is present, sitting on top of the stairs writing down the confession. In many versions both the trickster and his female accomplice are executed; in others they are jailed.

The only version resembling the Newfoundland form, a pistol being used in the dénouement, is again the tale from the Aran Isles. Here the maligned wife, who is not in male disguise, arranges for all the characters involved in the tale to meet and to tell their stories. The villainous sea captain agrees to tell his story only when the wife threatens to shoot him dead if he refuses to talk. When he confesses what he has done, the wife does not kill him, but instead she shoots the old hag who had betrayed her trust. In the Newfoundland version, however, it is the trickster who is shot, but the faithless servant girl, who has accepted his bribe reluctantly, remains unpunished and does not figure in the story again.

Ranke draws attention to a different and apparently older version of the theme of the wager on the wife's chastity. In this the villain approaches a woman he thinks is the wife, seduces her, and cuts off her finger with a ring on it as proof of the seduction. Although he has apparently won the bet, he is later proved to have failed when the real wife shows that her hands are unmaimed and reveals that another woman was substituted for her when the supposed seduction took place. In Great Britain this form of the tale is found in two literary versions, one in the Welsh *Mabinogion* and the other in a Scottish ballad.

Studies and Notes

Child, *Ballads*, 5, pp. 21-25, no. 268, headnote, and p. 23, note; Lee, *Sources*, pp. 42-57 (Day II, Novel 9); Bolte and Polívka, 3, p. 92, n. 1; Thompson, *The Folktale*, pp. 108-9; Ranke, *Folktales*, pp. 213-14, no. 38, notes; Spencer, *Stories*, pp. 25-28; Robe, *Index*, Type 882, pp. 141-42.

Canada

Lacourcière, Index, cites 33 Francophone versions of AT882 from Canada: 14 (New Brunswick), 18 (Quebec), 1 (Ontario).

United States

Fowke, *Folktales*, pp. 40-42, no. 7, trans. from French text in Barbeau, *JAF* 30 (1917), 123-25, heard from a French Canadian (Massachusetts).

Cf. Parsons, *Islands*, 1, pp. 177-80, no. 57 (with 315, 590), English trans. of Portuguese text, Cape Verde Islands, black (Massachusetts).

Zunser, *JAF* 48 (1935), 160, no. 4, Spanish tradition, in English (New Mexico).

Espinosa, *Folk-Tales*, p. 212, no. 70, English summary of Spanish text (New Mexico).

Parsons, *Tales*, pp. 141-47, no. 78, 2 versions, Taos Pueblo Indians (New Mexico).

Rael, *Cuentos*, pp. 659-60, 3 versions, English summaries of Spanish texts, no. 130 (New Mexico), no. 131 (Colorado), no. 132 (New Mexico).

Mexico

Aiken, *PTFS* 32 (1964), 8-12 (Chihuahua), and rpt. in Aiken, *Folktales*, pp. 115-19.

Foster, *Folklore and Beliefs*, pp. 233-34, no. 41, Sierra Popoluca Indian (Veracruz).

Parsons, *JAF* 45 (1932), 300-304, no. 13 (Oaxaca).

Wheeler, *Tales*, pp. 171-74, no. 71, pp. 174-81, no. 72, 2 versions, Spanish texts with English summaries (Jalisco).

The Caribbean and South America

Parsons, *Antilles*, 3, pp. 254-55, no. 254, English summary of French text, black (Trinidad).

Pino-Saavedra, *Folktales*, pp. 189-94, no. 37, with useful notes (Chile).

See Hansen, *Types*, Type 882, for reference to a text from the Dominican Republic.

See Robe, *Index*, Type 882, for reference to a text from Panama.

England

Briggs, *Dictionary*, A2, pp. 451-52, summary of unpublished text from *Thompson Notebooks*, Gypsy (England).

Shakespeare, *Cymbeline*, literary (England). For discussion see Spencer, *Stories*, pp. 25-28.

Wales
Cf. Guest, *Mabinogion,* pp. 267-81, "Taliesin," literary (Wales), and for a later trans. see Ford, *The Mabinogi,* pp. 167-77, "The Tale of Taliesin."

Scotland
Campbell, *Popular Tales,* 2, pp. 1-15, no. 18 (with 890), Gaelic text and English trans. (Islay).
Cf. Child, *Ballads,* 5, pp. 21-28, Child no. 268, "The Twa Knights," literary (Scotland), see discussion in headnote and further important parallels, p. 23, footnote.

Ireland
Larminie, *Folk-Tales,* pp. 115-29 (with cf. 611) (Co. Donegal).
Hunt, *Breffny,* pp. 47-64, no. 6 (Co. Cavan).
Ó Duilearga, *Béal.* 29 (1961), 144, no. 8 (with 890), English summary of Irish text (Co. Cork).
Ó Duilearga, *Béal.* 30 (1962), 53-56, no. 10 (Co. Clare).
Synge, *Aran Islands,* pp. 40-46 (with 890) (Co. Galway).
Irish Types, Type 882, 80 versions.

Continental Europe and Asia
Hodne, *Types,* AT882, 2 versions (Norway).
Webster, *Legends,* pp. 132-36 [bribed witch gets into house and steals wife's gold chain, which trickster uses as "proof"] (Basque).
Boccaccio, *Decameron,* pp. 117-27 (Day II, Novel 9), literary (Italy), see also the 1620 English trans. in Spencer, *Stories,* pp. 161-75.
Ranke, *Folktales,* pp. 90-94, no. 38, with useful notes, German (Czechoslovakia).
Groome, *Folk-Tales,* pp. 121-24, no. 33, with notes, Gypsy (Bukovina).
Dawkins, *MGAM,* pp. 438-41, no. 8, and p. 237, notes, Greek dialect text and English trans. (Turkey).
Cf. Afanas'ev, *Fairy Tales,* pp. 415-18 [girl maligned *before* marriage] (Russia).
Cf. Natesa Sastri, *Folk-Tales,* pp. 409-34, no. 38 (with 891) (Madras, India).
See Thompson and Roberts, *Types,* Type 882, for another Indian reference.

The Philippines
Fansler, *Tales,* pp. 248-57, no. 30, with notes.

46. JACK AND THE SLAVE ISLANDS[†]

Freeman Bennett
St. Pauls, Great Northern Peninsula
18 July 1970

AT882
TC964 71-50
Collectors: HH and Helen Halpert

Yeah.
[Int: What song are you going to sing?]
I don't know.

[Int: Yeah. You got a story you want to tell?]

Yes. I can tell ya a little story alright.

[Int: Alright.]

[*clears throat*] I can tell a little story well uh _ once upon a time ya know that's in _ olden times that's away back uh _ not in our days at all. That's uh...that was before Newfoundland was discovered. Well er...at them times see there...there was a rich man _ an' a poor man. Well _ he...he didn't want uh...the...his daughter _ to marry this **POOR** man. He didn't want that at all. He want er...his daughter to marry a rich man. Well very good. Now _ he had a servant there well he was a poor man. Well uh...now his daughter was gettin around with un. Well uh...the ol' feller got hold to it, well _ he was goin to turn un away. 'Cause he...he didn't want his daughter to marry un anyhow 'cause uh...he was too poor a man for her. Well uh...he turned un away. Well she decided _ she got fifty thousand dollars _ an' she carried [it] to un. "Now" she said "you take that fifty thousand dollars _ an' go to the States _ an' _ buy a...buy some land _ an' build a house an' start a business. An' when you gets it _ /fully/ under [way] _ I'll come. An' we'll be married."

Very good he took the fifty thousand dollars an' away he goes.* He went to the States an' he bought a...bought some land. An' _ he build his house. An' he start this...his business. Well uh...now the people 's around there uh...there wasn't so many people in the States as there was then...there was...there was now. An' uh the people around now well _ he was doin so good _ he was doin so good, well he took all the whole sway o' the place see. Well now they didn't like it. 'Cause he'd acome from...he belonged to England an' he come from England an' took the...the whole sway o' Americky well _ didn't like it, he uh...he was...had ships goin everywhere. Well she come _ an' they got married. Well now he had his uh...ships goin he had uh...three ships and _ he had they goin uh...one place to the other an' uh...one day the...all the ships got in together. An' this man uh...he went down on the pier, all his ships was in. An' _ he was walkin around on the pier an' talkin about uh...one thing an' another an' by an' by uh...he brought it up about the...women _ one feller did.

"Well" he said "I got a good woman." He said "There was never a wo...better woman borned" he said "than I got."

"Hm!" [*derisive tone*] he said "you got a good woman" he said "that's what **YOU** thinks!"

He said "Yes" he said "that's what I thinks." He said "An' I'll put up everything" he said "I got" _ he said "against it" he said "if you...you can find out anything about my woman." He said "An' I'll go aboard the ships an' stay tonight." Well very good he went aboard the ships an' stayed.

/ally/

*teller's wife coughs

Well now _ just about dark _ this feller goes up to his house. An' he knocked on the door _ an' the servant girl come out _ an' she opened the door. Asked un what he want. An' he said uh..."Will you put me in the...the...the missus's room" _ he said "behind the showcase?"

She said "No." She said "I won't do it."

"Well" he said "I give you two hundred dollars" he says "[if] you (only) put me in there."

"Well" she said "two hundred dollars" she said "a lot to turn down." An' _ she said "Yes" she said "I'll put ya in there." Very good she pay...she put un in the room _ behind the showcase. Well now _ when time come to go to bed she [*the wife*] went up...stairs _ up in her room. An' she undressed. An' _ she got in the bed, now she had a mole _ right under her left breast. Well now she got in the bed. Well now he was behind the showcase. Well now he...he seen this mole. An' uh _ after she got to sleep _ uh the servant girl _ let un out again. An' he went out.

Well now in the morning he walked down in the pier again an' uh...this feller come out. "Now" he said uh..."what can ya tell me" he said "about my woman?"

He said "I knows" he said "all I wants to know." [*quiet, knowing tone*]

He said "Well" he said "what do ya know?"

"Well" he said "for one thing" he said "your woman" he said "got a mole in under her left breast."

"Well" he said "God damn all women!" He said "You can take everything I got" _ he said "an' I'll go to the Slave Islands." Well very good.

He [*the winner of the bet*] went up _ an' he turned her out o' the house. Turned her out of her house. Now she didn't know what had happened see? She didn't know what happened. He turned her out of her house. Well now she was out on the street. An' she had nowhere to go. She didn't know what become of her husband _ an' what uh...what happened for he [*the winner of the bet*] come an' drive her out. Well uh...she was walkin along the street an' she...she walked up through the streets through the buildings an' _ she thought to herself well uh...the only chance she had is to go to...some door or 'nother see the...would they want ar servant girl.

So she went up to...one feller's door an' she knocked to the door. He come out an' he opened the door. An' uh...he bid her time o' day. An' ask her what she want. She said "I suppose" she said "you don't want nar servant girl?"

He said "Yes" he said "I wants a servant girl." He said "But I don't want YOU." He said "By the look o' you" he said "you got more money" he said "than I got."

She said "I got nothing" she says "only just what I'm standin in." An' then she up an' told him the story.

"Oh well" he said uh…"'cordin to that" he said "yes" he said "I'll take ya."

She said "I don't know where me husband is to" uh…she said "or I don't know what happened." An' she said "I got no place to go."

"Well" he said "I take ya in." Well he took her in there an' she was..soundin around an' see could she find out uh…what happened. An' uh…she couldn't find nothing out. An' she was there about _ a month. An' she said to him one day she said _ "If I had a suit o' sailor's clothes" _ she said "I'd uh…I'd put it on" she said "an' get me hair cutted off" _ she said "an' try to get a…cook aboard o' some o' the…the…the boats."

"Well" he said "I can get ya a suit o' sailor's clothes."

She said "I aint got no money to buy it."

"Well" he said "I'll buy it for ya."

Well he went an' he bought her a…suit o' clothes. An' she clipped her hair off. "Now" he said "I'll go down" he said "the ships is in." He said "I'll go down" he says "an' see" he said "he…if I can get a chance _ for you [to be] cook."

She said "Yes" she said "that's what I wants."

Well he went down. An' he walked out on the pier an' uh…one o' the captains was ashore there an' he said "Captain" he said "I suppose" he said uh…"you wouldn't want a cook?"

An' he said "Yes" he said "that's what I'm lookin for."

"Well now" he said "I got a man up there" he said "so good a cook" he said "you can't get no better cook" he said _ "I don't care where you goes." He said "You can't get no better cook than he is."

"Well" _ he said "tell un to come down" he said "I'll sign un on." He went up an' he told her. She went down. And _ she went aboard _ cook.

Well they went…they went out. They went out an' they was out for…a couple o' weeks. An' uh…by an' by it come dinner time. An' _ she called 'em down to their…their…to their dinner. An' they come down to their dinner an' 'twas a nice day _ an' she went up on deck. An' when she went up on deck _ the captain had everything _ on the cabin _ what he used to take the sun with see? All his charts an' everything.* Well now _ she goes to work _ 'twas a…'twas a…a foggy day _ she goes to work an' she took the sun _ an' how much water was in under _ an' how…how far we were…how far they was from land. An' she took it all. And she wrote it down see. Well now _ she went down in the…uh forecastle again. Well the captain come up. An' when he come up this is the first thing he seen. An' he looked at it. An' _ he called the mate over he said "Mate" he said "did you do that?"

He said "No" he said "Captain" he said "I never done it." He called all the sailors over. No _ nobody never done it. "Well" he said "someone had

*loud noise—
stove rattling

490

to do it." He said "I never done it." He said "Someone had to do it" he said "an' there's a smarter man aboard her" he said "than I is meself."

An' _ one o' the sailors said he said "Captain" he said uh…"that cook you got…we got down there" he said uh…"he seems like a wonderful smart man. HE might have adone it."

An' uh…captain said "Call un up." He called un up. An' he said "Cook" he said "did you do that?"

An' cook said "Yes" he said "I done it." He said "I been out" he said "about two weeks" he said "well gee" he said "I never asked" he said "where we was to." He said "Or how far we was from land" he said "or nothing" he said "an' I seen it all there on the cabin" he said "an' I didn't think" he said "'twas any harm" he said uh…"to take the sun."

"Not a bit" he said. "Not a bit. But my dear man" he said "you shouldn't be cookin." He said "You should be captain." He said "You're a smarter man" he said "than I is. Now" he said "when we goes back" _ he said "there's uh…another ship" he said "for me" _ he said "I'm supposed to take. Well" he said "I'll keep this one _ an'" he said "I'll give you that one" _ he said "when we goes back." Alright. Good enough.

So _ when they went back _ they was gone about a month _ when they got back _ they got back to…to the pier. Well all his ships got in. Well now this feller come down on the…come down on the pier see. An' he started in to tell his story _ how he got this stuff. An' he up uh…he told part of it. "Now" he said _ "when yous comes in the next time" he said "I'll tell yous the story." An' _ well now _ she was _ (?that was chasin her /thoughts/),   /draw/ she was kind o' thinkin now she was goin to find out where he was to see?

Well very good she took the…she took the other ship. An' they went out. Now they was keepin in companies _ an' uh…come thick [i.e., *foggy*]. An' uh…she lost sight of un. An' uh…he said uh…he said to the mate _ he said "I'd like to go" he said "to the Slave Islands."

An' uh…"Well" the mate said "if you'd like to go to the Slave Islands" he said "you're captain" he said "you can go I suppose."

And uh…"Well" he said "we'll go." Now she found out this is where her husband was to, to the Slave Islands.

Well they went to the Slave Islands. An' _ he went ashore _ an' he went to the head man o' the place. An' he said "Have you got a feller here" he said "by the name o' John? JACK" he said "we always called un but" he said uh…"John his name is."

He said "Yes" he said "he's here."

"Well" she said "I wants un."

"Oh no" he said "you can't have un." He said "He's one o' the best men" he said "I got here." He said "An' he's uh…he's the head man" he said "over the slaves." He said "An' I couldn't part with un."

"Well" she said "I got to have un." She said "I got to have un" she said "I'll give ya five hundred dollars" she said "if you'll gi' me that man."

"Well" he said "five hundred dollars" he says "is a lot to turn down." An' he said "If you'll gi' me five hundred dollars" he said "you...you can take un." So very good. He went off then an' he [*Jack*] come down.

Well now he didn't know her see. He didn't know her but sh...she knowed he soon as he come. Well she took un, she carried un aboard. An' she put un in...she locked un up in a room. "Now" she said "you stay there" _ she said "till I...takes ya out." An' now he still didn't know her an' didn't know what they was goin to do with un. Away he goes. Now the other...the other captain, the other ship _ got in a day the...day before un see. An' when he got in _ when he come in the...captain said to un he said "What happened" he said uh..."what happened" he said "for ya to be so long?"

He said "I got off o' me course." He said "Come thick" he said "an' I got off o' me course" he said "an' I was a long spell" he said "'fore I picked meself up [i.e., *got my bearings*]." He said "An' uh...that hove me behind."

He said "Yes" he said uh..."that's right." An' _ well now _ down comes this feller. When they got the...an' she went down below. An' she went to the room _ an' she _ took a revolverd. An' she said "Now" she said "take this revolverd" _ she said "an' come up on deck 'long wi' me." She said "An' when I tells you to fire" she said "you fire." Well now he STILL didn't know what she was goin to do see.

An' _ down comes this man an' _ "Now" he said "I promised to tell yous the story, well" he said "I'll tell yous the story now" he said _ "yous is _ here together" he said "I'll tell yous the story" he said "how I come with all that stuff. Well now" he said "this man" he said uh..."Jack his name was" he said "he come from this uh...from England" _ he said "an' he start the business here. Well" he said "he went ahead" he said "like a house afire." He said "An' he had ships goin everywhere. Well" he said "he walked down on the pier one day. And _ he was talkin about his woman." He said "An'...had a good woman." An' he said 'Yes' /I/ said 'that's what YOU thinks.'

'Why' he said 'what do you know about her?'

/I/ said 'I don't know nothing' /I/ said 'but I...I can know something.'

"Well" he said "well" he said "he put up everything he had" _ he said "against it." He said "An' I went up _ an' he went aboard the ships" _ he said "an' I went up" _ he said "to his house." He said "I knocked to his door. An' the servant girl come out. An' I ask her" he said "would she put me in the showcase. An' she told me no. And..." he said 'well' he said uh...'I'll give ya two hundred dollars if ya only put me in the showcase.' 'Well' she said _ 'two hundred dollars is a lot to turn down.' She said 'I'll put ya in there.'

/he/

/he/ /he/

492

"Well" he says "she's uh...she put me in the showcase." He said "An' the...the lady come up" he said "an' undressed" /he/ said "an' got in bed. Well" he said "she had a mole under her left breast. Now" he said "I don't...didn't know no more about the woman" he said "'an* [i.e., *than*] YOUS knows." He said "I didn't know nothing about her." He said "All I seen was this mole" he said "under her left breast. Well now" he said _ "I went down" _ he said "an' uh...servant girl let me out" he said "an' I went down" he said "next morning, well uh...he come up an' he asked me what did I know about his woman. An' he said 'Well' he said 'I knows all I wants to know.' He said uh...'Sh...your woman' he said 'got a mole' he said 'under her left breast.'

'Well' he said 'God damn all the women!' He said I'll...take everything I had' he said 'an' I'll go to the Slave Islands.'

Now" he said "I don't know no...didn't know more of un...know more about his woman" he said "'an...'an [i.e., *than*] yous knows."

"Now" she said "fire!" An' he fired. An' he killed un.

An' he got his place back again. As soon as he fired well uh...she told un who she was.

[Int: In other words he'd been blaming it...bla[ming]...thinking that she'd done wrong of some kind?]
Yeah. Yes.
[Int: Mm-hm. Mm-hm. The other fella just cheated him out of it.]
(Yeah).
[Int: What's this kind o' showcase?]
He...uh...in the...in the showcase.
[Int: Yeah. What...what is that?]
Well that...that's...that's a...that's a uh...a...a...piece wi'...with a glass into un see.
[Int: So he...]
He had the big showcase in there with a glass into un see. Well now he must ha' got somehow or 'nother to hide hisself _ to hide hisself the...the... the...[i.e., *to*] look out through somehow the [i.e., *to*] see this...see this mole under her left breast see. An' now he didn't know no more about the woman 'an...uh..'an [i.e., *than*] they knowed.
[Int: Where did you learn that story?]
I learned that story...I've aknowed that story _ oh I've aknowed that story sir ever since I been 'bout uh...ten or twelve year old.
[Int: Who told it first time? From whom did you learn it?]
Eh?
[Teller's wife: /?Who/]
[Int: Do you know who it was told it _ when you first learned it?]
No. I don't know. No.

/she/

*rep. 4

/(bool)/

493

[Int: Were there many storytellers when you were a young fella?]

Yes lot o' stories. Lot o' stories told when I was a young feller. I had a uncle _ I used to have a uncle an' I used to...I didn't used to stay home see. I always used to stay with he. Well night time _ night time them times 'twasn't houses like 'tis now, 'twas the ol' stoves an' _ old board floorin into 'em, well _ he'd lie down 'longside the stove an' I'd lie down 'longside of un. Then he'd start tellin me stories. Start tellin me stories an' singin 'em me songs see.

[Int: What was his name?]

Eh? Uh...uh Charl.

[Int: Charl...Bennett?]

Charles.

[Int: Charles Bennett?]

Charl Bennett yes. Charl Bennett. Yes.

[Int: Ah-hah. Mm-hm. What do you call thi[s]...does this story have a name?]

No. Not as I know for. I never...I ne...I...I...I don't know. I don't think [so].

Duration: 16 min., 23 sec.
Source: ?Charles Bennett (Benoit), (uncle), St. Pauls, Great Northern Peninsula.
Location: Sitting room of teller's house, afternoon.
Audience: Mrs. Rebecca Bennett (teller's wife), interviewers.

Context, Style, and Language: (For context see notes to No. 5).

After a little hesitation in which his wife encourages him and relays the interviewers' questions, Freeman Bennett launches quickly and enthusiastically into this story, settling down at ease with his guests in the quiet room, the silence broken only by the storyteller's voice, the occasional rattling of the wood stove, and the clock ticking away in the background. The tale again illustrates all the favorite aspects of his style, notably the marking of segments of the narrative by certain set phrases, the beginning of sentences with *An'* (often followed by a brief pause and/or hesitation form which heightens suspense and allows the teller time to think ahead), and the use of parallel motifs and phraseology, e.g., the stock response to the offer of money which occurs three times: "'two/five hundred dollars' she/he said/says 'is a lot to turn down.'" The elliptical style calls for explication at times, e.g., "if I can get a chance _ for you [to be] cook," but elsewhere the strong stress on individual words provides a useful contrast and assists the listener to focus attention on important points in the narrative. The context is cleverly localized in the preamble which sets the story in "olden times"—"before Newfoundland was discovered." The opening lines also include a hint in the phrase "not in our days at all" of more elaborate formulas found in other tales in this collection.

On the language side we find the pronunciation of *Americky* with lowered close front vowel in the final syllable, initial /t/ in *thick* (foggy—influenced, like *think* and other words with initial *th*, by Anglo-Irish), the loss of initial *th* in *than*, final offglide /d/ in *revolverd*, aphesis in *'nother*, and in the discussion following the tale the name *Charles* has its typical local pronunciation as two syllables, with schwa as the vowel of the second. The name is also abbreviated to *Charl*, probably preserving something of the original French pronunciation in the Benoit family of the older generation. Both forms of the name are common on the northwest coast of the Great Northern Peninsula. Dialectal vocabulary includes *good* used as an adverb; *sway* in the sense of "control" in "took the whole sway of" (cf. *OED Sway* sb. I. 5. Prevailing, overpowering or controlling influence); the pronoun *they* in object position in *he had they goin; he* in object position and following the preposition *for; ar* (any; see *DNE e'er* det), *picked meself up* (found my bearings, in the literal, nautical sense); and *hove* in the figurative sense of "put, threw" (cf. *OED Heave* v. I. 9). Note also the prepositional phrase *off o'* and the archaic and somewhat literary *bid her time o' day*. Present tense forms are *I is/tells, we goes*, while we also find the past tense *want* and the past participles *acome, cutted, adone, aknowed*, and the double negatives *don't want nar servant girl, can't get no better, nobody never done it*, and *didn't know no more*.

See also the notes to Nos. 4, 5, 6, 8, 37, 38, and 39.

Type and Motifs:

AT882. *The Wager on the Wife's Chastity.*

Z10.1. *Beginning formula.*

T91.5.1. *Rich girl in love with poor boy.*

T97. *Father opposed to daughter's marriage.*

N831. *Girl as helper.*

N15. *Chastity wager.*

N2.5. *Whole kingdom (all property) as wager.*

K2252. *Treacherous maidservant.*

K2112.1. *False tokens of woman's unfaithfulness.*

K92. *Gambling contest won by deception.*

Cf. R61. *Person sold into slavery.*

K1837. *Disguise of woman in man's clothes.*

F679. *Remarkable skill—miscellaneous [woman skilled as navigator].*

R152. *Wife rescues husband.*

Cf. J1141. *Confession obtained by a ruse.*

Q411.4. *Death as punishment for treachery.*

International Parallels: See No. 45.

47. JACK AND THE SLAVE ISLANDS[†]

Everett Bennett
St. Pauls, Great Northern Peninsula
31 August 1966

AT882
TC278 66-24
Collectors: HH and JW

Well once upon a time when I was a young feller you know _ there was two fellers...two more fellers _ Tom an'...Bill _ had a ship goin to foreign ports. They was married, the two o' them. An' they runned a business together. An' when they came back off their voyage _ their two women _ one had a...girl an' th' other a boy. Well they growed up to be...men an' women. An' one...the boy was called _ Bill after his father. An' his...father died. Well _ 'twas _ only young Bill now _ with the ol' man _ run the business.

So very good. He fell in love with the...this feller's daughter. So anyhow _ she was goin to school an' every day _ when she'd _ come home to dinner she go in an' have a time with...talk to Jack an' _ for JACK his name was, yes.

So anyhow she said uh..."Well Jack" she said uh..."you got to ask father" (she) said "if /he's/ satisfied [for you] to marry me...let you marry me." /she's/

"No need o' me askin" he said "he's not goina be satisfied." /he/

"Well" /she/ said "(there's) no harm to ask."

So anyhow _ when he came in the school that...in the...store that day he said uh..."Is you goina let me marry your daughter?"

Said "No Jack" he said "you'll never marry my daughter."

So very good. When she come out o' school in the evening she said uh..."Jack" she said "how ya get on?"

"Well like I told ya" he said "he told me (that)...I never get ya. But" he said "I'm goin to leave now." He said "An' I'm goin to uh...where was it...Cumberland _ [Teller's son: I don't know.] Cumberland." He said "An'...some day" he said "you may kind o'...come there."

So very good. He wasn't there long _ by god 'fore she got her escape an' she went. Well he got on _ wonderful _ while he was there, he had ships goin all parts o' the world. So they got married. This girl come an' she asked for such...this man there.

"Yeah."

Well she'd like to see un. He wasn't there long before _ the wedding _ to start an' they got married.

Well he was a man that done a good lot o' braggin you know and _ went down to the pier that night his ships was comin in an' he...said to his...woman when he was leavin uh..."Now I won't be back tonight" he said "I'm goin to stay aboard one o' the ships" he said "ships 'll be in tonight,

I won't be back." Well alright. She had _ waiting maids, servant girls an' everything.

So anyhow uh...he went down on the pier an' _ there was a feller there, one o' those devil-might-care fellers. He started in talkin about (how) well he's adone since he come in Cumberland an' _ had ships goin all parts. Yeah. An' uh...so anyhow "Yes" he said uh..."something else I'm goin to tell ya." He said "You got a fine whore" he said "up there on the hill too."

"Oh" he said "I don't know about that."

"Oh well" he said "I DO." He said "I'll bet you" he said "that _ everything you got here" he said "I can tell you" he said "what your wife is in the morning."

"Well alright go ahead."

(So) anyhow he stayed aboard the ship. An' never went up. So this feller went up an' he've got to the servant girl was there. An' he ask _ could he come in.

"No" she said. "You can't come in" she said uh..."master o' th' house is gone" she said "an' there's no men allowed in here when he's gone."

"Oh" he said _ "I GOT to get in." He said "I wants to get in" he said "an' get in the lady's room."

No she couldn't do that.

"Oh yes. You got to." He paid her a nice sum o' money to do it you know and _ anyhow she got in. /She/ let /him/ in. An' she [*the lady*] had a   /He/ /her/ showcase in her room. An' this is where he gets, in the showcase.

By an' by the lady come up an' _ goin to bed. Start pullin off her clothes. Now then he took remarks of all her clothes 'cordin as she pulled 'em off. An' he seen a mole _ on her left breast. Well he thought to hisself "That's good enough." Anyhow she got to bed an' got to sleep, the _ waiting maid let her out _ let un out.

So in the morning he went down on the pier an' uh...this feller was there.

An' he said "Well" he said "what d'ya know about my wife?"

He said "Like I told ya. Like I told ya" he said. He said "Your wife" he said "got on...stockins" he said "an' there's white rings around 'em." An' something else he told about her clothes an' he said "To make asure" he said uh..."she got a mole on her left breast."

"Well DAMN the women anyhow!" he said "I never wants to hear tell of another one" he said "I'm goin to the...to the Slave Islands" he said "an' be a slave the remainder o' me days."

Now then _ up this feller goes an' turned her out of her house. She didn't know what 'twas for. Drove her out on the street with nothing.

An' anyhow he took her over now, took all the vessels _ house _ land, everything.

*child talking
in back-
ground

So very good. He had ships now goin all parts. Her husband was gone, she didn't know where he was gone. An' uh...so anyhow _ she went round...town.* An' met a man, she asked un would he...did he want a servant girl.

He said "Yes." He said "I wants a servant girl" he said "but uh...I can't have a rich lady like you" he said "for a servant girl."

"Oh my dear man" she said "I'm not rich." She said "I'm poor" she said "all I got" she said "is what I'm stand in." She said "I...love to get a job."

"Oh well" he said "if you...come" he said "I'll take ye but" he says "I can't pay ya very big wages" oh she didn't mind that.

So anyhow after she'd been there with un quite a while _ she said one day to un she said uh..."I like [to] get a trip" she said "on a vessel _ somewheres." She said "I wonder could you get me a suit o' clothes" she said "sailor's clothes" she said "I dress in a sailor's clothes _ get [a] trip on a vessel."

"Well" he said "I can try." So he went down to the tailor's an' he got a suit o' clothes made up /for/ her. Fitted her just to the tee. So anyhow brought it up and _ he went down on the pier _ (she)...put on the clothes an' _ nice. Went down the pier an' there was a vessel there an' uh...he want a cook. (Happened to want) a cook.

An' he said uh..."Captain" he said "I got a nice young man up there to th' house" he said "pretty good cook too." He said "An' that's what he wants _ a job on the...on th' ocean."

"Well" he said "send un down." He sont him down. Ask would he come with un cook

He said "Yes" he said "that's what I've been waitin for."

Now this...devil-might-care feller was down on the wharf now. "Now" he said uh..."I tell yous" he said "the next trip I comes" he said "next trip yous comes back" he said "how I come to get this...outfit" he said "I got here."

So anyhow _ they was buildin a...they had a...buildin a new vessel now for the ol' captain. An' anyhow they was goin on the new one. So they was out sailin an'...she was cook. Called her "he" now, he was cook.

So one day _ she called 'em down to dinner an' she come on deck. When she come on deck she seen on the cabin...house _ the chart an' compass an' everything an'...pickin up the ship, find out where she was to an'...well she picked up...she picked up the ship _ found out where she was to an' _ took the courses off.

First thing the...captain seen when he come up _ was this down on the...cabin house. Called the mate, he said "You do that?"

"No." Said "I didn't do it."

"Well" he said "there's somebody have done it." He said "Somebody aboard this ship" he said "knows so much as I do or more."

An' the mate said "Well" he said uh..."captain" he said "that cook we got here" he says "seems like (a) pretty smart man."

"Yeah" he said "he do." He said "Ask un." So anyhow _ he asked un.

An' he said "Yes Captain." He said "I done that" he said "I been sailin with ya now quite a while" he said "an' I never...made it me business" he said "to ask you" he said "where we was to" he said "or nothing" he said "an' I seen all the fitout there" he said "an' I thought I'd...pick up the ship" he said "to see how far we was from land or see what course we was goin."

"Well" he said "an' you aboard of a ship" he said "cookin" he said "an' have navigation" he said "like you got."

"Oh yes" he said "I sooner be cookin" he said "than I'd...be at anything else."

"Well now" he said uh..."when I goes back off o' this trip they're building a new ship for me." He said "Have her ready." He said "I'll still take the ol' one. An' you'll...take the new one." Will he do that?

"Oh yes." He'd do that alright.

Anyhow when they got back off o' their trip an' uh...now this feller was goin to tell the roast [i.e., *the whole story*] this time. Come down on the wharf an' he...told the story.

An' uh...he said uh..."I knows nothing about the woman. Nothing whatever" he said "I got in a...showcase in her room" he said "an' I...took remarks of all her...clothes she pulled off" he said "an' _ to make the SURE thing" he said "I seen a mole on her left breast." He said "An' I come down" he said "an' I got un turned away from his house _ took all his ships" he said "an' he 'lowed he'd go to the Slave Islands an' be a slave the remainder of his days."

"Now" she thought to herself "that's my husband."

So anyhow they...got their ships ready, got loaded an'...'way to go. Two ships in company now.

So anyhow struck uh...storm, not much of a storm but 'twas kind of a fog, thick. They got _ astray from each other you know. An' he said to his mate _ he said "I'd like [to] go to Slave Islands."

"Hah well" he said "Captain" he said uh..."'tis up to you." (He) said "You got charge" she said "if you like to go to Slave Islands" he said "go." So anyhow he squared her away for the Slave Islands.

Went to the Slave Islands, he went ashore an' he asked the head man o' the slaves _ there's such a man there, callin of un by name

"Yeah." He was there. But he hadn't abeen no slave since he been there. He was a wonderful man an' he's too good a man to put for a slave. Well she'd like to see un.

Well they 'd..."You can see un but uh...you can't take un. Too good a man, we can't lose un."

"Well" she said "tis no harm to see un."

So anyhow she went to un then. She said uh…uh…"Could I take un aboard the ship? Take un 'board the ship" she said "for a hour or two" she said "an' I'll bring…uh…guarantee" she said "I'll bring /un/ back."

/a/

"Yeah." He could do that.

(So) anyhow she gets un. Gets him 'board the ship. Put un down in the cabin ‗ got un under way an' away to go.

And the other feller was in…the other ol' captain was in port two or three days. Gettin uneasy about (un). Didn't know where he was to.

"Oh well" he said uh…"we struck that uh…fog" he said "kind of a thick storm there" he said "an' we got off our course." Said "Leave us behind" he said "for a day or two."

"Oh yes" he said "that's alright."

So anyhow uh…now this feller [*Jack*] was down below, he didn't know what he was down there for. An' uh…they discharged their cargoes an' on their way back, now this is the time he was comin down and…tell the roast. So anyhow uh…when they was goin in port ‗ she went down.

"Now" she said "I want…" she said "when I calls you on deck" ‗ she give un a gun ‗ "when I calls you on deck" she said ‗ "an' tells you to fire" ‗ she

/we/

said "you fire." An' /he/ still didn't know what 'twas for.

So anyhow they got in port an' got tied up ‗ down he comes on the

*listener
coughs

wharf. Start tellin the (roast)* ‗ whole story now 'bout how he come to get…this feller turned away from his house an' ‗ get his…his wife turned out an' he get all his ships.

"But" he said "as for the woman" he said "I knows nothing about her." He said "No more than…any o' you men. But" he said "I seen this mole" he said "on her left breast" he said "an' uh…her husband thought I knowed ALL about her" he said "an' leaved her an' went to the Slave Islands. Said he'd go to Slave Islands an' be a slave the remainder of his days."

"Now" she said "fire."

/she/

Fired an' /he/ shot [un]. An' they was livin together in Cumberland an' had…best kind of a home when I leaved. [*laughter*] Four children (I think). [*laughter*]

[*recorder off*]*** oh I'd have agot somebody tell un you know, get somebody to tell 'em (sometimes).
[Int: Would they tell many like that?]
Oh yes. You'll get lots like that one time.
[Teller's son: Yeah.]
Oh I could set down one time [if] I haven't forgot 'em an' tell ya stories (here)…yes for…from that an' from six o'clock in the evenin [till] twelve o'clock in the night. But I forgot 'em now.
[*recorder off*] [Teller's son: ***stories. I did know one…]

I had a ol' uncle one time you know. Freeman an' me down there used to go down. Used to live down here an' we used to live up above. We go down Saturday evenings now. Livin by hisself he was, his woman was dead. One 'd lay...he'd lay round on the floor now an'...on one side an' the other on the other. He'd tell us stories then till we'd fall asleep the both of us. Tell away an ('em). He had some o' them hour an' a half long.

[Teller's son: Yeah.]

[*recorder off*]*** (that's all them you know). So LONG ago, I was only a boy then 'bout _ eight or nine year old I suppose.

[Int: But you learned them _ some o' them.]

Oh I learned them an' could tell 'em you know an' when I WAS tellin of 'em off an' on you know I wouldn't forget them see but now 'tis years ago since I told any stories. (Gist of it) goes out of me mind.

[*recorder off*]*** memory that I had perhaps forty year ago.

Duration: 13 min., 49 sec.

Source: John Roberts (Sally's Cove, Great Northern Peninsula), Lomond, Great Northern Peninsula (lumber camps), "round 1930."

Location: Kitchen of teller's house, afternoon.

Audience: Clarence Bennett (teller's son), members of his family, interviewers.

Context, Style, and Language: Clarence Bennett learned a number of his stories from his father and here we see his father asking him for confirmation of Jack's destination (Cumberland). When the confirmation is not forthcoming, his father reiterates the name with conviction nevertheless, as Clarence has not contradicted him or offered an alternative name.

This story is one of several told during this recording session in which father and son range widely over their repertoires. They sing songs, recite, and tell jokes, riddles, and toasts. For the most part they are alone with the interviewers, though children and other members of the family come in and out of the room from time to time.

Like "Hard Head" (Nos. 40 and 41) this story was learned from John Roberts and was told on two occasions by Everett Bennett, first in 1966 and again in 1970. The two versions are again closely parallel, at times almost word for word, but differ sufficiently in detail to make each telling distinctive and unique. For example, this first version names the brothers in the opening lines, the *devil-might-care feller* thinks to himself "That's good enough" when he gets enough evidence in the bedroom, and Jack vehemently forswears women after the evidence is given to him, while none of this appears in No. 48. In version one Jack asks the girl only once to marry him, but twice in version two, and tells her he is going to Cumberland whereas in version two she finds this out for herself. It makes clear that Jack's rival takes over his house, wife, and possessions, and includes more information and colorful dialogue when the captain is asked if he needs a cook. The lady is said to have white rings round her stockings, but red ones in version two, just as the sailor's clothes simply became men's clothes. The second version adds details about Jack selling his part of the business before

501

leaving for Cumberland, and the innocently amusing touch that he "didn't do much slavery" on the Slave Islands, and explains how the lady overhears that he has gone there so she is able to follow him. It also mentions that the lady has a lot of servants, and includes the rather curiously expressed liking which the captain has for the disguised lady: "the captain fell right in love with un for [i.e., *on behalf of*] his daughter." Version one whets the appetite of the audience for the revelation of the *devil-might-care* feller's trickery which is expected, and carried out, at the end of the first voyage and then expanded and explained further at the end of the second. The chronology of these events differs in No. 48 where the revelation is promised on the return from the second voyage, but when it is given it is unsatisfactory in its lack of detailed explanation, in the same way that in this version the narrative moves on very quickly through the account of the old and new ships. The two end formulas aiso differ slightly, and although both tales begin with the stock phrase *once upon a time* this first version facetiously adds "when I was a young feller you know" which, as in legends, gives an air of apparent authenticity by suggesting that the events took place in the teller's lifetime, and at the same time giving an exaggerated sense of his age and experience. The overall impression given by a close comparison of the two narratives is that the second version is somewhat less full and less well motivated than the first, although it proceeds more smoothly and at a faster pace.

The version presented here has many characteristics typical of this narrator, including the frequent punctuating expressions *So very good, (So) anyhow, (well) alright, by an' by,* and *he/she said* in the dialogue. He also often pauses and/or uses a hesitation form immediately after *he/she said* before the quoted speech begins. Jack is again portrayed as a quiet, phlegmatic man, slow to anger and restrained under provocation, as for example when he replies to the accusation that his wife is a whore by simply saying "Oh...I don't know about that."

In addition to the linguistic points noted under Nos. 11, 40, and 41, we find here the diphthong /ɐu/ in *yous* reduced to schwa in unstressed position in *I tell yous, sit* pronounced as *set,* and aphesis in *'lowed* and *'board.* Notable lexical items are *satisfied* in the sense of "agreeable" (cf. *OED* Satisfied ppl.a. 1); the dialectal *somewheres; remarks* in the sense of "notes or records" (see *OED* Remark sb.[1] 3.c. A mark or record of an observation. [This sense is designated obsolete, the last recorded non-dialectal use being in 1789]); *pick up* in the sense "find the position of (a ship)" (cf. *OED* Pick v.[1] VIII. 20. f.); the compound *fitout,* meaning equipment (see *DNE fit-out* n. 5), as distinct from *outfit,* meaning "property, possessions"—specifically ships and allied gear (cf. *DNE out-fit* n. 1 and *fit-out* n. 1); *roast,* in *blow the roast,* with the sense of "reveal the secret, tell the whole story, blow the gaff" (cf. *OED Blow* v.[1] III. 27, and *EDD ROAST* 8, obsolete, meaning "a rough jest"); *'lowed* in the sense "suppose, reckon, conclude" (cf. *OED Allow* v. 7 found in English and American dialects, and *EDD ALLOW* v. 1. To suppose. . . , cited from Ireland and the South Western and South Eastern counties of England); the unusual meaning of *showcase* which in this story can hardly refer to something in which the observer could be easily seen, although of course he would need to be able to observe from within this hiding-place; and the nautical expressions *cabin house, squared her away,* and *under way.* Present tense forms include *Is you, he do* (emphatic), *I calls/tells,* and in the past tense we have *runned, growed,*

502

and possibly *run, done, get* whose tense and/or function is ambiguous. Note also *agot* and *abeen*, transcribed here as past participles, but interpretable as reduced forms of *have got, have been*. The ambiguity of the addition of *a-* to such forms is especially obvious in *I'd have agot* and the strange word *asure* which seems to add initial schwa by analogy from past participle forms, but might equally well be a reduction of *her sure*, in which case the phrase *make her sure* would be glossed as *make it certain*, the pronoun *her* being used with neuter referent.

See also the notes to Nos. 11, 40, and 41.

Type and Motifs:
AT882. *The Wager on the Wife's Chastity.*
Z10.1. *Beginning formula.*
T97. *Father opposed to daughter's marriage.*
N15. *Chastity wager.*
N2.5. *Whole kingdom (all property) as wager.*
K2252. *Treacherous maidservant.*
K2112.1. *False tokens of woman's unfaithfulness.*
K92. *Gambling contest won by deception.*
Cf. R61. *Person sold into slavery.*
K1837. *Disguise of woman in man's clothes.*
F679. *Remarkable skill—miscellaneous [woman skilled as navigator].*
R152. *Wife rescues husband.*
Cf. J1141. *Confession obtained by a ruse.*
Q411.4. *Death as punishment for treachery.*
Z10.2. *End formula.*

International Parallels: See No. 45.

48. JACK AND THE SLAVE ISLANDS†

Everett Bennett   AT882
St. Pauls, Great Northern Peninsula   TC970 71-50
22 July 1970   Collector: HH

[Int: What do you call this one, Everett?]
I haven't got any...any...perfect name for this one. Uh...once upon a time there was two fellers _ two brothers _ an' they had a business. They was...married the (both) of them. An' they used to go on trips aboard of a vessel. An' they agreed _ if their two...women _ had two babies when they get back they would uh...marry 'em. So sure enough when they got back _ they had two babies _ boy an' a girl.

So anyhow _ Jack's father _ died _ when he was…quite young. An' Jack fell in love _ with his uncle's _ daughter. Oh right in love. She come down (to)…office every day an' have a talk to Jack an' _ she said "Jack" she said uh…"there's one thing you got to do." She said "You must ask…father if _ is he satisfied for me to marry ya."

"Yes" Jack said "I'll do that but _ I don't think it's any good."

So anyhow _ he come in th' office that day an' he said uh…"Uncle Tom" he said "is…you willin for me to marry your…daughter?"

"No Jack" he said. "You'll never marry my daughter."

Well when she came in th' evening _ "How ya get on?"

"Oh well like I said. He's not satisfied. Not satisfied for me to marry ya."

"Well" _ she said "ask un again" she said "Jack."

So a day or two after that _ he asked un again. An' he said "No Jack" he said "I told ya once before" he said _ "that I wasn't satisfied" he said "an' more I'm not."

"Well very good" Jack said. "Very good." He said "If you're not satisfied" he said _ "I'm sellin out" he said "I'm takin part of my business" he said "an' I'm goin away."

"Well you can do that" he said "Jack."

So anyhow _ bought…Jack's part o' business. Jack had a good bit o' money _ now, he sold his part the business. He went out in Cumberland. When he got in Cumberland _ well he settled down there an' he had _ lots o' money _ wonderful man, liked well amongst all the people. He had ships goin all foreign ports. So anyhow _ went on alright.

She found out where Jack was to. Girl found out where Jack was to. She went to Cumberland an' _ asked was there…such a man there by the name o' Jack uh…come there _ few years back. Oh yeah. He was there. Pretty wealthy man now. He had lots o' ships goin all foreign countries. Well she'd like to see un. Anyway they showed her where th' house was to an' [she] went up to the house an' uh…oh Jack was right pleased now, she was come. Well (they) was goin be married. An' they got married, now the people in Cumberland was…jealous over this. They didn't like this thing o' the girl come from another place an' married this man. They didn't like it.

So anyhow _ Jack was goin…ships 'd be comin in now the night. Told his wife. "Now" he said "I won't be back" he said "tonight" he said "I'll stay aboard _ one o' the boats tonight."

So anyhow _ there was a…one o' those _ devil-might-care fellers there. And _ he bet them _ people there that he could have a…turn from his wife. He said "I can have un" he said "turn from his wife" he said "by tomorrow morning."

"Oh how ya goin to do that?"

504

"Never mind. I'll do it."

Anyhow down comes Jack. Come aboard. Talk about how well he'd agot on since he got in Cumberland, had ships goin foreign ports an' _ this feller was there.

"Oh yes" he said. "You got a nice whore up there on the hill too."

"Oh" he said "I don't know that."

"Well" he said "I...I can...I can tell ya" he said. "I'll tell ya tomorrow morning" he said "what she's like."

"Alright" Jack said "go ahead. I'm satisfied."

Went up an' rapped to the door. Waiting maid come out _ servant girl.

An' _ "Oh" she said "you can't come in" she said _ "the _ master of th' house is gone" she said "there's no men allowed in here" /she/ said "after _ he's gone."   /he/

"Well -- I got to get in. Let me in _ an' put me in the lady's room."

So anyhow he paid her so much money to get in and _ got into...lady's room, sure enough she had a showcase in the room. This is where he got. By an' by she come [to] go to bed. [*coughs*] He took remarks of all her clothes when she pulled it off. An' he seen a mole on her left breast. [*clears throat*] So anyhow _ he got out now, she got to bed, he got out the room, 'way to go.

Went down aboard next morning.

"Well? What do ya know about me wife?"

He said "Like I told ya." Told about all the sto...uh...all the clothes she had on. Told /him/ what kind of stockings she had on. "Red rings" he said "around your wife's stockings." He said "An' to make it sure" he said "there's a mole on her left breast."   /her/

"Well damn the women" he said "anyhow!" He said "I'll _ leave her" he said uh..."go to the Slave Islands and be a slave the remainder o' me days." [*coughs*] [*aside:* ticklin now in my throat look.]

An'...so anyhow away he goes. Went to the Slave Islands. Well he was a slave but he _ didn't do much slavery, he was a...wonderful man an' they _ didn't give him much slavery to do. So anyhow _ she was still in Cumberland, didn't know what happened. Her husband was gone, didn't know what happened. An' _ down this feller come, now he had all...Jack's ships. Down this feller come an' _ on the pier an' started tellin of 'em about it.

Said "I got un to leave his wife." He said "An' he went to the Slave Islands." Very good. She knowed where he was to.

She shipped...she leaved her house _ an' went _ travellin. She come across a farmer. She asked un _ did he want a servant girl.

"Yeah. I wants a servant girl" he said "but you're too rich a girl _ for me to have for a servant girl."

"Oh no" she said "I'm not rich. All I got is what I…what I'm standin [in]."

Well he'd take her on. Took her on an' she was on now quite a while with un an' uh…/she/ said "I'd like to have a trip" _ she said. Said "Would you go down to the /pier/…uh…go down on the pier" she said "when the boats comes in an' see [if] you can get a place for me." Said "Tell 'em I'm a man."

/he/

/tay/

"Yeah." 'Way he goes. Went down, there was a boat comin in and _ come in and _ there was a man short. They want a cook.

Said "I got a good cook up there" he said "that's what he wants _ trip on a ship."

"Send him down."

So he went to the tailor's an' got a suit made for her an' dressed her all up in men's clothes an' away she goes. Come down. An' he…went aboard. He was a man now.

So they start. (Right) on the trip and _ oh he was such a _ nice smart-lookin man _ the captain fell right in love with un for his daughter now, he had a daughter the captain (did).

An' _ "Now" he said uh…"they're makin uh…they're buildin a…nother ship" he said "I'm havin 'nother _ new ship." [coughs] An' uh…he said "I'll take that one. I'll take th' ol' one, still take th' ol' one, you take the new one."

"Oh no." Couldn't do that.

So anyhow they went on the trip. Come back again _ an' _ he was goin _ new ship would be ready for the next time. So this got…man got…aboard. He uh…they called him up to dinner…called un down to dinner an' he come on deck. An' he seen anything…everything on the cabin what the captain had for pickin up the ship and seein where she was to an' takin her courses an' everything. He took the sun an' he picked up the vessel _ found out where she was to. By an' by they come up an' he went down _ forecastle.

First thing captain discovered. Said "Mate" he said "you do this?"

"No" he said.

"Well" he said "had to be you do it."

"No" he said "'twasn't."

Ask all the crew

"No."

The mate said uh…"Captain" he said "that cook we got" he said "seems like a pretty smart man."

Called un on deck. He said "You do this?"

He said "Yes captain" he said "I done it." Said "I been sailin with you quite a while now" he said "an' I never ask ye" he said "where we was to" he

506

said "or nothing at all" he said "an' I _ thought I'd pick her up" he said "an' find out _ where we was at."

"Well" he said "an' you goin around cook on the vessel" _ he said "an' _ can take a vessel" he said "any part the world." Ah yes he didn't like takin her (?o'course)

"Well now" he said "you got to take that new ship this time." Said "She's all ready."

When they got back _ give un the new ship an' cargo and _ crew. They start, two of 'em together. So they got out an' they _ struck a storm you know _ rough _ bad _ foggy. He got separated.

An' he said to his mate _ he said "I'd like [to] go to Slave Islands."

"Well" he said "you're...got charge o' the vessel" he said "[if] you'd like to go to Slave Islands" he said "go."

So anyhow he started to go to Slave Islands. Went an' anchored an' went ashore. Asked was there such a man there _ called him by name.

"Yeah."

Well she want un, no they couldn't part with un for ANYTHING.

"Oh" she said "I don't want un to keep" she said "I wants un...just take un aboard the ship" she said "an' I'll bring un back again." An' she got un. Got un aboard. She got un under board. Got un aboard _ away to go. Carried un away. She put un down...put un down in the cabin an' barred un in.

Oh he was...the other ol' feller was...couple of days in _ port where he...they had to go _ ahead of un. Oh he's right proud when he seen her come _ now. Thought he was lost.

"Oh no" he said "it come a little thick" he said "an' we got _ off o' course." So they _ discharged their cargo an' start back.

An' now this f...this _ bad feller _ he said "An' next time you comes back" he said _ "when yous comes back" he said "I'll tell ya what happened."

So anyhow they _ returned _ back home. An' he _ was down on the pier now. This feller [*Jack*] was locked down below. She went down. An' _ give un a gun.

"Now" she said uh..."you come on deck." Said "An' when I tells you to fire" she said "you fire."

He [*the bad feller*] said "How I come to get those vessels" _ he said "an' all this property" _ he said "I got in the lady's room" _ he said "an' I took marks of all her clothes 'cordin she pulled it off." He said "An' I seen a mole" he said "on her left breast."

When /he/ said that "Now" he said..."now" she said "fire." Fired an' shot un.　　　　　　　　　　　　　　　　　　　　　　　　　　　　/she/

An' when I leaved they was livin together an' they had four children I think. [*laughs*] That's the last of [it].

[Int: Where did you learn it?]

From Jack Roberts, Sally's Cove.

[*recorder off*] [Int: *** then we wouldn't have to worry about the length of it.]

He start talkin.

[Int: Who is this now?]

John Roberts of Sally's Cove. He started tellin us one Sunday after dinner. An' he told till supper time. An' he come out after supper – and he start tellin of un again. An' he never finished un. His son was into one o' th' other camps – an' he took sick. They come for un – an' he had to go and...in where his son was. An' the next Sunday – he finished that story. An' time he had un told – I knowed un all. But you know I never told that after I learned it see. An' I forgot it. Oh took him a full day...it'd take him a full day to tell un. An' I knowed un all every bit of un, I told un once or twice afterwards an' I give un right up, I – didn't bother.

[Int: How much of it would you remember?]

I can't remember none of un sir. Not one bit.

[Int: Yeah. You don't even remember what...sketch of it?]

No. Don't...can't...can't remember none of (un). Can't remember none.

[Int: How long ago was this?]

Oh that's 'bout uh...forty year ago I guess.

[Int: That would be about 1930?]

Round 19...19...round 1930 yeah. Yeah.

[Int: Where would you hear Jack tell these stories?]

In the lumber camps.

[Int: Oh. You mean you...he worked in the same camps where you were?]

Oh yes, worked in the same camp.

[Int: Where were the camps?]

Over on Lomond you know. When Lomond was workin. Lomond have camps then see, be crowds o' men. Forty or fifty men in the camps you see.

[Int: Mm-hm. What company was that?]

That's the...that was St. Lawrence. St. Lawrence Company. That's before the Bowaters took it over. Bowaters was...they sold to the Bowaters after that an' Bowaters took it over you see.

[Int: What did you work at...at in the camps?]

Oh cuttin wood.

Duration: 12 min., 53 sec.

Source: John Roberts (Sally's Cove, Great Northern Peninsula), Lomond, Great Northern Peninsula (lumber camps), "round 1930."

Location: Kitchen of teller's house.

Audience: Interviewer.

Context, Style, and Language: (For context see notes to No. 41).

This second version of the tale originally learned from John Roberts runs parallel with the version presented earlier (No. 47). Everett Bennett has no "perfect name," i.e., precise title, for the story, and no title was given by John Roberts in No. 45 or by Everett's brother, Freeman, in his version (No. 46). However, during an interview on 11 September 1971, Everett told the fieldworker who collected No. 48: "I don't hardly know the title of that one but you can put down 'The Slave Islands.'" Most of the typical features of Everett's style and language are to be seen here, including the opening formula "once upon a time" and the use of short and/or elliptical utterances in which function words, pronouns, and verbs are frequently omitted. The mixing and/or ambiguity of tenses which often accompany a compromise between direct and indirect speech are seen, for instance, near the beginning of the tale: "She come down (to)...office every day an' have a talk to Jack." As is usual in Newfoundland speech, /'forkasl/ has full vocalic quality in all three syllables, while the initial vowel is absent in *'twasn't,* the vowel of the definite article is lost in *th' evening,* and the singular pronoun *it* is used twice with the plural referent *clothes.* We also have the present tense *(they) comes,* and the use of the word *marks* in the obsolete sense of "notice," last recorded in 1823 (*OED Mark* sb.[1] *IV.* 20. Attention, notice).

See also the notes to Nos. 11, 40, 41, and **47.**

Type and Motifs:

AT882. *The Wager on the Wife's Chastity.*

Z10.1. *Beginning formula.*

P251.5. *Two brothers.*

T69.2. *Parents affiance children without their knowledge.*

T97. *Father opposed to daughter's marriage.*

N15. *Chastity wager.*

K2252. *Treacherous maidservant.*

K2112.1. *False tokens of woman's unfaithfulness.*

Cf. R61. *Person sold into slavery.*

K1837. *Disguise of woman in man's clothes.*

F679. *Remarkable skill—miscellaneous [woman skilled as navigator].*

R152. *Wife rescues husband.*

Cf. J1141. *Confession obtained by a ruse.*

Q411.4. *Death as punishment for treachery.*

Z10.2. *End formula.*

International Parallels: See No. 45.

Rebecca Bennett

49. THE FIDDLER'S BET[†]

Freeman and Rebecca Bennett
St. Pauls, Great Northern Peninsula
31 August 1966

Cf. AT882 [reversal]
TC282 66-24
Collectors: HH and JW

[Teller's wife: And do you know the one where...where we used to sing that...on the last of un.]
Hey?
[Teller's wife: Do you know that one where he used to sing on the last of un, where he says:
[*sings*]

> Be true my love, be true my love
> 'Tis only for one hour
> Be true my love, be true my love
> The ship and cargo's ours.

Oh yes that's uh...that's...that's...yes. Yes that's uh...the...the...that's...that's the feller that's er...where the feller bet this...uh...bet uh...the captain...uh...he could have two hours with his wife and she wouldn't know uh...an' he wouldn't know what she was. That is. That's uh...kind of a story an' a...an' a...an' a song all together.
[Teller's wife: Ah well ya know _ I never heard un.]
Hey?
·[Teller's wife: I never heard it.]
You never heard it?
[Teller's wife: No. I guess it's a smutty one.] [*laughs*]
[Int: Not too bad _ is it?]

No. No 'tis not uh...no 'tis not...'tis not uh...oh no 'tis not uh...blackguard ‿ nothing like that. No. Oh no. Fact is a feller see ‿ now there was a...feller HIS name was Jack. An' he was...uh married, he was livin in the...the city. An' there was a...a feller came in there uh...a captain ‿ he had a...a big ship see? An' he come to Jack's house uh...for the night see, he was goina board there. An' uh...he had his supper. An' they was talkin ‿ talkin about one thing an' another ‿ an' uh...good women an' bad women see? An' Jack said he said "Well" he said "I...I got a...a good woman."

He said "Yes" he said "Jack" he said "you might think you have."

"Oh yes" Jack said "I got a good woman."

He said "I bet ya ‿ " now Jack had a golden fiddle see?

He [Jack] said "I'll put my golden fiddle" he said "up arou[nd]...up against your ship an' cargo ‿ " he said "if you'll stay with my wife" he said "for two hours" he said "an' you won't know what she is."

"Alright" he said "Jack I'll bet ya." So he bet un.

"Now" he said uh..."Jack" he said "you go out" he said "in the other room" he said "an' shut the door."

"Oh yes" Jack said "I'll go out." So -- he went out. An' he start singin, now this is what he was singin: [sings]

> Be true me love, be true me love
> It's only for one hour
> Be true me love, be true me love
> The ship an' cargo's ours.
>
> Too late my love, too late my love
> His arms is around me middle
> He've done it once an' he's at it again
> You've alost your golden fiddle.

[laughs]

512

Too late my love, too late my love His arms is around me mid dle

He've done it once an' he's at it again You've a lost your golden fid dle."

When...when I'm by meself now uh...sot down or lied down by meself there's lots o' times they...they'll come in me mind see, a lot o' the stories but when...you wants to tell 'em, well you can't just remember it see?

[*recorder off*]*** Daresay I would if I could uh...if I was to think about it. Uh...you wasn't tapin of 'em but uh...I duh...I might have to stop in the story that uh...

[Int: That will be alright.]

to tell it see.

[Int: That would be alright.]

An' I...I don't [*recorder off*]*** don't believe I could tell it now.

Duration: 2 min., 11 sec.
Location: The darkening sitting room of the teller's house, in the late evening.
Audience: Male visitor, several children, interviewers.

Context, Style, and Language: (For context see notes to No. 4).

As with No. 46 this cante fable is prompted by Freeman Bennett's wife who sings one of the verses. This immediately reminds him of the story and he begins speaking during her singing as he starts to recall it. Mrs. Becky Bennett thinks that she may not have heard it because it is "a smutty one," although she herself evidently knows part of it. Freeman assures her that it is not "blackguard," i.e., vulgar or risqué. He also gives an apt definition of the cante fable as "kind of a story an'...a song all together." He tells it as a Jack tale and provides more context, background, and motivation for it than in most other versions of the tale in this collection.

See also the notes to Nos. 4, 5, 6, 8, 37, 38, 39, and 46.

Music: Both the teller and his wife pitch the song rather low in their respective vocal ranges. As a result each one's lowest three notes sound rather throaty and uncertain in intonation. The low pitching also appears to have prompted a small amount of melodic variation in bars 2, 6, and 7 of the wife's version by which means the melody is kept within an overall compass

513

of a minor tenth. The range of her husband's version, like that found in No. 51, extends to a perfect eleventh.

The jauntiness of the singing derives largely from the regularity and precision of the singer's rhythmic articulation. The latter is particularly apparent in those words which carry little or no voiced consonant or vowel, producing brief or nonexistent musical pitches but clear rhythmicizations.

The buildup to the narrator's humorous climax is effected partly through such musical means as the gradual quickening of the pace throughout stanza 2. The momentum is further increased in the second half of this stanza by the additional eighth notes, accommodating the text's extra syllables, and a pronounced glissando in bar 12.

The melody of "The Fiddler's Bet" song is well known as the first half of "The Girl I Left Behind Me," a tune of English or Irish provenance (Fuld, *The Book of World-Famous Music,* 1966; 1971, pp. 242-44). In Newfoundland, the tune is commonly found as mouth music and is associated with several songs and parodies, a number of which relate to the seal fishery (e.g., MUNFLA Tape, C1493, Murphy, *Songs Sung By Old Time Sealers,* 1925, p. 19; Doyle, *Old Time Songs and Poetry of Newfoundland,* 1955, p. 52). Despite the tune's widespread existence outside of the cante fable, neither the melody printed by Thomas D'Urfey for "The Merchant and the Fidler's Wife," *(Songs Compleat, Pleasant and Divertive,* 5, 1719; 1876, p. 77), nor that collected by Halpert in New Jersey ("The Cante Fable in New Jersey," *JAF* 55 (1942), 141), bears a close resemblance to "The Girl I Left Behind Me." It should be noted in passing, however, that the second half of the D'Urfey melody is based on the melodic progression which is also the opening melodic progression of "The Girl I Left Behind Me" and is associated with a version of "The Cruel Mother" (Karpeles, *Folk Songs from Newfoundland,* 1971, pp. 37-38) as well as several songs and parodies relating to the seal fishery.

Type and Motif:
     Cf. AT882 [reversal]. *The Wager on the Wife's Chastity.*
N15.1. *Chastity wager: woman succumbs.*

International Parallels: All of this small group of tales, Nos. 49-52, are fragmentary versions of a cante fable (tale with interspersed songs) that has been published in fuller texts from five places in the United States: New Jersey, Virginia, North Carolina, Missouri, and Idaho, and also reported from other parts of North America, including Ontario, New York, Ohio, and Kentucky.

For some years folklorists knew only American versions of this story. It was not till after 1952 that Halpert became aware of the long narrative song version published in D'Urfey's eighteenth-century collection of English songs, usually called *Pills to Purge Melancholy.* Subsequently he discovered a still earlier example, a cante fable text from the seventeenth century, in Wardroper, *Jest,* which reprints a text from Hicks, *Oxford Jests,* 1684. In both these English narratives the protagonist is a merchant who also owns the ship; in the American versions he is the ship's captain. In the summer of 1974, the details concerning the two English texts were passed on to Klaus Roth at the Sixth International Folk-Narrative

Research Congress in Helsinki. Roth later reprinted both the Hicks and D'Urfey texts in his excellent study of adultery Schwank ballads, Roth, *Ehebruchschwänke*.

Although the story is not recognized in the AT index, we have classified it tentatively as a reversal of AT882 because the plots of both sets of stories, Nos. 45-48 and 49-52, share the initial motivation, namely the betting of all the husband's property on the impeccable chastity of his wife.

In Nos. 45-48, the husband's trust is justified; in Nos. 49-52, however, by ironical contrast the wife succumbs to the seducer with remarkable speed and bluntly informs her husband that he has lost his bet along with his only property—his fiddle. In AT882 proper the chaste wife is indeed unjustly maligned. However, in those stories where the husband's fiddle is the only property which he wagers, his confidence in his wife is misplaced. We have therefore designated this tale Cf. AT882 [reversal].

This tentative classification runs counter to the views of several American collectors who have mistakenly classified this cante fable as a form of AT1360C, "Old Hildebrand." The error began with the two North Carolina texts, which Boggs listed as Version B in a group of tales he labeled "The Untrue Wife's Song." In reprinting one of these texts, Dorson accepted Boggs' classification and described it as an abbreviated form of Type 1360C. This classification was followed by the collectors of the Virginia and Idaho examples below. That it is mistaken can be seen by comparing the two stories in detail. Although both cante fables concern untrue wives who sing songs, the plot of AT1360C not only differs considerably from that of Cf. AT882 [reversal] but is also very much more complex.

Furthermore, since the story is not listed in the AT index, it is not found in the national folktale indexes based on the AT listing and so it is difficult to check whether it is known elsewhere in Europe. We strongly suspect that this dramatic exposition of a theme which has a long history in European satirical humor, namely the unwisdom of relying on a wife's chastity, will eventually be shown to have a wide distribution both in the British Isles and at least in western Europe.

Studies and Notes

Wardroper, *Jest*, pp. 54-55, no. 46 (rpt. from *Oxford Jests,* 1684); D'Urfey, *Songs,* 5, pp. 77-80; Boggs, *JAF* 47 (1934), 304, n.1, and 305, no. 24, Version B; Halpert, "The Cante Fable in New Jersey," *JAF* 55 (1942), 140-41, no. 3, with notes; Roth, *Ehebruchschwänke,* pp. 89-90, 373-75, E21, with notes.

United States

Halpert, *JAF* 55 (1942), 141-42, no. 3c, fragment (Brooklyn, New York).

Halpert, *JAF* 55 (1942), 140-41, nos. 3a, 3b, two versions from same informant (1 dictated, 1 recorded), second has tune (New Jersey), and rpt. of 3a with tune from 3b in Emrich, *Land,* pp. 394-95, and again rpt. of 3a [with insertion of misleading word "love" in first line] in Roth, *Ehebruchschwänke,* p. 375, no. E21.

Dance, *Shuckin',* pp. 147-48, no. 270, black (Virginia).

Boggs, *JAF* 47 (1934), 305, no. 24, B[1] and B[2], 2 versions (North Carolina), and rpt. of B[1] in Dorson, *Wind,* pp. 209-10.

Randolph, *Church House,* pp. 150-51, learned in Arkansas (Missouri), and mention of another unpublished Missouri text in note, p. 220.

Brunvand, *Northwest Folklore* 1, no. 2 (1966), 8-9 (Idaho).

The Halpert Folklore Collections include three further reports privately communicated following the publication of the New Jersey examples noted above. Professor J. Frederick Doering contributed a cante fable version he had collected in 1927 in Kitchener, Ontario; Dr. Edward N. Waters, of the Music Division in the Library of Congress, reported that he had heard the cante fable in Rochester, New York; and Dr. D. H. Daugherty recalled hearing the cante fable in his high school days in Crooksville, Ohio, and contributed a variation in the wife's song. In addition to these, a college student in Murray, Kentucky, contributed a long cante fable text in 1948, commenting that he had heard and told it many times in Carteret County, North Carolina, and Calloway County, Kentucky.

England

We have not located any published versions of this cante fable from oral tradition in England. For early literary versions see:

Wardroper, *Jest,* pp. 54-55, no. 46, in cante fable form, rpt. from Captain William Hicks, *Oxford Jests,* 5th ed., London, 1684, and again rpt. in Roth, *Ehebruchschwänke,* p. 373, no. E21.

D'Urfey, *Songs,* 5, pp. 77-80, "The Merchant and the Fidler's Wife," narrative song with tune, text only rpt. in Pinto and Rodway, *Muse,* pp. 282-84, no. 136, and text with tune rpt. in Roth, *Ehebruchschwänke,* pp. 373-74, no. E21.

50. THE FIDDLER'S BET[†]

Charles Hutchings
Cow Head, Great Northern Peninsula
24 August 1966

Cf. AT882 [reversal]
TC246 66-24
Collectors: HH and JW

[*recorder off*]*** a man and his wife see? An' the captain o' the boat _ told this man that he was goina _ have a time with his wife that night.

"Oh no" he said "you won't"

So they put up a bet see? He bet the cargo _ he put up the cargo for his bet _ an' the fellow _ [with the] wife he put up his fiddle see? Well [*laughs*] he's...anyway he lost his fiddle. [*laughs*]

[Int: Oh come on, you can tell more about it...] [*laughter*]

No. [*laughs*] No. [*laughs*] [*recorder off*] They were in ONE room an' she were in the other see?

[Int: Oh.]

An' she used to say _ he used to say to her: [*recites*]

> Prove true my love prove true my love _
> (If) 'tis only for one hour.
> Prove true my love prove true my love,
> The ship an' cargo will be ours.

An' it come back _ she says: [*recites*]

> Too late my love too late my love _ [*laughter*]
> His arms are round me middle.

[*laughter*] I won't say the rest anyway.

> You've lost your damn old fiddle.

[Int: An'...an'...lost...?]
Lost your damn old fiddle. [*laughter*]
[Int: And that...that you heard in the...where was it you heard that?]
I heard that down the Straits sir down at er...Sandy Cove I believe _ that
was. I thinks that's probably true.
[Int: Who...who was it? Do you remember who sang it? Who...?]
Oh er...fellow by name o' Lo Whalen _ belong Flower's Cove. I believe
he's dead now _ wouldn't say for sure but I think the man is dead now.
[Int: Whalen?]
Whalen _ Lo /Whalen/ his name was, belong to Flower's Cove. He was   /Welland/
cook for us.

Duration: 55 sec.
Source: Lo Whalen (Flowers Cove, Great Northern Peninsula), Sandy Cove, Great Northern
Peninsula.
Location: Kitchen of teller's house, late morning.
Audience: Mrs. Martha Hutchings (teller's wife), interviewers.

Context, Style, and Language: Charles and Martha Hutchings quickly make us feel very
welcome in their spotlessly clean and uncluttered kitchen, with its wood and oil stove, table,
daybed, and chairs. Mrs. Hutchings sits in a rocking chair throughout our visit, whether
singing, talking, or listening to the conversation. She and her husband obviously have a close
relationship and entertain each other in the evening by alternately singing songs. Before
recording we ask permission to move a loudly ticking clock from the room and this request
is immediately granted, with considerable amusement on all sides which helps to create an
even more relaxed and friendly interview situation. Although diffident at first, especially as
she normally sings in the evening, Mrs. Hutchings is soon persuaded to sing a few songs and
proves to have a very clear and attractive voice. Her husband, however, has recently been
ill and does not feel well enough to sing, although we discover he knows quite a number of
songs.

He is rather reluctant to tell this tale, evidently thinking it too risqué. After some
encouragement from one of the interviewers he summarizes it, but recites the song rather than
singing it, with further hesitation before reciting the final line—carefully omitting the two most

risqué lines which precede it. Consequently this fragmentary version is rather unsatisfactory but at least includes a brief preamble which gives some degree of context and motivation to the cante fable as a whole. Even this preamble, however, is circumspect in its euphemistic reference to the Captain's intentions: "he was goina _ have a time with his wife that night." Nevertheless, both the teller and his wife find the tale very amusing and laugh throughout the narration.

Mr. Hutchings' speech is of the West Country English type in its pronunciation features, and includes the common dialectal forms *she were, I believes,* and *I thinks.*

Type and Motif:

Cf. AT882 [reversal]. *The Wager on the Wife's Chastity.*
N15.1. *Chastity wager: woman succumbs.*

International Parallels: See no. 49.

51. THE FIDDLER'S BET[†]

Everett Bennett
St. Pauls, Great Northern Peninsula
24 August 1966

Cf. AT882 [reversal]
TC251 66-24
Collectors: HH and JW

[*recorder off*]*** lost his golden fiddle.
[Int: That's right]
[*recorder off*]*** [*sings*]

[Be true] me love _ be true me love
'Tis only for one hour
Be true me love be true me love
The ship an' cargo's ours.

[Male listener: Old Andy knows that.]

Too late me love too late me love
His arms are round me middle
(He've /adone/ this) once an' he's at it again   /adown/
You've alost your golden fiddle. [*laughter*]

Duration: 50 sec.

Location: Kitchen of John Edward Bennett's house, evening.

Audience: John Edward Bennett (teller's brother) and his wife, Clarence and Barbara Bennett (teller's son and daughter-in-law), Clyde Bennett and his wife, John Edward's daughter-in-law and her two children, Anthony Bryan (teller's son-in-law), interviewers.

Context, Style, and Language: (For context see notes to No. 11).

This cante fable was collected on two occasions from Everett Bennett, first on tape in 1966 and second taken down in handwritten form in 1971. The two versions are virtually identical, even down to the difficulty of transcribing the penultimate line. Contextualizing features are conspicuously lacking and the listener is left to gather the background from the two verses.

The version presented here was difficult to transcribe because of background noise on the tape which was recorded in a house full of people, including a number of children. Everett Bennett remembers it while trying to recall other stories and songs. He thoroughly enjoys singing it, and is laughing as he sings the last few words, the audience joining in with the laughter at the end.

See also the notes to Nos. 11, 40, 41, 47, and 48.

Music: As in No. 49, "The Fiddler's Bet" song is sung to the tune of "The Girl I Left Behind Me." It is, however, pitched appreciably higher than either of the versions in No. 49 and consequently all the notes lie comfortably within the singer's vocal range. The variability of the three-note melodic progression commencing bars 2, 6, 10, and 14 seems to indicate a degree of vocal agility, unlike the similarly placed melodic variation in No. 49 which, it has been suggested, results from vocal constraint.

The technique of speaking rather than singing all or part of a song's final line is quite common among folksingers in Newfoundland. In this performance, the last minute switch to speech causes the song's meter to become truncated and the final cadence to remain unresolved so that the listener is denied the rhythmic symmetry and tonal finality which the pattern of the music has led him to expect. Thus, the humor of the narrative is complemented by a twist in the musical structure which, coupled with the singer's own increasingly obvious merriment, helps to precipitate the appropriate audience response to the story—that of laughter.

Type and Motif:
Cf. AT882 [reversal]. *The Wager on the Wife's Chastity.*
N15.1. *Chastity wager: woman succumbs.*

International Parallels: See No. 49.

52. THE FIDDLER'S BET[†]

Everett Bennett
St. Pauls, Great Northern Peninsula
11 September 1971

Cf. AT882 [reversal]
HH Field Notebook
Collector: HH

That was a [bet] -- golden fiddle against [a] ship. [He says]:

Be true, me love, be true, me love,
'Tis only for one hour;
Be true, me love, be true, me love,
The ship and cargo is ours.

Now she said:

Too late, me love, too late, me love,
His arms is around my middle;
/If he/ /He've a/done it once, and he's at it again,
You've alost your golden fiddle.

Location: Kitchen of teller's house, morning.
Audience: Interviewer.

Context, Style, and Language: This second version of the brief cante fable differs from the first only in a few very minor details. However, it offers a little more information about the bet which is the motivation of the story, and while close examination will reveal some of the basic differences in noting down the tale by hand as distinct from transcribing it from tape, these are of little consequence here as the two versions are so brief and essentially the same.

See also the notes to Nos. 11, 40, 41, 47, 48, and **51.**

Type and Motif:
Cf. AT882 [reversal]. *The Wager on the Wife's Chastity.*
N15.1. *Chastity wager: woman succumbs.*

International Parallels: See No. 49.

53. THE BASKETMAKER

Freeman Bennett
St. Pauls, Great Northern Peninsula
31 August 1966

AT888A* + Cf. AT506
TC283 66-24
Collectors: HH and JW

[*recorder off*]*** That's the trouble see. There uh...I knows lots o' songs an'...an' stories but uh...they don't just come in me mind [Int. A: Yes.] at the time see? [*recorder off*] I knows what one that is an' I knowed that one one time. But I...I don't know un now. I knows...I knows that one...I...I knowed that one one time. [Int. A: Uh hm.] I knowed that story one time _ that uh...he...he had a...he had a door on his back yes. Yes. I...I knowed that story one time but I...I...I couldn't tell un to you now 'cause I...I can't mind. It's a long time ago since I thought about that story.
[*recorder off*]*** I knows that one about the robbers with the door _ alright. But I...I...I can't...I can't remember un now.
[*recorder off*]*** which one you means. [*recorder off*]*** [?I knowed] a lot o' stories one time an' uh...uh
[Int: You know a lot o' stories now!]
[*recorder off*]*** can't...just mind now, I used to know one about Hard Head one time. I was just tryin' to mind he. [*recorder off*]*** Yes I...I think I can mind another one to tell ya. Let's see now. (Alright). [*aside to Int. B:* oh my boy you're sick wi' smoke.] [*recorder off*]

One time...in olden times ya know _ in olden times _ now if you an' me was livin here _ I was livin here an' you was livin out there _ an' you had a...girl _ an' I had a son _ well now _ we would marry 'em when they was small children see? So very good. That's what they done. This...this

521

uh...feller. They was two farmers see? They was livin close 'longside, well one had a daughter an' the other one had a son. An' when they was born they married 'em see?

Well when they growed up _ to be big...boy an' a big girl well they...they took up goin together, well now they didn't know nothing about being married. Well they was...goin together goin to school. Well they...used to be goin together.

So very good uh...after they growed up _ a man an' woman _ she said uh...to.../Jack/ one day she said...he said to her, he said uh..."What about us gettin married?"

An' she said "Yes." She said uh..."I'm satisfied. But" she said uh..."go an' ask father" she said "tonight. If he said yes" she said "I will."

So very good. The next night _ that...night _ he got a bottle o' rum. [Though]t after his supper he'd get a bottle o' rum an' he'd go over an' give th' ol' man twothree drinks uh...he'd get his daughter for sure. Now he didn't know nothing about her bein married. He got a bottle o' rum an' he went over an' _ start talkin' to the ol' man an' he said _ "Have a drink o' rum?"

Well th' ol' man said "Yes" he said "I have a drink o' rum alright." He said "You got one." He took out the bottle an'...he start drinkin an' he start talkin. By an' by _ he said "I suppose" he said uh..."you wouldn't let me have me...have your daughter?"

And he said "Well now /Jack/" he said "I don't know" he said uh..."you got a trade?"

An' he said "No" he said "I got no trade."

"Oh well" he said "if you got no trade" he said uh..."I won't be able to let you have me daughter." He said "I...I said" he said uh..."when she was borned" he said "I wouldn't let no man have her unless they had a trade."

"Well" he said "I got no trade."

"Oh well" he said "you can't have her." Well now that knocked the good right out of un, well -- next evening when they got together well Jack told her, well _ he didn't know what to do.

"Well" she said "Jack" she said "you got to go an' ask un again _ uh.../Jack/."

And..."Oh" he said "no" he said "I'm not going back no more" he said "not going to ask no more" he said "'cause uh...uh...he won't let me have ya. He won't let us get married" he said "they would have to have [a] trade." He said "I'm not goin back an' ask no more."

(So) anyhow -- that day _ he was goin down the...the street _ an' he meet the...old Indian. She was come out with a big pile o' baskets see? An' _ she asked un did he want to buy a basket. An' he said "Yes" he said he think he would. Buyed the baskets from her an' he said "Now" he

/Bill/

/Bill/

/Bill/

said "how long" he said "do ya think" he said "('twould) take a man" he said "to learn to make they baskets?"

"Oh" she said "not very long" she said "I can learn ya" she said "how to make they baskets" she said "in a...in a week."

"Well" he said "now" he said "look" he said "I'll tell ya" he said "what I'll do." He said "I'll uh...give ya ten dollars" he said "if you'll learn me" he said "how to make they baskets."

"Oh well" she said "I'll do that."

Very good. Next day _ she come up. Th' old Indian come up an' Jack started in. He got some...he used to...the rind [o'] the birches see, they'd get the birches an' they strip uh...strips off of 'em like that an' they _ make the baskets see? An' get the dye an' dye 'em see and _ course 'twasn't very long _ 'fore begar Jack knowed how to make the baskets, you...he can make 'em just so good as the Indian.

Well now he thought to hisself he would make a basket an' he'd carry [un] over an' he'd give to the ol' feller. Well this is what he done, he got some dye an' he made oh he made a wonderful nice basket. An' he went over this night. An' went in.

"I got a basket here" he said "I brought ya" he said "for a present."

An' "My god" he said "/Jack/" he said "that's a nice basket."   /Bill/

He said "Yes" (he said) "it's a very good basket."

He said "I..."he said "I thought you told me" he said "you had no trade?"

"Oh well" [laughing tone] he said _ "that's not a trade at all."

"Oh yes" he said "'tis a trade." He said "I'm a farmer." He said "I'm a farmer" he said "I can't be a basketmaker." He said "You're a basketmaker" he said "you got a trade."

"Well" Jack said "yes" he said "I got (a) trade" he said "but I didn't think that was a trade at all."

"Oh yes" he said "that's a trade. Well" he said "Jack" he said "being as you got a trade" he said "yes" he says "you can have me daughter." Oh well now Jack was tickled to death.

Well Jack _ told her. Oh well _ the two of 'em was tickled to death, well next day they was married. An' _ [has a drink] after they got married, well now they was goin to spend their honeymoon see? And _ they went out uh...next morning they got up an' Jack said he said "We'll go out this morning" he said "an' we'll set down" he said "by the...by the seaside" he said "an' we'll watch the ships comin in" he said "the harbour" _ he said "for a hour." So that's what they done.

By an' by there was a big ship come in. An' _ she hove uh...she hove to. An' she put over a boat. An' she come ashore _ boat come ashore. An' he [the sailor]...said to Jack he said uh..."The captain" he said uh..."the captain" he said uh..."wants yous to come aboard" he said uh..."have dinner with un."

Well Jack said he...guessed 'twould be a very good trip. He said he...guessed they'd go aboard. So -- they went aboard. Took 'em down in the cabin. An' _ when they got 'em down in the cabin well they _ pulled her [*the ship*] off an' away they goes see.

When they come up on deck the two of 'em _ by god _ they was...there was uh...no sign o' land. Oh well now they was in a wonderful way. They was gone. An' _ blowed a nice breeze _ an' her hat blowed off see. An' blowed overboard. Well now they shoved over the boat to get her hat. Well Jack jumped in the boat _ to get her hat _ an' when he did _ course they chopped the line _ an' _ away they goes. Now Jack was off in the boat. Well now _ couldn't get in [i.e., *into harbour*].

So very good he thought to hisself well _ he wouldn't get in now. An' _ anyhow -- there was blowin a nice breeze. An' he sot down in the boat thinkin about what he was goin to do an' _ he was drivin [i.e., *drifting*] _ oh he was drivin fast. He sot down in the boat with his head down, well he didn't know what he was goin to do. Huh. God -- he looked up an' he _ seen some land. Well he was drivin awards the land. He was driving awards the land but he didn't know whe'r [i.e., *whether*] he was goin to get in there or no.

An' _ all at once _ all at once _ he heard something behind un. An' _ when he looked around _ there was a man climbin in over the stern of his boat. Now he looked at un. He didn't know...he didn't know who it was. He got up in the boat and he sat down in the boat. An' _ he said "Jack" he said "you're adrift."

He said "Yes." He said "I'm adrift" he said "an' I got no paddles" he said. "No way to get in." He said "An' I thought I seen some land there" he said "but I didn't...I didn't."

"Oh no" he said "there's no land" he said "you're a long ways" he said "from land."

Jack said he said "I [don't] know what I'm going to do" he said "I suppose" he said "I won't get in."

/tried/

"Well now" he said "Jack" _ he had a piece o'...he took a piece o' rope in his hand _ an' he /tied/ three knots in the piece o' rope. "Now" he said "Jack I got three knots tied in that piece o' rope. Now" he said "I'm goin to leave ya. Now" he said "after I leaves ya" he said "you untie one o' they knots" _ he said "an' you'll go pretty fast." An' he said "If uh...ya mightn't go fast enough" _ he said "if you don't go fast enough" he said "untie the second one. But" he said "whatever you does" he said "don't untie the last one." He said "'Cause if you unties the last one, well" he said uh..."she'll go in under water" he said "she'll be goin that fast." Huh! [*laughs*] He disappeared to Jack. Jack never seen un.

An' Jack thought to hisself well _ he sat down in the boat. He never...he never bothered to untie the knots, he sat there in the boat an'...(just looked at un). An' he was lookin at the rope an' he thought to hisself he'd untie a knot (to) see...see what she'd do. An' he untied a knot an' when he untied one o' the knots by god the boat start goin. Oh [*rising tone suggesting surprising speed*] she was goin pretty fast. Thought to hisself well he'd try another one. He untied another one an' when he untied the other one well she was goin oh _ she was almost flyin over the water. Away he goes.

An' _ 'twasn't very long _ before he had land in sight. An' _ god 'twasn't very long 'fore he _ got in handy enough to _ see 'twas land an' _ he got in harbour.

Now the day he got in th' harbour -- the ship got in _ with his woman into un. Well now he was in uh...the...city _ an' he had no uh...money. He had no money an' he...he didn't know what to do. An' he was hungry. An' he couldn't get nothing to eat. He thought to hisself if he had some dye _ he'd go back in the woods an' he'd rind some uh...birch an' he would make twothree baskets an' he might sell 'em. Oh _ he thought to hisself _ (an' said an') he thought to hisself "I believe I got a...bit o' money in me purse." He looked in an' he had...little bit o' money he had enough...he uh...made up enough that he bought some dye, twothree packs o' dye _ 'cause they used to dye...buy dye in packs them times. So he bought his dye an' he went back in the country. An' _ he rind some birches an' he made _ five or six baskets you know, that's all he had time to make 'cause he was gettin hungry. An' he dyed un, he made five or six basket[s] an' he come out in the city, well -- oh they was delighted with the baskets, he _ he have uh...uh he (hun[g] un) out only about a hour an' he had 'em all sold. Now he _ sold his baskets an' he _ stayed there that night. Now he had money enough to stay there that night _ an' then get his supper, stayed there that night an' _ bought some more dye an' next day he went back an' he made a whole turn [i.e., *load*] of 'em. An' _ he come out in the...city. An' he wasn't out very long 'fore he sold all THEM. Shoved his money in his pocket an' _ bought some more dye an' back he goes again. He made a lot o'...'nother lot an' come out, now when he...uh...made THIS lot an' came out _ well he come out in the same place, well now _ 'twasn't as easy to sell 'em see 'cause he'd asold a lot there. Well he was walkin down the street _ an' when he uh...walked down the street _ he's walkin down the street _ there was a big building as he was walking along uh...three storey high. An' he looked up...the building like that an' when he looked up _ he seen a woman standin up by the window _ an' she was lettin down a...spool o' thread an' she was lettin down a note on this spool o' thread see? An' uh...he watched the note. By an' by the note come down on the ground _ an' he went along an' he picked up the note _ an' he read un. An' when he read the note this was his woman. This was his woman, now she was uh...she had to marry the ca...she was...she had to marry the captain the night [i.e., *tonight*]. An' she said now she said uh...told un what time it'd be "Now" she said uh...uh..."you got to be there." Alright. He was GOINA be there.

Now he had a nice bit o' money. He went to the store an' he...he went down an' he sold his baskets _ he sold all his baskets an' he...he bought a suit o' clothes an' he went to...a boardin house...in a...t' house...an' he dressed hisself an' _ by an' by the weddin was comin off. An' _ he went down. He went down to th' house an' _ went in an' _ well captain he didn't know un. She knowed un...an' he...an' he...soon as he come in. He sot down an' they had their supper an' they was talkin an' _ one thing an' another an' by an' by uh...SHE said _ "I think" she said "'twould be alright" she said "to have a...story" she said. "I LOVE stories" she said an' uh..."I'd like to have a story."

An' uh...the captain said "Yes" he said "a story" he said "'d be alright."

She said "[If] anybody could tell a story" she said "I'd like to have a story" she says "just from a ol' sailor" she said "then [?about] sailin" she said. "A story" she said "he knows" she said "that'd be good story."

And captain said "Yes." He said "A story from a ol' sailor" he said "'d be alright."

An' she said "That's a old sailor down there" she said. "I believe" she said "he can tell a good story."

And he said "Well" he said "I...I don't know much about tellin stories" he said "I uh...stories" he said "is something I never told" he said "only about me OWNself" he said "when I was sailin."

"Oh well" the...captain said "that's the kind of a story we wants to hear"

So by god he up an' told this story about the...captain an' uh...about why they was off on their honeymoon ([ju]st told) it all out it an'...an' he said uh...when he got the story told he said "That's my woman there." He said "They...they sot me adrift" he said "out there" he said "an' that's my woman there" he said "he took me woman from me" he said "he's goin to marry her."

Well uh...there was three or four uh...police in there, well they jumped right up an' they put the handcuffs on un [*the captain*] right away an' took un out an' course...Jack got his woman back again.

[*recorder off*]*** baskets. That's "The Basketmaker."

[Int: "The Basketmaker" of course.]

Yes. That's "The Basketmaker." [*recorder off*]*** that's all of it.

Duration: 14 min., 36 sec.

Location: The darkening sitting room of the teller's house, in the late evening.

Audience: Mrs. Rebecca Bennett (teller's wife), male visitor, several children, interviewers.

Context, Style, and Language: (For context see notes to No. 4).

Because of the difficult recording conditions in the darkened room the tape recorder is switched on only when significant material is forthcoming, hence the somewhat fragmented preamble. Even in the half-light, however, Freeman Bennett notices that one of the interviewers seems to be avoiding a cloud of tobacco smoke, and he waves his hand to clear the air.

Apart from some confusion of the names *Jack* and *Bill* in the early stages, perhaps suggesting that there were two or more brothers in other versions, this narrative proceeds smoothly and without interruption. It includes the punctuating expressions *(So) very good, Alright, by an' by, he/she said* typical of this teller's style, and many sentences begin with the marker *Well,* signaling a new segment of the plot, while others begin with the continuity-marker *An',* often followed by a brief pause and/or hesitation form. The tale has some relevance to the local context in that Indian basket-sellers were well known in Newfoundland, but the teller builds on this by referring to the rinding of birch—an activity with which Newfoundlanders can readily identify, since birch rind is stripped and used for a variety of purposes in the province, including the covering of fish during the drying process and also for the insulating and waterproofing of buildings.

Items of linguistic interest include the lack of transitional /n/ and loss of initial aspirate in *a hour,* the pronunciation of *does* as /duːz/, the lack of plural inflection in *storey,* the reduction of *whether* to *whe'r, they* used as a demonstrative in object position, the Anglo-Irish asseveration *begar, drivin* (drifting; *DNE drive* v. 1), *breeze* (strong wind), *paddles* (oars; *DNE paddle* n. 1), *turn* (load; *DNE turn* n. 3), the present tense form *I leaves,* the past tense *meet, Buyed,* the past participle *asold* and the double negative *not goin back no more.*

See also the notes to Nos. 4, 5, 6, 8, 37, 38, 39, 46, and 49.

Types and Motifs:

AT888A*. *The Basket-maker* + Cf. AT506. *The Rescued Princess.*

Z10.1. *Beginning formula.*

T69.2. *Parents affiance children without their knowledge.*

T97. *Father opposed to daughter's marriage.*

H326.1. *Suitor test: aptness in handicrafts.*

Cf. N825.3. *Old woman helper.*

T100. *Marriage.*

R12.4. *Girl enticed into boat and abducted.*

S141. *Exposure in boat.*

Cf. R163. *Rescue by grateful dead man.*

D1282.1. *Magic knot.*

D2142.1.2. *Wind raised by loosing certain knots.*

Cf. R82. *Captive sends secret message (in orange or on handkerchief).*

K1816.0.3.1. *Hero in menial disguise at heroine's wedding.*

N681. *Husband (lover) arrives home just as wife (mistress) is to marry another.*

Cf. J1177.1. *Story told to discover thief: sundry tales.*

Q213. *Abduction punished.*

International Parallels: This single Newfoundland recension of AT888A*, so far as we can tell, is a unique English-language version. The AT index lists only three Irish references for this Type. Although *Irish Types* greatly enlarges the list of available versions, apparently none of them is in English. Similarly for the closely related story, AT949*, "Young Gentleman Learns Basketwork," the AT index cites only two Lithuanian versions.

In an essay on Irish Type 2412B, "The Man Who Had No Story," Almqvist (*Béal.* 37-38 [1969-70], 62) makes some interesting observations on the role of basketmaking in Ireland: ". . .The main character in the story is a basketmaker, a trade that many Irish farmers and fishermen took up as a sideline when it was impossible to eke out an existence from their main occupation. Selling the baskets often involved long journeys and contacts with many people. This provided excellent opportunities to tell and listen to stories. It is not at all surprising, then, that basketmakers frequently figure in Irish stories. A tale in which the hero is recognised by a special make of basket. . .[AT888A*]. . .is extraordinarily popular in Ireland."

The notion that an upper- or middle-class person would be wise to have a trade on which he could fall back if his circumstances suddenly changed appears to be a piece of conventional wisdom in Europe and elsewhere. We have cited below a few references to other tales in which this requirement also figures, i.e., that a man, no matter what his rank or financial status, must learn a trade before he may court a particular girl. In two of these stories, as soon as the intended lover demonstrates he can satisfy this requirement, he is allowed to marry the girl. In others his acquired skill in weaving also proves of practical benefit in his further adventures, like the skill in basketmaking in our Newfoundland tale.

According to the Type description, after the man learns the trade of basketmaking, his wife is abducted and he is cast adrift at sea. Our Newfoundland tale follows this sequence exactly and Jack is set adrift in a boat when he tries to retrieve his wife's hat which has blown overboard. This leads to adventures in which Jack is rescued by supernatural intervention. What is intriguing about this series of episodes is that Freeman Bennett, undoubtedly the most creative of all our storytellers, also uses them, though in a less elaborately detailed form, in AT506B (No. 96). The actual wording of the episodes in both stories is remarkably similar, as the reader will readily discover by even a cursory comparison. The similarities are so frequent as to suggest that this sequence comes naturally to the storyteller's mind at the point where Jack is cast adrift with no apparent hope of rescue, a situation that occurs in each of the two stories. This is yet another example of the storyteller's skill in combining and recombining "floating" episodes at appropriate points in different narratives.

Canada
Lacourcière, Index, cites 1 Francophone version of AT888A* from Canada: 1 (New Brunswick).

Ireland
Irish Handbook, p. 625, no. 15.
Irish Types 888A*, 65 versions.

The references that follow are not to AT888A* but to the related story AT949* discussed above.

United States

Cf. Hoogasian-Villa, *Tales,* pp. 348-50, no. 53 (cf. 949*) [Merchant who has no other trade is beggar for a day to win beggar's daughter as his wife], Armenian tradition, in English trans. (Michigan).

Continental Europe

Cf. Petrovitch, *Hero Tales,* pp. 366-69 [To marry girl Prince learns carpet-weaving as his trade. No further use made of this acquired skill in the plot of the story] (Serbia).

Cf. Khatchatrianz, *Folk Tales,* pp. 68-82 (949*) [To marry girl Prince learns to weave carpets as his trade. When imprisoned, weaves message to his wife in a carpet and she rescues him] (Armenia).

Cf. Kudian, *Apples,* pp. 40-43 [To marry girl King learns carpet weaving as his trade. When imprisoned, weaves message to his wife in carpet and is rescued] (Armenia).

Cf. Zheleznova, *Mountain,* pp. 164-80 [To marry girl man must learn a trade; learns to weave; wife reads message in brocade he wove and rescues imprisoned husband] (Armenia).

54. THE FAITHFUL WIFE[†]

Everett Bennett   AT891
St. Pauls, Great Northern Peninsula   TC251 66-24
24 August 1966   Collectors: HH and JW

[*recorder off*]*** he's just married ya see. Well he was goin for a trip. He's gone for...round nine, ten months. Now he's only just married he was...twitin [i.e., *teasing*] his wife you know about the men she was goina have while he was gone now, he was goin for nine or ten months. -- So anyhow _ very good.

She knowed the port he was goin to _ be to that night. She dresses up, gets a different rig you know an' _ everything dressed up now the real lady. Started off. Sure enough when she got [to] this place her hu...her husband was there. But he didn't know her. She was down on the pier an' by an' by the captain come ashore _ invites her aboard. "Come aboard?"

"Yeah." Went down the cabin and _ asked what about _ date for the night.

"Well" she said "yes" she said _ "if you can do one thing for me" she said "I'll have the night with ya." Well if was any way o' doin /it/ at all he was   /her/
goina do this now.

"Well I want half a dozen _ silver spoons" _ she says. "An' the 'nitials of your name _ put in the handles." Oh he could get that done. An' away he goes. (Gets) half a dozen spoons _ 'nitials of her name...of his name put in the handles o' the spoons.

So anyhow _ she starts back home now with her spoons the next morning. An' nine months _ between nine an' ten months from that _ [he] got back home. First thing he seen when he came in the house was a _ baby in the cot you see. "Ah! What was I tellin of ya when I leaved home what was goin to happen! Now" he said "I'm leavin ya" he said "an' I never wants to hear tell of ya no more."

"Oh" she said "there's one thing I wants for you to do 'fore you leaves" she said. "Have one more _ cup o' tea with me uh.../have/ one more lunch 'fore...'fore you leaves."

/not/

"Yes" he suppose he'd have that.

So anyhow she gets up two _ plates on the table an' sits in. Put down the spoons now. Took up the spoon. First thing he seen was his own 'nitials.

"Where in the heavens" he said "did you get THIS to?"

"Now" she said "what place was it you give 'em to me _ to." This was his own wife he'd had (the) night [with!]***[*recorder off*]

Duration: 2 min., 27 sec.
Location: Kitchen of John Edward Bennett's house, evening.
Audience: John Edward Bennett (teller's brother) and his wife, Clarence and Barbara Bennett (teller's son and daughter-in-law), Clyde Bennett and his wife, John Edward's daughter-in-law and her two children, Anthony Bryan (teller's son-in-law), interviewers.

Context, Style, and Language: (For context see notes to No. 11).

The opening few words of this story were lost as the tape recorder was being used only from time to time in this initial exploratory visit. Apart from this, however, the narrative runs smoothly and easily, with the punctuating expressions *So anyhow, very good, by an' by,* and *he/she said* again prominent, as are also the short elliptical sentences and the skillful variation of vocal quality—heard for example in the angry tones of self-vindication in the response of the husband to seeing the baby on his return home. Another typical feature of this narrator's style is also seen in the mingling of tenses, e.g., "the captain come ashore _ invites her aboard," and of direct and indirect speech, e.g., "'Come aboard?'/'Yeah.' Went down the cabin," etc., and "'Yes' he suppose he'd have that."

Dialectal forms include the lowered short close back round vowel in /spunz/ *(spoons)* typical of West Country English speech, aphesis in *'nitials,* the present participle *twitin* (teasing, taunting), in which the first syllable is pronounced *twite* (a variant recorded in *OED* from the sixteenth century with the spelling *twyte,* but see *EDD TWITE* v.[1] To reproach, taunt, reported only from Dorset and Somerset), *rig* (dress, clothing; see *DNE rig* n. 1), and the present tense *you leaves.*

See also the notes to Nos. 11, 40, 41, 47, 48, 51, and 52.

Type and Motifs:

AT891. *The Man Who Deserts His Wife and Sets Her the Task of Bearing Him a Child.*

K1814. *Woman in disguise wooed by her faithless husband.*
Cf. H1187. *Task left by departing husband for virgin wife to accomplish: have a son whose real mother she is and whose real father he is.*
Cf. H81. *Clandestine lover recognized by tokens.*

International Parallels: The AT title for this Type is misleading. Apart from the Boccaccio story noted below, which is also the source of Shakespeare's play, *All's Well That Ends Well,* only a few of the folktale versions, all of them from India, have the motif of the husband setting his deserted wife the task of "bearing him a child whose real father he is and whose real mother she is." It is worth noting that the task form of the narrative is also found in India in a Bihar woman's song.

In the usual form of this tale, a newly wed husband, either as revenge for some earlier action by the girl, or as punishment for her refusal to explain a challenging or taunting statement or threat that she had made, does not consummate their marriage (a fact implied but not clearly stated in the AT analysis), but instead goes away on a trip. Sometimes the husband has imprisoned his wife, but she escapes without his knowledge. The deserted wife is told or learns where he is going, precedes him there, and disguised, frequently as a courtesan, meets her husband, gains his love, sleeps with him, and gets certain gifts from him.

In some versions, when the wife knows she is pregnant, she leaves him, returns home, and bears his child. On his later return from his trip, to demonstrate that the child is his, she produces the love tokens he gave her. In several versions she meets and sleeps with her husband on three separate trips, eventually surprising him with his own three children, each of whom wears one of the gifts he made to his supposed mistress or mistresses. These identifying love tokens may be either personal possessions, such as his ring, jeweled dagger and headcloth, or some other quite distinctive gifts.

Why the newly married husband must leave immediately on a voyage without consummating the marriage is not explained in the Newfoundland tale. There is no suggestion that this is because of a lack of interest in his new wife (a reason that occurs in a few versions), or that his action is meant as a form of punishment for her. His teasing remarks that she will probably take lovers in his absence, implying that women cannot be trusted, apparently act as a challenge to his wife. The challenge thus serves a similar function in this narrative to that of the supposedly impossible task set for the wife by her deserting husband that she should bear him a child.

Similarly, the initialed silver teaspoons of the Newfoundland text function admirably as identifiable personal tokens of their love encounter. While at first glance initialed spoons are a strangely aristocratic item for a story from rural Newfoundland, we must also remember that there is a long European tradition of gifts of spoons as love or marriage tokens (see *HDA,* col. 1319, 11. 14-18).

In this Newfoundland tale, as in most other versions, the husband fails to recognize that the woman with whom he has an affair is his wife. In our western tradition most men are aware that a woman dressed for a party and with a changed hairstyle and makeup can look very different from the same woman in casual household garb. Nonetheless we may conjecture that in many traditions the fact that the husband thinks his wife is a stranger would probably be regarded as highly amusing by the storyteller's audience. Where the husband does see the resemblance to his wife, as in the delightful Greek version in Dawkins, *Modern,* and in the Sicilian version in Calvino, *Folktales,* the supposed stranger dismisses this by a sententious remark about resemblances being everywhere.

In the version found in Straparola, which differs in several respects from the usual form, the improbability of a husband failing to recognize his own wife is solved by witchcraft. The wife is transformed magically into the appearance of his mistress and takes the latter's place in her husband's bed. The problem of possible recognition does not even arise in the Boccaccio/Shakespeare version. The husband is introduced in the dark into the bedroom of the lady of whom he is enamored. Even on repeated nightly visits there is no light, so he cannot see that his wife has substituted herself for his supposed inamorata.

For the oral and literary examples of AT891 that we have found in English translation, we have indicated for each version: whether or not the husband assigned the task of the AT title; what tokens the wife secures; the number and sex of the offspring. Identifying tokens are occasionally lacking in several versions from the Indian subcontinent, but they are in fact not necessary: the woman's son carries out his mother's earlier threat and punishes his father. When she finally sees her husband again, she reminds him of the threat that she had made.

Except for one distantly related version from New Mexico, this tale has apparently not been found elsewhere in oral tradition either in North America or in the British Isles. Nor for that matter does it appear to be common anywhere in Europe: the AT index cites it only from Italy, Serbo-Croatia, and Greece.

The New Mexican version in Rael has tantalizing parallels with the standard form of AT891, but also several differences. The husband must go away for a long period of work, leaving his wife in his mother's care. The mother locks the girl in a room and never lets her out. As in the Straparola version, the devil comes to her aid, takes her out, and carries her swiftly to where her husband is. The devil, pretending the girl is his own wife, goes off to gamble for the night, leaving the woman with her actual husband. The husband fails to recognize his wife, but promptly "seduces" her and spends the night with her. Next morning he gives her a small trunk as a love gift. Afterward the devil carries the girl back into the locked room. When some time later the mother-in-law discovers that despite her imprisonment the wife is disgracefully pregnant, she sends for her son. When the son confronts his wife, she produces the trunk he gave her to prove to him that he is the father of her unborn child.

Studies and Notes

Lee, *Sources,* pp. 101-8 (Day III, Novel 9); Penzer, *Ocean,* 9, pp. 77-78, n. 2; Basile, *Pentamerone,* 2, p. 138 (Day V, Tale 6), notes; Dawkins, *Modern,* pp. 292-93, no. 45, headnote; Spencer, *Stories,* pp. 12-16.

United States

Cf. Rael, *Cuentos,* pp. 618-19, no. 25 [no task; small trunk; unborn child], English summary of Spanish text (New Mexico).

England
Shakespeare, *All's Well That Ends Well* [task; his ring; twin sons], literary.

Continental Europe
Calvino, *Folktales,* pp. 540-46, no. 151, English trans. of Pitrè's Sicilian text [no task; documents acknowledging each as his legal offspring; 2 sons, 1 daughter] (Italy). [Note that Laura Gonzenbach's German trans. of Pitrè's text is cited in the AT index and in a footnote in Penzer, *Ocean,* 9, pp. 77-78, n. 2.]

Boccaccio, *Decameron,* pp. 190-97 (Day III, Novel 9) [task; his ring; twin sons], literary (Italy).

Basile, *Pentamerone,* 2, pp. 134-38 (Day V, Diversion 6) [no task; pearl necklace, jewel for hair, gold chain with precious stones; 2 sons, 1 daughter], with notes, literary (Italy).

Cf. Straparola, *Nights,* 2, pp. 44-51 (Night VII, Fable 1) [no task; steals richly embroidered robe and pearl necklace from his room; 1 son, like his father, lacks little toe on one foot], literary (Italy).

Paton, *FL* 11 (1900), 336-39, no. 10 [no task; his dagger and ring, and a girl's dress; 2 sons, 1 daughter] (Greece).

Dawkins, *Modern,* pp. 292-98, no. 45 [no task; gold watch, gold walking stick, string of precious stones, and ring (plus dress of gold for woman); 2 sons, 1 daughter] (Greece).

Stevens, *Folk-Tales,* pp. 219-23, no. 40 [no task; his ring, jeweled dagger, and gold-broidered head kerchief; 2 sons, 1 daughter], pp. 231-45, no. 42 [no task; his ring, jeweled dagger, and scarf; 2 sons, 1 daughter], 2 versions (Iraq).

Bushnaq, *Folktales,* pp. 339-43 (with cf. 875, II, 875A, cf. 921) [no task; his dagger, prayer beads, and headcloth; 2 sons, 1 daughter], Arab tradition (Iraq).

Indian Subcontinent
Knowles, *Folk-Tales,* pp. 104-23 (with 1525) [no task; his ring and handkerchief; 1 son] (Kashmir).

Dhar, *Folk Tales,* pp. 37-45 (with 1525) [no task; they exchange rings; 1 son] (Kashmir).

Stokes, *Fairy Tales,* pp. 216-23, no. 28 (with 1730) [task; his cap and picture; 1 son] (Punjab).

Cf. Archer, *Songs,* pp. 143-45, no. 148 [in song form; task; his ring; 1 baby, sex not given] (Bihar).

Natesa Sastri, *Folk-Tales,* pp. 409-34, no. 38 (with 882) [task; his finger rings and earrings, and her lotus flower chastity token; 1 son] (Madras).

Penzer, *Ocean,* 9, pp. 77-85, no. 171G [no task; no tokens; 1 son], literary (India).

Parker, *Village* 2, pp. 81-87, no. 92 (with 1525), with notes [no task; no tokens; 1 son], 3, pp. 325-27, no. 249 [task; no tokens; 1 son], 2 versions (Ceylon).

See Thompson and Roberts, *Types,* Type 891, for additional references and analysis.

The Thompson and Roberts *Index* cites under AT891, though from a different edition, Bradley-Birt, *Fairy Tales,* pp. 53-59, no. 7 (with 510B) [no task] (Bengal). This tale, though it has the girl's threat and the unconsummated marriage, differs from the standard form in that no child is involved. The rejected girl in disguise makes her husband fall in love with her and only reveals herself as his wife after her threat has been fulfilled. For a somewhat related tale, see Ryder, *Ten Princes,* pp. 173-77, the tale of Nimbavati in "Mitragupta's Adventure," literary (India). In this a husband falls out of love with his wife. By pretending to be the daughter of his neighbor, she gets him to fall madly in love with her and they elope.